THE SIGNET BOOK OF
American Humor

REVISED EDITION

D1371286

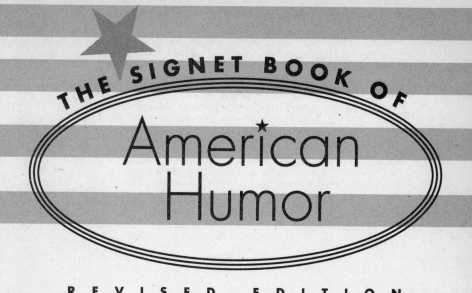

THE SIGNET BOOK OF

American Humor

REVISED EDITION

Edited and with a New Introduction
by Regina Barreca

NEW AMERICAN LIBRARY

New American Library
Published by New American Library, a division of
Penguin Group (USA) Inc., 375 Hudson Street,
New York, New York 10014, USA
Penguin Group (Canada), 10 Alcorn Avenue, Toronto, Ontario M4V 3B2, Canada
(a division of Pearson Penguin Canada Inc.)
Penguin Books Ltd., 80 Strand, London WC2R 0RL, England
Penguin Ireland, 25 St. Stephen's Green, Dublin 2, Ireland
(a division of Penguin Books Ltd.)
Penguin Books (Australia), 250 Camberwell Road, Camberwell, Victoria 3124, Australia
(a division of Pearson Australia Group Pty. Ltd.)
Penguin Books India Pvt. Ltd., 11 Community Centre, Panchsheel Park,
New Delhi - 110 017, India
Penguin Group (NZ), Cnr Airborne and Rosedale Roads,
Albany, Auckland 1310, New Zealand (a division of Pearson New Zealand Ltd.)
Penguin Books (South Africa) (Pty.) Ltd., 24 Sturdee Avenue, Rosebank,
Johannesburg 2196, South Africa

Penguin Books Ltd, Registered Offices:
80 Strand, London WC2R 0RL, England

First published by New American Library,
a division of Penguin Group (USA) Inc.

First Printing (Revised Edition), September 2004
10 9 8 7 6 5 4 3 2 1

Author copyrights and permissions can be found on pages 409–14.

 REGISTERED TRADEMARK—MARCA REGISTRADA

LIBRARY OF CONGRESS CATALOGING-IN-PUBLICATION DATA:

The Signet book of American humor/edited and with a new introduction
by Regina Barreca.—Rev. ed.
p. cm.
ISBN 0-451-21058-1
1. American wit and humor. I. Barreca, Regina.

PN6165.S54 2004
817.008—dc22   2004049884

Set in Bembo
Designed by Ginger Legato

Printed in the United States of America

This book is dedicated to my conspirators and stepsons,
Tim Meyer and Matthew Meyer,
who recognize, celebrate, and exploit the absurdities of life.
Here's to laughing and putting Dixie cups
over the eyes of the collective world.

Acknowledgments

Tracy Bernstein at New American Library deserves cheers, chocolates, balloons, and bouquets for her support of this book. Her intelligent, commonsense approach and contagious enthusiasm made the process of revision far more pleasurable than it had any right to be; to her I am hugely grateful.

In my office, stuck into a basement room at the University of Connecticut, graduate assistants past and present completed all the really demanding work—and they know I am not kidding when I declare as much. Mara Reisman and Barbara Campbell did the following (and more): researched author bios; found definitive texts; managed the tricky legwork of securing the copyrights and permissions; chased down elusive, out-of-print volumes; discovered secret addresses of famous authors. They also photocopied, kept files, and—perhaps most crucial to the ultimate success of the venture—refused to allow me to take any original documents away from the office itself for fear that I would lose them. Considerate, smart, and tenacious, they kept the project going even when the prospect was overwhelming. Barbara and Mara have my endless thanks. They deserve even more recognition than the occasional lunch of Indian food delivered by Wings Express can provide. In other words, Mara and Barbara deserve applause for their unflagging commitment to the completion of the book. Margaret Mitchell, who worked on the original edition, continues to have my gratitude for her research, scholarship, and keen critical insight.

Many of the contributors did me the great personal honor of permitting me to reprint their work for little or no cost. I also give them my sincere and humble thanks.

My husband, Michael Meyer (who knows a few things about laughing out loud), reminded me to have a good time even while I was working hard; his sons, Tim and Matthew, keep us from taking ourselves too seriously. It is a delight to dedicate this new edition to them.

Contents

Introduction

American Humor: Anything Goes

The best American humor is made up of stories, not jokes.

The best American humor is about life, loss, refusal, and recovery. It is not about two guys walking into a bar and finding a twelve-inch pianist, or a talking dog, or a one-legged hooker. The best humor America offers the world is not contained in limericks. (Don't search for the word "Nantucket"—it is not here.) What you will discover within these pages is material that remained funny fifteen minutes or a hundred fifty years after its debut—material that is slightly dangerous and more than slightly smart.

Written humor is about being smart: you have to be smart to write it and smart to get it.

Excessive, playful, blasphemous, indulgent, insurgent, and fiercely courageous, the writers presented here are drawn from a cross section of the population with one crucial thing in common: these writers found humor to be the shortest and most electric line between two—or more—points. They set about connecting the wires so the rest of us could hear the noise inside their heads. To them, nothing is sacred. Nothing scares them. The only thing they have to fear is the grim, tight-lipped, earnest specter of humorlessness itself. Maybe the words "wisecrack" and "smart-ass" reveal a greater understanding of how humor functions in our culture than we'd like to admit.

All great humor, regardless of country of origin, is about risk and privilege, but this volume is particularly American in nature for several reasons. What becomes clear from a close reading of several hundred years' worth of witty observations is that pretensions and affectation, whether homegrown or imported, are the American humorist's favorite fodder.

Humor maps the territory where absurdity, sexuality, and mortality meet, drawing together carnival, the carnal, and carnage.

The interplay between fear and desire is the perpetual human condition—

and, when seen from those certain angles most effectively employed by the humorist, really very funny. Fear of death and desire for death; fear of sex and desire for sex; how silly, after all. American writers often treat death and sexual union with humor—humor that ranges from the lightly ironic to the charmingly tasteless.

But what about people who are offended by such matters? What about the ones who pronounce in stern or shrill tones, "That's NOT funny?"

For one thing, the very phrase "That's not funny" is problematic. It is one of the lines most obviously reflective of a position of power. Who says it? Teachers, parents, bullies—any group that wishes to repress or control the reaction of a subordinate group. It is a phrase used only when people are already laughing. It is part of the mechanism of domination to forbid misrule, and comedy is characterized by misrule. It is part of the mechanism of control to prevent what is called "code switching" or "code mixing" except by express consent of the guardians of established order. Saying "That's not funny" really translates into saying "That's not right" and the split between what is funny and what is right is where the interesting material begins. Sex, death, and comedy all breach cultural taboos. Humor goes where others, angelic or not, fear to tread.

The contributors in this collection do not run away from what bothers them. Instead they run toward it—and trip over it. Some do a pratfall, some a subtle stumble, some an apoplectic version of Saint Vitus' dance, some a soft-shoe, but none—and this is the important part—remain on their knees.

And the readers' role in this spectacle? We laugh while we watch their antics. We stare, enthralled, during which time they pull the comfortable rug out from under us. This is their job.

If you start out being contented while reading humor, you'll end up fidgeting; if you start out restless, however, you'll be reassured when you notice what sprightly company you're in. Anybody with sense is relentless; anybody with a mind is very nearly always out of it. If most of the humor in this volume doesn't bother you, if it doesn't disturb you just a little bit, you're missing the point and ducking the very real punch in the punch line. Nothing bothers an American humorist more than seeing people comfortable when they should be uncomfortable.

These writers filter the anarchic and the subversive through the comic. The cultural critique offered by the humorist is directed at those above him or her, the ones running the show, the ones with bells, whistles, and whips at their command.

The Triumph of the Unofficial

James Kincaid, Aerol Arnold Professor of Literature at USC and author of *Annoying the Victorians*, declares in his essay "Who Is Relieved by the Idea of Comic Relief?" that we are sometimes tempted to dismiss comedy as unimportant because of the "most smothering of political conservatisms" urging us to see comedy as silly and trivial. We need to understand, he suggests, the way "official" culture frames comedy by applying to its structure and language a weary vocabulary of denigration—that swine guard the pearl. "[B]y coupling tragedy with the sublime . . . and aligning comedy with the mundane, the quotidian, and the material, we manage to muffle, even to erase, the most powerful narratives of illumination and liberation we have. . . . With comedy, nothing is sacrificed, nothing is lost; the discoordinate and the discontinuous are especially welcome."

Historians and critics of American humor and culture see this embrace of the defiant and anarchic as a particularly defining characteristic. When the country was new, American humor developed early as a defiant nose thumbing to the affectations and pretensions of those who remained on the other side of the Atlantic—especially those supercilious creatures who made a career of sniffing in derision at the upstarts. Europeans, especially the English, who visited and learned about America just so they could treat it with a more knowledgeable sense of contempt when they returned to the abnormally high ground they called home, were often the target of early humorists.

In her persuasive essay "What Is Humor? Why American Humor?" Nancy A. Walker makes the argument that "America in its early years was not so much described as it was invented. The habit of invention, closely tied to the habit of exaggeration, laid the groundwork for American humor. Long before the nineteenth century, Americans were known for their boastfulness and for their fondness for disguises. Aware of their own process of transformation from citizens of other countries to residents of a new land, settlers engaged in self-invention, and often tested out versions of a new reality on those new to the continent." She also argues that "American humor seemed to originate in . . . [the] story of the individual at odds with the rules of 'official' society—whether the Yankee peddler making his way by his wits . . . or the frontiersman spinning tales of his encounters with the wilderness. . . ."

One of the striking things about American humor is its focus on an important belief concerning national identity: nobody was born with the right to operate this country. Privilege should not be taken too seriously. The particularly distinctive characteristic of American humor emphasizes that the luck of the draw doesn't make you better or worse than others around you. If you think you're better, you're a self-righteous, self-deluded boor; if you think you're worse, you're a self-righteous, self-pitying chump.

The only way to win, the humorists show us, is to bet on this: we're all in it together. While we might disagree about what "it" is, or who "we" are, the maxim nevertheless holds true. In fact, the business of comedy is to satirize the pedantic and sphincter-tightening impulse to overdefine, separate, and factionalize. The American comic writer will show us that even at those moments when we're feeling desperately, despairingly alone, we're kidding ourselves if only we could see it; walk outside, and you'll inevitably meet forty million other desperately alienated outsiders, all of whom are pretty much chanting exactly the same ode of dejection.

The comic impulse at work, as so many of those who have written about it declare, brings us to the unavoidable conclusion that we are more alike than we are different. It doesn't much matter that we might not want to regard ourselves as inhabiting the same category as those we label yahoos and schnooks. Narrow it down to a pattern of national traits, however, and we see that we are formed by the same culture. (This makes most of us gulp in trepidation.) This is true even for those who believe that American culture has had an "impact" on their lives in much the same way, for example, as a dog can have an "impact" on a tree. Yet despite the fact that culture seems occasionally to want to separate us out, pair us off like socks, or collect us together like refuse for recycling, we're still in it together—and up to our eyeballs in it.

You Have a Problem with That?

One of the things we're all in it against, it becomes clear, is the bully. The figure of the bully cuts through American humor like a switchblade through cloth. What are the defining features of the bully? Bullies know they are right and insist on finding ways to make everyone else agree with their judgment. The bully doesn't have to be a belching, hirsute guy who traded in wit for weapons (although I wouldn't rule him out). The bully can also be an Iron Maiden of a second-grade teacher whose unstoppable voice scratches a hatred of penmanship into the soul.

Bullies persuade by pulling one up by the scruff of the neck, literally and/or metaphorically. They try to force others to dance their dance. They are the ones who preach the one-right-way-to-do-it creed, the everything-in-its-place litany, and the everyone-has-to-play-according-to-the-rules waltz. Bullies are masters and mistresses of obligation, responsibility, and duty, all of which they gleefully demand others fulfill accompanied by as much syco-phantic wriggling—and as little pleasure—as possible. Although they seem so inhuman that at times we fully expect them to drop down on all fours, bul-lies are often in positions of responsibility. Power make them drool with de-light; humor is one of the few things that make them cringe. This is one of the reasons humor is as important as it is in American culture.

Writers choose, of course, their own trademark bullies. This is when some members of the audience take a ringside seat while others duke it out. For example, male writers often focus on their wives, mothers, and girlfriends as bullies; the image of the domineering female (wielding frying pan, broom, or self-sacrifice as her weapon) grabbed hold of American humor's entrails from its infancy.

Naturally, female writers have often chosen their husbands, lovers, and sons as objects for witty whittling down. But they also direct their satiric gaze on male bosses, male government officials, male health-care providers, male religious leaders, male fashion designers—you can see that one is tempted to continue—as bullies, happily and easily coupling private and public bullying in one easy-to-open gender-biased package. Given the dearth of female bosses, government officials, etc., men have had to turn to their own kind for the purposes of humor.

This gender face-off pales in comparison with humor written by men and women of color, who have always been able to see the bully of Ameri-can racial inequality without needing any special lens. Aware that humor is one of the most effective ways to trick a fool into a display of his own piti-ful ignorance, craven viciousness, and ethical corruption, the American hu-mor writer of color insists that the bully unknowingly flaunts his own moral damnation.

And humor emerges from a variety of angles, sharpshooting from a vari-ety of perspectives. Writers from the Southern states see their New England counterparts as hilariously rigid, for example, while Northern writers con-struct their vision of the South with slyly disingenuous trepidation. Gay and lesbian writers often identify the bully by literalizing the definition of the "straight man" in their comedy. Liberals tease Conservatives; Conservatives mock Liberals. Cat fanciers snicker at dog walkers. Everybody makes fun of those from Long Island, but this is the only universal.

Although the targets appear unconnected, they remind us of other battles, fought over different turf but employing similar methods, ammunition, and aims. It turns out that superficially disparate struggles overlap if you see them from the slanted angle of the humorist; a potential battlefield of intellect and emotion is made into a playground for a dazzling, powerful, and ultimately useful juxtaposition of ideas.

But it refuses to be heavily didactic even as it leads to illumination. As Arthur Power Dudden's 1985 essay "American Humor" asserts, "American humor doesn't follow a formula, yet it separates itself cleanly from protest writings and systematic revolutionary doctrines. It attacks society's follies and fools indiscriminately, revealing in the process those shadowy highlights and lowlights between pretensions and achievements."

Successful as a Whole . . .

"America is successful as a whole," quipped Will Rogers. "But how successful is a hole?" Maybe you had to be there to laugh out loud, but the point remains an interesting one. If the "whole"—especially in humor—is made up of a series of holes, if the comic is concocted out of those very elements omitted by other forms of discourse, then humor is about what is left out—and about who is left out.

Humor laughs out loud, makes noise, and by so doing, makes trouble about issues rarely spoken of in polite conversation. Effective humor swivels a whole bank of klieg lights toward everything we've tried to hide, everything we resist examining. True, the once-hidden, unspoken, unexamined world might look garish under humor's first violent illumination, but after a while it becomes funny, then familiar, less terrifying, and therefore less powerful.

But not less dangerous—never less dangerous.

Yes, of Course, an Apology

Yet even the wide repertoire of wit provided by these pages won't satisfy every need. There are reasons for this and I'm going to tell you about them, so sit down. To say that this book had a modest budget is to underestimate the situation. Better to say the budget was so modest that it not only blushed when certain demands were made of it—it positively burst into tears as it wrung its poor little hands. Keeping in mind images of large-eyed little match girls and scrawny kittens, imagine this editor's chagrin at being told that she could not include some splendid and essential work of humor because she couldn't come up with sufficient dough to pay for the right to reprint.

Think about this editor wheedling and conniving, promising unspeakable acts in return for the favor of laying her anthologist's hands on a few funny words excerpted from the "property" held by this agent or that publisher. And then you'll no longer ask yourself why there aren't examples from some marvelous creators of humor, all of whom just happened to publish their work after 1919. I could give you a list of names and it would be practically as long as all of Dorothy Parker's virgins laid end to end.

While I won't mention names (for fear of being called in front of a grand jury), I will say that it's my belief a number of these writers would turn over in their graves, or weep in their penthouse beds, to find that they were being priced out of the humor-collection market. For example, I really wanted to include a dark horse favorite of mine, an author whose single successful work of humor, written in the thirties, has been out of print for something like forty years. The agents for her estate, who hold the rights to this piece, however, wanted literally thousands of dollars for a ten-page excerpt. This nice woman hasn't written anything new in a long, long time and so her prose is buried under newer material, almost invisible to the naked eye of the contemporary reader.

Wouldn't you think, therefore, that this woman would rather be recognized as an important figure in American humor, excerpted and properly identified, so that a new generation of readers could be so delighted by her malicious and whimsical prose that they would demand the book be brought back into print? Wouldn't you imagine that she'd want the book to lead to film adaptations, posthumous awards, and a grave festooned with flowers from admirers? Don't you think she'd want those words to be read? Me, I imagine the ghost of this writer trying to whack her agent over the head with an umbrella or perhaps a stick.

Not that I'm bitter.

And there are contemporary writers, cartoonists, and performers who should also be in this book, but who are kept locked up like fairy tale heroines, unable to let their hair down so that we can have access to them except through certain expensive windows. As a woman who makes most of her living by writing, I am (and please trust me on this) the last person on planet Earth to begrudge a humorist a dime if there is a dime being offered.

But I also know that I'm genuinely thrilled when literary types—the editors of a textbook, an anthology, a book of quotations, a calendar, a fortune cookie, whatever—want to take my work into their orbit, sending it out to audiences who might otherwise never have access to it. I hope they'll pay me a sort of "duty" for coming into my territory and taking a little bit of it with them, but I certainly wouldn't want them never to visit or be forced to walk out because the tariffs and fees were exorbitant.

That someone chooses to recognize your work is a privilege; if there's compensation, that's terrific. Everybody wins. But when the compensation demanded by corporate handlers for a cute eight-page article is the sort of figure usually kept in escrow to pay for a small yacht or a large foreign car, then compensation turns into punishment and restriction. Maybe I'm showing the one small part of myself that remains hopeful and naive, but I can't believe many authors (or creative folks of any persuasion) themselves know about or actually sanction this sort of limitation on the reach of their work.

So, basically, what I'm saying here is that if you don't find who you're looking for, it's not my fault. I knew you'd want them here, and I wanted exactly the same passage you wanted, but we're both going to have to live without them. It's sad, but even comedy is occasionally about loss. We must all be terribly brave.

Last Rights (and Wrongs)

Humor is indispensable; it is our most effective tool for insight and understanding as well as our most effective weapon against baseness and stupidity. But we need to make use of the best of it; humor does not work without our agency. Twain's Mysterious Stranger suggests as much:

> This multitude see the comic side of a thousand low-grade and trivial things—broad incongruities, mainly; grotesqueries, absurdities, evokers of the horselaugh. The ten thousand high-grade comicalities which exist in the world are sealed from their dull vision. Will a day come when the race will detect the funniness of these juvenilities and laugh at them—and by laughing at them destroy them? For your race, in its poverty, has unquestionably one really effective weapon—laughter. Power, money, persuasion, supplication, persecution—these can lift at a colossal humbug—push it a little—weaken it a little, century by century; but only laughter can blow it to rags and atoms at a blast. Against the assault of laughter nothing can stand.

American comedy embraces, at its white-hot core, cataclysmic upheavals and stupendously brave gestures of frivolity. This collection brings together under one aegis a chorus of voices which, under less auspicious circumstances, might be competing with rather than complementing one another. Its topics and issues—even the dangerous ones—can, at the best of moments, fall from humor's bag of tricks into our ordinary hands, where they can transform our lives.

We choose laughter at moments of crisis because the other alternatives are gnashing our teeth and rending our garments, neither of which has ever done anybody much good. The stories we tell ourselves—and maybe more important, the ones we tell one another—allow us to rattle the cage door. Sometimes we can rattle it hard enough to allow for escape; sometimes we rattle it so hard the cage itself falls away altogether.

Laughing together is as close as you can get to another person without actually touching, and sometimes laughter represents a closer tie than an embrace. We need laughter in our lives. Delightedly unwilling to be discouraged by the cultural and intellectual devices preventing us from seeing ourselves as we really are, the best humor is always part revelry, part revelation.

Stripping away both the mask and the fig leaf, humor refuses to genuflect before either fear or shame. It would rather be banished from the garden than trapped, unknowing or unwilling, within it. In so doing, the laughter it provides for its audience hints at the possibility of redemption.

Laughter is the sound you make when you are free.

—Regina Barreca
University of Connecticut

WORKS CITED

James Kincaid. "Who Is Relieved by the Idea of Comic Relief?" From a paper read at the 1991 meeting of the Modern Language Association.

Nancy A. Walker. "What Is Humor? Why American Humor?" in *What's So Funny? Humor in American Culture,* edited by Nancy A. Walker. Scholarly Resources, 1998.

Arthur Power Dudden. "American Humor." *American Quarterly* 37, 1985.

Mark Twain. *The Mysterious Stranger.* Signet Classics, 2003.

THE SIGNET BOOK OF

American Humor

REVISED EDITION

Bud Abbott and Lou Costello
(1897–1974) (1906–59)

Who's on First?

Abbott: All right, now whaddya want?

Costello: Now look, I'm the head of the sports department. I gotta know the baseball players' names. Do you know the guys' names?

Abbott: Oh sure.

Costello: So you go ahead and tell me some of their names.

Abbott: Well, I'll introduce you to the boys. You know sometimes nowadays they give ballplayers peculiar names.

Costello: You mean funny names.

Abbott: Nicknames, pet names, like Dizzy Dean—

Costello: His brother Daffy—

Abbott: Daffy Dean—

Costello: And their cousin!

Abbott: Who's that?

Costello: Goofy!

Abbott: Goofy, huh? Now let's see. We have on the bags—we have Who's on first, What's on second, I Don't Know's on third.

Costello: That's what I wanna find out.

Abbott: I say Who's on first, What's on second, I Don't Know's on third.

Costello: You know the fellows' names?

Abbott: Certainly!

Costello: Well then who's on first?

Abbott: Yes!

Costello: I mean the fellow's name!

Abbott: Who!

Costello: The guy on first!

Abbott: Who!

Costello: The first baseman!

Abbott: Who!

Costello: The guy playing first!

Abbott: Who is on first!

Costello: Now whaddya askin' me for?

Abbott: I'm telling you Who is on first.

3

Costello: Well, I'm asking YOU who's on first!

Abbott: That's the man's name.

Costello: That's who's name?

Abbott: Yes.

Costello: Well go ahead and tell me.

Abbott: Who.

Costello: The guy on first.

Abbott: Who!

Costello: The first baseman.

Abbott: Who is on first!

Costello: Have you got a contract with the first baseman?

Abbott: Absolutely.

Costello: Who signs the contract?

Abbott: Well, naturally!

Costello: When you pay off the first baseman every month, who gets the money?

Abbott: Every dollar. Why not? The man's entitled to it.

Costello: Who is?

Abbott: Yes. Sometimes his wife comes down and collects it.

Costello: Who's wife?

Abbott: Yes.

Costello: All I'm tryin' to find out is what's the guy's name on first base.

Abbott: Oh, no—wait a minute. Don't switch 'em around. What is on second base.

Costello: I'm not askin' you who's on second.

Abbott: Who is on first.

Costello: I don't know.

Abbott: He's on third—now we're not talkin' 'bout him.

Costello: Now how did I get on third base?

Abbott: You mentioned his name!

Costello: If I mentioned the third baseman's name, who did I say is playing third?

Abbott: No, Who's playing first.

Costello: Never mind first. I wanna know what's the guy's name on third.

Abbott: No, What's on second.

Costello: I'm not askin' you who's on second.

Abbott: Who's on first.

Costello: I don't know.

Abbott: He's on third.

Costello: Aaah! Would you please stay on third base and don't go off it?

Abbott: What was it you wanted?

Costello: Now who's playin' third base?

Abbott: Now why do you insist on putting Who on third base?

Costello: Why? Who am I putting over there?

Abbott: Yes. But we don't want him there.

Costello: What's the guy's name on third base?

Abbott: What belongs on second.

Costello: I'm not askin' you who's on second.

Abbott: Who's on first.

Costello: I don't know.

Abbott and Costello: THIRD BASE!

Costello: You got an outfield?

Abbott: Oh yes!

Costello: The left fielder's name?

Abbott: Why.

Costello: I don't know. I just thought I'd ask you.

Abbott: Well, I just thought I'd tell you.

Costello: All right then, tell me who's playin' left field.

Abbott: Who is playing fir—

Costello: STAY OUTTA THE INFIELD! I wanna know what's the left fielder's name.

Abbott: What's on second.

Costello: I'm not askin' you who's on second.

Abbott: Who's on first.

Costello: I don't know.

Abbott and Costello: THIRD BASE!

Costello: The left fielder's name?

Abbott: Why.

Costello: Because!

Abbott: Oh, he's center field.

Costello: Look, you gotta pitcher on this team?

Abbott: Now wouldn't this be a fine team without a pitcher?

Costello: The pitcher's name.

Abbott: Tomorrow.

Costello: You don't wanna tell me today?

Abbott: I'm tellin' you now.

Costello: Then go ahead.

Abbott: Tomorrow.

Costello: What time?

Abbott: What time what?

Costello: What time tomorrow are you going to tell me who's pitching?

Abbott: Now listen. Who is not pitching. Who is on fir—

Costello: I'll break your arm if you say, "Who's on first." I wanna know what's the pitcher's name.

Abbott: What's on second.

Costello: I don't know.

Abbott and Costello: THIRD BASE!

Costello: You got a catcher?

Abbott: Oh, absolutely.

Costello: The catcher's name.

Abbott: Today.

Costello: Today. And Tomorrow's pitching.

Abbott: Now you've got it.

Costello: All we've got is a couple of days on the team.

Abbott: Well, I can't help that.

Costello: Well, I'm a catcher too.

Abbott: I know that.

Costello: Now suppose that I'm catching, Tomorrow's pitching on my team, and their heavy hitter gets up.

Abbott: Yes.

Costello: Tomorrow throws the ball. The batter bunts the ball. When he bunts the ball, me being a good catcher, I wanna throw the guy out at first base. So I pick up the ball and throw it to who?

Abbott: Now that's the first thing you've said right.

Costello: I don't even know what I'm talkin' about!

Abbott: Well, that's all you have to do.

Costello: Is to throw the ball to first base.

Abbott: Yes.

Costello: Now who's got it?

Abbott: Naturally!

Costello: If I throw the ball to first base, somebody's gotta catch it. Now who caught it?

Abbott: Naturally!

Costello: Who caught it?

Abbott: Naturally.

Costello: Who?

Abbott: Naturally!

Costello: Naturally.

Abbott: Yes.

Costello: So I pick up the ball and I throw it to Naturally.

Abbott: NO, NO, NO! You throw the ball to first base and Who gets it.

Costello: Naturally.

Abbott: That's right. There we go.

Costello: So I pick up the ball and I throw it to Naturally.

Abbott: You don't!

Costello: I throw it to who?

Abbott: Naturally.

Costello: THAT'S WHAT I'M SAYING!

Abbott: You're not saying it that way.

Costello: I said I throw the ball to Naturally.

Abbott: You don't—you throw the ball to Who?

Costello: Naturally!

Abbott: Well, say that!

Costello: THAT'S WHAT I'M SAYING! I throw the ball to who?

Abbott: Naturally.

Costello: Ask me.

Abbott: You throw the ball to Who?

Costello: Naturally.

Abbott: That's it.

Costello: SAME AS YOU! I throw the ball to first base and who gets it?

Abbott: Naturally!

Costello: Who has it?

Abbott: Naturally!

Costello: HE BETTER HAVE IT! I throw the ball to first base. Whoever it is grabs the ball, so the guy runs to second. Who picks up the ball and throws it to What, What throws it to I Don't Know, I Don't Know throws it back to Tomorrow—triple play.

Abbott: Yes.

Costello: Another guy gets up. It's a long fly ball to Because. Why? I don't know. He's on third and I don't give a darn!

Abbott: What was that?

Costello: I said I don't give a darn!

Abbott: Oh, that's our shortstop.

Scott Adams
(Contemporary)

FROM *The Dilbert Principle*

Mandatory Self-Deprecation

I proudly include myself in the idiot category. Idiocy in the modern age isn't an all-encompassing, twenty-four-hour situation for most people. It's a condition that everybody slips into many times a day. Life is just too complicated to be smart all the time.

The other day I brought my pager to the repair center because it wouldn't work after I changed the battery. The repairman took the pager out of my hand, flipped open the battery door, turned the battery around, and handed the now functional pager back to me in one well-practiced motion. This took much of the joy out of my righteous indignation over the quality of their product. But the repairman seemed quite amused. And so did every other customer in the lobby.

On that day, in that situation, I was a complete idiot. Yet somehow I managed to operate a motor vehicle to the repair shop and back. It is a wondrous human characteristic to be able to slip into and out of idiocy many times a day without noticing the change or accidentally killing innocent bystanders in the process.

My Qualifications

Now that I've admitted that I can't replace the battery in my pager, you might wonder what makes me think I'm qualified to write this important book. I think you'll be impressed at my depth of experience and accomplishment:

1. I convinced a company to publish this book. That might not seem like much, but it's more than you did today. And it wasn't easy. I had to have lunch with people I didn't even know.

Making Them Wait

One of the most effective methods of humiliation used by managers is the practice of ignoring an underling who is in or near the manager's office while the manager pursues seemingly unimportant tasks. This sends a message that the employee has no human presence. It is similar to changing clothes in front of the family pet; the animal is watching but it couldn't possibly matter.

This tool of humiliation can be fine-tuned to any level simply by adjusting what activities are performed while the employee waits.

ACTIVITY	LEVEL OF HUMILIATION
Taking phone calls	Not so bad
Reading other things	Bad
Flossing	Very bad
Learning a foreign language	Very very bad

. . . a manager would never say, "I used my fork to eat a potato." A manager would say, "I utilized a multitined tool to process a starch resource." The two sentences mean almost the same thing, but the second one is obviously from a smarter person.

Running a Side Business from Your Cubicle

A cubicle is an excellent retail space, suitable for selling stuffed dolls, earrings, cosmetics, semiprecious gems, plant arrangements, household cleaning products, real estate, and vacation packages. Don't miss your opportunity to "moonlight," or as I like to call it, "fluorescentlight."

All you need is a tacky handmade sign on the outside of your cubicle that tells people you're open for business. A brochure or product sample can help lure people in.

You don't need high-quality merchandise. Let's be honest—if your co-workers were bright enough to know the difference between diamonds and monkey crap they wouldn't be working at your company. So don't waste a bunch of time on "quality." It's shelf space that matters, and you've got 180 cubic feet to play with. It's your chance to make some money while you're at work.

Theft of Office Supplies

Office supplies are an important part of your total compensation package. If God didn't want people to steal office supplies he wouldn't have given us briefcases, purses, and pockets. In fact, no major religion specifically bans the pilfering of office supplies.*

---

*Some religious scholars will debate my interpretation. But ultimately it's a matter of faith.

The only downside is the risk of being caught, disgraced, and imprisoned. But if you compare that to your current work situation I think you'll agree that it's not such a big deal.

The secret is to avoid getting too greedy. Office supplies are like compound interest—a little bit per day adds up over time. If you want some yellow sticky notes, don't take the whole box at once. Instead, use several sheets per day as page markers on documents that you're taking home. Later, carefully remove them and reassemble them into pads.

You can steal an unlimited amount of pens and pencils, but avoid the rookie mistake of continually asking the department secretary for the key to the supply closet. That attracts suspicion. Instead, steal supplies directly from your co-workers. Casually "borrow" their writing tools during meetings and never return them. Act naturally, and remember you can always laugh and claim it was a "reflex" if you get caught putting their stuff in your pocket.

Your co-workers will be trying to swipe your writing implements too. Defend your pens and pencils by conspicuously chewing on them during meetings. I've found that a few teeth marks are more effective than The Club in preventing theft.

If you have a home computer, say good-bye to purchasing your own diskettes. Stolen diskettes look exactly like work-related diskettes that are being taken home so you can "do a little work at night." The only practical limit on the number of diskettes you can steal is the net worth of the company you're stealing from. Your company will go broke if you steal too many diskettes. Nobody wins when that happens. That's why moderation is the key. After you have enough diskettes to back up your hard drive, and maybe shingle your house, think about cutting back.

Use Computers to Look Busy

Any time you use a computer it looks like "work" to the casual observer. You can send and receive personal e-mail, download pornography from the Internet, calculate your finances, and generally have a blast without doing anything remotely related to work. These aren't exactly the societal benefits that everybody expected from the computer revolution, but they're not bad either.

When you get caught by your boss—and you will get caught—your best defense is to claim you're teaching yourself to use the new software, thus saving valuable training dollars. You're not a loafer, you're a self-starter. Offer to show your boss what you learned. That will make your boss scurry away like a frightened salamander.*

---

*In laboratory tests, three out of four frightened salamanders were mistaken for supervisors.

★

The average life of an organization chart is six months. You can safely ignore any order from your boss that would take six months to complete. In other words, the environment will change before you have to do anything. You can just keep chewing leaves and scampering in the volcanic ash while new bosses come and go.

If you wait long enough, any bad idea will become extinct. And most good ideas too. So if you have time to master only one strategy, this is the one for you.

★

George Ade
(1866–1944)

The *Fable* of *What Happened* the *Night the Men Came* to the *Women's Club*

In a Progressive Little City claiming about twice the Population that the Census Enumerators could uncover, there was a Literary Club. It was one of these Clubs guaranteed to fit you out with Culture while you wait. Two or three Matrons, who were too Heavy for Light Amusements, but not old enough to remain at Home and Knit, organized the Club. Nearly every Woman in town rushed to get in, for fear somebody would say she hadn't been Asked.

The Club used to Round Up once a week at the Homes of Members. There would be a Paper, followed by a Discussion, after which somebody would Pour.

The Organization seemed to be a Winner. One Thing the Lady Clubbers were Dead Set On. They were going to have Harmony with an Upper Case H. They were out to cut a seven-foot Swath through English Literature from Beowulf to Bangs, inclusive, and no petty Jealousies or Bickerings would stand in the Way.

So while they were at the Club they would pull Kittenish Smiles at each other, and Applaud so as not to split the Gloves. Some times they would Kiss, too, but they always kept their Fingers crossed.

Of course, when they got off in Twos and Threes they would pull the little Meat-Axes out of the Reticules and hack a few Monograms, but that was to have been expected.

Everything considered, the Club was a Tremendous Go. At each Session the Lady President would announce the Subject for the next Meeting. For instance, she would say that Next Week they would take up Wyclif. Then every one would romp home to look in the Encyclopedia of Authors and find out who in the world Wyclif was. On the following Thursday they would have Wyclif down Pat, and be primed for a Discussion. They would talk about Wyclif as if he had been down to the House for Tea every evening that Week.

After the Club had been running for Six Months it was beginning to be Strong on Quotations and Dates. The Members knew that Mrs. Browning was the wife of Mr. Browning, that Milton had Trouble with his Eyes, and that Lord Byron wasn't all that he should have been, to say the Least. They began to feel their Intellectual Oats. In the meantime the Jeweler's Wife had designed a Club Badge.

The Club was doing such Notable Work that some of the Members thought they ought to have a Special Meeting and invite the Men. They wanted to put the Cap-Sheaf on a Profitable Season, and at the same time hand the Merited Rebuke to some of the Husbands and Brothers who had been making Funny Cracks.

It was decided to give the Star Programme at the Beadle Home, and after the Papers had been read then all the Men and Five Women who did not hold office could file through the Front Room and shake Hands with the President, the Vice-President, the Recording Secretary, the Corresponding Secretary, the Treasurer, and the members of the various Committees, all of whom were to line up and Receive.

The reason the Club decided to have the Brain Barbecue at the Beadle Home was that the Beadles had such beautiful big Rooms and Double Doors. There was more or less quiet Harpoon Work when the Announcement was made. Several of the Elderly Ones said that Josephine Beadle was not a Representative Member of the Club. She was Fair to look upon, but she was not pulling very hard for the Uplifting of the Sex. It was suspected that she came to the Meetings just to Kill Time and see what the Others were Wearing. She refused to buckle down to Literary Work, for she was a good deal more interested in the Bachelors who filled the Windows of the new Men's Club than she was in the Butler who wrote "Hudibras." So why should she have the Honor of entertaining the Club at the Annual Meeting? Unfortunately, the

Members who had the most Doing under their Bonnets were not the ones who could come to the Front with large Rooms that could be Thrown together, so the Beadle Home got the Great Event.

Every one in Town who carried a Pound of Social Influence showed up in his or her Other Clothes. Extra Chairs had to be brought in, and what with the Smilax and Club Colors it was very Swell, and the Maiden in the Lace Mitts who was going to write about it for the Weekly threw a couple of Spasms.

The Men were led in pulling at the Halters and with their Ears laid back. After they got into the Dressing Room they Stuck there until they had to be Shooed out. They did not know what they were going against, but they had their Suspicions. They managed to get Rear Seats or stand along the Wall so that they could execute the Quiet Sneak if Things got too Literary. The Women were too Flushed and Proud to Notice.

At 8:30 P.M. the Lady President stood out and began to read a few Pink Thoughts on "Woman's Destiny—Why Not?" Along toward 9:15, about the time the Lady President was beginning to show up Good and Earnest, Josephine Beadle, who was Circulating around on the Outskirts of the Throng to make sure that everybody was Happy, made a Discovery. She noticed that the Men standing along the Wall and in the Doorways were not more than sixty percent En Rapport with the Long Piece about Woman's Destiny. Now Josephine was right there to see that Everybody had a Nice Time, and she did not like to see the Prominent Business Men of the Town dying of Thirst or Leg Cramp or anything like that, so she gave two or three of them the Quiet Wink, and they tiptoed after her out to the Dining Room, where she offered Refreshments, and said they could slip out on the Side Porch and Smoke if they wanted to.

Probably they preferred to go back in the Front Room and hear some more about Woman's Destiny not.

As soon as they could master their Emotions and get control of their Voices, they told Josephine what they thought of her. They said she made the Good Samaritan look like a Cheap Criminal, and if she would only say the Word they would begin to put Ground Glass into the Food at Home. Then Josephine called them "Boys," which probably does not make a Hit with one who is on the sloping side of 48. More of the Men seemed to awake to the Fact that they were Overlooking something, so they came on the Velvet Foot back to the Dining Room and declared themselves In, and flocked around Josephine and called her "Josie" and "Joe." They didn't care. They were having a Pleasant Visit.

Josephine gave them Allopathic Slugs of the Size that they feed you in the Navy and then lower you into the Dingey and send you Ashore. Then she let them go out on the Porch to smoke. By the time the Lady President came to the last Page there were only two Men left in the Front room. One was Asleep and the other was Penned In.

The Women were Huffy. They went out to make the Men come in, and found them Bunched on the Porch listening to a Story that a Traveling Man had just brought to Town that Day.

Now the Plan was that during the Reception the Company would stand about in little Groups, and ask each other what Books they liked, and make it something on the order of a Salon. This Plan miscarried, because all the Men wanted to hear Rag Time played by Josephine, the Life-Saver. Josephine had to yield, and the Men all clustered around her to give their Moral Support. After one or two Selections, they felt sufficiently Keyed to begin to hit up those low-down Songs about Baby and Chickens and Razors. No one paid any Attention to the Lady President, who was off in a Corner holding an Indignation Meeting with the Secretary and the Vice-President.

When the Women began to sort out the Men and order them to start Home and all the Officers of the Club were giving Josephine the frosty Good Night, any one could see that there was Trouble ahead.

Next Day the Club held a Special Session and expelled Josephine for Conduct Unbecoming a Member, and Josephine sent Word to them as follows: "Rats."

Then the Men quietly got together and bought Josephine about a Thousand Dollars' Worth of American Beauty Roses to show that they were With her, and then Homes began to break up, and somebody started the Report that any-way it was the Lady President's Fault for having such a long and pokey Essay that wasn't hers at all, but had been Copied out of a Club Paper published in Detroit.

Before the next Meeting there were two Factions. The Lady President had gone to a Rest Cure, and the Meeting resolved itself into a good Cry and a general Smash-Up.

MORAL: *The only Literary Men are those who have to Work at it.*

Louisa May Alcott
(1832–88)

Transcendental Wild Oats

On the first day of June, 184–, a large wagon drawn by a small horse and containing a motley load, went lumbering over certain New England hills, with the pleasing accompaniments of wind, rain, and hail. A serene man with a serene child upon his knee was driving, or rather being driven, for the small horse had it all his own way. A brown boy with a William Penn style of countenance sat beside him, firmly embracing a bust of Socrates. Behind them was an energetic-looking woman, with a benevolent brow, satirical mouth, and eyes brimful of hope and courage. A baby reposed upon her lap, a mirror leaned against her knee, and a basket of provisions danced about her feet, as she struggled with a large, unruly umbrella. Two blue-eyed little girls, with hands full of childish treasures, sat under one old shawl, chatting happily together.

In front of this lively party stalked a tall, sharp-featured man, in a long blue cloak; and a fourth small girl trudged along beside him through the mud as if she rather enjoyed it.

The wind whistled over the bleak hills; the rain fell in a despondent drizzle, and twilight began to fall. But the calm man gazed as tranquilly into the fog as if he beheld a radiant bow of promise spanning the gray sky. The cheery woman tried to cover every one but herself with the big umbrella. The brown boy pillowed his head on the bald pate of Socrates and slumbered peacefully. The little girls sang lullabies to their dolls in soft, maternal murmurs. The sharp-nosed pedestrian marched steadily on, with the blue cloak streaming out behind him like a banner; and the lively infant splashed through the puddles with a ducklike satisfaction pleasant to behold.

Thus the modern pilgrims journeyed hopefully out of the old world, to found a new one in the wilderness.

The editors of the "Transcendental Tripod" had received from Messrs. Lion and Lamb (two of the aforesaid pilgrims) a communication from which the following statement is an extract;—

"We have made arrangements with the proprietor of an estate of about a hundred acres which liberates this tract from human ownership. Here we shall prosecute our effort to initiate a Family in harmony with the primitive instincts of man.

"Ordinary secular farming is not our object. Fruit, grain, pulse, herbs, flax, and other vegetable products, receiving assiduous attention, will afford ample manual occupation, and chaste supplies for the bodily needs. It is intended to adorn the pastures with orchards, and to supersede the labor of cattle by the spade and pruning-knife.

"Consecrated to human freedom, the land awaits the sober culture of devoted men. Beginning with small pecuniary means, this enterprise must be rooted in a reliance on the succors of an ever-bounteous Providence, whose vital affinities being secured by this union with uncorrupted fields and unworldly persons, the cares and injuries of a life of gain are avoided.

"The inner nature of each member of the Family is at no time neglected. Our plan contemplates all such disciplines, cultures, and habits as evidently conduce to the purifying of the inmates.

"Pledged to the spirit alone, the founders anticipate no hasty or numerous addition to their numbers. The kingdom of peace is entered only through the gates of self-denial; and felicity is the test and the reward of loyalty to the unswerving law of love."

This prospective Eden at present consisted of an old red farm-house, a dilapidated barn, many acres of meadow-land, and a grove. Ten ancient apple-trees were all the "chaste supply," which the place offered as yet; but in the firm belief that plenteous orchards were soon to be evoked from their inner consciousness, these sanguine founders had christened their domain Fruitlands.

Here Timon Lion intended to found a colony of Latter Day saints, who, under his patriarchal sway, should regenerate the world and glorify his name forever. Here Abel Lamb, with the devoutest faith in the high ideal which was to him a living truth, desired to plant a Paradise, where Beauty, Virtue, Justice and Love might live happily together, without the possibility of a serpent entering in. And here his wife, unconverted but faithful to the end, hoped, after many wanderings over the face of the earth, to find rest for herself and a home for her children.

"There is our new abode," announced the enthusiast, smiling with a satisfaction quite undamped by the drops dripping from his hat-brim, as they turned at length into a cart path that wound along a steep hillside into a barren-looking valley.

"A little difficult of access," observed his practical wife, as she endeavored to keep her various household goods from going overboard with every lurch of the laden ark.

"Like all good things. But those who earnestly desire, and patiently seek will soon find us," placidly responded the philosopher from the mud, through which he was now endeavoring to pilot the much-enduring horse.

"Truth lies at the bottom of a well, Sister Hope," said Brother Timon, pausing to detach his small comrade from a gate, whereon she was perched for a clearer gaze into futurity.

"That's the reason we so seldom get at it, I suppose," replied Mrs. Hope, making a vain clutch at the mirror, which a sudden jolt sent flying out of her hands.

"We want no false reflections here," said Timon, with a grim smile, as he crunched the fragments under foot in his onward march.

Sister Hope held her peace, and looked wistfully through the mist at her promised home. The old red house with a hospitable glimmer at its windows cheered her eyes; and considering the weather, was a fitter refuge than the sylvan bowers some of the more ardent souls might have preferred.

The new-comers were welcomed by one of the elect precious—a regenerate farmer, whose ideas of reform consisted chiefly in wearing white cotton raiment and shoes of untanned leather. This costume with a snowy beard, gave him a venerable, and at the same time a somewhat bridal appearance.

The goods and chattels of the society not having arrived, the weary family reposed before the fire on blocks of wood, while Brother Moses White regaled them on roasted potatoes, brown bread and water, in two plates, a tin pan, and one mug; his table service being limited. But, having cast the forms and vanities of a depraved world behind them, the elders welcomed hardship with the enthusiasm of new pioneers, and the children heartily enjoyed this foretaste of what they believed was to be a sort of perpetual picnic.

During the progress of this frugal meal, two more brothers appeared. One, a dark, melancholy man, clad in homespun, whose peculiar mission was to turn his name hind part before and use as few words as possible. The other was a blond, bearded Englishman, who expected to be saved by eating uncooked food and going without clothes. He had not yet adopted the primitive costume, however; but contented himself with meditatively chewing dry beans out of a basket.

"Every meal should be a sacrament, and the vessels used should be beautiful and symbolical," observed Brother Lamb, mildly, righting the tin pan slipping about on his knees. "I priced a silver service when in town, but it was too costly; so I got some graceful cups and vases of Britannia ware."

"Hardest things in the world to keep bright. Will whiting be allowed in the community?" inquired Sister Hope, with a housewife's interest in labor-saving institutions.

"Such trivial questions will be discussed at a more fitting time," answered Brother Timon, sharply, as he burnt his fingers with a very hot potato. "Neither sugar, molasses, milk, butter, cheese, nor flesh are to be used among us, for nothing is to be admitted which has caused wrong or death to man or beast."

"Our garments are to be linen till we learn to raise our own cotton or some substitute for woolen fabrics," added Brother Abel, blissfully basking in an imaginary future as warm and brilliant as the generous fire before him.

"Haou abaout shoes?" asked Brother Moses, surveying his own with interest.

"We must yield that point till we can manufacture an innocent substitute for leather. Bark, wood, or some durable fabric will be invented in time. Meanwhile, those who desire to carry out our idea to the fullest extent can go barefooted," said Lion, who liked extreme measures.

"I never will, nor let my girls," murmured rebellious Sister Hope, under her breath.

"Haow do you cattle'ate to treat the ten-acre lot? Ef things ain't 'tended to right smart, we shan't hev no crops," observed the practical patriarch in cotton.

"We shall spade it," replied Abel, in such perfect good faith that Moses said no more, though he indulged in a shake of the head as he glanced at hands that had held nothing heavier than a pen for years. He was a paternal old soul, and regarded the younger men as promising boys on a new sort of lark.

"What shall we do for lamps, if we cannot use any animal substance? I do hope light of some sort is to be thrown upon the enterprise," said Mrs. Lamb with anxiety, for in those days kerosene and camphene were not, and gas was unknown in the wilderness.

"We shall go without till we have discovered some vegetable oil or wax to serve us," replied Brother Timon, in a decided tone, which caused Sister Hope to resolve that her private lamp should always be trimmed, if not burning.

"Each member is to perform the work for which experience, strength and taste best fit him," continued Dictator Lion. "Thus drudgery and disorder will be avoided and harmony prevail. We shall rise at dawn, begin the day by bathing, followed by music, and then a chaste repast of fruit and bread. Each one finds congenial occupation until the meridian meal, when some deep-searching conversation gives rest to the body and development to the mind. Healthful labor again engages us till the last meal, when we assemble in social communion prolonged till sunset, when we retire to sweet repose, ready for the next day's activity."

"What part of the work do you incline to yourself?" asked Sister Hope, with a humorous glimmer in her keen eyes.

"I shall wait till it is made clear to me. Being in preference to doing is the great aim, and this comes to us rather by a resigned willingness than a wilful activity, which is a check to all divine growth," responded Brother Timon.

"I thought so." And Mrs. Lamb sighed audibly, for during the year he had spent in her family, Brother Timon had so faithfully carried out his idea of "being, not doing" that she had found his "divine growth" both an expensive and unsatisfactory process.

Here her husband struck into the conversation, his face shining with the light and joy of the splendid dreams and high ideals hovering before him.

"In these steps of reform, we do not rely so much on scientific reasoning, or physiological skill as on the spirit's dictates. The greater part of man's duty consists in leaving alone much that he now does. Shall I stimulate with tea, coffee, or wine? No. Shall I consume flesh? Not if I value health. Shall I subjugate cattle? Shall I claim property in any created thing? Shall I trade? Shall I adopt a form of religion? Shall I interest myself in politics? To how many of these questions,—could we ask them deeply enough—and could they be heard as having relation to our eternal welfare—would the response be 'Abstain'? "

A mild snore seemed to echo the last word of Abel's rhapsody, for Brother Moses had succumbed to mundane slumber and sat nodding like a massive ghost. Forest Absalom, the silent man, and John Pease, the English member, now departed to the barn; and Mrs. Lamb led her flock to a temporary fold, leaving the founders of the "Consociate Family" to build castles in the air till the fire went out and the symposium ended in smoke.

The furniture arrived next day, and was soon bestowed; for the principal property of the community consisted in books. To this rare library was devoted the best room in the house, and the few busts and pictures that still survived many flittings were added to beautify the sanctuary, for here the family was to meet for amusement, instruction, and worship.

Any housewife can imagine the emotions of Sister Hope, when she took possession of a large, dilapidated kitchen, containing an old stove and the peculiar stores out of which food was to be evolved for her little family of eleven. Cakes of maple sugar, dried peas and beans, barley and hominy, meal of all sorts, potatoes and dried fruits. No milk, butter, cheese, tea, or meat appeared. Even salt was considered a useless luxury and spice entirely forbidden by these lovers of Spartan simplicity. A ten years' experience of vegetarian vagaries had been good training for this new freak, and her sense of the ludicrous supported her through many trying scenes.

Unleavened bread, porridge and water for breakfast; bread, vegetables and water for dinner; bread, fruit and water for supper was the bill of fare ordained by the elders. No tea-pot profaned that sacred stove, no gory steak cried aloud for vengeance from her chaste gridiron; and only a brave woman's taste, time and temper were sacrificed on that domestic altar.

The vexed question of light was settled by buying a quantity of bayberry wax for candles; and, on discovering that no one knew how to make them, pine knots were introduced, to be used when absolutely necessary. Being summer, the evenings were not long, and the weary fraternity found it no great hardship to retire with the birds. The inner light was sufficient for most of them; but Mrs. Lamb rebelled. Evening was the only time she had to herself, and while the tired feet rested, the skilful hands mended torn frocks and little stockings, or anxious heart forgot its burdens in a book.

So "mother's lamp" burnt steadily, while the philosophers built a new heaven and earth by moonlight; and through all the metaphysical mists and philanthropic pyrotechnics of that period Sister Hope played her own little game of "throwing light," and none but the moths were the worse for it.

Such farming was probably never seen before since Adam delved. The band of brothers began by spading garden and field; but a few days of it lessened their ardor amazingly. Blistered hands and aching backs suggested the expediency of permitting the use of cattle till the workers were better fitted for noble toil by a summer of the new life.

Brother Moses brought a yoke of oxen from his farm—at least, the philosophers thought so till it was discovered that one of the animals was a cow; and Moses confessed that he "must be let down easy, for he couldn't live on garden sarse entirely."

Great was Dictator Lion's indignation at this lapse from virtue. But time pressed, the work must be done; so the meek cow was permitted to wear the yoke and the recreant brother continued to enjoy forbidden draughts in the barn, which dark proceeding caused the children to regard him as one set apart for destruction.

The sowing was equally peculiar, for owing to some mistake, the three brethren who devoted themselves to this graceful task, found when about half through the job that each had been sowing a different sort of grain in the same field; a mistake which caused much perplexity as it could not be remedied; but, after a long consultation, and a good deal of laughter, it was decided to say nothing and see what would come of it.

The garden was planted with a generous supply of useful roots and herbs; but, as manure was not allowed to profane the virgin soil, few of these vegetable treasures ever came up. Purslane reigned supreme, and the disappointed planters ate it philosophically, deciding that Nature knew what was best for them, and would generously supply their needs, if they could only learn to digest her "sallets" and wild roots.

The orchard was laid out, a little grafting done, new trees and vines set, regardless of the unfit season and entire ignorance of the husbandmen, who honestly believed that in the autumn they would reap a bounteous harvest.

Slowly things got into order, and rapidly rumors of the new experiment went abroad, causing many strange spirits to flock thither, for in those days communities were the fashion and transcendentalism raged wildly. Some came to look on and laugh, some to be supported in poetic idleness, a few to believe sincerely and work heartily. Each member was allowed to mount his favorite hobby, and ride it to his heart's content. Very queer were some of the riders, and very rampant some of the hobbies.

One youth, believing that language was of little consequence if the spirit was only right, startled newcomers by blandly greeting them with "Good-morning, damn you," and other remarks of an equally mixed order. A second irrepressible being held that all the emotions of the soul should be freely expressed, and illustrated his theory by antics that would have sent him to a lunatic asylum, if as an unregenerate wag said, he had not already been in one. When his spirit soared, he climbed trees and shouted; when doubt assailed him, he lay upon the floor and groaned lamentably. At joyful periods he raced, leaped and sang; when sad, he wept aloud; and when a great thought burst upon him in the watches of the night he crowed like a jocund cockerel, to the great delight of the children and the great annoyance of the elders. One musical brother fiddled whenever so moved, sang sentimentally to the four little girls, and put a music-box on the wall when he hoed corn.

Brother Pease ground away at his uncooked food, or browsed over the farm on sorrel, mint, green fruit, and new vegetables. Occasionally he took his walk abroad, airily attired in an unbleached cotton *poncho*, which was the nearest approach to the primeval costume he was allowed to indulge in. At midsummer he retired to the wilderness, to try his plan where the woodchucks were without prejudices and huckleberry bushes were hospitably full. A sunstroke unfortunately spoilt his plan, and he returned to semi-civilization a sadder and a wiser man.

Forest Absalom preserved his Pythagorean silence, cultivated his fine dark locks, and worked like a beaver, setting an excellent example of brotherly love, justice and fidelity by his upright life. He it was who helped overworked Sister Hope with her heavy washes, kneaded the endless succession of batches of bread, watched over the children, and did the many tasks left undone by the brethren who were so busy discussing and defining great duties that they forgot to perform the small ones.

Moses White patiently plodded about, "chorin' raound," as he called it, looking like an old-time patriarch, with his silver hair and flowing beard, and saving the community from many a mishap by his thrift and Yankee shrewdness.

Brother Lion domineered over the whole concern; for, having put the most money into the speculation, he was determined to make it pay—as if anything founded on an ideal basis could be expected to do so by any but enthusiasts.

Abel Lamb simply revelled in the Newness, firmly believing that his dream was to be beautifully realized, and in time, not only a little Fruitlands, but the whole earth be turned into a Happy Valley. He worked with every muscle of his body, for he was in deadly earnest. He taught with his whole head and heart;

planned and sacrificed, preached and prophesied, with a soul full of the purest as-
pirations, most unselfish purposes, and desires for a life devoted to God and man,
too high and tender to bear the rough usage of this world.

It was a little remarkable that only one woman ever joined this community.
Mrs. Lamb merely followed wherever her husband led,—"as ballast for his balloon," as she said in her bright way.

Miss Jane Gage was a stout lady of mature years, sentimental, amiable and lazy.
She wrote verse copiously, and had vague yearnings and graspings after the unknown, which led her to believe herself fitted for a higher sphere than any she
had yet adorned.

Having been a teacher, she was set to instructing the children in the common
branches. Each adult member took a turn at the infants; and, as each taught in his
own way, the result was a chronic state of chaos in the minds of these much afflicted innocents.

Sleep, food and poetic musings, were the desires of dear Jane's life, and she
shirked all duties as clogs upon her spirit's wings. Any thought of lending a hand
with the domestic drudgery, never occurred to her; and when to the question,
"Are there any beasts of burden on the place?" Mrs. Lamb answered, with a face
that told its own tale, "Only one woman!" the buxom Jane took no shame to
herself, but laughed at the joke, and let the stout-hearted sister tug on alone.

Unfortunately, the poor lady hankered after the flesh-pots, and endeavored to
stay herself with private sips of milk, crackers, and cheese, and on one dire occasion she partook of fish at a neighbor's table. One of the children reported this
sad lapse from virtue, and poor Jane was publicly reprimanded by Timon.

"I only took a little bit of the tail," sobbed the penitent poetess.

"Yes, but the whole fish had to be tortured and slain that you might tempt your
carnal appetite with one taste of the tail. Know ye not, consumers of flesh meat,
that ye are nourishing the wolf and tiger in your bosoms?"

At this awful question and the peal of laughter that arose from some of the
younger brethren, tickled by the ludicrous contrast between the stout sinner, the
stern judge, and the naughty satisfaction of the young detective, poor Jane fled
from the room to pack her trunk, and return to a world where fishes' tails were
not forbidden fruit.

Transcendental wild oats were sown broadcast that year, and the fame thereof
has not ceased in the land; for, futile as this crop seemed to outsiders, it bore an
invisible harvest, worth much to those who planted in earnest. As none of the
members of this particular community have ever recounted their experiences
before, a few of them may not be amiss, since the interest in these attempts has
never died out and Fruitlands was the most ideal of all these castles in Spain.

A new dress was invented, since cotton, silk and wool were forbidden as the
product of slave-labor, worm-slaughter, and sheep-robbery. Tunics and
trowsers of brown linen were the only wear. The women's skirts were longer,
and their straw hat-brims wider than the men's, and this was the only difference. Some persecution lent a charm to the costume, and the long-haired

linen-clad reformers quite enjoyed the mild martyrdom they endured when they left home. Money was abjured as the root of all evil. The produce of the land was to supply most of their wants, or to be exchanged for the few things they could not grow. This idea had its inconveniences; but self-denial was the fashion, and it was surprising how many things one could do without. When they desired to travel they walked, if possible, begged the loan of a vehicle, or boldly entered car or coach, and, stating their principles to the officials, took the consequences. Usually their dress, their earnest frankness, and gentle resolution won them a passage; but now and then they met with hard usage, and had the satisfaction of suffering for their principles.

On one of these penniless pilgrimages they took passage on a boat, and, when fare was demanded, artlessly offered to talk instead of pay. As the boat was well under way and they actually had not a cent, there was no help for it. So Brothers Lion and Lamb held forth to the assembled passengers in their most eloquent style. There must have been something effective in this conversation, for the listeners were moved to take up a contribution for these inspired lunatics, who preached peace on earth and good-will to man so earnestly, with empty pockets. A goodly sum was collected; but when the captain presented it the reformers proved that they were consistent even in their madness, for not a penny would they accept, saying, with a look at the group about them, whose indifference or contempt had changed to interest and respect, "You see how well we get on without money;" and so went serenely on their way, with their linen blouses flapping airily in the cold October wind.

They preached vegetarianism everywhere and resisted all temptations of the flesh, contentedly eating apples and bread at well-spread tables, and much afflicting hospitable hostesses by denouncing their food and taking away their appetites, discussing the "horrors of shambles," the "incorporation of the brute in man," and "on elegant abstinence the sign of a pure soul." But, when the perplexed or offended ladies asked what they should eat, they got in reply a bill of fare consisting of "bowls of sunrise for breakfast," "solar seeds of the sphere," "dishes from Plutarch's chaste table," and other viands equally hard to find in any modern market.

Reform conventions of all sorts were haunted by these brethren, who said many wise things and did many foolish ones. Unfortunately, these wanderings interfered with their harvests at home; but the rule was to do what the spirit moved, so they left their crops to Providence, and went a-reaping in wider, and, let us hope, more fruitful fields than their own. Luckily the earthly Providence who watched over Abel Lamb was at hand to glean the scanty crop yielded by the "uncorrupted land" which, "consecrated to human freedom," had received "the sober culture of devout men."

About the time the grain was ready to house, some call of the Oversoul wafted all the men away. An easterly storm was coming up and the yellow stacks were sure to be ruined. Then Sister Hope gathered her forces. Three little girls, one boy (Timon's son), and herself, harnessed to clothes-baskets and Russia-linen sheets, were the only teams she could command; but with these poor appliances the indomitable woman got in the grain and saved food for her young, with the instinct and energy of a mother-bird with a brood of hungry nestlings to feed.

This attempt at regeneration had its tragic as well as its comic side, though the world saw only the former.

With the first frosts, the butterflies, who had sunned themselves in the new light through the summer, took flight, leaving the few bees to see what honey they had stored for winter use. Precious little appeared beyond the satisfaction of a few months of holy living. At first it seemed as if a chance of holy dying also was to be offered them. Timon, much disgusted with the failure of the scheme, decided to retire to the Shakers, who seemed to be the only successful community going.

"What is to become of us?" asked Mrs. Hope, for Abel was heart-broken at the bursting of his lovely bubble.

"You can stay here, if you like, till a tenant is found. No more wood must be cut however, and no more corn ground. All I have must be sold to pay the debts of the concern, as the responsibility rests with me," was the cheering reply.

"Who is to pay us for what we have lost? I gave all I had—furniture, time, strength, six months of my children's lives,—and all are wasted. Abel gave himself body and soul, and is almost wrecked by hard work and disappointment. Are we to have no return for this, but left to starve and freeze in an old house, with winter at hand, no money, and hardly a friend left, for this wild scheme has alienated nearly all we had. You talk much about justice. Let us have a little, since there is nothing else left."

But the woman's appeal met with no reply but the old one: "It was an experiment. We all risked something, and must bear our losses as we can."

With this cold comfort, Timon departed with his son, and was absorbed into the Shaker brotherhood, where he soon found that the order of things was reversed, and it was all work and no play.

Then the tragedy began for the forsaken little family. Desolation and despair fell upon Abel. As his wife said, his new beliefs had alienated many friends. Some thought him mad, some unprincipled. Even the most kindly thought him a visionary, whom it was useless to help till he took more practical views of life. All stood aloof, saying, "Let him work out his own ideas, and see what they are worth."

He had tried, but it was a failure. The world was not ready for Utopia yet, and those who attempted to found it got only laughed at for their pains. In other days, men could sell all and give to the poor, lead lives devoted to holiness and high thought, and, after the persecution was over, find themselves honored as saints or martyrs. But in modern times these things are out of fashion. To live for one's principles, at all costs, is a dangerous speculation; and the failure of an ideal, no matter how humane and noble, is harder for the world to forgive and forget than bank robbery or the grand swindles of corrupt politicians.

Deep waters now for Abel, and for a time there seemed no passage through. Strength and spirits were exhausted by hard work and too much thought. Courage failed, when, looking about for help, he saw no sympathizing face, no hand outstretched to help him, no voice to say cheerily,—"We all make mistakes, and it takes many experiences to shape a life. Try again, and let us help you."

Every door was closed, every eye averted, every heart cold, and no way open whereby he might earn bread for his children. His principles would not permit him to do many things that others did; and in the few fields where conscience would allow him to work, who would employ a man who had flown in the face of society as he had done?

Then this dreamer, whose dream was the life of his life, resolved to carry out his idea to the bitter end. There seemed no place for him here,—no work, no friend. To go begging conditions was as ignoble as to go begging money. Better perish of want than sell one's soul for the sustenance of his body. Silently he lay down upon his bed, turned his face to the wall, and waited with pathetic patience for death to cut the knot which he could not untie. Days and nights went by, and neither food or water passed his lips. Soul and body were dumbly struggling together, and no word of complaint betrayed what either suffered. His wife, when tears and prayers were unavailing, sat down to wait the end with a mysterious awe and submission; for in this entire resignation of all things there was an eloquent significance to her who knew him as no other human being did.

"Leave all to God," was his belief; and, in this crisis the loving soul clung to this faith, sure that the All-wise Father would not desert this child who tried to live so near to him. Gathering her children about her she waited the issue of the tragedy that was being enacted in that solitary room, while the first snow fell outside untrodden by the footprints of a single friend.

But the strong angels who sustain and teach perplexed souls came and went, leaving no trace without, but working miracles within. For, when all other sentiments had faded into dimness, all other hopes died utterly; when the bitterness of death was nearly over, when body was past any pang of hunger or thirst, and soul stood ready to depart, the love that outlives all else refused to die. Head had bowed to defeat, hand had grown weary with heavy tasks, but heart could not grow cold to those who lived in its tender depths, even when death touched it.

"My faithful wife, my little girls,—they have not forsaken me, they are mine by ties that none can break. What right have I to leave them alone? What right to escape from the burden and sorrow I have helped to bring? This duty remains to me, and I must do it manfully. For their sakes, the world will forgive me in time; for their sakes, God will sustain me now."

Too feeble to rise, Abel groped for the food that always lay within his reach, and in the darkness and solitude of that memorable night, ate and drank what was to him the bread and wine of a new communion, a new dedication of heart and life to the duties that were left him when the dreams fled.

In the early dawn, when that sad wife crept fearfully to see what change had come to the patient face on the pillow, she saw it smiling at her, and heard a feeble voice cry out bravely, "Hope!"

What passed in that little room is not to be recorded except in the hearts of those who suffered and endured much for love's sake. Enough for us to know that soon the wan shadow of a man came forth, leaning on the arm that never failed him, to be welcomed and cherished by the children, who never forgot the experiences of that time.

"Hope" was the watchword now; and while the last log blazed on the hearth, the last bread and apples covered the table, the new commander, with recovered courage, said to her husband,—

"Leave all to God—and me. He has done his part; now I will do mine."

"But we have no money, dear."

"Yes, we have. I sold all we could spare, and have enough to take us away from this snow-bank."

"Where can we go?"

"I have engaged four rooms at our good neighbor's, Lovejoy. There we can live cheaply till spring. Then for new plans, and a home of our own, please God."

"But, Hope, your little store won't last long, and we have no friends."

"I can sew, and you can chop wood. Lovejoy offers you the same pay as he gives his other men; my old friend, Mrs. Truman will send me all the work I want; and my blessed brother stands by us to the end. Cheer up, dear heart, for while there is work and love in the world we shall not suffer."

"And while I have my good angel, Hope, I shall not despair, even if I wait another thirty years before I step beyond the circle of the sacred little world in which I have still a place to fill."

So one bleak December day, with their few possessions piled on an ox-sled, the rosy children perched a-top, and the parents trudging arm in arm behind, the exiles left their Eden and faced the world again.

"Ah, me! My happy dream! How much I leave behind that can never be mine again," said Abel, looking back at the lost Paradise, lying white and chill, in its shroud of snow.

"Yes, dear; but how much we bring away," answered brave-hearted Hope, glancing from husband to children.

"Poor Fruitlands! The name was as great a failure as the rest!" continued Abel, with a sigh, as a frostbitten apple fell from a leafless bough at his feet.

But the sigh changed to a smile, as his wife added, in a half-tender, half-satirical tone,—

"Don't you think that Apple Slump would be a better name for it, dear?"

Woody Allen
(Contemporary)

FROM *Without Feathers*

From The Scrolls

And the man sewed on to all his shirts a small alligator symbol and lo and behold, suddenly his merchandise moved like gangbusters, and there was much rejoicing while amongst his enemies there was wailing and gnashing of teeth, and one said, "The Lord is merciful. He maketh me to lie down in green pastures. The problem is, I can't get up."

LAWS AND PROVERBS

Doing abominations is against the law, particularly if the abominations are done while wearing a lobster bib.

The lion and the calf shall lie down together but the calf won't get much sleep.

Whosoever shall not fall by the sword or by famine, shall fall by pestilence so why bother shaving?

The wicked at heart probably know something.

Whosoever loveth wisdom is righteous but he that keepeth company with fowl is weird.

My Lord, my Lord! What hast Thou done, lately?

Regina Barreca
(Contemporary)

FROM *They Used to Call Me Snow White . . . But I Drifted*

. . . [T]he real shock came in the classroom, where I was often one of two or three women. One professor, I remember, always prefaced calling on me or any other woman in the class by asking "Miss Barreca, *as a woman,* what is your reading of this text?" I was profoundly embarrassed to be asked my opinion as a woman, since it seemed somehow less authoritative than being asked my opinion as a student or as a "general" reader. At first, I jokingly replied that I would be happy to answer "as a person," but that it was hard for me to answer as a woman. When the professor didn't so much as smile, I knew that tactic wouldn't work. Every time I raised my hand to answer a question, I was asked my opinion *as a woman.* It frustrated and angered me, because I wanted to be treated as an individual and not as a representative of a group.

It took months to understand that, in the eyes of this teacher, I'd always be a "miss" rather than just another, ordinary student. When I realized that there was no alternative, I figured I'd go with it, exaggerate the situation enough so that I could at least enjoy myself. So I started prefacing every answer with the phrase "As a woman, I think Shakespeare means . . . ," "As a woman, it strikes me that Tennyson's point is . . .". But then I figured, why stop at this? I started to say "As a woman, I think the weather's rather cold for June." "As a woman, I think I'll have the meatloaf for dinner." "As a woman, I think I'll go to bed early tonight." It started out as a joke, but as it caught on (a number of my friends started to use the same strategy to make the professors and guys in general hear how their remarks sounded), we started to examine further. Maybe we really were always speaking as a woman. Maybe there was no such thing as speaking as "just" a person. Maybe we always spoke as women whenever we spoke. Maybe this joke wasn't such a joke.

So that even as I stopped saying "As a woman, I believe such-and-such," I started thinking it. It occurred to me that nothing was neuter or neutral. I saw that my responses were in part determined by the fact of my gender—as well as by other factors, like my class and ethnicity. I didn't read novels about war in the same way a man would, for example, since I hadn't been brought up to consider going to war as a soldier as a possible future for myself. I hadn't played war games as a kid, I didn't find the idea of war engaging. It did not have "universal appeal," since it didn't appeal to me, a narcissistic but nevertheless compelling argument. In the same way that the male students complained that Jane Austen was obviously a second-rate writer because all she was interested in was marriage (Mark Twain once said that it was "a pity they let her die a natural death"), so I decided to assert that Hemingway's concern for bullfighting was no concern for an intelligent, insightful woman. Of what interest is bullfighting to the contemporary female reader? Hemingway was therefore second-rate, by their definition, since his subject matter had limited appeal and seemed gender specific. I learned to answer "Of course" when asked whether I responded to things as a female. I learned to accept that and even enjoyed discovering the ways in which my viewpoint differed from the perspective offered by my male peers.

FROM *The Hartford Courant*

Not-So-Evident Truths That Deserve Attention

Aunt Gina's Guide to 27 Truths You Might Not Want to Know But You Should Hear Anyway:

1. Some of us did not stop breaking out when we got through adolescence.
     Some of us did not stop breaking out when we got through menopause.
2. When you say, "My coworkers are just like family," you do not necessarily have to mean it in a nice way.
3. Forget grapes and nectar: Baked macaroni and cheese is the food of the gods.
4. "Missy" is not a flattering name for a section of retail clothing space designed to attract the adult female.
5. Very few couples can stay friends after a breakup if there is not a secret desire on the part of one of them to become lovers again.
6. Great satisfaction can be obtained by reading a paperback or magazine while taking a bubble bath on a cold afternoon.
7. Women are not taking over the workplace, despite mutterings of disgruntled troglodytes; we still make, on average, 68 cents on a man's dollar.
8. "Journaling" is not a word. If you want to be a writer, one of the first things you should know is the following: Do not make up verbs.

9. Almost nobody over the age of 18 months looks attractive in baby blue.
10. The important part of "step-parent" is "parent."
11. If there are no longer any remaining surfaces in your home upon which you can stencil and this worries you, you need to get out and volunteer someplace.
12. Men are not the only ones to admire the physiques of 19-year-olds of the opposite sex. Women just immediately say something like "Oh, he'd be great for my niece" in order not to sound like Blanche DuBois. It is not that we do not notice.
13. "Go easy on the eyeliner" is always good advice.
14. Cats purr even when they are nervous. What seems like an expression of pleasure might not always be exactly that.
15. Nicole Kidman should not suddenly be considered a great actress or a grande dame of the theater because she wore a nose made out of putty.
16. Tablecloths are meant to have things spilled on them. Towels are meant to be wiped on. Carpets are meant to be walked on. Dishes are meant to be eaten off of. If you have whole hunks of your house that should be specially lighted and kept under glass rather than used, get a silk rope and a sign that says "for display purposes only" but for heaven's sake, do not make other people (especially those people in your immediate family) feel guilty if they do not believe life should be lived under museum conditions.
17. George Gissing's novel *New Grub Street* and George Orwell's novel *Keep the Aspidistra Flying* are mandatory reading for anybody who aspires to write for a living. Skip the workbooks. Buy these. Read them every two years or so.
18. Everybody starts to conserve toilet paper when it's getting near the end of the roll.
19. Being nice to people—however spiritually and emotionally satisfying—guarantees only one thing: People will ask you to be nice to them again. It does not mean they will be nice to you.
20. Worrying about retaining water is important only if you are a boat.
21. Everyone who accepts second best actually knows, somewhere in his or her midnight heart, that second best is not good enough. This is true whether it is second best in love, in work or in expectation. To tell yourself that what you have is what you want when it is not will, eventually, corrode your soul. Be careful.
22. When you grow up without much money, buying your first washing machine is one of the deepest and most gratifying moments in life. You will never have to wash your pillowcases right after a stranger has washed his sneakers. It is worth working overtime to make this happen.
23. Everybody hopes that something wonderful will appear in the mail.

24. More women look like Kathy Bates than Farrah Fawcett. And more men look like Peter Boyle than Pierce Brosnan. Almost nobody looks like anyone you see on a screen who is under the age of 40, not even the people themselves.
25. Just because you are good at it does not mean you have to do it.
26. Even if you are self-contained, it does not mean you are invulnerable. Consider the egg.
27. Trust everyone, but cut the cards.

Thank God I'm A Middle-Aged Broad

Remember the John Denver song "Thank God I'm a Country Boy"? I want to write a new version: "Thank God I'm a Middle-Aged Broad."

I want to give thanks that I can be invisible when I want to be—I am in no danger of being evaluated as potential date material by guys in restaurants, at the supermarket or on the beach.

I no longer even worry about buying a bathing suit. Women of 46 could wear googly-eye glasses and spangles and carry swords on a beach and not be noticed.

I used to feel a little sad about this, remembering earlier days when it was sort of fun to be observed and appreciated as a young creature of my species. These days I am just happy to smear on the suntan lotion without wondering if I'll look dorky. I know I look dorky, but nobody else does because I am practically a stealth sunbather.

When you think about it, you realize that the only ones eyeing middle-aged women are other middle-aged women wondering, "Ohmygawd, do I look like *that?*"

I suggest that we reduce all sorts of tension by merely being more generous to our comrades. We could look at each other and think, "Isn't she brave to wear a suit without a full-support cup!" and applaud courage when we see it.

Because we are the only ones who will see it.

Life gets easier as you get older, if you do it right.

For years I wondered how I would look in the latest fashions. Not anymore. I wear what fits me. I have what no longer fits me professionally altered.

When I can't alter it anymore, I give it away. As a teenager, I bought all my clothes at thrift shops and wondered whose they were. As a middle-aged lady, I give my clothes to thrift shops and wonder whose they will become.

As you get older, you might also forget what it is like to be young or even to be around youngsters on a regular basis. It is healthful, I believe, to be reminded.

I was invited by one of my most remarkable former students to give a talk at the high school where she teaches. I was to give a short speech as part of a celebration for their honor students. Even though this is the busiest time of year in terms of both teaching and talking to outside groups, I accepted her invitation because I was enormously proud of the work she was doing—and because it had been a while since I talked in a school cafeteria.

When I got there, I remembered why it had been a long time since I talked in a school cafeteria.

(And I was simultaneously reminded of an undeniable fact that is nevertheless too often overlooked: The world, with all its kingdoms, does not contain enough money to pay teachers the salary they deserve. Whatever they are getting as pay should be instantly doubled. And if they work at a school where the hall monitors need to be armed, then their pay should be quintupled, and we should build their houses for them during our days off.)

What was this school like? This perfectly friendly, ordinary institution?

Hormones careened off the cinderblock walls. You could hear hearts beating and hearts breaking and hearts skipping a beat. In the tenth-grade class alone, there were girls who looked 12 and others who looked 27. There were boys who looked like cherubs and others who looked like extras from *Gladiator*.

I got up to the little podium to speak. Most of the kids were smiling and cheerful. But a small clot of students formed over to one side. They were already bored, before I even opened my mouth, and did not stop speaking even after I started. I used to be one of those kids. I know their M.O.

If I were younger, I might have been disheartened because I would have wanted them all to like me. Now all I wanted was for them to shut up. I stopped midsentence, announcing, "You need to be quiet now, OK?" and waited. They probably didn't join my fan club, but they no longer distracted me, meaning their classmates got a better talk.

As a middle-aged woman, you don't get observed, you don't get evaluated, you don't worry about whether everyone will love you. You simply do the best you can, knowing that is just fine.

Thank God I'm a middle-aged broad.

Why Do I Feel Guilty? Let Me Count The Ways

Nobody *likes* guilt, but many of us have it.

Sort of like cable.

Knowing in advance that I needed to write this column, I kept track during the week of my numerous occasions of guilt. Disappointingly, perhaps, they are different from occasions of sin. My list of what makes me feel guilty includes:

- Eating.
- Drinking.
- Sleeping.
- Talking on the telephone.
- Purchasing a copy of a tabloid because I started reading it on line at the supermarket checkout counter.

- Preferring *People* over *The New Yorker* (I refer here to the magazines, not to groups or individuals).
- Actually despising The *New Yorker*, especially the coy little insider pieces.
- Reading my horoscope before I read the news.
- Not reading all of the news.
- Not flossing.
- Not wearing sunscreen.
- Not insisting that my aged father live with us even though he does not want to.
- Not writing enough.
- Not exercising.
- Not meditating.
- Not gardening.
- Not having an organized closet.
- Not liking a movie recommended by a friend.
- Not wearing an outfit I bought last summer, having convinced myself that I could wear it year after year.
- Not letting my cats go outside, even though they would immediately be eaten by coyotes.
- Being wrong.
- Being right.
- Driving a non-earth-friendly vehicle.
- Purchasing coffee instead of making perfectly good coffee at home.
- Letting the water run so that it gets cold instead of having a bottle of cold water in the fridge.
- Dropping a paperback into the bath (while taking a bath, not as a critical comment).
- Snacking on foods containing trans-fatty acids, or transacid fatties, or whatever.
- Waking up early.
- Going to bed late.
- Buying mascara.
- Hating magical realism.
- Enjoying a cheeseburger.
- Not choosing to reuse towels at a hotel.
- Not sending a wedding gift in time for a bridal shower.
- Not sending a baby gift in time to a baby shower (different people).
- Not sending a baby gift in a timely fashion to the grandchild of good friends (happily part of yet another family) to receive the gift before he starts elementary school. Or law school, for that matter.
- Having written only half a sympathy letter to a friend whose sister died recently.
- Hating rhubarb.

- When dialing a company or service, always hitting "O" on the phone immediately, instead of "listening carefully" to the various options on the "menu which has recently changed" so that I get to speak to a live person.
- Being secretly glad that a male friend broke up with the long-term girlfriend I didn't like even though I never said I didn't like her.
- Snoring.

And this is a list compiled by a woman who considers herself relatively guilt-free. From a woman who is *far* from being a perfectionist. This is from a person who has worked on ridding herself of guilt. Years of therapy. Medication. Workshops. By a woman who feels guilty for talking about herself in the third person and so will now stop that horrible affectation. That's better.

OK, here's the tricky part: The idea of condemning yourself (or somebody else condemning you, causing you to accept their judgment and thereby "making" you feel bad) depends on the premise that you could have acted otherwise—that you could have behaved better. That you had a choice.

So I am free to feel guilt about my poor record on flossing and shower gifts, for example, while liberating myself from guilt concerning my instinctive dislike of rhubarb and *The New Yorker*. I cannot stop snoring or sleeping or eating, but I should finish that letter to the bereaved friend who won't mind one bit if it is late (and accept that feeling silly is my embarrassment kicking in, not her disappointed expectations), and perhaps I should think carefully before buying another gas-gobbling car.

Maybe the two most important things to remember about guilt are that: 1. guilt is neither a substitute for behaving better nor an antidote for having behaved badly; 2. it is something one does to oneself. Everybody knows the great line from Eleanor Roosevelt— "Nobody can make me feel inferior without my consent"—but it can also be applied to guilt: Nobody can make you feel guilty without your consent.

Instead of feeling guilty, stop doing what makes you feel bad. Or learn that, since you cannot act differently (if, indeed, that is true and not just an excuse—see the "rhubarb" example above), then accept it and deal with it. Do not celebrate your inner martyr—it's not your best feature.

Dave Barry
(Contemporary)

FROM *Dave Barry's Greatest Hits*

The Lesson of History

The difficult thing about studying history is that, except for Harold Stassen, everybody who knows anything about it firsthand is dead. This means that our only source of historical information is historians, who are useless because they keep changing everything around.

For example, I distinctly remember learning in fifth grade that the Civil War was caused by slavery. So did you, I bet. As far as I was concerned, this was an excellent explanation for the Civil War, the kind you could remember and pass along as an important historical lesson to your grandchildren. ("Gather 'round boys and girls, while Grandpa tells you what caused the Civil War. Slavery. Now go fetch Grandpa some more bourbon.")

Then one day in high school, out of the blue, a history teacher named Anthony Sabella told me that the Civil War was caused by economic factors. I still think this was a lie, and not just because Anthony Sabella once picked me up by my neck. I mean, today we have more economic factors than ever before, such as the Dow Jones Industrial Average, but you don't see the North and the South fighting each other, do you? Which is good, because the South has 96 percent of the nation's armed pickup trucks, whereas the North mainly has Fitness Centers, so it would be over in minutes.

DISCUSSION QUESTION: What kind of a name is "Dow" Jones? *Explain.*

Nevertheless, I had to pretend I thought the Civil War was caused by economic factors, or I never would have escaped from Mr. Sabella's class and got into college, where the history professors sneered openly at the primitive high-school-teacher notion that the Civil War had been caused by anything so obvious as economic factors. No, they said, the Civil War was caused by acculturalized regionalism. Or maybe it was romantic transcendentalism, or behavioristic naturalism, or structuralized functionalism. I learned hundreds of terms like these in college, and I no longer even vaguely remember what they mean. As far as I know, any one of them could have caused the Civil War. Maybe we should lock them all in a small room and deny them food and water until one of them confesses.

DISCUSSION QUESTION: Was the author "just kidding" when he made that last "off-the-wall" suggestion? Cite specific examples.

What is the cause of all this disagreement among the experts over basic historical issues? Economic factors. If you're a historian and you want to write a best-selling book, you have to come up with a new wrinkle. If you go to a publisher and say you want to write that Harry Truman was a blunt-spoken Missourian who made some unpopular decisions but was vindicated by history, the publisher will pick you up by your neck and toss you into the street, because there are already bales of such books on the market. But if you claim to have uncovered evidence that Harry Truman was a Soviet ballerina, before long you'll be on national morning television, answering earnest questions from David Hartman in a simulated living room.

DISCUSSION QUESTION: Don't you think David Hartman is just a little *too* avuncular? Why?

So I propose that we laypersons forget about historians and agree among ourselves to believe in a permanent set of historical facts once and for all. Specifically, I propose we use the facts contained in a book I found in my basement recently, called *Civilization Past and Present*, which was apparently one of my wife's high-school textbooks.

DISCUSSION QUESTION: Did she steal it? Or what?

Civilization Past and Present combines the advantage of having a snappy title with the advantage of ending in 1962, just before history starts to get really depressing. It's easy to understand, because my wife has underlined all the important words and phrases (*Germany*, for example). And it doesn't beat around the bush. For example, on page 599 it makes the following statement in plain black and white: "The causes of the American Civil War are complex."

Since some of you laypersons out there may not have *Civilization Past and Present* in your basements, here's a brief summary to tide you over until you can get your own copies:

HISTORY
5,000,000,000 B.C.–1962

After the Earth cooled, it formed an extremely fertile crescent containing primitive people such as the Hittites who believed in just the stupidest things you ever heard of. Then came Greece and Rome, followed by Asia. All of this came to a halt during the Middle Ages, which were caused by the Jutes and featured the following terms underlined by my wife: *the steward, the bailiff, and the reeve*. Next the Turks got way the hell over into France, after which there were towns. And the Magna Carta. Then France and England fought many wars that involved dates such as 1739 and were settled by the Treaty of Utrecht, which also was used to harness water power. By then the seeds had been sown for several World Wars and the Louisiana Purchase, but fortunately we now have a fairly peaceful atom. Now go fetch Grandpa some more bourbon.

DEFINE THE FOLLOWING: "Avuncular."

Read This First

Congratulations! You have purchased an extremely fine device that would give you thousands of years of trouble-free service, except that you undoubtedly will destroy it via some typical bonehead consumer maneuver. Which is why we ask you to PLEASE FOR GOD'S SAKE READ THIS OWNER'S MANUAL CAREFULLY BEFORE YOU UNPACK THE DEVICE. YOU ALREADY UNPACKED IT, DIDN'T YOU? YOU UN-PACKED IT AND PLUGGED IT IN AND TURNED IT ON AND FIDDLED WITH THE KNOBS, AND NOW YOUR CHILD, THE SAME CHILD WHO ONCE SHOVED A POLISH SAUSAGE INTO YOUR VIDEOCASSETTE RECORDER AND SET IT ON "FAST FORWARD," THIS CHILD ALSO IS FIDDLING WITH THE KNOBS, RIGHT? AND YOU'RE JUST STARTING TO READ THE INSTRUCTIONS, RIGHT??? WE MIGHT AS WELL JUST BREAK ALL THESE DEVICES RIGHT AT THE FACTORY BEFORE WE SHIP THEM OUT, YOU KNOW THAT?

We're sorry. We just get a little crazy sometimes, because we're always getting back "defective" merchandise where it turns out that the consumer inadvertently bathed the device in acid for six days. So, in writing these instructions, we naturally tend to assume that your skull is filled with dead insects, but we mean nothing by it. OK? Now let's talk about:

1. UNPACKING THE DEVICE: The device is encased in foam to protect it from the Shipping People, who like nothing more than to jab spears into the outgoing boxes. PLEASE INSPECT THE CONTENTS CARE-FULLY FOR GASHES OR IDA MAE BARKER'S ENGAGEMENT RING WHICH SHE LOST LAST WEEK, AND SHE THINKS MAYBE IT WAS WHILE SHE WAS PACKING DEVICES. Ida Mae really wants that ring back, because it is her only proof of engagement, and her fiancé, Stuart, is now seriously considering backing out on the whole thing inasmuch as he had consumed most of a bottle of Jim Beam in Quality Control when he decided to pop the question. It is not without irony that Ida Mae's last name is "Barker," if you get our drift.

   WARNING: DO NOT EVER AS LONG AS YOU LIVE THROW AWAY THE BOX OR ANY OF THE PIECES OF STYROFOAM, EVEN THE LITTLE ONES SHAPED LIKE PEANUTS.

   If you attempt to return the device to the store, and you are missing one single peanut, the store personnel will laugh in the chilling manner exhibited by Joseph Stalin just after he enslaved Eastern Europe. Besides the device, the box should contain:

   • Eight little rectangular snippets of paper that say: "WARNING."
   • A plastic packet containing four ⁵⁄₁₇" pilfer grommets and two chub-ended ⁶⁄₃" boxcar prawns.

   YOU WILL NEED TO SUPPLY: a matrix wrench and 60,000 feet of tram cable.

IF ANYTHING IS DAMAGED OR MISSING: You *immediately* should turn to your spouse and say: "Margaret, you know why this country can't make a car that can get all the way through the drive-thru at Burger King without a major transmission overhaul? Because nobody cares, that's why." (Warning: This Is Assuming Your Spouse's Name Is Margaret.)

2. PLUGGING IN THE DEVICE: The plug on this device represents the latest thinking of the electrical industry's Plug Mutation Group, which, in the continuing effort to prevent consumers from causing hazardous electrical current to flow through their appliances, developed the Three-Pronged Plug, then the Plug Where One Prong Is Bigger Than the Other. Your device is equipped with the revolutionary new Plug Whose Prongs Consist of Six Small Religious Figurines Made of Chocolate. DO NOT TRY TO PLUG IT IN! Lay it gently on the floor near an outlet, but out of direct sunlight, and clean it weekly with a damp handkerchief.

WARNING: WHEN YOU ARE LAYING THE PLUG ON THE FLOOR, DO NOT HOLD A SHARP OBJECT IN YOUR OTHER HAND AND TRIP OVER THE CORD AND POKE YOUR EYE OUT, AS THIS COULD VOID YOUR WARRANTY.

3. OPERATION OF THE DEVICE:

WARNING: WE MANUFACTURE ONLY THE ATTRACTIVE DESIGNER CASE. THE ACTUAL WORKING CENTRAL PARTS OF THE DEVICE ARE MANUFACTURED IN JAPAN. THE INSTRUCTIONS WERE TRANSLATED BY MRS. SHIRLEY PELTWATER OF ACCOUNTS RECEIVABLE, WHO HAS NEVER ACTUALLY BEEN TO JAPAN BUT DOES HAVE MOST OF *SHOGUN* ON TAPE.

INSTRUCTIONS: For results that can be the finest, it is our advising that: Never to hold these buttons two times!! Except the battery. Next, taking the (something) earth section may cause a large occurrence! However. If this is not a trouble, such rotation is a very maintenance action, as a kindly (something) viewpoint from Drawing B.

4. WARRANTY: Be it hereby known that this device, together with but not excluding all those certain parts thereunto, shall be warranted against all defects, failures, and malfunctions as shall occur between now and Thursday afternoon at shortly before 2, during which time the Manufacturer will, at no charge to the Owner, send the device to our Service People, who will emerge from their caves and engage in rituals designed to cleanse it of evil spirits. This warranty does not cover the attractive designer case.

WARNING: IT MAY BE A VIOLATION OF SOME LAW THAT MRS. SHIRLEY PELT-WATER HAS *SHOGUN* ON TAPE.

Lynda Barry
(Contemporary)

★ ★ ★

FROM *Down the Street*

LOVE ADVENTURE

LYNDA "I'M A HOG FOR YOU" BARRY © 1987

THERE WERE THESE VERY POPULAR BUSHES IN OUR NEIGHBORHOOD WHERE PRACTICALLY EVERY-ONE ON THE PLANET GOT THEIR FIRST KISS. ME AND DEENA SAID WE GOT OURS THERE TOO BY SOMEBODY'S COUSIN FROM IDAHO BUT IT WAS A LIE. WE HAD NEVER KISSED NO ONE.

NO ONE'S EVER GONNA KISS US MAN. AND NOBODY EVEN BELIEVES US ABOUT THAT GUY FROM IDAHO EITHER. WHO'D EVER KISS A GUY FROM IDAHO?

AT LEAST WE'RE NOT SLUTS.

SO?

WE TRIED TO COPY THE SENSUOUS LOOKS THAT MAKE A MAN HYPNOTISED AS SEEN ON T.V. AND IN OUR OPINION WE GOT THOSE LOOKS PERFECTED.

WHEN I FINALLY GOT MY FIRST KISS AND DEENA GOT HERS WE COULD NOT HELP BUT FEEL A CERTAIN ELEMENT OF DISAP-POINTMENT. WE COULD NOT EXPLAIN EXACTLY WHERE THIS FEELING CAME FROM AND NEITHER DID WE KNOW THAT WE WOULD SPEND THE NEXT TWENTY YEARS TRYING TO FIND OUT.

WELL HOW COME AFTER THEY KISSED US THEY START ACTING LIKE THEY DON'T EVEN LIKE US ANYMORE?

BECAUSE GUYS ARE STUPID.

THEN HOW COME WE STILL LIKE THEM?

I DON'T KNOW YET.

WE TRIED THEM OUT AT PARTIES BUT AS IT TURNED OUT THE GUYS OUR AGE WERE NOT AS SOPHISTICATED AS WE WERE.

YOU GUYS BEEN AT THE AQUARIUM OR SOMETHING?

I DON'T GET IT.

IS THIS SOME KIND OF DARE?

JUMP SHOT

BY LYNDA BOLD SOUL SISTER BARRY © 1988

THE TEENAGER NAME OF RICHARD COMES OUT LATE SOME NIGHTS TO SHOOT BASKETS ON OUR CORNER. YOU CAN WATCH HIM FROM MY BEDROOM WINDOW.

YOU CAN LAY ON THE BED AND HEAR THE BALL, THE PING PING OF IT AGAINST THE STREET BOUNCING. YOU CAN HEAR HIM WALK IT, THEN RUN IT AND DO HIS PERFECT HOOK SHOT.

BOUNCE, BOUNCE, BOUNCE, STOP. THE FAST NO-SOUND OF HIS FEET IN THE AIR, THE BALL FLYING UP, PAUSE, THEN WHAM-WHAM AGAINST THE BACK BOARD, A HIGH BOUNCE OFF THE RIM, HIM WHISPERING SON OF A BITCH.

HIM JUMPING UP ON THE CORNER, HIM JUMPING HIGH AND TURNING IN THE AIR UNDER A STREET LIGHT WITH A THOUSAND MILLION BUGS FLYING AROUND IT GOING WILD, WILD, WILD.

Robert Benchley
(1889–1945)

FROM *Chips Off the Old Benchley*

Tiptoeing Down Memory Lane

IN THE MANNER OF OUR OLDER LITERARY REMINISCERS

In these random wanderings down "Memory Lane" (as I call it—and who does not?) I am relying chiefly on a rather faulty faculty for reminiscence, a diary, belonging to somebody else, for 1890 (or rather the first three weeks of 1890, ending with a big blot) and some old bound volumes of *Harper's Round Table* for 1895–7 (1896 missing). For any discrepancies or downright lies, I beg the indulgence due an old man who has already become something of a bore.

Life in literary circles in New York during the late eighteen-nineties and early eighteen-seventies was quite different from literary life today. In the first place, more authors wore large mustaches and beards, which complicated things considerably. One might meet Walt Whitman (if one weren't careful) and think that it was Joachin Miller, except for the fact that Whitman lived in the East and Miller (thank God!) lived in the West. I remember on one occasion that Miller met Whitman in the lobby of the old Fifth Avenue Hotel (then just the plain Fifth Avenue Hotel, without the "old") and Miller said: "For a minute I thought you were Miller!" to which Whitman replied: "For a minute I thought you were Whitman!" It was a contretemps, all right. And not a very good one, either.

All of this made literary contacts very confusing in the old days, whereas today they are so simple that one may avoid them entirely by not going to teas or reading the book notes. I very well remember my first literary contact when I came to New York as a young boy of sixty-five in 1890. I had been out writing a novel, as all young boys were apt to do in those days, and came in, all hot and excited, to find Bret Harte, Frank Norris, Charles Warren Stoddard, and Irving Caesar waiting for me to talk over Mark Twain's latest story about the Drunken Frog of Calvados County. The last part of it hadn't come over the wire yet, so it didn't make much sense as a funny story, but we all laughed heartily at it because it was afterward to become so famous. I shall never forget Charles Dudley Warner's face as he laughed at it. It was terrible.

It was only a few weeks later that Mark Clemens ("Samuel Twain") asked me to lunch at the Century. I was very busy on my new book, and rather hated to leave off work as I hadn't even found my pencil, but my wife said that she thought that I ought to go as it would make such a nice tidbit for my memoirs later. I had also heard that the Century served a very delicious roast-beef hash, browned to a crisp, which was an added attraction. Sometime I must write a book of literary reminiscences about roast-beef hash browned to a crisp.

So I went. And was I bored! The hash was great, but Edmund Clarence Stedman, Henry Fuller, and Richard Watson Gilder all told the Drunken Frog story, and Mark Clemens ("Samuel Langhorne") acted it out, and what with beards and mustaches and jumpings up and down, I finally begged off and went to the Players' to meet J. I. C. Clark, Hamlin Garland, "Buster" West, and Dr. Johnson (who was not really dead at that time but only "playing possum").

I remember that it was on that day that I was an unwilling auditor to one of the most famous interplays of rapier wit which ever devastated a literary memoir. Nat Goodwin took me around to see a rehearsal of "All's Well That Ends All," where I met Sir Beerbohm Tree, who was in this country straightening out a little libel suit (he had accused William Winter of stealing one of his gags and Winter had retaliated with a suit claiming that the gag was no good anyway). Sir Beerbohm (Tree) was engaged at that moment in a controversy with Lester Wallack, so-named after Wallack's Theatre.

The two wits had been discussing something connected with the theatre (otherwise they wouldn't have been able to discuss at all) and Sir Beerbohm had said:

"All right, that's what *you* think!"

Wallack looked about him with a quizzical smile.

"Very well," he said, dryly, "if that's the way you feel about it."

Tree threw back his leonine head and glared.

"I see!" he said, and walked away.

It was a big day for repartee.

Early in January of that year (what year?) Walt Whitman confided to me that he was doing a play, to be called "Ten Nights in a Broad-brimmed Hat." I told him that it would never go, as there was no adagio dancer in it. He said that he felt that adagio dancing was going out, and that what the public wanted was something good and sexy without people actually throwing each other about. I never liked Whitman, because of his having once worked on a Brooklyn newspaper, but I told him that the only thing to do was to try it out in Newark and see how it went. I never heard anything more of the play—or of Whitman.

In my diary (or the diary that I am using) I find an entry: "Oct. 12th. This is the end! Filkins has gone too far." I am frankly mystified by this entry. So far as I know, there has been no character in our literary history by the name of Filkins (unless it was Ringold Lardner using another name) and I cannot understand just what bearing he has on this matter. If I had my wits about me, I should never include him in this biography. He means nothing.

It was just about this time that Ralph Waldo Emerson had been dead for ten years, so I never knew him. I did know a man named Emerson Cottner, however, which gives me a pretty good loophole for bringing the Sage of Concord (or was that Thoreau?) into these pages. Although I never knew Waldo Emerson (as we used to call him) I thought that he was all right.

During the fall before we went back to Hyannis to live, we were the center of quite a round of literary activity. I say "quite a round of literary activity." I mean that I went to the Century to a dinner given for William Dean Howells. It was a delightful occasion, and I got many names for my list, as well as two new overcoats. Horace Greeley, Richard Watson Gilder, Robert Underwood Johnson, Horace Watson Gilder, Richard Underwood Johnson, Robert Greeley, Otto H. Kahn, Charles Dudley Warner, Thomas Bailey Aldrich, Mrs. S. Standwood Menken (as *Columbia*). Music by the Yacht Club Boys.

I shall never forget an incident which occurred between Horace Watson Aldrich and Mark Twain ("Samuel Langhorne Gibson") during dinner. Twain got up and announced that owing to the limited capacity of the room, most of the people there would have to eat their dinners up in the Children's Room of the Century (for members under sixty). At this, Aldrich (or Gilder, as we used to call him), proposed a toast to "Our Absent Members," which J. A. B. Fuller, having only one leg, took personally, and stamped out of the room in a rage. It was delicious.

At Maybie's quip, a roar went up (which turned out to be from the furnace downstairs), but a great many of us, including Emily Dickinson (who, I thought, had never left Amherst, Mass., but who seemed to get around quite a bit for a recluse) all joined in the laughter, which was negligible. I shall never forget it, at least, not until this book gets proofread and off the presses. I think that my next book will be more in the nature of a serious history where I won't have to remember so many things.

And so we come to the end of the road. What lies beyond, what literary contacts are to be made, all must remain a mystery. (I might make a mystery story out of it, in fact.) There are so many figures in American life which do not come within the scope of this poor outline. But if I can hurry around and get some invitations, I may be able to add a few more names before the next issue. But by the next issue perhaps all my pretty little readers will have flown away. Frankly, I could hardly blame them.

Sic transit gloria mundi (as we used to call him).

Good Luck, and Try and Get It

You may think that you are not superstitious, but would you walk under a burning building? Would you hold a hammer in your left hand and bring it down on your right? Would you light three banknotes with one match? Probably not. But do you know why?

Most of the superstitions which we have today date back to the Middle Ages, when Superstition *was* something. In the Middle Ages they were superstition-poor they had so much. For several centuries there a man couldn't stoop over to lace up his shoon (middle-aged word for "shoes") in the morning without first throwing salt over his shoulder and wetting his finger in a distillation of wolfsbane. For every single thing they did in those days they had to do three other things first, and, by the end of the day, you know that runs into time. Often they never could get started on the real business at hand because they were so occupied in warding off the Evil Eye; and a man who really took care of himself and ran no chances might very well starve to death before he got through his warding-off exercises.

For instance, there was a thing called a "mandrake root" which was considered practically infallible for keeping naughty spirits at bay, but you had to go out and dig your own mandrake root. You couldn't say to your little boy while you were dressing: "Run out into the garden and pull up Daddy's mandrake root for him this morning." You had to go and dig it yourself. Furthermore, you had to dig it at midnight, or under just the right conditions of the moon, or it was no good. And, just to make things harder, you had to be deaf, otherwise you would hear the mandrake root shriek when you pulled it up, and, if you once heard that, you would fall down dead. People used to tie the root to a dog and then whistle from a safe distance where they couldn't hear the root complain. The dog would pull up the root in answering the whistle (as dirty a trick as ever was played on Man's Best Friend), hear the deadly scream and fall down dead in his tracks. Then the mandrake digger would rush up, grab the root, and tear off to the office. But, by this time, his office was probably in the hands of the sheriff or the water had overflowed the tub and dripped down into the room below, and there he was stuck with a mandrake root and a bill for $115.00.

Of course, today we know that there is no such thing as Bad Luck, but, just the same, there is no sense in making a fool of yourself. If, simply by walking around a ladder, you can humor some little gnome into not dogging your footsteps all day with a red-hot pea-shooter, then why be narrow-minded? Walk around the ladder, even though you laughingly say to yourself that you are spoiling that little gnome by being so indulgent. What harm can come from walking around the ladder, unless possibly you slip off into the gutter and sprain your ankle?

The reason why we feel an instinctive urge not to walk under a ladder is fairly interesting (only fairly), and perhaps it would be just as well if I told it to you. If you are superstitious about hearing stories about how superstitions arose, wet your right thumb and turn this page over once.

It seems that when William the Conqueror (or Lief the Unlucky, as he was known in the Greek version of the fable) first landed in England (you know the date as well as I do—1215 Magna Carta) he was very nervous for fear that a Certain Party had followed him from Normandy (his real reason for leaving). Every night he used to take a walk around the ramparts of his castle "just to get a breath of fresh air" as he said, but, as he had had nothing but fresh air all day, he fooled nobody. What he really was doing was taking a look to make sure that this Certain Party was not snooping around trying to find a way into the castle to get some evidence on him. One night he came upon a ladder placed up against the wall and, thinking to trap the intruder, he stood under this ladder, very close up against the stone work, to see if he could hear without being seen. It wasn't a ladder at all (he was pretty unfamiliar with the layout of the castle, having just come from Normandy) but a part of the drawbridge mechanism, and, just at that moment, the man in charge opened up the portcullis and pulled up the bridge to let in one of the menials who had been in town to a dance, and William the Conqueror was catapulted over backwards into the moat (from which all the water had been drawn that very evening to make room for fresh) and wrenched his back very badly. From that day on he gave orders for his bodyguard never to let him walk under a ladder *unless he was sure it was a ladder*. Gradually this last provision was dropped from the command and it became known as "William's Folly" to walk under *any* ladder. Gradually the "William's Folly" was dropped, and it became just a sap thing to do anyway. But we do not realize that the *original* form of this superstition was "Don't walk under a ladder unless you are sure that it *is* a ladder!" So, you see, we have just been overcautious all these years.

The practice among athletic teams of carrying along monkeys or owls as mascots comes from a very old custom of monkeys and owls carrying along athletic teams as mascots. The word "mascot" comes from the French *mascotte*, meaning little witch, but practically nobody today carries around a little witch to bring him good luck. In fact, a little witch would be a liability today, for it would mean just one more mouth to feed and one more railroad ticket to buy, even though you could probably get her on for half-fare.

But other things, usually inanimate, have taken the place of the little witch, and a great many people have odds and ends of crockery and bric-a-brac which they would not be without on any venture involving luck. (Name three ventures which do *not* involve luck.) These are sometimes called amulets, and range anywhere from a "lucky penny" (any penny at all is pretty lucky these days) to a small bust of some famous man. I once heard of a man who was carrying a trunk down stairs when a messenger boy came up to him and gave him a note saying that he had won a raffle. From that day on he considered the trunk his "lucky piece" and was afraid to go anywhere without it. This caused him no end of inconvenience and people stopped asking him to parties, but he still persisted in dragging the trunk with him wherever he went, always looking for another messenger boy to come up with another message of good-cheer. He finally hurt himself quite seriously, so that he couldn't take the trunk with him any more, and then he just stayed at home with the trunk. The last I heard he had not had any more good luck, but he laid it to the Depression.

Thus we see that, even in this enlightened day and age, the old medieval superstitions still persist in some form or other. Some of us go on feeling that if we sign our name on a little piece of paper, or cheque, we can get money from it. Others are perfectly convinced that if they go into a polling booth and push down a button they are having a part in running the government. If it isn't one sort of superstition it is another, and sometimes it is both.

FROM *The Benchley Roundup*

French for Americans

A HANDY COMPENDIUM FOR VISITORS TO PARIS

The following lessons and exercises are designed for the exclusive use of Americans traveling in France. They are based on the needs and behavior of Americans, as figured from the needs and behavior of 14,000 Americans last summer. We wish to acknowledge our indebtedness to American Express Co., 11 Rue Scribe, for some of our material.

The French Language

1. *Pronunciation*

Vowels	Pronounced
a	ong
e	ong
i	ong
o	ong
u	ong

2. *Accents*

The French language has three accents, the acute *e*, the grave *e*, and the circumflex *e*, all of which are omitted.

3. *Phrases most in demand by Americans*

English	French
Haven't you got any griddlecakes?	*N'avez-vous pas des griddlecakes?*
What kind of dump is this, anyhow?	*Quelle espèce de dump is this, anyhow?*
Do you call that coffee?	*Appelez-vous cela coffee?*
Where can I get a copy of the N.Y. Times?	*Où est le N.Y. Times?*
What's the matter? Don't you understand English?	*What's the matter? Don't you understand English?*
Of all the godam countries I ever saw.	*De tous le pays godams que j'ai vu.*
Hey there, driver, go slow!	*Hey there, chauffeur, allez lentement!*
Where's Sister?	*Où est Sister?*

English	French
How do I get to the Louvre from here?	Où est le Louvre?
Two hundred francs? In your hat.	Deux cents francs? Dans votre chapeau.
Where's Brother?	Où est Brother?
I haven't seen a good-looking woman yet.	Je n'ai pas vu une belle femme jusqu'à présent.
Where can I get laundry done by six tonight?	Où est le laundry?
Here is where we used to come when I was here during the War.	Ici est où nous used to come quand j'étais ici pendant la guerre.
Say, this is real beer all right!	Say, ceci est de la bière vrai!
Oh boy!	O boy!
Two weeks from tomorrow we sail for home.	Deux semaines from tomorrow nous sail for home.
Then when we land I'll go straight to Childs and get a cup of coffee and a glass of ice-water.	Sogleich wir zu hause sind, geh ich zum Childs und eine tasse kaffee und ein glass eiswasser kaufen.
Very well.	Très bien.
Leave it in my room.	Très bien.
Good night!	Très bien.
Where did Father go to?	Où est Papa?

Places in Paris for Americans to Visit

THE LOBBY OF THE RITZ

This is one of the most interesting places in Paris for the American tourist, for it is there that he meets a great many people from America. If he will stand by the potted palms in the corner he will surely find someone whom he knows before long and can enter into a conversation on how things are going at home.

THE AMERICAN EXPRESS CO., 11 RUE SCRIBE

Here again the American traveler will find surcease from the irritating French quality of most of the rest of Paris. If he comes here for his mail, he will hear the latest news of the baseball leagues, how the bathing is on the Maine coast, what the chances are for the Big Fight in September at the Polo Grounds, and whom Nora Bayes has married in August. There will be none of this unintelligible *French* jabber with which Paris has become so infested of late years. He will hear language spoken as it should be spoken, whether he came from Massachusetts or Iowa.

Where to Eat in Paris

HARTFORD LUNCH

There has been a Hartford Lunch opened at 115 Rue Lord Byron where the American epicure can get fried-egg sandwiches, Boston baked beans, coffee rings, and crullers almost as good as those he can get at home. The place is run by Martin Keefe, formerly of the Hartford Lunch in Fall River, Massachusetts, and is a mecca for those tourists who want good food well cooked.

UNITED STATES DRUG STORE

At the corner of Rue Bonsard and the Boulevard de Parteuille there is an excellent American drug store where are served frosted chocolates, ice-cream sodas, Coca-Cola, and pimento cheese sandwiches. A special feature which will recall the beloved homeland to Americans is the buying of soda checks *before* ordering.

French Currency

Here is something which is likely to give the American traveler no little trouble. In view of the fluctuating value of the franc, the following table should be memorized in order to insure against mistakes:

Day of Week	American value of Franc
Monday	5 cents
Tuesday	5.1 cents
Wednesday	4.9 cents
Thursday	1 lb. chestnuts
Friday	2½ yds. linoleum
Saturday	What-have-you

The proper procedure for Americans in making purchases is as follows:

1. Ascertain the value of the franc.
2. Make the purchase of whatever it is you want.
3. Ask *"Combien?"* (How much?)
4. Say *"Trop cher."* (What the hell!)
5. Try to understand the answer.
6. Pay the asking price and leave the shop swearing in English, American or other mother tongue.

Side Trips from Paris

There are many fascinating trips which may be made by the American sojourning in Paris which will relieve him of the tedium of his stay.

TRIP A.—Take the train at Paris for Havre and from there go by steamer to New York. The State of Maine Express leaves New York (Grand Central Station) at 7:30 P.M. and in the morning the traveler finds himself in Portland, Maine, from which many delightful excursions may be made up and down the rock-ribbed Atlantic coast.

TRIP B.—Entrain at Paris for Cherbourg, where there are frequent sailings westward. By the payment of a slight *pourboire* the ship's captain will put her in at the island of Nantucket, a quaint whaling center of olden times. Here you may roam among the moors and swim to your heart's content, unconscious of the fact that you are within a six-day run of the great city of Paris.

Ordinal Numbers and their Pronunciation

Numbers	*Pronounced*
1st. *le premier*	leh premyai
2nd. *le second*	leh zeggong
3rd. *le troisième*	leh trouazzeame
4th. *le quatrième*	leh kattreame
8th. *le huitième*	leh wheeteeame

Oh, well, you won't have occasion to use these much, anyway. Never mind them.

Other Words You Will Have Little Use For

Vernisser—to varnish, glaze.

Nuque—nape (of the neck).

Egriser—to grind diamonds.

Dromer—to make one's neck stiff from working at a sewing machine.

Rossignol—nightingale, picklock.

Ganache—lower jaw of a horse.

Serin—canary bird.

Pardon—I beg your pardon.

Opera Synopses

Some Sample Outlines of Grand Opera Plots for Home Study

I

DIE MEISTER-GENOSSENSCHAFT

SCENE: *The Forests of Germany.*
TIME: *Antiquity.*

CAST

STRUDEL, *God of Rain* ....Basso
SCHMALZ, *God of Slight Drizzle* ....Tenor
IMMERGLÜCK, *Goddess of the Six Primary Colors* ....Soprano
LUDWIG DAS EIWEISS, *the Knight of the Iron Duck* ....Baritone
THE WOODPECKER ....Soprano

ARGUMENT

The basis of "Die Meister-Genossenschaft" is an old legend of Germany which tells how the Whale got his Stomach.

ACT 1

The Rhine at Low Tide Just Below Weldschnoffen.—Immerglück has grown weary of always sitting on the same rock with the same fishes swimming by every day, and sends for Schwül to suggest something to do. Schwül asks her how she would like to have pass before her all the wonders of the world fashioned by the hand of man. She says, rotten. He then suggests that Ringblattz, son of Pflucht, be made to appear before her and fight a mortal combat with the Iron Duck. This pleases Immerglück and she summons to her the four dwarfs: Hot Water, Cold Water, Cool, and Cloudy. She bids them bring Ringblattz to her. They refuse, because Pflucht has at one time rescued them from being buried alive by acorns, and, in a rage, Immerglück strikes them all dead with a thunderbolt.

ACT 2

A Mountain Pass.—Repenting of her deed, Immerglück has sought advice of the giants, Offen and Besitz, and they tell her that she must procure the magic zither which confers upon its owner the power to go to sleep while apparently carrying on a conversation. This magic zither has been hidden for three hundred centuries in an old bureau drawer, guarded by the Iron Duck, and, although many have attempted to rescue it, all have died of a strange ailment just as success was within their grasp.

But Immerglück calls to her side Dampfboot, the tinsmith of the gods, and bids him make for her a tarnhelm or invisible cap which will enable her to talk to people without their understanding a word she says. For a dollar and a half extra Dampfboot throws in a magic ring which renders its wearer insensible. Thus armed, Immerglück starts out for Walhalla, humming to herself.

ACT 3

The Forest Before the Iron Duck's Bureau Drawer.—Merglitz, who has up till this time held his peace, now descends from a balloon and demands the release of Betty. It has been the will of Wotan that Merglitz and Betty should meet on earth and hate each other like poison, but Zweiback, the druggist of the gods, has disobeyed and concocted a love-potion which has rendered the young couple very unpleasant company. Wotan, enraged, destroys them with a protracted heat spell.

Encouraged by this sudden turn of affairs, Immerglück comes to earth in a boat drawn by four white Holsteins, and, seated alone on a rock, remembers aloud to herself the days when she was a girl. Pilgrims from Augenblick, on their way to worship at the shrine of Schmürr, hear the sound of reminiscence coming from the rock and stop in their march to sing a hymn of praise for the drying-up of the crops. They do not recognize Immerglück, as she has her hair done differently, and think that she is a beggar girl selling pencils.

In the meantime, Ragel, the papercutter of the gods, has fashioned himself a sword on the forge of Schmalz, and has called the weapon "Assistance-in-Emergency." Armed with "Assistance-in-Emergency" he comes to earth, determined to slay the Iron Duck and carry off the beautiful Irma.

But Frimsel overhears the plan and has a drink brewed which is given to Ragel in a golden goblet and which, when drunk, makes him forget his past and causes him to believe that he is Schnorr, the God of Fun. While laboring under this spell, Ragel has a funeral pyre built on the summit of a high mountain and, after lighting it, climbs on top of it with a mandolin which he plays until he is consumed.

Immerglück never marries.

II
IL MINNESTRONE
(PEASANT LOVE)

SCENE: *Venice and Old Point Comfort.*
TIME: *Early 16th Century.*

CAST

ALFONSO, *Duke of Minnestrone*		Baritone
PARTOLA, *a Peasant Girl*		Soprano
CLEANSO		Tenor
TURINO	*Young Noblemen of Venice*	Tenor
BOMBO		Basso

| LUDOVICO } | *Assassins in the Secret of Cafeteria Rusticana* | { Basso |
| ASTOLFO } | | { Methodist |

Townspeople, Cabbies, and Sparrows

ARGUMENT

"Il Minnestrone" is an allegory of the two sides of a man's nature (good and bad), ending at last in an awfully comical mess with everyone dead.

ACT 1

A Public Square, Ferrara.—During a peasant festival held to celebrate the sixth consecutive day of rain, Rudolpho, a young nobleman, sees Lilliano, daughter of the village bell-ringer, dancing along throwing artificial roses at herself. He asks of his secretary who the young woman is, and his secretary, in order to confuse Rudolpho and thereby win the hand of his ward, tells him that it is his (Rudolpho's) own mother, disguised for the festival. Rudolpho is astounded. He orders her arrest.

ACT 2

Banquet Hall in Gorgio's Palace.—Lilliano has not forgotten Breda, her old nurse, in spite of her troubles, and determines to avenge herself for the many insults she received in her youth by poisoning her (Breda). She therefore invites the old nurse to a banquet and poisons her. Presently a knock is heard. It is Ugolfo. He has come to carry away the body of Michelo and to leave an extra quart of pasteurized. Lilliano tells him that she no longer loves him, at which he goes away, dragging his feet sulkily.

ACT 3

In Front of Emilo's House.—Still thinking of the old man's curse, Borsa has an interview with Cleanso, believing him to be the Duke's wife. He tells him things can't go on as they are, and Cleanso stabs him. Just at this moment Betty comes rushing in from school and falls in a faint. Her worst fears have been realized. She has been insulted by Sigmundo, and presently dies of old age. In a fury, Ugolfo rushes out to kill Sigmundo and, as he does so, the dying Rosenblatt rises on one elbow and curses his mother.

III
LUCY DE LIMA

SCENE: *Wales.*
TIME: *1700 (Greenwich).*

CAST

WILLIAM WONT, *Lord of Glennnn* ....Basso
LUCY WAGSTAFF, *his daughter*..Soprano
BERTRAM, *her lover* ....Tenor

LORD ROGER, *friend of Bertram* ....Soprano

IRMA, *attendant to Lucy* ....Basso

Friends, Retainers, and Members of the local Lodge of Elks.

ARGUMENT

"Lucy de Lima" is founded on the well-known story by Boccaccio of the same name and address.

ACT 1

Gypsy Camp Near Waterbury.—The gypsies, led by Edith, go singing through the camp on the way to the fair. Following them comes Despard, the gypsy leader, carrying Ethel, whom he has just kidnapped from her father, who had previously just kidnapped her from her mother. Despard places Ethel on the ground and tells Mona, the old hag, to watch over her. Mona nurses a secret grudge against Despard for having once cut off her leg, and decides to change Ethel for Nettie, another kidnapped child. Ethel pleads with Mona to let her stay with Despard, for she has fallen in love with him on the ride over. But Mona is obdurate.

ACT 2

The Fair.—A crowd of sightseers and villagers is present. Roger appears, looking for Laura. He can not find her. Laura appears, looking for Roger. She can not find him. The gypsy queen approaches Roger and thrusts into his hand the locket stolen from Lord Brym. Roger looks at it and is frozen with astonishment, for it contains the portrait of his mother when she was in high school. He then realizes that Laura must be his sister, and starts out to find her.

ACT 3

Hall in the Castle.—Lucy is seen surrounded by every luxury, but her heart is sad. She has just been shown a forged letter from Stewart saying that he no longer loves her, and she remembers her old free life in the mountains and longs for another romp with Ravensbane and Wolfshead, her old pair of rompers. The guests begin to assemble for the wedding, each bringing a roast ox. They chide Lucy for not having her dress changed. Just at this moment the gypsy band bursts in and Cleon tells the wedding party that Elsie and not Edith is the child who was stolen from the summerhouse, showing the blood-stained derby as proof. At this, Lord Brym repents and gives his blessing on the pair, while the fishermen and their wives celebrate in the courtyard.

Jennifer Berman
(Contemporary)

FROM *Adult Children of Normal Parents*

Ambrose Bierce
(1842–1913 or –14)

FROM *The Cynic's Word Book*

A

ACQUAINTANCE, *n.* A person whom we know well enough to borrow from, but not well enough to lend to. A degree of friendship called slight when its object is poor or obscure, and "intimate" when he is rich or famous.

ACTUALLY, *adv.* Perhaps; possibly.

APOLOGIZE, *v.i.* To lay the foundation for a future offence.

APPEAL, *v.t.* In law, to put the dice into the box for another throw.

AVERSION, *n.* The feeling that one has for the plate after he has eaten its contents, madam.

B

BRUTE, *n.* See HUSBAND.

C

CALAMITY, *n.* A more than commonly plain and unmistakable reminder that the affairs of this life are not of our own ordering. Calamities are of two kinds: misfortune to ourselves, and good fortune to others.

COMPULSION, *n.* The eloquence of power.

CONGRATULATION, *n.* The civility of envy.

CONSOLATION, *n.* The knowledge that a better man is more unfortunate than yourself.

CONTEMPT, *n.* The feeling of a prudent man for an enemy who is too formidable safely to be opposed.

CONVENT, *n.* A place of retirement for women who wish for leisure to meditate upon the sin of idleness.

CORPORATION, *n.* An ingenious device for securing individual profit without individual responsibility.

D

DANCE, *v.i.* To leap about to the sound of tittering music, preferably with arms about your neighbor's wife or daughter. There are many kinds of dances, but all those requiring the participation of the two sexes have two characteristics in common: they are conspicuously innocent, and warmly loved by the guilty.

DAY, *n.* A period of twenty-four hours, mostly misspent. This period is divided into two parts, the day proper and the night, or day improper—the former devoted to sins of business, the latter consecrated to the other sort. These two kinds of social activity overlap.

DEBAUCHEE, *n.* One who has so earnestly pursued pleasure that he has had the misfortune to overtake it.

DEBT, *n.* An ingenious substitute for the chain and whip of the slave-driver.

F

FEMALE, *n.* One of the opposing, or unfair, sex.

FIDELITY, *n.* A virtue peculiar to those who are about to be betrayed.

G

GUILLOTINE, *n.* A machine which makes a Frenchman shrug his shoulders with good reason.

In his great work on *Divergent Lines of Racial Evolution*, the learned and ingenious Professor Brayfugle argues from the prevalence of this gesture—the shrug—among Frenchmen, that they are descended from turtles, and it is simply a survival of the habit of retracting the head inside the shell. It is with reluctance that I differ with so eminent an authority, but in my judgment (as more elaborately set forth and enforced in my work entitled *Hereditary Emotions*—lib. II, c. XI) the shrug is a poor foundation upon which to build so important a theory, for previously to the Revolution the gesture was unknown. I have not a doubt that it is directly referable to the terror inspired by the guillotine during the period of that instrument's awful activity.

H

HANDKERCHIEF, *n.* A small square of silk or linen, used in various ignoble offices about the face and especially serviceable at funerals to conceal the lack of tears. The handkerchief is of recent invention; our ancestors knew nothing of it and intrusted its duties to the sleeve. Shakespeare's introducing it into the play of "Othello" is an anachronism. Desdamona dried her nose with her coat-tails as Dr. Mary Walker and other reformers have done in our own day—an evidence that revolutions sometimes go backward.

HARANGUE, *n.* A speech by an opponent, who is known as an harang-outang.

HELPMATE, *n.* A wife, or bitter half.

HERS, *pron.* His.

I

IMBECILITY, *n.* A kind of divine inspiration, or sacred fire, affecting censorious critics of this dictionary.

L

LAUGHTER, *n.* An interior convulsion, producing a distortion of the features and accompanied by inarticulate noises. It is infectious and, though intermittent, incurable. Liability to attacks of laughter is one of the characteristics distinguishing man from the animals—these being not only inaccessible to the provocation of his example, but impregnable to the microbes having original jurisdiction in bestowal of the disease. Whether laughter could be imparted to animals by inoculation from the human patient is a question that has not been answered by experimentation. Dr. Weir Mitchell holds that the infectious character of laughter is due to instantaneous fermentation of *sputa* diffused in a spray. From this peculiarity he names the disorder *Convulsio spargens.*

Amy Bloom
(Contemporary)

In the Barcelona Cancer Center

"The Barcelona Cancer Center," Roy says. "Where are the tapas? Maybe there should be castanets at the nurses' station. Paella Valenciana everywhere you look." He puts his hands up into the air and clicks his fingers. Roy says this every time they come for chemotherapy. The Barcelona family made millions in real estate and donated several to St. Michael's; there is almost nothing worth curing that the Barcelonas have not given to. Mai ignores him; the person with cancer does not have to be amused. Ellie smiles widely at Roy. She has already had breast cancer and her job now is to help her best friend and her best friend's husband.

"How about the internationally renowned Sangria Treatment? Makes you forget your troubles." Roy stamps his sneakers, flamenco style. Since Mai's mastectomy, he has become whimsical and it does not become him. Mai knows Roy is doing the best he can and the only kindness she can offer is to not say, "You have been as dull as dishwater for twenty years. You don't have to change now." Ellie believes that all straight men should be like her father: stoic, handy and unimaginative. They should be dryly kind, completely without whimsy or faintly fabulous qualities. As far as Ellie's concerned, gay men can be full-blown birds of paradise, with or without homemaking skills. They can just lounge around in their marabou mules, saying witty, brittle things that reveal their hearts of gold. Ellie likes them that way, that's what they're for, to toss scarves over the world's lightbulbs, and straight men are for putting up sheetrock.

Mai sits between Roy and Ellie in the waiting room as if she's alone. Roy makes three cups of coffee from the waiting room kitchenette. The women don't drink theirs.

"This is disgusting," Roy says.

"I'll get us some from the lobby." Ellie loves the lobby's Java Joe coffee bar, a weirdly joyful pit stop, at the intersection of four different Barcelona family wings, with nothing but caffeine and sugar and attractively arranged fats and sugars; everyone who is not confined by an IV drip or a restricted diet eats there. Mai sips herbal tea all through chemo but Ellie goes up and back a few times, for a currant scone, for a cappuccino, for a mango smoothie. She is happy to spend three dollars on a muffin, grateful that she lives in a country in which no one thinks there's anything wrong or untoward about the AMA-approved pursuit of large profit at the expense of people's grief and health.

"This is great," says Roy. "Treats for me. Honey, look how she takes care of me. Yes, folks, *that's* a wife." This is supposed to be funny, because Ellie is a lesbian and therefore unlikely to be anyone's wife. If Ellie lived with another woman, neither Ellie nor Roy nor Mai would think of that woman as a wife. Ellie is pretty sure that her days of looking for a spouse are over; Mai thinks this, too, and used to imagine that when Roy died, at a suitable, but not horribly advanced age, of a swift-moving, but not painful disease, she and Ellie would retire to her parents' house in Oslo, or buy the little yellow house on Pearl Street in Provincetown that she and Ellie walked past on spring break twenty-one years ago. Now, it seems possible that Ellie will sit on a porch, slugging back brandy with some other old lady and that Roy will grow old with someone who has two breasts and a full head of hair.

Ellie prepares a little picnic on the seat next to Roy. Coffee the way he likes it and two different kinds of biscotti, a fist-sized apple fritter, two elephant ears sprinkling sugar everywhere and enough napkins to make this all bearable to Roy, who is two steps short of compulsive. Ellie presents the food-covered seat to Roy. He kisses her hand, which smells of coffee and antibacterial soap and of Ellie, for which he has no particular name. Mai has always smelled like clove; since November, she smells like seaweed and Roy, like a pregnant woman, has lost his taste for sushi, for lobster and for salt.

Elayne Boosler
(Contemporary)

FROM Punchline—*I Don't Get It*

In the movie *Punchline*, Tom Hanks is a medical student afraid of blood and Sally Field is a New Jersey housewife with three kids. Naturally, they become stand-up comics. . . .

Real comedy can't be learned; it comes from a need for justice. The best who stand up, stand up for something.

Great comics leave something wonderful behind when they leave the stage. Mr. Hanks's character is a self-described "hate stylist" whose crowning performance is a heartfelt diatribe against *debutantes*, of all things. It does not make the heart soar. And if this character is afraid of blood, he's really in the wrong business now.

Comedy is a blood sport. It flays the truth and spurts twisted logic. In America, people become comics because we don't have bullfighting.

Is it harder for women in comedy? It is after films like this. The housewife is introduced by the club owner as a woman with a chronic yeast infection, yet this purported natural wit says nothing in response. She does an apologetic routine that's a crude and embarrassed foray into cheap vibrator jokes and reverse sexism. In life, material like this gets booed off the stage. But the film's character—a complaining, asexual "comedienne" holding down the stereotype—wins the bake-off. And that's misleading, because comedy is very, very sexy when it's done right.

Mel Brooks and Carl Reiner
(Contemporary)

FROM *The 2000 Year Old Man*

Reiner: Sir, could you give us the secret of your longevity?

2000: Well, the major thing, the major thing, is that I never ever touch fried food. I don't eat it, I wouldn't look at it, and I don't touch it. And I never run for a bus. There'll always be another. Even if you're late for work, you know, I never run for a bus. I never ran, I just strolled, jaunty-jolly, walking to the bus stop.

★

Reiner: What was the means of transportation then?

2000: Mostly fear.

Reiner: Fear transported you?

2000: Fear, yes. You would see . . . an animal would growl, you'd go two miles in a minute. Fear would be the main propulsion.

Reiner: I think most people are interested in living a long and fruitful life, as you have.

2000: Yes. Fruit is good, too, you mentioned fruit. Yeah. Fruit kept me going for a hundred and forty years once when I was on a very strict diet. Mainly nectarines. I love that fruit. It's half a peach, half a plum, it's a hell of a fruit. I love it! Not too cold, not too hot, you know, just nice. Even a rotten one is good. That's how much I love them. I'd rather eat a rotten nectarine than a fine plum. What do you think of that? That's how much I loved them.

Claude Brown
(Contemporary)

FROM *Manchild in the Promised Land*

I always found Mrs. Rogers' visits hard to take. She was a very nice meddlesome old woman, but too godly to have around constantly. Poor Danny, he had to live with it. Mrs. Rogers had told Mama that Danny was so bad because his behavior was the Lord's way of testing her faith. Dad called Mrs. Rogers the "preacher woman." He believed that Mrs. Rogers was going against the Lord's Word and that this was the reason for her son's behavior. He had often said that "the Lord never told no woman to go out and preach the Gospel to nobody." Dad said that if the Lord had wanted a woman to preach, he would have chosen a woman to be one of his apostles.

On this day, Mrs. Rogers' advice was no different from the other times. After Mama had told Mrs. Rogers about what had happened in court, Mrs. Rogers began her usual sermon, saying, "Child, you just gotta pray, you just gotta pray and trust in the Lord." I always left the house at this point, because our house would be used as a practice pulpit for the next two or three hours.

As I ran down the stairs, I tried to imagine what was going on in the house. In a little while, Mrs. Rogers would be patting her foot real fast, and she would start talking real loud, clapping her hands, shaking her head, and every other word would be "Jesus" or "Lord." I wondered why Mrs. Rogers never got tired of talking about the Lord. Before Mrs. Rogers finished her private sermon, she would have Mama talking about the Lord and patting her feet. By the time Mrs. Rogers was ready to leave, she would have Mama promising to come to a church where she was preaching next Sunday. Mama would promise, and Mrs. Rogers would start telling her how good it is to be saved, to walk with Jesus, and to let God into your soul. Even though Mama knew Dad wasn't going to let her go to a sanctified church with that "jackleg preacher woman," she still promised to go. Dad always said, "All those sanctified people is just a bunch of old hypocrites, and none of 'em ain't a bit more saved than nobody else."

Mrs. Rogers never talked about saving Dad. She said, "That man got the devil in him," and I believed it. As a matter of fact, I had suspected something like that long before Mrs. Rogers did.

We had all been to Mrs. Rogers' Sunday sermon once. All of us except Dad. She was preaching that time in what looked like a church-apartment to me and a church-store to Carole. I think most of the people there were relatives of Mrs.

Rogers. All of her family was there except for Danny; he had escaped on the way to church. June, one of Mrs. Rogers' daughters, was playing an old, out-of-tune upright piano. Another one of Danny's sisters was banging two cymbals together and mumbling something about Jesus. She seemed to be in a trance. Mr. Rogers was shaking a tambourine and singing about Jesus with a faraway look in his eyes. Mrs. Rogers, who was dressed in a white robe, got up and started preaching. After Mrs. Rogers had been preaching for about fifteen minutes, an old lady got up and started screaming and shouting, "Help me, Lord Jesus!" She was still throwing her arms up and shouting for Jesus to help her when a younger woman jumped up and hollered, "Precious Lord Jesus, save me!" Mrs. Rogers' voice was getting louder all the time.

For two hours, she preached—and for two hours, people were getting up, shouting, jumping up and down, calling to Jesus for help and salvation, and falling out exhausted. Some of these "Holy Rollers," as Dad called them, would fall to the floor and start trembling rapidly; some of them even began to slobber on themselves. When I asked Mama what was wrong with those people and what they were doing on the floor, she told me that the "spirit" had hit them. When Carole heard this, she began to cry and wanted to get out of there before the spirit hit us. Mrs. Rogers had gone over to a man who was rolling on the floor, slobbering on himself, and babbling as if he were talking to the Lord. She held the man's hand very tight and told him repeatedly to walk with the Lord and not to fear Jesus. She was saying to the man, "Brother, say, 'Yes, Jesus; yes, Jesus.'" After a while, the man calmed down, and Mrs. Rogers said he had been saved.

Carole and Margie were frightened by these strange goings-on. I had been fascinated until now. But now this spirit thing had Mama jumping up and shouting. I joined Carole and Margie in a crying chorus, and the three of us started pulling on Mama. After Mama had jumped, clapped her hands and had her say about Jesus, she fell back in her chair, tired and sweating. One of Mrs. Rogers' blood sisters had started fanning Mama. Carole, Margie, and I had stopped crying, but we were still scared, because we didn't know if Mama was all right or not.

In the makeshift pulpit, Mrs. Rogers was looking real pleased with herself, probably thinking that she had saved a lot of people. I think Mrs. Rogers judged her sermon by the number of people who were hit by the spirit and fell down during her sermon. She cautioned the people who were saved about "back-slidin'" and told them about how happy they were going to be with Jesus in their lives. She also asked some of the old saved souls to "testify." After three or four saved souls had told about what a good friend Jesus had been to them, Mrs. Rogers began her third request for money. The ushers, who were also relatives of Mrs. Rogers, passed a china bowl down each row. Carole and Margie dropped the nickel that Mama had given to each of them in the bowl, then they turned and looked at me. Although that was the first time we had ever been to church together, they would have been surprised if I had put my nickel in the bowl. I didn't surprise them that day.

When Carole and Margie were busy telling Mama about me not putting my nickel in the bowl, I was pulling a chair from the aisle behind us. All the chairs in the place were kitchen chairs, and they weren't all the same size. Before I could get the chair into our aisle, a big fat shiny dark-skinned woman with a man's voice said, "Boy, leave dat chair 'lone." I was frightened by the heavy, commanding voice, but not as much as I was after I looked up and saw that great big old woman giving me the evil eye. My first thought was that she was a witch or a hag, whatever that was. I knew she couldn't be the boogeyman; not in church. But the longer I looked, the more I doubted her being anything other than the boogeyman. About thirty seconds later, when I had gotten my voice back, I meekly said, "Dat ain't your chair." The next thing I heard was the sound of Mama's hand falling heavily across my mouth. As I started crying, I heard Mama say, "What I tole you about sassin' ole people?" While I went on crying, Mama was telling me about the dangers of talking back to old people. I remember her saying, "If one of these ole people put the bad mouth on you, maybe you'll be satisfied."

For years afterward, the mention of church always reminded me of the day that we went to hear Mrs. Rogers preach. To me, a church was a church-apartment where somebody lined up a lot of kitchen chairs in a few rows, a preacher did a lot of shouting about the Lord, people jumped up and down until they got knocked down by the spirit, and Mrs. Rogers put bowls of money on a kitchen table and kept pointing to it and asking for more. It was a place where I had to stand up until I couldn't stand any more and then had to sit down on hard wooden chairs. The one good thing I got out of going to hear Mrs. Rogers preach was a new threat to use on Carole and Margie. Whenever Carole and Margie would threaten to tell on me, I told them that if they did, the spirit would hit them the way it hit those people in Mrs. Rogers' church-apartment.

Maybe Dad was right when he said Mrs. Rogers was just robbing people in the name of the Lord. Anyway, I felt pretty good about her not getting my nickel.

★

One day that same winter, Simms called everybody into the living room, where we used to have our house meetings. He told us that some girls were coming to Wiltwyck soon from a place called Vassar College and that they were going to teach us things like skiing, music, painting, and stuff like that. Simms said he expected us to treat those chicks better than the guys in the other houses, since we were older than the other guys. He had that "if you don't do right I'm gonna kick your ass" tone in his voice when he told us about the chicks from Vassar, but nobody cared much, because Simms hadn't hit a cat in a long time.

The first day the girls came to Wiltwyck, the cats in Aggrey swarmed all over them. In fact, everybody took to them right away. They were all white and not so hip, but most of them were real fine, so nobody cared about them being white and not being hip. It really wasn't hard to be nice to these chicks, because they were all real sweet. They were some of the nicest girls I had ever met, and some of them knew some things too. You could talk to them, and they could understand things. Every day, they would come to Wiltwyck early in the morning and stay until evening. One day, the girls from Vassar took us to the college for a picnic. It sure was a big place, and I never saw so many pretty girls in one place before in my life. There must have been about a million bicycles at that place. The girls said we could ride any of the bikes we wanted to, but we had to remember where we got them from and put them back when we finished. We really broke up some bikes that day. I saw Horse bring a bike back in five parts.

J.J. caused a girl to faint. He was coming down this steep hill real fast. There was a brick wall at the bottom, and J.J. couldn't steer too well. When J.J. hit the wall, he didn't get hurt, but the bike was all smashed up, and J.J went straight up into the air about fifteen feet. The girl was standing on the bridge, and when she heard the crash, she turned around just in time to see J.J. going up, and she fainted. When they woke her up, the girl said that she fainted because she thought sure the boy would be killed, but Rickets said that seeing a nigger flying through the air on the campus of Vassar College was enough to make any nice, respectable white girl faint. And sometimes Rickets knew what he was talking about.

Cathy, my piano teacher, was a big fine chick. She was white, but she was from China. Her father was a doctor or something in China, and she was born there and had lived there, but she was still white. She just came over here to go to Vassar College. She didn't speak Chinese or anything. As a matter of fact, she spoke real good English, and she was a sweet person, real big and real fine. Cathy ran over to J.J., who was lying there on the ground playing dead, and kneeled down beside him. She raised his head and put it in her lap and started screaming all over the place for somebody to get a doctor. I knew if she kept that up for long, they would never get J.J. up from there.

J.J. sneaked one eye open, looked up at those big breasts right over in his face, and started snuggling. I wanted to say, "Poor Cathy." She just shouldn't have done that. Somebody should have pulled her coat. I would have, but J.J. was a friend of mine, so I couldn't do that. After a while, she saw this cat opening one eye and getting closer, and I think she felt kind of foolish. So she threw his head off her lap and told him to get up. He laughed and got up. And everybody thought it was pretty funny.

But that wasn't the funniest thing that happened that day. The funniest thing was when we were in the music room and another girl screamed. We turned around to see what it was, and this girl was trying to jump up off a piano stool, because while she was playing the piano, somebody was under there playing with her legs. That was dear old Rickets. That's the way he was.

We had a lot of fun at Vassar College, and the girls were really something wonderful. I never would have thought that white girls could be so nice. Cats could look all up under their dresses and everything, and all they did was laugh.

We got along real fine with the girls until the day J.J. got lost in a snowstorm with the skiing teacher. They had searching parties out for them, lots of searching parties, all day long. But J.J. and the skiing teacher were lost in a blizzard for about four hours. Everybody in the world was wondering where they could be. But nobody found them. After the snowing was over, J.J. and the teacher came back, with smiles on their faces. They were happy, and I suppose everybody was happy—that is, everybody but Stilly and the rest of the staff. They were a little peeved. They wondered where in the world a nigger could be in a snowstorm with some pretty Norwegian skiing teacher. That's not supposed to happen to people from poor Negro backgrounds.

J.J. said he and the teacher had to stop in some barn for four hours to get out of the storm. All the cats up there envied J.J. that day. I kind of wished I had been caught in that storm too, because that teacher sure was something sweet . . . cute accent too.

After a while, I think they found out that it wasn't working. The guys got used to the girls, and they started treating them like mothers and sisters and that sort of thing. These were guys who cursed out mothers and sisters, and when they started treating these chicks like mothers and sisters, they were cursing them out too. One cat, Baldy, even had enough nerve to slap one of those girls. Now, everybody knew that perhaps you could curse them out or scream at them, but they also knew that no niggers were supposed to be slapping any girls from Vassar College. I guess we were supposed to be glad to even be able to say hello to them.

Then there was the Mac thing. Mac used to operate the movie camera for us on Thursday and Sunday nights. One day, while the girls from Vassar were at Wiltwyck, Mac got locked up in the movie booth with that same skiing teacher, and they had a lot of fun, I suppose, because they stayed in there a long time. Everybody started looking for Mac. He was supposed to be getting the cameras ready. They banged on the doors, they did everything, but nobody could find them. When Mac finally came out and they asked him where he'd been, he said, "In the movie booth." Somebody said, "Lawd, it's time to git these girls outta here."

They were all seniors in college, and when graduation time came around, they had to go. I think, in spite of everything, we missed them, and maybe they missed us too. That was the first time we'd ever known any Vassar girls, but I suppose that was the first time they'd ever known any poor little colored boys.

Charles Farrar Browne
(1834–67)

FROM *Artemus Ward, His Travels*

Affairs Round the Village Green

It isn't every one who has a village green to write about. I have one, although I have not seen much of it for some years past. I am back again, now. In the language of the duke who went round with a motto about him, "I am here!" and I fancy I am about as happy a peasant of the vale as ever garnished a melodrama, although I have not as yet danced on my village green, as the melo-dramatic peasant usually does on his. It was the case when Rosina Meadows left home.

The time rolls by serenely now—so serenely that I don't care what time it is, which is fortunate, because my watch is at present in the hands of those "men of New York who are called rioters." We met by chance, the usual way—certainly not by appointment—and I brought the interview to a close with all possible despatch. Assuring them that I wasn't Mr. Greeley, particularly, and that he had never boarded in the private family where I enjoy the comforts of a home, I tendered them my watch, and begged they would distribute it judiciously among the laboring classes, as I had seen the rioters styled in certain public prints.

Why should I loiter feverishly in Broadway, stabbing the hissing hot air with the splendid gold-headed cane that was presented to me by the citizens of Waukegan, Illinois, as a slight testimonial of their esteem? Why broil in my rooms? You said to me, Mrs. Gloverson, when I took possession of those rooms, that no matter how warm it might be, a breeze had a way of blowing into them, and that they were, withal, quite countryfied; but I am bound to say, Mrs. Gloverson, that there was nothing about them that ever reminded me, in the remotest degree, of daisies or new-mown hay. Thus, with sarcasm, do I smash the deceptive Gloverson.

Why stay in New York when I had a village green? I gave it up, the same as I would an intricate conundrum—and, in short, I am here.

Do I miss the glare and crash of the imperial thoroughfare? the milkman, the fiery, untamed omnibus horses, the soda fountains, Central Park, and those things? Yes, I do; and I can go on missing 'em for quite a spell, and enjoy it.

The village from which I write to you is small. It does not contain over forty houses, all told; but they are milk-white, with the greenest of blinds, and for the most part are shaded with beautiful elms and willows. To the right of us is a mountain—to the left a lake. The village nestles between. Of course it does. I never read a novel in my life in which the villages didn't nestle. Villages invariably. It is a kind of way they have.

We are away from the cars. The iron-horse, as my little sister aptly remarks in her composition On Nature, is never heard to shriek in our midst; and on the whole I am glad of it.

The villagers are kindly people. They are rather incoherent on the subject of the war, but not more so, perhaps, than are people elsewhere. One citizen, who used to sustain a good character, subscribed for the Weekly New York Herald, a few months since, and went to studying the military maps in that well-known journal for the fireside. I need not inform you that his intellect now totters, and he has mortgaged his farm. In a literary point of view we are rather bloodthirsty. A pamphlet edition of the life of a cheerful being, who slaughtered his wife and child, and then finished himself, is having an extensive sale just now.

We know little of Honoré de Balzac, and perhaps care less for Victor Hugo. M. Claés's grand search for the Absolute doesn't thrill us in the least; and Jean Valjean, gloomily picking his way through the sewers of Paris, with the spoony young man of the name of Marius upon his back, awakens no interest in our breasts. I say Jean Valjean picked his way gloomily, and I repeat it. No man, under those circumstances, could have skipped gaily. But this literary business, as the gentleman who married his colored chambermaid aptly observed, "is simply a matter of taste."

The store—I must not forget the store. It is an object of great interest to me. I usually encounter there, on sunny afternoons, an old Revolutionary soldier. You may possibly have read about "Another Revolutionary Soldier Gone," but this is one who hasn't gone, and, moreover, one who doesn't manifest the slightest intention of going. He distinctly remembers Washington, of course; they all do; but what I wish to call special attention to, is the fact that this Revolutionary soldier is one hundred years old, that his eyes are so good that he can read fine print without spectacles—he never used them, by the way—and his mind is perfectly clear. He is a little shaky in one of his legs, but otherwise he is as active as most men of forty-five, and his general health is excellent. He uses no tobacco, but for the last twenty years he has drunk one glass of liquor every day—no more, no less. He says he must have his tod. I had begun to have lurking suspicions about this Revolutionary soldier business, but here is an original Jacobs. But because a man can drink a glass of liquor a day, and live to be a hundred years old, my young readers must not infer that by drinking two glasses of liquor a day a man can live to be two hundred. "Which, I meanter say, it doesn't follor," as Joseph Gargery might observe.

This store, in which may constantly be found calico and nails, and fish, and tobacco in kegs, and snuff in bladders, is a venerable establishment. As long ago as 1814 it was an institution. The county troops, on their way to the defence of Portland, then menaced by British ships-of-war, were drawn up in front of this very store, and treated at the town's expense. Citizens will tell you how the clergyman refused to pray for the troops, because he considered the war an unholy one; and how a somewhat eccentric person, of dissolute habits, volunteered his services, stating that he once had an uncle who was a deacon, and he thought he could make a tolerable prayer, although it was rather out of his line; and how he prayed so long and absurdly that the Colonel ordered him under arrest, but that even while soldiers stood over him with gleaming bayonets, the reckless being sang a preposterous song about his grandmother's spotted calf, with its Ri-fol-lol-tiddery-i-do; after which he howled dismally.

And speaking of the store, reminds me of a little story. The author of "several successful comedies" has been among us, and the store was anxious to know who the stranger was. And therefore the store asked him.

"What do you follow, sir?" respectfully inquired the tradesman.

"I occasionally write for the stage, sir."

"Oh!" returned the tradesman, in a confused manner.

"He means," said an honest villager, with a desire to help the puzzled trades-man out, "he means that he writes the handbills for the stage drivers!"

I believe that story is new, although perhaps it is not of an uproariously mirthful character; but one hears stories at the store that are old enough, good-ness knows—stories which, no doubt, diverted Methuselah in the sunny days of his giddy and thoughtless boyhood.

There is an exciting scene at the store occasionally. Yesterday an athletic peas-ant, in a state of beer, smashed in a counter and emptied two tubs of butter on the floor. His father—a white-haired old man, who was a little boy when the Revolutionary war closed, but who doesn't remember Washington *much*, came round in the evening and settled for the damages. "My son," he said, "has con-siderable originality." I will mention that this same son once told me that he could lick me with one arm tied behind him, and I was so thoroughly satisfied he could, that I told him he needn't mind going for a rope.

Sometimes I go a-visiting to a farm-house, on which occasions the parlor is opened. The windows have been close-shut ever since the last visitor was there, and there is a dingy smell that I struggle as calmly as possible with, until I am led to the banquet of steaming hot biscuit and custard pie. If they would only let me sit in the dear old-fashioned kitchen, or on the door-stone—if they knew how dismally the new black furniture looked—but, never mind, I am not a reformer. No, I should rather think not.

Gloomy enough, this living on a farm, you perhaps say, in which case you are wrong. I can't exactly say that I pant to be an agriculturist, but I do know that in the main it is an independent, calmly happy sort of life. I can see how the pros-perous farmer can go joyously a-field with the rise of the sun, and how his heart may swell with pride over bounteous harvests and sleek oxen. And it must be rather jolly for him on winter evenings to sit before the bright kitchen fire and watch his rosy boys and girls as they study out the charades in the weekly paper, and gradually find out why my first is something that grows in a garden, and my second is a fish.

On the green hillside over yonder, there is a quivering of snowy drapery, and bright hair is flashing in the morning sunlight. It is recess, and the Seminary girls are running in the tall grass.

A goodly seminary to look at outside, certainly, although I am pained to learn, as I do on unprejudiced authority, that Mrs. Higgins, the Principal, is a tyrant, who seeks to crush the girls and trample upon them; but my sorrow is somewhat assuaged by learning that Skimmerhorn, the pianist, is perfectly splendid.

Looking at these girls reminds me that I, too, was once young—and where are the friends of my youth? I have found one of 'em, certainly. I saw him ride in the circus the other day on a bareback horse, and even now his name stares at me from yonder board-fence, in green, and blue, and red, and yellow letters. Dashington, the youth with whom I used to read the able orations of Cicero, and who, as a declaimer on exhibition days, used to wipe the rest of us boys pretty handsomely out—well, Dashington is identified with the halibut and cod interest—drives a fish-cart, in fact, from a certain town on the coast, back into the interior. Hurbertson, the utterly stupid boy—the lunkhead, who never had his lesson—he's about the ablest lawyer a sister State can boast. Mills is a newspaper man, and is just now editing a Major-General down South.

Singlinson, the sweet-voiced boy, whose face was always washed and who was real good, and who was never rude—*he* is in the penitentiary for putting his uncle's autograph to a financial document. Hawkins, the clergyman's son, is an actor, and Williamson, the good little boy who divided his bread and butter with the beggar-man, is a failing merchant, and makes money by it. Tom Slink, who used to smoke short-sixes and get acquainted with the little circus boys, is popularly supposed to be the proprietor of a cheap gaming establishment in Boston, where the beautiful but uncertain prop is nightly tossed. Be sure, the Army is represented by many of the friends of my youth, the most of whom have given a good account of themselves. But Chalmerson hasn't done much. No, Chalmerson is rather of a failure. He plays on the guitar and sings love songs. Not that he is a bad man. A kinder-hearted creature never lived, and they say he hasn't yet got over crying for his little curly-haired sister who died ever so long ago. But he knows nothing about business, politics, the world, and those things. He is dull at trade,—indeed, it is a common remark that "everybody cheats Chalmerson." He came to the party the other evening, and brought his guitar. They wouldn't have him for a tenor in the opera, certainly, for he is shaky in his upper notes; but if his simple melodies didn't gush straight from the heart, why were my trained eyes wet? And although some of the girls giggled, and some of the men seemed to pity him, I could not help fancying that poor Chalmerson was nearer heaven than any of us all!

George Carlin
(Contemporary)

FROM *Brain Droppings*

Things You Never See

- A puppet with a hard-on
- A butterfly with a swastika design
- The Latin word for *douche bag*
- Someone defecating in church
- A junkie with leisure time
- A serial killer with a light-up bow tie
- A mom-and-pop steel mill
- A shot glass full of carrot juice
- A bum with matching luggage
- Really interesting twins
- Condoms with pictures of the saints
- Two homosexuals who own a bait shop
- A pimp with a low profit margin
- A Rolls-Royce that's more than 50 percent primer paint

Baseball and Football

Baseball is different from any other sport; very different.

For instance, in most sports you score points or goals, in baseball you score runs.

In most sports the ball, or object, is put in play by the offensive team; in baseball the defensive team puts the ball in play, and only the defense is allowed to touch the ball. In fact, in baseball if an offensive player touches the ball intentionally, he's out; sometimes unintentionally, he's out.

Also: In football, basketball, soccer, volleyball, and all sports played with a ball, you score *with* the ball, and without the ball you can't score. In baseball the ball prevents you from scoring.

In most sports the team is run by a coach; in baseball the team is run by a manager; and only in baseball does the manager (or coach) wear the same clothing the players do. If you had ever seen John Madden in his Oakland Raiders football uniform, you would know the reason for this custom.

Now, I've mentioned football. Baseball and football are the two most popular spectator sports in this country. And, as such, it seems they ought to be able to tell us something about ourselves and our values. And maybe how those values have changed over the last 150 years. For those reasons, I enjoy comparing baseball and football:

Baseball is a nineteenth-century pastoral game.
Football is a twentieth-century technological struggle.

Baseball is played on a diamond, in a park. The baseball park!
Football is played on a gridiron, in a stadium, sometimes called Soldier Field or War Memorial Stadium.

Baseball begins in the spring, the season of new life.
Football begins in the fall, when everything is dying.

In football you wear a helmet.
In baseball you wear a cap.

Football is concerned with *downs*. "What down is it?"
Baseball is concerned with *ups*. "Who's up? Are you up? I'm not up! He's up!"

In football you receive a penalty.
In baseball you make an error.

In football the specialist comes in to kick.
In baseball the specialist comes in to relieve somebody.

Football has hitting, clipping, spearing, piling on, personal fouls, late hitting, and unnecessary roughness.
Baseball has the sacrifice.

Football is played in any kind of weather: Rain, snow, sleet, hail, fog . . . can't see the game, don't know if there is a game going on; mud on the field . . . can't read the uniforms, can't read the yard markers, the struggle will continue!
In baseball if it rains, we don't go out to play. "I can't go out! It's raining out!"

Baseball has the seventh-inning stretch.
Football has the two-minute warning.

Baseball has no time limit: "We don't know when it's gonna end!"
Football is rigidly timed, and it will end "even if we have to go to sudden death."

In baseball, during the game, in the stands, there's a kind of picnic feeling. Emotions may run high or low, but there's not that much unpleasantness.

In football, during the game in the stands, you can be sure that at least twenty-seven times you were perfectly capable of taking the life of a fellow human being.

And finally, the objectives of the two games are completely different:

In football the object is for the quarterback, otherwise known as the field general, to be on target with his aerial assault, riddling the defense by hitting his receivers with deadly accuracy in spite of the blitz, even if he has to use the shotgun. With short bullet passes and long bombs, he marches his troops into enemy territory, balancing this aerial assault with a sustained ground attack that punches holes in the forward wall of the enemy's defensive line.

In baseball the object is to go home! And to be safe! "I hope I'll be safe at home!"

Play Ball

Athletes like that physical shit. When they're pleased with each other they bump chests, butt heads, and bang forearms. Why don't they just punch each other in the fuckin' teeth? Wouldn't that be great? Teammates, I mean. After a touchdown pass, why doesn't the guy who caught the ball just go over and kick the quarterback right in the nuts? Same with a slam dunk in basketball. The guy who scores oughta grab a chair and beat the living shit out of the guy who fed him the ball. For about forty-five minutes. If this type of celebration were more common, the postgame show from the winners' locker room would be a lot livelier.

And I think there should be at least one sport where the object is to kill someone. A team sport. Deathball. Let's face it, athletes are mostly physical freaks with serious personality defects where competition is concerned, and they just love someone to "motivate" them. Well, what greater motivation can there be than trying to avoid being killed? It's a fuckin' natural! And for me, what could be more fun than watching one of these jackoffs motivate his ugly ass into an early grave every game?

Unnecessary Words

THERE IS A TENDENCY THESE DAYS TO COMPLICATE SPEECH
BY ADDING UNNECESSARY WORDS. THE FOLLOWING PHRASES
ALL CONTAIN AT LEAST ONE WORD TOO MANY.

emergency situation
shower activity
surgical procedure
boarding process
flotation device
hospital environment
fear factor
free of charge
knowledge base
forest setting
beverage items

prison setting
peace process
intensity level
belief system
seating area
sting operation
evacuation process
rehabilitation process
facial area
daily basis
blue in color

risk factor
crisis situation
leadership role
learning process
rain event
confidence level
healing process
standoff situation
shooting incident
planning process

There Are No Times That Don't Have Moments Like These

Since 1983, more than thirty people have been killed in post office shootings.
You know why? Because the price of stamps keeps changing. There's a lot of
pressure. "How much are they now, Rob? Twenty-nine? Thirty-two? I can't
keep track! Fuck it!" BANG BANG BANG BANG BANG BANG BANG
BANG BANG!!!

On Opening Day, the President doesn't throw *out* the first ball. He throws it
in. If he threw it out, it would land in the parking lot and someone would have
to go get it.

Roz Chast
(Contemporary)

★ ★ ★

FROM **The Four Elements**

Margaret Cho
(Contemporary)

FROM *I'm the One That I Want*

"The Wedding Fantasy" has been one of my most lasting and persistent day-dreams. They go back as far as T. Sean, my blue-eyed Texan beau, from when I was just twenty. I saw marrying him in quickie Vegas fashion. Smoking a ciga-rette in a pink shantung silk suit, '60s style, tapping my foot impatiently, holding a tiny bouquet of baby roses in a trembling gloved hand.

Curiously, I also saw our make-believe marriage fall apart, and me drunkenly stalking him into his next relationship. I fantasized about being found by his young son from his next marriage, passed out on their porch early in the morn-ing wearing a fur coat and pearls and nothing else, and clutching a broken cham-pagne glass—*That's Dad's first wife before Mommy. She's having some trouble letting go. Can I call the ambulance? Please? Please? Please?*

I saw getting married to Jude, a country-western crooner I had a brief affair with, just as clearly. That particular ceremony was held in a stone church in wine country, C&W all the way down to white cowboy boots. The justice o' the peace would be Col. Sanders, and he, of course, would also cater the event. Jude would sing to me, and all the girls would cry at the romance of it all and the fact that he was taken for good.

My fantasy wedding to Marcel, my last most horrible boyfriend, seemed far more real. We'd go to the South of France, to Provence, where he had attended a wedding years before. The theme would be turn-of-the-century peasant, and we would serve stone soup. There would be fiddles and tiny flowers weaved into my unruly mass of *Manon of the Spring* hair. All the men with their black vests and pocket watches like old-time bankers would lift the heavy oak table and set it outside in the field, where we would dance and drink the night away.

I never pictured my parents at these functions because they represented the awful truth, the bad shit, not that they were awful, bad, or shitty—they were just *real*, and I could not live without lying. They were the black watermelon seeds of my existence. I wanted to just have what I thought were the good parts of my life, seedless and sweet.

I got deeply into this fantasy, thinking I could go to 1900, that expensive bou-tique on Main that is open by appointment only, just to price antique cotton, to see what a dress would be like should this fantasy come true. I didn't want to lose my head about my wedding dress as many a young bride is known to do. There were so many new magazines to buy—*Bride's* and *Modern Bride* and such, just like *Vogue* but with a sense of purpose and direction. The gowns in there were ugly and puffy. I realized as always I'd have to go the vintage route, or perhaps design it myself.

I thought about the bridesmaid dresses. Lemon yellow granny dresses, sort of '70s Gibson girls with big bubbly bun hairdos, which of course they'd never wear again, but who cares? Who wears anything again? I saw myself in Victoriana, white gauze and delicate white lace and daisies in my bouquet, and the bridesmaids, my friends Siobhan, Ebby, and Marcel's sister Louise, in yellow to match the yolk of the daisy.

And suddenly, it wasn't a fantasy anymore, it was outright planning. Later, when the relationship went sour and I could barely stand the sight of Marcel, I still didn't want to break up because I had spent so much time on my fantasy. In fact, I was being held hostage by my fantasy. I was willing to let myself be miserable in this relationship, to stay with someone I hated, someone who tortured me every time he looked at me, talked to me, or touched me. I was going to endure a lifetime of hell for the pleasure of ONE IMAGINED DAY!!!!!!

No matter how hard it is, I am not going to fashion a wedding fantasy for my next crush. I will stop living life for a future happiness that does not and may never exist. I will live for now and stop wasting my time. Every moment I live can be as beautiful as a fantasy. Every second of life is precious. I vow to stop wasting my time on these dreams that turn my life into a nightmare. I vow to live, to be mindful, to pay attention to life and hold it hard to my heart. Every beat another second going by.

It was so hard then to not want to lose myself in the lacy, white emotions, the soft, womanly caresses of the bridal salon. I was insane, I was being a lunatic. Trying on wedding dresses, preparing for a wedding to someone who would never even call me back. But the ladies at the boutique didn't know that. They just wanted to help me be ready for my Special Day, the one I would remember for my entire life.

I tried on a dress, which didn't look good on me anyway. I went to wait outside for Sledge to pick me up. Curiously, he didn't think anything that I was doing was strange.

I was standing on a corner of Ventura Boulevard and this guy drove up and looked at me and then went and parked his car and walked back. He started talking to me and saying that I was attractive and asked what was I doing. It took me a long time to realize that he thought I was a prostitute! Sledge came roaring up in his Acura and I got into his car and he drove my crazy ass home.

James David Corrothers
(1869–1917)

An Indignation Dinner

Dey was hard times jes fo' Christmas round our neighborhood one year;
So we held a secret meetin', whah de white folks couldn't hear,
To 'scuss de situation, an' to see what could be done
Towa'd a fust-class Christmas dinneh an' a little Christmas fun.

Rufus Green, who called de meetin', ris an' said: "In dis here town,
An throughout de land, de white folks is a'tryin' to keep us down."
S' 'e: "Dey bought us, sold us, beat us; now dey 'buse us 'ca'se we's free;
But when dey tetch my stomach, dey's done gone too fur foh me!

"Is I right?" "You sho is, Rufus!" roared a dozen hungry throats.
"Ef you'd keep a mule a-wo'kin', don't you tamper wid his oats.
Dat's sense," continued Rufus. "But dese white folks nowadays
Has done got so close and stingy you can't live on what dey pays.

"Here 'tis Christmas-time, an', folkses, I's indignant 'nough to choke.
Whah's our Christmas dinneh comin' when we's mos' completely broke?
I can't hahdly 'fo'd a toothpick an' a glass o' water. Mad?
Say, I'm desp'ret! Dey jes better treat me nice, dese white folks had!"

Well, dey 'bused de white folks scan'lous, till old Pappy Simmons ris,
Leanin' on his cane to s'pote him, on account his rheumatis',
An' s' 'e: "Chillun, whut's dat wintry wind a-sighin' th'ough de street
'Bout yo' wasted summeh wages? But, no matter, we mus' eat.

"Now, I seed a beau'ful tuhkey on a certain gemmun's fahm.
He's a-growin' fat an' sassy, an' a-struttin' to a chahm.
Chickens, sheeps, hogs, sweet pertaters—all de craps is fine dis year;
All we needs is a committee foh to tote de goodies here."

Well, we lit right in an' voted dat it was a gran' idee,
An' de dinneh we had Christmas was worth trabblin' miles to see;
An' we eat a full an' plenty, big an' little, great an' small,
Not beca'se we was dishonest, but indignant, sah. Dat's all.

Bill Cosby
(Contemporary)

FROM *Love and Marriage*

Till Talk Do You Part

In her endless effort to bring her husband out of the cave, the American wife will tell him, "The problem with you is you are not in touch with your feelings." She will tell him this right after he has tried to shotput his son to dramatize some parental point for which mere language lacked clarity. She will tell him this right after he has kicked in the television set as a fitting response to an overtime field goal against his home team. A man can spend an entire morning creatively running amuck; and when he is finished and the foam on his lips has dried, his wife will say, "The problem with you is you are not in touch with your feelings."

Although I'm not a psychologist (my doctorate is in education, my BA in the quarter-mile), it has always seemed to me that I am nicely in touch with my feelings, one of which is an urge to bounce pass the next woman who tells me I am not in touch with my feelings. Of course, what women often mean by this charge is that men don't know how to cry; but crying isn't always an indication of genuine feeling. If it were, then Jimmy Swaggart and Tammy Faye Bakker would be sensitivity's king and queen.

I sometimes think that women may be too involved in revelation, that perhaps a marriage is strained by just four words: not *The children aren't yours* but *How was your day?* It is often too much pressure on a man to ask him to keep giving the six o'clock news, especially when the only thing to report is the weather. What, for example, is a dentist to say when his wife inquires, *How was your day?*

I did six fillings, four root canals, and a small child spat in my eye.

Maybe the best answer a husband can give to *How was your day?* is *I spent it dreading that question.* Or maybe the husband should draw first and ask his *wife, How was your day?* Then, however, he is liable to hear the four grimmest words of all:

I had the children.

Camille never has to be a district attorney with me, for she has a way to learn what I'm thinking that even allows me to have a good meal.

"If I ever want to find out anything about you," she has said, "I'll invite five of your friends to dinner and just listen in."

By communicating indirectly, sometimes through a basketball team, Camille and I have been able to keep the mystery in our marriage, a quality that the marriage manuals consider important. Of course, these manuals say that communication is important too; and so, the answer seems to be that a couple should communicate mysteriously, each one making sure that the other rarely knows what he is talking about. Every time that Camille and I exchange *That's not what I'm saying/Then what's your* point?, we are moving further into foggy paradise.

In this happy pursuit of marital mystery, Camille and I sometimes *almost* have a conversation, but then she thinks better of the idea.

"I want to talk to you," she told me one evening in the kitchen.

"Fine," I said. "Let's do it right after I finish these chili dogs. I don't want to distract my mouth right now."

A few minutes later and a few pounds heavier, I walked into the living room, where she was standing by the fireplace, a stunning portrait of a great lady about to hold forth. I hoped I was equal to the subject. I hoped it was the Cleveland Browns.

"Here I am for the talking," I said. "What was it you wanted?"

"*You* know what I wanted," she replied. "Let's just leave it at that."

And she turned and went up to the bedroom, no doubt for a meeting with Godot.

Because Camille and I have wisely left each other in the dark so often, our marriage has been rich in surprise. It is an atmosphere in which my son can come to me and say, "Dad, I've decided I want to be more involved in politics."

"That's good," I reply.

"So I'm dropping out of college, changing my name to Raul, and joining the Contras."

"Then I guess you'll be wanting some advance allowance."

"Yes, please. Either pesos or traveler's checks."

"You know, this is . . . well, I guess you'd have to call it a surprise. *I* didn't know you wanted to become a Nicaraguan guerrilla. At least not this *semester*."

"Well, *Mom* has known it for months."

"She has?"

"Yes, she even says the Contras are the ideal group for me because I'm always against everything. Dad, if you and Mom did more talking, you'd be ready with a going-away present for me."

My son did not understand, however, that there is a method in the intermittent and semicoherent exchanges of information that Camille and I have: we are trying not to use up the conversation allotted to our marriage. Unaware that this conversational allotment governs every marriage, most young couples do not pace their tongues and suddenly find themselves in three-month lulls.

The next time you're in a restaurant, study some couple that seems to have been married for more than ten years. Watch them exchanging long desperate looks, each of them hoping that the numbing silence will be broken by a good grease fire or a holdup. And each of them is about to be driven to think the unthinkable:

We should have brought the children.

★

Camille and I bring the children. In fact, people have said that we are prisoners of the children because we bring them everywhere we go, from Las Vegas to the South of France. However, I can recall six times in our marriage when we left the children home. *Seven* times if you count the night that Camille walked out on me and I went after her without bothering to get a sitter.

Nevertheless, I have to admit that whenever Camille has suggested that we go off without the children for longer than an hour and a half, I say either, "But it's always more *fun* with the children along" or "Just be patient, dear. In just nine or ten or fifteen years, they'll all be married or in the armed forces and then we'll have the house back. That's our reason to keep *living*."

However, early one summer in our thirteenth year of marriage, my mother offered to stay with the children for a week so that Camille and I could go on a little vacation alone and recapture the magic of the honeymoon we had always planned to take. For a moment, I had considered having my mother take Camille for a week and letting *me* go off with the children, whose interests were closer to mine; but then I yielded to my yen for adventure and decided to see if Camille and I could make it alone, operating under the handicap of having to talk only to each other.

"Darling," I had said to her, "what would you say if I told you that we're going to take a vacation without the children?"

"I'd say you're a liar," she replied.

"And usually you'd be right, but my mother just offered to stay with them so we can get to know each other again—unless there's someone else you'd rather get to know."

"No, you'll do. But I thought you said it's always more fun with the kids along."

"So it won't be our greatest vacation, but at least it'll be all ours. Just the two of us, dancing away from Fat Albert."

As the moment of our departure approached, Camille and I conceived some rules for this romantic escapade:

- There could be no mention of the children.
- No photographs, tapes of cuteness, or report cards could be taken along.
- No one could become pregnant or in any other way involved with kids.

And so, one afternoon in July, we turned our two girls and our boy over to my mother and then drove out to a charming old inn on eastern Long Island. A few minutes after arriving, as I zipped up the back of Camille's dress before taking her to an elegant dinner, I said, "You look so young and lovely. No one could ever tell that you had two kid . . . um, kidneys. Sorry."

"That's okay," she said. "I miss them too, those precious kidneys. And that spleen."

"Courage," I said. "We can make it."

In the dining room, we found a corner table, where I sat down and began desperately trying to think of things to talk about. So far, I had two: the plight of the dollar and the plight of the whale. I would have to pace myself with them or my mouth would be retired before the soup.

After a silence of no more than five or ten minutes, I tenderly placed my hand on Camille's and said, "Have I ever told you, my darling, that they should let the dollar float?"

"How you *talk*, lover," she demurely replied.

"And speaking of floating, this is a tough time to be a whale, don't you think?"

She smiled helplessly, and then I said, "You look so young and lovely tonight."

"You've said that already, but I don't mind. If my loveliness is the bottom of your barrel, you can go with it for a day or two."

The pressure was getting to me now. How *could* parents keep themselves from talking about their children? I decided that there should be a clinic where addicts could taper off, first looking at photos of their own children, then gradually at someone else's, and finally at slides of vasectomies.

Once our appetizers came, we began to chew our way through a seemingly endless lull. I thought about my oldest daughter often telling me not to talk with a mouthful of food and I congratulated myself on avoiding a demerit from Camille by keeping the thought unexpressed.

"You know, the Owls could go all the way this year," I finally said.

"Some new migration?" she replied.

"The *Temple Owls*. All the way."

"That would be nice. All the way where?"

As a bird-watcher, Camille was no better than Denise. Was *any* woman wise enough to follow my Owls?

After the meal a romantic mood was upon us, so hand in hand we walked down to the beach under a sky full of stars. We went almost to the water's edge, and for four or five minutes nothing was said; but neither of us was trying now, for we both were transported by the awesome beauty of the universe. At last, however, from somewhere deep in my soul, a thought emerged and was given voice.

"Just think," I said. "At this very moment, under these very stars, a little Cosby is wetting the bed." And then I piteously cried, "Oh, honey, I *tried*! You don't *know* how I tried!"

"Don't hate yourself," she said. "I was just about to suggest that we gather some shells for them."

Josephine Daskam
(1876–1961)

FROM *The Woman Who Caught the Idea*

There was once a Woman whose Fiancé had a Decided Theory regarding the most Desirable Characteristics of the Sexes. This Theory, in a Word, was that a Woman should be Like a Clinging Vine, while a Man should Resemble a Sturdy Oak. For Many Years, therefore, the Woman had Practiced Clinging with Great Success. One day, However, her Fiancé grew Critical of her Method . . .

So they Broke off the Engagement. The Fiancé found a Progressive and Stimulating Woman who Agreed to Criticize him and March Abreast of him. The only Trouble with this was that Not Only did she March Abreast, but it Seemed Probable that she would Get Ahead. Also she had a Work of Her Own, which sometimes Interfered with His. . . .

So he Returned to his Old Love and said, "Let All Be as it was Before."

"I am Afraid that can Not be," she replied, Sadly. "Since I Lost You I have Given Up Clinging, and I have Caught Your Idea. I had to Sympathize with Someone, so I have Taken Up a Work of My Own. Judging from your Tone I think you Would Fail to Comprehend it. The Century is Progressing and Things can Never Be as they Were Before."

This teaches us that It's Well to Be On with the Old Love Before you are Off with the New.

FROM *Smith College Stories*

The Education of Elizabeth

I
FROM MISS ELIZABETH STOCKTON TO MISS CAROLYN SAWYER

Lowell, Mass., Sept. 10, 189–.

My Dearest Carol: The thing we have both wished so much has happened! Papa has finally consented to let me go to college! It has taken a long time and a *great deal* of persuasion, and Mamma never cared *anything* about it, you know, herself. But I laid it before her in a way that I really am ashamed of! I never thought I'd do anything like it! But I *had* to, it seemed to me. I told her that she had often spoken of what a mistake Mrs. Hall made in letting Marjory come out so soon, and that I should *certainly* be unwilling to stay at Mrs. Meade's another year. I'm doing advanced work now, and I'm *terribly* bored. The girls all seem so very young, somehow! And I said that I couldn't come out till I was twenty-two, if I went to college. I teased so that she gave way, but we had a *terrible* siege with Papa. He is the *dearest* man in the world, but just a little *tiny* bit prejudiced, you know. He wants me to finish at Mrs. Meade's and then go abroad for a year or two. He wants me to do something with my music. But I told him of the *fine* Music School there was at Smith, and how much *harder* I should work there, *naturally*. He talked a good deal about the art advantages and travel and French—you know what I think about the *terrible narrowness* of a boarding-school education! It is *shameful*, that an intellectual girl of this century should be tied down to *French* and *Music*! And how can the scrappy little bit of gallery sight-seeing that I should do *possibly* equal four years of earnest, intelligent, *regular* college work? He said something about marriage—oh, dear! It is *horrible* that one should have to think of that! I told him, with a great deal of dignity and rather coldly, I'm afraid, that *my* life would be, I hoped, *something more* than the mere *evanescent glitter* of a *social butterfly*! I think it really impressed him. He said, "Oh, very well—very well!" So I'm coming, dearest, and you must write me all about what books I'd better get and just what I'd better know of the college

87

customs. I'm *so* glad you're on the campus. You know Uncle Wendell knows the President very well indeed—he was in college with him—and, somehow or other, I've got a room in the Lawrence, though we did n't expect it so soon! I feel inspired already when I think of the chapel and the big Science Building and that *beautiful* library! I've laid out a course of work that Miss Beverly—that's the literature teacher—thinks very ambitious, but I am afraid she doesn't realize the intention of a *college*, which is a little different, I suppose, from a *boarding-school* (!) I have planned to take sixteen hours for the four years. I must say I think it's rather absurd to limit a girl to that who *really* is *perfectly* able to do more. Perhaps you could see the Register—if that's what it is—and tell him I could just as well take eighteen, and then I could do that other Literature. I must go to try on something—really, it's very hard to convince Mamma that Smith is n't a *summer resort*! Good-by, dearest, we shall have such *beautiful* times together—I'm sure you'll be as excited as I am. We shall *for once* see as much of each other as we want to—I wish I could study with you! I'm coming up on the 8.20 Wednesday morning.

Devotedly yours,
ELIZABETH.

FROM MISS CAROLYN SAWYER
TO MISS ELIZABETH STOCKTON

Lake Forest, Ill., Sept. 17, 189–.

Dear Bess: I'm very glad you're coming up—it's the only place in the world. I'm not going to be able to meet you—I'm coming back late this year—Mrs. Harte is going to give our crowd a house-party at Lakemere. Isn't that gay? I met Arnold Ritch this summer. He knows you, he said. I never heard you speak of him. He's perfectly *smooth*—his tennis is all right, too. For heaven's sake, don't try to take sixteen hours—on the campus, too! It will break you all up. You'll get on the Glee Club, probably—bring up your songs, by the way—and you'll want to be on the Team. Have you got that blue organdie? You'll want something about like that, pretty soon. If you can help it, don't get one of those Bagdad things for your couch. I'm deadly sick of mine. Get that portière thing you used to have on the big chair at home. It's more individual. We're getting up a little dance for the 26th. If you know any man you could have up, you can come—it will be a good chance to meet some of the upper-class girls. We may not be able to have it, though. Don't tell Kate Saunders about this, please. She'd ask Lockwood over from Amherst, and I've promised Jessie Holden to ask him for her. We shall probably have Sue for class president this year—I'm glad of it, too. There will be a decent set of ushers. I suppose you'll want me for your senior for the sophomore-senior thing. I'll keep that if you wish. I shall get up by the 24th. I'm in the Morris. Don't forget your songs.

Yours in haste,

C. P. S.

FROM MRS. HENRY STOCKTON
TO MRS. JOHN SAWYER

Lowell, Mass., Sept. 23, 189–.

Dear Ella: In spite of great uncertainty on my part and actual unwillingness on her father's, Lizzie has started for Smith. It seems a large undertaking, for four years, and I must say I would rather have left her at Mrs. Meade's. But her heart is set on it, and it is very hard to deny her. She argues so, too; really, the child has great ability, I think. She fairly convinced me. It has always seemed to me that a girl with good social surroundings, a good home library, and an intellectual home atmosphere does very well with four years at so good a school as Mrs. Meade's, and a little travel afterwards. Lizzie has quite a little musical talent, too, and I should have liked her to devote more attention to that. Very frankly, I cannot say that I have been able to see any improvement in Carrie since she went away. I suppose it will wear off, but when I saw her this summer she had a manner that I did not like so well as her very pleasant air three—no, two—years ago. It seemed a curious mixture of youth and decision, that had, however, no maturity in it. Katharine Saunders, too, seems to me so utterly irresponsible for a young woman of twenty-one, and yet so almost arrogant. I expected she would know a great deal, as she studied Greek before she went, but she told me that she always skipped the Latin and Greek quotations in books! She seems to be studying nothing but French and Literature and History; her father could perfectly well have taught her all that, and was anxious to, but she would hear nothing of it. She wanted the college life, she said. Ah, well, I suppose the world has moved on since we read Livy at Miss Hopkins'! I picked up a Virgil of Lizzie's yesterday and was astonished to find how it all came back. We felt very learned, then, but now it is nothing.

I hope Carrie will be good to my little girl and help her perhaps with her lessons—not that I fear Lizzie will need very much help! Miss Beverly assures me that she has never trained a finer mind. Her essay on Jane Austen was highly praised by Dr. Strong, the rector of St. Mary's. Of course, dear Ella, you won't resent my criticism of Carrie—I should never dream of it with any one but an old and valued friend, and I shall gladly receive the same from you. But Lizzie has always been all that I could wish her.

Yours with love,

SARAH B. STOCKTON.

FROM MR. WILLIAM B. STOCKTON
TO MISS ELIZABETH STOCKTON

Boston, Mass., Oct. 16, 189–.

My Dear Niece: Your mother advises me of your having just entered Smith Academy. I had imagined that your previous schooling would have been sufficient, but doubtless your parents know best. Your mother seems a little alarmed as to your success, but I have reassured her. I trust the Stockton blood. Whatever your surroundings may be, you can never, I am sure, set yourself a higher model than your mother. I have never known her to lack the right word or action under any circumstances, and if you can learn that in your schooling, your friends and relatives will be more than satisfied.

I enclose my cheque for fifty dollars ($50), in case you should have any special demand on your purse not met by your regular allowance. I remember many such in my own schooldays. Wishing you success in your new life, I remain,

Your affectionate uncle,

WILLIAM B. STOCKTON.

FROM MISS ELIZABETH CRAIGIE
TO MISS ELIZABETH STOCKTON

New Haven, Conn., Oct. 21, 189–.

My Dear Elizabeth: Sarah tells me that you are going to college. I am sure I don't see why, but if you do, I suppose that is enough. Children are not what they used to be. It seems to me that four years at Mrs. Meade's should have been enough; neither your Aunt Hannah nor I ever went to college, though to be sure Hannah wanted to go to Mt. Holyoke Seminary once. I have never heard any one intimate that either of us was not sufficiently educated: I wonder that you could for one instant imagine such a thing! Not that I have any reason to suppose you ever did. However, that is neither here nor there. Your Aunt Hannah and I were intending to give you Mother's high shell-comb and her garnet set for Christmas. If you would prefer them now for any reason, you may have them. The comb is being polished and looks magnificent. An absurd thing to give a girl of your age, from my point of view. However, your Aunt Hannah thinks it best. I trust you will be very careful of your diet. It seemed to me that your complexion was not what it should have been when you came on this summer. I am convinced that it is nothing but the miscellaneous eating of cake and other sweets and over-education. There has been a young girl here from some college—I think it is Wellesley—and her complexion is disgraceful. Your Aunt Hannah and I never set up for beauties, but we had complexions of milk and roses, if I do say it. Hannah thinks that the garnets are unsuitable for you, but that is absurd. Mother was no older than you when she wore them, and looked very well, too, I have no doubt. I send you by express a box of Katy's doughnuts, the kind you like, very rich, and a chocolate cake. Also some salad and a loaf cake, Mrs. Harding's rule. I trust you will take sufficient exercise, and don't let your hands grow rough this winter. Nothing shows a lady so much as her hands. Would you like the garnets reset, or as Mother wore them? They are quite the style now, I understand. Hoping you will do well in your studies and keep well, I am,

> Yours lovingly,
> AUNT LIZZIE.

FROM MISS ELIZABETH STOCKTON TO MR. ARNOLD RITCH, JR.

Lawrence House, Northampton, Mass., Nov. 1, 189–.

My Dear Arnold: It is only fair to you to tell you that it can never be. No, never! When I—if I did (which I can hardly believe)—allowed you to think anything else, I was a mere child. Life looks very different to me, now. It is quite useless to ask me—I must say that I am surprised that you have spoken to Papa. Nor do I feel called upon to give my reasons. I shall always be a very, very good friend to you, however, and very, very much interested in you.

In the first place, I am, or at least you are, far too young. The American woman of today is younger than her grandmother. I mean, of course, younger than her grandmother is now. That is, than she was then. Also I doubt if I could ever love you as you think you do. Love me, I mean. I am not a man's woman. I much prefer women. Really, Arnold, it is very strange how men bore me now that I have known certain women. Women are so much more interesting, so much more fascinating, so much more exciting! This will probably seem strange to you, but the modern woman I am sure is rapidly getting not to need men at all! I have never seen so many beautiful red-haired girls before. One sits in front of me in chapel, and the light makes an aureole of glory about her head. I wrote a theme about it that is going to be in the *Monthly* for November.

I hope that you won't feel that our dear old friendship of so many years is in any way changed. I shall never forget certain things—

I am enjoying my work very much, though it is easier than I had thought it would be, and the life is different in many ways. If I did not think that Miss Sawyer had probably invited you, I should be very glad to have you come up for the Christmas concert, but I suppose it is useless to ask you. I had no idea you were so fond of tennis!

Your friend always,
ELIZABETH WOLFE STOCKTON.

FROM MR. HENRY STOCKTON TO MISS ELIZABETH STOCKTON

Lowell, Mass., Nov. 1, 189–.

My Dear Elizabeth: Yours received and read with my usual attention and interest. I am glad that your college life continues to be pleasant, and that you have found so many friends. I was much interested, too, in the photograph of Miss Hunter. I find the blue prints are more common than I had supposed, for I had imagined that they were something quite new. It is certainly very accommodating in your teachers to allow themselves to be so generally photographed. Your mother seemed much pleased with Miss Hunter, and glad that you were in the house with her and liked her so much. I was surprised to see her so young in appearance. I had very foolishly imagined the typical old style "schoolmarm," I suppose. But it seems that she was graduated only a few years ago, herself.

Now, my dear Elizabeth, I am going to speak to you very seriously. I trust that you will take it in good part and remember that nothing can be more to my interest than the real happiness and well-being of my daughter. The tone of your letters to both your mother and me has seemed for some weeks unsatisfactory. I mean that we have found in them a nervous, strained tone that troubles me exceedingly. I cannot see why you should close with such expressions as this (I copy verbatim): "Too tired to write more;" "All used up—lots of Latin to do—can only find time for a note;" "Tired to death because I'm not sleeping quite as well as usual, just now;" et cetera, et cetera.

I have been to see Mrs. Meade, and she assures me that your preparation was more than adequate: that your first year should prove very easy for you, *in Latin especially.* Now what does this mean? You left us well and strong, considering that you have always been a delicate girl. It was for that reason, as you know, that I particularly opposed your going to college.

But there is more. Mrs. Allen's daughter, Harriet, has been at home for some days to attend her sister's wedding. Your mother and I naturally seized the opportunity of inquiring after you, and after some questioning from us she admitted that you were not looking very well. She said that you seemed tired and were "going it a little too hard, perhaps." That seemed to me a remarkable expression to apply to a young girl! My endeavors to find out exactly what it meant resulted in nothing more explicit than that "Bess was trying to do too much."

Now, my dear girl, while we are naturally only too pleased that you should be striving to stand well in your classes, do not, I beg of you, imagine for one moment that any intellectual advancement you may win can compensate us or you for the loss of your health. You remember Cousin Will, who carried off six honors at Harvard and came home a nervous invalid. I fear that the Stockton temperament cannot stand the strain of too continued mental application.

I must stop now, to attend to some business matters, and I will add only this. Do not fail to remember my definite conditions, which have not altered since September. If you are not perfectly well at the Christmas holidays, you must remain with us. This may seem severe, but I am convinced, your mother also, that we shall be acting entirely for your good.

Yours aff.,
FATHER.

FROM MR. ARNOLD RITCH, SR., TO MISS MARION HUNTER

New York, N.Y., Nov. 4, 189–.

My Dear Miss Hunter: You may remember meeting, five years ago, in Paris, in the Louvre, an old American, who had the great pleasure of rendering you a trifling assistance in a somewhat embarrassing situation, and who had the further pleasure of crossing on the *Etruria* with you a month later. I was that man, and I remember that you said that if ever there should happen to be an occasion for it, you would be only too happy to return your imaginary debt.

If you really meant it, the occasion, strangely enough, has come. I know well enough from my lifelong friend, Richard Benton, whose family you have so often visited, that you are an extremely busy young woman, and I will state my case briefly. I never make half-confidences, and I rely implicitly on your discretion in the following clear statement. My only nephew and namesake, incidentally heir, has been for some time practically engaged to Miss Elizabeth Stockton, the daughter of an old friend. The engagement has been entirely satisfactory to all parties concerned, and was actually on the eve of announcement, when the young lady abruptly departed for Smith College.

My nephew is, though only twenty-four, unusually mature and thoroughly settled: he was deeply in love with the young lady and assures me that his sentiments were returned. She now quietly refuses him, and greatly to her parents' dissatisfaction announces that she intends remaining the four years and "graduating with her class," which seems a strong point with her.

Her father and I would gladly leave the affair to work itself out quietly, were it not for an unfortunate occurrence. Ritch, Jr. has been offered an extremely good opening in a Paris banking-house, which he must accept, if at all, immediately, and for six years. He is extremely broken up over the whole affair, and says that unless Elizabeth returns to her old relations with him, he will go. This will be in three weeks.

I am not so young as I was, and I cannot leave America again. I can only say that if the boy goes, my interest in life goes, to a great extent, with him. He does not mean to be selfish, but young people, you know, are harder than they think, and feel deeply and, for the moment, irrevocably. He says that he is certain that this is merely a fad on Miss Stockton's part, and that if he could see her for two weeks he would prove it. I should like to have him try.

This is my favor, Miss Hunter. Elizabeth respects and admires you more than any of her teachers. She quotes you frequently and seems influenced by you. Arnold has made me promise that I will not ask her parents to bring her home and that I will not write her. I will not. But can you do anything? It is rather absurd to ask you to conspire against your college, to give up one of your pupils: but you have a great many, and remember that I have but one nephew! It is all rather a comedy, but a sad one for me, if there is no change within three weeks, I assure you. They are only two headstrong children, but they can cause more than one heartache if they keep up their obstinacy. Elizabeth has forbidden Arnold to come to Northampton on the score of her work, and wild horses could not drag him there.

I offer no suggestion, I ask nothing definitely, I merely wonder if you meant what you said on the *Etruria,* and if your woman's wit, that must have managed so many young idiots, can manage these?

Yours faithfully,

ARNOLD M. RITCH.

FROM MISS MARION HUNTER
TO MRS. HENRY STOCKTON

Northampton, Mass., Nov. 7, 189–.

My Dear Mrs. Stockton: As you have certainly not forgotten that I assured you in the early fall of my interest, professionally and personally, in your daughter, you will need no further explanation, nor be at all alarmed, when I tell you that Elizabeth is a little overworked of late. In the house with her as I am, I see that she is trying to carry a little too much of our unfortunately famous "social life" in connection with her studies, where she is unwilling to lose a high grade. She entered so well prepared that she has nothing to fear from a short absence, and as she tells me that she does not sleep well at all of late, she will have no difficulty in getting an honorable furlough. Two weeks or so of rest and freedom from strain will set her up perfectly, I have no doubt, and she can return with perfect safety to her work, which is, I repeat, quite satisfactory.

Yours very cordially,
MARION HUNTER.

FROM MRS. HENRY STOCKTON
TO MISS ELIZABETH STOCKTON

(*Telegram*)

Lowell, Mass., Nov. 8.

Come home immediately will arrange with college and explain myself.

MOTHER.

FROM MISS MARION HUNTER
TO MISS CONSTANCE JACKSON

Northampton, Mass., Nov. 10, 189–.

Dear Con: I'm afraid it will be impossible for me to accept your seductive invitation for Thanksgiving. We're pulling the girls up a little sharply this year, and it would hardly do for me to come back late. But it *would* be good to hear a little music once more!

It was rather odd that you should have mentioned that idiotic affair of mine in Paris—the hero of it has just written me a long letter *apropos* of his nephew, who wants to marry that little Miss Stockton, whose Harvard cousin you knew so well. That portly squire of dames is actually simple and straightforward enough to suggest that I precipitate the damsel into the expectant arms of his nephew and heir apparent—he is used to getting his own way, certainly, and he writes a rather attractive letter. I owe him much (as you know) and if Elizabeth, who is a dear little thing and far too nice for the crowd she's getting in with—you knew Carol Sawyer, did n't you?—has such a weak-kneed interest in college as to be turned out of the way by a sight of the destined young gentleman, I fancy she would not have remained long with us in any case. She's a pretty creature and had cunning ways—I shall miss her in the house. For I don't believe she'll come back; she's not at all strong, and her parents are much worried about her health. It is more than probable that the Home will prove her sphere.

Personally, I don't mind stating that I would it were mine. When I consider how my days are spent——

You might not believe it, but they grow stupider and stupider. Perhaps I've been at it a bit too long, but I never saw such papers as these freshmen give one.

And they have begun singing four hymns in succession on Sunday morning! It's very hard—why they should select *Abide with Me* and *Lead, Kindly Light* for morning exercises and wail them both through to the bitter end every Sunday in the year is one of the local mysteries.

I must get at my papers, they cover everything. Remember me to Mr. Jackson; it was very kind of him to suggest it, but I must wait till Christmas for the Opera, I'm afraid. If I should not come back next year—and it is more than possible that I shan't—I may be in Boston. I hope in that case you won't have gone away.

Yours always,
M. I. HUNTER.

FROM MISS ELIZABETH STOCKTON TO MISS CAROLYN SAWYER

Lowell, Nov. 20.

Carol Dear: I am writing in a great hurry, as I have an engagement at four, to tell you that I have decided not to return to-day, as I intended. Will you get the key of 32 from Mrs. Driscoll, as Kitty goes home over Sunday, so it will be locked, and get out my mink collarette and my silver toilet things and my blanket wrapper, and I think there is twenty dollars in my handkerchief case. I am extremely disturbed and confused—when one is really responsible for anything one feels very much disturbed. Of course, I don't believe a word of it—it's all folly and nonsense—but still, six years is a long time. Of course, you don't know at all what I mean, dear, and I'm not sure I do either. I forgot to say that I'm probably not coming back to college this year. Mamma feels very worried about my health—you know I did n't sleep very well nights, and I used to dream about Livy. Anyway, she and Papa are going abroad early in the spring, and really, Carol, a college education is n't everything. If I were going to teach, you know, it would be different, but you see I was almost finished at Mrs. Meade's—I was taking advanced work—and it isn't as if I had had only the college preparation. Then, if we go abroad, I must do something with my French. You know there was simply *no* chance to practise conversation in such a large class, and I was forgetting it, which Arnold thinks would be a pity. He speaks very fine French himself. Then, you see, there'll be all the galleries and everything and the Sistine Madonna and the cathedrals—they're so educative—everybody admits that. It's hardly to be supposed that Geometry and Livy are really going to be as broadening to me as a year of travel with Papa and Mamma, is it? And though I never said anything to you about it, I really have felt for some time that there was something a little narrow about the college. They seem to think it is about all there is of life, you know, with the funny little dances and the teas and all that. Even that dear Miss Hunter is really *un peu gâtée* with it all—she thinks, I believe, that a college education is all there is for anybody. She told Mamma that I was n't well—she wanted me to keep my high grade. Oh! Carol! there are better things than grades! Life is a very much bigger thing than the campus even! I think, dear, that one really ought to consider very frankly just what we intend to do with our lives— if we are going to marry, we ought to try to make ourselves cultivated and broadminded, and in every way worthy to be—Oh, Carol, dearest, I'm terribly happy! It isn't settled, of course. I am utterly amazed that they all seem to think it is, but it isn't. Only probably if I still feel as I do now, when we get back, I shall ask you, dear, what we promised each other—to be my bridesmaid— the first one! I'm thinking of asking Sally and Grace and Eleanor— all our old set at Mrs. Meade's, you know. I think that pink, with a deep rose for hats and sashes, would look awfully well on all of you, don't you! It seems a long time since I was in Northampton: the girls seem very young and terribly serious over queer little lessons—or else trying to play they're interested in each other. Arnold says he thinks the attitude of so many women is bound to be unhealthy, and even in some cases a little morbid. I think he is quite right, don't you? After all, girls need some one besides themselves. I always thought that Mabel Towne was very bad for Katharine. Will you send, too, my Shelley and my selections from Keats? The way I neglected my reading—real reading, you know— oh! *c'était affreux!* I'm learning the loveliest song—Arnold is very fond of it:

Ninon, Ninon, que fais-tu de la vie?
L'heure s'enfuit, le jour succède au jour.
Rose ce soir, demain flètrie—
Comment vis-tu, toi qui n'as pas d'amour?

I'm going out now for a walk. I'm sure you'll like Arnold—I think you said you met him. He does n't remember you. Remember me to all the juniors I met, and if you see Ethel Henderson, tell her I'll write to her when I get time. Excuse this pointed pen—I'm learning to use it. Arnold hates a stub.

Yours always,
BETTY.

Ellen DeGeneres
(Contemporary)

FROM *My Point . . . and I Do Have One*

Nuns were very popular in the sixties. They must have had a good publicist then. They had *The Sound of Music*, about a nun. They had *The Singing Nun*—remember her? "Dominique a nique a nique a Dominique . . ." So they figure, "Hey, the nuns are popular, let's do a TV show." But I think it was just about nuns until they got the Network Notes. "Nuns are good. People will watch. But, couldn't they fly or something? People like flying."

I'm just surprised there were no copycat shows, like *The Swimming Rabbi* or *The Leaping Episcopalian*. Because, no matter how bizarre a show is, if it's popular, someone is going to try to imitate it. *Bewitched* came on and one year later it was *I Dream of Jeannie*. "No, they're different. On one she twitches her nose, on the other she blinks. But the most important thing is, one's a witch and the other's a genie. It's so different it's not even funny."

Other similar shows were *The Addams Family* and *The Munsters*, *Gilligan's Island* and *Lost in Space*, *Mr. Ed* and *My Mother the Car* (one is a talking horse, the other a talking car—they're both transportation); *Gunsmoke* and *60 Minutes* (well, they both have a bunch of guys and one girl).

My Mother the Car has to be the weirdest show ever. It even tops *The Flying Nun*. A man's mother dies and is reincarnated as a car. It *could* happen. I mean, a talking toaster or talking can opener, an ironing board or a Ping-Pong table—*those* would be ridiculous. But a talking car? That's much more likely.

Somewhere along the way to putting this show on the air, drugs had to be involved. It was the sixties. . . .

I think that part of my dilemma is that even though I want to have a baby, I don't want to *have* the baby. I can't imagine *hav*ing the baby. Giving birth is just so much pain. I know it's a beautiful child you end up with. I'm aware of that. But if I want a new washer and dryer, I wouldn't necessarily want to *have* a new washer and dryer, if you know what I mean (and if you don't, I really don't care to explain it in any more detail).

★

REAL FEARS VS. RIDICULOUS FEARS

Fear of earthquakes.	Fear of a pack of wild baby kittens dropping on your head as you are sleeping soundly in your bed at night.
Fear of flying.	Fear of losing control of the volume of your speech while saying something rude about someone sitting in front of you while at church.
Fear of speaking in public.	Fear of combing your hair so hard your head bleeds while your date is waiting in the front room.
Fear of high places.	Fear of having the uncontrollable urge of shaving not only your head, but the heads of everyone you meet.
Fear of dying.	Fear of eating way too many oranges for no apparent reason.

When you're a grown-up and you're up really late, it's still scary, isn't it? No matter how much you try to convince yourself it's cool, it's okay, you're imagining those little noises. It's scary. Whoever started all those boogeyman stories is a horrible person. It had to be started, obviously, by one guy—one guy telling a little kid a bedtime story. He just threw in the boogeyman. Clearly it caught on. I doubt there are royalties involved—if there are, he's probably feeling ripped off. Who knew it would turn out to be such a big hit? Maybe he could try to sue K. C. and the Sunshine Band. Although it's a different boogeyman, the song still scares me. Don't get me wrong—I danced to it just as much as the rest of you in 1975—but come on, someone sat down and wrote those lyrics. But I digress. My point . . . and I do have one, is that I still get scared at night. Every tiny creak, every little noise, I open my eyes real wide and listen with them. Have you noticed that? When it's dark and you can't see a thing, you open your eyes really wide and glance back and forth, like your eyes become your ears? Maybe it's just me.

You can tell a lot about a person by looking at the things that scare her or him (actually, I'm not really sure that's true, but since it's the premise of this story, I'll write it down and hope that nobody reads it too carefully). Sometimes what a person fears is actually the thing that they desire. For instance, if somebody is afraid of ice cream it could mean that they desire ice cream (hence the saying, I scream, you scream, we all scream for ice cream). However, if that person is allergic to ice cream, it probably means that they desire hives or some other type of rash.

Some people believe that it's a good idea to face your fears. I usually feel that it's much healthier to tie them up in a bag, drive out to the country, chuck them out your window, then drive home as fast as you can. But at the moment, I'm lying in bed in the middle of the night. I'm too tired to take a long drive. So, I will try looking into my heart to see what frightens me.

Ghosts. I'm afraid of ghosts. Do I really believe in ghosts? Sometimes I do. I watch these supernatural phenomenon shows about people who have seen doors and windows open and close and furniture move around the room. Sometimes I think, "Cool, I'd love to see that." But, most of the times, I wouldn't. I'd get kind of freaked out if a coffee table started dancing around, even if it was a goofy dance like the hokey-pokey.

The house I live in now might have a ghost: I think I've seen the guy. When I first moved into this house, strange things happened. I'd lock a door and a few minutes later I'd see that it was unlocked. A sliding door opened. It could've been the wind, you say. Well then, my skeptical friend, explain why there was a man standing in the middle of my bedroom dressed in some turn-of-the-century attire. Actually, it turns out that the man was my neighbor who got lost coming home from a costume party at Ernest Borgnine's house. But it could have been a ghost.

I'm also afraid of space aliens and spaceships. I'm scared that I'll be abducted by some UFO and then poked and prodded, which, from what I read, is what space aliens mostly do. Or what if they put some sort of chip in your brain that made you kill at their command or, even worse, made your favorite radio station the easy-listening one? What would be frightening, then, would be to come back and know that if you told anyone what happened to you, they'd think you were a nut. The only thing that scares me more than space aliens is the idea that there aren't any space aliens. We can't be the best that creation has to offer. I pray we're not all there is. If so, we're in big trouble.

Let's see, what else frightens me. Oh, I know. The scariest thing in the world almost happened to me the other day. Just thinking about it makes me break into a sweat (or maybe it's the hour and a half that I just spent on my treadmill that has caused me to break into a sweat; the important thing is that I'm sweating). Let me tell you about it. But first, a warning: If you are faint of heart, it would be a good idea to have a registered nurse nearby while you read this tale of near-terror. On the other hand, if you are a registered nurse, there's no need to have a faint-of-heart person with you. All they'd do is fidget around a lot and make you nervous.

I was at home, I was barefoot, I was about to put my shoes on . . . (Have I set the mood, is your heart beating fast?) Like a fool, I was just going to slip my foot into my shoe without looking. Luckily, at the last second I glanced down. In my shoe was . . . a huge spider—a big black-and-orange, hairy, crunchy spider. I almost put my foot right on it. Isn't that scary? Isn't that like something Stephen King would write? Stepping on a spider has to be the scariest thing in the world.

Actually, do you know what would be scarier? If, after putting on the one shoe I then recklessly put my foot in the other only to discover that it was teeming with . . . *hundreds* of spiders! All the babies were in there, a whole—let's see, it's a gaggle of geese, a school of fish, what is a group of spiders called? Oh, now I remember: a whole *snorkel* of spiders. That would be the scariest thing ever.

Unless, let's say you're out camping in the woods, or not even camping, or even in the woods; you're sleeping in your backyard. I don't know why. Maybe you like the great outdoors, but you want to be close to home in case somebody calls. Or maybe you had a fight with the person you live with, and you ended up yelling, "Okay, that does it. I'm sleeping in the backyard tonight!" It's only when you get back there that you realize it wasn't much of a threat. But you have too much pride to go and sleep inside (even though your dogs look at you from inside through the picture window with an expression that's a mixture of pity and confusion).

So (and this is the scary part), you're in the backyard and you're just about to doze off when you start feeling something kind of funny—not ha ha funny, but creepy, weird funny. So you look inside your sleeping bag and there's . . . a snake crawling up your leg. Aghhhhhhh! That just blows the spider thing away. It is not possible for there to be anything scarier than that.

Wait, I just thought of something more frightening. What if you're playing Frisbee on the beach and the person you're playing with (either a friend or someone kind of attractive who just happens to have a Frisbee, and you're flattered when they ask you to play with them—this part isn't important so you shouldn't be dwelling on it) throws the Frisbee way past you and you're furious because it's their fault, but you smile and yell, "I'll get it," and they say, "Okay." (Notice how I've managed to build up the suspense with some terse dialogue?)

Anyway, it turns out that the Frisbee has flown into one of those caves that you see at most beaches. Well, you go to get it and you realize that the Frisbee has gone farther down into the cave than you had thought. So you have to spelunk down into the abysmal depths of the pitch-black cave.

Finally, you reach what you assume is your Frisbee and you grab it, but it feels weird so you say, "Why is my Frisbee squishy?" So you squeeze it harder and you realize, "Hey, this isn't a Frisbee . . . it's a bat!"

Well, the bat starts making that *wee-bee-bee-bee* bat noise that bats make when you're squeezing them a little too hard (for more information on this read *Bats and the Sounds They Make When You Squeeze Them,* by Carney Pheek). So you start running as fast as you can out of the cave, but your screaming sets off thousands of bats—not a snorkel, that's only for spiders—a whole *Nipsy Russell* of bats, which start flying out after you. Now you're running through the sand, which is even harder than it sounds because you're wearing high heels (they look good with the swimsuit and slenderize your hips). So you're heading for the water thinking you'll be safe from the bats. But just before you submerge, a bat bites you on the ear. Oh man, those sharks can smell blood from miles away. So now you can see the shark fins swimming toward you. But you can't get out of the water because of the Nipsy Russell of bats. What a dilemma. It's like *The Pit and the Pendulum,* only different. I defy you to come up with something scarier than that. It's impossible.

Unless, say you're on a farm visiting your aunt . . . or whomever . . . and she calls out to you through the kitchen window, "Ellen, Ellen honey—would you mind going to look for that thing I misplaced?" And you don't even care what the thing is—because that guy's inside and he wants you to call him Uncle Larry and he's not your uncle and he's drunk all the time and he always wears those weird pajamas—but it's her life. So you go to look for that thing, and you think you see it in some bushes. You reach in to grab it, and you think you have it, but what you realize you're grabbing instead is (Oh my God!!!) a . . . lamb.

Okay, I admit that's not too scary by itself. But what if it's not just one lamb? What if it's a lot of lambs? What if it's a rack of lambs? That's pretty scary, huh? Because a lot of anything is scarier than one something.

Am I right? Think about it. One hundred poodles are scarier than one leopard. That's assuming, of course, that the leopard has no legs. You could come home, open the door, and see a leopard with no legs sitting in your living room. So what could it do? It's got no legs. It would be growling away, and you could sit right in front of it and make faces and touch its nose and "Woo" at it.

The only way a no-legged leopard could hurt you is if it fell out of a tree onto your head. I don't know how it got up the tree; maybe some of the other animals lifted it up there. But you have to admit when that leopard fell on you and clamped down on your head with its teeth, it would be pretty bad. You'd start running down the street yelling, "Help, help me, please."

And more often than not, you'd run into a big group of animal-rights activists, a *Naugahyde* of animal-rights activists. And, instead of helping, they'd probably throw red paint at you. You would scream out, "It's not a hat, it's a live animal! It's got no legs. I would never wear fur. I am wearing it against my will."

So now you've got a live leopard on your head and paint all over you as well. That is pretty darn terrifying. But you know, I don't want to diminish the spider in my shoe. Believe me, looking back, that was scary enough. I guess all I'm trying to say is you don't have to make stuff up; there are enough scary things in real life.

Joseph Dennie
(1768–1812)

Jack and Gill: A Scholarly Commentary

Among critical writers, it is a common remark that the fashion of the times has often given a temporary reputation to performances of very little merit, and neglected those much more deserving of applause. I shall endeavor to introduce to the nation a work, which, though of considerable elegance, has been strangely overlooked by the generality of the world. It has, of late, fallen into disrepute, chiefly from the simplicity of its style, which in this age of luxurious refinement, is deemed only a secondary beauty, and from its being the favorite of the young.

I must acknowledge that at first I doubted in what class of poetry it should be arranged. Its extreme shortness, and its uncommon metre, seemed to degrade it into a ballad, but its interesting subject, its unity of plan, and above all, its having a beginning, middle, and an end, decide its claim to the epic rank.

The opening is singularly beautiful:

JACK AND GILL

The first duty of the poet is to introduce his subject, and there is no part of poetry more difficult. Here our author is very happy: for instead of telling us, as an ordinary writer would have done, who were the ancestors of Jack and Gill, that the grandfather of Jack was a respectable farmer, that his mother kept a tavern at the sign of the Blue Bear; and that Gill's father was a Justice of the Peace, he introduces them to us at once in their proper persons.

I cannot help accounting it, too, as a circumstance honorable to the genius of the poet, that he does not in his opening call upon the Muse. This is an error into which Homer, and almost all the epic writers after him, have fallen; since by thus stating their case to the Muse, and desiring her to come to their assistance, they necessarily presuppose that she was absent, whereas there can be no surer sign of inspiration than for a muse to come unasked.

The personages being now seen, their situation is next to be discovered. Of this we are immediately informed in the subsequent line, when we are told:

JACK AND GILL
WENT UP A HILL.

Here the imagery is distinct, yet the description concise. The poet meant to inform us that two persons were going up a hill. Had the poet told us how the two heroes went up, whether in a cart or a wagon, and entered into the particulars which the subject involves, they would have been tedious, because superfluous.

These considerations may furnish us with the means of deciding a controversy, arising from a variation in the manuscripts; some of which have it *a* hill, and others *the* hill. As the description is in no other part local, I incline to the former reading. It has, indeed, been suggested that the hill here mentioned was Parnassus, and that the two persons are two poets, who, having overloaded Pegasus, the poor jaded creature was obliged to stop at the foot of the hill, whilst they ascended for water to recruit him. This interpretation, it is true, derives some countenance from the consideration that Jack and Gill were, in reality, as will appear in the course of the poem, going to draw water, and that there was on Parnassus such a place as Hippocrene, that is, a *horsepond,* at the top; but, on the whole, I think the text, as I have adopted it, to be the better reading.

Having ascertained the names and conditions of the parties, the reader naturally becomes inquisitive into their employment, and wishes to know whether their occupation is worthy of them.

JACK AND GILL
WENT UP A HILL
TO FETCH A BUCKET OF WATER.

Here we behold the plan gradually unfolding. We now discover their object, which we were before left to conjecture. Our acute author, instead of introducing a host of gods and goddesses, who might have impeded the journey of his heroes, by the intervention of the bucket, which is, as it ought to be, simple and conducive to the progress of the poem, has considerably improved on the ancient plan.

It has been objected that the employment of Jack and Gill is not sufficiently dignified for an epic poem; but, in answer to this, it must be remarked that it was the opinion of Socrates, and many other philosophers, that beauty should be estimated by utility, and surely the purpose of the heroes must have been beneficial. They ascended the rugged mountain to draw water, and drawing water is certainly more conducive to human happiness than drawing blood, as do the boasted heroes of the Iliad, or roving on the ocean and invading other men's property, as did the pious Aeneas.

Yes, they went to draw water. It might have been drawn for the purpose of culinary consumption; it might have been to quench the thirst of the harmless animals who relied upon them for support; it might have been to feed a sterile soil, and to revive the drooping plants, which they raised by their labors. Is not our author more judicious than Appollonius, who chooses for the heroes of his Argonautics a set of rascals, undertaking to steal a sheep skin? Do we not find the amiable Rebecca busy at the well? Does not one of the maidens in the Odyssey delight us by her diligence in the same situation?

But the descriptive part is now finished, and the author hastens to the catastrophe. At what part of the mountain the well was situated, what was the reason of the sad misfortune, or how the prudence of Jack foresook him, we are not informed, but so, alas! it happened:

JACK FELL DOWN—

Unfortunate Jack, at the moment when he was nimbly, for aught we know, going up the hill, perhaps at the moment when his toils were to cease, he made an heedless step, his centre of gravity fell beyond his base, and he tumbled. Buoyed by hope, we suppose his affliction not quite remediless, that his fall is an accident to which the wayfarers of this life are daily liable, and we anticipate his immediate rise to resume his labors. But:

JACK FELL DOWN
AND BROKE HIS CROWN—

Nothing now remains but to deplore the fate of the unhappy Jack. The mention of the *crown* has much perplexed the commentators. The learned Microphilus, in the 513th page of his "*Cursory Remarks*" on the poem, thinks he can find in it some allusion to the story of Alfred, who, he says, is known to have lived, during his concealment, in a mountainous country, and as he watched the cakes on the fire, might have been sent to bring water. But Microphilus' acute annotator, Vandergruten, has detected the fallacy of such a supposition, though he falls into an equal error in remarking that Jack might have carried a crown or a half crown-piece in his hand, which was fractured in the fall. My learned readers will doubtless agree with me in conjecturing that, as the crown is often used metaphorically for the head, and as that part is, or without any disparagement to the unfortunate sufferer, might have been, the heaviest, it was really his pericranium that sustained the damage.

Having seen the fate of Jack, we are anxious to know that of his companion. Alas!

AND GILL CAME TUMBLING AFTER.

Here the distress thickens on us. Unable to support the loss of his friend, he followed him, determined to share his disaster, and resolved that, as they had gone up together, they should not be separated as they came down.

In the midst of our afflictions, let us not, however, be unmindful of the poet's merit, which, on this occasion, is conspicuous. He evidently seems to have in view the excellent observation of Adam Smith, that our sympathy arises not from a view of the passion, but of the situation that excites it. Instead of unnecessary lamentation, he gives us the real state of the case; avoiding at the same time that minuteness of detail, which is so common among pathetic poets, and which, by dividing a passion and tearing it to rags, as Shakespeare says, destroys its force.

Of the bucket, we are told nothing, but it is probable that it fell with its supporters.

Let us conclude with a review of the poem's most prominent beauties. The subject is the *fall of man*. The heroes are men who did not commit a single fault, and whose misfortunes are to be imputed, not to indiscretion, but to destiny. The poet prudently clipped the wings of imagination, and repressed the extravagance of metaphorical decoration. All is simple, plain, consistent.

That part, too, without which poetry is useless sound, the moral, has not escaped the view of the poet. When we behold two young men, who but a short moment before stood up in all the pride of health, falling down a hill, how must we lament the instability of all things.

Phyllis Diller
(Contemporary)

FROM *The Complete Mother*

There Is Not Always Room For One More
Or
Have You Ever Noticed That Most Of
The People Who Favor Birth Control
Have Already Been Born?

When Fang and I got married he said, "In a couple of years we will hear the pitter patter of little footsteps." So I set traps. Nevertheless, I had chronic pregnancy, which is not surprising since even as a child I was accident prone. With me, birth control meant not having the kid until I got to the hospital. I was pregnant so often I felt like the bag on the vacuum cleaner. But you don't have to have so many children. There are three great methods of birth control. They are:

1. Thinking about what other people will say if you get pregnant again.
2. A garlic salami before retiring.
3. The pill.

Eleven million women in the world use birth control pills. They are called progressive. One billion women don't use birth control pills. They are called "Mama."

Of course, there are older types of contraceptives than the pill, but as of this writing, no one has figured out how to knit anything that works.

Doctors recommend birth control pills be taken the same time each day. Select the time of day when your children are at their worst—then it's easier to remember to take your pill.

That's The Glory Of Love
Or
How To Tell Your Husband

The 5 times I told Fang I was pregnant went like this:

1. I played a record of "Rockabye Baby" and he kissed me.
2. I said coyly: "The baby is going to have a playmate!" He said: "You bought a dog?"
3. I said: "Hey there! That silly stork is landing here again." We shook hands.
4. I said: "Guess what!" He shrugged his shoulders.
5. On the day I whispered to Fang, "We're going to have a fifth," he said: "Great! I'll get the ice and the mix."

I know you will want a novel way to tell your husband he is to become a father. Here are a few suggestions:

1. Write on the bathroom wall, "Margaret Sanger is a rat fink."
2. Say, "Is there room in your billfold for one more picture?"
3. "Honey, how would you like to get a little more value out of our babysitting money?"
4. "How would you like to see Father's Day work into something really big for you?"
5. "Don't you think it's too bad to put forth all that effort of setting a good example just for BILLY?"
6. "Would you like to meet somebody new?"

FROM *Phyllis Diller's Marriage Manual*

It might help you to be more satisfied with your mate if you remember that when you made the selection it was not multiple choice. I was sort of tricked into marrying. One night I was out with Fang and a girl said, "You better hang on to him." I thought I had a prize. I didn't know she meant that after one drink he falls down.

I always wondered how I could tell when the right one came along—but it was easy. He was the only one that came along.

Unfortunately, there is no way of looking up husbands in Consumer's Guide. For instance, Fang told me he was a self-made man. It wasn't until later that I discovered that he would have been wise to get some help. With him there's no question that it would have been better to have loved and lost.

POKER

1. As he is leaving, say, "Have fun. And if you win we'll get cough medicine for Barbie."
2. Say, "Don't hurry home. No matter how late it is, I'll be waiting up for you."
3. If you want a little extra attention, say, "Are you going to be using the .22 tonight?"
4. Ask him to fill the liquor cabinet before he goes.

And May The Best Man Emerge Victorious

1. Insist that your husband have regular checkups. It's much more enjoyable to fight with a mate in perfect health.
2. Fights should be carefully scheduled so as not to interfere with your favorite TV show or interrupt dinner hour at the police station.
3. No wound should be inflicted that cannot be covered by a standard size Band-Aid.
4. Nothing should be thrown that is bigger than a bread box. Have a few weapons handy but pie throwing is out of the question. Not only is it trite but, if you bake like I do, a direct hit with one of those things could kill you.

5. Remember, blood is not only thicker than water, it's much more difficult to get off the carpet.

Naturally these suggestions should be observed more strictly if you do not have a major medical insurance policy.

Ralph Ellison
(1914–94)

FROM *Invisible Man*

I fight my battle with Monopolated Light & Power. . . . It allows me to feel my vital aliveness. I also fight them for taking so much of my money before I learned to protect myself. In my hole in the basement there are exactly 1,369 lights. I've wired the entire ceiling, every inch of it. And not with fluorescent bulbs, but with the older, more-expensive-to-operate kind, the filament type. An act of sabotage, you know. I've already begun to wire the wall. A junk man I know, a man of vision, has supplied me with wire and sockets. Nothing, storm or flood, must get in the way of our need for light and ever more and brighter light. The truth is the light and light is the truth. When I finish all four walls, then I'll start on the floor. Just how that will go, I don't know. Yet when you have lived invisible as long as I have you develop a certain ingenuity. I'll solve the problem. And maybe I'll invent a gadget to place my coffee pot on the fire while I lie in bed, and even invent a gadget to warm my bed—like the fellow I saw in one of the picture magazines who made himself a gadget to warm his shoes! Though invisible, I am in the great American tradition of tinkers. That makes me kin to Ford, Edison and Franklin. Call me, since I have a theory and a concept, a "thinker-tinker." Yes, I'll warm my shoes; they need it, they're usually full of holes.

Ralph Waldo Emerson
(1803–82)

FROM *Journal*

June 23, 1838

I hate goodies. I hate goodness that preaches. Goodness that preaches undoes itself. A little electricity of virtue lurks here and there in kitchens and among the obscure, chiefly women, that flashes out occasional light and makes the existence of the thing still credible. But one had as gladly lief curse and swear as be guilty of this odious religion that watches the beef and watches the cider in the pitcher at table, that shuts the mouth hard at any remark it cannot twist nor wrench into a sermon, and preaches as long as itself and its hearer is awake. Goodies make us very bad. . . . We will almost sin to spite them. Better indulge yourself, feed fat, drink liquors, than go straitlaced for such cattle as these.

August, 1861

I am at a loss to understand why people hold Miss Austen's novels at so high a rate, which seem to me vulgar in tone, sterile in artistic invention, imprisoned in the wretched conventions of English society, without genius, wit, or knowledge of the world. Never was life so pinched and narrow. The one problem in the mind of the writer in both the stories I have read, *Persuasion*, and *Pride and Prejudice*, is marriageableness. All that interests in any character introduced is still this one, Has he or she money to marry with, and conditions conforming? 'Tis "the nympholepsy★ of a fond despair," say, rather, of an English boarding-house. Suicide is more respectable.

★Frenzy.

Nora Ephron
(Contemporary)

FROM *Heartburn*

It's hard when you don't like someone a friend marries. . . . [I]t means that even a simple flat inquiry like "How's Helen?" is taken amiss, since your friend always thinks that what you hope he's going to say is "Dead." You feel irritated because your darling friend has married beneath himself, and he feels irritated because you don't see the virtues of his beloved. Then, if your friend's marriage fails, he becomes even more irritated at you, because if you had been a real friend, you would have prevented him physically from making the mistake, you would have locked him up in a closet until the urge to get married had passed.

Vera said: "Why do you feel you have to turn everything into a story?"

So I told her why:

Because if I tell the story, I control the version.

Because if I tell the story, I can make you laugh, and I would rather have you laugh at me than feel sorry for me.

Because if I tell the story, it doesn't hurt as much.

Because if I tell the story, I can get on with it.

Blanche Farley
(Contemporary)

The Lover Not Taken

Committed to one, she wanted both
And, mulling it over, long she stood,
Alone on the road, loath
To leave, wanting to hide in the undergrowth.
This new guy, smooth as a yellow wood

Really turned her on. She liked his hair,
His smile. But the other, Jack, had a claim
On her already and she had to admit, he did wear
Well. In fact, to be perfectly fair,
He understood her. His long, lithe frame

Beside hers in the evening tenderly lay.
Still, if this blond guy dropped by someday,
Couldn't way just lead on to way?
No. For if way led on and Jack
Found out, she doubted if he would ever come back.

Oh, she turned with a sigh.
Somewhere ages and ages hence,
She might be telling this. "And I—"
She would say, "stood faithfully by."
But by then who would know the difference?

With that in mind, she took the fast way home,
The road by the pond, and phoned the blond.

Fanny Fern
(1811–72)

FROM *Fern Leaves from Fanny's Portfolio*

The Model Widower

Begins to think of No. 2 before the weed on his hat loses its first gloss;—may be seen assisting young girls to find a seat in church, or ordering carts off dry crossings, for pretty feet that are waiting to pass over;—is convinced he "never was made to live alone;"—his "children must be looked after," or, if he has not any, he would like to be looked after—himself;—draws a deep sigh every time a dress rustles past, with a female woman in it;—is very particular about the polish of his boots and the fit of his gloves;—thinks he looks very interesting in black;—don't walk out in public much with his children; when he does, takes the *youngest*;—revives his old taste for moonlight and poetry;—pities single men with all his heart; wonders how they contrive to exist!—reproves little John for saying "Pa" so loud, when he meets him in the street;—sets his face against the practice of women's going home "alone and unprotected" from evening meeting;—tells the widows his heart aches for them!—wonders which, of all the damsels he sees, he shall make up his mind to marry;—is sorry he shall be obliged to disappoint them all but one!—has long since preferred orange-blossoms to the cypress-wreath;—starts up, some fine day, and refurnishes his house from garret to cellar;—hangs his first wife's portrait in the attic,—shrouded in an old blanket,—and marries a playmate for his oldest daughter.

Mistaken Philanthropy

"Don't moralize to a man who is on his back;—help him up, set him firmly on his feet, and then give him advice and means."

There's an old-fashioned, verdant piece of wisdom, altogether unsuited for the enlightened age we live in; fished up, probably, from some musty old newspaper, edited by some eccentric man troubled with that inconvenient appendage called a heart! Don't pay any attention to it. If a poor wretch—male or female—comes to you for charity, whether allied to you by your own mother, or mother Eve, put on the most stoical, "get thee behind me," expression you can muster. Listen to him with the air of a man who "thanks God he is not as other men are." If the story carry conviction with it, and truth and sorrow go hand in hand, button your coat up tighter over your pocket-book, and give him a piece of—good advice! If you know anything about him, try to rake up some imprudence or mistake he may have made in the course of his life, and bring that up as a reason why you can't give him anything more substantial, and tell him that his present condition is probably a salutary discipline for those same peccadilloes!—ask him more questions than there are in the Assembly's Catechism, about his private history, and when you've pumped him high and dry, try to teach him—on an empty stomach—the "duty of submission." If the tear of wounded sensibility begins to flood the eye, and a hopeless look of discouragement settles down upon the face, "wish him well," and turn your back upon him as quick as possible.

Should you at any time be seized with an unexpected spasm of generosity, and make up your mind to bestow some worn-out old garment, that will hardly hold together till the recipient gets it home, you've bought him, body and soul, of course; and are entitled to the gratitude of a life-time! If he ever presumes to think differently from you, after that, he is an "ungrateful wretch," and "ought to suffer." As to the "golden rule," that was made in old times; everything is changed now; it is not suited to our meridian.

People should not *get* poor; if they do, you don't want to be bothered with it. It is disagreeable; it hinders your digestion. You would rather see Dives than Lazarus; and, it is my opinion, your taste will be gratified in that particular,—in the other world, if not in this!

Important for Married Men

"The Budget says, that a lady lost the use of her tongue for nearly a week the other day, from eating too many tomatoes. The price of this indispensable vegetable will, no doubt, rise in consequence."

No it won't! There is nothing in this world—with one exception—that gentlemen love so well as to hear women talk to each other. You are sitting *tête-à-tête* with Moses, at your domestic fireside. A lady friend comes in; she is bright, and witty, and agreeable. You have both a tremendous budget of feminine *"bon mots"* and good things to share with each other. The question is, how to get rid of Moses. You hint that there is a great political meeting at Tammany Hall, on which occasion Cass, or whoever is god of your husband's political idolatry, is going to speak. He don't stir a peg. Then you adroitly raise the window-curtain, and speak of the beauty of the night, and how many gentlemen are out with cigars in their mouths. It don't "end in—smoke!" Then you ask him "if he has carried the morning's paper over to his mother!" He is as deaf as a "post!" Finally, in despair, you get into the remotest corner of the room, and commence operations, leaving Moses to his corner and his book, for fear of disturbing(?) him.

Kitty tells you a most excruciating story, and you tell her another; and you laugh till the tears start. Well, now you just creep slily round Moses' chair, and take a peep at him. St. Cecilia! if that book is not upside down, and his mouth stretched from ear to ear! He has swallowed every word with the avidity of a cat over her first mouse banquet; and yet, if you did not face him up with that up- side-down book, he would persist he had been reading the funniest book alive! And so he has, but it was not bound in "calf" or "sheep-skin!"

Owls Kill Humming-Birds

"We are not to suppose that the oak wants stability because its light and changeable leaves dance to the music of the breeze;—nor are we to conclude that a man wants solidity and strength of mind because he may exhibit an occasional playfulness and levity."

No, indeed! So, if you have the bump of mirthfulness developed, don't marry a tombstone. You come skipping into the parlor, with your heart as light as a feather, and your brain full of merry fancies. There he sits! stupid—solemn—and forbidding.

You go up and lay your hand on his arm; he's magnetized about as much as if an omnibus-driver had punched him in the ribs for his fare; and looks in your face with the same expression he'd wear if contemplating his ledger.

You turn away and take up a newspaper. There's a witty paragraph; your first impulse is to read it aloud to him. No use! He wouldn't see through it till the middle of next week. Well, as a sort of escape-valve to your *ennui,* you sit down to the piano and dash off a waltz; he interrupts you with a request for a dirge.

Your little child comes in,—Heaven bless her!—and utters some one of those innocent pettinesses which are always dropping like pearls from children's mouths. You look to see him catch her up and give her a smothering kiss. Not he! He's too dignified!

Altogether, he's about as genial as the north side of a meeting-house. And so you go plodding through life with him to the dead-march of his own leaden thoughts. You revel in the sunbeams; he likes the shadows. You are on the hill- tops; he is in the plains. Had the world been made to his order, earth, sea, and sky would have been one universal pall—not a green thing in it except himself! No vine would "cling," no breeze "dally," no zephyr "woo." Flowers and children, women and squirrels, would never have existed. The sun would have been quenched out for being too mercurial, and we should have crept through life by the light of the pale, cold moon!

No—no—make no such shipwreck of yourself. Marry a man who is not too ascetic to enjoy a good, merry laugh. Owls kill humming-birds.

A Law More Nice Than Just

After all, having tried it I affirm that nothing reconciles a woman quicker to her femininity than an experiment in male apparel, although I still maintain that she should not be forbidden by law to adopt it when necessity requires; at least, not till the practice is amended by which a female clerk, who performs her duty equally well with a male clerk, receives less salary, simply because she is a woman.

To have to jump on to the cars when in motion, and scramble yourself on to the platform as best you may without a helping hand; to be nudged roughly in the ribs by the conductor with, "your fare, sir?" to have your pretty little toes trod on, and no healing "beg your pardon," applied to the smart; to have all those nice-looking men who used to make you such crushing bows, and give you such insinuating smiles, pass you without the slightest interest in your coat tails, and perhaps push you against the wall or into the gutter, with a word tabooed by the clergy. In fine, to dispense with all those delicious little politenesses (for men are great bears to each other) to which one has been accustomed, and yet feel no inclination to take advantage of one's corduroys and secure an equivalent by making interest with the "fair sex," stale to you as a thrice-told tale. Isn't *that* a situation?

To be subject to the promptings of that unstifleable feminine desire for adornment, which is right and lovely within proper limits, and yet have no field for your operations. To have to conceal your silken hair, and yet be forbidden a becoming moustache, or whiskers, or beard—(all hail beards, I say!). To choke up your nice throat with a disguising cravat; to hide your bust (I trust no Miss Nancy is blushing) under a baggy vest. To have nobody ask you to ice cream, and yet be forbidden, by your horrible disgust of tobacco, to smoke. To have a gentleman ask you "the time sir?" when you are new to the geography of your watch-pocket. To accede to an invitation to test your "heft," by sitting down in one of those street-weighing chairs, and have one of the male bystanders, taking hold of your foot, remark, "Halloo, sir, you must not rest these upon the ground while you are being weighed"; and go grinning away in your coat-sleeve at your truly feminine faux pas.

And yet—and yet—to be able to step over the ferry-boat chain when you are in a distracted hurry, like any other fellow, without waiting for that tedious unhooking process, and quietly to enjoy your triumph over scores of impatient-waiting crushed petticoats behind you; to taste that nice lager beer "on draught"; to pick up contraband bits of science in a Medical Museum, forbidden to crinoline, and hold conversations with intelligent men, who supposing you to be a man, consequently talk sense to you. That is worth while.

Take it all in all, though, I thank the gods I am a woman. I had rather be loved than make love; though I could beat the makers of it, out and out, if I did not think it my duty to refrain out of regard to their feelings, and the final disappointment of the deluded women! But—oh, dear, I want to do such a quantity of "improper" things, that there is not the slightest real harm in doing. I want to see and know a thousand things which are forbidden to flounces—custom only can tell why—I can't. I want the free use of my ankles, for this summer at least, to take a journey; I want to climb and wade, and tramp about, without giving a thought to my clothes; without carrying about with me a long procession of trunks and boxes, which are the inevitable penalty of femininity as at present appareled. I hate a Bloomer, such as we have seen—words are weak to say how much; I hate myself as much in a man's dress; and yet I want to run my fingers through my cropped hair some fine morning without the bore of dressing it; put on some sort of loose blouse affair—it must be pretty, though—and a pair of Turkish trousers—*not* Bloomers—and a cap, or hat—and start; nary a trunk— "nary" a bandbox. Wouldn't that be fine? But propriety scowls and says, "ain't you ashamed of yourself, Fanny Fern?" *Yes, I am,* Miss Nancy. I *am* ashamed of myself, that I haven't the courage to carry out what would be so eminently convenient, and right, and proper under the circumstances. I am ashamed of myself that I sit like a fool on the piazza of some hotel every season, gazing at some distant mountain, which every pulse and muscle of my body, and every faculty of my soul, are urging me to climb, that I may "see the kingdoms of the earth and the glory of them." I *am* ashamed of myself that you, Miss Nancy, with your uplifted forefinger and your pursed-up mouth, should keep me out of a dress in which only I can hope to do such things. Can't I make a compromise with you, Miss Nancy? for I'm getting restless, as these lovely summer days pass on. I'd write you such long accounts of beautiful things, Miss Nancy—things which God made for female as well as male eyes to see; and I should come home so strong and healthy, Miss Nancy—a freckle or two, perhaps—but who cares? O-h-n-o-w, Miss Nancy, d-o—Pshaw! you cross old termagant! May Lucifer fly away wid ye.

FROM *The Life & Beauties of Fanny Fern*

A Whisper to Romantic Young Ladies

"A crust of bread, a pitcher of water, a thatched roof, and love,— there's happiness for you."

Girls! *that's a humbug!* The very *thought* of it makes me groan. It's all moonshine. In fact, men and moonshine in my dictionary are synonymous.

"Water and a crust! RATHER spare diet! May do for the honey-moon. Don't make much difference *then,* whether you eat shavings or sardines—but when you return to *substantials,* and your wedding dress is put away in a trunk for the benefit of posterity, if you can get your husband to *smile* on anything short of a 'sirloin' or a roast turkey, you are a lucky woman.

"Don't every married woman know that a man is as savage as a New Zealander when he's hungry? and when he comes home to an empty cup-board and meets a dozen little piping mouths, (necessary accompaniments of 'cottages' and 'love,') clamorous for supper, *'Love* will have the *sulks,'* or my name isn't Fanny. Lovers have a trick of getting disenchanted, too, when they see their Aramintas with dresses pinned up round the waist, hair powdered with sweeping, faces scowled up over the wash-tub, and soap-suds dripping from red elbows.

"We know these little accidents never happen in novels—where the heroine is always 'dressed in white, with a rose-bud in her hair,' and lives on blossoms and May dew! There are no wash-tubs or gridirons in *her* cottage; *her* children are born cherubim, with a seraphic contempt for dirt pies and molasses. *She* re-mains 'a beauty' to the end of the chapter, and 'steps out' just in time to antici-pate her first gray hair; her husband drawing his last breath at the same time, as a dutiful husband *should;* and not falling into the unromantic error of outliving his grief, and marrying a second time!

"But this humdrum life, girls, is another affair, with its washing and ironing and cleaning days, when children expect boxed ears, and visitors picked-up din-ners. All the 'romance' there is in it, you can put under a three-cent piece!

"St. Paul says they who marry do well enough, but they who *don't* marry do WELL-ER! Sensible man that. Nevertheless, had *I* flourished in those times, I would have undertaken to change his sentiments; for those old-fashioned gentle-men were worth running after.

"One half the women marry for fear they shall be old maids. Now I'd like to know why an old maid is to be snubbed, any more than an old bach-elor? Old bachelors receive 'the mitten,' occasionally, and old maids have been known to *outlive several 'offers.'* They are both useful in their way—particularly old bachelors!

"Now *I* intend to be an old maid; and I shall found a mutual accommoda-tion society, and admit old bachelors honorary members. They shall wait on *us* evenings, and we'll hem their pocket handker*chers* and mend their gloves. No *boys under thirty* to be admitted. Irreproachable dickeys, immaculate shirt-bosoms and faultless boots *indispensable.* Gentlemen always to sit on the *opposite* side of the room—no refreshments but *ices! Instant expulsion* the consequence of the first attempt at love-making! No allusion to be made to Moore or By-ron! The little *'bye-laws'* of the society *not* to be published! Moonlight eve-nings, the sisters are not at home! the moon being considered, from time immemorial, an unprincipled magnetiser!"

"Don't Disturb Him!"

"If your husband looks grave, let him alone; don't disturb or annoy him."

Oh, pshaw! when I'm married, the soberer my husband looked, the more fun I'd rattle about his ears. *'Don't disturb him!'* I guess so! I'd salt his coffee—and pepper his tea—and sugar his beef-steak—and tread on his toes—and hide his newspaper—and sew up his pockets—and put pins in his slippers—and dip his cigars in water—and I wouldn't stop for the Great Mogul, till I had shortened his long face to my liking. Certainly he'd 'get vexed,' there wouldn't be any fun in teasing him if he didn't, and that would give his melancholy blood a good healthful start, and his eyes would snap and sparkle, and he'd say, 'Fanny, WILL you be quiet or not?' and I should laugh, and pull his whiskers, and say, decidedly, *'Not!'* and then I should tell him he hadn't the slightest idea how handsome he looked when he was vexed, and then he would pretend not to hear the compliment—but would pull up his dickey, and take a sly peep in the glass (for all that!) and then he'd begin to grow amiable, and get off his stilts, and be just as agreeable all the rest of the evening *as if he wasn't my husband,* and all because I didn't follow that stupid bit of advice 'to let him alone.' Just imagine ME, Fanny, sitting down on a cricket in the corner, with my forefinger in my mouth, looking out the sides of my eyes, and waiting till that man got ready to speak to me! You can see at once it would be—be—— Well, the amount of it is, I *shouldn't do it*!

Fannie Flagg
(Contemporary)

FROM *Fried Green Tomatoes at the Whistle Stop Café*

About ten years ago, when Ed had started seeing a woman he worked with down at the insurance company, she had attended a group called The Complete Woman, to try and save her marriage. She wasn't sure she loved Ed all that much, but she loved him just enough to not want to lose him. Besides, what would she do? She had lived with him as long as she had lived with her parents. The organization believed that women could find complete happiness if they, in turn, would dedicate their entire lives to just making their man happy.

Their leader had informed them that all the rich and successful career women out there who appeared to be so happy were, in reality, terribly lonely and miserable and secretly envied them their happy Christian homes.

It was a stretch to imagine that Barbara Walters might want to give it all up for Ed Couch, but Evelyn tried her hardest. Of course, even though she was not religious, it was a comfort to know that the Bible backed her up in being a doormat. Hadn't the apostle St. Paul said for women not to usurp power over the men, but to be in silence?

So, hoping she was on the right track, she started up the ladder on *The Ten Steps to Complete Happiness*. She tried step number one and met Ed at the front door nude, wrapped in Saran wrap. But Ed had been horrified: He'd jumped inside the house and slammed the door. "Jesus Christ, Evelyn! What if I had been the paper boy? Have you gone insane?"

Jeff Foxworthy
(Contemporary)

FROM *No Shirt, No Shoes . . . No Problem!*

Technique is everything.

First you kiss for three hours. Then you move your arm up on her arm. The goal is to have the inside of your arm accidentally brush the outside of her breast. If she doesn't shift away, you may move on. "Okay, wait a couple of minutes and bring the arm back . . . Oops, bumped it again. Still okay. Okay, now let's see if we can put our hand on her side, between her waist and her chest. Still doing okay . . ."

The whole procedure is like monitoring a space launch.

"Okay, let's gently ease the hand up. T-minus-8, 7, 6, 5, 4, move, grab." Many times that's when a young woman will launch a preprogrammed counterattack and stop your hand, or move it back to its original position. With any luck her primary systems will fail and her secondary systems will be forced to take over, and your hand will be cleared for takeoff.

Often, I would proceed to T-minus-four seconds and reverse course and start again, with ever so slight variations. It was confusing and satisfying. The idea was to wear a girl down. Eventually, they got damn tired of stopping you.

Too bad it never dawned on us that perhaps our objects of desire might have *wanted* what we wanted as well.

As I matured sexually and socially and began dating regularly, I made some important discoveries. For example, girls in the country were easier targets than girls in the city. Girls in the city had other stuff to do. They could go to a movie, they could go to the mall. Girls in the country didn't have a whole lot to look forward to. So whenever I went on vacation or down to the farm, I immediately began looking for prospects.

I figured that out the summer between the ninth and tenth grades, when I went to Pawpaw's farm in South Carolina. I met a girl who was the friend of a friend and we were all going to ride horses. She was cute, with blunt-cut blond hair. After a morning on horseback, she and I tied our mounts outside my uncle's trailer. No one was home. We went inside to get something to drink, settled down into the sofa, and she shifted right toward me.

I liked to think I was just too charming. On the other hand maybe she figured that making out with me was better than cleaning up after the horses, or the usual country pastime of staring all afternoon at a tree. Like I said, there wasn't much to do. Anyway, she pretty quickly let me put my hand inside her shirt. Not only did I feel it, I saw it. It was so cute. You know how you open up a blanket and you see a puppy for the first time? So innocent, and it's looking right up at you. That's all we did, but it was enough.

Later Uncle Bob and I milked the cows and talked. Uncle Bob said, "Hey, you guys were gone for quite a while," he said, with a devious chuckle. My mind churned. Suddenly I had my first shot at actually getting a man's approval.

"Oh, yeah. Yeah." Remember, this is my *uncle Bob.* And we're *milking* a cow.

"So, how was it?"

"Good. Good," I lied. "Really good."

"Did you . . . ?"

"Oh, sure. Sure."

"You dawg."

His reaction taught me an important lesson: Lying works. I'm just glad Bob wasn't so impressed that he wanted to demonstrate any advanced techniques on the cow.

★

We always hear how men like to swap tales of a graphic sexual nature in the locker room. This is completely true. However, we can be more subtle. Occasionally we simply like to brag about our hot moves.

Whining is always at the top of the list.

He: *Please, sugar dumpling, please.*
She: *No. Uh-uh. No way.*
He: *But my girlfriend just don't understand me like you do.*
She: *Then break up with her.*
He: *Cain't. She's also my maw.*
She: *You're sick!*
He: *Me? Sick? You did it with your cousin!*
She: *I know. But he's nice.*
He: *But sweetie . . .*

Even though this example is assumed to be true only in select regions of the country, guys everywhere are *still* pathetic. They prove it every year at spring break. My most vivid memory is of five guys crammed into a Camaro, going to Fort Lauderdale or Daytona Beach, saying, "We're gonna get some. We're gonna get some." Then six days later, "Next year. *Next year* we're gonna get some."

Nobody ever got lucky. It took me two or three spring breaks to finally figure out what I'd been doing wrong. Like everyone else, I'd been too overeager. Hollering things at women didn't work. And for most women projectile vomiting has never been a turn-on. Finally, I tried a different tactic. When we all went into some place selling quarter drinks, I let the guys roam the bar while I sat by myself at a table and acted uninterested. Within five minutes I had eight coeds saying, "Why are you just sitting here? What's wrong with you?"

Anything that works.

Travis Tritt's road manager showed me the all-time best way to pick up a woman. We did a show at the Omni for the Super Bowl when it was last in Atlanta. I noticed that he had on two different cowboy boots: one was red lizard, the other tan buckskin. I said, "Why do you have on two different boots?"

He said, "I've gotten more women doing this than I can handle. All I have to do is go out dressed like this to a bar. I don't have to say a word. Women just come up to me and go, 'Why do you have on two different boots?' *They* start the conversation."

Like I said, anything that works.

★

Men are hounds. We think nothing of dating someone who just broke up with our best friend. I once asked a friend if I could date his ex. He said, "Don't you recall me telling you about her chasing me through the parking lot with a butcher knife?"

"Yeah," I said, "but she's *really* good-looking."

★

Roommates are tough. You've got to pick someone you can beat up on because you never get along with everybody always. Even if you shared an apartment with the Pope, I guarantee that three weeks into it you'd be going, "Hey, you mind picking up the cape, man? And quit leaving the papal miter on the kitchen counter."

I've always looked for a roommate with a sense of humor, someone roughly like me, only different. I'm not so sure living with myself is any piece of cake. You definitely don't want someone wilder than you are. You want the same degree of wildness. If you're the wild one you'll feel like you're living with your Aunt Florence while he's holding a naked Twister Bingo session in his bedroom—or worse, in the living room, where you can see it all. You both need to stagger in side by side. The *Odd Couple* approach never works.

An ideal roommate has a horny sister. Or *is* someone's horny sister. Or is one and has one. Or knows one. I'm just kidding around here.

Paying the rent on time is also a good quality.

One person to absolutely avoid as a roommate is an ex-wife, no matter what sick circumstances drive you to again share the same living space. First, you don't want to be around when she's getting phone calls from other guys. Second, she doesn't want to be around while you're burning her clothes.

No matter how you fare during these days of swine and losers, I promise that you will soon miss the times when you were wild and free and living with someone you could just move out on at any time. Maybe for no other reason than that I'm a sentimental guy, about five years ago I got nostalgic for the apartment life. Then Gregg got pregnant. She ate all my food and threw up once a day. It was just like having a roommate all over again.

Redd Foxx
(1922–91)

FROM **Redd Foxx, B.S.**

I've just composed a love song, it's called "I love you, darling, if you never have any cash money in your pocket book during your entire life in this world. But I *won't* be with you, darling . . . if you never have any cash money in your pocket book during your entire life in this world or anywhere else you might go with nothing. 'Cause I don't need nobody to help me do bad. I can starve to death by myself, sugar. So try and forget me. But always remember I love you more than any woman I've ever known in my life, 'cause that night I went up to your house and got drunk you didn't mess with none of the money that was left in my wallet 'cause you must have known, *deep down in your heart,* if I'd a come to and found some of my hard-earned money gone, I'd a went home and got a two-by-four that I been soaking in motor oil since 1953. And I'd a came back searching for you, and found you anywhere on earth with any of the money in your bag, I'd a took my greasy two-by-four, knowing that it would not break, bend, or splinter, and try to cave your skull in with it . . . cha–cha–cha."

Al Franken
(Contemporary)

FROM *Oh, the Things I Know!*

Oh, the Things You'll Keep Telling Yourself!

Time for a reality check. You're going to have some setbacks. Time for a reality check of that reality check. "Setbacks" is just a nice word for "failures."

When confronted with failure, you will undoubtably tell yourself something like "You learn more from failure than you do from success." The *next* time you fail, you will probably say to yourself again, "You learn more from failure than you do from success." By the third time you fail, you may start to think, "Why am I failing so often if I am supposedly learning so much from these failures?" Most likely, that will be just a passing thought, and you will seek solace in your old standby, "You learn more from failure than you do from success," or some version thereof, like "Failure is a better teacher than success" or "Show me a man who is a success, and I'll show you a man who has failed a dozen times."

That last one is good for your next nine failures. After which you may begin to wonder whether telling yourself this sort of thing over and over is really getting you anywhere.

Most of the things people keep telling themselves, while temporarily encouraging, are simply untrue. Take, for example, that popular adage "You learn more from failure than you do from success." Let me give you an example from my own life, which, unlike the other examples from my life in this book, is an actual true example of something that really happened to me.

In 1995, I wrote and starred in the film *Stuart Saves His Family*. It was a failure as defined by the Hollywood powers-that-be, in that it lost millions of dollars for Paramount instead of making millions of dollars for the studio. Now, I am very proud of the movie, and if I had to do it over again, I wouldn't change a thing, except perhaps whatever it was that made it a failure.

But to tell you the truth, I did learn a few things from my failure. I learned, for example, that I would probably never again have the opportunity to star in a movie, a piece of information that can officially be categorized as utterly useless, because there is no way to act upon it. I also learned that writing is not for me. I have approached every writing project since then with dread. And it is only due to dire financial necessity that I have undertaken writing projects like this one.

On the other hand, had the movie been a huge success and won the Academy Award for Best Picture that year instead of *Braveheart* (which was, frankly, overrated), I would have been "hot" instead of "cold." All sorts of opportunities would have presented themselves. I could have been in many more movies and learned how to act better. Who knows? I might have been able to direct a movie. Perhaps one about submarines. Think of all the stuff I would have learned about submarines if I had to direct a whole movie about them.

A single success would have entitled me to make a half dozen failures. And even if I didn't learn as much from those failures as I would have from successes, I would have learned something because there would have been six of them.

Or I might have made a witty or memorable speech when I accepted my Academy Award, like Roberto Benigni. That would have been fun.

Think of all the things I could have learned from success. So be careful when you find yourself repeatedly telling yourself something encouraging that probably isn't true. Like "It's lonelier at the top." In my experience people at the top are immensely popular. Who do you think is more likely to get his phone call returned: Intel chairman Andy Grove or a homeless man?

Here's another phrase to be extremely wary of: "Every time one door closes, another door opens." Very often when one door closes, another does open. A trapdoor, leading directly to that lonely place at the bottom.

Here's a phrase that often makes people at funerals even more miserable than they already are: "God doesn't give you any more than you can handle." There's nothing worse than feeling guilty about going crazy.

But I don't mean to be entirely negative. There are pessimistic phrases that are equally untrue. For example, "Nice guys finish last." Believe me, there are plenty of unsuccessful assholes. And being a winner doesn't automatically make you a prick. Many nice guys have finished on top, like Tom Hanks and . . . Well, I'm sure there are others. Oh, yes. There's Oprah. She's very nice.

CHAPTER SUMMARY

So why do we keep telling ourselves these useless bromides and soothing falsehoods? In reality, they're a form of denial. Next time you confront a failure, ask yourself, "What really happened here? Is it possible that there is absolutely nothing to be learned from this experience?" If the answer is yes, don't waste valuable time trying to invent a lesson where none may exist. If there is something to be learned, fine. But that's no reason to be especially grateful for having had to learn it the hard way.

Benjamin Franklin
(1706–90)

Model of a Letter of Recommendation of a Person You Are Unacquainted With

PARIS, *April 2, 1777.*

Sir,—The bearer of this, who is going to America, presses me to give him a letter of recommendation, though I know nothing of him, not even his name. This may seem extraordinary, but I assure you it is not uncommon here. Sometimes, indeed, one unknown person brings another equally unknown, to recommend him; and sometimes they recommend one another! As to this gentleman, I must refer you to himself for his character and merits, with which he is certainly better acquainted than I can possibly be. I recommend him, however, to those civilities which every stranger, of whom one knows no harm, has a right to; and I request you will do him all the favour that, on further acquaintance, you shall find him to deserve. I have the honour to be, etc.

Benjamin Franklin

On Selecting a Mistress

[Philadelphia,] 25 June 1745

To★★★★

My Dear Friend:

I know of no medicine fit to diminish the violent natural inclinations you mention; and if I did, I think I should not communicate it to you. Marriage is the proper remedy. It is the most natural state of man, and therefore the state in which you are most likely to find solid happiness. Your reasons against entering into it at present appear to me not well founded. The circumstantial advantages you have in view by postponing it, are not only uncertain, but they are small in comparison with that of the thing itself, the being married and settled. It is the man and woman united that make the compleat human being. Separate, she wants his force of body and strength of reason; he, her softness, sensibility and acute discernment. Together they are more likely to succeed in the world. A single man has not nearly the value he would have in the state of union. If you get a prudent, healthy wife, your industry in your profession, with her good economy, will be a fortune sufficient.

But if you will not take this counsel and persist in thinking a commerce with the sex inevitable, then I repeat my former advice, that in all your amours you should prefer old women to young ones.

You call this a paradox and demand my reasons. They are these:

1. Because they have more knowledge of the world, and their minds are better stored with observations, their conversation is more improving, and most lastingly agreeable.

2. Because when women cease to be handsome they study to be good. To maintain their influence over men, they supply the diminution of beauty by an augmentation of utility. They learn to do a thousand services small and great, and are the most tender and useful of friends when you are sick. Thus they continue amiable. And hence there is hardly such a thing to be found as an old woman who is not a good woman.

3. Because there is no hazard of children, which irregularly produced may be attended with much inconvenience.

4. Because through more experience they are more prudent and discreet in conducting an intrigue to prevent suspicion. The commerce with them is therefore safer with regard to your reputation. And with regard to theirs, if the affair should happen to be

known, considerate people might be rather inclined to excuse an
old woman, who would kindly take care of a young man, form
his manners by her good counsels, and prevent his ruining his
health and fortune among mercenary prostitutes.

5. Because in every animal that walks upright, the deficiency of the
fluids that fill the muscles appears first in the highest part. The
face first grows lank and wrinkled; then the neck; then the breast
and arms; the lower parts continuing to the last as lump as ever:
so that covering all above with a basket, and regarding only what
is below the girdle, it is impossible of two women to know an old
one from a young one. And as in the dark all cats are grey, the
pleasure of corporal enjoyment with an old woman is at least
equal, and frequently superior; every knack being, by practice, capable of improvement.

6. Because the sin is less. The debauching a virgin may be her ruin,
and make her for life unhappy.

7. Because the compunction is less. The having made a young girl
miserable may give you frequent bitter reflection; none of which
can attend the making an old woman happy.

8thly & lastly. They are so grateful!

Thus much for my paradox. But still I advise you to marry
directly; being sincerely

Your affectionate Friend,
Benjamin Franklin

A Petition of the Left Hand

To Those Who Have the Superintendency of Education

I address myself to all the friends of youth, and conjure them to direct their
compassionate regards to my unhappy fate, in order to remove the prejudices of
which I am the victim. There are twin sisters of us; and the two eyes of man do
not more resemble, nor are capable of being upon better terms with each other,
than my sister and myself, were it not for the partiality of our parents, who make
the most injurious distinctions between us. From my infancy I have been led to
consider my sister as a being of a more elevated rank. I was suffered to grow up
without the least instruction, while nothing was spared in her education.

She had masters to teach her writing, drawing, music, and other accomplishments; but if by chance I touched a pencil, a pen, or a needle, I was bitterly rebuked; and more than once I have been beaten for being awkward, and wanting a graceful manner. It is true, my sister associated me with her upon some occasions; but she always made a point of taking the lead, calling upon me only from necessity, or to figure by her side.

But conceive not, sirs, that my complaints are instigated merely by vanity. No; my uneasiness is occasioned by an object much more serious. It is the practice in our family, that the whole business of providing for its subsistence falls upon my sister and myself. If any indisposition should attack my sister,— and I mention it in confidence upon this occasion, that she is subject to the gout, the rheumatism, and cramp, without making mention of other accidents,—what would be the fate of our poor family?

Must not the regret of our parents be excessive, at having placed so great a difference between sisters who are so perfectly equal? Alas! we must perish from distress; for it would not be in my power even to scrawl a suppliant petition for relief, having been obliged to employ the hand of another in transcribing the request which I have now the honour to prefer to you.

Condescend, sirs, to make my parents sensible of the injustice of an exclusive tenderness, and of the necessity of distributing their care and affection among all their children equally. I am, with a profound respect, sirs, your obedient servant,

THE LEFT HAND.
Benjamin Franklin.

Adrianne Frost
(Contemporary)

Easter Is Cancelled

I am reproductive free.
It sounds like it should be a positive thing. "I'm drug free." "I'm lice free." "I'm reproductive free." In 1988, I was diagnosed with endometriosis, which means that the lining of my uterus decided to grow on my other reproductive organs. I guess it got lonely. The uterus is generally a party-free atmosphere, where it is widely known that the ovaries, the cervix and fallopian tubes are a hotbed of thrills. While I appreciate that the lining of my uterus was excited to bond, have a Heiny and do the hair and nails of the rest of my female organs, for me this was not a good thing. It began to cause extreme pain. I had

thirteen surgeries total. The laparoscopies gave me the smiley scar above the pubis. And the laparotomies produced the belly button grin below the navel. It warms my heart to know that my scars can indicate my happiness even when I am unable. Which is good considering the Ziegfeld Follies of physicians I've had to deal with (cue music):

Dr. Padgett:
Well, you've got endometriosis. I'm going to do a laparoscopy and laser it off. First, we'll void you of everything you've ever eaten *in your life*. Also, we are going to send the *angriest* nurse we have to do the enema. Then we'll shave you. Not your legs. And with all of our advanced technology, we will use a single blade razor and bowl of water, like you're in a Merchant-Ivory film. I'm sorry to say we won't give you a heart or French landing strip, no; we will leave you with a goatee. You will be the Maynard G. Krebs of vaginas. But good news: then the pain'll be gone! (*later*) The endometriosis has returned. Also, your uterus is tilting back towards your spine, so I'm going to cut some ligaments to create a cradle, returning your uterus to its upright position. I am going to put you on a drug called Danazol. It's a relatively new drug and there are a few side effects: breast reduction, hot flashes, weight gain, hirsutism, clitoral atrophy and severe mood swings. And you have to change your name to Steve. But it'll ensure the disease never returns. It only costs $145.00 a month . . . for six months. Then the pain'll be gone!!

Dr. Davis:
You have *severe* endometriosis. I'm going to do a laparotomy and laser it off, then I'm going to cut the nerves behind the uterus that send pain signals to the brain. Then we'll put you on a monthly injection called Lupron that will induce menopause and forbid the disease from returning and it only costs $365.00 per injection. For six months. Then, the pain'll really, really be gone. (*later, laughing*) You can't possibly still be having pain. It's phantom pain: like when a man loses his leg and still feels the leg there. Give it time. (*Incredulously*) You can't possibly be having pain!

Dr. Padgett: (Nervously)
Let's try Provera injections. You'll go through menopause for about six months, but it's only injected every other month and it's only $120.00 per injection. No pain after that, no way.

Dr. Belina:
You have adenomyosis. The endometriosis has bled through the walls of your uterus and latched onto your internal organs, including the bladder, colon and sciatica nerve. I'm going to take out the uterus, cervix and try to save one or both ovaries. Then I'm going to keep you in the hospital for 5 days and administer steroids intravenously to speed healing along with daily whirlpools and general pampering. That's what I did for Liza. It comes out to about $35,000 for

everything. (*With absolute certainty*) But you will be pain free. How do I know? Because I am your Lord and Savior Jesus Christ.

Dr. Coady: (*Condescendingly*)

Well, of *course* you have pain. You still have one ovary left, and the endometriosis will continue to grow as long as the lone ovary is producing estrogen. There's a new drug called Zoladex. It's a small pill injected into the stomach every month for six months. Hot flashes, weight gain, mood swings, $400.00, no pain, no pain, no pain. Also, cut back on your dairy.

Dr. Padgett: (*Excited*)

Well, it's a good thing we did this laparoscopy! You had an ovarian cyst the size of my head (*holding it up next to his head*). Look at that! It's **huge**! I got rid of the ovary, too. It was all messed up. Now, we'll put you on estrogen, which will replace your lost hormones and cause all kinds of side effects **and** give you a higher risk of breast cancer! But say "Bye, bye pain!"

Dr. Bla, Bla, Dr. God, Dr. Bored, Dr. Disbelief, DR, DR, DR:

You have endometriosis, adenomyosis, parasites, fibromyalgia, a bleeding ulcer, chronic fatigue syndrome, adhesions, scar tissue, a yeast infection, pelvic inflammatory disease, irritable bowel syndrome, phantom pain, a bacterial infection, ovarian cysts, a lazy bladder, diverticulitis, a severe pelvic infection, a tilted uterus, an angry cervix and a troll living in your colon.

Dr. Adrianne:

Well, now there's no eggs in the basket. I suppose for some people being without reproductive organs is a positive thing. "No cramps, no periods, no PMS! And with no period, comes no weight gain or bloating." I went from a size 6 to a sixteen. From Cindy Crawford to Della Reese. Now I'm "Full Figured," like I've reached my intake. And I will never be able to trick a man into marrying me. I have always been confused, however, as to why God gave me birthing hips but took away my uterus.

Lewis Burke Frumkes
(Contemporary)

FROM *How to Raise Your I.Q. by Eating Gifted Children*

Scientists have long suspected a link between eating gifted children and raising the I.Q., but until recently no one has been able to prove it. Now scientists believe they have found evidence to support their theory. Two teams of researchers, one on a diet of gifted children, the other on a placebo, have turned in amazing results. The team eating only gifted children succeeded in raising their I.Q.s an average of fifteen points over a period of two years, while the placebo group remains as stupid as ever.

The implications are enormous. Not only may it be possible in the future to raise one's I.Q. by ingesting an occasional gifted child (there are approximately 2½ million in the U.S. alone, 5 million drumsticks, etc.), but it may provide ecologists with a partial solution to runaway population.

Nevertheless, conservationists are up in arms. You can't have people running around just plucking children off the street, they say; not every child is gifted. It could turn into offspringacide.

Scientists are careful to point out that while studies have shown gifted children to be larger and more attractive in the main than ordinary children, not every large, attractive child is gifted. "Frequently a plump, juicy-looking child is just well fed," says Dr. Heraldic Leap, director of Gifted Studies at Johns Hopkins University. He urges potential consumers to be sure the child they eat is indeed gifted if they expect to see any appreciable increase in their intelligence.

How can you be sure the child you eat is gifted?

Dr. Leap suggests acquiring your child from Mensa, the Bronx High School of Science, or any of the reputable rapid advance classes found in most major cities. Or, he says, obtain a certificate from the child's school verifying that he or she has scored in the top 2 percent on any standardized intelligence test. Most schools are very good about this and will go out of their way to provide documentation. Finally, he adds, "Gifted children just taste different."

The following recipes were supplied by the educational psychology department of Columbia Teachers College.

Gifted Child En Papillote
(six servings)

En papillote means roughly baked in a bag. Thus you will need sufficient aluminum foil to wrap completely around your children.

3 moderately gifted children,
   I.Q.s 130–140
broth or lightly salted bath water
2 pounds butter
2 quarts of flour
½ gallon Coppertone lotion
1 gallon Tropical Blend oil
1 dozen eggs beaten

handful of cayenne pepper
handful of mace or nutmeg
handful of ground chives
bucket of finely chopped
   mushrooms
salt and freshly ground pepper
   to taste

1. Place the 3 gifted children in a small tub and add bath water barely to cover. Add hot water, reduce the heat, cover and simmer gently until the kids are pink enough to pinch, 25–40 minutes, depending on the size of your gifted children. Remove the children from the bath and cool. Carefully skin the kids with a court order.
2. Preheat solarium to hot.
3. Cut 3 pieces of aluminum foil large enough to make a body reflector for each child and spread the foil with half the butter.
4. In an enormous skillet or pan blend the other ingredients into a saucy lotion.
5. Place each child in the center of each square of foil and ladle some sauce-lotion over the top. Fold the edges of the foil and seal tightly by crimping the edges. Arrange on baking sheet and bake 10 minutes. Serve wrapped in the foil. Pale kids will require less cooking time.

Gifted Child Fricassee

Not for the squeamish. (See Cooking Gifted Children and Chickens, Terman-Perdue.)

Barbecued Gifted Child

½ dozen gifted children
flour

6 broom handles
Johnson and Johnson marinade

Lightly dust the gifted children in flour and douse with marinade. Attach each child to a broom handle and proceed to barbecue as you would an ordinary child.

Gifted Child with Rosemary

4 gifted children
1 handful salt
1 pound butter

4 children named
 Rosemary
1 dozen onions chopped
1 pint of vinegar

Allow children to play in the other ingredients overnight. Then pair each gifted child with a Rosemary, sauté lightly, and serve.

Charlotte Perkins Gilman
(1860–1935)

Queer People

The people people work with best
 Are often very queer,
The people people own by birth
 Quite shock your first idea;
The people people choose for friends

 Your common sense appall,
But the people people marry
 Are the queerest ones of all.

William Goldman
(Contemporary)

FROM *The Princess Bride*

It's one of my biggest memories of my father reading. I had pneumonia, remember, but I was a little better now, and madly caught up in the book, and one
thing you know when you're ten is that, no matter what, there's gonna be a
happy ending. They can sweat all they want to scare you, the authors, but back
of it all you know, you just have no doubt, that in the long run justice is going to
win out. And Westley and Buttercup—well, they had their troubles, sure, but
they were going to get married and live happily ever after. I would have bet the
family fortune if I'd found a sucker big enough to take me on.

Well, when my father got through with that sentence where the wedding was
sandwiched between the ministers' meeting and the treasury whatever, I said,
'You read that wrong.'

My father's this little bald barber—remember that too? And kind of illiterate.
Well, you just don't challenge a guy who has trouble reading and say he's read
something incorrectly, because that's really threatening. 'I'm doing the reading,'
he said.

'I know that but you got it wrong. She didn't marry that rotten Humperdinck.
She marries Westley.'

'It says right here,' my father began, a little huffy, and he starts going over it
again.

'You must have skipped a page then. Something. Get it right, huh?'

By now he was more than a tiny bit upset. 'I skipped nothing. I read the
words. The words are there, I read them, good night,' and off he went.

'Hey please, no,' I called after him, but he's stubborn, and, next thing, my
mother was in saying, 'Your father says his throat is too sore; I told him not to
read so much,' and she tucked and fluffed me and no matter how I battled, it was
over. No more story till the next day.

I spent that whole night thinking Buttercup married Humperdinck. It just
rocked me. How can I explain it, but the world didn't work that way. Good got
attracted to good, evil you flushed down the john and that was that. But their
marriage—I couldn't make it jibe. God, did I work at it. First I thought that
probably Buttercup had this fantastic effect on Humperdinck and turned him
into a kind of Westley, or maybe Westley and Humperdinck turned out to be
long-lost brothers and Humperdinck was so happy to get his brother back he
said, 'Look, Westley, I didn't realize who you were when I married her so what

I'll do is I'll divorce her and you marry her and that way we'll all be happy.' To this day I don't think I was ever more creative.

But it didn't take. Something was wrong and I couldn't lose it. Suddenly there was this discontent gnawing away until it had a place big enough to settle in and then it curled up and stayed there and it's still inside me lurking as I write this now.

The next night, when my father went back to reading and the marriage turned out to have been Buttercup's dream, I screamed 'I knew it, all along I knew it,' and my father said, 'So you're happy now, it's all right now, we can please continue?' and I said 'Go' and he did.

But I wasn't happy. Oh my ears were happy, I guess, my story sense was happy, my heart too, but in my, I suppose you have to call it 'soul', there was that damn discontent shaking its dark head.

All this was never explained to me till I was in my teens and there was this great woman who lived in my home town, Edith Neisser, dead now, and she wrote terrific books about how we screw up our children—*Brothers and Sisters* was one of her books, *The Eldest Child* was another. Published by Harper. Edith doesn't need the plug, seeing, like I said, as she's no longer with us, but if there are any amongst you who are worried that maybe you're not being perfect parents, pick up one of Edith's books while there's still time. I knew her 'cause her kid Ed got his haircuts from my pop, and she was this writer and by my teens I knew, secretly, that was the life for me too, except I couldn't tell anybody. It was too embarrassing—barber's sons, if they hustled, maybe got to be IBM salesmen, but writers? No way. Don't ask me how, but eventually Edith discovered my shhhhhh ambition and from then on, sometimes, we would talk. And I remember once we were having iced tea on the Neisser porch and talking and just outside the porch was their badminton court and I was watching some kids play badminton and Ed had just shellacked me, and as I left the court for the porch, he said, 'Don't worry, it'll all work out, you'll get me next time' and I nodded, and then Ed said, 'And if you don't, you'll beat me at something else.'

I went to the porch and sipped iced tea and Edith was reading this book and she didn't put it down when she said, 'That's not necessarily true, you know.'

I said, 'How do you mean?'

And that's when she put her book down. And looked at me. And said it: 'Life isn't fair, Bill. We tell our children that it is, but it's a terrible thing to do. It's not only a lie, it's a cruel lie. Life is not fair, and it never has been, and it's never going to be.'

Would you believe that for me right then it was like one of those comic books where the lightbulb goes on over Mandrake the Magician's head? 'It isn't!' I said, so loud I really startled her. 'You're right. It's not fair.' I was so happy if I'd known how to dance, I'd have started dancing. 'Isn't that great, isn't it just terrific?' I think along about here Edith must have thought I was well on my way toward being bonkers.

But it meant so much to me to have it said and out and free and flying—that was the discontent I endured the night my father stopped reading, I realized right then. That was the reconciliation I was trying to make and couldn't.

And that's what I think this book's about. All those Columbia experts can spiel all they want about the delicious satire; they're crazy. This book says 'life isn't fair' and I'm telling you, one and all, you better believe it. I got a fat spoiled son—he's not gonna nab Miss Rheingold. And he's always gonna be fat, even if he gets skinny he'll still be fat and he'll still be spoiled and life will never be enough to make him happy, and that's my fault maybe—make it all my fault, if you want—the point is, we're not created equal, for the rich they sing, life isn't fair. I got a cold wife; she's brilliant, she's stimulating, she's terrific; there's no love; that's okay too, just so long as we don't keep expecting everything to somehow even out for us before we die.

Look. (Grownups skip this paragraph.) I'm not about to tell you this book has a tragic ending, I already said in the very first line how it was my favorite in all the world. But there's a lot of bad stuff coming up, torture you've already been prepared for, but there's worse. There's death coming up, and you better understand this: some of the wrong people die. Be ready for it. This isn't Curious George Uses the Potty. Nobody warned me and it was my own fault (you'll see what I mean in a little) and that was my mistake, so I'm not letting it happen to you. The wrong people die, some of them, and the reason is this; life is not fair. Forget all the garbage your parents put out. Remember Morgenstern. You'll be a lot happier.

Mark Halliday
(Contemporary)

Graded Paper

On the whole this is quite successful work:
your main argument about the poet's ambivalence—
how he loves the very things he attacks—
is mostly persuasive and always engaging.

At the same time,
              there are spots
where your thinking becomes, for me,
alarmingly opaque, and your syntax seems to jump
backwards through unnecessary hoops,
as on p. 2 where you speak of "precognitive awareness
not yet disestablished by the shell that encrusts
each thing that a person actually says"
or at the top of p. 5 where your discussion of
"subverbal undertow miming the subversion of self-belief
woven counter to desire's outreach"
leaves me groping for firmer footholds.
(I'd have said it differently,
or rather, said something else.)
And when you say that women "could not fulfill themselves" (p. 6)
"in that era" (only forty years ago, after all!)
are you so sure that the situation is so different today?
Also, how does Whitman bluff his way into
your penultimate paragraph? He is the *last* poet
I would have quoted in this context!
What plausible way of behaving
does the passage you quote represent? Don't you think
literature should ultimately reveal possibilities for *action*?

Please notice how I've repaired your use of semicolons.

And yet, despite what may seem my cranky response,
I do admire the freshness of
your thinking and your style; there is
a vitality here; your sentences thrust themselves forward
with a confidence as impressive as it is cheeky. . . .
You are not
            me, finally,
and though this is an awkward problem, involving
the inescapable fact that you are so young, so young
it is also a delightful provocation.

Margaret Halsey
(1910–97)

FROM *With Malice Toward Some*

Today, when one of my blanks said OCCUPATION, I wrote down *none*, though I suspected this would not do. A severe but courteous official confirmed this impression. So I crossed it out and wrote *parasite*, which, not to be too delicate about it, is what I am. This made the official relax a little and he himself put *housewife* in what space there was left. "Be a prince," I said. "Make it *typhoid carrier*." But he only smiled and blotted out *parasite* so that it would not show.

I am a big girl now and too old to believe in Shakespeare.

We left the suitcases and went out to eat, as—if the smell in the corridors was any indication—it was Human Sacrifice Night at the hotel. Three-quarters of an hour of walking failed to disclose a restaurant which was still open. Just as I was saying tragically that we would have to go back to the room and eat toothpaste, Henry noticed a place of decidedly humble aspect which seemed in two minds about closing up. We hurried in, and an absent-minded waitress gave us a pot of tea, supplemented after fifteen minutes by a piece of steak which had evidently been put to bed for the night and resented being disturbed.

Humility is not my forte, and whenever I dwell for any length of time on my own shortcomings, they gradually begin to seem mild, harmless, rather engaging little things, not at all like the staring defects in other people's characters.

★

American men look at women when (they think) the women are not aware of it; Englishmen do not look at them at all; but Frenchmen look at them with such thoroughness and intensity that you half expect them to approach and ask dubiously, "Is it washable?"

Lynn Harris
(Contemporary)

Worrywarts and All

When I found out that the American reporter who'd been abducted by the Serbs was my dear old friend David Rohde, I remained surprisingly calm.

Why?

Not because I wasn't worried about him, but because I didn't know how to worry about him. I already have worry software in my brain for everyday things, like minor illness and travel during inclement weather. You call, send cards, monitor the Weather Channel, look up telltale symptoms ("fatigue") in *Our Bodies, Our Selves*, whatnot.

But political imprisonment in Bosnia? I didn't know where to start.

Only one person would know what to do: my mother. My mother is the best worrier I know. Her worrying is epic, Olympic, encyclopedic. People in the hospital, on transatlantic flights, at midlife crossroads—all of them jostle for a spot on her elite Worry List. She knows everything: the chemical composition of the pesticide on your apple, the link between yogurt and breast cancer ("Eat only Stonyfield Farms," she once intoned cryptically), how far away you should sit from household appliances (notably, computers) that emit hazardous electromagnetic rays. When I moved to Brooklyn, she bought me two canisters—one for my bike—of pepper spray. She responds to any mention of the Brooklyn Blades, my women's ice hockey team, with an update on the condition of the Boston University player who recently wound up paralyzed from the neck down. She e-mails me about the latest in vitamin research (B6 is in; beta-carotene is out). (True story: I'd originally written "fish oil is in," but when mom happened to see a draft of this column while I was visiting home, she crossed it out and wrote in "B6.")

Problem was, when I heard that David had been taken prisoner, my parents were away in Argentina. Quite a project, the hostage crisis, for a novice worrier.

It crossed my mind to call my friend Kent's Aunt Barb, the only person who may have my mother beat, at least in terms of international worry protocol. When Kent went to China for a year, Aunt Barb devised a code that would elude the eyes of censoring captors. If Kent signed his letters with his first name, all was well. But if he used his middle name, she'd know he was in trouble. Kent then went to work for the CIA, so Barb really had her hands full.

Luckily, by the time I summoned the courage to call David's family, he'd just been released. (And a few months later, David won a Pulitzer for his efforts. I think his mom should have gotten one, too. By the way, he now covers Brooklyn—including the war-torn Park Slope Food Co-Op—for the *Times*—)

You have to realize that asking my mother for worrying assistance represents quite a breakthrough in our relationship, since I had long ago resolved never to be like her. As you can imagine, her worrying cramped my style during my formative years. She insisted on dropping me off right in front of school dances to make sure I "got there okay." If my destination eluded direct surveillance, I had to call when I got there. Curfews were set not so much in Eastern Standard Time, but rather in Guilt Mean Time ("You know I won't sleep until I hear you come in").

Then I went to college. My mother didn't always know where I was, what I was doing, and whether or not I washed my hands with anti-bacterial soap before and after I did it. And she didn't ask. I was becoming free to start living—and worrying—on my own.

So one night, I was lying there waiting for my then-boyfriend to come in from a rehearsal (don't worry, Mom, it was only once, and he brought a sleeping bag). It was getting later and later, and I was getting madder and madder. I began to rehearse all the stinging, guilt-tipped barbs I'd hurl at him: "Where have you been . . . I was worried . . . You could have called . . . You know I won't sleep until I hear you come in . . ."

I sat up in bed. Oh, my God. It had happened.

I've fought it, but it's only gotten worse. I have developed an acute fear of raw chicken and now trail my housemate Jason around the kitchen with Comet and the "chicken" cutting board. I am trying to convince my housemate Chris to eat more vegetables, especially green leafy anti-carcinogens. In our apartment, I have instituted The Noon Rule: whoever "doesn't come home" must call by noon the next day so the others know [not] to worry. I tsk-tsk at bicyclists and in-line skaters without helmets. If I forget to say "Drive carefully," it occurs to me that if there is an accident, it will be my fault. After I did a reporting assignment in a pediatric emergency room, every stove-top saucepan, moving vehicle, and untied shoelace became, in my eyes, an instrument of death.

I reached my worry zenith the day I went on an ice-skating outing with a group of under-served kids. We had to herd them through the busy subway and along the Central Park South sidewalk, across the street, and into Wollman Rink in Central Park—and then let them loose to navigate on untied skates with blades that couldn't cut butter. Can you imagine? My heart nearly stopped every time one of our young charges stepped off the curb.

And as I raced around the rink from kid to kid, picking one up and tightening another's laces, I felt the cells on the back of my head starting to divide into two sharp eyes.

It was time to tell my mother what had happened. I told her about my day and apologized for making fun of her all those years, assuming she'd welcome her heir with open arms to the world of worriers.

I was wrong.

Triumphant, mocking, satisfied, she responded, "Ha, ha."

So I guess we're equal. Almost. My mother has now gone on to worry that I'm worrying too much. "I wish sometimes you could relax," she tells me, with no trace of irony. Yes, she's still the master, but I'm learning. And when she's worrying about me, I'm still her testy daughter. This kidnapped-reporter thing does give me a little mileage in that regard, I must say. Now, if I ever get another perilous reporting assignment in, God forbid, the NYPD vs. FDNY hockey game, or the food co-op, I can say, "Relax, Mom, it's not like I'm sneaking into Srebrenica! . . . Oh, and by the way, how far away from my computer am I supposed to be sitting?"

Bret Harte
(1836–1902)

The Haunted Man

A Christmas Story by Ch–r–s D–ck–n–s

PART I
THE FIRST PHANTOM

Don't tell me that it wasn't a knocker. I had seen it often enough, and I ought to know. So ought the three o'clock beer, in dirty high-lows, swinging himself over the railing, or executing a demoniacal jig upon the doorstep; so ought the butcher, although butchers as a general thing are scornful of such trifles; so ought the postman, to whom knockers of the most extravagant description were merely human weaknesses, that were to be pitied and used. And so ought, for the matter of that, etc., etc., etc.

But then it was *such* a knocker. A wild, extravagant, and utterly incomprehensible knocker. A knocker so mysterious and suspicious that Policeman X 37, first coming upon it, felt inclined to take it instantly in custody, but compromised with his professional instincts by sharply and sternly noting it with an eye that admitted of no nonsense, but confidently expected to detect its secret yet. An ugly knocker; a knocker with a hard, human face, that was a type of the harder human face within. A human face that held between its teeth a brazen rod. So hereafter, in the mysterious future should be held, etc., etc.

But if the knocker had a fierce human aspect in the glare of day, you should have seen it at night, when it peered out of the gathering shadows and suggested an ambushed figure; when the light of the street lamps fell upon it, and wrought a play of sinister expression in its hard outlines; when it seemed to wink meaningly at a shrouded figure who, as the night fell darkly, crept up the steps and passed into the mysterious house; when the swinging door disclosed a black passage into which the figure seemed to lose itself and become a part of the mysterious gloom; when the night grew boisterous and the fierce wind made furious charges at the knocker, as if to wrench it off and carry it away in triumph. Such a night as this.

It was a wild and pitiless wind. A wind that had commenced life as a gentle country zephyr, but wandering through manufacturing towns had become de- moralised, and reaching the city had plunged into extravagant dissipation and wild excesses. A roistering wind that indulged in Bacchanalian shouts on the street corners, that knocked off the hats from the heads of helpless passengers, and then fulfilled its duties by speeding away, like all young prodigals,—to sea.

He sat alone in a gloomy library listening to the wind that roared in the chimney. Around him novels and story-books were strewn thickly; in his lap he held one with its pages freshly cut, and turned the leaves wearily until his eyes rested upon a portrait in its frontispiece. And as the wind howled the more fiercely, and the darkness without fell blacker, a strange and fateful likeness to that portrait appeared above his chair and leaned upon his shoulder. The Haunted Man gazed at the portrait and sighed. The figure gazed at the portrait and sighed too.

"Here again?" said the Haunted Man.

"Here again," it repeated in a low voice.

"Another novel?"

"Another novel."

"The old story?"

"The old story."

"I see a child," said the Haunted Man, gazing from the pages of the book into the fire,—"a most unnatural child, a model infant. It is prematurely old and philosophic. It dies in poverty to slow music. It dies surrounded by luxury to slow music. It dies with an accompaniment of golden water and rattling carts to slow music. Previous to its decease it makes a will; it repeats the Lord's Prayer, it kissed the 'boofer lady.' That child"——

"Is mine," said the phantom.

"I see a good woman, undersized. I see several charming women, but they are all undersized. They are more or less imbecile and idiotic, but always fascinating and undersized. They wear coquettish caps and aprons. I observe that feminine virtue is invariably below the medium height, and that it is always babyish and infantine. These women"——

"Are mine."

"I see a haughty, proud, and wicked lady. She is tall and queenly. I remark that all proud and wicked women are tall and queenly. That woman"——

"Is mine," said the phantom, wringing his hands.

"I see several things continually impending. I observe that whenever an accident, a murder, or death is about to happen, there is something in the furniture, in the locality, in the atmosphere, that foreshadows and suggests it's years in advance. I cannot say that in real life I have noticed it,—the perception of this surprising fact belongs"——

"To me!" said the phantom. The Haunted Man continued, in a despairing tone—

"I see the influence of this in the magazines and daily papers; I see weak imitators rise up and enfeeble the world with senseless formula. I am getting tired of it. It won't do, Charles! It won't do!" and the Haunted Man buried his head in his hands and groaned. The figure looked down upon him sternly: the portrait in the frontispiece frowned as he gazed.

"Wretched man," said the phantom, "and how have these things affected you?"

"Once I laughed and cried, but then I was younger. Now, I would forget them if I could."

"Have then your wish. And take this with you, man whom I renounce. From this day henceforth you shall live with those whom I displace. Without forgetting me, 'twill be your lot to walk through life as if we had not met. But first, you shall survey these scenes that henceforth must be yours. At one to-night, prepare to meet the phantom I have raised. Farewell!"

The sound of its voice seemed to fade away with the dying wind, and the Haunted Man was alone. But the firelight flickered gaily, and the light danced on the walls, making grotesque figures of the furniture.

"Ha, ha!" said the Haunted Man, rubbing his hands gleefully; "now for a whiskey punch and a cigar."

Cynthia Heimel
(Contemporary)

FROM *If You Can't Live Without Me, Why Aren't You Dead Yet?*

Swinging Through England

Not that this is really what the column is about, but fourteen years ago, when I was a slip of a girl living in England, I fell (thud) in love and had my heart broken for the first time. Oh, it was awful, I was so seriously besotted, sure my feelings were returned, and then it turned out he was one of those guys who make girls fall for them, just to see if they can do it. It was my first exposure to this virulent species of tick, and I never totally recovered. In fact, we keep in touch, John and I. Saw each other last week.

But mainly I went to England to see the girls. Do you know that English girls are the greatest? Not only are they crisp, and witty, and have those rose-petal complexions, and are all completely mad, but they are *definite* about things. No shilly-shallying, no ambivalence, these girls give the most complicated of human situations *names*.

"Well, did he have the boy disease?" Felicity demanded when I related my travails with a certain guy. We were eating spaghetti carbonara in the magnificently cluttered kitchen of Louisa's house in Bayswater, the kind of place where you go through the entrance hall and suddenly think, "Wait a minute, wasn't that a Cézanne I just walked by?" Anyway, the boy disease?

"You know," said Felicity (brunette, stunning), "when everything's just great and you're having a wonderful time and then he suddenly becomes very weird and disappears. It's epidemic nowadays. I believe it was first isolated by Natalia Schiffrin, who noticed that if her friends were looking starry-eyed and walking on air one week, they were bound to be hollow-eyed, pale, and listless the next. Apparently boys are being disappointing in droves these days."

"But why?" I wondered.

"No one knows," Louisa (blond, gorgeous) said. "Perhaps it has something to do with Chernobyl. Now, do we all want chocolate and cream? Or shall we just drink another bottle of wine?"

The next day I called John, my nemesis. "Delightful that you're here," he said. "Unfortunately tonight I'm going to the Hurlingham Club, tomorrow I'm off to Regent's Park, and on Thursday it's the Proms. Lunch, I'm afraid."

"Fuck you!" I cried. "You, the one who broke my heart, can't stop being posh for a minute to see me?" No I didn't, really. "Lunch will be lovely," I said.

"Fuck him," I said to the girls. "I'm not going."

"Go and be horrible to him, which will make him fall madly in love," Felicity said.

"Felicity is such a man," Sue (Ursula Andress lookalike) giggled.

"No, she's not, she's a woman," I said, noticing her breasts.

"She's right. I am a man," said Felicity. "But you don't know Will Wenham's famous theory?" she asked me.

"It's perfectly simple," said Louisa. "All women are either girls, women, or men. And all men are either men, boys, or hairdressers. Stop looking like a dead halibut."

"You've lost me," I said. "Give examples."

"Sigourney Weaver is a man. Jane Fonda is a man. Diane Keaton is a girl," said Louisa. "Jessica Lange is a woman. Mel Gibson is a boy, Clint Eastwood is a man. Cary Grant was a hairdresser."

"How dare you!" I said.

"No, it's perfectly okay. There's nothing wrong with being a hairdresser, and it has nothing to do with sexual orientation," said Felicity. "Very good people are hairdressers. Louisa's father is a hairdresser, and he's a great man."

"My father is not a hairdresser!" said Louisa, shocked. "My father is God."

"Of course he is," said Felicity, "but he's still a hairdresser. He knows about color, and clothes, and cares if his hair's a fright."

"Perhaps he's a creature," said Sue.

Creatures, it seems, defy description completely, and are the best of all.

"He's a hairdresser," said Felicity, "and thank God he is. Most men are boys. Men who are men are probably the best, but almost impossible to find."

"Whereas I, although female, am definitely a man," said Louisa, shifting her gorgeous legs coquettishly, "I even have the boy disease, that's how much a man I am. I get madly interested in someone, pursue him to the ends of the earth, and the moment he shows some sort of interest, I think, 'Hang on, I'm not sure I really like the way you wear your pinstriped shirts all buttoned up, and the way you breathe gets on my nerves.' And I leave them. I can't help it."

"You're a bunch of loonies," I decided.

"We're not, it's an exact science," Sue said. "We've studied it for years. We even know that girls tend to have women for daughters."

"What am I?" I asked.

"You're a woman."

"Well, it's true, my mother was a girl."

"You see, then," said Louisa. "The more you study this, the more your life will fall into place."

It did. I went to lunch. John has just turned forty. His temples are graying. He told me about his love life. "I'm involved with an architect. She was married in May 1989. In June 1989 I kissed her in a garden in Clapham. In January 1990, she left her husband."

"And now, of course, you don't want her anymore."

"Well, it is a bit of a problem." He creased his face into seriousness but couldn't hide the gleam in his eye, and I felt chilled. But then the light dawned. "You're a boy," I thought to myself. "I can see you in the sandbox, red face, poncy little sailor suit and lollipop, only wanting the other children's toys, taking them away, and then losing interest."

In the bus going home, the conductor was tidying his receipts fussily, he was such a hairdresser. So was the waiter at the Indian restaurant who kept realigning the glasses.

The day before I was to leave, a fellow phoned and offered me a trip to St. Moritz, where I would stay and be pampered in the best hotel. He would take care of everything.

"A man," I thought, terrified.

Take a Career Woman, Please

There's something we've got to talk about. I thought it was all settled years ago, 1975 maybe, when men and women were in the throes of ironing out their differences. Way before we figured out who opened the door for whom, who got to call whom for a date, whose orgasm was most important, I thought we'd already sorted out the money thing.

So I'm on the phone with this guy the other day. This guy is so smart and successful, he is a guy at the top of his profession, and his profession demands utmost perception about human relationships. So you could have knocked me over with a beansprout when he says, "I think when women went into business, men felt a great loss."

"Is this a joke?" I asked. "What's the punchline?"

"No, listen," he said urgently. "I don't think men will ever recover, it was really a blow."

"When you say business, do you mean like executive women, like Wall Street bankers and such, the ones who dress in suits and seem hard and cold and not what you'd consider feminine? Are you decrying a loss of billowing skirts and soft hair and womanliness? You don't want women to appear as shorter men?"

"No," he said. "I mean all kinds of business."

"You mean women just generally working for a living? Like . . . me, even?"

"I shouldn't have brought this up. I don't mean anything."

"I want to know. Tell."

"Well," he said. "I think men want to care for women. Take care of them. It's very important to us. We deeply miss it."

"What do you miss, the subservience? Being in control? I don't get it. What do you miss?"

"I don't know!" he wailed, and I felt my heart break into a million pieces. And listen, I told him. It is my new policy to tell things to men without anger, because anger begets anger, and this guy, well this is a great guy who was telling me the truth I didn't want to hear.

"This breaks my heart," I said, "because the very thing that I need most, that I could never give up, that is most essential to my existence, this is the very thing that hurts you, that causes a deep and unsurmountable rift between us. I need to take care of myself. I need to be financially independent."

"Oh, God, don't listen to me. What do I know?" he asked.

But he knows. I see it all over the place.

I see it in the faces of men when I'm standing at the bus stop at night. If a woman stands at the bus stop at night in Manhattan, she looks vulnerable and financially needy. I stand there and am amazed to notice the sharp interest men take. They don't leer. Their faces say, "I want to know you. Maybe you're the one for me." It's very weird. If I am instead hailing a cab, they don't even see me, I don't exist.

And I see it in the lives and relationships of friends and acquaintances. Get a job, your husband hates you. Get a good job, your husband leaves you. Get a stupendous job, your husband leaves you for a teenager.

Oh, don't mutter. Maybe not you. Men are all different. Some men positively thrive and grow sleek on their women's successes. But more and more, men's resentment and anger are rearing their ignoble heads. This is not exactly what I had in mind for 1989.

I vaguely understand how men feel. I get a small dose of it when I consider my kid. He's growing up and away from me, becoming independent, as he should. But of course I hate it. I hate losing him. I want the familial bond snug and undisturbed. Whenever I panic over this awful separation, a tiny voice in my brain says, "But babe, you hold the purse strings—he's totally dependent." And my brain breathes a small ugly sigh of relief. He *has* to stick by me.

Is it that men (not you, surely) are afraid of losing us? Afraid that we'll just pick ourselves up and run off when we start getting a regular paycheck? Does it cause intense insecurity? This seems reasonable. We want to bind those we love to us by any means we can, fair or foul. And it can easily happen that a woman with financial independence *will* run off, for any number of good or bad reasons, so I understand such a man's feelings.

Nevertheless, I want to explain my own. It would be easiest if you went to the video store and rented *His Girl Friday*. This movie is a total witfest, pure entertainment, I've seen it at least twenty times. It concerns an ace reporter, Hildy, who wants a "normal" life, so she's quitting her job and marrying Ralph Bellamy. But somehow, just as she is leaving, she is embroiled in *one last story*. She can't help herself, the story, involving murder, is too good to resist. At a crucial moment, just when she must get on the train with her fiancé or forfeit all, Hildy sees the sheriff, who has essential information. She goes after him. He runs away. She runs after him and, with a giant leap, she grabs him around the legs and tackles him.

Now, this is a great comedic moment, the audience piss themselves laughing. Not me, I burst into tears every time.

Do you see? She can't help herself, she has to do a good job! Even deeper than her need for normalcy, for marriage, is this wellspring of commitment to the work she loves. Instinct takes over and she runs like a gazelle.

Or go see *Working Girl*. Many people dislike this movie because Sigourney Weaver plays a career woman/scheming bitch. I don't mind this. At the end Melanie Griffith gets her own office and doesn't have to bring anybody coffee anymore. This of course brings me to tears.

All human beings, even women, have a deep need to perform their work with as much creativity and competence as they can muster. It fulfills us, we feel complete and satisfied. Work can be housekeeping and child-rearing—convenient for all concerned. It can be selling junk bonds. Anything. (Listen, when I write what I consider a good joke, I feel the adrenaline rush from my toes to the top of my head.)

A human being who is deprived of her work, her destiny, becomes despondent. She ends up wearing her pajamas all day.

So when a woman goes to work, try not to take it personally. We do it not to hurt men, or to take something from men. It's not about men at all. We do it because we have to.

FROM *When Your Phone Doesn't Ring, It'll Be Me*

Fathers and Daughters: A Pop Quiz

Four of my close friends are pregnant. All of them are having girls. Extrapolating outward, this clearly means that 30 percent of women of childbearing age are at this very moment pregnant with girls. And the burning question is: Will these innocent tiny fetuses grow up to become young women every bit as confused and fucked up as my friends and I?

I do not want to see our future women awash with neuroses, low self-esteem and double messages. To curtail this eventuality, I have prepared a little quiz you can all take to see if you'd make a good dad. Go ahead, make my day.

1. Every time I turn on a talk show or read a book or newspaper, the topic of incest/child abuse smacks me in the face. Although I had no idea that incest/child abuse is our new national pastime, my own feelings about it are:

   a. A man feeds and clothes and cares for his children and they owe him something. They owe him everything. They are *his* children and whatever he chooses to do with them is his business.

   b. I was beat up and abused regularly by my own father and I hate him for it. I am a boiling cauldron of rage. I hope to God I don't do anything like that to my own children. I'm kind of pretty sure I won't.

   c. Some kids are always flaunting themselves in front of you, they're just asking for it.

   d. It's not so bad if it's a niece or second cousin or something.

Yup, that was a trick question designed to weed out the psychos amongst you. If you even contemplated a, b, c, or d, you are never allowed to be a father. Immediately begin ten years of intensive psychotherapy or shoot yourself.

2. I have heard that a child's self-image is initially (and usually indelibly) shaped by her parents' feedback. My daughter is pretty, good in math, scared of riding her bike, always climbing trees, and obsessed with weird, punk clothing. To give her a positive self-image

   a. I would tell her she is beautiful, gorgeous, a real knockout, a heartbreaker.

   b. I would work with her every day to help her learn to ride her bike.

   c. Every time she got an A in math I'd give her a special treat.

   d. I'd tell her she cannot climb trees unless with a grown-up, I'd play math games with her, I'd let the bike rust, I'd give her a specified clothing allowance and let her wear whatever the hell she wants.

If you answered a, you're doing what countless fathers before you have done: You've focused on your daughter's appearance instead of her intrinsic self-worth. She will become crazed about her looks and let her inner self atrophy. If she grows up to be plain, she will feel worthless. If she grows up to be pretty, she will constantly need reassurance yet still feel worthless. If she grows up to be Brigitte Bardot reincarnated, she will become an arrogant, spoiled, man-teaser who will revel in her stunningness until her looks start to fade, when she will try to kill herself.

If you answered b, you're ignoring all her positive aspects and rubbing her nose in her weakness. She will grow up lacking confidence, always sure that whatever she does well is not nearly as important as her failures. Plan on plenty of therapy bills.

If you answered c, you're a lousy party-pooper. Before you know it, she'll stop having fun with math and start feeling pressured to please you. Let her have her own successes and enjoy them with her, let her have her failures and commiserate with her. Don't be Bob Barker.

If you answered d, you're a fab parent. You know that children need reasonable limits to feel safe and loved, you know that if you let her climb trees unsupervised she'd think, "Jeez, they really want to get rid of me." Letting her wear whatever she wants tells her no matter how weird she is, you love her anyway. And children, trust me, usually think they are incredibly weird.

3. My daughter is leaving for summer camp tomorrow. I want her to go out to dinner with the family. She wants to spend her last night with her friends. My response is
   a. "You'll have dinner with us, young lady, and like it."
   b. "I can't believe, after all your mother and I have done for you, that you don't want to be with us."
   c. "Honey, are you sure I can't guilt-trip you into being with us?"
   d. "Oh, who cares what the hell you do?"

If you answered a, you'll be doing a perfectly fine parent thing. She'll be miserable and hate you all through dinner, and then be really thrilled to get away from you the next day.

If you answered b, you're causing more trouble than you can even imagine. One of the most difficult issues of childhood is separating from one's parents. By guilt-tripping her, she'll not only be afraid of leaving you for her own sake, but now you've given her the added burden of your happiness. She'll feel she is destroying you by leaving and will end up a bitter and twisted human, either running away when she is sixteen or living at home until she is fifty.

If you answered c, you are a gifted parent. You are not only acknowledging that you are in a position to misuse your power over your child, you are showing that you have weakness, and are therefore not God. You're making a joke about the serious problem of separation and becoming your kid's ally instead of her enemy. Someday I hope to be just like you.

If you answered d, your kid, with everykid's fragile ego, will believe you. Is that what you want?

4. Wait a minute, I don't have space for question four. This column has run totally away with me. Okay, just some final words: Don't ever use the word "ladylike." Don't ever say, "Only boys can do that." Don't encourage your boys to be strong and assertive and your daughters to be meek and submissive. And whatever you do, do not take your child to cocktail parties and force everyone to make a great big fuss.

FROM *Get Your Tongue Out of My Mouth, I'm Kissing You Good-bye*

What's a Guy to Do?

I'm still trying to figure out why men are in such trouble.

Oh, come on, you know you are. You're bewildered, insecure, and terribly nervous. You're confused not only about how to act with women, but how to relate to the entire world. You've been buffeted by constant social and sexual conflicts and have lost control of all inner equilibrium.

I see you on talk shows attempting to explain yourself to audiences of sneering women. I see you pouring into twelve-step meetings, where you try to cry in front of people. But worst of all, I'm starting to see you at bookstores furtively buying self-help books.

The buying of a self-help book is the most desperate of all human acts. It means you've lost your mind completely: You've entrusted your mental health to a self-aggrandizing twit with a psychology degree and a yen for a yacht. It means you're having a major identity crisis.

Women did this a while ago, when our sex was having an identity crisis that lasted for oh, a decade. We didn't know who we were supposed to be, so we mainlined annoying tomes like *Women Who Love Too Much*. But then along came Anita Hill. She was the ignition that switched on everywoman's brain. Before Anita, we were all whining,

What's wrong with me? Where can I find a book to fix me? After Anita, we all decided, "Wait a minute! It isn't me after all! Women are *still* being fucked over in our society!"

We're feeling much better now, thank you.

But men are feeling worse. You've been through a lot of identity-battering in the last twenty years:

First, you had to unlearn everything you were ever taught about women when feminism came along. You thought that you were supposed to grow up, get married, and immediately become the captain of the ship, the breadwinner. All that responsibility was scary, but a man had to do what a man had to do.

Then you were told that that was all wrong and how dare you? It was time to give up half your power to women or else.

Some of you became recalcitrant pigs, but many of you tried. You tried to be sensitive, you tried to learn the new language of women, you tried to gently abdicate your heavy mantle of responsibility, you tried to treat women as equal.

Then you were told that that was all wrong and how come you were all such wimps? What woman wanted a man she could walk all over?

So then you all bought motorcycle jackets and grew little ponytails and sported a three-day growth of beard and tried to be neotough. The message was "No broad better push me around, and if she does, well, I'll . . . I'll be sensitive and caring."

That didn't work, because women were going through their aforementioned crisis around then and nothing you did pleased us. Nothing.

Then along came Robert Bly and the masculinist movement and suddenly many of you found yourself spending nights in the woods, sweating and beating drums. Or at least reading about it.

But that felt just too goofy, and you had bigger problems. The economy plunged disastrously and many people lost jobs. Maybe not you. But maybe you soon. Plus women were charging you with sexual harassment and date rape. Maybe not you. But maybe you soon.

At this point in history, does it feel like you can't do anything right?

It's time to realize that there's nothing wrong with you. Well, there's plenty wrong with *some* of you. Men who abuse women, men who take the anger in their souls out on women, men who think of women as sex objects to be used and discarded should not even be allowed to be called men. But most of you are well-meaning but hopelessly befuddled.

So you're buying self-help books, you're blaming yourselves for your own unhappiness, you think you have some fatal flaw that reading some book will put right.

But it's not you. Society is fucking you over. Society has taken away all possible role models.

The last role model you had was "breadwinner, captain of the family." You could go ahead and become that, or you could become some kind of James Dean/Jack Nicholson guy and rebel against everything and run away. Either choice gave you a built-in structure in your attitudes toward women: You were either totally responsible or totally irresponsible. Either choice was sanctioned by society.

Now these choices have been systematically destroyed and replaced with nothing. There's nothing you're supposed to be, there's nothing to rebel against being.

You're working in a void, without identity, and the only messages you receive are negative: Don't be a pig, don't be a wimp.

Many of you have taken refuge in careers, defining yourselves solely by your jobs. This doesn't work anymore either. You're having heart attacks, you're getting fired.

Okay, I'm not a man. But I have been through a period of my life where it was either reinvent yourself or kill yourself. And I say it's time for a masculine revolution.

This means you've got to stop listening to anybody. Stop listening to a society which tells you you're powerful when in fact a couple of rich guys control everything. Stop listening to beer commercials which instruct you to be a moron. Stop listening to women who don't know what the hell they want but want you to give it to them anyway. Follow your best instincts. Figure out what's important to you.

Maybe you could reinvent the concept of fatherhood. Everybody seems to be decrying the lack of fathers, nobody seems to know what fathers are supposed to do. Maybe you can drop that heavy cloak of "manliness" that keeps you acting silent and strong when you want to be gossipy and playful.

Oh, don't listen to me, either. Just make it up as you go along. Just stop moping before we all go insane.

O. Henry
(1862–1910)

The Ransom of Red Chief

It looked like a good thing: but wait till I tell you. We were down South, in Alabama—Bill Driscoll and myself—when this kidnapping idea struck us. It was, as Bill afterward expressed it, "during a moment of temporary mental apparition"; but we didn't find that out till later.

There was a town down there, as flat as a flannel-cake, and called Summit, of course. It contained inhabitants of as undeleterious and self-satisfied a class of peasantry as ever clustered around a Maypole.

Bill and me had a joint capital of about six hundred dollars, and we needed just two thousand dollars more to pull off a fraudulent town-lot scheme in Western Illinois with. We talked it over on the front steps of the hotel. Philoprogenitiveness, says we, is strong in semi-rural communities; therefore, and for other reasons, a kidnapping project ought to do better there than in the radius of newspapers that send reporters out in plain clothes to stir up talk about such things. We knew that Summit couldn't get after us with anything stronger than constables and, maybe, some lackadaisical bloodhounds and a diatribe or two in the *Weekly Farmers' Budget*. So, it looked good.

We selected for our victim the only child of a prominent citizen named Ebenezer Dorset. The father was respectable and tight, a mortgage fancier and a stern, upright collection-plate passer and forecloser. The kid was a boy of ten, with bas-relief freckles, and hair the color of the cover of the magazine you buy at the news-stand when you want to catch a train. Bill and me figured that

Ebenezer would melt down for a ransom of two thousand dollars to a cent. But wait till I tell you.

About two miles from Summit was a little mountain, covered with a dense cedar brake. On the rear elevation of this mountain was a cave. There we stored provisions.

One evening after sundown, we drove in a buggy past old Dorset's house. The kid was in the street, throwing rocks at a kitten on the opposite fence.

"Hey, little boy!" says Bill, "would you like to have a bag of candy and a nice ride?"

The boy catches Bill neatly in the eye with a piece of brick.

"That will cost the old man an extra five hundred dollars," says Bill, climbing over the wheel.

That boy put up a fight like a welter-weight cinnamon bear; but, at last, we got him down in the bottom of the buggy and drove away. We took him up to the cave, and I hitched the horse in the cedar brake. After dark I drove the buggy to the little village, three miles away, where we had hired it, and walked back to the mountain.

Bill was pasting court-plaster over the scratches and bruises on his features. There was a fire burning behind the big rock at the entrance of the cave, and the boy was watching a pot of boiling coffee, with two buzzard tail-feathers stuck in his red hair. He points a stick at me when I come up, and says:

"Ha! cursed paleface, do you dare to enter the camp of Red Chief, the terror of the plains?"

"He's all right now," says Bill, rolling up his trousers and examining some bruises on his shins. "We're playing Indian. We're making Buffalo Bill's show look like magic-lantern views of Palestine in the town hall. I'm Old Hank, the Trapper, Red Chief's captive, and I'm to be scalped at daybreak. By Geronimo! that kid can kick hard."

Yes, sir, that boy seemed to be having the time of his life. The fun of camping out in a cave had made him forget that he was a captive himself. He immediately christened me Snake-eye, the Spy, and announced that, when his braves returned from the warpath, I was to be broiled at the stake at the rising of the sun.

Then we had supper; and he filled his mouth full of bacon and bread and gravy, and began to talk. He made a during-dinner speech something like this:

"I like this fine. I never camped out before; but I had a pet 'possum once, and I was nine last birthday. I hate to go to school. Rats ate up sixteen of Jimmy Talbot's aunt's speckled hen's eggs. Are there any real Indians in these woods? I want some more gravy. Does the trees moving make the wind blow? We had five puppies. What makes your nose so red, Hank? My father has lots of money. Are the stars hot? I whipped Ed Walker twice, Saturday. I don't like girls. You dassent catch toads unless with a string. Do oxen make any noise? Why are oranges round? Have you got beds to sleep on in this cave? Amos Murray has got six toes. A parrot can talk, but a monkey or a fish can't. How many does it take to make twelve?"

Every few minutes he would remember that he was a pesky redskin, and pick up his stick rifle and tiptoe to the mouth of the cave to rubber for the scouts of the hated paleface. Now and then he would let out a war-whoop that made Old Hank the Trapper shiver. That boy had Bill terrorized from the start.

"Red Chief," says I to the kid, "would you like to go home?"

"Aw, what for?" says he. "I don't have any fun at home. I hate to go to school. I like to camp out. You won't take me back home again, Snake-eye, will you?"

"Not right away," says I. "We'll stay here in the cave awhile."

"All right!" says he. "That'll be fine. I never had such fun in all my life."

We went to bed about eleven o'clock. We spread down some wide blankets and quilts and put Red Chief between us. We weren't afraid he'd run away. He kept us awake for three hours, jumping up and reaching for his rifle and screeching: "Hist! pard," in mine and Bill's ears, as the fancied crackle of a twig or the rustle of a leaf revealed to his young imagination the stealthy approach of the outlaw band. At last, I fell into a troubled sleep, and dreamed that I had been kidnapped and chained to a tree by a ferocious pirate with red hair.

Just at daybreak, I was awakened by a series of awful screams from Bill. They weren't yells, or howls, or shouts, or whoops, or yawps, such as you'd expect from a manly set of vocal organs—they were simply indecent, terrifying, humiliating screams, such as women emit when they see ghosts or caterpillars. It's an awful thing to hear a strong, desperate, fat man scream incontinently in a cave at daybreak.

I jumped up to see what the matter was. Red Chief was sitting on Bill's chest, with one hand twined in Bill's hair. In the other he had the sharp case-knife we used for slicing bacon; and he was industriously and realistically trying to take Bill's scalp, according to the sentence that had been pronounced upon him the evening before.

I got the knife away from the kid and made him lie down again. But, from that moment, Bill's spirit was broken. He laid down on his side of the bed, but he never closed an eye again in sleep as long as that boy was with us. I dozed off for a while, but along toward sun-up I remembered that Red Chief had said I was to be burned at the stake at the rising of the sun. I wasn't nervous or afraid; but I sat up and lit my pipe and leaned against a rock.

"What you getting up so soon for, Sam?" asked Bill.

"Me?" says I. "Oh, I got a kind of pain in my shoulder. I thought sitting up would rest it."

"You're a liar!" says Bill. "You're afraid. You was to be burned at sunrise, and you was afraid he'd do it. And he would, too, if he could find a match. Ain't it awful, Sam? Do you think anybody will pay out money to get a little imp like that back home?"

"Sure," said I. "A rowdy kid like that is just the kind that parents dote on. Now, you and the Chief get up and cook breakfast, while I go up on the top of this mountain and reconnoitre."

I went up on the peak of the little mountain and ran my eye over the contiguous vicinity. Over towards Summit I expected to see the sturdy yeomanry of the village armed with scythes and pitchforks beating the countryside for the dastardly kidnappers. But what I saw was a peaceful landscape dotted with one man ploughing with a dun mule. Nobody was dragging the creek; no couriers dashed hither and yon, bringing tidings of no news to the distracted parents. There was a sylvan attitude of somnolent sleepiness pervading that section of the external outward surface of Alabama that lay exposed to my view. "Perhaps," says I to myself, "it has not yet been discovered that the wolves have borne away the tender lambkin from the fold. Heaven help the wolves!" says I, and I went down the mountain to breakfast.

When I got to the cave I found Bill backed up against the side of it, breathing hard, and the boy threatening to smash him with a rock half as big as a cocoanut.

"He put a red-hot boiled potato down my back," explained Bill, "and then mashed it with his foot; and I boxed his ears. Have you got a gun about you, Sam?"

I took the rock away from the boy and kind of patched up the argument. "I'll fix you," says the kid to Bill. "No man ever yet struck the Red Chief but he got paid for it. You better beware!"

After breakfast the kid takes a piece of leather with strings wrapped around it out of his pocket and goes outside the cave unwinding it.

"What's he up to now?" says Bill, anxiously. "You don't think he'll run away, do you, Sam?"

"No fear of it," says I. "He don't seem to be much of a home body. But we've got to fix up some plan about the ransom. There don't seem to be much excitement around Summit on account of his disappearance; but maybe they haven't realized yet that he's gone. His folks may think he's spending the night with Aunt Jane or one of the neighbors. Anyhow, he'll be missed to-day. To-night we must get a message to his father demanding the two thousand dollars for his return."

Just then we heard a kind of war-whoop, such as David might have emitted when he knocked out the champion Goliath. It was a sling that Red Chief had pulled out of his pocket, and he was whirling it around his head.

I dodged, and heard a heavy thud and a kind of a sigh from Bill, like a horse gives out when you take his saddle off. A niggerhead rock the size of an egg had caught Bill just behind his left ear. He loosened himself all over and fell in the fire across the frying pan of hot water for washing the dishes. I dragged him out and poured cold water on his head for half an hour.

By and by, Bill sits up and feels behind his ear and says: "Sam, do you know who my favorite Biblical character is?"

"Take it easy," says I. "You'll come to your senses presently."

"King Herod," says he. "You won't go away and leave me here alone, will you, Sam?"

I went out and caught that boy and shook him until his freckles rattled.

"If you don't behave," says I, "I'll take you straight home. Now, are you going to be good, or not?"

"I was only funning," says he, sullenly. "I didn't mean to hurt Old Hank. But what did he hit me for? I'll behave, Snake-eye, if you won't send me home, and if you'll let me play the Black Scout to-day."

"I don't know the game," says I. "That's for you and Mr. Bill to decide. He's your playmate for the day. I'm going away for a while, on business. Now, you come in and make friends with him and say you are sorry for hurting him, or home you go, at once."

I made him and Bill shake hands, and then I took Bill aside and told him I was going to Poplar Grove, a little village three miles from the cave, and find out what I could about how the kidnapping had been regarded in Summit. Also, I thought it best to send a peremptory letter to old man Dorset that day, demanding the ransom and dictating how it should be paid.

"You know, Sam," says Bill, "I've stood by you without batting an eye in earthquakes, fire and blood—in poker games, dynamite outrages, police raids, train robberies, and cyclones. I never lost my nerve yet till we kidnapped that two-legged skyrocket of a kid. He's got me going. You won't leave me long with him, will you, Sam?"

"I'll be back some time this afternoon," says I. "You must keep the boy amused and quiet till I return. And now we'll write the letter to old Dorset."

Bill and I got paper and pencil and worked on the letter while Red Chief, with a blanket wrapped around him, strutted up and down, guarding the mouth of the cave. Bill begged me tearfully to make the ransom fifteen hundred dollars instead of two thousand. "I ain't attempting," says he, "to decry the celebrated moral aspect of parental affection, but we're dealing with humans, and it ain't human for anybody to give up two thousand dollars for that forty-pound chunk of freckled wildcat. I'm willing to take a chance at fifteen hundred dollars. You can charge the difference up to me."

So, to relieve Bill, I acceded, and we collaborated a letter that ran this way:

EBENEZER DORSET, ESQ.:

We have your boy concealed in a place far from Summit. It is useless for you or the most skillful detectives to attempt to find him. Absolutely, the only terms on which you can have him restored to you are these: We demand fifteen hundred dollars in large bills for his return; the money to be left at midnight to-night at the same spot and in the same box as your reply—as hereinafter described. If you agree to these terms, send your answer in writing by a solitary messenger to-night at half-past eight o'clock. After crossing Owl Creek on the road to Poplar Grove, there are three large trees about a hundred yards apart, close to the fence of the wheat field on the right-hand side. At the bottom of the fence-post, opposite the third tree, will be found a small pasteboard box.

The messenger will place the answer in this box and return immediately to Summit.

If you attempt any treachery or fail to comply with our demand as stated, you will never see your boy again.

If you pay the money as demanded, he will be returned to you safe and well within three hours. These terms are final, and if you do not accede to them no further communication will be attempted.

TWO DESPERATE MEN.

I addressed this letter to Dorset, and put it in my pocket. As I was about to start, the kid comes up to me and says:

"Aw, Snake-eye, you said I could play the Black Scout while you was gone."

"Play it, of course," says I. "Mr. Bill will play with you. What kind of a game is it?"

"I'm the Black Scout," says Red Chief, "and I have to ride to the stockade to warn the settlers that the Indians are coming. I'm tired of playing Indian myself. I want to be the Black Scout."

"All right," says I. "It sounds harmless to me. I guess Mr. Bill will help you foil the pesky savages."

"What am I to do?" asks Bill, looking at the kid suspiciously.

"You are the hoss," says Black Scout. "Get down on your hands and knees. How can I ride to the stockade without a hoss?"

"You'd better keep him interested," said I, "till we get the scheme going. Loosen up."

Bill gets down on his all fours, and a look comes in his eye like a rabbit's when you catch it in a trap.

"How far is it to the stockade, kid?" he asks, in a husky manner of voice.

"Ninety miles," says the Black Scout. "And you have to hump yourself to get there on time. Whoa, now!"

The Black Scout jumps on Bill's back and digs his heels in his side.

"For Heaven's sake," says Bill, "hurry back, Sam, as soon as you can. I wish we hadn't made the ransom more than a thousand. Say, you quit kicking me or I'll get up and warm you good."

I walked over to Poplar Grove and sat around the post-office and store, talking with the chaw-bacons that came in to trade. One whisker-ando says that he hears Summit is all upset on account of Elder Ebenezer Dorset's boy having been lost or stolen. That was all I wanted to know. I bought some smoking tobacco, referred casually to the price of black-eyed peas, posted my letter surreptitiously, and came away. The postmaster said the mail-carrier would come by in an hour to take the mail to Summit.

When I got back to the cave Bill and the boy were not to be found. I explored the vicinity of the cave, and risked a yodel or two, but there was no response.

So I lighted my pipe and sat down on a mossy bank to await developments.

In about half an hour I heard the bushes rustle, and Bill wobbled out into the little glade in front of the cave. Behind him was the kid, stepping softly like a scout, with a broad grin on his face. Bill stopped, took off his hat, and wiped his face with a red handkerchief. The kid stopped about eight feet behind him.

"Sam," says Bill, "I suppose you'll think I'm a renegade, but I couldn't help it. I'm a grown person with masculine proclivities and habits of self-defense, but there is a time when all systems of egotism and predominance fail. The boy is gone. I sent him home. All is off. There was martyrs in old times," goes on Bill, "that suffered death rather than give up the particular graft they enjoyed. None of 'em ever was subjugated to such supernatural tortures as I have been. I tried to be faithful to our articles of depredation; but there came a limit."

"What's the trouble, Bill?" I asks him.

"I was rode," says Bill, "the ninety miles to the stockade, not barring an inch. Then, when the settlers was rescued, I was given oats. Sand ain't a palatable substitute. And then, for an hour I had to try to explain to him why there was nothin' in holes, how a road can run both ways, and what makes the grass green. I tell you, Sam, a human can only stand so much. I takes him by the neck of his clothes and drags him down the mountain. On the way he kicks my legs black and blue from the knees down; and I've got to have two or three bites on my thumb and hand cauterized.

"But he's gone"—continues Bill—"gone home. I showed him the road to Summit and kicked him about eight feet nearer there at one kick. I'm sorry we lose the ransom; but it was either that or Bill Driscoll to the madhouse."

Bill is puffing and blowing, but there is a look of ineffable peace and growing content on his rose-pink features.

"Bill," says I, "there isn't any heart disease in your family, is there?"

"No," says Bill, "nothing chronic except malaria and accidents. Why?"

"Then you might turn around," says I, "and have a look behind you."

Bill turns and sees the boy, and loses his complexion and sits down plump on the ground and begins to pluck aimlessly at grass and little sticks. For an hour I was afraid of his mind. And then I told him that my scheme was to put the whole job through immediately and that we would get the ransom and be off with it by midnight if old Dorset fell in with our proposition. So Bill braced up enough to give the kid a weak sort of a smile and a promise to play the Russian in a Japanese war with him as soon as he felt a little better.

I had a scheme for collecting that ransom without danger of being caught by counterplots that ought to commend itself to professional kidnappers. The tree under which the answer was to be left—and the money later on—was close to the road fence with big, bare fields on all sides. If a gang of constables should be watching for any one to come for the note, they could see him a long way off crossing the fields or in the road. But no, sirree! At half-past eight I was up in that tree as well hidden as a tree toad, waiting for the messenger to arrive.

Exactly on time, a half-grown boy rides up the road on a bicycle, locates the pasteboard box at the foot of the fence-post, slips a folded piece of paper into it, and pedals away again back toward Summit.

I waited an hour and then concluded the thing was square. I slid down the tree, got the note, slipped along the fence till I struck the woods, and was back at the cave in another half an hour. I opened the note, got near the lantern, and read it to Bill. It was written with a pen in a crabbed hand, and the sum and substance of it was this:

TWO DESPERATE MEN.

Gentlemen: I received your letter to-day by post, in regard to the ransom you ask for the return of my son. I think you are a little high in your demands, and I hereby make you a counter-proposition, which I am inclined to believe you will accept. You bring Johnny home and pay me two hundred and fifty dollars in cash, and I agree to take him off your hands. You had better come at night, for the neighbors believe he is lost, and I couldn't be responsible for what they would do to anybody they saw bringing him back. Very respectfully,

EBENEZER DORSET.

"Great pirates of Penzance," says I; "of all the impudent—"

But I glanced at Bill, and hesitated. He had the most appealing look in his eyes I ever saw on the face of a dumb or a talking brute.

"Sam," says he, "what's two hundred and fifty dollars, after all? We've got the money. One more night of this kid will send me to a bed in Bedlam. Besides being a thorough gentleman, I think Mr. Dorset is a spendthrift for making us such a liberal offer. You ain't going to let the chance go, are you?"

"Tell you the truth, Bill," says I, "this little he ewe lamb has somewhat got on my nerves too. We'll take him home, pay the ransom, and make our getaway."

We took him home that night. We got him to go by telling him that his father had bought a silver-mounted rifle and a pair of moccasins for him, and we were to hunt bears the next day.

It was just twelve o'clock when we knocked at Ebenezer's front door. Just at the moment when I should have been abstracting the fifteen hundred dollars from the box under the tree, according to the original proposition, Bill was counting out two hundred and fifty dollars into Dorset's hand.

When the kid found out we were going to leave him at home he started up a howl like a calliope and fastened himself as tight as a leech to Bill's leg. His father peeled him away gradually, like a porous plaster.

"How long can you hold him?" asks Bill.

"I'm not as strong as I used to be," says old Dorset, "but I think I can promise you ten minutes."

"Enough," says Bill. "In ten minutes I shall cross the Central, Southern, and Middle Western States, and be legging it trippingly for the Canadian border."

And, as dark as it was, and as fat as Bill was, and as good a runner as I am, he was a good mile and a half out of Summit before I could catch up with him.

Nicole Hollander
(Contemporary)

FROM *Female Problems*

Eeek! It's Kathie Lee

WHAT
WAS
THAT
NoiSe?

I fear exercise, flying, great heights, walking around alone at night, musical comedy, small dark places, roaches and mice, cash machines that run out of money, sudden noises, new neighbors, cocktail parties, foreign languages, stolen credit cards, credit bureaus, the IRS, bombs at airports, airline food, bingo, stuffing from inside the turkey, dentists, highway construction, vicious dogs, gangs of eight-year-old boys, nursing homes, dense forests, getting locked out of my apartment without shoes, deserts, empty highways, pierced nipples, abandoned motels, running out of gas, miniskirts, spiked heels, mold, Republicans, killer bees, spit on the sidewalk, Fundamentalists, graffiti, snowstorms, cold weather, humidity, gum disease, telephone calls after 9:00 P.M., large bodies of water, people who talk a lot, mysterious tinfoil packages in the back of the refrigerator, the FBI, shy people, washing machines that overflow, frozen pipes, walking across an open field during a thunderstorm, ant invasions, piles of ironing, sudden attacks of lust, electrical outlets, tomatoes without flavor, mobile homes during a hurricane, runaway horses, maps, cruise control, hockey pucks, masseuses who crack your neck, getting trapped in a sauna, car jackers, men in suits, crying babies, cruel landlords, crooked mechanics, Freddy Krueger, insurance companies, needles, tongue depressors, plastic bags, and Florida. . . . But please, O powerful one, O ruler of the body, please don't make me fear hot dogs with everything, on a poppyseed bun; ice cream laced with chocolate and nuts; thick steaks; garlic bread with butter; two eggs over easy with bacon, hash browns, and a side of sausage; or meat loaf with gravy.

Notes from the traveler Who Whines

I Like to
tRAVeL
IN MY
BATHRoBe.

Well, a really bad trip is where you die, am I right? Anything less: dysentery, loss of your passport, bugged hotel rooms, insects the size of ponies, mud slides, frostbite, and outright rudeness are the stuff of good stories when you get back home. The recollection of near disaster is the only thing that will remove the glassy look from a friend's eyes as you recount your trip to Afghanistan or Iowa. Well, I'm not doing it. It's not worth it.

James Morris was with Edmund Hillary when he reached the summit of Mount Everest. That same intrepid man later had a sex change operation and became Jan Morris. Fearful journeys, both, but Ms. Morris is addicted to exploring and has never had a bad experience.

I have had bad experiences in Elmhurst, Illinois. Like soufflé, I do not travel well. I whine. My IQ goes down. I forget to look both ways. I can get lost taking a new way home from the office. London defeated me. I panic over trifles. I became comatose in a hotel in Santa Monica because there was an odd stain on the ceiling and the spreads felt clammy. I had to be half-carried to the plane. (A plane, oh my God, I'm on a plane. Well, it was either that or live in Santa Monica forever.)

So I am unable to visit the rain forest, take a solo trip around the globe in a tiny boat, or see the pyramids in old Algiers. I will never exchange courteous speech and gifts with chieftains in Samoa or get a haircut in Kashmir. If I were by profession a governess, you would not find me in a forbidding mansion on a moor in a windswept corner of England, even though I was down on my luck and the master of the house was terribly good-looking and stern.

I am an armchair traveler of a very limited kind. I like to read books about awful trips. I loved *Forgotten Fatherland*. The author searches for the lost colony of Elisabeth Nietzsche in Paraguay and suffers mightily from aggressive biting insects and a diet composed solely of protein. The English seem to excel at this kind of writing. Bless them. I keep a copy of *Bad Trips* (edited by Keith Fraser) at my bedside. I leaf through it when I feel the urge to travel. It calms me and confirms to me the rightness of my abject wimpiness. Even for armchair traveling I impose strict limits. I don't watch films in which young people are imprisoned in Turkey for minor drug offenses or where women disguise themselves in chadors and escape with their daughters from alien cultures. Makes me nervous.

Most trips involve plane travel. I hate that. A friend of mine was offered a free trip to Uzbekistan. She couldn't pass it up. Well, who could? Many of us have longed to go to a theater festival in Uzbekistan all our adult lives. She said she thought of me when, on the second or fifth leg of the journey, her plane, experiencing mechanical difficulties, landed at an unmarked airfield. After quite a while, in which no one in authority communicated anything and the passengers were not allowed off the aircraft, a long ladder was placed against the wing. A man climbed up the ladder and hit something sharply with a hammer and they took off again.

FROM *The Whole Enchilada*

Marietta Holley
(1836–1926)

FROM *The Widder Doodle's Courtship*

I Wish I Was a Widder
by Betsey Bobbet

Oh, "Gimlet," back again I float
    With broken wings, a weary bard;
I cannot write as once I wrote,
    I have to work so very hard.
So hard my lot, so tossed about,
My muse is fairly tuckered out.

My muse aforesaid, once hath flown,
    But now her back is broke, and breast;
And yet she fain would crumble down
    On "Gimlet" pages she would rest;
And sing plain words as there she's sot
Haply they'll rhyme, and haply not.

I spake plain words in former days,
    No guile I showed, clear was my plan;
My gole it matrimony was.
    My earthly aim it was a man.
I gained my man, I won my gole,
Alas, I feel not as I fole.

Yes, ringing through my maiden thought
    This clear voice rose, "Oh come up higher"
To speak plain truth with cander fraught,
    To married be, was my desire.
Now sweeter still this lot doth seem
To be a widder is my theme.

For toil hath claimed me for her own,
    In wedlock I have found no ease;

I've cleaned and washed for neighbors round;
　　And took my pay in beans and pease;
In boiling sap no rest I took
Or husking corn in barn and stook.

Or picking wool from house to house,
　　White-washing, painting, papering,
In stretching carpets, boiling souse,
　　E'en picking hops it hath a sting
For spiders there assembled be,
Mosqueetoes, bugs, and etcetree.

I have to work, oh! very hard;
　　Old Toil, I know your breadth, and length.
I'm tired to death; and in one word
　　I have to work beyond my strength,
And mortal men are very tough
To get along with—nasty, rough.

Yes, tribulation's doomed to her
　　Who weds a man, without no doubt
In peace a man is singuler
　　His ways, they are past finding out,
And oh! the wrath of mortal males
To paint their ire, earth's language fails.

And thirteen children in our home
　　Their buttons rend, their clothes they burst.
Much bread and such do they consume;
　　Of children they do seem the worst;
And Simon and I do disagree,
He's prone to sin continualee.

On Marriage

"Good land!" says I, "is marryin' the only theme that anybody can lay holt of?" says I, "it seems to me it would be the best way to lay holt of duty now, and then, if a bo come, lay holt of him. If they ketch a bo with such a hook as they are a-fishin' with now, what kind of a bo will it be? Nobody but a fool would lay holt of a hook baited with dime novels and pups. Learn your girls to be industrious, and to respect themselves. They can't now, Delila Ann, I know they can't. No woman can feel honorable and reverential toward themselves, when they are foldin' their useless hands over their empty souls, waitin' for some man, no matter who, to marry 'em and support 'em. When in the agony of suspense and fear, they have narrowed down to this one theme, all their hopes and prayers, Good Lord; *anybody!*

"But when a woman lays holt of life in a noble, earnest way, when she is dutiful, and cheerful, and industrious, God-fearin', and self-respectin', though the world sinks, there is a rock under her feet that won't let her down far enough to hurt her any. If love comes to her to brighten her pathway, so much the better. She will be ready to receive them royally, and keep him when she gets him. Some folks don't know how to use love worth a cent. But no matter whether she be single or double, I am not afraid of her future."

On Competition

Tirzah Ann burst right out a-crying, and says she:

"Mother, one week's more rest would have tuckered me completely out; I should have died off."

I wiped my own spectacles, I was so affected, and says I, in choked up axents:

"You know I told you just how it would be; I told you you wus happy enough to home, and you hadn't better go off in search of rest or of pleasure."

And says she, breakin' right down agin, "One week more of such pleasure and recreation, would have been my death blow."

Says I, "I believe it, I believe you; you couldn't have stood another mite of rest and recreation, without it's killin' of you—anybody can see that by lookin' at your mean." But says I, knowin' it wus my duty to be calm, "It is all over now, Tirzah Ann; you hain't got to go through it again; you must try to overcome your feelin's. Tell your ma all about it. Mebby it will do you good, in the words of the him, 'Speak, and let the worst be known, Speakin' may relieve you.'"

And I see, indeed, that she needed relief. Wall, she up and told me the hull on it. And I found out that Mrs. Skidmore wus to the bottom of it all—she, and Tirzah Ann's ambition. I could see that them two wus to blame for the hull on it.

Mrs. Skidmore is the wife of the other lawyer in Janesville; they moved there in the spring. She wus awful big feelin', and wus determined from the first to lead the fashion—tried to be awful genteel and put on sights of airs.

And Tirzah Ann bein' ambitious, and knowin' that she looked a good deal better than Mrs. Skidmore did, and knew as much agin, and knowin' that Whitfield wus a better lawyer than her husband wus, and twice as well off, wusn't goin' to stand none of her airs. Mrs. Skidmore seemed to sort o' look down on Tirzah Ann, for she never felt as I did on that subject.

Now, if anybody wants to feel above me, I look on it in this light, I filosofize on it in this way: it probably does them some good, and it don't do me a mite of hurt, so I let 'em feel. I have always made a practice of it—it don't disturb me the width of a horse-hair. Because somebody feels as if they wus better than I am, that don't make 'em so; if it did, I should probably get up more interest on the subject. . . .

"Such folks have to put on more airs than them that have got sunthin' to feel big over." Says I, "It is reeson and filosify that if anybody has got a uncommon intellect, or beauty, or wealth, they don't, as a general thing, put on the airs that them do that hain't got nothin'; they don't *have* to; they have got sunthin' to hold 'em up—they can stand without airs. But when anybody hain't got no intellect, nor riches, nor nothin'—when they hain't got nothin' only jest air to hold 'em up, it stands to reeson that they have got to have a good deal of it."

I had studied it all out, so it wus as plain to me as anything. But Tirzah Ann couldn't see it in that light, and would get as mad as a hen at Mrs. Skidmore ever sense they came to Janesville, and was bound she shouldn't go by her and out-do her. And so when Mrs. Skidmore gin it out in Janesville that she and her husband wus a goin' away for the summer, for rest and pleasure, Tirzah Ann said to herself that she and her husband would go for rest and pleasure, if they both died in the attempt. Wall, three days before they started, Tirzah Ann found that Mrs. Skidmore had got one dress more than she had, and a polenay, so she went to the store and got the material and ingredients, and sot up day and night a-makin' of 'em up; it most killed her a-hurryin' so.

Wall, they started the same day, and went to the same place the Skidmores did—a fashionable summer resort—and put up to the same tavern, to rest and recreate. But Mrs. Skidmore bein' a healthy, raw-boned woman, could stand as much agin rest as Tirzah Ann could. Why, Tirzah Ann says the rest wus enough to wear out a leather wemen, and how she stood it for two weeks wus more than she could tell. You see she wusn't used to hard work. I had always favored her and gone ahead with the work myself, and Whitfield had been as careful of her, and as good as a woman to help her, and the rest came tough on it; it wus dretful hard on her to be put through so.

You see she had to dress up two or three times a day, and keep the babe dressed up slick. And she had to promenade down to the waterin'-place, and drink jist such a time, and it went against her stomach, and almost upset her every time. And she had to go a-ridin', and out on the water in boats and yots, and that made her sick, too, and had to play erokey, and be up till midnight to parties. You see she had to do all this, ruther than let Mrs. Skidmore get in ahead on her, and do more than she did, and be more genteel than she wus, and rest more.

And then the town bein' full, and runnin' over, they wus cooped up in a little mite of a room up three flights of stairs; that in itself, wus enough to wear Tirzah Ann out; she never could climb stairs worth a cent. And their room wus very small, and the air close, nearly tight, and hot as an oven; they wus used to great, cool, airy rooms to hum; and the babe couldn't stand the hotness and the tightness, and she began to enjoy poor health, and cried most all the time, and that wore on Tirzah Ann; and to hum, the babe could play round in the yard all day a'most, but here she hung right on to her ma.

And then the rooms on one side of 'em wus occupied by a young man a-learnin' to play on the flute; he had been disappointed in love, and he would try to make up tunes as he went along sort o' tragedy style, and dirge-like, the most unearthly and woe-begone sounds, they say, that they ever heard or heard on. They say it wus enough to make anybody's blood run cold in their veins to hear 'em; he kept his room most of the time, and played day and night. He had ruther be alone day times and play, than go into company, and nights he couldn't sleep, so he would set up and play. They wus sorry for him, they said they wus; they knew his mind must be in a awful state, and his sufferin's intense, or he couldn't harrow up anybody's feelin's so. But that didn't make it more the easier for them.

Tirzah Ann and Whitfield both says that tongue can't never tell the sufferin's they underwent from that flute, and their feelin's for that young man; they expected every day to hear he had made way with himself, his agony seemed so great, and he would groan and rithe so fearful, when he was playin'.

And the room on the other side of 'em wus occupied by a young woman who owned a melodien; she went into company a good deal, and her spells of playin' and singin' would come on after she had got home from parties. She had a good many bo's, and wus happy dispositioned naturally; and they said some nights, it would seem as if there wouldn't be no end to her playin' and singin' love songs, and performin' quiet pieces, polkys, and waltzes, and such. Tirzah Ann and Whitfield are both good-hearted as they can be, and they said they didn't want to throw no shade over young hearts; they had been young themselves not much more than two years ago; they knew by experience what it wus to be sentimental, and they felt to sympathize with the gladness and highlarity of a young heart, and they didn't want to do nothin' to break it up. But still it came tough on 'em—dretful. I s'pose the sufferin's couldn't be told that they suffered from them two musicianers. And the babe not bein' used to such rackets, nights, would get skairt, and almost go into hysterick fits. And two or three nights, Tirzah Ann had 'em, too—the hystericks. I don't know what kept Whitfield up; he says no money would tempt him to go through it again; I s'pose she almost tore him to pieces; but she wasn't to blame, she didn't know what she was a-doin'.

It hain't no use to blame Tirzah Ann now, after it is all over with; but she sees it plain enough now, and she's a-sufferin' from the effects of it, her tryin' to keep up with Mrs. Skidmore, and do all she done. And there is where her morals get all run down, and Whitfield's, too.

Langston Hughes
(1902–67)

FROM *Laughing to Keep from Crying*

We all ordered fish and settled down comfortably to shocking our white friends with tales about how many Negroes there were passing for white all over America. We were determined to *épater le bourgeois* real good via this white couple we had cornered, when the woman leaned over the table in the midst of our dissertations and said, "Listen, gentlemen, you needn't spread the word, but me and my husband aren't white either. We've just been *passing* for white for the last fifteen years."

"What?"

"We're colored, too, just like you," said the husband. "But it's better passing for white because we make more money."

All at once we dropped our professionally self-conscious "Negro" manners, became natural, ate fish, and talked and kidded freely like colored folks do when there are no white folks around. . . . After the fish we went to two or three more night spots and drank until five o'clock in the morning.

Finally we put the light-colored people in a taxi heading downtown. They turned to shout a last good-by. The cab was just about to move off, when the woman called to the driver to stop.

She leaned out the window and said with a grin, "Listen, boys! I hate to confuse you again. But, to tell the truth, my husband and I aren't really colored at all. We're white. We just thought we'd kid you by passing for colored a little while—just as you said Negroes sometimes pass for white."

She laughed as they sped off toward Central Park.

Zora Neale Hurston
(1891–1960)

FROM *Their Eyes Were Watching God*

The more people in there the more ridicule he poured over her body to point attention away from his own. So one day Steve Mixon wanted some chewing tobacco and Janie cut it wrong. She hated that tobacco knife anyway. It worked very stiff. She fumbled with the thing and cut way away from the mark. Mixon didn't mind. He held it up for a joke to tease Janie a little.

"Looka heah, Brother Mayor, whut yo' wife done took and done." It was cut comical, so everybody laughed at it. "Uh woman and uh knife—no kind of uh knife, don't b'long tuhgether." There was some more good-natured laughter at the expense of women.

Jody didn't laugh. He hurried across from the post office side and took the plug of tobacco away from Mixon and cut it again. Cut it exactly on the mark and glared at Janie.

"I god amighty! A woman can stay round uh store till she get old as Methusalem and still can't cut a little thing like a plug of tobacco! Don't stand dere rollin' yo' pop eyes at me wid yo' rump hangin' nearly to yo' knees!"

A big laugh started off in the store but people got to thinking and stopped. It was funny if you looked at it right quick, but it got pitiful if you thought about it awhile. It was like somebody snatched off part of a woman's clothes while she wasn't looking and the streets were crowded. Then too, Janie took the middle of the floor to talk right into Jody's face, and that was something that hadn't been done before.

"Stop mixin' up mah doings wid mah looks, Jody. When you git through tellin' me how tuh cut uh plug uh tobacco, then you kin tell me whether mah behind is on straight or not."

"Wha—whut's dat you say, Janie? You must be out yo' head."

"Naw, Ah ain't outa mah head neither."

"You must be. Talkin' any such language as dat."

"You de one started talkin' under people's clothes. Not me."

"Whut's de matter wid you, nohow? You ain't no young girl to be gettin' all insulted 'bout yo' looks. You ain't no young courtin' gal. You'se uh ole woman, nearly forty."

"Yeah, Ah'm nearly forty and you'se already fifty. How come you can't talk about dat sometimes instead of always pointin' at me?"

"T'ain't no use in gettin' all mad, Janie, 'cause Ah mention you ain't no young gal no mo'. Nobody in heah ain't lookin' for no wife outa yuh. Old as you is."

"Naw, Ah ain't no young gal no mo' but den Ah ain't no old woman neither. Ah reckon Ah looks mah age too. But Ah'm uh woman every inch of me, and Ah know it. Dat's uh whole lot more'n *you* kin say. You big-bellies round here and put out a lot of brag, but 'tain't nothin' to it but yo' big voice. Humph! Talkin' 'bout *me* lookin' old! When you pull down yo' britches, you look lak de change uh life."

"Great God from Zion!" Sam Watson gasped. "Y'all really playin' de dozens tuhnight."

Molly Ivins
(Contemporary)

FROM *You Got to Dance with Them What Brung You*

Folks Aren't Really Good at Heart? I'm Not Giving Up

The municipal motto of Northfield, Minnesota, is "Cows, Colleges and Contentment." Honest. Last year they had a contest to think up a new motto and, after some civic thought, decided to keep "Cows, Colleges and Contentment."

So as we veer rhetorically toward the apocalypse as various social prophets mutter direly about the growth of the underclass, the unraveling of the social fabric, the brutalization of consciousness, and other pesky problems, you'll be happy to know that somewhere the sun is shining, somewhere the skies are bright, somewhere the children are laughing, et cetera. In Northfield, Minnesota, for one.

Having just survived a heavy dose of apocalyptic rhetoric the other night in New York City, I was especially glad to land where all the children are above average. Not that Minnesota is problem-free: on the front page of Friday's Minneapolis *Star Tribune*, we find enumerated three certifiable cases in which the Monied Special Interests have triumphed over the Will of the People in Minnesota in recent years. Three, count 'em—on the fingers of one hand.

The proximate cause of the current bout of apocalyptic analysis is that this year is the fiftieth anniversary of practically everything. As such, it's a handy vantage point for surveying as depressing a half-century of history as recorded time can offer. The last half of the twentieth century is never going to rank as a humanist high point; the fact that it was supposed to be the American Century is only further case for depression.

It started with a Holocaust. Have you heard the interviews with the soldiers who first liberated Dachau? And it is ending with two more, Rwanda and Bosnia, about which no one is doing much of anything. In between, we've spent fifty years in denial about Hiroshima and Nagasaki, managed to get involved in a ten-year war we now acknowledge was "terribly wrong," and built enough nuclear weapons to blow up the earth and everyone on it several times over. We can't even sit around and gloat about the Soviets because they've disbanded themselves.

If it weren't for the automatic teller machine and the self-cleaning garlic press, we'd have no evidence of progress at all—and I know people who think ATM's are part of a plot to prevent people from getting to know one another.

As an inveterate optimist, I hate arguing optimism versus pessimism, especially with people who are well informed. Let's face it: The evidence is always on the side of the pessimists. In fact, one of the few pro-optimism arguments that works is to point out that things can always get worse, which means we should be cheerful right now, because now will eventually turn out to be the Good Old Days.

Going onto a college campus these days—or even facing a junior-high audience for that matter—involves some tricky juggling. Telling kids to go forth and change the world may not be fair. On the other hand, telling them they're bound to have a hard time and shouldn't get their hopes up is not a peppy message.

Katha Pollitt, the feminist sage, observes that it's rather a shame that Americans have had to shed so many illusions during the last fifty years, mostly illusions about our own innocence and power. But she believes that it's a shame in the same sense that it's a shame that smoking causes cancer. It's too bad, but there it is. Are we not better off without illusions? Better off facing the very real limits on our national power and, certainly, the limits on our national innocence?

I suspect she's right; she often is. But I don't believe that recognizing the evil we have done in the course of our endless efforts to maintain our good opinion of ourselves means we must dislike ourselves. Rather an alarming number of Americans already don't like their fellow Americans—with good cause, they would all maintain. We seem to have gone from the old stereotype of Americans as fat, dumb, and happy to a new stereotype of fat, dumb, and unhappy.

After the bleak consideration of the last fifty years at the New York colloquium, one member of the audience was so depressed that she stood up and read Anne Frank's beautiful statement that ends, "I still believe that people are really good at heart."

"So look what happened to Anne Frank" is the obvious response. God bless the child, but her death is enough to make anyone doubt that people are really good at heart. There is a kind of bitterness that one finds among Holocaust survivors that is unanswerable. One of them, interviewed in the documentary *Shoah* and asked what was in his heart, said: "If you could open my breast and lick my heart, you would be poisoned and die from the bitterness of it."

They are entitled to their bitterness. The rest of us are not.

Erica Jong
(Contemporary)

FROM **Fear of Flying**

We drove to the hotel and said goodbye. How hypocritical to go upstairs with a man you don't want to fuck, leave the one you do sitting there alone, and then, in a state of great excitement, fuck the one you don't want to fuck while pretending he's the one you do. That's called fidelity. That's called monogamy. That's called civilization and its discontents.

I was a little appalled at my own promiscuity, that I could go from one man to another and feel so glowing and intoxicated. I knew I would have to pay for it later with the guilt and misery which I alone know how to give myself in such good measure. But right now I was happy. I felt properly appreciated for the first time. Do two men perhaps add up to one whole person?

Besides I really believed in pursuing a long-standing and deep relationship with one person. I could easily see the sterility of hopping from bed to bed and having shallow affairs with lots of shallow people. I had had the unutterably dismal experience of waking up in bed with a man I couldn't bear to talk to—and that was certainly no liberation either. But still, there just didn't seem to be any way to get the best of both exuberance and stability into your life. The fact that greater minds than mine had pondered these issues and come up with no very clear answers didn't comfort me much either. It only made me feel that my concerns were banal and commonplace. If I were really an exceptional person, I thought, I wouldn't spend hours worrying my head about marriage and adultery. I would just go out and snatch life with both hands and feel no remorse or guilt for anything. My guilt only showed how thoroughly bourgeois and contemptible I was. All my worrying this sad old bone only showed my ordinariness.

Judith Katz
(Contemporary)

FROM Running Fiercely Toward a High Thin Sound

Sarah reached up and pinched my cheek. "So you're the maid of honor. Let me set you ladies up in dressing room three."

It took me a minute to remember they were talking about me, that I was the honor maiden. Nonetheless, when Sarah led us to a far corner of the bridal boutique, I followed. Sarah jingled a huge ring of keys and unlocked a white door. "You go in and make yourselves comfortable. Mimi will be in to fit you in a minute."

"It's lovely, isn't it?" my mother gestured broadly at the small private room. Mirrors covered three walls, a white shag rug was on the floor. The furniture was early Barbie doll—two plump white hassocks and a satin couch.

"I hope you have a decent bra on," my mother said as I unbuttoned my shirt. I suddenly couldn't remember if I had on any bra at all, but before I could pull my shirt back on the door swung open and there stood Mimi, who must have been Sarah's depressed twin. She had a tape measure around her neck, a long pink dress slung over one arm, and a pair of white linen pumps clutched between her thick fingers. Sighing deeply, Mimi hung the dress on a chrome hook and set the shoes down at my feet. Then she knelt in front of me and with the help of a shoe horn slipped my foot into one of the pumps.

"Like a glove," Mimi said as she got me into the other shoe.

"I don't think I can walk." I stood and wobbled from one end of the dressing room to another.

"A little practice, you'll be fine," my mother said.

"Besides, you'll kick them off as soon as the dancing starts."

I was surprised to hear my sister Electa's voice. She hadn't said a word since we got into the department store.

"She won't kick them off," my mother argued.

"I probably will," I answered, disturbed at the whine in my voice, "but still, I have to walk down the aisle—"

"Don't worry, Janie, we've got a nice strong best man for you to lean on when it comes to that." Electa winked conspiratorially.

Best man? I never even considered I'd have to wobble on some strange guy's arm on top of every other thing. "But I still have to stand up at the altar teetering—"

"For God's sake," burst my mother, "the heel is only half inch—less than that. You can practice standing. It won't kill you—"

"I could break my neck," I said softly.

"Yes, think of the headlines," Electa said, "FEMINIST SISTER DIES IN TRAGIC HIGH HEEL ACCIDENT: 'I DIDN'T THINK IT COULD HAPPEN HERE' SAYS SHOCKED BRIDE."

"Alright, Electa, cut the comedy," my mother said. "Mimi, the shoes fit. Let's try the dress."

"*Oi*, the dress."

"It's not gonna kill you to wear a dress and heels and look like a *mencsh* for five hours."

"It totally contradicts my political world view."

"Stop talking nonsense. Mimi! The dress."

The dress was worse than I'd imagined. The sleeves were sheer, the bodice and hem frilly. I cringed at the thought of wearing it in public. "Electa, this is a real girly outfit."

"I know, Jane. I'm sorry, but it's the best of what they're offering this year."

"What's wrong with it?" my mother wanted to know. "A dress is for girls to wear. What were you expecting? Lace overalls?"

"It's just so—"

"Feminine?" my mother sneered. "Look, we haven't got all day. Try it on."

I slipped out of the rest of my clothes. To my relief, I had remembered to wear a bra and if it wasn't clean, my mother didn't notice. I climbed into the dress, which pinched at the waist as my mother zipped it.

"It's too small, Ma."

She pulled up at the zipper, and my sister Electa empathetically held her breath. Mimi the seamstress evilly fingered the pins in the cushion on her wrist.

"It really doesn't fit," I said weakly.

"It fits. With a different bra—you know, it wouldn't hurt to lose a few pounds before the wedding anyway . . . *oi* . . . there." My mother triumphantly slipped the zipper all the way shut. I saw myself in the three dressing room mirrors. I recognized the face, but I couldn't place the body anywhere. "Ma, if I turn purple because I can't breathe it's gonna spoil the effect."

"You only have to wear it once. It's fine."

"I'm gonna faint."

"Alright, we can let it out, can't we, Mimi? Jane, take it off."

Mimi unzipped, and I dutifully stepped out of the dress.

My mother snatched the dress out of Mimi's hands and carefully examined the seams. "There's plenty here to play with."

"Ma," Electa looked our mother in the eye, "let Jane try the next size."

"It will fit like a tent."

"Please, can we try the next size?" Electa asked the seamstress directly, bypassing my mother, taking matters into her own bride-to-be hands.

Mimi returned in a few minutes bearing another gown exactly like the first but bigger. I numbly climbed into it. It zipped like a charm but hung oddly in strange places.

"What did I tell you," my mother said triumphantly, "a tent."

Electa again went over my mother's head. "Mimi, what's easier? To take in or let out?"

"In my professional opinion, it would be easier to find a style that fit the young lady to begin with."

A tear formed in the corner of my eye. Electa sat back in her chair with her head in her hands. "This is impossible. I can't find one dress that looks good on five different women!"

"Try the smaller size again."

"Ma, I can't fit in the smaller size."

"*Can't* means *won't*."

I stood looking at myself in the larger dress. I pressed my eyes in to hold back a fit of crying. Electa touched my shoulder. "Really, Jane, it's not so bad."

"The smaller one is better," my mother said flatly. "Jane, try the smaller one just one last time."

I stood paralyzed in the middle of the dressing room.

"Really," said my mother, "I just want to prove a point. Please step into this."

She held the dress open like an envelope. I looked at Electa who looked at Mimi who silently washed her hands of the entire matter. Then Mimi unzipped the bigger gown and held it while I carefully stepped out.

The other women held their breath as I wedged myself into the first dress. My mother once again tugged at the zipper.

"It's gonna rip."

My mother squeezed the flesh of my back in under the zipper and yanked. "I could use a little cooperation. Pull your tummy in."

"It's in as far as it will go."

"Mommy," Electa pulled herself up to her full height, which in the space of the dressing room was rather impressive. "I'm not going to watch you torture Jane one more minute. Jane, you put on the large dress. Mimi, you pin it."

My mother threw up her hands and sat in a corner where she sulked until the pinning was complete. Normally I would have been nervous that she was going to lapse into her depression again, but right now I had troubles of my own.

"It's not my fault I can't fit into a size-eleven dress."

"No comment," my mother muttered.

She was still alive, and I was an adolescent again. The fluorescent light made my skin green, my teeth yellow, my face puffy and full of tear streaks. I wobbled in my white linen pumps while Mimi took pin after pin from her pin cushion wrist watch, poked, adjusted, and sighed.

At last, the seamstress got up off her knees. She dusted her hands and opened them to my reflection in the mirror. "You look like a million," she said.

Even through the straight pins, I could see that the dress looked better, although it was nothing I would ever choose for myself.

I picked my way out of the dress. My mother said, "Don't scratch yourself. If you get blood on that dress it's ruined."

I put my own clothes on but still could not recognize myself in the bridal boutique mirrors.

"You look exhausted," said my mother. "C'mon. I'm gonna buy you girls some lunch."

Bel Kaufman
(Contemporary)

FROM *Up the Down Staircase*

A Doze of English

In answer to your question what we got out of English so far I am answering that so far I got without a doubt nothing out of English. Teachers were sourcastic sourpuses or nervous wrecks. Half the time they were from other subjects or only subs. One term we had 9 different subs in English. Once when Dr. Bester took our class I got a glimpse of what it's all about but being the Head he isn't allowed to teach.

Also no place to learn. Last term we had no desks to write only wet slabs from the fawcets because our English was in the Science Lab and before that we had no chairs because of being held in Gym where we had to squatt.

Even the regulars Mrs. Lewis made it so boreing I wore myself out yawning, and Mr. Loomis (a Math) hated teaching and us. Teachers try to make us feel lower than themselves, maybe this is because they feel lower than outside people. One teacher told me to get out of the room and never come back, which I did.

A Cutter

What I got out of it is Litterature and Books. Also some Potery. And just before a test—a doze of English. Having Boys in class dis-tracks me from my English. Better luck next time.

Linda Rosen

In Miss Pastorfeilds class I really enjoyed it we had these modren methods like Amature Hour and Gussing Games in rows with a scorekepper and to draw stick figures to show the different charactors in the different books and Speling Hospital and Punctuation Trafic and Sentence Baseball with prizes for all thats the way to really learn English.

A True Student

I only learned one thing and that is a "quotion mark" I know a "quotion mark" upside down and that's all this one teacher thaught. I had one well not to mention no names and she was mad for "grammar" mistakes, Miss Lewis loved to pick on me! With Pasterfield we "dramatized" everything in sight and my last was a bug on "Democricy", we spent all our time voting on what to do and no time to do it.

Only once I had a teacher that was any good but she got "sick" and left. I hope this term with you will be good because you seem to be "alive" though it's too early to tell.

Chas. H. Robbins

I hate to think back on all my English years except one teacher I will never forget because when my note book wasn't so good (it was mostly in pencil) instead of telling me to do it over in ink she just told me to put renforcements on the holes and that will be enough. The next day she asked me did I put renforcements in. When I said I did she didn't even look she just said she'd take my word for it. That gave me a warm feeling inside because it was the first time a teacher took a pupil's word without asking to see if it was true. Most of the time they don't even know your name.

Me

In two years of H.S. Eng. I learned
1. How to read a newspaper
A. Headlines
2. How to outline
3. Comparises of authors (Hawthore)
4. And S. Marner

They shouldn't give S. Marners out. We would prefer a teen age book like Lollita better.

Teenager

During my many years of frequenting school I was well satisfied with my instruction. English is a very important language to study, especially if it's the language we speak daily. Since most of us are in High School, we are interested in getting an English education. I believe English to have been of grave importance to me and I will try in my next future to increase my knowledge. English outshines all my other subjects. I've always had good marks because I am a worker and I feel that anything a teacher tells me is of benefit to me. Speaking, which is my specialty, composition, which also attracts my attention, writing perfect sentences with punctuation where it really belongs, and many others which are of grave importance have been taught to me with excellent results. I was likewise impressed by the good work of my classmates. I hope to achieve further progress in my chosen program of study with an excellent teacher like yourself.

Harry A. Kagan
(The Students Choice)

Being your new around here you should know I made a bargian with all my teachers, if I don't bother them they won't bother me. So from now on I'm not writting any more for you.

the Hawk

★

In my 16 year life span so far I've had my share of almost every type of teacher but one I shall ne'er forget was in elementary (6th grade) because with her I had to watch my peas and ques. She was so strict she gave us homework every night and tried to pound it into our heads but it's the way she did the pounding that makes her different. She took a real interest and brought out our good and bad points. She stayed in every day after school so we could come in and ask her questions about the work. She militarized us and sometimes whacked us but for all her strictness a strange thing happened at the end of the term: every one gathered around her and kissed her.

But high school seems harder, speeches, speeches, that's all we hear.

Dropout

What I learned in English is to doodle. It's such a boring subject I just sat and doodled the hours away. Sometimes I wore sunglasses in class to sleep.

Doodlebug

★

I don't look at a teacher as a thing but as a person like myself & I accepted many teachers with their faults & tried to conscentrate on their Dr. Jekile side. But some are just not cut out to be teachers—too old and nervous & the way she taught you just couldn't understand it. She was the talker. If she didn't talk about her sisters or next door neighbors she talked about the generation of to-day & we couldn't get a word in edgewise. She was one of those that make big plans at the beginning of the term & never get around to it. They act like they're doing you the greatest favor, with sarcastic remarks like "The nerve of some peoples children!" The answer was actually scared out of us even if we knew it. When we did answer she gave us no credit but said "It's about time you learned something!" Whenever I laughed or excuse me burped in class quite acidentally I would be pulled out to sit in some remote corner of the school.

A Bashful Nobody

★

I had Dr. Bester for one week while my regular teacher took a rest cure and we liked him but I feel he developed a false character to cover up. This false character consisted of a stern face and remarks but every one saw a good teacher shining through the false window of sterness. He roused our somewhat hidden interest in English and we all worked our head off for him.

Carole Blanca

I once had an English teacher in another school that not only treated me as a student but as she would her own sons. She gave me clothes that her son had outgrown. The clothes that were given to me were in good condition.

Frank Allen

In Junior High we had a brand new teacher of English, he was so young he couldn't manage the class at all, we didn't listen to a word he said even when he shouted. One day while he had a chalk fight with a kid the kids all left the room one by one. Well, instead of going out to the hall to see if we were there he put on his coat, took his umbrella swung it over his shoulder and marched out of the room whistling. He didn't say a word to us. You can probably guess that we were replaced by a new teacher.

That is the one English that stands out in my head.

The only teacher I had who didn't make us feel so bad about ourselves. That's Mrs. Schachter. She was plain with us and she made everything seem easy which it isn't. She even liked us. Every since I have pleaded on bended knee to get her back but to no availl. I wish I went to a school with big sunny windows with trees in them and no one talks behind your back. Where the teacher would be more of a friend and not have favorites just because some one is better.

Vivian Paine

As long as you asked here is my list:
Miss Pastorfield lets us walk all over her
Mrs. Lewis they should retire her
Mr. Barringer is a big show off
Mrs. Schachter OK
Miss Barrett should be a movie stare
Mr. Loomis ignorammis
You may not agree but that's my opion.

While attending Jr. H.S. I ran across a teacher who enjoyed himself and didn't mind being a teacher. His way of teaching was simple, he taught with pride and always understood his pupils even if they couldn't explain themselves. He wasn't a dictating teacher but in some magic way we always behaved ourselves. I learned everything I know about English from this nobel man. He made me feel the earth around me, he was like wine except that he didn't give high marks. I frequently went to his room during lunch, we played darts, we ate lunch he brought for us and he would help us with what he could even in other subjects like science. In the summer we went to the park with him and played baseball. This teacher and I still correspond with each other by writing letters.

grateful student

English is a personal subject that should be taught by men. Too many females in the schools and they're all no good.

Rusty

In my other school I was more of a Majority because the Whites were only these few kids but the education they dished out wasn't so good. Here they tried to integrate me but it didn't take.

I'm not what you call an "A" student but I don't mind school at lease it takes me away from home but the teachers are too prejudice they are mostly Whites and I never got a fair mark out of them.

I'm not exactly a book reader but I didn't mind it so much untill the teachers started in they ruined it for me. I got no advantage out of diograms and spelling words to write ten times only a waist of good paper. Semicollons also don't stick to my head. It's not right to be pick on all the time!

Edward Williams, Esq.

What I learned. What I hope to achieve.

So far I've learned words with meanings, words without meanings, oral words, spelling words, parts of speech and a test every Friday. I hope to achieve a grasp on literature and life.

Sophomore

A kaleidoscope. A crazy quilt. An ever-shifting pattern. Shapes and shadows that come and go, leaving no echo behind, no ripple on the water where no stone was ever dropped. Such is my remembrance of the lost and vanished years of English, from whence I arise, all creativity stifled, yet a Phoenix with hope reborn each term anew. Will it be different this term? Will I be encouraged, guided, inspired? The question, poised on the spear of Time, is still unanswered. (I was supposed to be in Mrs. Schachter's Creative Writing class but because of a conflict with Physics 2, I couldn't get in.)

Elizabeth Ellis

Its not necesery to study english because, what's the use of it big deal so we never make society so what? We're still living aren't we who needs it, studying another language it would be much better, for example take books it's alright when you see it in the movies, and the words oh, they really get me. It's a bunch of nonsense.

(Frankly I would prefer a teacher freely telling me I'm no good in english then giving me dirty looks in the hall.)

Disgusted

Dribs & Drabs, McBeth one week Moby Dick next, a quotation mark, oral debates on Should Parents be Strict? Should Girls Wear Jeans? The mistakes I made in elementary school I still make. I hope to achieve correction.

Stander

I think after you learn to speak English in kindergarden the subject should be droped. Ha–ha! Grammer should be outlawed! Coma sentences should be bared from the language! Oral talks are to embarrassing for those not gifted with "gab". Writen work causes many errors in gr. & sp! Reading books are to hard to answer questions on it! (I like English with no strain on my brain!) Also on the dislike side of English I can put the constant anoyance of certain students who horsed around. I can put myself in that catagory because I horsed around and I didn't benefit myself one bit and probly anoyed the class! However we must take the good with the bad and know our whole life will not be a bed of roses!

Lou Martin

Grammar & Shakes.—Phooey!
Essays—a lot of gossip.
Ivanho is for the Birds.
George Elliot stinks, even though he is a lady.

Why did you ask this question? To show that *you* can do the job better? You teachers are all alike, dishing out crap and expecting us to swallow it and then give it back to you, nice and neat, with a place in it for the mark to go in. But you're even phonier than the others because you put on this act—being a dame you know how—and you stand there pretending that you give a damn. Who you kidding?

We're dirt to you, just like you're dirt to the fatheads and whistle-blowers who run this jail, and they're dirt to the swindlers and horn-tooters who run the school system.

Except for one man in this whole school no one has ever given a damn about me, and it's the same at home and in the street outside. You probably don't care for my language, so you can give me a zero in Vocabulary.

Anyhow I'm quitting at the end of this term and joining the dogs eating dogs eating other dogs in the great big lousy world you're all educating us for. I sure as hell got myself an education. Though it's not in any syllabus. But you're the one who's stuck here. Don't worry, you'll find plenty of others willing to play your game of baah, baah, little lost lambs, come back to school. But trot in step, double file. And you'll get your nice clean diplomas served on crap. Yummy.

I trust this answers your question.

Joe Ferone

Joe—Though your vocabulary is colorful, certain words would be more effective if used sparingly. You express yourself vividly and well, and your metaphors—from dogs to lambs—are apt. I would tend to give you a considerably higher mark than you give yourself, and I am not speaking of English.

There is some truth in what you say, but you are far too intelligent to cling to a view as narrow as yours. As for your indictment of me—in this country one is innocent until proved guilty. Why not give me the chance any suspect gets? I think we should have a talk. Can you see me after school today?

S. Barrett

★

I don't understand them big words you use, and I'm busy after school. Every day. You'll have to prove yourself on your own time.

Joe

(P.S. I wish I could believe you.)

Garrison Keillor
(Contemporary)

Marooned

I remember exactly when the marriage took a weird turn. I was on the examining table with my shorts draped around my ankles and my tail pointing high in the air and Dr. Miller surveying my colon through a cold steel periscope and making *hmmmm* sounds, his ballpoint pen scratching on a notepad, and at this delicate moment, he said, softly, "Do I strike you as a selfish person?"

"No . . . why?" I asked. The periscope felt like it was about six feet up me and I'm only five-foot-eight.

"I took a personal-inventory test in that book about getting ahead that everybody's reading—you know, the book that I heard you're related to the author of," he said. According to the test, he said, he was rather selfish.

I groaned, feeling the excavation of the Holland Tunnel within me, but of course I knew which book he meant. My dumbbell brother-in-law Dave's book, that's which one.

He told me Dave's book had meant a lot to him. "I never buy books other than science fiction," he confided, "but my partner Jamie gave it to me for my birthday and I opened it up and I couldn't put the rascal down. Heck of a book." Meanwhile, *the periscope was way up there in my hinder, probing parts of me I had been unaware of until now.* "He says that what holds us back is fear, and that fear is selfish, and that getting ahead is a problem of *getting outside yourself*," and he gave the periscope a little nudge for emphasis. "You have to really *focus* on a goal outside yourself in order to succeed. My goal is to open a restaurant. Jamie's a wonderful cook. Chinese and Mexican, what do you think?"

I felt sore afterward. I went home and told Julie that a person as dim as my proctologist was exactly who Dave's book was aimed at, one ream job deserves another, and so forth. I was steamed.

She said, "You've always resented Dave, Danny, and you know why? I'll tell you why. Because your life is in Park and the key isn't even in the ignition. You're totally into negativity, Danny. You stopped growing twenty-six years ago. And how would I know? Because I'm your wife, that's how I know."

Twenty-six years ago I graduated from the University of Minnesota journalism school with honors, the editor of the Minnesota *Daily,* and got a job as a professional copywriter at a Minneapolis ad agency. Dave Grebe was a clerk in his dad's stationery store, peddling birthday cards. He and I played basketball on a Lutheran church team; that's how I met his sister Julie; she picked him up after the game because he'd lost his driver's license for drunk driving. He was twenty, big and porky and none too bright, just like now. "I'd sure like to get the heck out of stationery, I hate the smell of it, mucilage especially, and the damn perfume, it's like someone vomited after eating fruit," Dave remarked to me more than once.

So I was not too surprised when, one fine day, Dave walked away from his job and shaved his head clean and moved to a commune in south Minneapolis, living with sixteen other disciples of the Serene Master Diego Tua, putting on the sandals of humility and the pale-green robe of constant renewal. "I have left your world, Danny," he told me on the phone.

Julie, who had become my wife, thought that Dave "just needed to get away for a while." I pointed out to her that the Tuans were fanatics who roamed the airport jingling bells and droning and whanging on drums, collecting money to support their master and his many wives and concubines. The Tuans believed that they held the secrets of the universe and everyone else was vermin.

Julie thought they were Buddhists of some sort.

"They could be Buddhists or nudists or used-car salesmen who like to dress up in gowns, but whatever they are, they're working your brother like a puppet on a string."

She thought that Dave was only doing what he felt was best for him. Subject closed. So I did double duty for a few years—was a copywriter *and* kept the Grebe stationery store going—and Dave went around droning and whanging and dinging and making a holy nuisance of himself.

"We are God's roadblocks," said the Happy Master, Diego himself, "warning the people that the bridge is washed out." His real name was Tim U. Apthed; he chose the name Diego, *Die—ego,* and crunched his initials into a surname, and founded a church for jerks. My agency, Curry, Cosset, Dorn, flew me to Atlanta or Boston or Chicago occasionally, and I'd come running through the terminal to catch a plane and hear the drums and bells and there were the Tuans in the middle of the concourse, holding up their signs, "Your Life Is a Lie," and chanting. "Only two ways, one false, one true. Only one life, which way are you? Back! back! turn away from your lies! And God will give you a beautiful surprise!" and I'd be trying to squeeze through the crowd of shaven men including my blissful brother-in-law and get on board the plane. It was like Run, Sheep, Run.

"Well, when he talks about people being so materialistic, I think he has a good point," said Julie.

Then, fifteen years ago, Mr. Grebe died of a cerebral hemorrhage—clapped his hand to his forehead one morning and said, "Oh mercy. Call Ann and tell her I'll be late," and fell over dead onto the ballpoint-pen rack. The rest of us were living in the felt-tip era but Mr. Grebe never gave up on ballpoints, which worked better on carbon paper, he explained patiently, ignoring the fact that photocopying had replaced carbons. The family was devastated at the loss of this vacuous and bewildered man. They mourned for weeks, during which I was the bulwark, arranging the funeral, paying the bills, ordering stock, and Dave sat in a corner weeping. They never found out who Ann was.

Dave left the Tuans and let his hair grow out and went to work at the Wm. Grebe Stationery Shop. Every few days he'd call up and say, "I don't know how I can ever make it up to everyone for the terrible things I've done."

You get sick of remorse when it becomes a broken record. Dave kept saying, "You've been so great, Danny, and I've been a jerk. I don't know why God lets me live." After a few months of it, I told him that I didn't know either but that he could take his guilt and put it where the sun don't shine. He reported this to Julie. She vindictively canceled our vacation trip to the Bahamas. "I can never forgive you for saying that to my brother," she said, and she was right, she couldn't.

Meanwhile, Dave, who once had renounced material things, took over Wm. Grebe, stocked it with felt tips and expanded into malls and branched out into discount bookselling, got rich in about three years, and became one smooth guy: bought a Hasselblad camera, Finnish furniture, a Steinway, a Martin guitar, four Harleys, a Peterbilt truck, an original Monet (*Girl with Light Hair*), and next thing I knew he was going around giving pep talks to Kiwanis clubs, and then, he wrote his book about getting ahead, *Never Buy a Bottle of Rat Poison That Comes with Gift Coupons*. It sold more copies than there are rats in Rio (millions). He turned Tuanism inside out and restated it in capitalist terms, and made low cash flow seem like a denial of God's love.

On the same day that an interview with Dave appeared on the front page of *The Wall Street Journal*, I got canned at the agency. Twenty-five years I had labored at Curry, Cosset, Dorn, and on a Monday morning, as I sharpened my No. 2 pencil, a twenty-nine-year-old guy in a red bow tie leaned over the wall of my work cubicle and said, "The folks at Chippy called and cut back on the campaign, Danny, I'm going to have to let you go for a while."

"Are you sure?" That's all I could think to say. A quarter-century with the company—"Are you sure?" He was sure.

I crawled home, bleeding, and Julie was glued to the TV, watching Dave talk about the irrelevance of suffering. It was a videotape, not a live appearance, but even so, she did not turn it off when she heard my tragic news. She said, "That's too bad," and then, "I'm so proud of him. This is one of his new videotapes. He's going to put out twelve of them. He just seems to touch a chord in people, don't you think? People can't help but respond to him. It's a natural gift." She recommended that I study *Rat Poison* to give me the confidence to find a new job and wait for his next book, *How to Find Your Rear End Without Using Both Hands*.

"Your brother," I said, "is one of the world's biggest b.s.ers."

This was when Julie decided that we needed to face up to my problems. "You are a dark cloud in my life, Danny. A small dark cloud," she said.

I don't know what she meant by that. I'm a happy guy who loves life, it's just that I have a moony face. A guy can't help it that his face won't light up. Inside, I'm like a kid with a new bike. Though being flushed down the toilet while your brother-in-law is getting rich certainly puts a crimp in a guy's hose. Dave was hot. I was dead. For twenty-five years, I had been a happy guy who created dancing ketchup commercials, who made high-fiber bran flakes *witty*, who wrote those coffee commercials in which the husband and wife share a golden moment over a cup of java. I brought lucidity to capitalism, and Dave brought gibberish, and he walked off with the prize.

The next day, Julie told me that Dave thought we should go away and be alone and he'd given her fifteen thousand dollars so we could charter a fifty-foot schooner for a two-week cruise off Antigua, where we could try to put the marriage back together.

"Fifteen thousand dollars would come in handy in other ways than blowing it on a cruise," I pointed out. "We could invest it. I'm unemployed, you know."

"Aren't you willing to invest in our marriage?" she said.

"We could *buy* a boat for that kind of money and sail every weekend." She said that fifteen thousand wasn't enough to pay her to get into a boat with me at the tiller.

"Remember the time we drifted powerless down the Mississippi because you put oil in the gas tank? Remember how you tried to rig up an overcoat on an oar to make a sail? Remember how we drifted toward that oncoming coal barge and stood and waved our arms and cried out in our pitiful voices?"

Ten years had not dimmed her memory of that afternoon.

So off we flew to Antigua.

We flew first-class, in those wide upholstered seats, where everything is sparkly and fresh and lemony and candles flicker on the serving cart. A painful reminder of how cheery life can be for the very rich, people like Dave. The flight attendants wore gold-paisley sarongs slit up the side and pink-passion lipstick, they were Barnard graduates (*cum laude*) in humanities, and they set a vase of fresh roses on my table, along with the seviche and salmon loaf and crab puffs with Mornay sauce, and they leaned over me, their perfect college-educated breasts hanging prettily in place, and they whispered, "You've got a nice butt. You ever read Kant?" I knew that they only flirted with me because I was holding a first-class ticket; I wanted to say, "I'm forty-seven, I'm broke, ashamed, in pain, on the verge of divorce, and sponging off a despised relative. I've hit bottom, babes. Buzz off."

We stayed one night at Jumby Bay, dropping a bundle, and headed off by cab to the Lucky Lovers Marina, and there, at the end of the dock, lay the *Susy Q*. I put my arm around Julie, who was shivering despite the bright sunshine and eighty-five degrees.

"Is that a schooner or a ketch?" I said.

"It's a yawl," she replied. It was hard not to notice the frayed rigging and rusted hardware, the oil slick around the stern, the sail in a big heap on deck, and what appeared to be sneaker treadmarks along the side of the hull. But we had put down a deposit of fifteen hundred dollars already, so we banished doubt from our minds.

"Hello! Anybody below?" I hollered. There was a muffled *yo,* and a beautiful young man poked up his head from the cockpit and smiled. His golden curls framed his Grecian-god-like face, his deep tan set off by a green T-shirt that said "Montana . . . The Big Sky." He was Rusty, our captain, he said. "I was just making your bed downstairs. Come on down. Your room's up front!"

This struck me as odd, that he said *downstairs* instead of *below decks,* and I mentioned this to Julie as we stowed our bags in the cabin. "How can you get upset about poor word choice when our marriage is on the rocks?" she asked.

The *Susy Q* cleared port and sailed west toward Sansevar Trist, and she and I sat below discussing our marriage, which I have always believed is not a good idea for Julie and me. My experience tells me that we should shoot eight-ball, sit in a hot tub, go to the zoo, rake the lawn, spread warm oil on each other's bodies, do anything but talk about our marriage, but she is a fan of those articles like "How Lousy Is Your Marriage: A 10-Minute Quiz That Could Help You Improve It" and of course the first question is, "Are you and your husband able to sit down and discuss your differences calmly and reasonably?" *No! Of course not! Are you kidding? Who discusses these things without screaming? Name one person!* So she launched off on a reasonable discussion of differences, and two minutes later we're screeching and hissing and slamming doors so hard the pictures fall off the walls. We simply are unable to discuss our marriage—does that make us terrible people? Our marriage is like the Electoral College: it works okay if you don't think about it.

"Do you love me?" Julie asked, as the boat rocked in the swell, Rusty thumping around on deck overhead.

"How do you mean that?"

"I mean, is it worth it to try to stick together? Marriages have their rough passages. It's only worth it if there's love. If there isn't why waste time trying to patch this up."

"Do you love me?"

"I asked first."

"How come I'm the one who has to say if I love you or not? Why is it always up to me?"

There was a loud thump above, like somebody kicking the side, and then Rusty let out a cry, "Oh shoot!" I poked my head up out of the hatch. "It's the steering thing," he said. The tiller had broken off and was now bobbing in our wake. I told him to lash an oar in its place and come around and retrieve the tiller, and I ducked back down into the cabin. Julie was sitting on the bunk, her back to the bulkhead, her trim brown legs drawn up.

"I better go up and help Rusty," I said.

"You can't run away, Danny," she said. "It's a simple question. Do you love me or not? What's so hard about that?"

I flopped down on the chair. "Why can't we *converse* about this in a calm friendly way instead of getting into a shouting match over every little thing—"

"A little thing," she said. "Our love. A little thing. Oh right. Sure. Great way to start off a vacation. Our love, a little thing."

There was a loud *cra-a-a-ack* above, like a sequoia falling, and a muffled splash. I stuck my head up. The sail was gone, and the mast. "I was gonna turn right and the whole thing broke and fell off," he said, shaking his head. "Boy, that was something!" He shrugged and grinned, like he'd just burned the toast. "Oh well, we still got a motor." I told him to come about and retrieve the sail and mast and then head for port.

I told Julie that we had serious problems above and maybe we should postpone our talk. She said we had been postponing it for twenty years.

I was about to tell her how full of balloon juice she was, and then I heard the motor turn over, a dry raspy sound, like gravel going down a chute, and I realized the *Susy Q* was going nowhere. Still, it wasn't as aggravating as Miss Priss there, sitting and telling me about my marriage.

"Dave recommended a great book to me and it opened my eyes. *The Silent Chrysalis*. I read it twice. Danny, in some way my love for you is a symptom of my denial of myself, an attempt to make myself invisible."

The starter cranked over once and wheezed and coughed a deep dry cough.

Julie's eyes locked with mine. "We need to change that love from something angry to a *mature* love," she said. "I can't use you as an instrument of my self-hatred."

"What is that supposed to mean?" I asked.

"Dave thinks you're trapped in a lingering infantile narcissism, like a lot of guys. I don't know. I can't speak to that. Only you can."

How does a stationery-store clerk suddenly become the expert on American men? I wondered, but then Rusty's face appeared in the hatch, a mite taut around the eyes. "We may have to ditch the boat in a minute, you guys. We're coming real close to the reef, I think. The water looks sort of bubbly out there."

Julie grabbed my arm when I got up to go topside. "You're not going to just walk away from this one, Danny. You're going to face up to what's wrong, which is your selfishness. Your selfishness is a *fact*, Danny. Let's stop denying it. Let's deal with it."

Rusty's voice was hoarse. "Come on, folks."

I poked my head up. The Great Navigator had an odd horrified expression on his face, and his chin was aquiver. He wore an orange life jacket. "Want me to take the helm?" I asked.

"No helm left to take, and there's big jagged rocks up ahead, folks, so if you see a cushion, better grab on to it. This is not a test."

There was a distant roar of waves that was not as distant as before.

I ducked down and told Julie we were about to abandon ship. "If you can't deal with the truth, Danny, then I can't be married to you," said Julie, softly. "I don't want a marriage based on a lie."

I was just about to tell her that she wouldn't have that problem much longer, when there was a jagged ripping tearing crunching sound from just below our feet, and the boat lurched to a dead stop. Water began boiling up from below. I grabbed Julie and hoisted her through the hatch, grabbed a carry-on bag and a couple cushions, and took Julie by the hand, and we jumped into the water. Rusty was already on shore, waving to us. It was shallow, all right; the water frothed around our feet on the jagged coral, but it wasn't too hard wading in to shore, a beautiful white sandy beach that curved around and around a very pretty island—uninhabited, we soon discovered. "Well," said Rusty, "looks like you guys may get a little more than two weeks. Nice place, too." And he glanced down at Julie. Her T-shirt was wet from the surf, and her breasts shone through. He looked at her a long time, I thought.

We made a hut from palm fronds and the jibsail. Julie had brought her purse and suntan oil and four books about marriage and communication, and I had dragged in our suitcase and a bottle of Campari, and Rusty had salvaged the oregano, sweet basil, rosemary, chives, coriander, cayenne pepper, paprika, orange zest, nutmeg, cinnamon, pine nuts, bay leaf, marjoram, tarragon, caraway, and saffron.

"The boat sinks and you rescue the spice rack?" I cried. "You're the captain and your boat goes down and you come ashore with the spice rack?"

Rusty looked at Julie. "Just because we're marooned on an island doesn't mean the food has to be bland and tasteless," he said.

She nodded. "It's no dumber than bringing a bottle of Campari. You don't like Campari," she said. "You only like beer."

And an hour later, Julie had made beds out of pine boughs and Rusty had carved a salad bowl from a stump and tossed a salad in it—"Just some ferns and breadfruit and hearts of palm," he said. He had also baked a kelp casserole over an open fire. Julie thought it was the best salad in salad history. Actually, it was okay. "And this casserole!" she cried. "I have never tasted kelp that tasted like this kelp tastes. What's the secret?"

"Paprika," he said.

Julie couldn't get over it. She said, "Danny couldn't even boil an egg. I kept offering to teach him, but he never wanted to learn."

It was hard not to notice that she was talking about me in the past tense.

"No, Danny couldn't have made a salad like this in a million years. Are you kidding? Not him," she chortled. "No, no, no, no, no."

We sat under the palm tree as the sun went down, and Julie and Rusty talked about the American novel, how they didn't care for Updike, who had never written strong women characters and was hung up on male menopause and had no ear for dialogue.

"No ear for dialogue?" I cried.

"No ear for dialogue," she said.

"John Updike? No ear for dialogue? Are you kidding me? Updike? That's what you said, right? Updike? His dialogue? No ear?"

"He has none," she said.

"None. Updike."

"Right."

"I can't believe this," I said. "You're sitting here under this palm tree and saying the John Updike—*the* John Updike, who wrote the Rabbit books—that he has no ear for *dialogue*? Tell me something. If John Updike has no ear for dialogue, then who do you think *does* have an ear for dialogue?"

Rusty looked at Julie. "Maya Angelou. Alice Walker. Doris Lessing," he said.

"Doris Lessing," I said.

"Yes," she said. "Doris Lessing."

"An ear for dialogue," I said. I stood up. "You know, I must be going deaf, but I could swear you just said Doris Lessing. Or did you say Arthur Schlesinger?" I kicked a little dirt toward Rusty.

"I said, Doris Lessing," he said.

It was the first of many discussions where I was in the minority. One morning, over a dried-seaweed breakfast, Julie said she thought there is such a thing as a "masculine personality" and that it is basically controlling and violent. Rusty agreed. "But some of us are working to change that," he said. Julie felt that men are inherently competitive, i.e. linear, hierarchical, and women are circular, i.e. radiant. "I never thought of it that way before," said Rusty. Julie and Rusty started meditating together every morning, sitting on the beach facing the east. "Hey, mind if I sit in?" I said, cheerfully.

Julie squinted up at me. "I think you'd block the unity of the experience," she said.

Rusty nodded.

"Well, far be it from me to block anyone's unity," I said, and walked away.

That night, Julie and Rusty were cooking a bark soup and she looked up at me and said, "Rusty is such an inspiration. I'm glad this happened."

I grabbed her arm. "This numbskull who ran the boat onto the rock is an inspiration?"

Rusty confronted me later that night, after Julie went to sleep. "I've decided to take Julie away from you," he said. "You two do nothing but fight, and she's obviously attracted to me, so if she and I paired up, at least there'd be two happy people on this island. It makes more sense that way. Two out of three isn't bad. So why don't you go and sleep in the jungle someplace. This tent is for Julie and me."

I said, "Okay, you're right," and I turned and bent down and picked up my

Campari bottle and then whirled and swung it straight up into his nuts and he staggered back and I threw a handful of dirt in his eyes. He bent down, blinded, and I kicked him as hard as I could in the gut, and he went *whooomph*, like a needle sliding across a record, and down he went, and I picked him up and threw him into the ocean and suddenly the water was whipped to a froth by thousands of tiny carnivorous fish and the frenzy went on for half a minute and subsided and whatever was left of Rusty sank bubbling to the bottom.

It wasn't the Zen way but it got the job done.

Julie was distraught in the morning. She dashed around the island screaming his name. "What have you done to him, Danny?" she shrieked.

"He fell in the water and the fish ate him," I said.

"You killed him!"

"Nothing ever dies. He is at one with the fish."

Two weeks later, when the big cruise ship saw us and anchored a half-mile to leeward and sent in a launch to take us off, Julie had calmed down and was almost ready to talk to me again. I could tell. I yelled up to her where she sat on the ledge of the rocky promontory, "You know something? I think the secret of marriage is that you can't change the person you love. You have to love that person the way he or she is. Well, here I am!"

"You got that out of a book," she called back. It was the first time she'd spoken to me in two weeks.

A man in officer whites with big tufts of hair on his chest was on the launch. He said, "You the couple who went down with the *Susy Q*? Where's the captain?"

"He drowned," I said. Julie said nothing. She still has said nothing about Rusty to me at all, and nothing about our marriage, but we have had sex more often than any time since we were twenty-four. It has been nice. I definitely think there is a vital connection between anger and an exciting sex life.

When we got back to the States, I saw a newspaper in the Newark airport with a picture of Dave on the front page glowering at the photographer and trying to stiff-arm him. He had been arrested for fondling a couple of fifteen-year-old girls in his swimming pool at his birthday party and was charged with six counts of sexual assault. I chuckled, but it was a low chuckle, and Julie didn't hear it. We were back two days and a publisher offered me $50,000 for a book about our "desert-island" experience. "Nah," I said, "nothing happened. Worst part was having to go around in a wet bathing suit." Since returning, I have done little except be a help and a support to Dave and Julie and the whole Grebe family. I have been a monster of pity and understanding and quiet strength. I have been there for them every moment in their terrible suffering. Dave sat weeping in our kitchen and told us, "I've been under so much stress, and it was like it was somebody else unfastening those girls' straps, and I was only watching." I said, "Don't feel you have to talk about it." He told me that he didn't know what he would ever do without the strength I gave him in this awful crisis. "It's my pleasure," I said, sincerely.

Florynce Kennedy
(1916–2000)

One-Liners

When a male heckler called out "Are you a lesbian?" she immediately replied, "Are you my alternative?"

There's a lady in the dentist's chair who is pretty nervous about what's going on. The dentist works on her for about three minutes and all of a sudden he realizes that she has managed to obtain a very tight grip on his testicles, and she's squeezing just short of agony. So he stops and says, "What is this?" and she says, "We are not going to hurt each other, are we, Doctor?"

I'm just a loud-mouthed middle-aged colored lady . . . and a lot of people think I'm crazy. Maybe you do too, but I never stop to wonder why I'm not like other people. The mystery to me is why more people aren't like me.

★

When women began wearing pants there was a tremendous backlash. I can remember—I was still practicing law at that time—going to court in pants and the judge's remarking that I wasn't properly dressed, that the next time I came to court I should be dressed like a lawyer. He's sitting there in a long black dress gathered at the yoke, and I said, "Judge, if you won't talk about what I'm wearing, I won't talk about what you're wearing."

Jean Kerr
(Contemporary)

FROM *How I Got to Be Perfect*

Can This Romance Be Saved?

LOLITA AND HUMBERT CONSULT
A MARRIAGE COUNSELOR

It was a mistake to read Vladimir Nabokov's *Lolita* and the "Can This Marriage Be Saved?" column in the *Ladies' Home Journal* on the same evening. The total effect was a little confusing.

The counselor interviews Humbert, and reports his side of the story:

Humbert was a tall, graying man. The natural pallor of his skin was perhaps accentuated by the drabness of his present garb. With his quiet, old-world charm he made me welcome in the cells and spoke quite readily of his broken romance.

"Doctor, picture—if you will—my darling, my nymphet, my Lolita, her scrawny, brown, twelve-year-old legs splashed all over with daubs of Mercurochrome, which spread like roses under the little white wings of Band-Aids.

"To watch her sit at the kitchen table and play jacks was to know what Aristotle meant by pity and terror and to feel with Oedipus, arriving blind and gutted at Colonus. The jacks in her grubby paws flew into the air like little prisms of silver, like stars. And when sometimes it happened, as often it did, that the small rubber ball dropped from her hands into the butter dish (my darling was not very well co-ordinated), the stream of four-letter words that poured from her adorable mouth would have dazzled a fishmonger.

"Ah, Lolita—the snap, snap, splat of her bubble gum (she chewed twelve hours a day, my lamb did) will echo down the corridors of all my dreams. Even in hell (*is* there a hell, shall we talk theology, Doctor?) I will be bedeviled (forgive the pun; it was intended) by visions of the precious one who curled up so sweetly in my lap after I gave her five dollars.

"My conscience, that wary censor, that watchdog of memory, permits me to recall only the happy hours, when Lolita lay at my feet poring over movie magazines and munching candied apples (alas, she often brought these—the apples—to bed). Her bright eyes sparkled as she gorged herself on pictures of pulchritudinous Rock or Tab or Guy (surely I invent these names) here photographed in a limed-oak study, there caught spread-armed and godlike on a surfboard.

"It has been suggested that after her mother's most timely demise I forced my attentions on this angel-nymphet. (Idle roomers beget idle rumors.) But I swear to you that I did no more than kidnap her from that summer camp, right under the toothy smiles of the lady counselors (fat, middle-aged sows, all of them, twenty-two or older). It was little Lolita, accomplished beyond her years, who seduced poor old Humbert. It was the fly, if you will, who gobbled up the spider. You must remember that I was worn down from poring over scholarly journals (did you know, dear Doctor, that Dante's Beatrice was a nymphet of thirteen?) and weakened by the atrociously poor food provided by the series of mental institutions to which I was periodically committed. On the other hand, my little lamb chop was in fighting trim, lean and lithe from playing hopscotch. Oh, Lolita, oh those nights, *mon Dieu!* (that's French, Doctor; I'm a very educated fellow).

"Imagine my horror when my darling, who—what is the vulgar phrase?—who had it made, who had handsome, hairy Humbert in the palm of her tiny hand, left, scrammed, vamoosed, ran off. And ran off, would you believe it, with the first fat, balding slob who promised her a glimpse of Hamburger Heaven. And I, all alone, bewailed my outcast state and troubled the deaf deities with my burping, noisy grief. Ah, laugh if you will, but hath not a pervert eyes, hands, senses, passions, and affections? Do you wonder that I killed him?

"And here I am, behind bars which contain me and enclose me like my own parentheses. Yesterday and yesterday and yesterday I was always her victim, Doctor. An unlikely story, you say, and yet you may have observed how it sells."

The counselor interviews Lolita, and reports her side of the story:

I would not say that my first interview with twelve-year-old Lolita was entirely successful. In the first place, she was busy manipulating her Yo-Yo and seemed reluctant to talk. After I had gained her confidence, she opened up a little.

"Look, Doc, it was a nightmare from the beginning. The night he swiped me from that camp and took me to the motel, do you know what he did to me? First of all, you've gotta get the picture that there's nothing in this room but the double bed and one bureau. So what happens? Humbert takes the three big drawers for his stuff and leaves me with those two little tiny drawers on top. I couldn't even get all my hair ribbons in. Was I burned up!

"I'll say this. He could be sweet enough when he wanted to. But as soon as we got out of bed in the morning, my troubles began. Boy did he overwork the togetherness bit. All this jazz about 'sharing' nearly drove me out of my little pink mind. If I went out on the front sidewalk to skip rope, *he* had to skip rope. We had to cut down the clothesline to get a rope big enough for him. Boy, you should have seen him, huffing and puffing and getting his big clodhoppers all tangled up in the rope. If I had an onion sandwich, you bet your life Big Daddy had to have an onion sandwich. He'd pile on the onions and then, as soon as he got it all down, he'd turn absolutely green and have to drink *gallons* of Bromo-Seltzer. All this time he'd be groaning and saying, 'You see, mah puhteet, I'd do anything for you—anything.' I'd come right out and tell him, 'Look, Pops, if you wanna do me a real favor, go to the movies and leave me alone for two hours.' Then he'd start to cry and say I was just trying to get rid of him. That guy cried so much he should have had windshield wipers for those glasses.

"But the worst of all was the way he hogged things. On Sunday morning, who used to toddle out in his pajamas and grab all the funnies first? Mr. Geritol. Of course by the time I got hold of them, they were an absolute mess. He used to pretend that he just wanted to know what I was reading. But he didn't fool me. A forty-year-old yakking it up over Moon Mullins—I ask you. If you want the inside story, Doc, I'm looking for a more mature man."

The counselor gives his advice:

At first glance it seemed as though these two people were poles apart. To begin with, there was the vast difference in their ages. Obviously it was difficult for an experienced girl like Lolita to put up with Humbert's childishness.

However, as our interviews continued, I was quick to notice that they had a number of important things in common. For instance, Humbert, as a child, suffered from an "absent" mother. That is to say, his mother died when he was eighteen months old, and so, quite naturally, he hated her. As a counselor, I was able to show Humbert that his rebellious attitude stemmed in large part from the fact that, as a child, he lacked that symbol of sensual pleasure, the cookie jar. Resentful at being abandoned by his mother, he was trying to penalize all other women who, in his fantasies, became "cookies." Humbert was quick to acknowledge the truth of my diagnosis. "Doctor," he said, "that's a new one on me."

Lolita, on the other hand, had a "present" mother who danced attendance on her night and day. Naturally she hated her. The mother, with that obtuseness so often found among females of the lower middle classes, made a fetish of propriety. Consequently, she was unsympathetic to twelve-year-old Lolita's valiant efforts to form a sexual alliance with an older man. And, what was worse, she constantly interfered with Lolita's natural development by saying things like "Don't leave the soap in the bathtub" or "Get your fingers out of the plate." Is it any wonder that Lolita has spent her whole life trying to get her fingers in the plate?

The solution for this pair did not come all at once. But as our sessions drew to a close I felt that the future looked brighter for both of them. Lolita has agreed to stop bringing candied apples to bed. (The onion sandwiches are no longer a problem; since Lolita's gall bladder operation she is no longer able to tolerate raw onions.)

On his side, Humbert has agreed to stay in prison. With time off for good behavior, he can look forward to a parole in forty-five years. At this time he will be eighty-five and should be sufficiently mature to shoulder his responsibilities.

Lolita will wait. (I have decided to take her into my home as a ward.) In the meantime, she is optimistic. As she herself expressed it, "With my luck, he'll get out of the clink."

Good luck to you both, Lolita and Humbert.

Out of Town with a Show

OR WHAT TO DO UNTIL THE PSYCHIATRIST COMES

I used to love to go out of town with a show—you miss so much at home. Oh, the exhilaration of being in Philadelphia just as the air is turning nippy, and knowing that somebody else back in Larchmont will have to find the storm windows. Indeed when I was younger and still in love with room service, I felt, like any other red-blooded American housewife, that a whole day spent rewriting the first act was a small price to pay for the privilege of having somebody else make my breakfast and bring it up to me on a tray. I don't know just when the truth caught up with me. But I have noticed recently that the mere thought of going to Boston with a musical causes me to tremble and drop small objects.

Many people have asked me—well, my father has asked me several times—why playwrights have to take a show out of town to try it out. Can't they tell anything from rehearsals?

The truth is that the playwright learns a great deal from rehearsals. He learns that the play is brave, haunting, luminous, tender, and hilarious, and that a cardboard container of coffee sent in from the delicatessen costs thirty cents. Everybody tells him how great the play is—the producer's secretary, the press agent's wife, the leading lady's mother. In fact, after spending only twenty minutes peering at a rehearsal from the back of an empty theater, they are so choked up with the magic of it all that they can barely vocalize. They squeeze the author's trembling hand and mutter hoarsely, "This is it, Sam—it can't miss." Not wishing to dispel the universal euphoria, Sam dismisses as unlikely his own secret theory that the play was badly cast, is being badly directed, and may have been badly written. Soon he is making discreet inquiries as to when the balloting closes for the Pulitzer Prize, and finally he comes home to tell his wife, "Honey, I don't see how it can miss."

And that's why he goes to Philadelphia: so he can see how it can miss.

Out of town the first thing he is up against is Murphy's Law. In Abe Burrows' definition, Murphy's Law states simply: if something *can* go wrong, it will. Now you wouldn't think it to look at me, but I just happen to be the world's expert on the things that can go wrong out of town. That's why I've taken up finger painting. The doctor says it will help me to forget. But while I can still remember, I would like to point out a few of the simpler rules for survival, for those of you who may be thinking of writing a play. And it's no use pretending that you have no intention of writing a play. There are distraught playwrights locked away in the Touraine Hotel this minute who, as recently as last year, were decently and profitably employed by Young and Rubicam or the Chock Full o' Nuts Company.

Learn to Cope with Room Service

We will start with the idea that the play will have to be entirely rewritten (there is no other possibility). This means that you will have to spend twenty-two hours out of every day closeted in a small hotel room with a rented typewriter and a very bad reproduction of a Utrillo.

Entombed as he is, the playwright usually makes the foolish mistake of supposing that he can count on room service to sustain the slender thread of life. This is patently ridiculous, as anyone who has ever waited three hours for two pots of black coffee will know. The thing to do is to bring along a couple of Care packages, or even a tin of biscuits. This will eliminate that air of panic which brings out the beast in room service, and will allow you to order with the proper air of detachment. With any luck, you may stun the girl on the other end of the wire into instant action. A good method is to begin by asking her what day it is. Greet the news that it is Thursday with real appreciation. Then say, in an offhand, casual way, "Thursday, eh? Well, look, sometime over the weekend send me up a chicken sandwich, but there's no rush, I won't be checking out until the end of the month." Sometimes you'll get it in ten minutes.

The worst possible thing you can do, however, is to throw yourself on her mercy and suggest that you are dying of starvation. I know one playwright who swears he could have fixed that play if he hadn't spent all his time calling to inquire what had happened to his breakfast. And a pitiful sight he was, too—a large man of fifty-four shrieking into the telephone, "Yeah, yeah, yeah—I'm the scrambled eggs in 412!" Many writers of comedies exhaust their best energies composing humorous insults to hurl at room service (one I know went so far as to send a large funeral wreath to the kitchen "in memory of all those who have passed away in the last twenty-four hours"). I've never been up to anything so daring or original. I'm not the rugged type, and in the total absence of food, sleep, and clean laundry I tend to sink into childish incoherence. I take the phone in faltering hand and say, with what I assume in my enfeebled state to be dignity, "Hello, Room Service, is this Room Service—well, you're the *worst Room Service I ever met!*"

I know one hotel in Philadelphia (name supplied on request) in which there is only one possible way to get room service. If you take off your clothes, climb into the shower, and begin to lather, the boy will start banging on the door with your tray. You will go through a great many bath towels in this way, which will lead to further quarreling with the maid, but at least you'll get something to eat.

Stay Out of the Lobby

Most authors waste a great deal of valuable energy slinking about the lobby during intermissions in a foolish effort to overhear the comments of the paying customers. They do this, mind you, even on those occasions when the audience has coughed and muttered throughout the entire first act with an animosity that has caused the actors to fear for their safety and the producer to leave town. Even in these circumstances the playwright somehow imagines that he will overhear a tall, distinguished man (clearly a United States senator) say to his companion, "Egad, Helen, it's plays like this that make theatergoing worth while."

Alas, this never happens. The people who attend the theater in tryout towns do not seem to recognize their obligation to discuss what they have just seen. Indeed, there is something downright perverse in the way they persist in believing that they are free to chat about their own affairs. Should you rub shoulders with a vivacious group out on the sidewalk, all you'll hear is a lady saying, "That's Jim for you, he *will* drink manhattans when he knows how I hate to drive the station wagon."

When I was in Philadelphia some years ago with a comedy called *King of Hearts*, I brushed so close to so many strangers that it's a wonder I wasn't arrested for soliciting. However, in two weeks of eavesdropping I heard only one remark that was in any way relevant to the show. This happened when a lady got up after the first act with dismay written all over her perplexed face. She turned to her husband and said plaintively, "George, this *can't* be *Dial M for Murder*!"

Even this wasn't as devastating as the experience a friend of mine had in Wilmington. It was opening night of his new melodrama, and after the second act he flew to his lookout in the lobby, where he was rewarded by hearing two couples actually discussing the play. "Well, Bill," asked the first man, "how do you like it?" My friend held his breath. Bill's answer was not long in coming. "You'd better ask Grace," he said, "she stayed awake."

Another reason authors should stay out of the lobby is that they look so terrible. Our playwright friend Sam, who is normally so natty that he has actually posed for a vodka advertisement, will turn up in the Shubert lobby in Philadelphia looking as unshaven, unkempt, and unstrung as the end man in a police lineup. In this condition he will strike terror into the hearts of the visiting investors, who will conclude that he is not likely to live long enough to finish the rewrite. He will also come under the inspection of some acquaintance who will take the trouble to write to his poor old mother and announce, "Sam is hitting the bottle again, or else he's got hepatitis."

One season I spent three weeks in Boston with a musical, and of course went rapidly to seed. Now, a certain random, helter-skelter look is absolutely native to me. But on this occasion I sank into a really spectacular state of disrepair. I looked like a wire-service photo that would go nicely under the caption "She Survived Death March." Dear friends would take me aside and say, "I know all about the second act, but you do have a comb, don't you?" In any case it was clear that in my derelict condition I couldn't be seen moping about the lobby, so I used to stand behind a pillar that was additionally sheltered by a large palm. It was in this retreat that I was accosted one night by a young man I had never seen before but who was evidently a classmate of my brother's. "Well, hel-lo!" he said, all sunny smiles of recognition, "aren't you Frankie's sister, Jean Kerr?" I was quite naturally outraged. "Nonsense," I said, summoning all the dignity I could muster, "she's a much younger person."

Insist That All Midnight Conferences Be Held in Somebody Else's Hotel Room

Each night after the performance it is customary for all members of the production staff to meet with the author to discuss the somber past, the doubtful future, and the plain fact that the new comedy scene which just went into the show is falling rather flatter than the old one. This session, coming as it does at the end of a perfect day, may loosen your last grip on sanity. It is nevertheless obligatory. The producer insists upon it because he is still trying to persuade you to cut that God-awful scene at the end of the first act and because he is reluctant to go down to the bar and join his friends who have come from New York to see the show. (The friends will say, "I'm gonna level with you, Lou—close it," which is why, in the theater, auld acquaintance are oft forgot and never brought to mind.) And most playwrights accept the inevitable nightly post-mortem because they have learned that it is one tenth of one per cent less taxing to talk about the rewrite than to do the rewrite.

However, all of this talking should definitely be done in the producer's suite. Should the merry little band assemble in your room, not only will you have to sign the tab for all those chicken sandwiches and all that scotch, but, what is more to the point, you will have cut off your escape hatch.

Sooner or later as soft voices die and tempers rise, the director (or maybe the producer) will see fit to add to the many true remarks spoken in jest. "Look, Sam," he will say, still smiling, "we all know the first act is lousy—what you don't seem to realize is that the *second* act stinks." At this moment you should be free to arise and go without a backward glance. It might take twenty minutes if you have to throw them all out of your room.

These nuggets of advice I am dispensing so freely are all, as you can see, concerned with protecting the sanity of the playwright. Playwrights are an unstable crew at best, and they tend to become unglued in the face of the most trivial mishaps. I remember one who was carted right back to Menninger's because, at the climactic moment of his play, the bit player who had to call for the police cried out loudly and clearly, "Help! There's been a murder—call the poloose!"

But if the author, standing at the back of the house gnashing his teeth, is painfully aware that the leading man has just answered the telephone before it rang, the audience tends to remain blissfully unconscious of technical mishaps, unless, of course, the leading lady actually tumbles off the stage into the first row of the orchestra. In this connection I recall an experience I had while tending an ailing musical in Philadelphia. For complicated reasons of the plot there was a big snowstorm effect at the finale of the show. One night the ropes that controlled the snow bags (enormous canvas bags filled with tiny pellets of white paper) somehow became intertwined with the ropes that pulled up the main curtain, so that from the beginning of the second act it snowed—gently, evenly, peacefully, down through the crystal chandeliers of the ballroom, all over the sunny farm scene, without pause during the nightclub scene, it snowed on the just and unjust alike. Indeed, the prodigal flurries continued right up to the moment, at the very end of the show, when the leading lady had to say, "It's snowing, Max." She said the line looking up to the empty heavens, because by that time, naturally, we were fresh out of snow—and I sat there with my face buried in my hands, praying for guidance. When I dashed outside, still feeling murderous, I stumbled into a friend who was seeing the show for the first time. "Oh, Lord," I said, "you would have to catch this performance. Of course things go wrong every night, but this—this is the worst, the absolute worst!" He surprised me by being entirely philosophical about the whole matter. "You worry too much," he said, patting my shoulder. "Sure I noticed she was flat on that first song, but I don't think anybody else did."

By the way, many of the problems that cause faintness and loss of appetite out of town begin with simple mistakes in casting. Some performers that should never, in any circumstances, be cast are:

1. Known alcoholics. You will have trouble enough with the unknown ones.

2. Small children. It's not just that, unless, happily, they are orphans, you will have to cope with their mothers. Much worse is the fact that children, being quicker, brighter, and in a better state of preservation than their elders, can and do memorize the entire script in three days. Thereafter they conceive it to be their civic duty to prompt the star any time and every time he seems to be groping for a word. This unwise practice not only exposes the child to unsuitable language but, in general, lowers the morale and defeats the efforts of the director to create a tight ship with a happy crew.

3. Dogs. Dogs, of course, don't have mothers, which makes them a little easier to deal with, though not much. I was once connected with a production that required the services of a large English sheepdog. We began rehearsals with a beast that was supposed to be so highly trained that I imagined he would be able to do the rewrite. As it turned out, he was not trained even in the conventional sense. The circumstances over which he had no control eventually elicited howls of outrage from the manager of the theater in which we were rehearsing and resulted in our being urged—in the most intemperate language imaginable—to "go hire another hall." Furthermore, this same unfortunate animal had a tendency to bite the actors during performance, which not only lost him audience sympathy but lost us several actors.

He was replaced out of town by an enchanting dog who, unlike her predecessor, was well adjusted and secure, and limited her nibbling to the bits of liver we deposited at various key points on the set. However, she commanded a salary that was well in excess of that paid to most of the company, a circumstance which did not endear her to the other performers, several of whom claimed that, in any case, she had a habit of scratching her ears on their best lines. (I don't think she did this deliberately, but then you never know; and so far as these actors were concerned, they were already unhinged from having to compete with two very cute child actors who crept into any hearts conceivably left vacant by that dog.)

In addition to talking about the pitfalls that must be side-stepped, I might say a word about the really bad moments that may be inevitable. Many playwrights have recorded their despair at being required to attend the premature closing in New York. And this is a very grim occasion for the playwright. Since objectivity doesn't begin to set in for about six months, he still doesn't grasp what happened. The play may be a poor thing, alas, but it's his own, and around the dear ruin each wish of his heart is entwined verdantly still.

To me, however, there is a worse moment. This occurs during one of the final performances out of town, after all of the changes have been made. You stand at the back of the house and observe the results of all the work, all the sleepless nights, the conferences, the rehearsals, the arguments. And the show is better, oh, definitely better, and the audience seems to be enjoying it. You should be happy—and then, suddenly, you experience a brief but exquisitely painful moment of clarity in which you realize that what you are seeing is not really the show you had in mind at all.

This always reminds me of a story about a friend of mine. One Easter she had to prepare dinner for fifteen people, counting children and relatives. For reasons of economy she decided to make a ham loaf instead of the traditional baked ham. Obviously it was going to be four times the trouble, since the recipe for the ham loaf was extremely elaborate: there were a dozen different ingredients and the whole thing had to be made in advance and allowed to "set" overnight in pineapple juice. But she went gamely ahead, convinced that she was going to produce something tastier than baked ham, if not indeed a gourmet's dish. As she took the square pink loaf out of the oven, a sinister thought crossed her mind. She cut off a little slice and tasted it, her worst suspicions confirmed. In tears she flew out of the kitchen to find her husband. "Oh, Frank," she said, "do you know what I've *got*? I've got Spam!"

All I can say is God love you, honey, if you're in Philadelphia and you've got Spam.

The Conversation Gap

Of course, I have no statistics, and nobody ever tells me anything. But I suspect one reason marriages break up is that some wives, after spending a full hour in rich, deeply shared silence with the beloved, are apt to remark, "In heaven's name, *say* something, will you?"

The problem stems quite naturally from the fact that women speak because they wish to speak, whereas a man speaks only when driven to speech by something outside himself—like, for instance, he can't find any clean socks, or he has just read in a headline that Con Edison is asking for a new rate increase. A wife who really feels cheerful and chatty early in the morning (a circumstance that can be explained only by a faulty metabolism) can always inveigle her husband into conversation by using a little imagination and by learning to snap up cues. She might say, "Speaking of clean socks reminds me, did you read Anatole Broyard's review of *Humboldt's Gift*?" Now he's on the spot. He has to say something, even if it is only to comment on the total absence of any connection between his socks and *Humboldt's Gift*.

I have a rather engaging little trick for stirring my own husband into statement. I just quote a few lines from the balcony scene of *Romeo and Juliet*.

"He speaks," I say in mock lyrical tones, "but he says nothing. What of that? His eyes discourses. I will answer *it*." Thus prodded, he is apt to say things he will have to retract later, but there are risks to everything.

Actually, if you had wanted a husband who would be a stimulating conversationalist, you should have married a mechanic or even a gardener—certainly not an author or a professional man or, last of all, a lecturer. When we got married, my husband was a lecturer and professor of drama and I used to imagine the stimulating, intellectual conversation we were going to have at breakfast. Like this:

Me: That play last night was interesting, didn't you think?
Him: Very. Of course, the author is still heavily in debt to Chekhov—the despairing protagonist, the shackling environment, the complete stasis in the third act, and, of course, the total absence of climax.
Me: Yes, he has an almost kinetic sense of atmosphere, but he never licked the story line.
Him: Licked it? He should have joined it.
             (Appreciative chuckles all around)

This, however, is a transcript of the actual conversation:

Him: (Despairingly) I'll bet this is diet bread.
Me: What's the matter with diet bread?
Him: (After a pause) Everything. Why don't we eat things other people eat?
Me: Such as—
Him: (Passionately) Those flat sticky things with jam inside them. Or muffins. Why don't we ever have muffins?
Me: (Evenly) Very well, dear, we'll have muffins.
Him: (Suspiciously) Oh, I know you. You'll get diet muffins.

We really should have our own radio show.

It's interesting to observe the phenomenon that will cause a husband who hasn't opened his yap in weeks suddenly to find the gift of speech. Just order a new coat that differs in any way at all from the last five coats you have owned and watch Big Chief Still Waters blossom into Alistair Cooke, a veritable fount of articulation. "Yes, I know it's the new style, but we haven't got a space ship yet. Oh, I see, all the fullness in the back is *supposed* to make you look as if you're standing in a head wind! Well, never mind. It'll be economical, anyway—in the summer you can take it to the beach and use it as a cabana." Etc.

There is a cure for this. Just take him with you when you go to Bonwit Teller's. Once you deposit him on that chaste Empire sofa in Misses' Suits, his whole attitude will change—not to mention his pulse, temperature, and rate of breathing. Precisely what causes men to go into shock in Bonwit's I can't imagine. My husband keeps looking from right to left in a state of ashen panic, as though he feared at any moment one of those elegant salesladies was going to snatch him and set his hair. But at any rate he brings a more judicious attitude to the subject of high style. "Yeah, yeah," he mutters at my first appearance from the depths of the dressing room, "it looks great, let's get out of here."

Some men do most of their talking at the movies ("Good Lord, I knew I was in for *Moby Dick*, but you didn't say there was going to be forty minutes of cartoons!"). My father is a man like that. The most he has spoken in thirty years was on a certain unfortunate occasion when my mother (who can't remember the titles of movies) took him for the second time in three weeks to see Bob Hope in *Son of Paleface*.

But let's get down to cases:

How to Talk to a Man When He's Snoring

When I speak of snoring I do not refer to the simple, rhythmic snorp-bleet, snorp-bleet to which every loyal, understanding wife should adjust. I am here talking of snoring which has the range and crescendo of a musical composition—where you can actually detect a verse, two choruses, and a release. I used to give my husband a gentle shove and whisper, "Honey, turn over—you're snoring." The result was that he turned over and in two minutes was snoring louder than before, while I lay awake for hours planning a separation and wondering what we were going to do about the children and all those monogrammed towels.

Then I learned the trick, which is to get the snorer interested. Don't make statements. Ask questions. Shake him and say, "Darling, what are you trying to say?" Eventually, after a few incoherent "huh, huhs" and "what, whats," he'll ask, "What do you mean, what am I trying to say?" After a few more equally pointless questions and answers he will be so cross that it will be at least fourteen minutes before he'll be able to snore again, giving you ample time to get to sleep first.

How to Talk to a Man in a Fashionable Restaurant

I once read an interview with the Duchess of Windsor in which she said that she and the Duke hated to eat in public restaurants because they had to converse so animatedly and affect such feverish interest in each other—lest rumors start that they were estranged—that she never could enjoy a bite of her dinner. It ought to be (but somehow it isn't) helpful to tell yourself that you're not the Duchess of Windsor and that nobody is even the tiniest bit interested in whether you and your husband have spoken since 1963. The point is that in a restaurant (like Sardi's, for instance) where you are surrounded by the tinkling laughter of beautiful models engaged in vivacious conversation with movie actors, you do feel somehow that you can't just sit there, specters at the feast, looking like two people who have just learned that their 1976 income tax return is being investigated. Of course there are lots of things on your mind that you could say ("Well, you saw that Chris got D in Health Habits again," or, "The exterminator says our new bugs are silverfish") but this doesn't seem to be the time or the place.

A couple I knew have solved the problem beautifully. She just tells him the story of "The Three Bears," a narrative which is admirable for the purpose because of its many rising inflections. And he helps her out by occasionally interjecting a remark like "By George, you mean she ate every last bite of the baby bear's porridge?" Do try it some time. Anybody overhearing you will conclude that you are discussing a new television spectacular—either that, or you're both a little bit dotty. If you should be concerned about this aspect of the matter, or if you should happen to intercept a stunned glance from the waiter, you can always drop in a covering remark like "Woody Allen—*there's* your Baby Bear!"

How to Talk to a Man When He's Taking a Shower

Here you have a captive audience and an ideal opportunity to tell a husband a number of things that you don't want him to hear. (Later on you can say, "Of course, I told you, you just don't listen!") There is no limit to the amount of unwelcome information you can get off your chest at one clip in these circumstances: "The man from Macy's was here and I took thirty dollars out of your wallet," and "Betty called, she and George are going to drop in," and "This is our weekend to take care of the school rabbit."

How to Talk to a Man on the Telephone, Long Distance

When a man calls you from Tulsa, he invariably makes the mistake of calling either from a public bar or from his mother's living room. Neither setting is exactly conducive to a free exchange of ideas. There, within earshot of his fellow revelers or his mother, he can hardly say the one thing you want to hear, which is that he misses you terribly, it's been a nightmare, a nightmare! And he's never going to make a trip alone again. For that matter, you can't tell him you miss him either, because the children are there with you and they become downright alarmed at any hint that their parents have preserved this degrading adolescent attachment so far into senility. So, if you're not careful, it's going to be a total loss of five dollars and eighty-five cents.

Don't, whatever you do, launch into that foolish litany of last-minute health bulletins: "Yes, I'm fine, yes, Chris is fine, yes, Gilbert is fine, etc." Let it be understood in advance that if one of the children should be rushed to the hospital for an emergency appendectomy, you'll mention it.

Use the time to clear up some matter that has really been troubling you. Explain that you finally saw *The Bridge on the River Kwai* on television and that it was marvelous, marvelous, but you didn't understand the ending. Get him to explain it. Did Alec Guinness mean to set off that dynamite or didn't he? What about William Holden? Who really killed him? This is important. When William Holden gets shot, a woman wants to know the facts. Later, when you hang up, you may discover that you've forgotten to ask what time his plane arrives at La Guardia, but the call won't have been a total loss.

How to Talk to a Man Before a Party

There are two occasions when a wife absolutely expects that a loyal husband will cleave to her side: when she's having a baby and when she's having a party. (It's interesting to note that the announcements on both occasions always seem to imply that these are joint projects, but, when it comes right down to it, who has that baby and who has that party? You do.) No one expects a husband to go out in the kitchen and stuff eggs, but he might try being a moral support during that horrible, hollow half hour before the first guest arrives. There you are, wandering aimlessly about from ashtray to ashtray, suddenly feeling as strange and as lost as if you had just checked into a motel in downtown Pittsburgh. And one of the reasons you can't rely on your husband for a comforting remark is that this is precisely the moment he chooses to lay a few asphalt tiles on the floor of the rumpus room.

If you should stand on your rights and say "Don't you disappear anywhere at all, just stay right here!" he will eventually lighten the tension by muttering "Great Scott, you forgot limes!" What he should say, of course, is something soothing like "Darling, you look charming in that dress. It reminds me of the night we met, do you remember? You were dancing with Hugh, and I came in with Connie and Leo . . ."

The last time we had a party I suggested this constructive line of conversation to my husband. He claimed that he'd once said something very similar, and what I said was "In heaven's name, stop chattering about the night we met and go get some ice."

How to Talk to a Man After You've Told Him That if He Doesn't Stop Fiddling with That Old Toaster He Is Going to Blow a Fuse, and He Does.

There is no way. Just light a candle and count ten or your blessings, whichever is greater.

James Kincaid
(Contemporary)

FROM *Eroticism Is a Two-Way Street, and I'm Working Both Sides*

Maturity, you and I agree, is, at bottom, an erotic realism, the graceful and becoming acknowledgment that Sophia Loren will not, after all these years, come to the door and tear our clothes from us, right off us, all of them. No, she won't. Had she been likely to do so, she would have done it by now. She isn't coming. Stop thinking about whether she should have come or whether she would have come had she had any sense or all the time you wasted preparing for her or whether you are not justified in writing her a very angry letter. We (You and I) are mature and have put away childish things. We laugh at the idea of Sophia Loren coming to our door, though she is still so heart-stoppingly beautiful and would have such a good time with us were she somehow only to drop by when she is here and she wouldn't after all have to stay so long (she is often in Los Angeles, you know, and so am I).

One qualification: the teachers of the very young are often knockouts, men and women alike. Gorgeous kindergarten teachers are the rule; but they become progressively less thinkable as sexual partners as the students get older and more capable of thinking that sexual partners are what they'd like to have. By junior high it's a mockery, by high school preposterous. Graduate education is an exposure to full-scale god-awful revulsion; it's a wonder the highly educated propagate. Those who go on to be deans and presidents enter another species altogether, a reptilian order where cross-fertilization with the human is not to be thought on.

Alan King
(1927–2004)

FROM # Help! I'm a Prisoner in a Chinese Bakery

After You Say "I Do" . . . You Don't

Has it ever occurred to you that the greatest loves of history and literature had one thing in common? The boy and the girl never got married. . . .

Not only don't they get married, they virtually never see each other. The lovers are always kept apart by family, society, wars, crusades, the black plague, or they're married to someone else. If you want to read about love and marriage, you've gotta go out and buy two separate books.

Romeo and Juliet, they got married. They spent one night together and the next day he committed suicide. Then she committed suicide. I'm trying to figure out what went on in that bedroom. . . .

I don't ever remember being single. My wife and I were kids together. . . . We grew up in the same slum together. . . .

I remember how much her father was against our marriage. He wanted her to marry a doctor, and, now that I look back on it, he was right. She should have married a doctor. It's the only way I could ever have gotten even with the medical profession. Furthermore, her father didn't want her to get married below her station. Jeanette's station was Fourteenth Street, and I had to get off at Eighth Street. That was six blocks below her station. . . .

He had one more standard question. They've always gotta ask it. It's part of the ritual.

"Will you support my daughter in the manner to which she's accustomed?"

"Sure," I replied. "We're moving in with you."

Tony Kornheiser
(Contemporary)

FROM **Pumping Irony**

Chic Coffee: Say It Ain't So, Joe

In the '50s, the craze was ice cream. Every weekend the family went out for ice-cream sundaes and banana splits, and then your dad dropped dead at forty-eight, his arteries all plumped up like kielbasa, and so we reconsidered our diets and opted for something less frivolous and more nourishing, and in the '60s, the craze was . . . pizza. Pizza was also horrible for your health, inasmuch as it consisted essentially of bread (for useless bulk) and cheese (for circulatory blockage), tomato paste (for color), yeast (for infections), and those red-and-yellow-flake peppers (for boils and blisters on the roof of the mouth). Eventually, diet gurus began to enter our lives, and in the '70s, the craze was salad bars, which featured "three-bean salad" (garbanzo, fatouli, and ganoozi beans) and other fine ethnic delicacies you would not feed a hamster. No one really liked salad bars, other than the manufacturer of Plexiglas sneeze guards. In the '80s, the fad was enterprises dedicated to the production and sales of fresh chocolate chip cookies, as though chocolate chip cookies were some product of great quality and sophistication in which absolute freshness was required for the true connoisseur, as opposed to some brown glob that tastes perfectly good when it comes in a bag from Keebler.

Now it's coffee.

People actually go *out* for coffee. Like it's a movie. Like it's entertainment.

All across America, every store that goes out of business is replaced by a Starbucks or a Quartermaine's or some other fancy coffee chain featuring this week's special: Peruvian Monkeyfoot Decaf. (Which comes, by the way, with a thick foamy head that would make Budweiser jealous, and takes up two-thirds of the cup, so when you pierce the canopy of foam, you realize you've paid four dollars for two sips. Which is why they call it Star-BUCKS.)

Fran Lebowitz
(Contemporary)

⋆ ★ ⋆

FROM *Social Studies*

Things

To put it rather bluntly, I am not the type who wants to go back to the land—I am the type who wants to go back to the hotel. This state of affairs is at least partially due to the fact that nature and I have so little in common. We don't go to the same restaurants, laugh at the same jokes or, most significant, see the same people. . . .

First of all, nature is by and large to be found out of doors, a location where, it cannot be argued, there are never enough comfortable chairs. Secondly, for fully half of the time it is day out there, a situation created by just the sort of harsh overhead lighting that is so unflattering to the heavy smoker. Lastly, and most pertinent to this discourse, is the fact that natural things are by their very definition wild, unkempt and more often than not crawling with bugs. Quite obviously, then, natural things are just the kind of things that one does not strive to acquire. *Objets d'art* are one thing; *objets d'nature* are not.

Jay Leno, with Bill Zehme
(Contemporary)

⋆ ★ ⋆

FROM *Leading with My Chin*

I was never one to respond well to being yelled at. Fortunately, there wasn't that much yelling in our house. My father would raise his voice, but because he was partially deaf, I figured he just wanted me to *understand* him more clearly. The one time I truly infuriated him was just a few weeks after I'd gotten my driver's license. I had been out driving my mom's '64 Ford Falcon and I turned a corner at a ridiculously high speed. Suddenly, the car rolled over, crushed the roof, then rolled back over onto all four wheels. I was okay, but the headroom was now approximately four inches. I still managed to drive the car home, then went inside and sheepishly told my dad, "Oh, I, uh, had a little accident with the car."

He was very calm. "All right," he said, "let's take a look." He was expecting maybe a broken taillight or a little ding on the fender. We stepped outside and—

"WHAT THE HELL HAPPENED HERE?!"

When you're a kid, you try to diminish your crimes. So I just said, "Uh, the car fell over."

"WHAT DO YOU MEAN IT FELL OVER?! HOW THE HELL DOES A CAR FALL OVER? IT'S SITTING THERE AND THEN IT FELL OVER? IS THAT WHAT YOU'RE TELLING ME?"

"Well, it was slippery and I was on a corner—"

"THE CAR ROLLED OVER ON THE ROOF! THAT IS NOT A DENT!"

And, of course, my mother, who knew nothing about cars, came out and said, "Maybe the car did just fall over . . ."

"IT DIDN'T FALL OVER! THE BOY WAS SPEEDING!"

"Well," Mom said, "it *could* have fallen over."

That was the angriest I ever made my father. And it didn't help that he developed a slight stoop from driving it in to the body shop.

As I've mentioned, my brother, Pat, is ten years older than me. When I was in high school, he was drafted into the army and sent to Vietnam. We all wanted to keep his spirits up over there, but nobody in the family was much of a letter writer. So my father had the idea to get a tape recorder and ship him voice messages. We went to the electronics store and got one of the new miniature reel-to-reel machines that barely predated cassettes. My father said to the clerk, "My boy is over in Vietnam and we want to send him taped greetings from the family!"

The clerk asked, "How long a tape do you want—fifteen minutes?"

"*Fifteen minutes!* We wouldn't even finish saying hello in fifteen minutes! What's your *longest* tape?"

"Ninety minutes."

"That's more like it! Give me four of those!"

So we brought home the recorder and the tapes and a year's supply of batteries. My father set up everything on the kitchen table and called my mom and me into the room. Very excitedly, he announced, "Okay, now we're all gonna talk to Pat!" He pressed the start button and, in his own inimitable way, began:

"HELLO, PAT! EVERYTHING HERE IS GOOD! I'M FINE! YOUR MOTHER'S FINE! HERE'S YOUR BROTHER! JAMIE, TALK TO PAT!"

I stepped forward: "Hey, Pat! How you doing? Hope you're okay! Be careful over there! Here's Mom!"

Mom bent over the machine and said, "Hello, Pat! Take care of yourself now! Don't do anything silly!"

Then my dad came back: "HEY, WHERE'S BRUCE THE DOG? BRING BRUCE OVER HERE AND MAKE HIM BARK FOR PAT!"

Bruce barked: "Roof roof! Roof roof!"

Then, of course, my father had to point out, "THAT'S THE DOG THERE, PAT! THAT'S BRUCE THE DOG! ALL RIGHT! LET'S PLAY IT BACK!"

We listened to all of about three minutes we put on this ninety-minute tape. The next day, the same thing: "PAT, EVERYTHING IS GOOD! NOT MUCH ELSE IS GOING ON! HERE'S THE DOG!"

"Roof roof! Roof roof!"

After a few weeks, there was no more than nine minutes of tape filled and it was mostly the dog barking. Finally, my father said, "Oh, let's just send the tape! What the hell!" So we shipped the whole contraption off to my brother. Thinking back, I have a feeling he might have preferred a few letters.

Having a brother in Vietnam was, of course, a very frightening experience, as many families know. All you can do is hope that no bad news comes. I remember watching television with my mom and dad one Sunday night when we heard a car pull into our driveway. Then we heard the car door open and footsteps coming up the walk. Next our screen door opened and it sounded like something had been thrown into the house. This was all very ominous. My father went to check and came back holding a telegram. Without opening it, he laid the telegram on the dining room table and just stared at it. My mother and I saw this and, slowly, we all sat down around the table, looking at the telegram. Nobody said anything for ten minutes. We just sat there, feeling kind of sick and very scared. Finally, my father reached for the telegram and slit it open. He cleared his throat and began to read aloud:

"*Dear Mr. Leno: You are invited to Wentworth Chevrolet to view the exciting new Caprice Classic!*"

My father was furious! He never drove a Chevrolet again for the rest of his life.

Oklahoma! Where the comic came sweepin' down the plain! So many unforgettable images to recall:

Going through Oklahoma City, I asked somebody for a restaurant recommendation. He said, "Hey, aren't you Eye-talian? We've got one of the best Eye-talian restaurants here! In fact, the owner's from Iowa!" I went there and saw the red-checked tablecloths and wine bottles along the wall. All of which looked promising. I ordered spaghetti and meatballs. Then the waiter asked, "You want fries with that? It comes with fries, you know." So I got the fries, plus three slices of Wonder Bread for sopping marinara. As they say, "When in Oklahoma City, do as the Romans do!"

(This, by the way, was vastly preferable to a place in West Virginia, where the menu listed something called a Wop Salad. The waiter there explained that it was a regular salad made with Italian dressing. I said, "Oh, of course! How foolish of me not to know that!" Then there was the old diner in Des Moines that hung signs boasting: PIZZA—THE NEWEST TASTE TREAT! YOU CAN EAT IT WITH YOUR HANDS!)

David Letterman
(Contemporary)

Top Ten Good Things About Being Named George W. Bush

10. Read my lips: I never pay taxes.
9. I receive courtesy calls whenever Cheney has a heart attack.
8. I always get the Presidential Suite at Motel 6 in downtown Cleveland.
7. After sex, my wife hums "Hail to the Chief."
6. Whenever I get bored, I call the Texas Department of Corrections and have them execute a guy.
5. Last week, I used an improperly addressed Halliburton contribution to buy myself a trampoline.
4. I've been cleaning up on Denny's "Presidents Eat Free" promotion.
3. Amusing late-night phone calls from a drunk Tony Blair.
2. People are pleasantly surprised that I'm not an idiot.
1. The president offered me ten grand for a copy of my military records.

Top Ten Signs You've Hired a Bad Department Store Santa

10. He wears the Santa costume all year round.
9. Tells salesgirls that "Me and Mrs. Claus have an understanding."
8. After every toy request says, "Yeah, right."
7. Tries unsuccessfully to hide the fact that he's wearing handcuffs.
6. Charges $5.95 for the first minute; $2.95, each additional minute.
5. Every day around ten a.m., throws up on the down escalator.
4. Keeps sending elves out for more vermouth.
3. Whether they want it or not, gives every kid a crew cut.
2. Keeps reminiscing about his vice presidency under George Bush.
1. He's packin' heat.

Anita Loos
(1893–1981)

FROM *Gentlemen Prefer Blondes*

Dorothy said that she did not say anything more about me being a debutant at Little Rock, because after all Dorothy knows that I really did not make any debut in Little Rock, because just when it was time to make my debut, my gentleman friend Mr. Jennings became shot, and after the trial was over and all of the Jury had let me off, I was really much too fatigued to make any debut.

So then Dorothy said, why don't we throw a party now and you can become a debutant now and put them all in their place, because it seems that Dorothy is dying for a party. So that is really the first sensible suggestion that Dorothy has made yet, because I think that every girl who is engaged to a gentleman who has a fine old family like Henry, had really ought to be a debutant. So I told her to come right over and we would plan my debut but we would keep it very, very quiet and give it tomorrow night, because if Henry heard I was making my debut he would come up from Pennsylvania and he would practically spoil the party, because all Henry has to do to spoil a party is to arrive at it.

So Dorothy came over and we planned my debut. So first we decided to have some engraved invitations engraved, but it always takes quite a little time to have invitations engraved, and it would really be foolish because all of the gentlemen we were going to invite to my debut were all members of the Racquet Club, so I could just write out a notice that I was having a debut and give it to Willie Gwynn and have Willie Gwynn post it on the Racquet Club board.

So Willie Gwynn posted it on the club board and then he called me up and he told me that he had never seen so much enthusiasm since the Dempsey-Firpo fight, and he said that the whole Racquet Club would be there in a body. So then we had to plan about what girls we would ask to my debut. Because I have not seemed to meet so many society women yet because of course a girl does not meet society women until her debut is all over, and then all the society women all come and call on a debutant. But I know practically all of the society men, because practically all of the society men belong to the Racquet Club, so after I have the Racquet Club at my debut, all I have to do to take my real place in society is to meet their mothers and sisters, because I know practically all of their sweethearts now.

But I always seem to think that it is delightful to have quite a lot of girls at a party, if a girl has quite a lot of gentlemen at a party, and it is quite delightful to have all the girls from the Follies, but I really could not invite them because, after all, they are not in my set. So then I thought it all over and I thought that even if it was not etiquette to invite them to a party, it really would be etiquette to hire them to come to a party and be entertainers, and after they were entertainers they could mix in to the party and it really would not be a social error.

So then the telephone rang and Dorothy answered it and it seems that it was Joe Sanguinetti, who is almost the official bootlegger for the whole Racquet Club, and Joe said he had heard about my debut and if he could come to my debut and bring his club which is the Silver Spray Social Club of Brooklyn, he would supply all of the liquor and he would guarantee to practically run the rum fleet up to the front door.

So Dorothy told him he could come, and she hung up the telephone before she told me his proposition, and I became quite angry with Dorothy because, after all, the Silver Spray Social Club is not even mentioned in the Social Register and it has no place at a girl's debut. But Dorothy said by the time the party got into swing, anyone would have to be a genius if he could tell whether he belonged to the Racquet Club, the Silver Spray Social Club, or the Knights of Pythias. But I really was almost sorry that I asked Dorothy to help plan my debut, except that Dorothy is very good to have at a party if the police come in, because Dorothy always knows how to manage the police, and I never knew a policeman yet who did not finish up by being madly in love with Dorothy. So then Dorothy called up all of the reporters on all of the newspapers and invited them all to my debut, so they could see it with their own eyes.

So Dorothy says that she is going to see to it that my debut lands on the front page of all of the newspapers, if we have to commit a murder to do it.

June 19th:

Well, it has been three days since my debut party started but I finally got tired and left the party last night and went to bed because I always seem to lose all of my interest in a party after a few days, but Dorothy never loses her interest in a party and when I woke up this morning Dorothy was just saying goodbye to some of the guests. I mean Dorothy seems to have quite a lot of vitality, because the last guests of the party were guests we picked up when the party went to take a swim at Long Beach the day before yesterday, and they were practically fresh, but Dorothy had gone clear through the party from beginning to end without even stopping to go to a Turkish bath as most of the gentlemen had to do. So my debut has really been very novel, because quite a lot of the guests who finished up at my debut were not the same guests that started out at it, and it is really quite novel for a girl to have so many different kinds of gentlemen at her debut.

Willie Gwynn's sister was having a dance at the Gwynn estate on Long Island, and Willie Gwynn said that all of the eligible gentlemen in New York were conspicuous by their absents at his sister's party, because they were all at my party. So it seems as if I am really going to be quite a famous hostess if I can just bring my mind to the point of being Mrs. Henry Spoffard, Jr.

FROM *But Gentlemen Marry Brunettes*

Well, just going into the old Breene family mansion on Fifth Avenue, ought to make a girl feel as if she was getting somewheres. Because you have to be shown through three separate doors, and the first two of them are *iron*. But when Charlie showed Dorothy through them, all Dorothy could think of was that the Breene family were giving themselves three separate chances to throw her out, and she began to lose some of her self-possession.

Well, after they got past the third door, the butler started to lead them through quite a long, hollow hallway that had nothing to relieve it but some life size crockery baby elephants that only made Dorothy feel more unimpressive. But they finally reached the old family libery, and under an electric lamp, sat the father of Charlie Breene. But Dorothy says that, after all that suspence, Charlie's Father was not such a climax. I mean, he is the kind of a gentleman who has never done anything in his life, either one way or another. And the Breene family were always holding him up to Charlie as an example of what he could keep from doing if he would only concentrate his mind on it.

Well, Dorothy looked Mr. Breene over, and she began to feel quite a little better. And Mr. Breene told Dorothy that he was pleased to meet her, because somebody had taken him to a Follies once five years ago, and he really could not remember when he had ever had such an enjoyable evening. So Dorothy spoke up and said, "If you feel that way about it, why don't you take a long chance, and try going again?" So Mr. Breene said that that was really quite a bright idea, and he wondered why he had never thought of it.

And while he was wondering, Mrs. Breene came in. Well, Mrs. Breene was really more than sweet to Dorothy, for she made conversation just as if Dorothy were an equal. And first she asked Dorothy her opinion of quite a few rare old first editions of anteek classic books they had in their libery. And when Mrs. Breene asks for an opinion, she is always polite enough to stop, and wait for a reply. But Dorothy did not have any, and the atmosphere became quite strained. I mean, Dorothy does not know enough about etiquette to know that any time a girl feels like she has nothing to say, the best thing to do is to ask for a glass of water. And asking for a glass of water, where it was quite inconvenient to find one, would have made Dorothy feel quite important.

Well, after Mrs. Breene saw that Dorothy had become as uncomfortable as she could be in a libery, she invited her into the Art gallery, to show her a new picture she just bought by the famous Spanish artist called Zuluago. And Mrs. Breene told Dorothy to look it over carefully, and then tell her what she thought of its' "chiarusquero." Well, Dorothy had practically no thoughts on the subjeck, but she suddenly got quite a bright idea, and asked Charlie what *he* thought of it. So Charlie spoke up and said, "By Jove, I don't know what it is." Well, of course, it made Mrs. Breene look quite small that any son of hers was so uncultured. So she really had to bite her lip. But she became sweeter than ever to Dorothy and told her that she had arranged quite a little surprise for her. And the surprise was that she had invited Jefferson Breene, the famous uncle of Charlie, who is not only the head of the whole Breene family, but one of the most impressive Americans of the Age, to come and look her over at dinner.

Well, while they were waiting for Jefferson Breene to arrive and look Dorothy over, the famous debutant, Muriel Devanant came in and did it. Well, Muriel seemed to be delighted with Dorothy from the start, for she greeted her in quite a hearty tone, and shook Dorothy's hand in quite a strong grasp that Dorothy says reminded her of a homesick Elk meeting one of his kind in some foreign climb. But the way that Dorothy acted was the depths of being uncultured. For she backed away from Muriel, in defence, and began to look toward an exit. So finally even Charlie noted her disturbants, and he got Dorothy off on one side, and wanted to know if anything was the matter. And Dorothy said "Nothing that an earthquake couldn't clear up." But Charlie did not understand what she was getting at. And he began to look at Dorothy askance.

Well, finally it seemed to be dinner time, and Mrs. Breene said they would not wait for Mr. Jefferson Breene, because when a gentleman holds the affairs of the Nation in his pocket, he is likely to be late at any moment. So Mrs. Breene led them through 5 or 6 large size salons with quite slippery floors and small Armenian rugs, and Dorothy says that the only difference between her and Eliza crossing the ice, was that Mrs. Breene had forgotten to order blood hounds.

Well, Dorothy said they finally arrived at the old oaken dining room, where the table was all laid out in her honor, to look like a funeral. And just as they were sitting down, the great Jefferson Breene himself came in. But when he made his entrants, Dorothy realized that she had already met him, at the apartment of a girl in the Follies called Gloria. Only at the apartment of Gloria he went under the nom de plume of Mr. Jones. Well, when Jefferson Breene was intraduced to Dorothy he was really quite surprised. But he did not seem to want to mention their previous acquaintence before the family. So he said "grace" instead.

Well, during dinner, Jefferson Breene gave Dorothy quite a confidential talk about the evils of modern life, and he finally brought up the subjeck of having met Dorothy at Gloria's apartment. So he explained to Dorothy that his interest in Gloria was to help a girl from doing wrong. Because he said that he had a theory that if gentlemen would give girls expensive apartments, and automobiles and jewelry as a reward to *keep* from doing wrong, instead of visa versa, the world would really be a better place. So he told Dorothy that that was what he was doing to Gloria. But Dorothy held her tongue, because she says the only reply she could think up to that old bird, couldn't be spoken out loud in a refined home.

Well, then Mrs. Breene started in to ask Dorothy questions about the habits of girls in the Follies. Because it seems that Mrs. Breene was so broad minded, that she did not care how much she learned about Life. But Dorothy says that Mrs. Breene had the idea that Follies girls were about the same as red ants, and Dorothy did not know enough about red ants to answer her questions. Well, Dorothy tried to give Charlie a sign to think up a quick excuse to get out as soon as dinner was over. But Charlie did not understand, because it seems that he thought they were giving Dorothy a pleasant evening.

Well, dinner was no sooner over than the string quartet arrived. And then Society people began to pour in for the musical evening. And Mrs. Breene was so sweet to Dorothy that she picked out the most titled aristocrats to introduce her to, even if Dorothy did not know what to call them. But instead of taking the opertunity of making friends, Dorothy only let everybody see her misery. And the kind of an expression that Dorothy wears on her face when she is on the verge of standing more than she can bear, almost gives a person the impression that she is cross eyed. So the Society people began to leave Dorothy severly alone. And Mrs. Breene kept Charlie busy putting small gilt chairs all over the salon so that he could not join Dorothy and keep her company. And every time he looked at Dorothy across the salon, she was sitting all alone, looking quite unpopular, with a very unbecoming expression on her countenance. And I am really afraid that Charlie was beginning to wonder.

Well, finally Mrs. Breene came over to Dorothy and told her that she ought to smile, and enjoy herself and join in the conversation. But Dorothy does not know how to make an effort, and smile in Society, like the rest of us have to do. And finally the string quartet started in to play something that was called on the program a Bach Fudge, and Dorothy started to feel even worse.

But by this time, Mrs. Breene's own troubles began. Because nothing that Mrs. Breene could do would make those music lovers keep quiet. And just as soon as she got one set to hold their tongues in the hall, another set would start talking about themselves in the salon. And Mrs. Breene would have to crowd her way through all the gilt chairs, to tell them to "Hush!"

But, by that time, the music lovers in the hall would be at it again. And Mrs. Breene would try to hush them at a distants. But it was really like water rolling off of a duck's back. So then she would have to make her way back through all the gilt chairs in order to hush them again in the hallway. And she had to work like a Trojan, without really getting anywheres. And the looks of the string quartet kept getting blacker and blacker.

And finally things even got worse. Because somebody discovered that the butler was laying out champagne in the libery. And a regular Exodus started to occur in that direction, until there were only 4 people left in the salon, and they were the string quartet. So Mrs. Breene became almost frantick. And she rushed toward the libery, but by the time she got there, it was jammed to the door with music lovers. Well, she finally worked her way through the crowd, and told them that the champagne would *not* be opened until the music was over, so they might just as well make up their minds to listen to the string quartet. So she pushed them all out and locked the door, and they finally decided to go back to the salon and be quiet. But Mrs. Breene did not know that one of the guests was locked up in the libery with the butler and all of that champagne. And, of course, the guest that was locked up, was Dorothy.

Well, it seems that the butler and Dorothy started right in to become friendly. For he was in quite a Bolshivistic state of mind himself, because, by rights it should have been his night out. And it seems that he was a German butler who loved music, so he had bought himself a ticket to Lowangrin at the opera. But, of course, he had to give it up. And he could not even hear the string quartet, because they had to shut the libery door on account of the way the guests behaved. So he seemed to think that, in this world, it was only the wealthy who were allowed to love music. So he and Dorothy took a drink to forget their troubles.

Well, the champagne was of the very best, so they had some more, and the first thing Dorothy knew, she began to cheer up and feel better. And Dorothy says, that by the time the string quartet got through their program, she had reached a state where she could have been happy in a swamp. So she emerged from the libery and made her way back through the party, smiling to the right and left, and greeting people heartily that she had not even had an intraduction to.

Well, when she reached the salon, it seems that Dorothy decided to do a dance of some new step she had learned in the Follies. I mean, nobody had even asked her, but strange to say, instead of everybody being annoyed, they were all delighted. And they started to applaud. So then Dorothy decided to sing the comick version of a song that some of the girls had composed in the privacy of their own dressing room, that was not even meant to be sung in the Follies, much less a salon. But instead of being shocked, those music lovers were even more delighted, and they started to crowd back into the salon in such large numbers that the string quartet, that was trying its best to get out of the salon, nearly had its shello smashed.

Well, Dorothy became the Life of the party. And Charlie Breene stood by in pride and watched her with the love light in his eyes. And Mrs. Breene finally had to step in and take Dorothy by the arm, and make her stop. Because she told her guest that they must not allow the dear child to overtax herself.

Well, then Dorothy started to say "good-night" to her Hostess, and quite a few guests still crowded around to listen, because by this time Dorothy had gained quite a little reputation as a "Bon Mot." So Mrs. Breene was really more than sweet to Dorothy, and she took her by the hand, and seemed to want to hold quite a little conversation. But Dorothy could not understand what she was saying because Mrs. Breene could not seem to help from breaking out into French. Well, Dorothy had learned quite a few Mexican words when she was in the Southern part of California, so Dorothy says she came right back at her in Mexican. But Dorothy really ought not to have talked Mexican to such a refined Social leader as Mrs. Breene, because hardly any society leaders know Mexican, and Dorothy was so ignorant that she did not know that it is the depths of low breeding to hold a conversation in Mexican, when the one you are holding it with does not understand the Mexican language.

Well, Dorothy says she finally told Mrs. Breene, in Mexican, to "help herself to the chili," and then she took Charlie by the hand and bowed herself out. And the last she saw of Mrs. Breene, she was standing in the midst of guests who admired Dorothy, gritting her teeth, and telling Charlie that he must bring his little friend again some time.

Well, when they got out, Charlie was in the seventh Heaven, because it was the first time that his Mother had ever approved of any Follies girl enough to ask her to come again. And everybody else was so full of enthusiasm about Dorothy, that Charlie was very, very proud. So he asked her to become his bride.

Well, Dorothy, as usual, was skeptical. Because she had gotten an idea that Mrs. Breene's enthusiasm was forced, and might break down before the alter. So she asked Charlie for time to think the proposition over. But Dorothy says that she really was intreeged by the idea of being able to return Mrs. Breene's hospitality by inviting *her* to their wedding breakfast. So, I mean, sometimes even a girl like Dorothy gets an impults that is sweet.

"Moms" Mabley
(1894–1975)

FROM Stand-up Routines

One day she was sitting on the porch and I said, "Granny, how old does a woman get before she don't want no more boyfriends?" (She was around 106 then.) She said, "I don't know, Honey. You have to ask somebody older than me." She said, "A woman is a woman as long as she lives; there's a certain time in a man's life when he has to go to a place called over the hill."

★

Now his sporting days are over, and his tail light is out,
And what used to be his sex appeal now is just his water spout.
So that's the story, alas and alack,
When he's squeezed out the toothpaste, he just can't squeeze it back.

So if we want to make whoopie, don't wait until—
We get—over the hill, over the hill.

★

My daddy liked him so I had to marry that old man. My daddy should have married him; he the one liked him (*laughter*). The nearest thing to death you ever seen in your life. His shadow weighed more than he did. He got out of breath threading a needle. And UGLY! He was so ugly he hurt my feelings. . . . He was so ugly he had to tip up on a glass to get a drink of water. . . . I thought he never would die. . . . I shouldn't talk like that about him though. He's dead. They say you shouldn't say nothing about the dead unless you can say something good. He's dead, GOOD!

My slogan is if it don't fit don't force it. In other words, if you can't make it, don't fake it. Let somebody else take it. . . . I'd rather pay a young man's way from here to California than to tell an old man the distance. . . . Don't get me wrong, it ain't no disgrace to come from the South. But it's a disgrace to go back down there.

Merrill Markoe
(Contemporary)

FROM *What the Dogs Have Taught Me and Other Amazing Things I've Learned*

Stupid Women, Stupid Choices

Put on alert by my foolproof "dumb-movie sensory system"—a highly developed sixth sense that reminds me to stay away from movies with titles containing numbers or accompanied by the words *produced by Simpson and Bruckheimer*—I had been purposely avoiding *Pretty Woman*. But *Pretty Woman* was the thing that wouldn't die. I kept seeing ads that called it "the feel-good hit of the season." And then it was rereleased so everyone would have a chance to see it *again*. And then came a barrage of new ads proclaiming that at long last the movie was available on videocassette.

Finally, I started to hear that ten-year-old girls were watching it over and over, and this was when I began to get concerned, because my own ten-year-old-girl fantasy fixations were the early starting point for a whole lot of trouble later on. So I gave in and saw the darn thing, and my short review is this: It really sucks and it pissed me off.

To recap briefly, the amazingly appealing Julia Roberts plays the most improbable hooker in the history of unlikely TV and movie hookers. She might as well have been portraying the Bean Goddess from Neptune, so unhookerlike is her character. (In fact, what we have here is the first true Disney hooker! The story could almost have been serialized on the old *Mickey Mouse Club* with Annette in the starring role!)

Anyway, here's the hooker dressed like Rocker Barbie, leading a life just a tad less brutal, alienating or problematic than that of any cosmetics counter saleswoman when she encounters repressed, handsome, egomaniac john Richard Gere. This man has just been dumped by his girlfriend because, she says, she is "sick of being at his beck and call." So he decides to hire this (wink, wink) *hooker* to be his temporary social companion. And as it turns out, not only does she not have any kind of a "beck and call" problem, something about this situation causes her to blossom, flower and *thrive!* Even though he never offers her anything in the way of emotional interaction, that doesn't affect her *incredible joie de vivre!* Because she's just so darned full of this drug-free, childlike wonderment at life! Wow! A hotel lobby! Yikes! Room service! A hat! A dress! A *really big* bathtub! Oh, my God! Pinch me! I'm dreaming!

Because this is a movie, she pretty soon falls in love with this guy. And now, when he offers to *pay* her to stay, she is hurt and packs up to leave. "It's just not good enough anymore," she says to him. "I want *the whole fairy tale!!*" (And I'm thinking to myself, *Excuse me, but where was I when they rewrote the fairy tale to start, "Once upon a time, in a land far, far away, there was this hooker . . .".?*)

Anyway, these are the easy, lighthearted reasons to hate the movie. That it is evil and loathsome to glorify hooking and sociopathic men is kind of obvious. But the ending was the final straw. Moved to the kind of white-knight behavior that I have never seen exhibited, even in the name of love, by a human male of any race, creed or religion anywhere except in a movie, the Richard Gere character shows up at the last minute to *rescue* Julia Roberts and bring us to the super-disgusting last line. As he lifts her into his arms, she says, "And now I'll rescue you right back."

That was when the uncontrollable barfing started for me. Because I knew that the guys who made this movie were all patting themselves on the back, thinking that the line added some kind of Nineties contemporary woman's egalitarian spin to the proceedings. I really got revved up, thinking about the insanity of that mainstay of Hollywood romantic plot devices: *rescuing*.

(You: "Gee, Merrill is certainly very grumpy today. I wonder if she's getting enough potassium and magnesium.")

It's certainly a time-honored tradition to have women be the *rescued* party. (Cinderella and Sleeping Beauty spring to mind.) But the fantasies that had the tightest hold on me involved the woman as the *rescuer*. In my preteen years I went repeatedly to see *West Side Story* because I had the hots for all the (wink, wink) teenage gang members. They were the first versions of a fantasy prototype that I have always found a real winner—I speak of the wounded, brooding, tough-guy loner with the mysterious tragic past, running, ever running, from unjust circumstances, his sad eyes the only clue to the horrible lack of love that has driven him to unfortunate acts of rage, rebellion, and self-destruction. Now he is hurt, and dangerous to everyone except that one woman whose love might make a difference. It is she he can come to in the middle of the night as he hides from the "authorities" who have wronged him. Together they will walk through the turbulent weather, joint observers of life's cruelties, until he kisses her with such ferocity that she has no choice but to devote her very being to trying to save him.

Various versions of this scenario accompanied me through my girlhood in the form of James Dean, Clint Eastwood or even the young Bob Dylan; then, more recently, Sean Penn, Gary Oldman or Johnny Depp. (Girlhood nothing; I was mesmerized *last weekend* by the several male cast members who have been doing this dance on *Twin Peaks*.) And that got me to thinking, *Who are these guys playing? Who are these wounded, brooding guys in real life?* Finally, I realized that wounded, brooding loners in real life are the emotionally crippled, paranoid, narcissistic guys with drug and alcohol and commitment problems who drove the woman of the Eighties into a frenzy, writing, reading and buying that endless series of bestselling books with the long, annoying titles. I refer, of course, to the *Men Who Hate Women and the Women Who Love Them*, etc., genre.

Just about all these books are devoted to the premise that rescuing is not only futile, it is *impossible* (because someone can rescue himself, but no one can rescue another person). These books contain chapter after chapter of advice on how to rebuild your decimated life and your shattered self-esteem—just two of the cute little by-products of your full-out rescuing attempt. In fact, in the past decade we have become a nation of Twelve-Step Programs (AA, ACOA, CODA, etc.), each set up to instruct participants in how to regain their sanity and stop rescuing.

(You again: "Gee, Merrill really *is* grumpy today. I'll bet she isn't getting enough vitamin B complex. Someone should check.")

If the characters in *Pretty Woman* had lived real people's lives, here is how the story would have continued after the movie. Longing to feel more legitimate, the Julia Roberts character would succeed in getting the Richard Gere character to marry her. And, feeling more legitimized, she would begin to build a sense of identity, power and self-worth, all of which would become threatening to the

Richard Gere character even though she would be imagining that it made her more appealing. After all, the only reason she never moved in this direction before was her unfortunate social circumstances. Of course, she also loses interest in being at his beck and call, which is maybe when she notices that he has begun to withdraw emotionally. But who can blame him? He feels hurt and betrayed. This is not the woman he married. And so he secretly starts searching for another naive, joie-de-vivre-driven, beck-and-call girl to serve his needs. In other words, if I am not mistaken, *Pretty Woman* turns into the story of Donald and Ivana Trump and Marla Maples!

Well! Now that I have proven how pernicious this whole rescuing business can be (in fact, it's even at the core of that most pathetic of female situations—waiting for the unhappily trapped married man), then what, oh what, you are probably wondering, are we to put in its place? How do we rebuild our romantic fantasies? Well, I think there is a solution. And, as they say on the sitcoms, "It's kinda crazy but it just might work."

Here it is: Entertain the notion that the rescuing isn't what we crave. After all, there's a lot of *work*. Couldn't it be the theatrical behavior? All of those appealing facial expressions and great moves are being totally wasted on the wrong bunch of guys. And so I call for a national retraining program in which pleasant, good-natured accountants and management trainees can learn to pout and brood and wear leather jackets. One class could be devoted to the dramatic uses of staring into nature—the pounding surf, the driving rain, the howling wind. Learn which seasonal precipitate is right for you.

In other words, if we could just get the good, well-intentioned but dowdy guys to take all this over, it would be a whole lot easier and more doable than trying to get women like me to stop falling in love with the screwed-up, weaselly guys who use that behavior to such good effect.

Well, it's just an idea. I'm off now to see about some kind of meditation plan and maybe consult with a dietician.

An Insider's Guide to the American Woman

The first item in my collection of the greatest irritants of the early Nineties is the June 1990 issue of *Esquire* featuring "The Secret Life of the American Wife." On the cover is a partially clothed woman, anatomically labeled with such questions as "HER LIPS: Can you trust what they say?" and "HER BRA: What *really* keeps it up?"

I'm not surprised to learn that men are still mystified by women. Certainly women are still utterly baffled by men. But what I found so infuriating this time around was the type of thing the (presumably college-educated) editors and writers were pretending to find so gosh-darned unfathomable. And their approach! So *retro*, so Fifties, so "Honey, now dry those tears and how about we take you downtown and buy you something sparkly?"

The lead article ("Your Wife: An Owner's Manual") offered pseudoscientific dissections of such feminine mysteries as "HER HANDBAG: Its capacity and contents" and "HER PLUMBING: General Diagnostics." If this is how far men have come in their knowledge of women—to wide-eyed wonderment at the contents of her purse and dumbfounded speechlessness at the thought of "female plumbing"—well, I personally think now is as good a time as any to throw in the towel.

My suggestion to men is, *Stop trying* to comprehend that which is clearly too complicated for you. Let me kindly state that it no longer really matters whether or not you understand. I just don't think you should worry your pretty little heads about it for another moment. Instead, simply *memorize* the following information and blindly incorporate it into your thinking, much as one might deal with an elusive scientific concept, such as $E = mc^2$.

MERRILL'S FUN FACTS TO KNOW AND TELL ABOUT WOMEN

I. WOMEN AND THE ENGLISH LANGUAGE. To a woman, the words "I had a great time. I'll call you" translate roughly to mean, "He said he had a great time. He'll call me." So, if you *say* those words, expect to *make* a call to the woman to whom you have said them. If this does not fit into your plans, *do not say those words*. (I know this is confusing. Just memorize it and do it. There's nothing more to discuss.)

Women have other quirky language-oriented notions. For instance, to a woman the words "I love you" represent a heartfelt expression of the intensely fond feelings you have for her. At least, this kind of thing will be what the woman has in mind when *she* utters the words, and so she will not be pleased if your response is "Thank you" or "I know."

There is an interesting truth behind some of this that may be hard to grasp: Women *like* to talk about personal things. In fact, they actually *listen* when a man does just that. Why? Well, because women believe that a conversation can go beyond a simple exchange of sports scores! Yes! They do! In fact, women who meet for the first time on a checkout line will often have more intimate conversations with each other than they have had with men to whom they have been married for two or three decades. They do this voluntarily! Why? Because they find it *enjoyable*!

Now that you understand this, realize that the answer to "Hi, honey. What did you do today?" is *not* "I don't know. Nothing."

II. WOMEN AND FOOD. Most women are on a diet, thinking about going on a diet or wondering if they should think about going on a diet. In a free-market economy, a majority of women will order a salad on a majority of dining-out occasions. If a man wishes a woman to change her eating habits and make them more like his own, he need only repackage the food he would like to see eaten as a salad. For example, most women would feel okay about sitting down to a hot-fudge-sundae salad or a pizza salad.

It is not necessary to inquire whether a woman would like something for dessert. The answer is, *yes*, she *would* like something for dessert, but she would like *you* to order it so she can pick at it with her fork. She does not want you to call attention to this by saying, "If you wanted a dessert, why didn't you order one?" You must understand, she *has* the dessert she wants. The dessert she wants is contained *within* yours!

Bear in mind also that she wants you to keep pace with her and prefers you to eat at least half of your dessert because she does *not* want the responsibility of having eaten most of it.

III. THEIR ENTERTAINMENT NEEDS. Unlike men, most women are not endlessly in search of opportunities to watch things crash and blow up. Women tend to prefer movies teeming with human intrigue and personal foible to movies where someone breaks through a plate glass window with a car, or breaks a plate glass window with his fist, or breaks someone's head with his fist in a car, or breaks someone's fist with a plate glass window. We're just wacky that way.

IV. WOMEN'S ABLUTIONS (and why they take so long). The amount of time a woman takes to prepare for a date with a man is in direct proportion to the amount of time she has spent observing that man staring saucer-eyed at other women who have put in at least the aforementioned amount of preparation time on their date. If a man would like to see one decrease, so too must the other.

V. THEIR PLUMBING. How much should you know? Women are the ones who do not have a penis and did not even have to undergo painful penis-removal surgery to accomplish this. As a result, they will require more frequent stops on a long car trip.

Once a month women find themselves strangely depressed and taking a long hard look at where they've made a wrong turn in life. They will ruminate over such dilemmas as "Perhaps the reason I'm depressed is that I really need to find a better job, but I guess I'm afraid to change because I have such low self-esteem, which comes from my childhood when my mother always used to tell me blah blah blah blah blah." Then they realize they have just gotten their period, which snuck up on them in the form of a mood change. So if you get involved with a woman, don't be surprised when you find it sneaking up on you as well.

There are very simple ways to give a woman an orgasm. These involve specific manipulations of "the plumbing." If you suspect that you don't know what you're doing but think you are bluffing effectively and/or you notice that it is taking more than a half hour, please be advised that you're fooling *no* one. It's just that most women are too polite and too concerned about the frailties of the male ego to say anything. So ask the owner of "the plumbing" to provide you with some helpful tips!!! And save everyone involved a couple of long, painful hours!!! And by the way . . . if you *do* suspect that you don't know what you're doing, for God's sake, don't do it *harder*.

VI. WOMEN AND LOVE. I have heard men say that they don't mind the idea of breast implants in a woman because, after all, big breasts are big breasts.

(Actually what I have heard men say is slightly coarser.) On the other hand, I have never met a woman who would rather be with a man in a toupee than a bald man.

This ability to accept and embrace the less-than-ideal, this generosity of spirit, has a downside—the tendency to be attracted to psychos. We know better, we're not proud of this, and we have spent decades learning that we would *really* rather be with nice men. But any man who has a problem attracting women because they think he is too nice would do well to augment his usual behavior with anguished exhalations of barely controlled rage.

In case you haven't noticed, women take sex just a tad more personally than do guys. For a woman, the only working definition of a one-night stand is a night spent with a guy who turned out to be a total weenie. The degree of any date's success can be easily determined by the degree of obsession it causes in the woman. If you would like to test this, introduce yourself to some of her good friends. If they aren't already sick of hearing your name, *the date didn't go that well.*

Once women are in love, they can be easily manipulated because they're so overwhelmed with feelings of insecurity. Many will happily take responsibility for everything that goes wrong, as in: "If he isn't happy it's my fault" and "If I'm not happy it's my fault."

Now that you know this, be a good guy and don't take unfair advantage. *Own up to stuff you know is your fault.* You might as well, anyway, because there is still another female phenomenon that ensures you'll be living on borrowed time if you don't.

VII. WOMEN AND THERAPY. Women are naturally attracted to therapy. Yes, it's true! If they don't get expensive one-on-one counseling, they will read self-help books and magazine articles or listen to radio and TV shows that discuss these issues or talk to and get advice from their friends who have done some or all of the above. Women do this because therapy actually involves so many of the things they enjoy: personal idiosyncrasy, a chance to talk dramatically about themselves and a good starting point for future conversations with friends or anyone they might meet in the checkout line.

VIII. THEIR PURSES, THEIR BRAS. A woman learns at a young age that she will be expected to carry the equivalent of a suitcase everywhere she goes for the rest of her life. And so she plans accordingly, secure in the knowledge that she will permanently have at her disposal anything, under a certain size, she might need in an emergency. This means that no matter what unexpected event or disaster she encounters, a woman will always have enough makeup to look really cute.

As far as the bra goes . . . give me a break, okay? *Give me a fucking break.*

The Marx Brothers

FROM *A Night at the Opera*

Groucho: I just remembered—I came back here looking for somebody. You don't know who it is, do you?

Chico: Funny—it just slipped my mind.

Groucho (*Snapping his fingers*): I remember now—the greatest tenor in the world, that's what I'm after!

Chico: That's funny. I am his manager.

Groucho: Whose manager?

Chico: The greatest tenor in the world.

Groucho: The fellow that sings at the opera here?

Chico: Sure!

Groucho: What's his name?

Chico: What do you care? Some Italian name—I can't pronounce it. What you want with him?

Groucho: Well, I'd like to offer him a job. Would he be interested?

Chico: I don't know, but *I'm* interested. That's the main thing. What sort of job?

Groucho: With the New York Opera. America is waiting to hear him sing.

Chico: Well, he can sing loud, but he can't sing that loud.

Groucho: Well, I think we can get America to meet him halfway. The main thing is, can he sail tomorrow night?

Chico: If you pay him enough money, he can sail *last* night. How much you pay him?

Groucho (*Aside*): Let's see—a thousand dollars a night. I'm entitled to a little profit. (*To* Chico) How about ten dollars a night?

(Chico *laughs scornfully.*)

Chico: Ten dollars! . . . (*A quick change of mood*) All right. I'll take it.

Groucho: That's fine. Of course, I want a ten percent commission for putting the deal over.

Chico: And I get ten percent as his manager.

Groucho: Well, that leaves eight dollars. Say he sings once a week—that's eight dollars a week clear profit for him.

Chico (*Considering a week*): He sends five dollars home to his mother.

Groucho: Well, that still leaves him three dollars.

Chico: Three dollars. Can he live in New York on that?

Groucho: Like a prince—of course, he won't be able to eat, but he can live like a prince. Oh, I forgot to tell you. He'll have to pay income tax on that three dollars.

Chico: Income tax?

Groucho: Yes, there's a federal tax and the state tax and there may be a city tax. And, naturally, a sales tax.

Chico: How much does that all come to?

Groucho: Well, I figure if he doesn't sing too often, he can break even.

Chico: All right. We'll take it.

Groucho (*Holding contract farther and farther away*): I can read, but I can't see it. If my arms were a little longer, I could read it . . . Ah, here we are. Now pay attention to this first clause. (*Reads*) "The party of the first part shall be known in this contract as the party of the first part." How do you like that? Pretty neat, eh?

Chico: No, that'sa no good.

Groucho (*Indignantly*): What's the matter with it?

Chico (*Conciliatorily*): I don't know—let's hear it again.

Groucho: "The party of the first part shall be known in this contract as the party of the first part."

Chico: It sounds a little better this time.

Groucho: Well, it grows on you. Want to hear it once more?

Chico: Only the first part.

Groucho: The *party* of the first part?

Chico: No. The *first part* of the party of the first part.

Groucho: Well, it says, "The first part of the party of the first part shall be known in this contract—" Look! Why should we quarrel about a thing like that? (*He tears off the offending clause*) We'll take it right out.

Chico (*Tearing the same clause out of his contract*): Sure, it's too long anyhow. Now what have we got left?

Groucho: Well, I've got about a foot and a half . . . Now, then: "The party of the second part shall be known in this contract as the party of the second part."

Chico: Well, I don't know. I don't like the second party, either.

Groucho: You should have come to the first party. We didn't get home till around four in the morning. (*Slight pause*) I was blind for three days.

Chico: Look, couldn't the first part of the second party be the second part of the first party? Then we got something.

Julio Marzán
(Contemporary)

Ethnic Poetry

The ethnic poet said: "The earth is maybe
a huge maraca / and the sun a trombone /
and life / is to move your ass /to slow beats."
The ethnic audience roasted a suckling pig.

The ethnic poet said: "Oh thank Goddy, Goddy /
I be me, my toenails curled downward /
deep, deep, deep into Mama earth."
The ethnic audience shook strands of sea shells.

The ethnic poet said: "The sun was created black /
so we should imagine light / and also dream /
a walrus emerging from the broken ice."
The ethnic audience beat on sealskin drums.

The ethnic poet said: "Reproductive organs /
Eagles nesting California redwoods /
Shut up and listen to my ancestors."
The ethnic audience ate fried bread and honey.

The ethnic poet said: "Something there is that
doesn't love a wall / That sends
the frozen-ground-swell under it."
The ethnic audience deeply understood humanity.

Jackie Mason
(Contemporary)

Jackie Mason on Starbucks

Starbucks is the best example of a phony status symbol that means nothing, but people will still pay 10× as much for because there are French words all over the place. You want coffee in a coffee shop, that's 60 cents. But at Starbucks, Café Latte: $3.50. Café Crémier: $4.50. Café Suisse: $9.50. For each French word, another four dollars. Why does a little cream in coffee make it worth $3.50? Go into any coffee shop; they'll give you all the cream you want until you're blue in the face. Forty million people are walking around in coffee shops with jars of cream: "Here's all the cream you want!" And it's still 60 cents. You know why? Because it's called "coffee." If it's Café Latte—$4.50. You want cinnamon in your coffee? Ask for cinnamon in a coffee shop; they'll give you all the cinnamon you want. Do they ask you for more money because it's cinnamon? It's the same price for cinnamon in your coffee as for coffee without cinnamon—60 cents, that's it. But not in Starbucks. Over there, it's Cinnamonnier—$9.50.

You want a refill in a regular coffee shop, they'll give you all the refills you want until you drop dead. You can come in when you're 27 and keep drinking coffee until you're 98. And they'll start begging you: "Here, you want more coffee, you want more, you want more?" Do you know that you can't get a refill at Starbucks? A refill is a dollar fifty. Two refills, $4.50. Three refills, $19.50. So, for four cups of coffee—$350. And it's burnt coffee. It's burnt coffee at Starbucks, let's be honest about it. If you get burnt coffee in a coffee shop, you call a cop. You say, "It's the bottom of the pot. I don't drink from the bottom of the pot." But when it's burnt at Starbucks, they say, "Oh, it's a blend. It's a blend. It's a special bean from Argentina . . ." The bean is in your head.

And there're no chairs in those Starbucks. Instead, they have these high stools. You ever see these stools? You haven't been on a chair that high since you were two. Seventy-three-year-old Jews are climbing and climbing to get to the top of the chair. And when they get to the top, they can't even drink the coffee because there's 12 people around one little table, and everybody's saying, "Excuse me, excuse me, excuse me, excuse me . . ." Then they can't get off the chair. Old Jews are begging Gentiles, "Mister, could you get me off this?" Do you remember what a cafeteria was? In poor neighborhoods all over this country, they went to a cafeteria because there were no waiters and no service. And so poor people could save money on a tip. Cafeterias didn't have regular tables or chairs either. They gave coffee to you in a cardboard cup. So because of that, you paid less for the coffee. You got less, so you paid less. It's all the same as Starbucks—no chairs, no service, a cardboard cup for your coffee—except in Starbucks, the less you get, the more it costs. By the time they give you nothing, it's worth four times as much. Am I exaggerating? Did you ever try to buy a cookie in Starbucks? Buy a cookie in a regular coffee shop. You can tear down a building with that cookie. And the whole cookie is 60 cents. At Starbucks, you're going to have to hire a detective to find that cookie, and it's $9.50. And you can't put butter on it because they want extra. Do you know that if you buy a bagel, you pay extra for cream cheese in Starbucks? Cream cheese, another 60 cents. A knife to put it on, 32 cents. If it reaches the bagel, 48 cents. That bagel costs you $312. And they don't give you the butter or the cream cheese. They don't give it to you. They tell you where it is. "Oh, you want butter? It's over there. Cream cheese? Over here. Sugar? Sugar is here." Now you become your own waiter. You walk around with a tray. "I'll take the cookie. Where's the butter? The butter's here. Where's the cream cheese? The cream cheese is there." You walked around for an hour and a half selecting items, and then the guy at the cash register has a glass in front of him that says "Tips." You're waiting on tables for an hour, and you owe him money. Then there's a sign that says please clean it up when you're finished. They don't give you a waiter or a busboy. Now you've become the janitor. Now you have to start cleaning up the place. Old Jews are walking around cleaning up Starbucks. "Oh, he's got dirt too? Wait, I'll clean this up." They clean up the place for an hour and a half.

If I said to you, "I have a great idea for a business. I'll open a whole new type of a coffee shop. A whole new type. Instead of 60 cents for coffee, I'll charge $2.50, $3.50, $4.50, and $5.50. Not only that, I'll have no tables, no chairs, no water, no busboy, and you'll clean it up for 20 minutes after you're finished," would you say to me, "That's the greatest idea for a business I ever heard! We can open a chain of these all over the world!" No, you would put me right into a sanitarium. Starbucks can only get away with it because they have French titles for everything, Nazi-bastard son of a bitches. And I say this with the highest respect, because I don't like to talk about people.

H. L. Mencken
(1880–1956)

FROM *Prejudices: First Series*

The Blushful Mystery

1
SEX HYGIENE

The literature of sex hygiene, once so scanty and so timorous, now piles mountain high. There are at least a dozen formidable series of books of instruction for inquirers of all ages, beginning with "What Every Child of Ten Should Know" and ending with "What a Woman of Forty-five Should Know," and they all sell amazingly. Scores of diligent authors, some medical, some clerical and some merely shrewdly chautauqual, grow rich at the industry of composing them. One of these amateur Havelock Ellises had the honor, during the last century, of instructing me in the elements of the sacred sciences. He was then the pastor of a fourth-rate church in a decaying neighborhood and I was sent to his Sunday-school in response to some obscure notion that the agony of it would improve me. Presently he disappeared, and for a long while I heard nothing about him. Then he came into sudden prominence as the author of such a series of handbooks and as the chief stockholder, it would seem, in the publishing house printing them. By the time he died, a few years ago, he had been so well rewarded by a just God that he was able to leave funds to establish a missionary college in some remote and heathen land.

This holy man, I believe, was honest, and took his platitudinous compositions quite seriously. Regarding other contributors to the literature it may be said without malice that their altruism is obviously corrupted by a good deal of hocus-pocus. Some of them lecture in the chautauquas, peddling their books before and after charming the yokels. Others, being members of the faculty, seem to carry on medical practice on the side. Yet others are kept in profitable jobs by the salacious old men who finance vice crusades. It is hard to draw the line between the mere thrifty enthusiast and the downright fraud. So, too, with the actual vice crusaders. The books of the latter, like the sex hygiene books, are often sold, not as wisdom, but as pornography. True enough, they are always displayed in the show-window of the small-town Methodist Book Concern—but you will also find them in the back-rooms of dubious second-hand book-stores, side by side with the familiar scarlet-backed editions of Rabelais, Margaret of Navarre and Balzac's "Droll Tales." Some time ago, in a book advertisement headed "Snappy Fiction," I found announcements of "My Battles With Vice," by Virginia Brooks—and "Life of My Heart," by Victoria Cross. The former was described by the publisher as a record of "personal experiences in the fight against the gray wolves and love pirates of modern society." The book was offered to all comers by mail. One may easily imagine the effects of such an offer.

But even the most serious and honest of the sex hygiene volumes are probably futile, for they are all founded upon a pedagogical error. That is to say, they are all founded upon an attempt to explain a romantic mystery in terms of an exact science. Nothing could be more absurd: as well attempt to interpret Beethoven in terms of mathematical physics—as many a fatuous contrapuntist, indeed, has tried to do. The mystery of sex presents itself to the young, not as a scientific problem to be solved, but as a romantic emotion to be accounted for. The only result of the current endeavor to explain its phenomena by seeking parallels in botany is to make botany obscene. . . .

2
ART AND SEX

One of the favorite notions of the Puritan mullahs who specialize in this moral pornography is that the sex instinct, if suitably repressed, may be "sublimated" into the higher sorts of idealism, and especially into aesthetic idealism. That notion is to be found in all their books; upon it they ground the theory that the enforcement of chastity by a huge force of spies, stool pigeons and police would convert the republic into a nation of incomparable uplifters, forward-lookers and artists. All this, of course, is simply pious fudge. If the notion were actually sound, then all the great artists of the world would come from the ranks of the hermetically repressed, *i.e.*, from the ranks of Puritan old maids, male and female. But the truth is, as every one knows, that the great artists of the world are never Puritans, and seldom even ordinarily respectable. No virtuous man—that is, virtuous in the Y.M.C.A. sense—has ever painted a picture worth looking at, or written a symphony worth hearing, or a book worth reading, and it is highly improbable that the thing has ever been done by a virtuous woman. The actual effect of repression, lamentable though it may be, is to destroy idealism altogether. The Puritan, for all his pretensions, is the worst of materialists. Passed through his sordid and unimaginative mind, even the stupendous romance of sex is reduced to a disgusting transaction in physiology. As artist he is thus hopeless; as well expect an auctioneer to qualify for the Sistine Chapel choir. All he ever achieves, taking pen or brush in hand, is a feeble burlesque of his betters, all of whom, by his hog's theology, are doomed to hell.

3
A LOSS TO ROMANCE

Perhaps the worst thing that this sex hygiene nonsense has accomplished is the thing mourned by Agnes Repplier in "The Repeal of Reticence." In America, at least, innocence has been killed, and romance has been sadly wounded by the same discharge of smutty artillery. The flapper is no longer naïve and charming; she goes to the altar of God with a learned and even cynical glitter in her eye. The veriest school-girl of to-day, fed upon Forel, Sylvanus Stall, Reginald Wright Kauffman and the Freud books, knows as much as the midwife of 1885, and spends a good deal more time discharging and disseminating her information. All this, of course, is highly embarrassing to the more romantic and ingenuous sort of men, of whom I have the honor to be one. We are constantly in the position of General Mitchener in Shaw's one-acter, "Press Cuttings," when he begs Mrs. Farrell, the talkative charwoman, to reserve her confidences for her medical adviser. One often wonders, indeed, what women now talk of to doctors. . . .

Please do not misunderstand me here. I do not object to this New Freedom on moral grounds, but on aesthetic grounds. In the relations between the sexes all beauty is founded upon romance, all romance is founded upon mystery, and all mystery is founded upon ignorance, or, failing that, upon the deliberate denial of the known truth. To be in love is merely to be in a state of perceptual anesthesia—to mistake an ordinary young man for a Greek god or an ordinary young woman for a goddess. But how can this condition of mind survive the deadly matter-of-factness which sex hygiene and the new science of eugenics impose? How can a woman continue to believe in the honor, courage and loving tenderness of a man after she has learned, perhaps by affidavit, that his haemoglobin count is 117%, that he is free from sugar and albumen, that his blood pressure is 112/79 and that his Wassermann reaction is negative? . . . Moreover, all this new-fangled "frankness" tends to dam up, at least for civilized adults, one of the principal well-springs of art, to wit, impropriety. What is neither hidden nor forbidden is seldom very charming. If women, continuing their present tendency to its logical goal, end by going stark naked, there will be no more poets and painters, but only dermatologists and photographers. . . .

4
SEX ON THE STAGE

The effort to convert the theater into a forum of solemn sex discussion is another abhorrent by-product of the sex hygiene rumble-bumble. Fortunately, it seems to be failing. A few years ago, crowds flocked to see Brieux's "Les Avariés," but to-day it is forgotten, and its successors are all obscure. The movement originated in Germany with the production of Frank Wedekind's "Frühlings Erwachen." The Germans gaped and twisted in their seats for a season or two, and then abandoned sex as a horror and went back to sex as a comedy. This last is what it actually should be, at least in the theater. The theater is no place for painful speculation; it is a place for diverting representation. Its best and truest sex plays are not such overstrained shockers as "Le Mariage d'Olympe" and "Damaged Goods," but such penetrating and excellent comedies as "Much Ado About Nothing" and "The Taming of the Shrew." In "Much Ado" we have an accurate and unforgettable picture of the way in which the normal male of the human species is brought to the altar—that is, by the way of appealing to his hollow vanity, the way of capitalizing his native and ineradicable asininity. And in "The Taming of the Shrew" we have a picture of the way in which the average woman, having so snared him, is purged of her resultant vainglory and bombast, and thus reduced to decent discipline and decorum, that the marriage may go on in solid tranquillity.

The whole drama of sex, in real life, as well as on the stage, revolves around those two enterprises. One-half of it consists of pitting the native intelligence of women against the native sentimentality of men, and the other half consists of bringing women into a reasonable order, that their superiority may not be too horribly obvious. To the first division belong the dramas of courtship, and a good many of those of marital conflict. In each case the essential drama is not a tragedy but a comedy—nay, a farce. In each case the conflict is not between imperishable verities but between mere vanities and pretensions. This is the essence of the comic: the unmasking of fraud, its destruction by worse fraud. Marriage, as we know it in Christendom, though its utility is obvious and its necessity is at least arguable, is just such a series of frauds. It begins with the fraud that the impulse to it is lofty, unearthly and disinterested. It proceeds to the fraud that both parties are equally eager for it and equally benefited by it—which actually happens only when two Mondays come together. And it rests thereafter upon the fraud that what is once agreeable (or tolerable) remains agreeable ever thereafter—that I shall be exactly the same man in 1938 that I am to-day, and that my wife will be the same woman, and intrigued by the merits of the same man. This last assumption is so outrageous that, on purely evidential and logical grounds, not even the most sentimental person would support it. It thus becomes necessary to reënforce it by attaching to it the concept of honor. That is to say, it is held up, not on the ground that it is actually true, but on the ground that a recognition of its truth is part of the bargain made at the altar, and that repudiation of this bargain would be dishonorable. Here we have honor, which is based upon a sense of the deepest and most inviolable truth, brought in to support something admittedly not true. Here, in other words, we have a situation in comedy, almost exactly parallel to that in which a colored bishop whoops "Onward, Christian Soldiers!" like a calliope in order to drown out the crowing of the rooster concealed beneath his chasuble.

In all plays of the sort that are regarded as "strong" and "significant" in Greenwich Village, in the finishing schools and by the newspaper critics, connubial infidelity is the chief theme. Smith, having a wife, Mrs. Smith, betrays her love and trust by running off with Miss Rabinowitz, his stenographer. Or Mrs. Brown, detecting her husband, Mr. Brown, in lamentable proceedings with a neighbor, the grass widow Kraus, forgives him and continues to be true to him in consideration of her children, Fred, Pansy and Little Fern. Both situations produce a great deal of eye-rolling and snuffling among the softies aforesaid. Yet neither contains the slightest touch of tragedy, and neither at bottom is even honest. Both, on the contrary, are based upon an assumption that is unsound and ridiculous—the assumption, to wit, that the position of the injured wife is grounded upon the highest idealism—that the injury she suffers is directed at her lofty and impeccable spirit—that it leaves her standing in an heroic attitude. All this, soberly examined, is found to be untrue. The, fact is that her moving impulse is simply a desire to cut a good figure before her world—in brief, that plain vanity is what animates her.

This public expectation that she will endure and renounce is itself hollow and sentimental, and so much so that it can seldom stand much strain. If, for example, her heroism goes beyond a certain modest point—if she carries it to the extent of complete abnegation and self-sacrifice—her reward is not that she is thought heroic, but that she is thought weak and foolish. And if, by any chance, the external pressure upon her is removed and she is left to go on with her alleged idealism alone—if, say, her recreant husband dies and some new suitor enters to dispute the theory of her deathless fidelity—then it is regarded as down-right insane for her to continue playing her artificial part.

In frank comedy we see the situation more accurately dealt with and hence more honestly and more instructively. Instead of depicting one party as revolting against the assumption of eternal fidelity melodramatically and the other as facing the revolt heroically and tragically, we have both criticizing it by a good-humored flouting of it—not necessarily by act, but by attitude. This attitude is normal and sensible. It rests upon genuine human traits and tendencies. It is sound, natural and honest. It gives the comedy of the stage a high validity that the bombastic fustian of the stage can never show, all the sophomores to the contrary notwithstanding.

When I speak of infidelity, of course, I do not mean only the gross infidelity of "strong" sex plays and the divorce courts, but that lighter infidelity which relieves and makes bearable the burdens of theoretical fidelity—in brief, the natural reaction of human nature against an artificial and preposterous assumption. The assumption is that a sexual choice, once made, is irrevocable—more, that all desire to revoke it, even transiently, disappears. The fact is that no human choice can ever be of that irrevocable character, and that the very existence of such an assumption is a constant provocation to challenge it and rebel against it.

What we have in marriage actually—or in any other such contract—is a constant war between the impulse to give that rebellion objective reality and a social pressure which puts a premium on submission. The rebel, if he strikes out, at once collides with a solid wall, the bricks of which are made up of the social assumption of his docility, and the mortar of which is the frozen sentimentality of his own lost yesterday—his fatuous assumption that what was once agreeable to him would be always agreeable to him. Here we have the very essence of comedy—a situation almost exactly parallel to that of the pompous old gentleman who kicks a plug hat lying on the sidewalk, and stumps his toe against the cobblestone within.

Under the whole of the conventional assumption reposes an assumption even more foolish, to wit, that sexual choice is regulated by some transcendental process, that a mysterious accuracy gets into it, that it is limited by impenetrable powers, that there is for every man one certain woman. This sentimentality not only underlies the theory of marriage, but is also the chief apology for divorce. Nothing could be more ridiculous. The truth is that marriages in Christendom are determined, not by elective affinities, but by the most trivial accidents, and that the issue of those accidents is relatively unimportant. That is to say, a normal man could be happy with any one of at least two dozen women of his acquaintance, and a man specially fitted to accept the false assumptions of marriage could be happy with almost any presentable woman of his race, class and age. He is married to Marie instead of to Gladys because Marie definitely decided to marry him, whereas Gladys vacillated between him and some other. And Marie decided to marry him instead of some other, not because the impulse was irresistibly stronger, but simply because the thing seemed more feasible. In such choices, at least among women, there is often not even any self-delusion. They see the facts clearly, and even if, later on, they are swathed in sentimental trappings, the revelation is not entirely obliterated.

Here we have comedy double distilled—a combat of pretensions, on the one side, perhaps, risen to self-hallucination, but on the other side more or less uneasily conscious and deliberate. This is the true soul of high farce. This is something not to snuffle over but to roar at.

Alice Duer Miller
(1874–1942)

FROM *Are Women People?*

Our Own Twelve Anti-Suffragist Reasons

1. Because no woman will leave her domestic duties to vote.
2. Because no woman who may vote will attend to her domestic duties.
3. Because it will make dissension between husband and wife.
4. Because every woman will vote as her husband tells her to.

5. Because bad women will corrupt politics.
6. Because bad politics will corrupt women.
7. Because women have no power of organization.
8. Because women will form a solid party and out-vote men.
9. Because men and women are so different that they must stick to different duties.
10. Because men and women are so much alike that men, with one vote each, can represent their own views and ours too.
11. Because women cannot use force.
12. Because the militants did use force.

Why We Oppose Pockets for Women

1. Because pockets are not a natural right.
2. Because the great majority of women do not want pockets. If they did they would have them.
3. Because whenever women have had pockets they have not used them.
4. Because women are required to carry enough things as it is, without the additional burden of pockets.
5. Because it would make dissension between husband and wife as to whose pockets were to be filled.
6. Because it would destroy man's chivalry toward woman, if he did not have to carry all her things in his pockets.
7. Because men are men, and women are women. We must not fly in the face of nature.
8. Because pockets have been used by men to carry tobacco, pipes, whiskey flasks, chewing gum and compromising letters. We see no reason to suppose that women would use them more wisely.

Why We Oppose Women Travelling in Railway Trains

1. Because travelling in trains is not a natural right.
2. Because our great-grandmothers never asked to travel in trains.
3. Because woman's place is the home, not the train.
4. Because it is unnecessary; there is no point reached by a train that cannot be reached on foot.
5. Because it will double the work of conductors, engineers and brakemen who are already overburdened.
6. Because men smoke and play cards in trains. Is there any reason to believe that women will behave better?

Why We Oppose Votes for Men

1. Because man's place is the armory.
2. Because no really manly man wants to settle any question otherwise than by fighting about it.
3. Because if men should adopt peaceable methods women will no longer look up to them.
4. Because men will lose their charm if they step out of their natural sphere and interest themselves in other matters than feats of arms, uniforms and drums.
5. Because men are too emotional to vote. Their conduct at baseball games and political conventions shows this, while their innate tendency to appeal to force renders them peculiarly unfit for the task of government.

The Universal Answer

Oh, there you go again,
Invading man's domain!
It's Nature's laws, you know, you are defying.
Don't fancy that you can
Be really like a man,
So what's the use of all this fuss and trying?
It seems to me so clear,
That women's highest sphere
Is being loving wives and patient mothers.
Oh can't you be content
To be as you were meant?
For { souls
{ books belong to husbands and to
{ votes [brothers.

What Every Woman Must Not Say

"I don't pretend I'm clever," he remarked, "or very wise,"
And at this she murmured, "Really," with the right polite surprise.
"But women," he continued, "I must own I understand;
Women are a contradiction—honorable and underhand—
Constant as the star Polaris, yet as changeable as Fate,
Always flying what they long for, always seeking what they hate."
"Don't you think," began the lady, but he cut her short: "I see
That you take it personally—women always do," said he.
"You will pardon me for saying every woman is the same,
Always greedy for approval, always sensitive to blame;

Sweet and passionate are women; weak in mind, though strong in soul;
Even you admit, I fancy, that they have no self-control?"
"No, I don't admit they haven't," said the patient lady then,
"Or they could not sit and listen to the nonsense talked by men."

Dennis Miller
(Contemporary)

FROM *The Rants*

Dysfunction

Why did Johnny fail in school? Why did Johnny start hanging out with heroin addicts? Why did Johnny get caught boosting stereo equipment? Why did he go to the big house? And why was he released two years later and then apprehended with a Mannlicher Carcano in a hotel room overlooking the President's motorcade route?

Well, Johnny will tell you, in this week's *People* magazine, that his problems are all about the fact that when he was five years old he was in the school play, and, get this, Mummy arrived ten minutes late. You see, Mummy disempowered him. Mummy ruined Johnny's life.

Now I don't want to get off on a rant here, but thanks to the notion of the dysfunctional family, every zipperhead in this country can now tap themselves with the Freudian wand and in a flash go from failed frog to misunderstood prince. Tad tubby? Mummy mistakenly thought food was love. You say you're angry? Must have been your brother's midnight wedgie raids. Huh?

Or maybe you haven't fulfilled your sappy little junior high daydream about being the greatest person on earth, hailed by all, from the lowliest bootlick to the richest barons of industry—And you just know it would have happened if only your selfish parents hadn't totally ruined your self-esteem by obsessing on paying the bills instead of obsessing on paying attention to you and your silly, talentless antics on the diving board at the public pool.

Listen—folks, we all have dashed hopes, mere figments of futures crushed by graduations, jobs, marriages—reality. Sure, it's tough waking up from a deep REM delirium starring you as the focal point of the universe to an Eraserhead reality in which you're the condiment guy at Der Wienerschnitzel. But you know something, that shouldn't give rise to this shrieking cacophony of blame.

Every day we get a new escape hatch from the psychiatric community: Co-dependency, addictive personalities, inherited personality disorder, multiple personality learning disorder, no personality whatsoever disorder, fetal membrane subcutaneous infectious submissive sexuality dislocator, Epstein Roseanne Barr . . . for Christ's sake, we are going over a Niagara of psychobabble in a barrel full of holes.

We have become a country of ragged recidivists dedicated to the proposition that all parents are created equally bad and the progeny/progenitor dynamic should be the landfill for all our personal shortcomings.

And if you're deep enough in denial to actually think that you did have a happy childhood, then your shrink will tell you, you must be forgetting something.

"Think back, think back, way back . . . would some drugs help you remember? . . . Maybe a subtle question or two will help jog your memory, like . . . did your auntie Hortense ever make you take a bath with her? Did your own father ever put his mouth on your stomach and blow? And what for, if not to humiliate you? Sure, there you go, there's a good reason why your friends make more money than you.

"Hey, Jinky, you shouldn't feel bad about flunking out of school and getting fired from the trampoline center. It's not your fault. It all goes back to when you were an embryo.

"Don't you feel better knowing that all your problems were laid on you, man? All right, we have to stop now, Mr. Jinkelstein. That'll be a hundred and eighty bucks. And now that we know you have more personal baggage than Joan Collins on safari, I think you should start coming in twice a day for the next four Olympics or so because I need to pay off my Lamborghini."

Look, I'm not insensitive to the real victims of abuse, the human casualties of alcoholic neglect. There are people out there who have been dealt absolutely fucking brutal cards, and it breaks your heart.

But you cannot join that club solely through intellectual legerdemain. Let's be honest; too many unhappy, unfilled people see the bulletproof excuse of dysfunction lying there and pick it up like a cudgel to ward off any personal responsibility for their lives. And as long as we continue to allow people to make the easy turn and casually claim that they're victims, they will never even make the effort to Fitzcarraldo the boat over the mountain and achieve true personal victory.

Of course, that's just my opinion. I could be in denial.

Margaret Mitchell
(1900–49)

FROM *Gone with the Wind*

A startling thought this, that a woman could handle business matters as well as or better than a man, a revolutionary thought to Scarlett who had been reared in the tradition that men were omniscient and women none too bright. Of course, she had discovered that this was not altogether true but the pleasant fiction still stuck in her mind. Never before had she put this remarkable idea into words. She sat quite still, with the heavy book across her lap, her mouth a little open with surprise, thinking that during the lean months at Tara she had done a man's work and done it well. She had been brought up to believe that a woman alone could accomplish nothing, yet she had managed a plantation without men to help her until Will came. Why, why, her mind stuttered, I believe women could manage everything in the world without men's help.

Pat Mora
(Contemporary)

FROM *Aunt Carmen's Book of Practical Saints*

Prayer to the Saints
Oración a los Santos

At sixteen I began to pray to you, old friends,
    for a handsome man who would never stray.
        Devoutly, I'd say,
Saint Peter the Apostle,
    please grant me this miracle,
Saint Raphael, the Archangel,
    remove every obstacle,
San José, dear father,
    may he frown at liquor,
Saint Clare,
    for Mother, could he be a millionaire,
Saint John Nepomuk,
    my few faults may he overlook,
Santa María Magdalena,
    que a veces me sirva mi cena,
Saint Christopher,
    may he my figure prefer,
Our Lady of Remedies,
    could he avoid my father's frugalities,
Saint Francis,
    please don't make him a pessimist,
Saint Anne,
    could he be a very handsome man,
Saint Anthony,
    may he know the art of flattery,
Santa Bárbara, protector against lightning,
    make him good at dancing,

247

Saint Genevieve,
    may he never plot to deceive,
Saint Blaise,
    let him shower me with praise,
Saint Jerome,
    have him build me my dream-home,
San Pascual,
    como él que no haya igual,
Saint Patrick,
    could he be a lovesick Catholic,
Saint Gertrude the great,
    forgive me, but make him passionate,
Saint Lucy,
    suggest he kiss me secretly,
Saint Martin,
    may my smile turn him to gelatin,
Santa Teresita,
    que me traiga florecitas,
Saint Agnes,
    make him love me with wild excess,
Saint James,
    por favor, nudge him this love to proclaim,
Saint Rose,
    have him soon propose,
Saint Elizabeth,
    may we celebrate our fiftieth,
Saint Jude,
    let me soon be wooed,
Saint Stephen,
    please remind all the santos
            to find me a husband soon. Ah, men.
Amen.

Ogden Nash
(1902–71)

FROM *Good Intentions*

Not George Washington's, Not Abraham Lincoln's, But Mine

Well, here I am thirty-eight,
Well, I certainly thought I'd have longer to wait.
You just stop in for a couple of beers,
And gosh, there go thirty-seven years.
Well, it has certainly been fun,
But I certainly thought I'd have got a lot more done.
Why if I had been really waked up and alive,
I could have been a Congressman since I was twenty-one or President since I
    was thirty-five.
I guess I know the reason my accomplishments are so measly:
I don't comprehend very easily.
It finally dawned on me that in life's race I was off to a delayed start
When at the age of thirty-three I had to be told that I could swim faster if I'd
    keep my fingers together instead of spreading them apart,
And I was convinced that precociousness was not the chief of my faults
When it was only last winter that I discovered that the name of that waltz that
    skaters waltz to is "The Skaters' Waltz."
After thirty-seven years I find myself the kind of man that anybody can sell any-
    thing to,
And nobody will ever tell anything to.
Whenever people get up a party of which I am to be a member to see some pic-
    ture which I don't want to see because I am uninterested in the situation that
    Scarlett and Mr. Chips are estranged over,
Why my head is what it is arranged over.
Contrariwise, I myself not only can't sell anybody anything,
I can't even ever tell anybody anything.
I have never yet had a good gossip bomb all poised and ready to burst
That somebody hasn't already told everybody first.
Yes, my career to date has certainly been a fiasco;
It would not have made a thrilling dramatic production for the late Oliver Mo-
    rosco or the late David Belasco.

But in spite of the fact that my career has been a fiasco to date,
Why I am very proud and happy to be thirty-eight.

Bill Nye
(1850–96)

FROM *Bill Nye and Boomerang*

Suggestions for a School of Journalism

A number of friends having personally asked me to express an opinion upon the matter of an established school of journalism, as spoken of by ex-Mayor Henry C. Robinson, of Hartford, Connecticut, and many more through the West who are strangers to me personally, having written me to give my views upon the subject, I have consented in so far that I will undertake a simple synopsis of what the course should embrace.

I most heartily indorse the movement, if it may be called such at this early stage. Knowing a little of the intricacies of this branch of the profession, I am going to state fully my belief as to its importance, and the necessity for a thorough training upon it. We meet almost everywhere newspaper men who are totally unfitted for the high office of public educators through the all-powerful press. The woods is full of them. We know that not one out of a thousand of those who are to-day classed as journalists is fit for that position.

I know that to be the case, because people tell me so.

I cannot call to mind to-day, in all my wide journalistic acquaintance, a solitary man who has not been pronounced an ass by one or more of my fellow-men. This is indeed a terrible state of affairs.

In many instances these harsh criticisms are made by those who do not know, without submitting themselves to a tremendous mental strain, the difference between a "lower case" q and the old Calvinistic doctrine of unanimous damnation, but that makes no difference; the true journalist should strive to please the masses. He should make his whole life a study of human nature and an earnest effort to serve the great reading world collectively and individually.

This requires a man, of course, with similar characteristics and the same general information possessed by the Almighty, but who would be willing to work at a much more moderate salary.

The reader will instantly see how difficult it is to obtain this class of men. Outside of the mental giant who writes these lines and two or three others, per- haps——

But never mind. I leave a grateful world to say that, while I map out a plan for the ambitious young journalist who might be entering upon the broad arena of newspaperdom, and preparing himself at a regularly established school for that purpose.

Let the first two years be devoted to meditation and prayer. This will prepare the young editor for the surprise and consequent profanity which in a few years he may experience when he finds in his boss editorial that God is spelled with a little g, and the peroration of the article has been taken out and carefully locked up between a death notice and the announcement of the birth of a cross-eyed infant.

The ensuing five years should be spent in becoming familiar with the surpris- ing and mirth-provoking orthography of the English language.

Then would follow three years devoted to practice with dumb bells, sand bags and slung shots, in order to become an athlete. I have found in my own journal- istic history more cause for regret over my neglect of this branch than any other. I am a pretty good runner, but aside from that I regret to say that as an athlete I am not a dazzling success.

The above course of intermediate training would fit the student to enter upon the regular curriculum.

Then set aside ten years for learning the typographical art perfectly, so that when visitors wish to look at the composing room, and ask the editor to explain the use of the "hell box," he will not have to blush and tell a gauzy lie about its being a composing stick. Let the young journalist study the mysteries of type setting, distributing, press work, gallies, italic, shooting sticks, type lice and other mechanical implements of the printer's department.

Five years should be spent in learning to properly read and correct proof, as well as how to mark it on the margin like a Chinese map of the Gunnison country.

At least fifteen years should then be devoted to the study of American politics and the whole civil service. This time could be extended five years with great profit to the careful student who wishes, of course, to know thoroughly the names and records of all public men, together with the relative political strength of each party.

He should then take a medical course and learn how to bind up contusions, apply arnica, court plaster or bandages, plug up bullet holes and prospect through the human system for buck shot. The reason of this course which should embrace five years of close study, is apparent to the thinking mind.

Ten years should then be devoted to the study of law. No thorough metropol- itan editor wants to enter upon his profession without knowing the difference between a writ of *mandamus* and other styles of profanity. He should thoroughly understand the entire system of American jurisprudence, and be as familiar with the more recent decisions of the courts as New York people are with the semi-annual letter of Governor Seymour declining the Presidency.

The student will by this time begin to see what is required of him and will enter with greater zeal upon his adopted profession.

He will now enter upon a theological course of ten years. He can then write a telling editorial on the great question of What We Shall Do To Be Saved without mixing up Calvin and Tom Paine with Judas Iscariot and Ben Butler.

The closing ten years of the regular course might be profitably used in learning a practical knowledge of cutting cord wood, baking beans, making shirts, lecturing, turning double handsprings, preaching the gospel, learning how to make a good adhesive paste that will not sour in hot weather, learning the art of scissors grinding, punctuation, capitalization, prosody, plain sewing, music, dancing, sculpting, etiquette, how to win the affections of the opposite sex, the ten commandments, every man his own teacher on the violin, croquet, rules of the prize ring, parlor magic, civil engineering, decorative art, calsomining, bicycling, base ball, hydraulics, botany, poker, calisthenics, high-low jack, international law, faro, rhetoric, fifteen-ball pool, drawing and painting, mule skinning, vocal music, horsemanship, plastering, bull whacking, etc., etc., etc.

At the age of 95 the student will have lost that wild, reckless and impulsive style so common among younger and less experienced journalists. He will emerge from the school with a light heart and a knowledge-box loaded up to the muzzle with the most useful information.

The hey day and the springtime of life will, of course, be past, but the graduate will have nothing to worry him any more, except the horrible question which is ever rising up before the journalist, as to whether he shall put his money into government four per cents or purchase real estate in some growing town.

FROM *Baled Hay*

Fun of Being a Publisher

Being a publisher is not all sunshine, joy and johnny-jump-ups, although the gentle and tractable reader may at times think so.

A letter was received two years ago by the publishers of this book, on the outside of which was the request to the "P. Master of Chicago to give to the most reliable man in Chicago and oblige."

The P. Master thereupon gave the letter to Messrs. Belford, Clarke & Co., who have sent it to me as a literary curiosity. I want it to go down to posterity, so I put it in this great work. I simply change the names, and where words are too obscure, doctor them up a little:

BUTLER, Bates county, Mo., Jan. the 2, 1881.

I have a novle fresh and pure from the pen, wich I would like to be examined by you. I wish to bring it before the public the ensuing summer. I have wrote a good deal for the press, and always with great success. I wrote once an article on the growth of pie plant wich was copied fur and wide. You may have heard of me through my poem on "The Cold, Damp Sea or the Murmuring Wave and its Sad Kerplunk."

I dashed it off one summer day for the Scabtown *Herald*.

In it, I enter the fair field of fancy and with exquisite word-painting, I lead the reader on and on till he forgets that breakfast is ready, and follows the thrilling career of Algonquin and his own fair-haired Sciataca through page after page of delirious joy and poetic rithum.

In this novle, I have wove a woof of possibilities, criss-crossed with pictures of my own wild, unfettered fancy, which makes it a work at once truthful and yet sufficiently unnatural to make it egorly sot for by the great reading world.

The plot of the novle is this:

Algonquin is a poor artist, who paints lovely sunsets and things, nights, and cuts cordwood during the day, struggling to win a competence so that he can sue for the hand of Sciataca, the wealthy daughter of a plumber.

She does not love him much, and treats him coldly; but he perseveres till one of his exquisite pictures is egorly snapt up by a wealthy man at $2. The man afterwards turns out to be Sciataca's pa.

He says unkind things of Algonquin, and intimates that he is a better artist in four-foot wood than he is as a sunset man. He says that Algonquin is more of a Michael Angelo in basswood than anywhere else, and puts a wet blanket on Sciataca's love for Algonquin.

Then Sciataca grows colder than ever to Algonquin, and engages herself to a wealthy journalist.

Just as the wedding is about to take place, Algonquin finds that he is by birth an Ohio man. Sciataca repents and marries her first love. He secures the appointment of governor of Wyoming, and they remove to Cheyenne.

Then there are many little bursts of pictureskness and other things that I would like to see in print.

I send also a picture of myself which I would like to have in the book. Tell the artist to tone down the freckles so that the features may be seen by the observer, and put on a diamond pin, so that it will have the appearance of wealth, which the author of a book generally wears.

It is not wrote very good, but that won't make any difference when it is in print.

When the reading public begins to devour it, and the scads come rolling in, you can deduct enough for to pay your expenses of printing and pressing, and send me the balance by post-office money order. Please get it on the market as soon as possible, as I need a Swiss muzzlin and some other togs suitable to my position in liturary circles.

Yours truly, LUELLA BLINKER.

What Is Literature?

A squash-nosed scientist from away up the creek, asks, "What is literature?" Cast your eye over these logic-imbued columns, you sun-dried savant from the remote precincts. Drink at the never-failing BOOMERANG springs of forgotten lore, you dropsical wart of a false and erroneous civilization. Read our "Address to the Duke of Stinking Water," or the "Ode to the Busted Snoot of a Shattered Venus De-Milo," if you want to fill up your thirsty soul with high-priced literature. Don't go around hungering for literary pie while your eyes are closed and your capacious ears are filled with bales of hay.

Table Manners of Children

Young children who have to wait till older people have eaten all there is in the house, should not open the dining-room door during the meal and ask the host if he is going to eat all day. It makes the company feel ill at ease, and lays up wrath in the parents' heart.

Children should not appear displeased with the regular courses at dinner, and then fill up on pie. Eat the less expensive food first, and then organize a picnic in the preserves afterward.

Do not close out the last of your soup by taking the plate in your mouth and pouring the liquid down your childish neck. You might spill it on your bosom, and it enlarges and distorts the mouth unnecessarily.

When asked what part of the fowl you prefer, do not say you will take the part that goes over the fence last. This remark is very humorous, but the rising generation ought to originate some new table jokes that will be worthy of the age in which we live.

Children should early learn the use of the fork, and how to handle it. This knowledge can be acquired by allowing them to pry up the carpet tacks with this instrument, and other little exercises, such as the parent mind may suggest.

The child should be taught at once not to wave his bread around over the table, while in conversation, or to fill his mouth full of potatoes, and then converse in a rich tone of voice with some one out in the yard. He might get his dinner down his trachea and cause his parents great anxiety.

In picking up a plate or saucer filled with soup or with moist food, the child should be taught not to parboil his thumb in the contents of the dish, and to avoid swallowing soup bones or other indigestible debris.

Toothpicks are generally the last course, and children should not be permitted to pick their teeth and kick the table through the other exercises. While grace is being said at table, children should know that it is a breach of good breeding to smouge fruit cake just because their parents' heads are bowed down, and their attention for the moment turned in another direction. Children ought not to be permitted to find fault with the dinner, or fool with the cat while they are eating. Boys should, before going to the table, empty all the frogs and grasshoppers out of their pockets, or those insects might crawl out during the festivities, and jump into the gravy.

If a fly wades into your jelly up to his gambrels, do not mash him with your spoon before all the guests, as death is at all times depressing to those who are at dinner, and retards digestion. Take the fly out carefully, with what naturally adheres to his person, and wipe him on the table cloth. It will demonstrate your perfect command of yourself, and afford much amusement for the company. Do not stand up in your chair and try to spear a roll with your fork. It is not good manners to do so, and you might slip and bust your crust, by so doing. Say "thank you," and "much obliged," and "beg pardon," wherever you can work in these remarks, as it throws people off their guard, and gives you an opportunity to get in your work on the pastry and other bric-a-brac near you at the time.

Dorothy Parker
(1893–1967)

FROM *Complete Stories*

The Garter

There it goes! That would be. That would happen to me. I haven't got enough trouble. Here I am, a poor, lone orphan, stuck for the evening at this foul party where I don't know a soul. And now my garter has to go and break. That's the kind of thing they think up to do to me. Let's see, what shall we have happen to her now? Well, suppose we make her garter break; of course, it's an old gag, but it's always pretty sure-fire. A lot they've got to do, raking up grammar-school jokes to play on a poor, heartsick orphan, alone in the midst of a crowd. That's the bitterest kind of loneliness there is, too. Anybody'll tell you that. Anybody that wouldn't tell you that is a rotten egg.

This couldn't have happened to me in the perfumed sanctity of my boudoir. Or even in the comparative privacy of the taxi. Oh, no. That would have been too good. It must wait until I'm cornered, like a frightened rat, in a room full of strangers. And the dressing-room forty yards away—it might as well be Sheridan. I would get that kind of break. Break, break, break, on thy cold gray stones, O sea, and I would that my tongue could utter the thoughts that arise in me. Boy, do I would that it could! I'd have this room emptied in thirty seconds, flat.

Thank God I was sitting down when the crash came. There's a commentary on existence for you. There's a glimpse of the depths to which a human being can sink. All I have to be thankful for in this world is that I was sitting down when my garter busted. Count your blessings over, name them one by one, and it will surprise you what the Lord hath done. Yeah. I see.

What is a person supposed to do in a case like this? What would Napoleon have done? I've got to keep a cool head on my shoulders. I've got to be practical. I've got to make plans. The thing to do is to avert a panic at all costs. Tell the orchestra for God's sake to keep on playing. Dance, you jazz-mad puppets of fate, and pay no attention to me. I'm all right. Wounded? Nay, sire, I'm healthy. Oh, I'm great.

The only course I see open is to sit here and hold on to it, so my stocking won't come slithering down around my ankle. Just sit here and sit here and sit here. There's a rosy future. Summer will come, and bright, bitter Autumn, and jolly old King Winter. And here I'll be, hanging on to this damned thing. Love and fame will pass me by, and I shall never know the sacred, awful joy of holding a tiny, warm body in my grateful arms. I may not set down imperishable words for posterity to marvel over; there will be for me nor travel nor riches nor wise, new friends, nor glittering adventure, nor the sweet fruition of my gracious womanhood. Ah, hell.

Won't it be nice for my lucky hosts, when everybody else goes home, and I'm still sitting here? I wonder if I'll ever get to know them well enough to hang my blushing head and whisper my little secret to them. I suppose we'll have to get pretty much used to one another. I'll probably live a long time; there won't be much wear on my system, sitting here, year in, year out, holding my stocking up. Maybe they could find a use for me, after a while. They could hang hats on me, or use my lap for an ash-tray. I wonder if their lease is up, the first of October. No, no, no, now I won't hear a word of it; you all go right ahead and move, and leave me here for the new tenants. Maybe the landlord will do me over for them. I expect my clothes will turn yellow, like Miss Havisham's, in *Great Expectations*, by Charles Dickens, an English novelist, 1812–1870. Miss Havisham had a broken heart, and I've got a broken garter. The Frustration Girls. The Frustration Girls on an Island, The Frustration Girls at the World's Fair, The Frustration Girls and Their Ice-Boat, The Frustration Girls at the House of All Nations. That's enough of that. I don't want to play that any more.

To think of a promising young life blocked, halted, shattered by a garter! In happier times, I might have been able to use the word "garter" in a sentence. Nearer, my garter thee, nearer to thee. It doesn't matter; my life's over, anyway. I wonder how they'll be able to tell when I'm dead. It will be a very thin line of distinction between me sitting here holding my stocking, and just a regulation dead body. A dead, damp, moist, unpleasant body. That's from *Nicholas Nickleby*. What am I having, anyway—An Evening with Dickens? Well, it's the best I'll get, from now on.

If I had my life to live over again, I'd wear corsets; corsets with lots of firm, true, tough, loyal-hearted garters attached to them all the way around. You'd be safe with them; they wouldn't let you down. I wouldn't trust a round garter again as far as I could see it. I or anybody else. Never trust a round garter or a Wall Street man. That's what life has taught me. That's what I've got out of all this living. If I could have just one more chance, I'd wear corsets. Or else I'd go without stockings, and play I was the eternal Summer girl. Once they wouldn't let me in the Casino at Monte Carlo because I didn't have any stockings on. So I went and found my stockings, and then came back and lost my shirt. Dottie's Travel Diary: or Highways and Byways in Picturesque Monaco, by One of Them. I wish I were in Monte Carlo right this minute. I wish I were in Carcassonne. Hell, it would look like a million dollars to me to be on St. Helena.

I certainly must be cutting a wide swath through this party. I'm making my personality felt. Creeping into every heart, that's what I'm doing. Oh, have you met Dorothy Parker? What's she like? Oh, she's terrible. God, she's poisonous. Sits in a corner and sulks all evening—never opens her yap. Dumbest woman you ever saw in your life. You know, they say she doesn't write a word of her stuff. They say she pays this poor little guy, that lives in some tenement on the lower East Side, ten dollars a week to write it and she just signs her name to it. He has to do it, the poor devil, to help support a crippled mother and five brothers and sisters; he makes buttonholes in the daytime. Oh, she's terrible.

Little do they know, the blind fools, that I'm all full of tenderness and affection, and just aching to give and give and give. All they can see is this unfortunate exterior. There's a man looking at it now. All right, baby, go on and look your head off. Funny, isn't it? Look pretty silly, don't I, sitting here holding my knee? Yes, and I'm the only one that's going to hold it, too. What do you think of that, sweetheart?

Heaven send that no one comes over here and tries to make friends with me. That's the first time I ever wished that, in all my life. What shall I do if anyone comes over? Suppose they try to shake hands with me. Suppose somebody asks me to dance. I'll just have to rock my head and say, "No spik Ingles," that's all. Can this be me, praying that nobody will come near me? And when I was getting dressed, I thought, "Maybe this will be the night that romance will come into my life." Oh, if I only had the use of both my hands, I'd just cover my face and cry my heart out.

That man, that man who was looking! He's coming over! Oh, now what? I can't say, "Sir, I have not the dubious pleasure of your acquaintance." I'm rotten at that sort of thing. I can't answer him in perfect French. Lord knows I can't get up and walk haughtily away. I wonder how he'd take it if I told him all. He looks a little too Brooks Brothers to be really understanding. The better they look, the more they think you are trying to get new with them, if you talk of Real Things, Things That Matter. Maybe he'd think I was just eccentric. Maybe he's got a humane streak, somewhere underneath. Maybe he's got a sister or a mother or something. Maybe he'll turn out to be one of Nature's noblemen.

How do you do? Listen, what would you do if you were I, and . . . ?

The Little Hours

Now what's this? What's the object of all this darkness all over me? They haven't gone and buried me alive while my back was turned, have they? Ah, now would you think they'd do a thing like that! Oh, no, I know what it is. I'm awake. That's it. I've waked up in the middle of the night. Well, isn't that nice. Isn't that simply ideal. Twenty minutes past four, sharp, and here's Baby wide-eyed as a marigold. Look at this, will you? At the time when all decent people are just going to bed, I must wake up. There's no way things can ever come out even, under this system. This is as rank as injustice is ever likely to get. This is what brings about hatred and bloodshed, that's what *this* does.

Yes, and you want to know what got me into this mess? Going to bed at ten o'clock, that's what. That spells ruin. T-e-n-space-o-apostrophe-c-l-o-c-k: ruin. Early to bed, and you'll wish you were dead. Bed before eleven, nuts before seven. Bed before morning, sailors give warning. Ten o'clock, after a quiet evening of reading. Reading—there's an institution for you. Why, I'd turn on the light and read, right this minute, if reading weren't what contributed toward driving me here. I'll show it. God, the bitter misery that reading works in this world! Everybody knows that—everybody who *is* everybody. All the best minds have been off reading for years. Look at the swing La Rochefoucauld took at it. He said that if nobody had ever learned to read, very few people would be in love. There was a man for you, and that's what *he* thought of it. Good for you, La Rochefoucauld; nice going, boy. I wish I'd never learned to read. I wish I'd never learned to take off my clothes. Then I wouldn't have been caught in this jam at half-past four in the morning. If nobody had ever learned to undress, very few people would be in love. No, his is better. Oh, well, it's a man's world.

La Rochefoucauld, indeed, lying quiet as a mouse, and me tossing and turning here! This is no time to be getting all steamed up about La Rochefoucauld. It's only a question of minutes before I'm going to be pretty darned good and sick of La Rochefoucauld, once and for all. La Rochefoucauld this and La Rochefoucauld that. Yes, well, let me tell you that if nobody had ever learned to quote, very few people would be in love with La Rochefoucauld. I bet you I don't know ten souls who read him without a middleman. People pick up those scholarly little essays that start off "Was it not that lovable old cynic, La Rochefoucauld, who said . . ." and then they go around claiming to know the master backwards. Pack of illiterates, that's all they are. All right, let them keep their La Rochefoucauld, and see if I care. I'll stick to La Fontaine. Only I'd be better company if I could quit thinking that La Fontaine married Alfred Lunt.

I don't know what I'm doing mucking about with a lot of French authors at this hour, anyway. First thing you know, I'll be reciting *Fleurs du Mal* to myself, and then I'll be little more good to anybody. And I'll stay off Verlaine too; he was always chasing Rimbauds. A person would be better off with La Rochefoucauld, even. Oh, damn La Rochefoucauld. The big Frog. I'll thank him to keep out of my head. What's he doing there, anyhow? What's La Rochefoucauld to me, or he to Hecuba? Why, I don't even know the man's first name, that's how close I ever was to *him*. What am I supposed to be, a hostess to La Rochefoucauld? That's what *he* thinks. Sez he. Well, he's only wasting his time, hanging around here. I can't help him. The only other thing I can remember his saying is that there is always something a little pleasing to us in the misfortunes of even our dearest friends. That cleans me all up with Monsieur La Rochefoucauld. *Maintenant c'est fini, ça.*

Dearest friends. A sweet lot of dearest friends *I've* got. All of them lying in swinish stupors, while I'm practically up and about. All of them stretched sodden through these, the fairest hours of the day, when man should be at his most productive. Produce, produce, produce, for I tell you the night is coming. Carlyle said that. Yes, and a fine one *he* was, to go shooting off his face on production. *Oh*, Thomas Carli-yill, what I know about *you*-oo! No, that will be enough of that. I'm not going to start fretting about Carlyle, at this stage of the game. What did he ever do that was so great, besides founding a college for Indians? (That one ought to make him spin.) Let him keep his face out of this, if he knows what's good for him. I've got enough trouble with that lovable old cynic, La Rochefoucauld—him and the misfortunes of his dearest friends!

The first thing I've got to do is get out and ship me up a complete new set of dearest friends; that's the first thing. Everything else can wait. And will somebody please kindly be so good as to inform me how I am ever going to meet up with any new people when my entire scheme of living is out of joint—when I'm the only living being awake while the rest of the world lies sleeping? I've got to get this thing adjusted. I must try to get back to sleep right now. I've got to conform to the rotten little standards of this sluggard civilization. People needn't feel that they have to change their ruinous habits and come my way. Oh, no, no; no, indeed. Not at all. I'll go theirs. If that isn't the woman of it for you! Always having to do what somebody else wants, like it or not. Never able to murmur a suggestion of her own.

And what suggestion has anyone to murmur as to how I am going to drift lightly back to slumber? Here I am, awake as high noon what with all this milling and pitching around with La Rochefoucauld. I really can't be expected to drop everything and start counting sheep, at my age. I hate sheep. Untender it may be in me, but all my life I've hated sheep. It amounts to a phobia, the way I hate them. I can tell the minute there's one in the room. They needn't think that I am going to lie here in the dark and count their unpleasant little faces for them; I wouldn't do it if I didn't fall asleep again until the middle of next August. Suppose they never get counted—what's the worst that can happen? If the number of imaginary sheep in this world remains a matter of guesswork, who is richer or poorer for it? No, sir; *I'm* not their scorekeeper. Let them count themselves, if they're so crazy mad after mathematics. Let them do their own dirty work. Coming around here, at this time of day, and asking me to count them! And not even *real* sheep, at that. Why, it's the most preposterous thing I ever heard in my life.

But there must be *something* I could count. Let's see. No, I already know by heart how many fingers I have. I could count my bills, I suppose. I could count the things I didn't do yesterday that I should have done. I could count the things I should do today that I'm not going to do. I'm never going to accomplish anything; that's perfectly clear to me. I'm never going to be famous. My name will never be writ large on the roster of Those Who Do Things. I don't do anything. Not one single thing. I used to bite my nails, but I don't even do that any more. I don't amount to the powder to blow me to hell. I've turned out to be nothing but a bit of flotsam. Flotsam and leave 'em—that's me from now on. Oh, it's all terrible.

Well. This way lies galloping melancholia. Maybe it's because this is the zero hour. This is the time the swooning soul hangs pendant and vertiginous between the new day and the old, nor dares confront the one or summon back the other. This is the time when all things, known and hidden, are iron to weight the spirit; when all ways, traveled or virgin, fall away from the stumbling feet, when all before the straining eyes is black. Blackness now, everywhere is blackness. This is the time of abomination, the dreadful hour of the victorious dark. For it is always darkest— Was it not that lovable old cynic, La Rochefoucauld, who said that it is always darkest before the deluge?

There. Now you see, don't you? Here we are again, practically back where we started. La Rochefoucauld, we are here. Ah, come on, son—how about your going your way and letting me go mine? I've got my work cut out for me right here; I've got all this sleeping to do. Think how I am going to look by daylight if this keeps up. I'll be a seamy sight for all those rested, clear-eyed, fresh-faced dearest friends of mine—the rats! My *dear*, whatever have you been doing; I thought you were so good lately. Oh, I was helling around with La Rochefoucauld till all hours; we couldn't stop laughing about your misfortunes. No, this is getting too thick, really. It isn't right to have this happen to a person, just because she went to bed at ten o'clock once in her life. Honest, I won't ever do it again. I'll go straight, after this. I'll never go to bed again, if I can only sleep now. If I can tear my mind away from a certain French cynic, *circa* 1650, and slip into lovely oblivion. 1650. I bet I look as if I'd been awake since then.

How do people go to sleep? I'm afraid I've lost the knack. I might try busting myself smartly over the temple with the night-light. I might repeat to myself, slowly and soothingly, a list of quotations beautiful from minds profound; if I can remember any of the damn things. That might do it. And it ought effectually to bar that visiting foreigner that's been hanging around ever since twenty minutes past four. Yes, that's what I'll do. Only wait till I turn the pillow; it feels as if La Rochefoucauld had crawled inside the slip.

Now let's see—where shall we start? Why—er—let's see. Oh, yes, I know one. This above all, to thine own self be true and it must follow, as the night the day, thou canst not then be false to any man. Now they're off. And once they get started, they ought to come like hot cakes. Let's see. Ah, what avail the sceptered race and what the form divine, when every virtue, every grace, Rose Aylmer, all were thine. Let's see. They also serve who only stand and wait. If Winter comes, can Spring be far behind? Lilies that fester smell far worse than weeds. Silent upon a peak in Darien. Mrs. Porter and her daughter wash their feet in soda-water. And Agatha's Arth is a hug-the-hearth, but my true love is false. Why did you die when lambs were cropping, you should have died when apples were dropping. Shall be together, breathe, and ride, so one day more am I deified, who knows but the world will end tonight. And he shall hear the stroke of eight and not the stroke of nine. They are not long, the weeping and the laughter; love and desire and hate I think will have no portion in us after we pass the gate. But none, I think, do there embrace. I think that I shall never see a poem lovely as a tree. I think I will not hang myself today. Ay tank Ay go home now.

Let's see. Solitude is the safeguard of mediocrity and the stern companion of genius. Consistency is the hobgoblin of little minds. Something is emotion re-membered in tranquility. A cynic is one who knows the price of everything and the value of nothing. That lovable old cynic is one who—oops, there's King Charles's head again. I've got to watch myself. Let's see. Circumstantial evidence is a trout in the milk. Any stigma will do to beat a dogma. If you would learn what God thinks about money, you have only to look at those to whom He has given it. If nobody had ever learned to read, very few people—

All right. That fixes it. I throw in the towel right now. I know when I'm licked. There'll be no more of this nonsense; I'm going to turn on the light and read my head off. Till the next ten o'clock, if I feel like it. And what does La Rochefoucauld want to make of that? Oh, he *will*, eh? Yes, he will! He and who else? La Rochefoucauld and *what* very few people?

Sam Pickering, Jr.
(Contemporary)

FROM *Living to Prowl*

Book Tour

Reading occasionally influences life. In the *Hartford Courant* I read an article describing a book tour made by Kaye Gibbons. To publicize her novel *Sights Unseen*, Gibbons visited thirty cities. *Walkabout Year*, my latest collection of essays, appeared in early October. "Damn," I said to Vicki, putting the paper down on the kitchen table, "I bet my Australia book would sell better if I went on a tour." "Then go on one," Vicki said, bending over and slipping a tray of cinnamon buns into the oven. I followed Vicki's advice. I walked out of the kitchen into the hall. From a hook in the closet, I removed the Akubra hat that I bought in Cairns three years ago. Then I strolled through the woods to the Cup of Sun, the first stop on my tour. I drank two cups of coffee, ate a bran muffin, and talked to Mary, Ellen, George, and Roger. Later that morning Eliza played soccer at Spring Hill. I wore the hat to the game. "Just in from the outback?" Chuck said when he saw me. "No," I said, "I'm on a book tour, and this is my second appearance." "Oh," Chuck said, pausing before asking, "Do you think the girls will win today?" "Yes," I said. I watched the game. The girls won 4–0. When I returned home, I hung the Akubra back on the hook in the closet. The tour was over, or at least the actual tour ended. My imaginary tour, however, was in full swing, stretching not just through thirty cities but through all my days, not only shaping sights unseen but so quickening them that they cast bright shadows across the hours.

Children force parents to see clearly. In a family the sun often rises and sets at high noon, preventing parents from dreaming and transforming shadows into the stuff of life. Recently the president of the United States spoke at the University of Connecticut. "Daddy," Eliza said at dinner one night, "the parents of lots of my friends received invitations to meet the president. You write books. Why weren't you invited?" Before I answered, Edward spoke. "Many people write books," he said; "Dad's not important." Edward told the truth, something that brings book tours to abrupt ends. Because my applications are always rejected, I no longer apply for literary fellowships. Now, instead of becoming gloomy as I fill out forms and realize that no matter my words the applications will fail, I only dream of success. I imagine the pages fellowships will enable me to write. When I get up from my desk after not completing an application, I feel invigorated. I am ready to wander hill and field and spinning loops through the air turn falling leaves into necklaces, strings of jewels: yellow sugar maple and black locust, crimson red maple, orange hickory, and bronze beech. Keeping imagination vital is not easy. This fall I turned down two speaking engagements because the fees offered were modest. In contrast I agreed to speak on four occasions for free. "The honorariums were so low they made me feel ordinary," I explained to Vicki. "When a person doesn't receive a fee, he is free to create an imaginary self. Money does not define him and reduce him to the everyday." "But," Edward said when I finished the explanation, "if you made the speeches, you would earn enough to buy Mommy the new refrigerator she wants."

Writers whose tours take them to faraway places meet lots of literary folk. On my tour I met only one other writer, and that was Eliza. On Eliza's desk I found an account of Hungry Bert, a young vole who spent his summer playing games instead of stocking a larder for the winter. During the first week of winter Bert stripped the shelves of his storeroom. Forced to leave his burrow to search for food, Bert suffered from the cold. " 'Just look at my hands; they are frozen,' Bert exclaimed; 'even the marrow of my bones is blue from cold!' 'That's what you get from playing kick-the-acorn instead of collecting insects for the winter!' cried a goose, flying south." Luck enabled Bert to survive "the winter of '93," as Eliza phrased it. Early in the fall a squirrel abandoned a flea-infested nest. In a corner of the nest Bert discovered a cache of acorns.

In late September fleas infested our yard. In jumping from the grass to George and Penny, they hopped into dinner table conversation. From there they bounced into Eliza's writings. While cleaning Eliza's room, I found a poem under the bed. The poem was entitled "Poppies." "The poppies grow gaily out upon the green, / Their colors are sapphires and a rosy sheen. / They bob and dance so gracefully in the blowing breeze, / While listening to the music and singing with the fleas. / If I were but a poppy in a field of grass, / I know a flute I'd play, not a horn of brass."

After book tours writers often get mail. Despite the appearance of *Walkabout Year*, I received few letters this fall. Only after my tour ended did the mail bring letters that touched on writing matters. One day I received two letters. Announcing the publication of a magazine devoted to elementary school matters, the first letter began, "Dear Literature Professional." An old friend and a literary amateur who had written a box of books wrote the second letter. Some time ago he suffered a stroke, and I wrote him, wishing him good health and describing the happy hours I spent watching the children play soccer. "Your soccer-parent days remind me of my son and me years ago," my friend said. "Now all my grandchildren are college graduates and ready to improve an imperfect world. Alas."

Unlike most writers on tour, schedule did not buckle me tightly to place and time. "Your tour," Vicki said, "sounds more like a detour." "Yes," I said, "that's the best kind of tour." One morning I drifted through Carthage, Tennessee. I didn't sign copies of my book, but I learned that Alice Blair, the fairest bud ever to bloom in the gritty soil around Mayflower, had married William Whicker from Nashville. Whicker was from a wealthy family. He grew up in a big house on Craighead and graduated from Wallace School after which he spent two lean years at Vanderbilt. Rich men often make poor husbands, and Whicker did not appreciate Alice, thinking her roots ran shallower than those of people blossoming in West Nashville. One night after she labored over dinner, Alice asked, "Darling, do I cook as well as your mother?" "My dear girl," Whicker responded, turning his fork sideways and digging at a kernel of corn lodged next to the first premolar on the left side of his face, "I come from an old and distinguished family. My mother was not a cook." Old and distinguished the Whickers may have been; brainy they were not. Before the wedding Whicker's brother Baxley visited the Blairs in Mayflower. Alice's father Nunnley was a deacon in the local church. On Sunday night Baxley accompanied Nunnley to a meeting of the church vestry. A parishioner had left the church a substantial bequest, and the vestry debated whether to spend the money on a chandelier or on a piano. Out of courtesy the vestry solicited Baxley's opinion. "If I was you," Baxley said, excavating a seam of golden wax running through his inner ear, "I'd buy a piano. You are mighty deep in the country, and you aren't going to find anybody out here who can play a chandelier."

Carthage itself enjoyed Indian summer, that quiet time between the last of the summer camp meetings and the first of the winter revivals. Taking advantage of the theological calm, Slubey Garts started a collection of sermons. "Folks tell that you are writing a book," Googoo Hooberry said to Slubey one afternoon. "Yes," Slubey answered, "although I'm just a poor weak worm creeping after Christ, I'm trying to do a little something at it." "Well," Googoo said, "keep going. You have just as much right to make a book as them that knows how." Slubey had not progressed far when I visited Carthage. He had decided on a title, written part of an invocation, and filled a spiral notebook with jottings. The title was *Like to a Saltlick,* the phrase being taken from "Come back to Christ like a saltlick," an invitation Slubey often issued during services at the Tabernacle of Love, spreading his arms wide, gazing upward, and staggering slightly, looking like, Turlow Gutheridge said, "he was carrying a giant turnip to the Smith County Fair."

Slubey liked music. He often said, "You can lead a congregation to the collection plate but without some whooping and hollering they'll just stand there." In the invocation Slubey combined his affection for music with what he thought was the dangerous spread of Catholicism in Tennessee, particularly in Nashville. "After Nashville, Carthage; after Carthage, the world," Proverbs Goforth declared one Sunday. In the invocation Slubey stated that *papist* and *Romanist* disagreed not only with his soul but also with his ear. In order to make his prose more euphonic and more pleasing to God and man, he was changing, he wrote, the *-ist* ending of *papist* and *Romanist* to *-ite*, thus producing *papite* and *Romanite.* "Christ did not build his cathedral on a cabbage stump, but on words," Slubey said, explaining that in changing *-ist* to *-ite* he was following "the divine pencil." "Edomites, Moabites, and Ammonites," he said, wandered the Holy Land, "not Edomists, Moabists, and Ammonists." "Elijah was a Tishbite, not a Tishbist; Ephron was a Hittite, not a Hittist, and Bildad was a Shuite, not a Shuist." I told Slubey that I didn't think linguists would adopt his changes. But I could be wrong. After I told Josh about Slubey's proposal, he embraced the notion wholeheartedly and immediately began calling Communists, Communites, and feminists, feminites.

Despite the invocation Slubey's notes implied that the book would contain only one critique of papite practices. Under the heading "Relics and Bamboozle" appeared a list, "pickled tongues, candied noses, and ears in aspic" followed by "the hook that caught the great fish which swallowed Jonah, the bag from one of Pharaoh's lean kine, and three hairs from the tail of the ass that Jesus rode into Jerusalem." The rest of the sermons appeared to be standard moral fare. Under "Anger," Slubey wrote, "Describe the red-mouthed man." Beneath "Spewing Hate" *Humility* appeared, followed by "bowing to a dwarf will not prevent a man from standing up again." On another page, one that I assumed referred to Gluttony, he wrote, "John the Baptist fed on locusts, but today people are not satisfied with chocolate-covered raspberries or strawberries; they want chocolate-covered watermelons." "Lazy folks," he wrote on the next page, "water the horse with the milk bucket. In spring they don't drain fields, and instead of corn they raise frogs." Under "Ravages of Cupid," he warned, "bedroom slippers are made out of banana skins. Only wingtips can ferry the soul over the bottomless ocean of corruption." Watery metaphors lay beached throughout Slubey's notes. "Many lewdsters," he wrote, "awash on the flood of sin consider sending a note to God in a bottle, begging for help and forgiveness. Alas, wine fills all the bottles in their basements, and instead of praying to God they worship drink and sink under the waves." On the same page appeared an anecdote. Although Slubey ran a pencil through the names, I was able to decipher "Horace Armitage" and "Enos Mayfield's Inn." Horace, it seems, appeared at the inn late one Saturday night. Drunk and short of money, he slapped a Gideon Bible on the bar "as security for drink." When Enos refused to accept the bible, Horace was incensed. "Why you refuse God's own word!" he shouted, staggering toward the door. "You must be an infidel."

My tour did not flow smoothly. Fatherhood forced me to return to Storrs for soccer games. On the Sunday of Columbus Day weekend, I got up at six o'clock in order to drive Edward to Lebanon for a tournament that began at eight. I returned home at 6:45 that evening, Eliza's last game having started in Willimantic at 5:10 in the afternoon. Sarah Dorr was Eliza's best friend. Sarah played on the same team as Eliza, and often I drove the girls to games. Afterward they enjoyed insulting each other, Eliza calling Sarah "doorknob" and Sarah responding with "nosepicker." When soccer did not kick books out of mind, Josh burst into my office. "Great god!" he exclaimed last Tuesday. "The woods are full of men in drag and carrying guns. Don't think about going on one of your inspirational little rambles now." "In drag?" I asked. "Yes," he said, "flaming queens in gray and green outfits." "Camouflage," I said; "the men are hunters dressed in camouflage." "No!" Josh shouted. "Soldiers wear camouflage, and no war is being fought in Mansfield. The men are queens." Early in October myth was on Josh's mind. "Remember Pygmalion," he said, "the sculptor who carved a statue of a beautiful woman and then fell so in love with his creation that he kissed it, whereupon the gods blessed him and turned her into flesh and blood?" "Sure," I said. "Supposedly, Pygmalion and his bride lived happily ever after." "Well," Josh continued, "that wouldn't happen in today's feminite environment. Now the statue would accuse Pygmalion of sexual harassment and sue him for kissing without permission."

Josh is fond of silly stories, and yesterday he insisted upon my listening to an account of a mother snake and her nineteen snakelings. The snakelings spent days practicing hissing, perfecting their technique in a pit dug for them by their mother. One day when the mother had to slither out to crawl a couple of errands, she sent her children to the den of Mrs. Pot, a neighbor. Mrs. Pot was out of her den, but when she returned and found the snakelings hissing in her pit, she sent them home. When they crawled through the front hole, the babies' mother asked why they came home so soon. "Mrs. Pot sent us," the snakelings cried. "Why that ungrateful coluber," the mother exclaimed. "Who assisted her the last time she suffered from ecdysis and couldn't see? Who nursed her when she bruised her fangs against the heel of man? Who does Mrs. Pot think she is? Her family is new to this range. Who showed her all the vole runs? Why I remember when the Pots didn't have a pit to hiss in."

I had heard Josh's story before. Instead of boring, however, repetition reassures, implying that life is comfortably circular, not linear. Yesterday's event will be tomorrow's happening, and no regimen of zeal or moral earnestness can alter the cycle. Rather than thrusting forward into the unknown, carrying banners proclaiming "progress" and "development," the person who believes life circular can relax, and riding the wheel of days, marvel at the dust pitched up by spinning time. On my tour I traveled a familiar October landscape. Fields appeared shaved, the corn stalks chopped into silage. From Horsebarn Hill the land rumpled outward in embers, trees flaming red and orange through ashy mists. In depressions between rows of stalks, lamb's quarters glowed, the stems claret and the flowers purple. Low bush huckleberry spilled down a slope in a red haze. Beneath leaves yellow crystals glittered like small sparks. In woods hayscented and New York ferns crumpled. Color leached out of fronds, transforming them into ghostly remnants of the green that rolled like water through spring. Down the hill behind the sheep barn cinnamon ferns turned ochre, looking as if they had been burned by a damp fire, cindered and rusted at the same time. Bundles of satiny sweet everlasting glowed in the dull light. Bushy and purple-stemmed asters drifted across vision looking as fragile as cirrus clouds. Canada geese honked overhead, the sound almost too familiar to hear. In contrast calls of crows jerked into awareness like wrenches tugging frozen bolts. A collar of alders pressed against the woods. Resembling gauze bandages, woolly aphids wrapped around twigs. The larvae of striped alder sawfly clung in circles to the margins of leaves and on cold mornings glistened like glazed doughnuts.

Leaves bunched across the forest floor in shag rugs. The foliage thinned. The woods turned yellow, and shadows became wispy. As sunlight sifted through black birch and sugar maple, it lost body and absorbing color floated lightly over the understory like a throw of weary lace. Thickets of spicebush turned hollows yellow. Along the border of the woods, green dried out of beaked hazelnut. For a moment the leaves turned yellow. Then splotches spread across them like measles, at first appearing red and proud but then shrinking into brown crust.

Because I had no appointments, I drifted across days. Instead of signing books, I looked for, if not the signatures, at least traces of others. On a dead star-nosed mole flies laid eggs in clutches, resembling bundles of shiny white spindles. Sagging on a spicebush were three heart-shaped balloons, all with "Happy Anniversary" printed on them. A hedge of pink hibiscus blossomed across the front of one balloon. On the second balloon horticultural artists forced peonies out of season and into the company of chicory and goldenrod. A wicker basket opened like a ventricle on the last balloon. Roses burst over the rim of the basket in scarlet spurts while in the middle of the basket a dove huddled on a nest, an anniversary being a time when home is where the heart is and when feeling pulses stronger than thought.

I followed whim through days. One damp morning I watched leaves drizzle into the Fenton River. Some surfed the air, riding up over a finger of breeze then quickly dipping and coasting into the water. Others swung through circles resembling drops tossed out by a sprinkler. Some leaves from red maples turned like corkscrews. Others with long stems fell like arrows. The river was low, and leaves drifted slowly downstream, bunching against rocks and ledges, and in worn bends rumpling together, resembling quilts pushed against headboards. Hemlocks grew along the riverbank, and needles hooked leaves, seeming to reel them in and wear them as ornaments. I walked up from the river to the raspberry field. A woodcock broke cover and flying low circled behind me. A flock of yellow-rumped warblers hurried through the scrub. Sulfur shelf fungus bloomed on a log. The leaves of staghorn sumac resembled artists' palettes running with color, green near the stems, deep orange in the middle, and red at the tips. Northern red oak grew at the edge of the field. Color swept out from then drew back into the big leaves, shimmering, making me think Neats Foot oil had been rubbed into them. White pines towered behind the oaks. Tops of the trees were green, but nearer the ground branches had broken off, and the trunks resembled heavy culverts, at their bases needles oozing out in an overflow of orange.

To see how season signed October I toured at different times. Early in the morning fibrous mists floated over lowlands. A tuft of reed canary grass resembled a scythe, the panicle bending the stem into a blade. Inside the curve hung a spider web, droplets of water silver on the silk, creating the illusion of motion, making the grass swish through the air. A bumblebee quivered chilled and dying on top of a field thistle. Seeds spilled out of milkweed in damp mats, resembling sheets of water that had frozen, melted, and frozen again, this last time into cloudy sheaves. At midday I forced my hands into open milkweed pods. The pods felt warm and oily. Sometimes I shook stalks, and a frolic of clouds blew out of the pods. Below the white hairs seeds hung swollen, arches of yellow at the bases of the hairs curving over them like minute rainbows. On Queen Anne's lace umbrels folded inward so seeds could dry. Lady bugs nested in the umbrels, the prickly seeds blankets around them. I did not tell Josh or Slubey about touring early October. Queen Anne's lace, Josh would have warned, was just the bit of nifty to spice up the gowns of men trolling the woods with guns and dressed fit to kill, hoping for a slice of the old venison. Slubey would have preached to me, accusing me of turning nature into god. I can hear Slubey now. "Instead of listening to the rustle of leaves, harken to the rustle of angels' wings."

Book tours, as Slubey might have put it, "pry open the portals of the head." At the end of a tour writers return home, having seen and heard the stuff of new stories. One evening during the middle of my tour, I drove Eliza to soccer practice. As I drove along the dirt road past the town dump, Eliza asked a question. "Daddy," she said, "what is Communism?" "Communism was," I said, "a theory of government. Like all theories it promised people better lives." I explained that the gap between theory and practice was vast, primarily, I said, because humans were flawed creatures. Self always got in the way when people tried to implement theory. "Instead of being our brothers' keepers," I said, "we have become our brothers' exploiters." "Communism," I continued, promised "a fairer distribution of income. If the United States were Communist country," I said, "I would not have the money to send you to Camp Wohelo in Maine each summer. But then some of the poor children in Hartford might have better lives." "That doesn't sound bad to me, Daddy," Eliza said. "I don't know why Americans hate Communism so much."

The practice field was four miles from our house, so I stayed at the field and talked to parents. Most parents were threads from the same financial and social fabric: doctors, teachers, lawyers, and artists. A few parents did not have means, however. On the weekend Eliza's team was scheduled to play in a tournament. The entrance fee for the tournament was fifteen dollars a child. "Is Sally looking forward to the tournament?" I said to a mother. "She'd like to play," the mother answered slowly, "but we can't come up with the fifteen dollars. Bill broke his arm six weeks ago. He hasn't worked since, and we don't have insurance." Sally played in the tournament. Afterward she baked me an apple pie. The pie was sweet. Still, as I ate it, my mind scrolled back to the conversation with Eliza. "Fifteen dollars," I thought, "from each according to his abilities. To each according to his need. Communites could teach us a lesson."

The narrative weather changed rapidly during my tour. While some stories were cloudy, others were sunny. The morning after the tournament I went to the Cup of Sun, and Ellen told me a story about Robbie, the five-year-old son of a friend. This fall Robbie started kindergarten. When he got on the bus the first day, he asked the bus driver his name. "Just call me Mr. Bus Driver," the man said. "Isn't it wonderful, Daddy," Robbie said to his father later, "that Mr. and Mrs. Driver named their little boy Bus, and when he grew up, he became a bus driver?" "Yes, son," the father said, "that's wonderful." As children age, stories told about them remain wondrous, albeit the tone changes. Edward's soccer team played most games on a field below the middle school. Parents parked cars at the school. We sat on a railing at the edge of the parking lot, watched the games, and talked about our children, then life itself. Twelve and thirteen, the boys on the team had grown prickly. "Ryan," a mother recounted, "never wears shoes out of the locker room. Last Wednesday when the temperature was below freezing, he walked barefoot across the parking lot. When he got to the car, he said, 'Boy, I'm cold.' 'Maybe, if you wore your shoes, you would be warmer,' I suggested. 'Why are you always trying to ruin my life!' he shouted, getting into the backseat and slamming the door."

Halloween is a week away, and at the Cup of Sun this morning, friends and I dallied through muffins and coffee, talking about costumes. One year when I was a graduate student, I bought several pairs of inflatable buttocks. I strapped them to my chest and backside and went to a party as an ass. Another time I purchased a plague of rubber flies. I glued a swarm to my face. Afterward I attached threads to the wings of another swarm and hung them from the brim of a battered Cavanaugh hat. Then I went to a party as Fly Face, a character from the Dick Tracy comic strip. "Costumes are fun," Mary said; "years ago a friend convinced his sweetheart to dress like a girl scout for a Halloween party. She put the outfit on in my friend's apartment, and they never got to the party." "Sort of like your book tour," George said; "you never got out of Mansfield." "Still, I bet you had almost as much fun as that scout master," Ellen said. "More," I said. "I had much more fun."

Sylvia Plath
(1932–63)

FROM *The Bell Jar*

He said, "Esther, have you ever seen a man?"

"No," I said. "Only statues."

"Well, don't you think you would like to see me?"

I didn't know what to say. My mother and my grandmother had started hinting around to me a lot lately about what a fine, clean boy Buddy Willard was, coming from such a fine, clean family, and how everybody at church thought he was a model person, so kind to his parents and to older people. . . .

"Well, all right, I guess so," I said.

I stared at Buddy while he unzipped his chino pants . . . and then took off his underpants that were made of something like nylon fishnet.

"They're cool," he explained, "and my mother says they wash easily."

Then he just stood there in front of me and I kept staring at him. The only thing I could think of was turkey neck and turkey gizzards and I felt very depressed.

Buddy seemed hurt I didn't say anything. "I think you ought to get used to me like this," he said. "Now let me see you."

But undressing in front of Buddy suddenly appealed to me about as much as having my Posture Picture taken at college, where you have to stand naked in front of a camera, knowing all the time that a picture of you stark naked, both full view and side view, is going into the college gym files to be marked A B C or D depending on how straight you are.

"Oh, some other time," I said.

Edgar Allan Poe
(1809–49)

How to Write a Blackwood Article

In the name of the Prophet—figs!
CRY OF TURKISH FIG-PEDLER

I presume everybody has heard of me. My name is the Signora Psyche Zenobia. This I know to be a fact. Nobody but my enemies ever calls me Suky Snobbs. I have been assured that Suky is but a vulgar corruption of Psyche, which is good Greek, and means "the soul" (that's me, I'm *all* soul), and sometimes "a butterfly," which latter meaning undoubtedly alludes to my appearance in my new crimson satin dress, with the sky-blue Arabian *mantelet*, and the trimmings of green *agraf-fas*, and the seven flounces of orange-colored *auriculas*. As for Snobbs—any person who should look at me would be instantly aware that my name wasn't Snobbs. Miss Tabitha Turnip propagated that report through sheer envy. Tabitha Turnip indeed! Oh, the little wretch! But what can we expect from a turnip? Wonder if she remembers the old adage about "blood out of a turnip, etc."

(Mem.: put her in mind of it the first opportunity.) (Mem.: again—pull her nose.) Where was I! Ah! I have been assured that Snobbs is a mere corruption of Zenobia, and that Zenobia was a queen (so am I. Dr. Moneypenny always calls me the Queen of Hearts), and that Zenobia, as well as Psyche, is good Greek, and that my father was "a Greek," and that consequently I have a right to our patronymic, which is Zenobia, and not by any means Snobbs. Nobody but Tabitha Turnip calls me Suky Snobbs. I am the Signora Psyche Zenobia.

As I said before, everybody has heard of me. I am that very Signora Psyche Zenobia so justly celebrated as corresponding secretary to the "Philadelphia, Regular, Exchange, Tea, Total, Young, Belles, Lettres, Universal, Experimental, Bibliographical, Association, To, Civilize, Humanity." Dr. Moneypenny made the title for us, and says he chose it because it sounded big, like an empty rumpun-cheon. (A vulgar man that sometimes, but he's deep.) We all sign the initials of the society after our names, in the fashion of the R.S.A., Royal Society of Arts—the S.D.U.K., Society for the Diffusion of Useful Knowledge, etc., etc. Dr. Money-penny says that S stands for *stale*, and that D.U.K. spells duck (but it don't), and that S.D.U.K. stands for Stale Duck, and not for Lord Brougham's Society; but then Dr. Moneypenny is such a queer man that I am never sure when he is tell-ing me the truth. At any rate we always add to our names the initials. P.R.E.T.T.Y.B.L.U.E.B.A.T.C.H.—that is to say, Philadelphia, Regular, Ex-change, Tea, Total, Young, Belles, Lettres, Universal, Experimental, Bibliographi-cal, Association, To, Civilize, Humanity—one letter for each word, which is a decided improvement upon Lord Brougham. Dr. Moneypenny will have it that our initials give our true character, but for my life, I can't see what he means.

Notwithstanding the good offices of the Doctor, and the strenuous exertions of the Association to get itself into notice, it met with no very great success un-til I joined it. The truth is, members indulged in too flippant a tone of discus-sion. The papers read every Saturday evening were characterized less by depth than buffoonery. They were all whipped syllabub. There was no investigation of first causes, first principles. There was no investigation of anything at all. There was no attention paid to that great point, the "fitness of things." In short, there was no fine writing like this. It was low—very! No profundity, no reading, no metaphysics, nothing which the learned call spirituality and which the unlearned choose to stigmatize as cant. (Dr. M. says I ought to spell "cant" with a capital K—but I know better.)

When I joined the Society it was my endeavor to introduce a better style of thinking and writing, and all the world knows how well I have succeeded. We get up as good papers now in the P.R.E.T.T.Y.B.L.U.E.B.A.T.C.H. as any to be found even in "Blackwood." I say "Blackwood," because I have been assured that the finest writing, upon every subject, is to be discovered in the pages of that justly celebrated magazine. We now take it for our model upon all themes, and are getting into rapid notice accordingly. And, after all, it's not so very diffi-cult a matter to compose an article of the genuine "Blackwood" stamp, if one only goes properly about it. Of course I don't speak of the political articles.

Everybody knows how *they* are managed, since Dr. Moneypenny explained it. Mr. Blackwood has a pair of tailor's-shears, and three apprentices who stand by him for orders. One hands him the "Times" another the "Examiner," and a third a Gulley's "New Compendium of Slang-Whang." Mr. B— merely cuts out and intersperses. It is soon done: nothing but "Examiner," "Slang-Whang," and "Times;" then "Times," "Slang-Whang," and "Examiner;" and then "Time," "Examiner," and "Slang-Whang."

But the chief merit of the magazine lies in its miscellaneous articles; and the best of these come under the head of what Dr. Moneypenny calls the *bizarreries* (whatever that may mean) and what everybody else calls the *intensities*. This is a species of writing which I have long known how to appreciate, although it is only since my late visit to Mr. Blackwood (deputed by the Society) that I have been made aware of the exact method of composition. This method is very simple, but not so much so as the politics. Upon my calling at Mr. B—'s, and making known to him the wishes of the Society, he received me with great civility, took me into his study and gave me a clear explanation of the whole process.

"My dear madam," said he, evidently struck with my majestic appearance, for I had on the crimson satin, with the green *agraffas*, and orange-colored *auriculas*, "my *dear* madam," said he, "sit down. The matter stands thus. In the first place, your writer of intensities must have very black ink, and a very big pen, with a very blunt nib. And, mark me, Miss Psyche Zenobia!" he continued, after a pause, with the most impressive energy and solemnity of manner, "mark me!— *that pen*—*must*—*never be mended!* Herein, madam, lies the secret, the soul, of intensity. I assume upon myself to say, that no individual, of however great genius, ever wrote with a good pen—understand me—a good article. You may take it for granted that when manuscript can be read it is never worth reading. This is a leading principle in our faith, to which if you cannot readily assent, our conference is at an end."

He paused. But, of course, as I had no wish to put an end to the conference, I assented to a proposition so very obvious, and one, too, of whose truth I had all along been sufficiently aware. He seemed pleased, and went on with his instructions.

"It may appear invidious in me, Miss Psyche Zenobia, to refer you to any article, or set of articles, in the way of model or study; yet perhaps I may as well call your attention to a few cases. Let me see. There was 'The Dead Alive,' a capital thing! the record of a gentleman's sensations when entombed before the breath was out of his body; full of taste, terror, sentiment, metaphysics, and erudition. You would have sworn that the writer had been born and brought up in a coffin. Then we had the 'Confessions of an Opium-eater'—fine, very fine!—glorious imagination—deep philosophy—acute speculation—plenty of fire and fury, and a good spicing of the decidedly unintelligible. That was a nice bit of flummery, and went down the throats of the people delightfully. They would have it that Coleridge wrote the paper—but not so. It was composed by my pet baboon, Juniper, over a rummer of Hollands and water, 'hot, without sugar.' " (This I could scarcely have believed had it been anybody but Mr. Blackwood, who assured me of it.) "Then there was 'The Involuntary Experimentalist,' all about a gentleman who got baked in an oven, and came out alive and well, although certainly done to a turn. And then there was 'The Diary of a Late Physician,' where the merit lay in a good rant, and indifferent Greek—both of them taking things with the public. And then there was 'The Man in the Bell,' a paper, by the bye, Miss Zenobia, which I cannot sufficiently recommend to your attention. It is the history of a young person who goes to sleep under the clapper of a church bell, and is awakened by its tolling for a funeral. The sound drives him mad, and, accordingly, pulling out his tablets, he gives a record of his sensations. Sensations are the great things, after all. Should you ever be drowned or hung, be sure and make a note of your sensations; they will be worth to you ten guineas a sheet. If you wish to write forcibly, Miss Zenobia, pay minute attention to the sensations."

"That I certainly will, Mr. Blackwood," said I.

"Good!" he replied. "I see you are a pupil after my own heart. But I must put you *au fait* to the details necessary in composing what may be denominated a genuine 'Blackwood' article of the sensation stamp, the kind which you will understand me to say I consider the best of all purposes.

"The first thing requisite is to get yourself into such a scrape as no one ever got into before. The oven, for instance,—that was a good hit. But if you have no oven or big bell at hand, and if you cannot conveniently tumble out of a balloon, or be swallowed up in an earthquake, or get stuck fast in a chimney, you will have to be contented with simply imagining some similar misadventure. I should prefer, however, that you have the actual fact to bear you out. Nothing so well assists the fancy as an experimental knowledge of the matter in hand. 'Truth is strange,' you know, 'stranger than fiction'—besides being more to the purpose."

Here I assured him I had an excellent pair of garters, and would go and hang myself forthwith.

"Good!" he replied, "do so; although hanging is somewhat hackneyed. Perhaps you might do better. Take a dose of Brandreth's pills, and then give us your sensations. However, my instructions will apply equally well to any variety of misadventure, and on your way home you may easily get knocked in the head, or run over by an omnibus, or bitten by a mad dog, or drowned in a gutter. But to proceed.

"Having determined upon your subject, you must next consider the tone, or manner, of your narration. There is the tone didactic, the tone enthusiastic, the tone natural—all commonplace enough. But then there is the tone laconic, or curt, which has lately come much into use. It consists in short sentences. Somehow thus: Can't be too brief. Can't be too snappish. Always a full stop. And never a paragraph.

"Then there is the tone elevated, diffusive, and interjectional. Some of our best novelists patronize this tone. The words must be all in a whirl, like a humming top, and make a noise very similar, which answers remarkably well instead of meaning. This is the best of all possible styles where the writer is in too great a hurry to think.

"The tone metaphysical is also a good one. If you know any big words this is your chance for them. Talk of the Ionic and Eleatic schools—of Archytas, Gorgias, and Alcmæon. Say something about objectivity and subjectivity. Be sure and abuse a man named Locke. Turn up your nose at things in general, and when you let slip anything a little *too* absurd, you need not be at the trouble of scratching it out, but just add a foot-note, and say that you are indebted for the above profound observation to the *Kritik der reinen Vernunft*, or to the *Metaphysische Anfangsgrunde der Naturwissenschaft*. This will look erudite and—and—and frank.

"There are various other tones of equal celebrity, but I shall mention only two more, the tone transcendental and the tone heterogeneous. In the former the merit consists in seeing into the nature of affairs a very great deal farther than anybody else. This second sight is very efficient when properly managed. A little reading of the 'Dial' will carry you a great way. Eschew, in this case, big words; get them as small as possible, and write them upside down. Look over Channing's poems and quote what he says about a 'fat little man with a delusive show of Can.' Put in something about the Supernatural Oneness. Don't say a syllable about the Infernal Twoness. Above all, study innuendo. Hint everything—assert nothing. If you feel inclined to say 'bread and butter,' do not by any means say it outright. You may say anything and everything *approaching* to 'bread and butter.' You may hint at buckwheat cake, or you may even go so far as to insinuate oatmeal porridge, but if bread and butter be your real meaning, be cautious, my *dear* Miss Psyche, not on any account to say 'bread and butter'!"

I assured him that I should never say it again as long as I lived. He kissed me, and continued:

"As for the tone heterogeneous, it is merely a judicious mixture, in equal proportions, of all the other tones in the world, and is consequently made up of everything deep, great, odd, piquant, pertinent, and pretty.

"Let us suppose now you have determined upon your incidents and tone. The most important portion—in fact, the soul of the whole business, is yet to be attended to; I allude to *the filling up*. It is not to be supposed that a lady, or gentleman either, has been leading the life of a bookworm. And yet above all things it is necessary that your article have an air of erudition, or at least afford evidence of extensive general reading. Now I'll put you in the way of accomplishing this point. See here!" (pulling down some three or four ordinary-looking volumes, and opening them at random). "By casting your eye down almost any page of any book in the world, you will be able to perceive at once a host of little scraps of either learning or *bel-esprit-ism,* which are the very thing for the spicing of a 'Blackwood' article. You might as well note down a few while I read them to you. I shall make two divisions: first, *Piquant Facts for the Manufacture of Similes; and second, Piquant Expressions to be introduced as occasion may require.* Write now!"—and I wrote as he dictated.

"PIQUANT FACTS FOR SIMILES. 'There were originally but three

Muses—Melete, Mneme, Aœde—meditation, memory, and singing.' You may make a great deal of that little fact if properly worked. You see it is not generally known, and looks *recherché*. You must be careful and give the thing with a downright improviso air.

"Again. 'The river Alpheus passed beneath the sea, and emerged without injury to the purity of its waters.' Rather stale that, to be sure, but, if properly dressed and dished up, will look quite as fresh as ever.

"Here is something better. 'The Persian Iris appears to some persons to possess a sweet and very powerful perfume, while to others it is perfectly scentless.' Fine that, and very delicate! Turn it about a little, and it will do wonders. We'll have something else in the botanical line. There's nothing goes down so well, especially with the help of a little Latin. Write!

" 'The *Epidendrum Flos Aeris,* of Java, bears a very beautiful flower, and will live when pulled up by the roots. The natives suspend it by a cord from the ceiling, and enjoy its fragrance for years.' That's capital! That will do for the Similes. Now for the Piquant Expressions.

"PIQUANT EXPRESSIONS. *The venerable Chinese novel Ju-Kiao-Li.'* Good! By introducing these few words with dexterity you will evince your intimate acquaintance with the language and literature of the Chinese. With the aid of this you may possibly get along without either Arabic, or Sanskrit, or Chickasaw. There is no passing muster, however, without Spanish, Italian, German, Latin, and Greek. I must look you out a little specimen of each. Any scrap will answer, because you must depend upon your own ingenuity to make it fit into your article. Now write!

" '*Aussi tendre que Zaïre'*—as tender as Zaïre—French. Alludes to the frequent repetition of the phrase, *la tendre Zaïre,* in the French tragedy of that name. Properly introduced, will show not only your knowledge of the language, but your general reading and wit. You can say, for instance, that the chicken you were eating (write an article about being choked to death by a chicken-bone) was not altogether *aussi tendre que Zaïre*. Write!

> *'Ven muerts tan ascondida,*
> *Que no te sienta venir,*
> *Porque el plazer del morir*
> *No me torne à dar la vida.'*

That's Spanish, from Miguel de Cervantes. 'Come quickly, O death! but be sure and don't let me see you coming, lest the pleasure I shall feel at your appearance should unfortunately bring me back again to life.' This you may slip in quite *à propos* when you are struggling in the last agonies with the chicken-bone. Write!

> *'Il pover' huomo che non sen' era accorto,*
> *Andava combattendo, ed era morto.'*

That's Italian, you perceive—from Ariosto. It means that a great hero, in the heat of combat, not perceiving that he had been fairly killed, continued to fight valiantly, dead as he was. The application of this to your own case is obvious; for I trust, Miss Psyche, that you will not neglect to kick for at least an hour and a half after you have been choked to death by that chicken-bone. Please to write!

'Und sterb' ich doch, so sterb' ich denn
Durch sie—durch sie!'

That's German—from Schiller. 'And if I die, at least I die—for thee—for thee!' Here it is clear that you are apostrophizing the *cause* of your disaster, the chicken. Indeed what gentleman (or lady either) of sense, *wouldn't* die, I should like to know, for a well-fattened capon of the right Molucca breed, stuffed with capers and mushrooms, and served up in a salad-bowl, with orange-jellies *en mosaïques*. Write! (You can get them that way at Tortoni's.)—Write, if you please!

"Here is a nice little Latin phrase, and rare one (one can't be too *recherché* or brief in one's Latin, it's getting so common)—*ignoratio elenchi*. He has committed an *ignoratio elenchi*, that is to say, he has understood the words of your proposition, but not the idea. The man was a *fool*, you see. Some poor fellow whom you addressed while choking with that chicken-bone, and who therefore didn't precisely understand what you were talking about. Throw the *ignoratio elenchi* in his teeth, and at once you have him annihilated. If he dare to reply, you can tell him from Lucan (here it is) that speeches are mere *anemonæ verborum*, anemone words. The anemone, with great brilliance, has no smell. Or, if he begin to bluster, you may be down upon him with *insomnia Jovis*, reveries of Jupiter—a phrase which Silius Italicus (see here!) applies to thoughts pompous and inflated. This will be sure and cut him to the heart. He can do nothing but roll over and die. Will you be kind enough to write?

"In Greek we must have something pretty—from Demosthenes, for example. Ἀυήρ δ φεύ γων και πάλιυ μαχαήσε'''ται. (Aner o pheugon kai palin makesetai.) There is a tolerably good translation of it in 'Hudibras'—

'For he that flies may fight again,
Which he can never do that's slain.'

In a 'Blackwood' article nothing makes so fine a show as your Greek. The very letters have an air of profundity about them. Only observe, madam, the astute look of that Epsilon! That Phi ought certainly to be a bishop! Was ever there a smarter fellow than that Omicron? Just twig that Tau! In short, there is nothing like Greek for a genuine sensation-paper. In the present case your application is the most obvious thing in the world. Rap out the sentence, with a huge oath, and by way of ultimatum at the good-for-nothing dunder-headed villain who couldn't understand your plain English in relation to the chicken-bone. He'll take the hint and be off, you may depend upon it."

These were all the instructions Mr. B— could afford me upon the topic of question, but I felt they would be entirely sufficient. I was, at length, able to write a genuine "Blackwood" article, and determined to do it forthwith. In taking leave of me, Mr. B— made a proposition for the purchase of the paper when written; but, as he could offer me only fifty guineas a sheet, I thought it better to let our society have it than sacrifice it for so paltry a sum. Notwithstanding this niggardly spirit, however, the gentleman showed his consideration for me in all other respects, and indeed treated me with the greatest civility. His parting words made a deep impression upon my heart, and I hope I shall always remember them with gratitude.

"My dear Miss Zenobia," he said, while the tears stood in his eyes, "is there *any*thing else I can do to promote the success of your laudable undertaking? Let me reflect! It is just possible that you may not be able, so soon as convenient, to—to—get yourself drowned, or—choked with a chicken-bone, or—or hung,—or bitten by a—but stay! Now I think me of it, there are a couple of very excellent bull-dogs in the yard—fine fellows, I assure you—savage, and all that—indeed just the thing for your money—they'll have you eaten up, *auriculas* and all, in less than five minutes (here's my watch!)—and then only think of the sensations! Here! I say—Tom!—Peter!—Dick, you villain!—let out those"—but as I was really in a great hurry, and had not another moment to spare, I was reluctantly forced to expedite my departure, and accordingly took leave *at once*— somewhat more abruptly, I admit, than strict courtesy would have otherwise allowed. . . .

Libby Reid
(Contemporary)

FROM *You Don't Have to Pet to Be Popular*

FROM *Do You Hate Your Hips More Than Nuclear War?*

Can YOU Qualify for

VIRGINITY RE-CERTIFICATION?

TAKE THIS SIMPLE

TEST

AND FIND OUT!

YES NO
☐ ☐ I haven't had a real boyfriend in 2 years

YES NO
☐ ☐ My most fullfilling emotional attachment is with my cat

YES NO
☐ ☐ Saturday nights I like to stay home alone, eat chocolate, and dwell on my problems

YES NO
☐ ☐ ERECTION means CONSTRUCTION

ANSWERS: If you think you deserve your virginity back, it's yours! CONGRATULATIONS!

This document certifies (YOUR NAME)_____ as a born again VIRGIN. All previous bad romantic encounters declared Null and Void. Go forth and begin anew.

OFFICIAL SEAL of the State of UNREQUITED LOVE

WITNESS

Dr. Betterlucknextline GOVERNOR

Agnes Repplier
(1855–1950)

FROM *Essays in Miniature*

Battle of the Babies

A warfare has been raging in our midst, the echoes of which have hardly yet died sullenly away upon either side of the Atlantic. It has been a bloodless and un-Homeric strife, not without humorous side-issues, as when Pistol and Bardolph and Fluellen come to cheer our anxious spirits at the siege of Harfleur. Its first guns were heard in New York, where a modest periodical, devoted to the training of parents, opened fire upon those time-honored nursery legends which are presumably dear to the hearts of all rightly constituted babies. The leader of this gallant foray protested vehemently against all fairy tales of a mournful or sanguinary cast, and her denunciation necessarily included many stories which have for generations been familiar to every little child. She rejected *Red Riding Hood*, because her own infancy was haunted and embittered by the evil behavior of the wolf; she would have none of *Bluebeard*, because he was a wholesale fiend and murderer; she would not even allow the pretty *Babes in the Wood*, because they tell a tale of coldhearted cruelty and of helpless suffering; while all fierce narratives of giants and ogres and magicians were to be banished ruthlessly from our shelves. Verily, reading will be but gentle sport in the virtuous days to come.

Now it chanced that this serious protest against nursery lore fell into the hands of Mr. Andrew Lang, the most lighthearted and conservative of critics, and partial withal to tales of bloodshed and adventure. How could it be otherwise with one reared on the bleak border land, and familiar from infancy with the wild border legends that Sir Walter knew and loved; with stories of Thomas the Rhymer, and the plundering Hardens, and the black witches of Loch Awe! It was natural that with the echoes of the old savage strife ringing in his ears, and with the memories of the dour Scottish bogies and warlocks lingering in his heart, Mr. Lang could but indifferently sympathize with those anxious parents who think the stories of Bluebeard and Jack the Giant Killer too shocking for infant ears to hear. Our grandmothers, he declared, were not ferocious old ladies, yet they told us these tales, and many more which we were none the worse for hearing. "Not to know them is to be sadly ignorant, and to miss that which all people have relished in all ages." Moreover, it is apparent to him, and indeed to most of us, that we cannot take even our earliest steps in the world of literature, or in the shaded paths of knowledge, without encountering suffering and sin in some shape; while, as we advance a little further, these grisly forms fly ever on before. "Cain," remarks Mr. Lang, "killed Abel. The flood drowned quite a number of persons: David was not a stainless knight, and Henry VIII was nearly as bad as Bluebeard. Several deserving gentlemen were killed at Marathon. Front de Bœuf came to an end shocking to sensibility, and to Mr. Ruskin." The *Arabian Nights, Pilgrim's Progress, Paul and Virginia*—all the dear old nursery favorites must, under the new dispensation, be banished from our midst; and the rising generation of prigs must be nourished exclusively on *Little Lord Fauntleroy*, and other carefully selected specimens of milk-and-water diet.

The prospect hardly seems inviting; but as the English guns rattled merrily away in behalf of English tradition, they were promptly met by an answering roar from this side of the water. A Boston paper rushed gallantly to the defense of the New York periodical, and gave Mr. Lang—to use a pet expression of his own— "his kail through the reek." American children, it appears, are too sensitively organized to endure the unredeemed ferocity of the old fairy stories. The British child may sleep soundly in its little cot after hearing about the Babes in the Wood; the American infant is prematurely saddened by such unmerited misfortune. "If a consensus of American mothers could be taken," says the Boston writer, "our English critic might be infinitely disgusted to know in how many nurseries these cruel tales must be changed, or not told at all to the children of less savage generations. No mother nowadays tells them in their unmitigated brutality."

Is this true, I wonder, and are our supersensitive babies reared perforce on the optimistic version of Red Riding Hood, where the wolf is cut open by the woodman, and the little girl and her grandmother jump out, safe and sound? Their New England champion speaks of the "intolerable misery"—a very strong phrase—which he suffered in infancy from having his nurse tell him of the Babes in the Wood; while the Scriptural stories were apparently every whit as unbearable and heartbreaking. "I remember," he says, "two children, strong, brave man and woman now, who in righteous rage plucked the Slaughter of the Innocents out from the family Bible." This was a radical measure, to say the least, and if many little boys and girls started in to expurgate the Scriptures in such liberal fashion, the holy book would soon present a sadly mutilated appearance. Moreover, it seems to me that such an anecdote, narrated with admirable assurance, reveals very painfully the lack of a fine and delicate spirituality in the religious training of children; of that grace and distinction which are akin to saintship, and are united so charmingly in those to whom truth has been inseparably associated with beauty. There is a painting by Ghirlandaio hanging over the altar in the chapel of the Foundling Asylum in Florence. It represents the Adoration of the Magi, and kneeling by the side of the Wise Men is a little group of the Holy Innocents, their tiny garments stained with blood, their hands clasped in prayer; while the Divine Child turns from his mother's embraces, and from the kings' rich gifts to greet the little companions who have yielded up their spotless lives for him. Now, surely those lean, brown Florentine orphans, who have always before their eyes this beautiful and tender picture, absorb through it alone a religious sentiment unfelt by American children who are familiar only with the ugly and inane prints of American Sunday-schools, in which I have known the line, "My soul doth magnify the Lord," to be illustrated by a man with a magnifying-glass in his hand. Possibly our Sunday-school scholars, being more accurately instructed as to dates, could inform the little Florentines that the Innocents were not slaughtered until after the Magi had returned to the East. But no child who had looked day after day upon Ghirlandaio's lovely picture—more appealing in its pathos than Holman Hunt's brilliant and jocund Triumph of the Innocents—could desire to pluck "in righteous rage" that chapter from the Bible. He would have at least some dim and imperfect conception of the spiritual meaning, the spiritual joy, which underlie the pain and horror of the story.

This reflection will help us in some measure to come to a decision, when we return to the vexed problem of nursery tales and legends. I believe it is as well to cultivate a child's emotions as to cultivate his manners or his morals, and the first step in such a direction is necessarily taken through the stories told him in infancy. If a consensus of mothers would reject the good old fairy tales "in their unmitigated brutality," a consensus of men of letters would render a different verdict; and such men, who have been children in their time, and who look back with wistful delight upon the familiar figures who were their earliest friends, are entitled to an opinion in the case. How admirable was the "righteous rage" of Charles Lamb, when he wanted to buy some of these same brutal fairy stories for the little Coleridges, and could find nothing but the correct and commonplace literature which his whole soul abhorred! "Mrs. Barbauld's and Mrs. Trimmer's nonsense lay in piles about," he wrote indignantly to papa Coleridge, "and have banished all the old classics of the nursery. Knowledge, insignificant and vapid as Mrs. Barbauld's books convey, must, it seems, come to a child in the shape of knowledge; and his empty noddle must be turned with conceit of his own powers when he has learnt that a horse is an animal, and that Billy is better than a horse, and such like; instead of that beautiful interest in wild tales which made the child a man, while all the time he suspected himself to be no bigger than a child."

Just such a wild tale, fantastic rather than beautiful, haunted Châteaubriand all his life—the story of Count Combourg's wooden leg, which, three hundred years after its owner's death, was seen at night walking solemnly down the steep turret stairs, attended by a huge black cat. Not at all the kind of story we would select to tell a child nowadays. By no means! Even the little Châteaubriand heard it from peasant lips. Yet in after years, when he had fought the battle of life, and fought it with success; when he had grown gray, and illustrious, and disillusioned, and melancholy, what should come back to his mind, with its old pleasant flavor of terror and mystery, but the vision of Count Combourg's wooden leg taking its midnight constitutional, with the black cat stepping softly on before? So he notes it gravely down in his Memoirs, just as Scott notes in his diary the pranks of Whippity Stourie, the Scotch bogie that steals at night into open nursery windows; and just as Heine, in gay, sunlit Paris, recalls with joy the dark, sweet, sombre tales of the witch and fairy haunted forests of Germany.

These are impressions worth recording, and they are only a few out of many which may be gathered from similar sources. That which is vital in literature or tradition, which has survived the obscurity and wreckage of the past, whether as legend, or ballad, or mere nursery rhyme, has survived in right of some intrinsic merit of its own, and will not be snuffed out of existence by any of our precautionary or hygienic measures. We could not banish Bluebeard if we would. He is as immortal as Hamlet, and when hundreds of years shall have passed over this uncomfortably enlightened world, the children of the future—who, thank Heaven, can never, with all our efforts, be born grown up—will still tremble at the bloodstained key, and rejoice when the big brave brothers come galloping up the road. We could not even rid ourselves of Mother Goose, though she, too, has her mortal enemies, who protest periodically against her cruelty and grossness. We could not drive Punch and Judy from our midst, though Mr. Punch's derelictions have been the subject of much serious and adverse criticism. It is not by such barbarous rhymes or by such brutal spectacles that we teach a child the lessons of integrity and gentleness, explain our nursery moralists, and probably they are correct. Moreover, Bluebeard does not teach a lesson of conjugal felicity, and Cinderella is full of the world's vanities, and Puss in Boots is one long record of triumphant effrontery and deception. An honest and self-respecting lad would have explained to the king that he was not the Marquis of Carabas at all; that he had no desire to profit by his cat's ingenious falsehoods, and no weak ambition to connect himself with the aristocracy. Such a hero would be a credit to our modern schoolrooms, and lift a load of care from the shoulders of our modern critics. Only the children would have none of him, but would turn wistfully back to those brave old tales which are their inheritance from a splendid past, and of which no hand shall rob them.

FROM *Counter-Currents*

I pick up a very serious and very well-written book on the Brontë sisters, and am told that if I would "touch the very heart of the mystery that was Charlotte Brontë" (I had never been aware that there was anything mysterious about this famous lady), I will find it—save the mark!—in her passionate love for children.

"We are face to face here, not with a want, but with an abyss, depth beyond depth of tenderness, arid longing, and frustration; with a passion that found no clear voice in her works because it was one with the elemental nature in her, undefined, unuttered, unutterable!"

It was certainly unuttered. It was not even hinted at in Miss Brontë's novels, nor in her voluminous correspondence. Her attitude toward children—so far as it found expression—was the arid but pardonable attitude of one who had been their reluctant caretaker and teacher. If, as we are now told, "there were moments when it was pain for Charlotte to see the children born of and possessed by other women," there were certainly hours—so much she makes clear to us— in which the business of looking after them wearied her beyond her powers of endurance. It is true that Miss Brontë said a few, a very few friendly words about these little people. She did not, like Swift, propose that babies should be cooked and eaten. But this temperate regard, this restricted benevolence, gives us no excuse for wallowing in sentiment at her expense.

Chris Rock
(Contemporary)

FROM *Rock This!*

We All Look the Same in the Dark

White people don't know how to tell the difference between one black man and another. If they could, we'd all get along. It would solve everything. But to the white man, we're all the same.

Trouble.

They see two black men together and it's a crowd. A dangerous mob. To white people, even Ed Bradley and Bryant Gumbel hanging out, waiting to cross the street together, is potentially scary. Clarence Thomas in an Adidas warm-up suit will *not* get a cab in Washington, D.C. He *will* get followed around in the mall while he tries to check out athletic footwear.

White people are so blind that they can't even tell the difference between me and a larger-than-life character like Suge Knight. But my friends, there's a **BIG FUCKING DIFFERENCE.** You can tell just by looking that one of us is not to be fucked with.

Blacks, however, can immediately distinguish between white guys. For instance: Pauly Shore and J.F.K., Jr.

See what I mean? You know immediately.

Why is this so? Because blacks have *had* to learn to differentiate. We're confronted by white faces on TV. We pay our rent to a white guy. We work for white guys. White people don't have to know anything about black people to survive. They can go their whole lives and never even know a black person.

Black people have gone to the Olympics for years, representing America. Not black people, but America. That's the problem with black people. We want to be down. We want to be cool. When other ethnic groups get dissed they form their *own* communities.

Chinese people came over here. They got dissed. They said, "Fuck you! We got Chinatown. All right? Our own thing."

Italian people came over here. They got dissed. They said, "You man, fuck you! Little Italy. All right? We got our own thing."

You ever heard of Little Africa?

Didn't think so.

Little Africa is the GHETTO.

Let's see: I don't think we created the ghetto on purpose.

Black people have it bad. At least the Chinese and Italians have their own restaurants.

That's right. We don't even have our own food. Soul food is *not* black food. It's just some nasty shit they fed to the slaves. You think a ham hock tasted good the first time the white man shoved it in our faces? No. We had to cover it in seasoning to make it work. Black people don't even have salad dressing— and *everybody* has salad dressing, even Paul Newman. Our salad dressing is hot sauce.

Mommy? Can I Say "Nigger?"

I just said "nigger" a whole lot. You probably think I shouldn't use the N-word, but that rule is just for white folks. Any black person can say "nigger" and get away with it. It's true. It's like calling your kid an idiot. Only *you* can call your kid that. Someone else calls your kid an idiot, there's a fight.

Yet some white people still wonder why black people can say "nigger" and they can't. Believe it or not, it's a very common question. I hear it all the time.

White person: Chris, can I say "nigger?"
Me: Why would you even *want* to?
White person: I don't mean anything *bad* by it. I've traveled the world. I got a yacht, I fucked Raquel Welch. Now, if I could just say "nigger," everything would be complete.
Me: No. After I smack you upside the head everything will be complete.

"Nigger" is one of those words, like "fuck," that means different things depending on how you use it.

"I love you, nigger." Good.

"You're my nigger." That's nice.

"Shut up, nigger!" Not so good.

"I'm going to kill you, nigger." You better run.

Of course, "nigger" is just a word. White people could call us anything, like "butter."

"Hey, you fucking butter! Pick that cotton, butter!"

The problem is that then they wouldn't be able to use the word "butter" for anything else. But they've got to use *something*. Next thing you know, white folks are sitting around the breakfast table with their eggs and toast, saying, "You're kidding. I can't believe it's *not* nigger."

School Daze

Hand-in-hand with my size, the experience that probably shaped my life most was being bused to school starting when I was seven years old.

It wasn't only me. Black kids in New York City and around the country got bused. That's what time it was in America. All of us were supposedly heading off to a better education. A lot of people looked at busing as this great thing:

"Ooh, we get to go to *white* schools."

I got bused from Bed-Stuy to a white school in a poor white neighborhood: Gerretson Beach, Brooklyn. It was even worse than where I lived. My parents assumed I'd get a better education in a better neighborhood. What I actually got was a worse education in a worse neighborhood. And a whole bunch of ass-whippings.

Nobody was glad to see me.

Busing's tough. I had to get up every morning at 6:00 a.m. to go to school to compete with white kids who didn't have to wake up until 8:00 a.m.

That's not fair.

One teacher said, "Oh, Chris can't read."

I thought, "No. Chris is fucking tired."

It was also hard being the only black kid in my class. Whenever they would do that lesson on slavery, everyone would turn around and look at me.

Talk about your fucking stereotypes!

(And sometimes a teacher would come to me when she was in a particular jam after school: "Mr. Rock, it appears I have locked my keys in my car. Could you help me get them out?")

Everybody knew my name. Most kids want to be popular. But not that kind of popular. I felt like Franklin in the "Peanuts" comic strip.

I've watched those "Peanuts" specials for twenty-something years, and they never let Franklin say anything. Every other character had an identifiable trait. Charlie was awkward. Lucy was a bitch. Linus was co-dependent. Schroeder loved music. Peppermint Patty was a lesbian. That's right, Peppermint Patty was a lesbian. (I'm sure if you could ask her what her favorite song is, she'd say "Constant Craving.") Anyway, they never gave Franklin anything to say.

Come on, Charles Schulz, help us out here. Give him something. Maybe a Jamaican accent.

"Hey, Charlie Brown, mon, le's go get some curry goat."

You know what's really sad, they didn't invite Franklin to any of the parties. They invited the dog, though. Snoopy would be dancing his ass off. But Franklin was barred.

This is the guy I related to. Of course, Franklin had the good fortune to be in a cartoon.

This was my real life.

Guys were always hitting me. Everybody called me nigger. The guys would put a lot of stank in it, like "Ya fuckin' nigger." The girls would be nice. They

would say, "Hi, Nigger," like it was a nickname. It caused some mild psycholog-
ical damage. I couldn't tie my shoes until I was 9, I wet the bed until I was 13,
and I still can't go to sleep without Mommy making sure the Boogie Man isn't
under the bed.

Kids are the cruelest, meanest, nastiest people on Earth. Don't put anything
past them. When the Pan Am jet blew up, people were talking about terrorists. I
said, "Those fucking kids."

Nobody knows who killed Kennedy.

I say, ask a kid.

Will Rogers
(1879–1935)

FROM *The Writings of Will Rogers*

The Older We Men Get, the More Cuckoo We Are

All I know is just what I read in the papers. Say did a fashion Magazine ever fall
into your hands? I don't mean a woman's fashion one, Lord we have all spent
half our life looking at "Laungerie" adds. But what I mean did a men's fashion
Magazine ever drop across your trail? Well my Wife dug one up somewhere, and
she has got a pretty good sense of humor, and I heard her giggling at this thing,
and asked what it was, and I am telling you that it was a great big prosperous
Magazine. There must be flocks of 'em that take that stuff serious.

Now if you have ever landed a good job, couldent seem to grab off your second million, couldent get so tropical with the Ladies, why it was because maby
you dident have on the following, as that is given in the Magazine as the "Real
ultra Calf's brains": "Black jacket single breasted, fairly shapely, it buttons with
two medium wide notch lapels. The waist coat is double breasted, narrow in its
lap, with a likable roll in its collar, and a much waisted look. Below the jacket and
waistcoat, are mull grey trousers without pleats or turn ups. These have a double
stripe. One line of white the other of biscuit color. The stripes are far enough
apart to not jarr. The boots are black, the lowers are varnished with deGniche
varnish, mixed with a little claret to make the enameled more brilliant, and pli-
able, the button tops are of dull finish French calfskin."

Now you farmers that's been hollering for relief, maby that's what the matter
with you, you havent had this "deGniche varnish mixed with a little claret."

That may be just the Mary McHaughen bill you are looking for. It says: "Below the waistcoat and jacket appear the trousers." Now you Democrats that havent got anywhere in years maby you havent been wearing your trousers below your waistcoat. In fact some of you maby havent had trousers either above or below. They say the boots are black, and then it says they button. Did you ever see a button boot? It looks like the buttons would catch on the brush when you are riding through the mosquite. There is one place in there where it says it has a "waisted look." Say I have been in style all my life and dident know it if that waisted look means what it says.

Did you ever have trousers with a biscuit colored stripe? Say there is not two women that make biscuits the same color, so any stripe is biscuit colored. And then it says, "The stripes of Biscuit and white are not close enough to jarr." Now just how close will one stripe jarr another one? Some will jarr evidently quicker than others, so you got to be careful, you may have on a pair of pants, and you feel something funny and it's your pants jarring. They are just liable to jarr right off you can't tell. There is nothing worse than a jarring pair of pants.

It tells about how the men of Palm Beach that are "Well dressed" change five times a day. "Green is the color that has made it's appearance in men's jackets, Lovatts blue green, grey greens, lapels are of a stubby character, as made by English tailors, small patterned neckwear in foulard continues." So watch your jackets. Lack of a pea green jacket has held many a good man back. Now don't by any chance throw away your old foulard ties, they are going to get some mileage out of them. You take a good small pattern tie on a smooth neck, and it ought to do from two to five hundred cocktails without showing wear. Of course on a rough neck, it will gradually wear itself frayed at the edges.

Have you given any thought much to your bathrobe? There is a thing that you must decide on. They have "bright colored terry robes, and elaborate designs, and solid color contrasted trimmings." Those are mostly worn by men that buy on margins. I have become so discouraged over the selection of my bathrobe that I sometimes think I will just get out of the tub and get right into my clothes, like I have been doing, and not monkey with one of the things.

There is a new cocoanut straw hat that is being worn by just a few of the very smartly dressed men of Palm Beach and Nassau: It's got a high "puggarree" band and a "careless" curl to the brim. Maby it will help you get your Ford order through quicker if you only had a touch of "Puggarree" to your old lid.

Now boneheads like you and I can't imagine sane people taking all this junk serious, but they do. Why if a tie has one more dot in it than the one worn by Tony Biddle, their day is spoiled. Talk about women being vain, and always primping, why say men will make a sucker out of any woman when it comes to thinking he is about the grapes, a Corset manufacturer told me that if it was not for men's corsets they would have to go out of business. Can you imagine a big hulk going in getting a corset fitted? No Sir, we can't laugh at the women any more. Men are getting their nails manicured, and even pointed and colored. They are henna'ing their hair. They are watching their diet. They are reducing everything but their head. And the funny part the older and the funnier looking they are the more Cuckoo they are. They will be rougeing their lips, and powdering their noses next.

Here is an ad in the Magazine that you will get a kick out of. "From the Montmarte, Hollywood's most fashionable Cafe, rendevoux of the smart set of Hollywood. Where the stars dine and dance comes the exclusive styles that go into Hollywood Clothes, Styles that are swagger, flattering, chosen by men to whom appearance is everything painstakingly tailored in selected fabrics, $20.00 and $25.00. A few extra Ultra at $30.00."

Maby that's what has kept you out of the movies you dident have one of those "Extra Ultra suits" at $30.00. Then there is some "Snappy" top coats at $8.00. Cost you more to check 'em than it would to buy 'em, but I am telling you men are watching their styles. That's why they all look so funny.

The Lady Mosquito Is Busy, Thanks

Well all I know is just what I read in the papers. We are always reading statistics and figures. Half of America do nothing but prepare Propaganda for the other half to read. Insurance Companies have Guys figure out the very day you will die. (In fact they won't insure till they have it investigated and find out.) Then you like a Sucker go bet them you will live longer than that. The Government can tell you how much wheat is going to be raised next year.

Everyone is figured out down to a Gnat's tooth according to some kind of statistics. Course nobody knows if the figures are right or not, you have no way of checking up on 'em. But just the other day a fellow in Atlantic City, New Jersey come through with some statistics that really ought to set us all thinking. It wasent one of those "The average working Girl makes $33 a week spends $10 for board $12 for silk stockings and the rest for lip sticks."

This was professor Thomas J. Headlee, Dr. Professor and Chief "Entomologist." (That word will stop you ignorant ones. But we got a fifty-fifty break I don't know what it means either.)

Well he delivered this address at a Convention of the New Jersey Exterminators Association duly assembled in the very heart of the Mosquito belt. So I gather from that that an Entomologist is a man that has devoted his life to a study that must include this Jersey product. He has either given his life's work for or against the Mosquito. Now it's not only what this fellow said that is of such vital interest to all of us. It's the surprise that New Jersey had such an organization called, "The New Jersey Mosquito Exterminators Inc." Anyone who has ever visited that State could not possibly understand how there could be an organization devoted to the annihalition of those Komical little rascals. And if they have got such a Society what have they been doing? Where have they been exterminating and when?

But you see that's what they been doing is holding dinners. All you do in America nowadays is get a name for some kind of Organization, then you start holding dinners. An Organization without a dinner is just impossible. Now the only Mosquitos exterminated was at the dinner. Well during the scratching and shipping and singing of the mosquitos at this Dinner, Mr. Headlee read off the following authoritative statistics.

"The normal productivity of one lone Female house Mosquito in one year is 159,875,000,000 offspring."

Now you statistic hounds get that. (There is four sets of those three figures.) So according to my remembrance of Ray's "elementary" Arithmatic, that runs us up into the Billions. So that first 159 you see there ain't nothing but BILLIONS. Now just wait and let that soak in awhile, 159 billions of offsprings.

You Mothers that think you have done something for your race when you have brought into the World two to 8 or 10 young Hyenas, you certainly can't boast after reading what the Female Mosquito has done to leave her imprint on the ankles of humanity. Now I don't know what was done at the dinner about it. Perhaps they all signed a pledge to all go out and during the coming year to exterminate as early in the season as possible one Female Mosquito, thereby lessening the yearly yield by 158 billion.

Now wait a minute. You ain't heard nothing yet. "Only half of these, or 79,937,500,000 should be counted as Pests, for they are the active, buzzing, biting, and egg laying females. The others are mere Males which do not bite and are harmless. These figures which are based on the known rate of Mosquito reproduction and which disregard infantile mortality, indicate the urgent need for control measures that begin early in the season."

Now Women, what have you got to say for yourselves? Get that, the Males are harmless, they don't bite, Buzz or lay eggs. That's great. It makes me proud I am a Male. That fellow Kipling had it right when he wrote, (or maby it was Shakespeare, or Lady Astor, or somebody over there) "The Female of the Specie is more deadly than the Male." Women denied it then and there was a great mess raised about it. But this Jersey entomologist has finally got the dope on 'em.

Now we are getting down to the "Nubbin" or main part and like all Speakers he dident explain that. It is this. He told you to "go out and exterminate a Female as early in life as possible." But he dident tell you how to distinguish the female from the Male. You are liable to go out with the best intentions in the World and kill one, and what might it turn out to be but an innocent Male. A poor Male Mosquito, that had never done a soul a wrong all its life. It had never sung to you, it had never bit you, it had never laid eggs on you. In fact it had gone through life acting in a Gentlemanly way, and here it is killed. Why? Because you havent been taught to distinguish the sex. He has given up his life this poor Mosquito has just as a Martyr to the ignorance of the human race.

What we need is Literature of two kinds. One to teach us readily to realize the sex, and the other is Pamphlets for the Female Mosquitos on Birth Control. Show them that they are not only doing their part but they are going over their Quota. Teach them that the days of the big families in Mosquitos are past, that what we want is "Fewer and better Mosquitos." Try and get 'em to move out of

Jersey and to Fifth and Park Avenue New York and let 'em see there that being prolific in offsprings is only for the "Lower Classes."

Don't try to kill off the females. Educate 'em up to modern ways. They are not so crazy about laying eggs, it's just because they think it's their duty to do it. Course the whole thing is kinder mysterious to me. I don't see how the Female can be the one that Lays all the eggs; raises all the young, does all the biting, and still has time to sing. Now some of these must kinder overlap. Now they can't bite and sing at the same time. We know that from experience. They generally don't start singing about it till the biting is over, then they crow about it. If the biting hasent been good they won't sing. I have noticed that.

Now when do they find time to raise all these children? There must be times when they can't be singing or biting. Now the way this Entomologist has left us now about the only way we have left open to do is watch a Mosquito till he bites you and then destroy him. (I mean her.) In other words, if he bites you he is a Her, and if he sings, he is a Her. Watch him and see if he lays an egg, then it's a Her.

But if he just sits around all day and don't do anything, why about the only conclusion we can come to is that it is a HE. Don't kill him, he does no harm, he just sits and revels in the accomplishments of his Wife. So when you find a Male the best thing to do is just to sit there and wait till his Wife comes between bites. "How does the Male live?" That's what they going to take up at the next dinner.

Helen Rowland
(1875–1950)

FROM *Reflections of a Bachelor Girl*

Kissing a girl, without first telling her that you love her, is as small and mean as letting a salesman take you for a free ride in an automobile when you have no intention of buying it.

★

Flinging yourself at a man's head is like flinging a bone at a cat; it doesn't fascinate him, it frightens him.

Men say they admire a woman with high ideals and principles; but it's the kind with high heels and dimples that a wife hesitates to introduce to her husband.

Never worry for fear you have broken a man's heart; at the worst it is only sprained and a week's rest will put it in perfect working condition again.

Nothing can exceed the grace and tenderness with which men make love—in novels—except the off-hand commonplaceness with which they do it in real life.

About the only sign of personal individuality that the average woman is allowed to retain after she marries is her toothbrush.

A man seldom discovers that he hasn't married his affinity until his wife begins to get crow's feet around the eyes.

Odd how a man always gets remorse confused with reform; a cold bath, a dose of bromo-selzer, and his wife's forgiveness will make him feel so moral that he will begin to patronize you.

Husbands are like the pictures in the anti-fat advertisements—so different before and after taking.

★

There are moments when the meanest of women may feel a sisterly sympathy for her husband's first wife.

★

A woman may have a great deal of difficulty getting married the first time, but after that it's easy, because where one man leads the others will follow like a flock of sheep.

When you see what some girls marry, you realize how they must hate to work for a living.

There is no such thing as a confirmed bachelor in the countries where harems are fashionable.

It isn't tying himself to one woman that a man dreads when he thinks of marrying; it's separating himself from all the others.

It's the men who are least particular about their own morals who are the most particular about a woman's; if Satan should come up here seeking a wife, he would probably demand an angel with gilt wings instead of a nice congenial little devil.

What do they know—about one another that makes every man who kisses a girl warn her so darkly and impressively not to trust any of the others?

Poverty is only a relative affair, after all; it is X minus the things you want.

The woman who is wedded to an art and also to a man pays the full penalty for that kind of bigamy.

Some men are born for marriage, some achieve marriage; but all of them live in the deadly fear that marriage is going to be thrust upon them.

A summer resort is a place where a man will resort to anything from croquet to cocktails for amusement and where a girl will resort to anything from a half-grown boy to an aged paralytic for an escort.

When a man becomes a confirmed old bachelor it is not because he has never met the one woman he could live with, but because he has never met the one woman he couldn't live without.

Don't fancy a man is serious merely because he treats you to French dinners and talks sentiment; wait until he begins to take you to cheap tables d'hôte and talks economy.

★

It is one of the mockeries of matrimony that the moment two people begin to be awfully courteous to one another round the house it is a sign they are awfully mad.

FROM *Book of Flirts*

Marvellous, oh, my Daughter, is the way of a man with women; for every man hath a *method* and each his favorite *stunt*. And the stunt that he hath found to work successfully with one damsel shall be practised upon each in turn, even unto the finest details thereof.

Behold, one man shall come unto thee saying:

"How foolish are the sentimentalists! But, as for *me*, my motives are altruistic and disinterested; and a woman's *friendship* is what I most desire." Yet, I charge thee, seek among his women "friends" and thou shalt not find an *homely* damsel in all their number.

For this is the *platonic* stunt. . . .

Yet observe how still another seeketh to be more subtle.

Mark how he sitteth afar off and talketh of love in the *abstract*; how he calleth three times a week, yet remaineth always *impersonal*; how he praiseth the shape of thine hand and admireth thy rings, yet toucheth not so much as the *tips* of thy fingers.

"Lo," he thinketh in his heart, "I shall keep her guessing. Yea, I shall wrack her soul with thoughts of how I may be brought to subjection. And when she can no longer contain her curiosity, then will she seek to *lure* me, and I shall gather her in mine arms."

And this is the *elusive* stunt.

. . . Each of these is but as a chainstitch unto a rose pattern, beside him that playeth the *frankly devoted*.

For all women are unto him as one woman—and that one *putty*.

FROM *It Must Be Thrilling to Be a Man*

It must be thrilling to be a man!

It must be wonderful always to get the best food, the best service and all the waiter's attention. . . .

It must be wonderful to feel that your morals are not your own responsibility, and that it is up to some woman to "guide you to heaven." . . .

It must be thrilling to know that you will always be "as young as you feel," and that you will be fascinating just as long as you have a few strands of hair left to plaster across your forehead.

It must be comforting to face forty without the slightest fear that you will be out of the "vamping" class—and to believe at fifty that a girl of nineteen loves you for yourself alone!

It must be consoling to know that, no matter how poor or plain, or passé you may be, you can always find some woman willing to dine with you, flirt with you—and even to marry you! . . .

It must be delightful to be able to carry all your belongings in your pockets, instead of having to struggle with a hand-bag, a vanity case, a change-purse, and half a dozen other pieces of "junk." . . .

It must be wonderful to know that, when you die, if you have managed to keep out of jail and the newspaper, everybody will speak of you as a "good man."

It must be wonderful to have someone believe everything you tell her!

It must be *wonderful* to be a man!

Charles Schulz
(1922–2000)

⭐ ⭐ ⭐

FROM **Classic Peanuts**

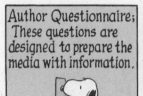

Author Questionnaire; These questions are designed to prepare the media with information.

Author's name *Snoopy*
Residence *Just a doghouse.*
Phone *unlisted*

Birth *See records at Daisy Hill Puppy Farm.*
Citizenship *Papers misplaced. These things happen.*

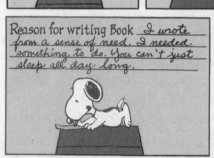

Reason for writing Book *I wrote from a sense of need. I needed something to do. You can't just sleep all day long.*

I was one of eight Beagles. We had a happy life. Lots to eat and a good cage; although looking out at the world through chicken wire can get to you after awhile.

Married *Almost once, but that's a long story.*

Schools and Colleges attended *Obedience School dropout.*

Suggestions for Promotion *If you don't promote my book, I'll get another publisher so fast it will make your head spin.*

I LIKE FILLING OUT QUESTIONNAIRES!

297

David Sedaris
(Contemporary)

FROM *Me Talk Pretty One Day*

Today's Special

It is his birthday, and Hugh and I are seated in a New York restaurant, awaiting the arrival of our fifteen-word entrées. He looks very nice, dressed in the suit and sweater that have always belonged to him. As for me, I own only my shoes, pants, shirt, and tie. My jacket belongs to the restaurant and was offered as a loan by the maître d', who apparently thought I would feel more comfortable dressed to lead a high-school marching band.

I'm worrying the thick gold braids decorating my sleeves when the waiter presents us with what he calls "a little something to amuse the palette." Roughly the size and color of a Band-Aid, the amusement floats on a shallow, muddy puddle of sauce and is topped with a sprig of greenery.

"And this would be . . . what, exactly?" Hugh asks.

"This," the waiter announces, "is our raw Atlantic swordfish served in a dark chocolate gravy and garnished with fresh mint."

"Not again," I say. "Can't you guys come up with something a little less conventional?"

"Love your jacket," the waiter whispers.

As a rule, I'm no great fan of eating out in New York restaurants. It's hard to love a place that's outlawed smoking but finds it perfectly acceptable to serve raw fish in a bath of chocolate. There are no normal restaurants left, at least in our neighborhood. The diners have all been taken over by precious little bistros boasting a menu of indigenous American cuisine. They call these meals "traditional," yet they're rarely the American dishes I remember. The patty melt has been pushed aside in favor of the herb-encrusted medallions of baby artichoke hearts, which never leave me thinking, Oh, right, those! I wonder if they're as good as the ones my mom used to make.

Part of the problem is that we live in the wrong part of town. SoHo is not a macaroni salad kind of place. This is where the world's brightest young talents come to braise carmelized racks of corn-fed songbirds or offer up their famous knuckle of flash-seared crappie served with a collar of chided ginger and cornered by a tribe of kiln-roasted Chilean toadstools, teased with a warm spray of clarified musk oil. Even when they promise something simple, they've got to tart it up—the meatloaf has been poached in seawater, or there are figs in the tuna salad. If cooking is an art, I think we're in our Dada phase.

I've never thought of myself as a particularly finicky eater, but it's hard to be a good sport when each dish seems to include no fewer than a dozen ingredients, one of which I'm bound to dislike. I'd order the skirt steak with a medley of suffocated peaches, but I'm put off by the aspirin sauce. The sea scallops look good until I'm told they're served in a broth of malt liquor and mummified litchi nuts. What I really want is a cigarette, and I'm always searching the menu in the hope that some courageous young chef has finally recognized tobacco as a vegetable. Bake it, steam it, grill it, or stuff it into littleneck clams, I just need something familiar that I can hold on to.

When the waiter brings our entrées, I have no idea which plate might be mine. In yesterday's restaurants it was possible both to visualize and to recognize your meal. There were always subtle differences, but for the most part, a lamb chop tended to maintain its basic shape. That is to say that it looked choplike. It had a handle made of bone and a teardrop of meat hugged by a thin rind of fat. Apparently, though, that was too predictable. Order the modern lamb chop, and it's likely to look no different than your companion's order of shackled pompano. The current food is always arranged into a senseless, vertical tower. No longer content to recline, it now reaches for the sky, much like the high-rise buildings lining our city streets. It's as if the plates were valuable parcels of land and the chef had purchased one small lot and unlimited air rights. Hugh's saffron linguini resembles a miniature turban, topped with architectural spires of shrimp. It stands there in the center while the rest of the vast, empty plate looks as though it's been leased out as a possible parking lot. I had ordered the steak, which, bowing to the same minimalist fashion, is served without the bone, the thin slices of beef stacked to resemble a funeral pyre. The potatoes I'd been expecting have apparently either been clarified to an essence or were used to stoke the grill.

"Maybe," Hugh says, "they're inside your tower of meat."

This is what we have been reduced to. Hugh blows the yucca pollen off his blackened shrimp while I push back the sleeves of my borrowed sport coat and search the meat tower for my promised potatoes.

"There they are, right there." Hugh uses his fork to point out what could easily be mistaken for five cavity-riddled molars. The dark spots must be my vegetable.

Because I am both a glutton and a masochist, my standard complaint, "That was so bad," is always followed by "And there was so little of it!"

Our plates are cleared, and we are presented with dessert menus. I learn that spiced ham is no longer considered just a luncheon meat and that even back issues of *Smithsonian* can be turned into sorbets.

"I just couldn't," I say to the waiter when he recommends the white chocolate and wild loganberry couscous.

"If we're counting calories, I could have the chef serve it without the crème fraîche."

"No," I say. "Really, I just couldn't."

We ask for the check, explaining that we have a movie to catch. It's only a ten-minute walk to the theater, but I'm antsy because I'd like to get something to eat before the show. They'll have loads of food at the concession stand, but I don't believe in mixing meat with my movies. Luckily there's a hot dog cart not too far out of our way.

Friends always say, "How can you eat those? I read in the paper that they're made from hog's lips."

"And . . . ?"

"And hearts and eyelids."

That, to my mind, is only three ingredients and constitutes a refreshing change of pace. I order mine with nothing but mustard, and am thrilled to watch the vendor present my hot dog in a horizontal position. So simple and timeless that I can recognize it, immediately, as food.

Henry W. Shaw
(1818–85)

Amerikans

Amerikans love caustick things; they would prefer turpentine tew colone-water, if they had tew drink either.

So with their relish of humor; they must hav it on the half-shell with cayenne.

An Englishman wants hiz fun smothered deep in mint sauce, and he iz willin tew wait till next day before he tastes it.

If you tickle or convince an Amerikan yu hav got tew do it quick.

An Amerikan luvs tew laff, but he don't luv tew make a bizzness ov it; he works, eats, and haw-haws on a canter.

I guess the English hav more wit, and the Amerikans more humor.

We havn't had time, yet, tew bile down our humor and git the wit out ov it:

The English are better punsters, but i konsider punning a sort ov literary prosti-tushun in which future happynesz iz swopped oph for the plezzure ov the moment.

Thare iz one thing i hav noticed: evryboddy that writes expeckts tew be wize or witty—so duz evrybody expect tew be saved when they die; but thare iz good reason tew beleave that the goats hereafter will be in the majority, just az the sheep are here.

Don't forget *one* thing, yu hav got tew be wize before yu kan be witty; and don't forget *two* things, a single paragraff haz made sum men immortal, while a volume haz bin wuss than a pile-driver tew others—but what would Amerikans dew if it want for their sensashuns?

Sumthing new, sumthing startling iz necessary for us az a people, and it don't make mutch matter what it iz—a huge defalkashun—a red elephant—or Jersee clams with pearls in them will answer if nothing better offers.

Englishmen all laff at us for our sensashuns, and sum ov them fret about it, and spred their feathers in distress for us, az a fond and foolish old hen, who haz hatched out a setting ov ducks' eggs, will stand on the banks ov a mill pond, wringing her hands in agony to see her brood pitch in and take a sail. *She* kant understand it, but the *Ducks* know awl about it.

N.B.—Yu kan bet 50 dollars the Ducks know all about it.

N.B.—Yu kan bet 50 dollars more that it makes no difference who hatches out an Amerikan, the fust thing he will do, iz to pitch into sumthin.

N.B.—No more bets at present.

Jean Shepherd
(1921–99)

FROM *Wanda Hickey's Night of Golden Memories and Other Disasters*

Now we were deep in the heart of the thrill-ride section of the fair. The Ferris wheel reached high up into the dark sky, its spokes outlined in colored light bulbs, jerking upward and stopping and jerking and jerking upward again. It loomed over us like a huge illuminated snowflake.

"I wanna go on the Ferris wheel!" Randy whined for the 317th time. This time, he was not to be denied.

My father bought a ticket from the man in the little booth. Off my brother went through the turnstile and into a wobbly car the color of a grape. A minute later, he was laughing down at us and sticking his tongue out as he swept up ecstatically into the night. Every few seconds, the wheel would stop and unload a car. We stood around and waved every time he went past.

Finally, the grape car stopped at the bottom. We could see the attendant in blue coveralls swing the gate open. He seemed to be arguing with the occupant. The attendant finally hollered out to the guy in the box office:

"HEY, JAKE! THIS KID WON'T GET OUT!"

"Oh, fer Chrissake, what now?" the old man muttered.

"NOW, YOU GET OUT. YOU HAD ENOUGH," said the attendant.

"WHAAAAAAAA!"

The attendant reached in and wrenched him out, fighting and kicking every inch of the way. My father took over the battle, dragging him out into the midway.

"I WANNA GO ON AGAIN!!" he screamed, but to no avail.

The big wheel started up without him as we moved on to the next attraction, Randy struggling at every step.

We tried to hurry past a merry-go-round swarming with little kids and mothers, but it was no use. Randy threatened to throw himself under it if he didn't get to ride on it. I stood with my father as he whirled round and round beside my mother, sitting on a black swan with a yellow beak. He tried to do a headstand as *The Man on the Flying Trapeze* played over and over and over and over. After the sixth ride, we managed to pull him off. He emerged slightly pale but still game. We ate a red candy cane apiece, thus setting the stage for total disaster.

My father never went on rides unless they were real gut busters. He had ventured unflinchingly onto roller coasters so violent as to turn away strong men, quaking in fear. He spotted one of his old favorites, an evil contraption known as the Whirligig Rocket Whip. We had been warned of its presence long before we arrived on the scene. Screams of horror and the flashing light of the emergency ambulance led us to the killer ride of them all.

At every fair or amusement park, there is one ride that is the yokel equivalent of the main bull ring in Madrid. This is where callow-faced youths and gorilla-armed icemen prove their virility to their admiring women. The Rocket Whip was a classic of its kind. It consisted of two bullet-shaped cars, one yellow, one red, attached to the ends of rotating arms. It revolved simultaneously clockwise and up and down. At the same time, the individual cars rotated in their own orbits. The old man, spotting the Rocket Whip, strained forward like a fire horse smelling smoke.

"Are you sure you should go on that?" My mother held back.

"Aw, come on. It'll do the kids good. Blow the stink off 'em." She didn't answer, just gazed up in fear at the mechanical devil that was now about to take on passengers. The yellow car rested near the ground, its wire-mesh door invitingly open.

He bought three tickets from the operator, who sat near the turnstile in a rocking chair, the control lever at his side.

"Let's go, kids."

We piled into the car. It was simplicity itself; two hard metal seats and a bar that clamped down over the laps of the occupants, so that their bodies didn't become actually dismembered. We sat stationary for a long moment. High above us, the occupants of the red car gazed down at us—upside down—waiting for Thor's hammer to descend.

The man yanked the lever and it began. Slowly at first, we began to spin. The landscape outside our wire-mesh cage blurred as we gained speed. We leaped skyward, up, up; paused briefly at the top of the arc at what looked like thousands of feet above ground level, then plunged straight down. Just as we neared the earth, we were whipped upward again. By this time, the car, caught by enormous forces, had begun spinning centrifugally on its own. We were trapped in a giant cream separator.

There were brief flashes of dark sky, flashing lights, gaping throngs, my old man's rolling eyes, his straw hat sailing around the interior of the car.

"Oh, no, fer Chrissake!" he yelled. A shower of loose change—quarters, nickels, dimes, pennies—sprayed out of his pockets, filled the car for an instant and was gone, spun out into the night.

"Oh, Jesus Christ! No!" he yelled again, as his brown-and-white marbled Wearever fountain pen with his name on it, given to him by the bowling team, flew out of his pocket and disappeared into the night.

Higher and higher we flew, swooping low to scream upward again. My kid brother, chalk white, whimpered piteously. I hung onto the iron bar, certain that my last hour had arrived. My head thumped the back of the car steadily as it spun.

"Ain't this fun, kids? Wow, what a ride!" shouted the old man, sweating profusely. He made a grab for his hat as it sailed past.

"Wave to Ma, kids! There she is!"

It was then that the operator turned the power on full. Everything that had gone before was only a warm-up. Our necks snapped back as the Rocket Whip accelerated. I was not touching the seat at any point. Jack-knifed over the bar, I saw that one of my shoes had been wrenched off my foot. At that moment, with no warning, my kid brother let it all go. His entire day's accumulation of goodies, now marinated and pungent, gushed out in a geyser. The car spun crazily. The air was filled with atomized spray of everything he had ingested for the past 24 hours. Down we swooped.

"My new pongee shirt!"

Soaked from head to foot, the old man struggled frantically in his seat to get out of the line of fire. It was no use. I felt it coming, too. I closed my eyes and the vacuum forces of outer space just dragged it all out of me like a suction pump. From a million miles away, I heard my old man shouting something, but it didn't matter. All I knew was that if I didn't hold onto that bar, it would be all over.

We gradually spun to a stop and finally the wire-mesh door opened. My feet touched the blessed earth. On rubbery legs, clinging weakly together, the three of us tottered past the turnstile as other victims were clamped into the torture chamber we had just left.

"Great ride, eh, folks? I left you on a little longer, 'cause I could see the kids was really enjoyin' it," said the operator, pocketing the last of my father's change as we passed through the turnstile.

"Thanks. It sure was great," said the old man with a weak smile, a bent cigarette hanging from his lips. He always judged a ride by how sick it made him. The nausea quotient of the Rocket Whip was about as high as they come.

We sat on a bench for a while to let the breeze dry off the old man's shirt, and so that our eyes could get back into focus. From all around us we could hear the whoops and hollers of people going up and down and sideways on the other rides.

There was one across from the Rocket Whip that my kid brother, who had great recuperative powers, *had* to go on. We didn't have the strength to stop him. It was a big barrel made out of some kind of shiny metal and it spun around like a cocktail shaker on its side. The people were screaming and yelling; their skirts were flying up, their shoes falling off. Randy loved it. We hung around and waited until they threw him out.

Allan Sherman
(1924–73)

FROM *The Rape of the A.P.E.**

. . . American language, an exquisitely forked tongue which enabled the speaker to remain always polite and smiling, though his message be lethal. *Basic APE* was a brilliant code, a shorthand route to competitive success. We all became fluent in it; some of us managed to be eloquent.

Basic APE	*English Translation*
She's a nice girl.	She's got buck teeth.
She's a nice girl with a great personality.	She's also crossed-eyed.

---

*A.P.E.: American Puritan Ethic

Betty Smith
(1896–1972)

FROM *A Tree Grows in Brooklyn*

In the summer of that same year, Johnny got the notion that his children were growing up ignorant of the great ocean that washed the shores of Brooklyn. Johnny felt that they ought to go out to sea in a ship. So he decided to take them for a rowboat ride at Canarsie and do a little deep-sea fishing on the side. He had never gone fishing and he'd never been in a rowboat. But that's the idea he got.

Weirdly tied up with this idea, and by a reasoning process known only to Johnny, was the idea of taking Little Tilly along on the trip. Little Tilly was the four-year-old child of neighbors whom he had never met. In fact, he had never seen Little Tilly but he got this idea that he had to make something up to her on account of her brother Gussie. It all tied up with the notion of going to Canarsie.

Gussie, a boy of six, was a murky legend in the neighborhood. A tough little hellion, with an over-developed underlip, he had been born like other babies and nursed at his mother's great breasts. But there, all resemblance to any child, living or dead, ceased. His mother tried to wean him when he was nine months old but Gussie wouldn't stand for it. Denied the breast, he refused a bottle, food or water. He lay in his crib and whimpered. His mother, fearful that he would starve, resumed nursing him. He sucked contentedly, refusing all other food, and lived off his mother's milk until he was nearly two years old. The milk stopped then because his mother was with child again. Gussie sulked and bided his time for nine long months. He refused cow's milk in any form or container and took to drinking black coffee.

Little Tilly was born and the mother flowed with milk again. Gussie went into hysterics the first time he saw the baby nursing. He lay on the floor, screaming and banging his head. He wouldn't eat for four days and he refused to go to the toilet. He got haggard and his mother got frightened. She thought it wouldn't do any harm to give him the breast just once. That was her big mistake. He was like a dope fiend getting the stuff after a long period of deprivation. He wouldn't let go.

He took all of his mother's milk from that time on and Little Tilly, a sickly baby, had to go on the bottle.

Gussie was three years old at this time and big for his age. Like other boys, he wore knee pants and heavy shoes with brass toe tips. As soon as he saw his mother unbutton her dress, he ran to her. He stood up while nursing, an elbow on his mother's knee, his feet crossed jauntily and his eyes roving around the room. Standing to nurse was not such a remarkable feat as his mother's breasts were mountainous and practically rested in her lap when released. Gussie was indeed a fearful sight nursing that way and he looked not unlike a man with his foot on a bar rail, smoking a fat pale cigar.

The neighbors found out about Gussie and discussed his pathological state in hushed whispers. Gussie's father got so that he wouldn't sleep with his wife; he said that she bred monsters. The poor woman figured and figured on a way to wean Gussie. He *was* too big to nurse, she decided. He was going for four. She was afraid his second teeth wouldn't come in straight.

One day she took a can of stove blackening and the brush and closed herself in the bedroom where she copiously blackened her left breast with the stove polish. With a lipstick she drew a wide ugly mouth with frightening teeth in the vicinity of the nipple. She buttoned her dress and went into the kitchen and sat in her nursing rocker near the window. When Gussie saw her, he threw the dice, with which he had been playing, under the washtubs and trotted over for feeding. He crossed his feet, planted his elbow on her knee and waited.

"Gussie want tiddy?" asked his mother wheedlingly.

"Yup!"

"All right. Gussie's gonna get nice tiddy."

Suddenly she ripped open her dress and thrust the horribly made-up breast into his face. Gussie was paralyzed with fright for a moment, then he ran away screaming and hid under the bed where he stayed for twenty-four hours. He came out at last, trembling. He went back to drinking black coffee and shuddered every time his eyes went to his mother's bosom. Gussie was weaned.

The mother reported her success all over the neighborhood. It started a new fashion in weaning called, "Giving the baby the Gussie."

Johnny heard the story and contemptuously dismissed Gussie from his mind. He was concerned about Little Tilly. He thought she had been cheated out of something very important and might grow up thwarted. He got a notion that a boat ride off the Canarsie shore might wipe out some of the wrong her unnatural brother had done her. He sent Francie around to ask could Little Tilly go with them. The harassed mother consented happily.

The next Sunday, Johnny and the three children set out for Canarsie. Francie was eleven years old, Neeley ten and Little Tilly well past three. Johnny wore his tuxedo and derby and a fresh collar and dicky. Francie and Neeley wore their everyday clothes. Little Tilly's mother, in honor of the day, had dressed her up in a cheap but fancy lace dress trimmed with dark pink ribbon.

On the trolley ride out, they sat in the front seat and Johnny made friends with the motorman and they talked politics. They got off at the last stop which was Canarsie and found their way to a little wharf on which was a tiny shack; a couple of water-logged rowboats bobbed up and down on the frayed ropes which held them to the wharf. A sign over the shack read:

"Fishing tackle and boats for rent."

Underneath was a bigger sign which said:

FRESH FISH TO TAKE HOME FOR SALE HERE.

Johnny negotiated with the man and, as was his way, made a friend of him. The man invited him into the shack for an eye opener saying that he himself only used the stuff for a night cap.

While Johnny was inside getting his eyes opened, Neeley and Francie pondered how a night cap could also be an eye opener. Little Tilly stood there in her lace dress and said nothing.

Johnny came out with a fishing pole and a rusty tin can filled with worms in mud. The friendly man untied the rope from the least sorry of the rowboats, put the rope in Johnny's hand, wished him luck and went back to his shack.

Johnny put the fishing stuff into the bottom of the boat and helped the children in. Then he crouched on the wharf, the bit of rope in his hand and gave instructions about boats.

"There is always a wrong and a right way to get on a boat," said Johnny, who had never been on any boat except an excursion boat once. "The right way is to give the boat a shove and then jump in it before it drifts out to sea. Like this."

He straightened up, pushed the boat from him, leaped . . . and fell into the water. The petrified children stared at him. A second before, papa had been standing on the dock above them. Now he was below them in the water. The water came to his neck and his small waxed mustache and derby hat were in the clear. His derby was still straight on his forehead. Johnny, as surprised as the children, stared at them a moment before he said:

"Don't any of you damned kids dare to laugh!"

He climbed into the boat almost upsetting it. They didn't dare laugh aloud but Francie laughed so hard inside that her ribs hurt. Neeley was afraid to look at his sister. He knew that if their eyes met, he'd burst out laughing. Little Tilly said nothing. Johnny's collar and dicky were a sodden paperish mess. He stripped them off and threw them overboard. He rowed out to sea waveringly, but with silent dignity. When he came to what he thought was a likely spot, he announced that he was going to "drop anchor." The children were disappointed when they discovered that the romantic phrase simply meant that you threw a lump of iron attached to a rope overboard.

Horrified, they watched papa squeamishly impale a muddy worm on the hook. The fishing started. It consisted in baiting the hook, casting it dramatically, waiting awhile, pulling it up minus worm and fish and starting the whole thing over again.

The sun grew bright and hot. Johnny's tuxedo dried to a stiff wrinkled greenish outfit. The children started to get a whopping case of sunburn. After what seemed hours, papa announced to their intense relief and happiness that it was time to eat. He wound up the tackle, put it away, pulled up the anchor and made for the wharf. The boat seemed to go in a circle which made the wharf get further away. Finally they made shore a few hundred yards further down. Johnny tied up the boat, told the children to wait in it and went ashore. He said he was going to treat them to a nice lunch.

He came back after a while walking sideways, carrying hot dogs, huckleberry pie and strawberry pop. They sat in the rocking boat tied to the rotting wharf, looked down into the slimy green water that smelled of decaying fish, and ate. Johnny had had a few drinks ashore which made him sorry that he had hollered at the kids. He told them they could laugh at his falling into the water if they wanted to. But somehow, they couldn't bring up a laugh. The time was past for that. Papa was very cheerful, Francie thought.

"This is the life," he said. "Away from the maddening crowd. Ah, there's nothing like going down to the sea in a ship. We're getting away from it all," he ended up cryptically.

After their amazing lunch, Johnny rowed them out to sea again. Perspiration poured down from under his derby and the wax in the points of his mustache melted causing the neat adornment to change into disorganized hair on his upper lip. He felt fine. He sang lustily as he rowed:

Sailing, sailing, over the bounding main.

He rowed and rowed and kept going around in a circle and never did get out to sea. Eventually his hands got so blistered that he didn't feel like rowing any more. Dramatically he announced that he was going to pull for the shore. He pulled and pulled and finally made it by rowing in smaller and smaller circles and making the circles come near the wharf. He never noticed that the three children were pea green in the spots where they were not beet red from the sunburn. If he had only known it, the hot dogs, huckleberry pie, strawberry pop and worms squirming on the hook weren't doing them much good.

At the wharf, he leaped to the dock and the children followed his example. All made it excepting Tilly who fell into the water. Johnny threw himself flat on the dock, reached in and fished her out. Little Tilly stood there, her lace dress wet and ruined, but she said nothing. Although it was a broiling hot day, Johnny peeled off his tuxedo jacket, knelt down and wrapped it around the child. The arms dragged in the sand. Then Johnny took her up in his arms and strode up and down the dock patting her back soothingly and singing her a lullaby. Little Tilly didn't understand a thing of all that happened that day. She didn't understand why she had been put into a boat, why she had fallen into the water or why the man was making such a fuss over her. She said nothing.

When Johnny felt that she was comforted, he set her down and went into the shack where he had either an eye opener or a night cap. He bought three flounders from the man for a quarter. He came out with the wet fish wrapped in a newspaper. He told his children that he had promised to bring home some fresh-caught fish to mama.

"The principal thing," said papa, "is that I am bringing home fish that were caught at Canarsie. It makes no difference who caught them. The point is that we went fishing and we're bringing home fish."

His children knew that he wanted mama to think he caught the fish. Papa didn't ask them to lie. He just asked them not to be too fussy about the truth. The children understood.

They boarded one of those trolley cars that had two long benches facing each other. They made a queer row. First there was Johnny in green wrinkled salt-stiff pants, an undershirt full of big holes, a derby hat and a disorderly mustache. Next came Little Tilly swallowed up in his coat with salt water dripping from under it and forming a brackish pool on the floor. Francie and Neeley came next. Their faces were brick red and they sat very rigid trying not to be sick.

People got on the car, sat across from them and stared curiously. Johnny sat upright, the fish in his lap, trying not to think of the holes in his exposed undershirt. He looked over the heads of the passengers pretending to study an Ex-Lax advertisement.

More people got on, the car got crowded but no one would sit next to them. Finally one of the fish worked its way out of the sodden newspaper and fell on the floor where it lay slimily in the dust. It was too much for Little Tilly. She looked into the fish's glazed eye, said nothing but vomited silently and thoroughly all over Johnny's tuxedo jacket. Francie and Neeley, as if waiting for that cue, also threw up. Johnny sat there with two exposed fish in his lap, one at his feet and kept staring at the ad. He didn't know what else to do.

When the grisly trip was ended, Johnny took Tilly home feeling that his was the responsibility of explaining. The mother never gave him a chance to explain. She screamed when she saw her dripping be-fouled child. She snatched the coat off, threw it into Johnny's face and called him a Jack-the-Ripper. Johnny tried and tried to explain but she wouldn't listen. Little Tilly said nothing. Finally Johnny got a word in edgewise.

"Lady, I think your little girl has lost her speech."

Whereupon the mother went into hysterics. "You did it, you did it," she screamed at Johnny.

"Can't you make her say something?"

The mother grabbed the child and shook her and shook her. "Speak!" She screamed. "Say something." Finally Little Tilly opened her mouth, smiled happily and said,

"T'anks."

Katie gave Johnny a tongue lashing and said that he wasn't fit to have children. The children in question were alternating between the chills and hot flashes of a bad case of sunburn. Katie nearly cried when she saw the ruin of Johnny's only suit. It would cost a dollar to get it cleaned, steamed and pressed and she knew it would never be the same again. As for the fish, they were found to be in an advanced state of decay and had to be thrown into the garbage can.

The children went to bed. Between chills and fever and bouts of nausea, they buried their heads under the covers and laughed silently and bed-shakingly at the remembrance of papa standing in the water.

Johnny sat at the kitchen window until far into the night trying to figure out why everything had been so wrong. He had sung many a song about ships and going down to the sea in them with a heave ho and a heave to. He wondered why it hadn't turned out the way it said in songs. The children should have returned exhilarated and with a deep and abiding love for the sea and he should have returned with a fine mess of fish. Why, oh why hadn't it turned out the way it did in a song? Why did there have to be his blistered hands and his spoiled suit and sunburn and rotting fish and nausea? Why didn't Little Tilly's mother understand the intention and overlook the result? He couldn't figure it out—he couldn't figure it out.

The songs of the sea had betrayed him.

Gloria Steinem
(Contemporary)

FROM *Outrageous Acts and Everyday Rebellions*

If Men Could Menstruate

So what would happen if suddenly, magically, men could menstruate and women could not?

Clearly, menstruation would become an enviable, boast-worthy, masculine event:

Men would brag about how long and how much.

Young boys would talk about it as the envied beginning of manhood. Gifts, religious ceremonies, family dinners, and stag parties would mark the day.

To prevent monthly work loss among the powerful, Congress would fund a National Institute of Dysmenorrhea. Doctors would research little about heart attacks, from which men were hormonally protected, but everything about cramps.

Sanitary supplies would be federally funded and free. Of course, some men would still pay for the prestige of such commercial brands as Paul Newman Tampons, Muhammad Ali's Rope-a-Dope Pads, John Wayne Maxi Pads, and Joe Namath Jock Shields—"For Those Light Bachelor Days."

Statistical surveys would show that men did better in sports and won more Olympic medals during their periods.

Generals, right-wing politicians, and religious fundamentalists would cite menstruation ("*men*-struation") as proof that only men could serve God and country in combat ("You have to give blood to take blood"), occupy high political office ("Can women be properly fierce without a monthly cycle governed by the planet Mars?"), be priests, ministers, God Himself ("He gave this blood for our sins"), or rabbis ("Without a monthly purge of impurities, women are unclean").

Male liberals or radicals, however, would insist that women are equal, just different; and that any woman could join their ranks if only she were willing to recognize the primacy of menstrual rights ("Everything else is a single issue") or self-inflict a major wound every month ("You *must* give blood for the revolution").

Street guys would invent slang ("He's a three-pad man") and "give fives" on the corner with some exchange like "Man, you lookin' *good*!"

"Yeah, man, I'm on the rag!"

TV shows would treat the subject openly. (*Happy Days:* Richie and Potsie try to convince Fonzie that he is still "The Fonz," though he has missed two periods in a row. *Hill Street Blues:* The whole precinct hits the same cycle.) So would newspapers. (SUMMER SHARK SCARE THREATENS MENSTRUATING MEN. JUDGE CITES MONTHLIES IN PARDONING RAPIST.)

Men would convince women that sex was *more* pleasurable at "that time of the month." Lesbians would be said to fear blood and therefore life itself, though all they needed was a good menstruating man.

Medical schools would limit women's entry ("they might faint at the sight of blood").

Of course, intellectuals would offer the most moral and logical arguments. Without that biological gift for measuring the cycles of the moon and planets, how could a woman master any discipline that demanded a sense of time, space, mathematics—or the ability to measure anything at all? In philosophy and religion, how could women compensate for being disconnected from the rhythm of the universe? Or for their lack of symbolic death and resurrection every month?

Menopause would be celebrated as a positive event, the symbol that men had accumulated enough years of cyclical wisdom to need no more.

Liberal males in every field would try to be kind. The fact that "these people" have no gift for measuring life, the liberals would explain, should be punishment enough.

Pam Stone
(Contemporary)

On Female Problems

I'm not much of a Southern belle. Southern women tend to be real demure. They don't like to talk about anything graphic. I had a girlfriend who told me she was in the hospital for female problems. I said, "Get real! What does that mean?" She says, "You know, *female* problems." I said, "What? You can't parallel park? You can't get credit?"

Frank Sullivan
(1892–1976)

The Cliché Expert Testifies on Literary Criticism

Q—Mr. Arbuthnot, you are an expert in the use of the cliché as applied to literary criticism?

A—I am told that I am, sir.

Q—We shall soon find out. What is this object, marked Exhibit A, which I hold?

A—That is a book.

Q—Good. What kind of book is it?

A—It is a minor American classic. Truly a prose epic.

Q—And what kind of document is it?

A—It is a valuable human document.

Q—Very good, Mr. Arbuthnot. Please continue.

A—It is a book in which the results of painstaking—or scholarly—research are embodied and it should interest all thoughtful readers. This reviewer could not put it down.

312

Q—Why not?

A—Because of its penetrating insight into the ever-present problem of international relationships. It is a sincere and moving study of an American family against the background of a small college town, and it is also a vivid and full-blooded portrayal of the life of that true child of nature, the Southern Negro.

Q—How is it written?

A—It is written with sympathy, pathos, and kindly humor. It throws a clear light on a little-understood subject and is well worth reading.

Q—How is it illustrated?

A—Profusely. It is original in conception, devoid of sentimentality, highly informative, consistently witty, and rich in color. Place it on your required-reading list.

Q—Why?

A—Because it strikes a new note in fiction. Mystery and suspense crowd its pages. The author has done an encyclopedic job of blending fact and fiction, and the result is an authentic drama of social revolution, a definite contribution to proletarian literature, and an important addition to frontier literature.

Q—Told with a wealth of what?

A—Told with a wealth of detail.

Q—And how portrayed?

A—Realistically portrayed, in staccato prose. For sheer brilliance of style there has been nothing like it since *Moby Dick*. Rarely does a narrative move at such a fast pace.

Q—What is it a shrewd comment on?

A—The American scene. It marks a red-letter day in American literature. It is capital entertainment.

Q—What pervades it?

A—A faint tinge of irony.

Q—And how is it translated?

A—Ably. It is a penetrating study in abnormal psychology, and unlike most scientific works, it is written in language understandable to the layman. It belongs in the front rank of modern picaresque literature. Ideology.

Q—I beg your pardon?

A—I said ideology. Also catharsis, and nuances of feeling.

Q—What about them?

A—Well, they have to come in somewhere.

Q—I see. Now, to return to the minor American classic, Mr. Arbuthnot. Would you call it a subtle and arresting piece of work?

A—Certainly I would. Why do you suppose I'm an expert in the use of the cliché? I'd also call it an honest attempt to depict, a remarkable first novel, a veritable masterpiece, a genuine contribution to literature, a really fine study in contemporary manners, a thrilling saga of life in frontier days, and the most impressive study of degeneration since Zola. It bids fair to go down as one of the great biographies of all time, including *Moby Dick*. In short, it has unusual merit.

Q—How does it augur?

A—It augurs well for the future of the author.

Q—And how does it end?

A—It ends upon a distinct note of despair. It is a work of art.

Q—I'm glad you liked it, Mr. Arbuthnot.

A—Who said I liked it?

Q—Well, didn't you like it?

A—Certainly not.

Q—Why not?

A—Because it is, one fears, mawkishly sentimental and, one regrets, faintly pretentious. It is destructive rather than constructive. Curiously enough, it does not carry conviction. Strangely enough, it lacks depth. Oddly enough, the denouement is weak. It is to be regretted that the title is rather misleading and it need hardly be pointed out that the book as a whole lacks cohesion and sparkle. I am very much afraid, one regrets, that it falls definitely into the hammock school of fiction. And of course, like all first novels, it is autobiographical. Frankly, it doesn't quite come off.

Q—I'm glad you told me. I won't buy it.

A—Ah, but in spite of its faults it contains much of real value, and in the opinion of the present reviewer it would be the long-awaited great American novel except for one serious defect.

Q—What is that?

A—It lacks an index.

Q—Mr. Arbuthnot, it is easy to see that you have earned your spurs in the field of literary criticism. So much for the book. Now, observe this object I hold here in my hand, marked Exhibit B. What is it?

A—That? *That* is an *author*.

Q—Whose are those italics, Mr. Arbuthnot?

A—The italics are mine.

Q—What kind of author is this?

A—A promising young author who will bear watching.

Q—What does he write?

A—Powerful first novels. Or important first novels.

Q—What kind of story-teller is he?

A—He's a born story-teller.

Q—What kind of satirist is he?

A—A satirist of the first order.

Q—Tell us more about this interesting creature.

A—Well, he cannot be lightly dismissed. He is undoubtedly to be reckoned with, one feels, as a definite force in American literature.

Q—Why?

A—Because his work plainly shows the influence of Joyce, Hemingway, Proust, Gertrude Stein, and Virginia Woolf. Here is an authentic talent from which we may expect great things, for he is a writer of no mean ability and he knows whereof he writes.

Q—So what do you do?

A—So I hail him. And I acclaim him. He has a keen ear for the spoken word. He also has a flair. He sets out to tell. He deals with themes, or handles them. He captures moods. His execution is brilliant, his insight is poetic, his restraint is admirable, and he has a sense of values. He writes hard-bitten, full-bodied, fine-grained novels of the soil, with a telling use of the American language. There is something almost uncanny in his ability to look into men's souls. Not since *Moby Dick* has an American author displayed such a knowledge of human nature. And he paints a vivid word picture and works on a vast canvas.

Q—How?

A—With consummate artistry. He writes with commendable frankness.

Q—Using what kind of style?

A—Using a limpid prose style. He has a real freshness of approach that stamps him as an artist in the true sense of the word. He culls his material, and his niche in the hall of literary fame seems secure.

Q—I'm glad you like him, Mr. Arbuthnot.

A—But I don't.

Q—No? Why not?

A—Because his talent is plainly superficial and ephemeral. He has an unfortunate habit of allowing his personality to obtrude. His book is badly documented, and not the least of his many irritating mannerisms is his addiction to inexcusable typographical errors. His book is full of clichés, and he does not make his characters live and feel and breathe. And he writes with one eye on Hollywood.

Q—You mean to tell me that a cad like that has the audacity to call himself an author?

A—Well, now, don't be too hard on him. Although he decidedly does not justify his early promise, it is as yet too early to evaluate his work. Want to know about the plot?

Q—Yes, indeed. What about the plot?

A—The plot is like Mae West.

Q—I give up. Why?

A—Because it is well rounded and fully developed. But unlike Mae West, it is marred by structural weaknesses.

Q—What kind of structural weaknesses?

A—Inherent structural weaknesses. It is motivated, of course. And its threads are cunningly woven into a harmonious texture by the deft hand of a skilled literary craftsman.

Q—Just one thing more, Mr. Arbuthnot. How many kinds of readers are there?

A—Four: casual, average, gentle, and constant.

Q—Mr. Arbuthnot, I think that about finishes. I can't thank you enough for having come here today to help us out.

A—It has been a pleasure—a vivid, fascinating, significant, vigorous, timely, urbane, breath-taking, mature, adequate, nostalgic, unforgettable, gripping, articulate, engrossing, poignant, and adult pleasure to be of service to you, sir.

Linda Sunshine
(Contemporary)

FROM *Women Who Date Too Much (And Those Who Should Be So Lucky)*

The Woman Who Mistook Her Blind Date for a Potential Husband

Everyone knows that the best policy is to not expect miracles from life. "I didn't want to be rich," Kate (Mrs. Zero) Mostel once claimed, "I just wanted enough to get the couch reupholstered."

Still, when you go out on a blind date, it's hard not to entertain the following fantasy:

The doorbell rings. You get up from your dressing table, take one last lingering look at yourself in the mirror, and nod with approval. You open the front door.

He stands in the doorway, but you can barely see his face behind all of those enormous yellow roses he's holding in his hands. He presents you with the bouquet.

He is incredibly tall and looks like a cross between William Hurt, Tom Cruise, and the guy you loved madly in sixth grade.

His crooked smile reveals his vulnerability, a great set of real white teeth, and a neat dimple in his left cheek.

He is rendered speechless by your beauty and falls instantly in love with you.

The next day, you discover he is a millionaire brain surgeon/criminal lawyer who pilots his own Lear jet and owns an oceanfront summer house in Southampton.

Say hello to your dream blind date.

Say good-bye to reality.

The blind date is genuine proof that truth is stranger than fiction. The facts speak for themselves:

A perfect stranger calls you up. You have an extremely uncomfortable conversation, which you both pretend to enjoy. He asks you to see a movie that you have no interest in seeing. You worry about what to wear, what he'll look like, and whether you'll have anything to talk to him about.

In your heart of hearts, you know you will have a terrible time, the date will be a total washout. But, still, you have an anxiety attack if your hair frizzes while you are getting ready for him to arrive.

Your tendency during this initial stage of anxiety is to curse the friend or relative responsible for arranging the date. Try to avoid hating this person.

It is best to remember that the people who set you up on a blind date have the best of intentions, really they do. You need to keep this in mind, because the truth is you can never, never believe what anyone tells you when they describe the person you are being fixed up with.

If you're told, for instance, that your blind date looks like a movie star; you're not told that the movie star is Meat Loaf.

If you're told that your blind date is a great catch, you're not told that his wife's alimony lawyer has been trying to catch the guy for months.

If you're told this is a match made in heaven; you're not told it was on an off-day.

If you're told your blind date is an old-fashioned guy, you're not told that this applies mainly to his clothes.

But, hey! You're single, and although your phone rings constantly, it's always your mother calling you.

It is a well-known fact, by the way, that the worst blind dates, bar none, are those arranged by your mother. It doesn't matter whether the guy is a district attorney, a genius, a best-selling writer. If your mother found him, he's a geek.

Regardless, you want to take advantage of every opportunity, so you accept blind date after blind date. Eventually, however, your inner psyche begins to rebel.

Your cousin Rhonda offers to fix you up with her brother's accountant, but instead you choose to stay home and watch *St. Elsewhere.*

Your best friend meets a great new guy and you forget to ask: Does he have any single friends?

You make a firm decision that blind dating is not for you. You begin to consider the alternatives: celibacy or surrogate dating.

Judy Tenuta
(Contemporary)

FROM *The Power of Judyism*

All the great love stories are based on some poor pining plankton who can't pounce on the petite princess of his dreams. Look at *Wuthering Heights*. Do you think for one minute that if Cathy surrendered to Heathcliff he would be half as crazy about her? No way. He was in love with his fantasy of that floozie. Even after Cathy marries some society squid that she doesn't love, Heathcliff pursues her and says, "Cathy, nothing can come between our love; not even you." What a great line. Women the world over dream about such passionate prose from some pumped-up parasite.

Cathy says, "Heathcliff, I'm married. Why did you come after me?"

He says, "Because you willed it."

Could you hemorrhage, heifers?

Heathcliff repeats, "I'm here because you willed it, Cathy." How could she not melt? I'm yelling, "Cathy, you fool, lay down already, loosen your lovesick loins." But Cathy is no fool, she knows that as a true romantic, giving in to love would be the death of lust. So she spurns Heathcliff again and he is even more mental about possessing her.

Why can't we petite flowers in the real world find a passionate love puppy like Heathcliff? Because they do not exist. Neither do Romeos or Othellos. These guys can afford to be passionate about their Juliets and Desdemonas because they don't have to earn a living like every other mortal toad.

James Thurber and E. B. White
(1896–1961) (1899–1985)

FROM *Is Sex Necessary? Or, Why You Feel the Way You Do*

The Sexual Revolution: Being a Rather Complete Survey of the Entire Sexual Scene

The sexual revolution began with Man's discovery that he was not attractive to Woman, as such. The lion had his mane, the peacock his gorgeous plumage, but Man found himself in a three-button sack suit. His masculine appearance not only failed to excite Woman, but in many cases it only served to bore her. The result was that Man found it necessary to develop attractive personal traits to off-set his dull appearance. He learned to say funny things. He learned to smoke, and blow smoke rings. He learned to earn money. This would have been a solution to his difficulty, but in the course of making himself attractive to Woman by developing himself mentally, he inadvertently became so intelligent an animal that he saw how comical the whole situation was.

Thus, at the very start of the sexual revolution, Man faced one very definite problem: in becoming mentally "aware," he had become intellectually critical, and had discovered that it was increasingly difficult to make up his mind whether he really desired any one woman, however capable he was of getting her. It was the heyday of monogamy, and in order to contemplate marriage, it was necessary for a man to decide on One Particular Woman. This he found next to impossible, for the reason that he had unconsciously set up so many mental barriers and hazards.

Let me mention a few.

(1) The fear that his fiancée might get fat inside of a few years. To any mentally alert man, this thought was a strong deterrent. Quite often the man met the girl's parents. He would quickly size up her mother and make a mental calculation as to how long it would be before the daughter was in the same boat. Somehow, it took the bloom off the romance. If he was not fortunate enough to meet the parents of the young lady, he was quite apt to note things about her own conformation that seemed prophetic. A slight thickness in the neck, a trace of rotundity in the bosom, a touch too much ankle. In these portents he found much discomfort, and was quite likely to call the engagement off.

(2) The use of a word, phrase, or punctuation mark by his fiancée that annoyed him. In these early days of the sex awakening, it was not at all uncommon to find examples of the girl's using some slight phrase which had a grating effect. It was often the case that the man was literarily inclined—because literary inclinations were early found to be advantageous in sex, almost as advantageous, in fact, as the peacock's tail—and if this was the case the man was doubly sensitive to the curious little crudities, niceties, whimsies, and circumlocutions which women were afflicted with. I am thinking at the moment of the case of a young man who, in his junior year in college, had found the girl he believed ideal for him to marry, and then one day learned, quite by accident, that she was in the habit of using the word "Howdy" as a form of salutation. He did not like "Howdy," although he did not know why. Days and nights he spent trying to reconcile himself to the idea of it, weighing the young lady's extreme beauty and affability against her one flaw. In the end he decided he could not stomach it, and broke the troth.

(3) Difference in height. If a man fell in love with a woman taller than himself (which sometimes happened), he became morose from dwelling on the objections to such an alliance. This particular situation usually had a way of settling itself automatically: there were so many reasons, real or imaginary, why the man felt that the marriage was impossible, that just the mere business of thinking about them broke him in health and he died, leaving a margin of several weeks before the date of the wedding.

(4) The suspicion that if he waited twenty-four hours, or possibly less, he would likely find a lady even more ideally suited to his taste than his fiancée. Every man entertained such a suspicion. Entertained it royally. He was greatly strengthened in his belief by the fact that he kept catching a fleeting glimpse of this imaginary person—in restaurants, in stores, in trains. To deny the possibility of her existence would be, he felt, to do a grave injustice to her, to himself, and to his fiancée. Man's unflinching desire to give himself and everybody else a square deal was the cause of much of his disturbance. Man had become, you see, a thinking being. He had come to know enough about permutations and combinations to realize that with millions of Caucasian females to choose from, the chances of his choosing the ideal mate were almost zero.

So matters went. Man, we have seen, had begun to develop himself so that he would be attractive to Woman, and in doing so had made Woman of doubtful attraction to *him*. He had become independent. He had become critical. He had become scared. Sex was awakening and it was all Man could do to keep from laughing.

Woman, on her part, saw dimly what was going on in the world. She saw it through the sweet haze of Dream. She caught glimpses of it in the mirror of her Narcissistic soul.★ Woman was at the crossroads. She had many ways open

---

★This is the first mention in this article of Narcissism. You'll hear more about it, don't worry.

to her, but she chose one: *she chose to imitate Man.* At a time when sex was in transition, she had the bad judgment to begin a career of independence for herself, in direct imitation of her well-meaning mate. She took up smoking. She began to earn money (not much, but some). She drank. She subordinated domesticity to individuality—of which she had very little. She attained to a certain independence, a cringing independence, a wistful, half-regretful state. Men and women both became slightly regretful: men regretted that they had no purple tail to begin with, women that they had ever been fools enough to go to work. Women now "understood life," but life had been so much more agreeable in its original mystery.

And now we come to Sex.* Woman, observing that her mate went out of his way to make himself entertaining, rightly surmised that sex had something to do with it. From that she logically concluded that sex was recreational rather than procreational. (The small, hardy band of girls who failed to get this point were responsible for the popularity of women's field hockey in this country, 1911–1921.) As though in a vision, the "right to be sexual" came to women. They fell to with a will. For thousands of years they had been content merely to be amiable, and now they were going to be sexual. The transition from amiability to sexuality was revolutionary.† It presented a terrific problem to Woman, because in acquiring and assuming the habits that tended to give her an equality with Man, she discovered that she necessarily became a good deal *like* Man. The more she got like him, the less he saw in her. (Or so he liked to think, anyway.) Just as soon as she began to put her own sex on an even basis, she found that he lost interest. Her essential Narcissism (pleasure of looking in a mirror) was met by his Begonia-ism (concept of the potted plant). Things got so that Woman spent *all* her time admiring herself in mirrors, and Man, discouraged, devoted himself quietly to raising begonias, which are fairly easy to raise. Sex atrophied.

But, as I say, sex was in the transition stage. Woman soon began to outgrow her Narcissism and was satisfied to snatch quick glances of herself in make-shift mirrors, such as the backs of watches, the shiny fenders of automobiles, plate-glass windows, subway weighing machines, and such. Convinced that sex was not sin, she set out joyously to study it. How hard she studied has recently been apparent, even to persons who read only a few books a year.

New York became the capital of the sexual revolution. It was conveniently located, had a magnificent harbor,‡ a high mortality rate, and some of the queerest-shaped apartments to be found anywhere. There are apartments in New York in which one must step across an open bathtub in going from the kitchen to the bedroom; any unusual layout like that arouses sexual desire and brings people pouring into New York from other cities. New York became the Mecca

---

*Are you glad?

†Zaner claims it was also amusing.

‡New York has one of the finest harbors in the world.

for young ladies from the South and from the Middle West whose minds were not quite made up about sexual freedom, but who thought that if they could once get to New York and into an irregular apartment, the answer might come to them.

Their mothers were against it.

"Now what can you get in New York that you can't get right here at home?" their mothers said.

"Concerts, new plays, and the opera," the daughters invariably replied. There has never, to my knowledge, been a case of a young lady telling her mother that she wanted to go to New York because she was seeking an outlet for her erotic eagerness. It was always concerts that she wanted. Often it turned out to be concerts that she got.

When she arrived in New York and secured her unfurnished apartment (usually in West Fourth Street), her mental elation was so great and her activity in making parchment lamp shades so unabating that for the first couple of weeks she let sex go. Women are notoriously apt to get off the track; no man ever was diverted from the gratification of his desires by a parchment lamp shade. At any rate, the young lady was so tired at night she could hardly keep her eyes open, much less her mind. Furthermore, she was beginning to have *Schmalhausen* trouble. *Schmalhausen* trouble is a common ailment among girls in their twenties. It usually attacks girls who have taken a small apartment (*schmalhausen*) and are reading the behaviorism essays of Samuel D. Schmalhausen. The effect of sitting within narrow walls and absorbing a wide viewpoint breaks down their health. The pain that they suffer during this period is caused by their discovery of the lyrical duality, or two-sidedness, of life—a discovery that unbalances all sensitive young ladies in whom sex cries for expression. Even in a New York apartment there are two sides to everything, and this particularly applies to a girl's potential sexuality.★

Let me explain this duality.

The very fact that the young lady had settled in the vicinity of Sheridan Square indicates that there was a strong vein of poetry in her. She saw life (and sex) through a lyrical haze which tended to accentuate its beauty by softening its truths. The whole purpose and scheme of poetry is to heighten the tenderness and essential goodness of life by a musical elaboration of its traditional worth.† Well, when the young lady allowed the lyrical possibilities of love to work on her mind, it made her mad to remember how candid she had been the night before in discussing contraception with the commercial artist who lived downstairs. It grew to be a big question in her own mind, just what her emancipation ought to consist of: whether it meant having lemon skins and gin stoppers in the washbasin and talking freely of exhibitionism and voyeurism,

---

★Girls with a bad case of Schmalhausen sometimes saw as many as three sides to sex.
†See Tithridge's "Poetry," but don't read it.

or whether it meant being the recipient of some overwhelmingly beautiful passion which her poetical soul still prescribed but which she knew couldn't exist because she was so widely read. To stall for time she would make another lamp shade.

Days slipped by. Always there was conflict in her soul. She had plunged into the "candor régime" whole-heartedly; she could enter a roomful of people and say almost anything at all. She also went in for nudity—another outlet for sex eagerness. She dallied in the bath, lay around the apartment without any clothes on, appeared scantily clad at her door when the laundryman called to collect, and week-ends went swimming naked in the moonlight with other young people. (Incidentally, when she saw what a man looked like without any clothes on, the old *Schmalhausen* trouble came back stronger than ever.)

By and by, because of this very uncertainty of soul, a kind of orderliness of habit crept into her life. Unable to decide whether sex was the poem she half believed it to be or the casual episode she had schooled herself to think it was, she compromised by practically giving sex the air. She now held a good job and was earning well. Candor and nudity, with an occasional bit of exhibitionism, began to satisfy her completely. She was growing older. The apartment was nicely decorated now and teeming with lamp shades. She held some good in- dustrial stocks and had developed an ambition to write. She became content to be literary rather than sexual. She became, in other words, that most dangerous of all by-products of the Sexual Revolution—a biologico-cultural type. She had a way of leading young men on into exhilarating topics, and sitting with them in provocative attitudes, and then putting on her hat and going quietly home to bed. In short, New York was now home to this girl, this biologico-cultural lady, and she was in a fair way to step placidly into a good old-fashioned marriage when the right man came along.

And he usually did, the poor yap.

John Trumbull
(1750–1831)

FROM **The Progress of Dulness, 1772–1773**

A College Education

Two years thus spent in gathering knowledge,
The lad sets forth t'unlade at college,
While down his sire and priest attend him,
To introduce and recommend him;
Or if detain'd, a letter's sent
Of much apocryphal content,
To set him forth, how dull soever,
As very learn'd and very clever;
A genius of first emission,
With burning love for erudition;
So studious he'll outwatch the moon
And think the planets set too soon.
He had but little time to fit in;
Examination too must frighten.
Depend upon't he must do well,
He knows much more than he can tell;
Admit him, and in little space
He'll beat his rivals in the race;
His father's incomes are but small,
He comes now, if he comes at all.
    So said, so done, at college now
He enters well, no matter how;
New scenes awhile his fancy please,
But all must yield to love of ease.
In the same round condemn'd each day,
To study, read, recite and pray;
To make his hours of business double—
He can't endure th' increasing trouble;
And finds at length, as times grow pressing,
All plagues are easier than his lesson.
With sleepy eyes and count'nance heavy,
With much excuse of *non paravi*,

324

Much absence, *tardes* and *egresses*,
The college-evil on him seizes.
Then ev'ry book, which ought to please,
Stirs up the seeds of dire disease;
Greek spoils his eyes, the print's so fine,
Grown dim with study, or with wine;
Of Tully's Latin much afraid,
Each page, he calls the doctor's aid;
While geometry, with lines so crooked,
Sprains all his wits to overlook it.
His sickness puts on every name
Its cause and uses still the same;
'Tis tooth-ache, cholic, gout or stone,
With phases various as the moon;
But though through all the body spread,
Still makes its cap'tal seat, the head.
In all diseases, 'tis expected,
The weakest parts be most infected.

Mark Twain
(1835–1910)

Speech on the Babies

[At the banquet, in Chicago, given by the army of the Tennessee to their first commander, General U. S. Grant, November 1879. The fifteenth regular toast was "The Babies—as they comfort us in our sorrows, let us not forget them in our festivities."]

I like that. We have not all had the good fortune to be ladies. We have not all been generals, or poets, or statesmen; but when the toast works down to the babies, we stand on common ground. It is a shame that for a thousand years the world's banquets have utterly ignored the baby, as if he didn't amount to anything. If you will stop and think a minute—if you will go back fifty or one hundred years to your early married life, and recontemplate your first baby—you will remember that he amounted to a good deal, and even something over. You soldiers all know that when that little fellow arrived at family headquarters you had to hand in your resignation. He took entire command. You became his lackey, his mere body-servant, and you had to stand around too. He was not a commander who made allowances for time, distance, weather, or anything else. You had to execute his orders whether it was possible or not. And there was only one form of marching in his manual of tactics, and that was the double-quick. He treated you with every sort of insolence and disrespect, and the bravest of you didn't dare say a word. You could face the death-storm at Donelson and Vicksburg, and give back blow for blow; but when he clawed your whiskers, and pulled your hair, and twisted your nose, you had to take it. When the thunders of war were sounding in your ears, you set your faces toward the batteries and advanced with steady tread; but when he turned on the terrors of his war-whoop, you advanced in the other direction, and mighty glad of the chance too. When he called for soothing-syrup, did you venture to throw out any side remarks about certain services being unbecoming an officer and a gentleman? No. You got up and *got* it. When he ordered his pap-bottle, and it was not warm, did you talk back? Not you. You went to work and *warmed* it. You even descended so far in your menial office as to take a suck at that warm, insipid stuff yourself, to see if it was right—three parts water to one of milk, and a touch of sugar to modify the colic, and a drop of peppermint to kill those immortal hiccoughs. I can taste the stuff yet. And how many things you learned as you went along! Sentimental young folks still take stock in that beautiful old saying, that when the baby smiles in his sleep, it is because the angels are whispering to him. Very pretty, but too thin—simply wind on the stomach, my friends. If the baby proposed to take a walk at his usual hour, two o'clock in the morning, didn't you rise up promptly and remark, with a mental addition which would not improve a Sunday-school book *much*, that that was the very thing you were about to propose yourself?

Oh! you were under good discipline, and as you went fluttering up and down the room in your undress uniform, you not only prattled undignified baby-talk, but even turned up your martial voices and tried to *sing*!—"Rock-a-by baby in the tree-top," for instance. What a spectacle for an army of the Tennessee! And what an affliction for the neighbours, too; for it is not everybody within a mile around that likes military music at three in the morning. And when you had been keeping this sort of thing up two or three hours, and your little velvet-head intimated that nothing suited him like exercise and noise, what did you do? ("Go on!") You simply *went* on until you dropped in the last ditch. The idea that a *baby* doesn't *amount* to anything! Why, *one* baby is just a house and a front yard full by itself. *One* baby can furnish more business than you and your whole Interior Department can attend to. He is enterprising, irrepressible, brimful of lawless activities. Do what you please, you can't make him stay on the reservation. Sufficient unto the day is one baby. As long as you are in your right mind don't you ever pray for twins. Twins amount to a permanent riot, and there ain't any real difference between triplets and an insurrection.

Yes, it was high time for a toast-master to recognise the importance of the babies. Think what is in store for the present crop! Fifty years from now we shall all be dead, I trust, and then this flag, if it still survive (and let us hope it may), will be floating over a Republic numbering 200,000,000 souls, according to the settled laws of our increase. Our present schooner of State will have grown into a political leviathan—a *Great Eastern*. The cradled babies of to-day will be on deck. Let them be well trained, for we are going to leave a big contract on their hands.

Among the three or four million cradles now rocking in the land are some which this nation would preserve for ages as sacred things, if we could know which ones they are. In one of these cradles the unconscious Farragut of the future is at this moment teething—think of it!—and putting in a world of dead earnest, unarticulated, but perfectly justifiable profanity over it, too. In another the future renowned astronomer is blinking at the shining Milky Way with but a languid interest—poor little chap!—and wondering what has become of that other one they call the wet-nurse. In another the future great historian is lying—and doubtless will continue to lie until his earthly mission is ended. In another the future president is busying himself with no profounder problem of state than what the mischief has become of his hair so early; and in a mighty array of other cradles there are now some 60,000 future office-seekers, getting ready to furnish him occasion to grapple with that same old problem a second time. And in still one more cradle, somewhere under the flag, the future illustrious commander-in-chief of the American armies is so little burdened with his approaching grandeurs and responsibilities as to be giving his whole strategic mind at this moment to trying to find out some way to get his big toe into his mouth—an achievement which, meaning no disrespect, the illustrious guest of this evening turned *his* entire attention to some fifty-six years ago; and if the child is but a prophecy of the man, there are mighty few who will doubt that he *succeeded*.

Fenimore Cooper's Literary Offenses

The Pathfinder and The Deerslayer stand at the head of Cooper's novels as artistic creations. There are others of his works which contain parts as perfect as are to be found in these, and scenes even more thrilling. Not one can be compared with either of them as a finished whole.

The defects in both of these tales are comparatively slight. They were pure works of art. *Prof. Lounsbury.*

The five tales reveal an extraordinary fullness of invention.

. . . One of the very greatest characters in fiction, Natty Bumppo. . . .

> The craft of the woodsman, the tricks of the trapper, all the delicate art of the forest, were familiar to Cooper from his youth up. *Prof. Brander Matthews.*

> Cooper is the greatest artist in the domain of romantic fiction yet produced by America. *Wilkie Collins.*

It seems to me that it was far from right for the Professor of English Literature in Yale, the Professor of English Literature in Columbia, and Wilkie Collins to deliver opinions on Cooper's literature without having read some of it. It would have been much more decorous to keep silent and let persons talk who have read Cooper.

Cooper's art has some defects. In one place in *Deerslayer*, and in the restricted space of two-thirds of a page Cooper has scored 114 offenses against literary art out of a possible 115. It breaks the record.

There are nineteen rules governing literary art in the domain of romantic fiction—some say twenty-two. In *Deerslayer* Cooper violated eighteen of them. These eighteen require:

1. That a tale shall accomplish something and arrive somewhere. But the *Deerslayer* tale accomplishes nothing and arrives in the air.
2. They require that the episodes of a tale shall be necessary parts of the tale, and shall help to develop it. But as the *Deerslayer* tale is not a tale, and accomplishes nothing and arrives nowhere, the episodes have no rightful place in the work, since there was nothing for them to develop.
3. They require that the personages in a tale shall be alive, except in the case of corpses, and that always the reader shall be able to tell the corpses from the others. But this detail has often been overlooked in the *Deerslayer* tale.
4. They require that the personages in a tale, both dead and alive, shall exhibit a sufficient excuse for being there. But this detail also has been overlooked in the *Deerslayer* tale.
5. They require that when the personages of a tale deal in conversation, the talk shall sound like human talk, and be talk such as human beings would be likely to talk in the given circumstances, and have a discoverable meaning, also a discoverable purpose, and a show of relevancy, and remain in the neighborhood of the subject in hand, and be interesting to the reader, and help out the tale, and stop when the people cannot think of anything more to say. But this requirement has been ignored from the beginning of the *Deerslayer* tale to the end of it.
6. They require that when the author describes the character of a personage in his tale, the conduct and conversation of that personage shall justify said description. But this law gets little or no attention in the *Deerslayer* tale, as Natty Bumppo's case will amply prove.

7. They require that when a personage talks like an illustrated, gilt-edged, tree-calf, hand-tooled, seven-dollar Friendship's Offering in the beginning of a paragraph, he shall not talk like a negro minstrel in the end of it. But this rule is flung down and danced upon in the *Deerslayer* tale.
8. They require that crass stupidities shall not be played upon the reader as "the craft of the woodsman, the delicate art of the forest," by either the author or the people in the tale. But this rule is persistently violated in the *Deerslayer* tale.
9. They require that the personages of a tale shall confine themselves to possibilities and let miracles alone; or, if they venture a miracle, the author must so plausibly set it forth as to make it look possible and reasonable. But these rules are not respected in the *Deerslayer* tale.
10. They require that the author shall make the reader feel a deep interest in the personages of his tale and in their fate; and that he shall make the reader love the good people in the tale and hate the bad ones. But the reader of the *Deerslayer* tale dislikes the good people in it, is indifferent to the others, and wishes they would all get drowned together.
11. They require that the characters in a tale shall be so clearly defined that the reader can tell beforehand what each will do in a given emergency. But in the *Deerslayer* tale this rule is vacated.

In addition to these large rules there are some little ones. These require that the author shall

12. *Say* what he is proposing to say, not merely come near it.
13. Use the right word, not its second cousin.
14. Eschew surplusage.
15. Not omit necessary details.
16. Avoid slovenliness of form.
17. Use good grammar.
18. Employ a simple and straightforward style.

Even these seven are coldly and persistently violated in the *Deerslayer* tale.

Cooper's gift in the way of invention was not a rich endowment; but such as it was he liked to work it, he was pleased with the effects, and indeed he did some quite sweet things with it. In his little box of stage-properties he kept six or eight cunning devices, tricks, artifices for his savages and woodsmen to deceive and circumvent each other with and he was never so happy as when he was working these innocent things and seeing them go. A favorite one was to make a moccasined person tread in the tracks of the moccasined enemy, and thus hide his own trail. Cooper wore out barrels and barrels of moccasins in working that trick. Another stage-property that he pulled out of his box pretty frequently was his broken twig. He prized his broken twig above all the rest of his effects, and worked it the hardest. It is a restful chapter in any book of his when somebody doesn't step on a dry twig and alarm all the reds and whites for two hundred yards around. Every time a Cooper person is in peril, and absolute silence is worth four dollars a minute, he is sure to step on a dry twig. There may be a hundred handier things to step on, but that wouldn't satisfy Cooper. Cooper requires him to turn out and find a dry twig; and if he can't do it, go and borrow one. In fact, the Leather-stocking Series ought to have been called the Broken Twig Series.

I am sorry there is not room to put in a few dozen instances of the delicate art of the forest, as practised by Natty Bumppo and some of the other Cooper-ian experts. Perhaps we may venture two or three samples. Cooper was a sailor—a naval officer; yet he gravely tells us how a vessel, driving toward a lee shore in a gale, is steered for a particular spot by her skipper because he knows of an *undertow* there which will hold her back against the gale and save her. For just pure woodcraft, or sailorcraft, or whatever it is, isn't that neat? For several years Cooper was daily in the society of artillery, and he ought to have noticed that when a cannon-ball strikes the ground it either buries itself or skips a hun-dred feet or so; skips again a hundred feet or so—and so on, till finally it gets tired and rolls. Now in one place he loses some "females"—as he always calls women—in the edge of a wood near a plain at night in a fog, on purpose to give Bumppo a chance to show off the delicate art of the forest before the reader. These mislaid people are hunting for a fort. They hear a cannon-blast, and a cannon-ball presently comes rolling into the wood and stops at their feet. To the females this suggests nothing. The case is very different with the ad-mirable Bumppo. I wish I may never know peace again if he doesn't strike out promptly and *follow the track* of that cannon-ball across the plain through the dense fog and find the fort. Isn't it a daisy? If Cooper had any real knowledge of Nature's ways of doing things, he had a most delicate art in concealing the fact. For instance: one of his acute Indian experts, Chingachgook (pronounced Chicago, I think), has lost the trail of a person he is tracking through the forest. Apparently that trail is hopelessly lost. Neither you nor I could ever have guessed out the way to find it. It was very different with Chicago. Chicago was not stumped for long. He turned a running stream out of its course, and there, in the slush in its old bed, were that person's moccasin tracks. The current did not wash them away, as it would have done in all other cases—no, even the eternal laws of Nature have to vacate when Cooper wants to put up a delicate job of woodcraft on the reader.

We must be a little wary when Brander Matthews tells us that Cooper's books "reveal an extraordinary fullness of invention." As a rule, I am quite willing to accept Brander Matthews's literary judgments and applaud his lucid and graceful phrasing of them; but that particular statement needs to be taken with a few tons of salt. Bless your heart, Cooper hadn't any more invention than a horse; and I don't mean a high-class horse, either; I mean a clothes-horse. It would be very difficult to find a really clever "situation" in Cooper's books, and still more dif-ficult to find one of any kind which he has failed to render absurd by his han-dling of it. Look at the episodes of "the caves"; and at the celebrated scuffle between Magua and those others on the table-land a few days later; and at Hurry Harry's queer water-transit from the castle to the ark; and at Deerslayer's half-hour with his first corpse; and at the quarrel between Hurry Harry and Deerslayer later; and at—but choose for yourself; you can't go amiss.

If Cooper had been an observer his inventive faculty would have worked better; not more interestingly, but more rationally, more plausibly. Cooper's proudest creations in the way of "situations" suffer noticeably from the absence of the observer's protecting gift. Cooper's eye was splendidly inaccurate. Cooper seldom saw anything correctly. He saw nearly all things as through a glass eye, darkly. Of course a man who cannot see the commonest little everyday matters accurately is working at a disadvantage when he is constructing a "situation." In the *Deerslayer* tale Cooper has a stream which is fifty feet wide where it flows out of a lake; it presently narrows to twenty as it meanders along for no given reason, and yet when a stream acts like that it ought to be required to explain itself. Fourteen pages later the width of the brook's outlet from the lake has suddenly shrunk thirty feet, and become "the narrowest part of the stream." This shrinkage is not accounted for. The stream has bends in it, a sure indication that it has alluvial banks and cuts them; yet these bends are only thirty and fifty feet long. If Cooper had been a nice and punctilious observer he would have noticed that the bends were oftener nine hundred feet long than short of it.

Cooper made the exit of that stream fifty feet wide, in the first place, for no particular reason; in the second place, he narrowed it to less than twenty to accommodate some Indians. He bends a "sapling" to the form of an arch over this narrow passage, and conceals six Indians in its foliage. They are "laying" for a settler's scow or ark which is coming up the stream on its way to the lake; it is being hauled against the stiff current by a rope whose stationary end is anchored in the lake; its rate of progress cannot be more than a mile an hour. Cooper describes the ark, but pretty obscurely. In the matter of dimensions "it was little more than a modern canal-boat." Let us guess, then, that it was about one hundred and forty feet long. It was of "greater breadth than common." Let us guess, then, that it was about sixteen feet wide. This leviathan had been prowling down bends which were but a third as long as itself, and scraping between banks where it had only two feet of space to spare on each side. We cannot too much admire this miracle. A low-roofed log dwelling occupies "two-thirds of the ark's length"—a dwelling ninety feet long and sixteen feet wide, let us say—a kind of vestibule train. The dwelling has two rooms—each forty-five feet long and sixteen feet wide, let us guess. One of them is the bedroom of the Hutter girls, Judith and Hetty; the other is the parlor in the daytime, at night it is papa's bedchamber. The ark is arriving at the stream's exit now, whose width has been reduced to less than twenty feet to accommodate the Indians—say to eighteen. There is a foot to spare on each side of the boat. Did the Indians notice that there was going to be a tight squeeze there? Did they notice that they could make money by climbing down out of that arched sapling and just stepping aboard when the ark scraped by? No, other Indians would have noticed these things, but Cooper's Indians never notice anything. Cooper thinks they are marvelous creatures for noticing, but he was almost always in error about his Indians. There was seldom a sane one among them.

The ark is one hundred and forty-feet long; the dwelling is ninety feet long. The idea of the Indians is to drop softly and secretly from the arched sapling to the dwelling as the ark creeps along under it at the rate of a mile an hour, and butcher the family. It will take the ark a minute and a half to pass under. It will take the ninety-foot dwelling a minute to pass under. Now, then, what did the six Indians do? It would take you thirty years to guess, and even then you would have to give it up, I believe. Therefore, I will tell you what the Indians did. Their chief, a person of quite extraordinary intellect for a Cooper Indian, warily watched the canal-boat as it squeezed along under him, and when he had got his calculations fined down to exactly the right shade, as he judged, he let go and dropped. And *missed the house!* That is actually what he did. He missed the house, and landed in the stern of the scow. It was not much of a fall, yet it knocked him silly. He lay there unconscious. If the house had been ninety-seven feet long he would have made the trip. The fault was Cooper's not his. The error lay in the construction of the house. Cooper was no architect.

There still remained in the roost five Indians. The boat has passed under and is now out of their reach. Let me explain what the five did—you would not be able to reason it out for yourself. No. 1 jumped for the boat, but fell in the water astern of it. Then No. 2 jumped for the boat, but fell in the water still farther astern of it. Then No. 3 jumped for the boat, and fell a good way astern of it. Then No. 4 jumped for the boat, and fell in the water *away* astern. Then even No. 5 made a jump for the boat—for he was a Cooper Indian. In the matter of intellect, the difference between a Cooper Indian and the Indian that stands in front of a cigar-shop is not spacious. The scow episode is really a sublime burst of invention; but it does not thrill, because the inaccuracy of the details throws a sort of air of factitiousness and general improbability over it. This comes of Cooper's inadequacy as an observer.

The reader will find some examples of Cooper's high talent for inaccurate observation in the account of the shooting-match in *The Pathfinder*.

> A common wrought nail was driven lightly into the target, its head having been first touched with paint.

The color of the paint is not stated—an important omission, but Cooper deals freely in important omissions. No, after all, it was not an important omission; for this nail-head is a *hundred yards from* the marksmen, and could not be seen by them at that distance, no matter what its color might be. How far can the best eyes see a common house-fly? A hundred yards? It is quite impossible. Very well; eyes that cannot see a house-fly that is a hundred yards away cannot see an ordinary nail-head at that distance, for the size of the two objects is the same. It takes a keen eye to see a fly or a nail-head at fifty yards—one hundred and fifty feet. Can the reader do it?

The nail was lightly driven, its head painted, and game called. Then the Cooper miracles began. The bullet of the first marksman chipped an edge of the nail-head; the next man's bullet drove the nail a little way into the target—and removed all the paint. Haven't the miracles gone far enough now? Not to suit Cooper; for the purpose of this whole scheme is to show off his prodigy, Deerslayer-Hawkeye-Long-Rifle-Leatherstocking-Pathfinder-Bumppo before the ladies.

> "Be all ready to clench it, boys!" cried the Pathfinder, stepping into his friend's tracks the instant they were vacant. "Never mind a new nail; I can see that, though the paint is gone, and what I can see I can hit at a hundred yards, though it were only a mosquito's eye. Be ready to clench!"
>
> The rifle cracked, the bullet sped its way, and the head of the nail was buried in the wood, covered by the piece of flattened lead.

There, you see, is a man who could hunt flies with a rifle, and command a ducal salary in a Wild West show today if we had him back with us.

The recorded feat is certainly surprising just as it stands; but it is not surprising enough for Cooper. Cooper adds a touch. He has made Pathfinder do this miracle with another man's rifle; and not only that, but Pathfinder did not have even the advantage of loading it himself. He had everything against him, and yet he made that impossible shot; and not only made it, but did it with absolute confidence, saying, "Be ready to clench." Now a person like that would have undertaken that same feat with a brickbat, and with Cooper to help he would have achieved it, too.

Pathfinder showed off handsomely that day before the ladies. His very first feat was a thing which no Wild West show can touch. He was standing with the group of marksmen, observing—a hundred yards from the target, mind; one Jasper raised his rifle and drove the center of the bull's-eye. Then the Quartermaster fired. The target exhibited no result this time. There was a laugh. "It's a dead miss," said Major Lundie. Pathfinder waited an impressive moment or two; then said, in that calm, indifferent, know-it-all way of his, "No, Major, he has covered Jasper's bullet, as will be seen if any one will take the trouble to examine the target."

Wasn't it remarkable! How *could* he see that little pellet fly through the air and enter that distant bullet-hole? Yet that is what he did; for nothing is impossible to a Cooper person. Did any of those people have any deep-seated doubts about this thing? No; for that would imply sanity, and these were all Cooper people.

> The respect for Pathfinder's skill and for his *quickness and accuracy of sight* [the italics are mine] was so profound and general, that the

instant he made this declaration the spectators began to distrust their own opinions, and a dozen rushed to the target in order to ascertain the fact. There, sure enough, it was found that the Quartermaster's bullet had gone through the hole made by Jasper's, and that, too, so accurately as to require a minute examination to be certain of the circumstance, which, however, was soon clearly established by discovering one bullet over the other in the stump against which the target was placed.

They made a "minute" examination; but never mind, how could they know that there were two bullets in that hole without digging the latest one out? for neither probe nor eyesight could prove the presence of any more than one bullet. Did they dig? No; as we shall see. It is the Pathfinder's turn now; he steps out before the ladies, takes aim, and fires.

"If one dared to hint at such a thing," cried Major Duncan, "I should say that the Pathfinder has also missed the target!"

As nobody had missed it yet, the "also" was not necessary; but never mind about that, for the Pathfinder is going to speak.

"No, no, Major," said he, confidently, "that *would* be a risky declaration. I didn't load the piece, and can't say what was in it; but if it was lead, you will find the bullet driving down those of the Quartermaster and Jasper, else is not my name Pathfinder."

A shout from the target announced the truth of this assertion.

Is the miracle sufficient as it stands? Not for Cooper. The Pathfinder speaks again, as he "now slowly advances toward the stage occupied by the females":

"That's not all, boys, that's not all; if you find the target touched at all, I'll own a miss. The Quartermaster cut the wood, but you'll find no wood cut by that last messenger."

The miracle is at last complete. He knew—doubtless *saw*—at the distance of a hundred yards—that his bullet had passed into the hole *without fraying the edges*. There were now three bullets in that one hole—three bullets embedded processionally in the body of the stump back of the target. Everybody knew this—somehow or other—and yet nobody had dug any of them out to make sure. Cooper is not a close observer, but he is interesting. He is certainly always that, no matter what happens. And he is more interesting when he is not noticing what he is about than when he is. This is a considerable merit.

The conversations in the Cooper books have a curious sound in our modern ears. To believe that such talk really ever came out of people's mouths would be to believe that there was a time when time was of no value to a person who thought he had something to say; when it was the custom to spread a two-minute remark out to ten; when a man's mouth was a rolling-mill, and busied itself all day long in turning four-foot pigs of thought into thirty-foot bars of conversational railroad iron by attenuation; when subjects were seldom faithfully stuck to, but the talk wandered all around and arrived nowhere; when conversations consisted mainly of irrelevancies, with here and there a relevancy, a relevancy with an embarrassed look, as not being able to explain how it got there.

Cooper was certainly not a master in the construction of dialogue. Inaccurate observation defeated him here as it defeated him in so many other enterprises of his. He even failed to notice that the man who talks corrupt English six days in the week must and will talk it on the seventh, and can't help himself. In the *Deerslayer* story he lets Deerslayer talk the showiest kind of book-talk sometimes, and at other times the basest of base dialects. For instance, when some one asks him if he has a sweetheart, and if so, where she abides, this is his majestic answer:

> "She's in the forest—hanging from the boughs of the trees, in a soft rain—in the dew on the open grass—the clouds that float about in the blue heavens—the birds that sing in the woods—the sweet springs where I slake my thirst—and in all the other glorious gifts that come from God's Providence!"

And he preceded that, a little before, with this:

> "It consarns me as all things that touches a fri'nd consarns a fri'nd."

And this is another of his remarks:

> "If I was Injin born, now, I might tell of this, or carry in the scalp and boast of the expl'ite afore the whole tribe; or if my inimy had only been a bear"—[and so on].

We cannot imagine such a thing as a veteran Scotch Commander-in-Chief comporting himself in the field like a windy melodramatic actor, but Cooper could. One one occasion Alice and Cora were being chased by the French through a fog in the neighborhood of their father's fort:

> *"Point de quartier aux coquins!"* cried an eager pursuer, who seemed to direct the operations of the enemy.
> "Stand firm and be ready, my gallant 60ths!" suddenly exclaimed a voice above them; "wait to see the enemy; fire low, and sweep the glacis."
> "Father! father!" exclaimed a piercing cry from out the mist; "it is I! Alice! thy own Elsie! spare, O! save your daughters!"
> "Hold!" shouted the former speaker, in the awful tones of parental agony, the

sound reaching even to the woods, and rolling back in solemn echo. " 'Tis she! God has restored me my children! Throw open the sally-port; to the field, 60ths, to the field! pull not a trigger, lest ye kill my lambs! Drive off these dogs of France with your steel!"

Cooper's word-sense was singularly dull. When a person has a poor ear for music he will flat and sharp right along without knowing it. He keeps near the tune, but it is *not* the tune. When a person has a poor ear for words, the result is a literary flatting and sharping; you perceive what he is intending to say, but you also perceive that he doesn't *say* it. This is Cooper. He was not a word-musician. His ear was satisfied with the *approximate* word. I will furnish some circumstantial evidence in support of this charge. My instances are gathered from half a dozen pages of the tale called *Deerslayer*. He uses "verbal" for "oral"; "precision" for "facility"; "phenomena" for "marvels"; "necessary" for "prede-termined"; "unsophisticated" for "primitive"; "preparation" for "expectancy"; "rebuked" for "subdued"; "dependent on" for "resulting from"; "fact" for "condition"; "fact" for "conjecture"; "precaution" for "caution"; "explain" for "determine"; "mortified" for "disappointed"; "meretricious" for "factitious"; "materially" for "considerably"; "decreasing" for "deepening"; "increasing" for "disappearing"; "embedded" for "inclosed"; "treacherous" for "hostile"; "stood" for "stooped"; "softened" for "replaced"; "rejoined" for "remarked"; "situation" for "condition"; "different" for "differing"; "insensible" for "unsentient"; "brevity" for "celerity"; "distrusted" for "suspicious"; "mental imbecility" for "imbecility"; "eyes" for "sight"; "counteracting" for "opposing"; "funeral obse-quies" for "obsequies."

There have been daring people in the world who claimed that Cooper could write English, but they are all dead now—all dead but Lounsbury. I don't re-member that Lounsbury makes the claim in so many words, still he makes it, for he says that *Deerslayer* is a "pure work of art." Pure, in that connection, means faultless—faultless in all details—and language is a detail. If Mr. Lounsbury had only compared Cooper's English with the English which he writes himself—but it is plain that he didn't; and so it is likely that he imagines until this day that Cooper's is as clean and compact as his own. Now I feel sure, deep down in my heart, that Cooper wrote about the poorest English that exists in our language, and that the English of *Deerslayer* is the very worst that even Cooper ever wrote.

I may be mistaken, but it does seem to me that *Deerslayer* is not a work of art in any sense; it does seem to me that it is destitute of every detail that goes to the making of a work of art; in truth, it seems to me that *Deerslayer* is just simply a literary *delirium tremens*.

A work of art? It has no invention; it has no order, system, sequence, or result; it has no life-likeness, no thrill, no stir, no seeming of reality; its characters are confusedly drawn, and by their acts and words they prove that they are not the sort of people the author claims they are; its humor is pathetic; its pathos is funny; its conversations are—oh! indescribable; its love-scenes odious; its English a crime against the language.

Counting these out, what is left is Art. I think we must all admit that.★

A Cooper Indian who has been washed is a poor thing, and commonplace; it is the Cooper Indian in his paint that thrills. Cooper's extra words are Cooper's paint—his paint, his feathers, his tomahawk, his warwhoop.

In the two-thirds of a page elsewhere referred to, wherein Cooper scored 114 literary transgressions out of a possible 115, he appears before us with all his things on. As follows, the italics are mine—they indicate violations of Rule 14:

In a minute he was once fastened to the tree, *a helpless object of any insult or wrong that might be offered. So eagerly did every one now act, that nothing was said.* The fire was immediately lighted *in the pile, and the end of all was anxiously expected.*

It was not the intention of the Hurons *absolutely* to destroy *the life of* their victim by *means of* fire. They designed merely to put his *physical* fortitude to the severest proofs it could endure, short of that extremity. In the end, they fully intended to carry his scalp into their village, but it was their wish first to break down his resolution, and to reduce him to *the level of* a complaining sufferer. With this view, the pile of brush *and branches* had been placed at a *proper* distance, *or one* at which it was thought the heat would soon become intolerable, though *it might* not *be* immediately dangerous. *As often happened, however, on these occasions,* this distance had been miscalculated, and the flames *began to wave their forked tongues in a proximity to the face of the victim that* would have proved fatal in another instant had not Hetty rushed through the crowd, armed with a stick, and scattered the blazing pile *in a dozen directions.* More than one hand was raised to strike the *presumptuous* intruder to the earth; but the chiefs prevented the blows by reminding their *irritated* followers of the state of her mind. Hetty, herself, was insensible to the risk she ran; but, *as soon as she had performed this bold act, she* stood looking about her in frowning resentment, as if to rebuke the *crowd of attentive savages for their cruelty.*

'God bless you, dear*est sister,* for that brave and ready act,' murmured Judith, *herself unnerved so much as to be incapable of exertion;* 'Heaven itself has sent you on its holy errand.'

Number of words, 320; necessary ones, 220; words wasted by the generous spendthrift, 100.

In our day those 100 unnecessary words would have to come out. We will

---

★At this point, the original published version of the Cooper essay ends. But the late Bernard De Voto announced in *The New England Quarterly* for September 1946 that Twain had conceived of the essay as Number 1 in a series of "Studies in Literary Criticism," supposedly prepared by "Mark Twain, M.A., Professor of Belles Lettres in the Veterinary College of Arizona," and that in publishing it separately he had cut the last seven paragraphs. The second essay in the series, which was never finished, develops some of Twain's most interesting objections to Cooper.

take them out presently and make the episode approximate the modern require-ment in the matter of compression.

If we may consider each unnecessary word in Cooper's report of that barbe-cue a separate and individual violation of Rule 14, then that rule is violated 100 times in that report. Other rules are violated in it. Rule 12, two instances; ★ Rule 13, three instances;† Rule 15, one instance;‡ Rule 16, two instances;§ Rule 17, one or two little instances;‖ the Report in its entirety is an offense against Rule 18#—also against Rule 16. Total score, about 114 violations of the laws of liter-ary art out of a possible 115.

Let us now bring forward the Report again, with the most of the unnecessary words knocked out. By departing from Cooper's style and manner, all the facts could be put into 150 words, and the effects heightened at the same time—this is manifest, of course—but that would not be desirable. We must stick to Cooper's language as closely as we can:

> In a minute he was once more fastened to the tree. The fire was immediately lighted. It was not the intention of the Hurons to de-stroy Deerslayer's life by fire; they designed merely to put his forti-tude to the severest proofs it could endure short of that extremity. In the end, they fully intended to take his life, but it was their wish first to break down his resolution and reduce him to a complaining suf-ferer. With this view the pile of brush had been placed at a distance at which it was thought the heat would soon become intolerable, without being immediately dangerous. But this distance had been miscalculated; the fire was so close to the victim that he would have been fatally burned in another instant if Hetty had not rushed through the crowd and scattered the brands with a stick. More than one Indian raised his hand to strike her down but the chiefs saved her by reminding them of the state of her mind. Hetty herself was insensible to the risk she ran; she stood looking about her in frown-ing resentment, as if to rebuke the savages for their cruelty.
>
> 'God bless you, dear!' cried Judith, 'for that brave and ready act. Heaven itself has sent you on its holy errand, and you shall have a chromo.'

Number of words, 220—and the facts are all in.

★Rule 12: "*Say* what he is proposing to say, not merely come near it."
†Rule 13: "Use the right word, not its second cousin."
‡Rule 15: "Not omit necessary details."
§Rule 16: "Avoid slovenliness of forms."
‖Rule 17: "Use good grammar."
#Rule 18: "Employ a simple and straightforward style."

II

Young Gentlemen: In studying Cooper you will find it profitable to study him in detail—word by word, sentence by sentence. For every sentence of his is interesting. Interesting because of its make-up; its peculiar make-up, its original make-up. Let us examine a sentence or two, and see. Here is a passage from Chapter XI of *The Last of the Mohicans,* one of the most famous and most ad-·mired of Cooper's books:

> Notwithstanding the swiftness of their flight, one of the Indians had found an opportunity to strike a straggling fawn with an arrow, and had borne the more preferable fragments of the victim, patiently on his shoulders, to the stopping-place. Without any aid from the science of cookery, he was immediately employed in common with his fellows, in gorging himself with this digestible sustenance. Magua alone sat apart, without participating in the revolting meal, and apparently buried in the deepest thought.

This little paragraph is full of matter for reflection and inquiry. The remark about the swiftness of the flight was unnecessary, as it was merely put in to forestall the possible objection of some over-particular reader that the Indian couldn't have found the needed "opportunity" while fleeing swiftly. The reader would not have made that objection. He would care nothing about having that small matter explained and justified. But that is Cooper's way; frequently he will explain and justify little things that do not need it and then make up for this by as frequently failing to explain important ones that do need it. For instance he allowed that astute and cautious person, Deerslayer-Hawkeye, to throw his rifle heedlessly down and leave it lying on the ground where some hostile Indians would presently be sure to find it—a rifle prized by that person above all things else in the earth—and the reader gets no word of explanation of that strange act. There was a reason, but it wouldn't bear exposure. Cooper meant to get a fine dramatic effect out of the finding of the rifle by the Indians, and he accomplished this at the happy time; but all the same, Hawkeye could have hidden the rifle in a quarter of a minute where the Indians could not have found it. Cooper couldn't think of any way to explain why Hawkeye didn't do that, so he just shirked the difficulty and did not explain at all. In another place Cooper allowed Heyward to shoot at an Indian with a pistol that wasn't loaded—and grants us not a word of explanation to how the man did it.

No, the remark about the swiftness of their flight was not necessary; neither was the one which said that the Indian found an opportunity; neither was the one which said he *struck* the fawn; neither was the one which explained that it was a "straggling" fawn; neither was the one which said the striking was done with an arrow; neither was the one which said the Indian bore the "fragments"; nor the remark that they were preferable fragments; nor the remark that they were *more* preferable fragments; nor the explanation that they were fragments of the "victim"; nor the over-particular explanation that specifies the Indian's "shoulders" as the part of him that supported the fragments; nor the statement that the Indian bore the fragments patiently. None of those details has any value. We don't care what the Indian struck the fawn with; we don't care whether it was a straggling fawn or an unstraggling one; we don't care which fragments the Indian saved; we don't care why he saved the "more" preferable ones when the merely preferable ones would have amounted to just the same thing and couldn't have been told from the more preferable ones by anybody, dead or alive; we don't care whether the Indian carried them on his shoulders or in his handkerchief; and finally, we don't care whether he carried them patiently or struck for higher pay and shorter hours. We are indifferent to that Indian and all his affairs.

There was only one fact in that long sentence that was worth stating, and it could have been squeezed into these few words—and with advantage to the narrative, too:

"During the flight one of the Indians had killed a fawn, and he brought it into camp." You will notice that "During the flight one of the Indians had killed a fawn and he brought it into camp," is more straightforward and businesslike, and less mincing and smirky, than it is to say "Notwithstanding the swiftness of their flight, one of the Indians had found an opportunity to strike a straggling fawn with an arrow, and had borne the more preferable fragments of the victim; patiently on his shoulders, to the stopping-place." You will notice that the form "During the flight one of the Indians had killed a fawn and he brought it into camp" holds up its chin and moves to the front with the steady stride of a grenadier, whereas the form "Notwithstanding the swiftness of their flight, one of the Indians had found an opportunity to strike a straggling fawn with an arrow, and had borne the more preferable fragments of the victim, patiently on his shoulders, to the stopping-place," simpers along with an airy, complacent, monkey-with-a-parasol gait which is not suited to the transportation of raw meat.

I beg to remind you that an author's way of setting forth a matter is called his Style, and that an author's style is a main part of his equipment for business. The style of some authors has variety in it, but Cooper's style is remarkable for the absence of this feature. Cooper's style is always grand and stately and noble. Style may be likened to an army, the author to its general, the book to the campaign. Some authors proportion an attacking force to the strength or weakness, the importance or unimportance, of the object to be attacked; but Cooper doesn't. It doesn't make any difference to Cooper whether the object of attack is a hundred thousand men or a cow; he hurls his entire force against it. He comes thundering down with all his battalions at his back, cavalry in the van, artillery on the flanks, infantry massed in the middle, forty bands braying, a thousand banners streaming in the wind; and whether the object be an army or a cow you will see him come marching sublimely in, at the end of the engagement, bearing the more preferable fragments of the victim patiently on his shoulders, to the stopping-place. Cooper's style is grand, awful, beautiful; but it is sacred to

Cooper, it is his very own, and no student of the Veterinary College of Arizona will be allowed to filch it from him.

In one of his chapters Cooper throws an ungentle slur at one Gamut because he is not exact enough in his choice of words. But Cooper has that failing himself, as was remarked in our first Lecture. If the Indian had "struck" the fawn with a brick, or with a club, or with his fist, no one could find fault with the word used. And one cannot find much fault when he strikes it with an arrow; still it sounds affected, and it might have been a little better to lean to simplicity and say he shot it with an arrow.

"Fragments" is well enough, perhaps, when one is speaking of the parts of a dismembered deer, yet it hasn't just exactly the right sound—and sound is something; in fact sound is a good deal. It makes the difference between good music and poor music, and it can sometimes make the difference between good literature and indifferent literature. "Fragments" sounds all right when we are talking about the wreckage of a breakable thing that has been smashed: it also sounds all right when applied to cat's-meat; but when we use it to describe large hunks and chunks like the fore- and hind-quarters of a fawn, it grates upon the fastidious ear.

"Without any aid from the science of cookery, he was immediately employed, in common with his fellows, in gorging himself with this digestible sustenance."

This was a mere statistic; just a mere cold, colorless statistic; yet you see Cooper has made a chromo out of it. To use another figure, he has clothed a humble statistic in flowing, voluminous and costly raiment, whereas both good taste and economy suggest that he ought to have saved these splendors for a king, and dressed the humble statistic in a simple breech-clout. Cooper spent twenty-four words here on a thing not really worth more than eight. We will reduce the statistic to its proper proportions and state it in this way:

"He and the others ate the meat raw."

"Digestible sustenance" is a handsome phrase, but it was out of place there, because we do not know these Indians or care for them; and so it cannot interest us to know whether the meat was going to agree with them or not. Details which do not assist a story are better left out.

"Magua alone sat apart, without participating in the revolting meal," is a statement which we understand, but that is our merit, not Cooper's. Cooper is not clear. He does not say who it is that is revolted by the meal. It is really Cooper himself, but there is nothing in the statement to indicate that it isn't Magua. Magua is an Indian and likes raw meat.

The word "alone" could have been left out and space saved. It has no value where it is.

I must come back with some frequency, in the course of these Lectures, to the matter of Cooper's inaccuracy as an Observer. In this way I shall hope to persuade you that it is well to look at a thing carefully before you try to describe it; but I shall rest you between times with other matters and thus try to avoid over-fatiguing you with that detail of our theme. In *The Last of the Mohi-*

cans Cooper gets up a stirring "situation" on an island flanked by great cataracts—a lofty island with steep sides—a sort of tongue which projects downstream from the midst of the divided waterfall. There are caverns in this mass of rock, and a party of Cooper people hide themselves in one of these to get away from some hostile Indians. There is a small exit at each end of this cavern. These exits are closed with blankets and the light excluded. The exploring hostiles back themselves up against the blankets and rave and rage in a blood-curdling way, but they are Cooper Indians and of course fail to discover the blankets; so they presently go away baffled and disappointed. Alice, in her gratitude for this deliverance, flings herself on her knee to return thanks. The darkness in there must have been pretty solid; yet if we may believe Cooper, it was a darkness which could not have been told from daylight; for here are some nice details which were visible in it:

"Both Heyward and the more tempered Cora witnessed the act of involuntary emotion with powerful sympathy, the former secretly believing that piety had never worn a form so lovely as it had now assumed in the youthful person of Alice. Her eyes were radiant with the glow of grateful feelings; the flush of her beauty was again seated on her cheeks, and her whole soul seemed ready and anxious to pour out its thanksgivings, through the medium of her eloquent features. But when her lips moved, the words they should have uttered appeared frozen by some new and sudden chill. Her bloom gave place to the paleness of death; her soft and melting eyes grew hard, and seemed contracting with horror; while those hands which she had raised, clasped in each other, towards heaven, dropped in horizontal lines before her, the fingers pointed forward in convulsed motion."

It is a case of strikingly inexact observation. Heyward and the more tempered Cora could not have seen the half of it in the dark that way.

I must call your attention to certain details of this work of art which invite particular examination. "Involuntary" is surplusage, and violates Rule 14.★ All emotion is involuntary when genuine, and then the qualifying term is not needed; a qualifying term is needed only when the emotion is pumped-up and ungenuine. "Secretly" is surplusage, too; because Heyward was not believing out loud, but all to himself; and a person cannot believe a thing all to himself without doing it privately. I do not approve of the word "seated," to describe the process of locating a flush. No one can seat a flush. A flush is not a deposit on an exterior surface, it is a something which squashes out from within.

I cannot approve of the word "new." If Alice had had an old chill, formerly, it would be all right to distinguish this one from that one by calling this one the new chill; but she had not had any old chill, this one was the only chill she had had, up till now, and so the tacit reference to an old anterior chill is unwarranted and misleading. And I do not altogether like the phrase "while those hands which she had raised." It seems to imply that she had some other hands—some other

---

★Rule 14: "Eschew surplusage."

ones which she had put on a shelf a minute so as to give her a better chance to raise those ones; but it is not true; she had only the one pair. The phrase is in the last degree misleading. But I like to see her extend these ones in front of her and work the fingers. I think that that is a very good effect. And it would have almost doubled the effect if the more tempered Cora had done it some, too.

John Updike
(Contemporary)

FROM *Museums and Women and Other Stories*

Under the Microscope

It was not his kind of pond; the water tasted slightly acid. He was a Cyclops, the commonest of copepods, and this crowd seemed exotically cladoceran—stylish water-fleas with transparent carapaces, all shimmer and bubbles and twitch. His hostess, a magnificent Daphnia fully an eighth of an inch tall, her heart and cephalic ganglion visibly pulsing, welcomed him with a lavish gesture of her ciliate, branching antennae; for a moment he feared she would eat him. Instead she offered him a platter of living

desmids. They were bright green in color and shaped like crescents, hourglasses, omens. "Who do you know here?" Her voice was a distinct constant above the din. "Everybody knows *you,* of course. They've read your books." His books, taken all together, with generous margins, would easily have fitted on the period that ends this sentence.

The Cyclops modestly grimaced, answered "No one," and turned to a young specimen of water-mite, probably *Hydrachna geographica,* still bearing ruddy traces of the larval stage. "Have you been here long?" he asked, meaning less the party than the pond.

"Long enough." Her answer came as swiftly as a reflex. "I go back to the surface now and then; we breathe air, you know."

"Oh I know, I envy you." He noticed she had only six legs. She was newly hatched, then. Between her eyes, arranged in two pairs, he counted a fifth, in the middle, and wondered if in her he might find his own central single optic amplified and confirmed. His antennules yearned to touch her red spots; he wanted to ask her, *What do you see?* Young as she was, partially formed, she appeared, alerted by his abrupt confession of envy, ready to respond to any question, however presuming.

But at that moment a monstrous fairy shrimp, an inch in length and extravagantly tinted blue, green, and bronze, swam by on its back, and the water shuddered. Furious, the Cyclops asked the water-mite, "Who invites *them*? They're not even in our scale."

She shrugged permissively, showing that indeed she had been here long enough. "They're entomostracans," she said, "just like Daphnia. They amuse her."

"They're going to eat her up," the Cyclops predicted.

Though she laughed, her fifth eye gazed steadily into his wide lone one. "But isn't that what we all want? Subconsciously, of course."

"Of course."

An elegant, melancholy flatworm was passing *hors d'œuvres*. The Cyclops took some diatoms, cracked their delicate shells of silica, and ate them. They tasted golden brown. Growing hungrier, he pushed through to the serving table and had a Volvox in algae dip. A shrill little rotifer, his head cilia whirling, his three-toothed mastax chattering, leaped up before him, saying, with the mixture of put-on and pleading characteristic of this pond, "I wead all your wunnaful books, and I have

a wittle bag of pomes I wote myself, and I would wove it, *wove* it if you would wead them and wecommend them to a big bad pubwisher!" At a loss for a civil answer, the Cyclops considered the rotifer silently, then ate him. He tasted slightly acid.

The party was thickening. A host of protozoans drifted in on a raft of sphagnum moss: a trumpet-shaped Stentor, apparently famous and interlocked with a lanky, bleached Spirostomum; a claque of paramœcia, swishing back and forth tickling the crustacea on the backs of their knees; an old Voticella, a plantlike animalcule as dreary, the Cyclops thought, as the batch of puffs rooted to the flap of last year's *succès d'estime*. The kitchen was crammed with ostracods and flagellates engaged in mutually consuming conversation, and over in a corner, beneath an African mask, a great brown hydra, the real thing, attached by its sticky foot to the hissing steam radiator, rhythmically swung its tentacles here and there until one of them touched, in the circle of admirers, something appetizing; then the poison sacs exploded, the other tentacles contracted, and the prey was stuffed into the hydra's swollen coelenteron, which gluttony had stretched to a transparency that veiled the preceding meals like polyethylene film protecting a rack of dry-cleaned suits. Hairy with bacteria, a Simocephalus was munching a rapt nematode. The fairy shrimps, having multiplied, their crimson tails glowing with hæmoglobin, came cruising in from the empty bedrooms. The party was thinning.

Suddenly fearful, fearing he had lost her forever, the Cyclops searched for the water-mite, and found her miserably crouching in a corner, quite drunk, her seventh and eighth legs almost sprouted. "What do you see?" he now dared ask.

"Too much," she answered swiftly. "Everything. Oh, it's horrible, horrible."

Out of mercy as much as appetite, he ate her. She felt prickly inside him. Hurriedly— the rooms were almost depleted, it was late—he sought his hostess. She was by the doorway, her antennae frazzled from waving goodbye, but still magnificent, Daphnia, her cara-

pace a liquid shimmer of psychedelic pastel. "Don't go," she commanded, expanding, "I have a *minus*cule favor to ask. Now that my children, all thirteen billion of them, thank God, are off at school, I've taken a part-time editing job, and my first real break is this manuscript I'd be *so* grateful to have you read and comment on, whatever comes into your head, I admit it's a little long, maybe you can skim the part where Napoleon invades Russia, but it's the first *effort* by a perfectly delightful midge larva I know you'd enjoy meeting—"

"I'd adore to, but I can't," he said, explaining, "my eye. I can't afford to strain it, I have only this one . . ." He trailed off, he felt, feebly. He was beginning to feel permeable, acidic.

"You poor dear," Daphnia solemnly pronounced, and ate him.

And the next instant, a fairy shrimp, oaring by inverted, casually gathered her into the trough between his eleven pairs of undulating gill-feet and passed her toward his brazen mouth. Her scream, tinier than even the dot on the "i," was unobserved.

Judith Viorst
(Contemporary)

FROM *How Did I Get to Be 40 & Other Atrocities*

Self-Improvement Program

I've finished six pillows in Needlepoint,
And I'm reading Jane Austen and Kant,
And I'm up to the pork with black beans in
    Advanced Chinese Cooking.
I don't have to struggle to find myself
For I already know what I want.
I want to be healthy and wise and extremely good-looking.

I'm learning new glazes in Pottery Class,
And I'm playing new chords in Guitar,
And in Yoga I'm starting to master the lotus position.
I don't have to ponder priorities
For I already know what they are:
To be good-looking, healthy, and wise,
And adored in addition.

I'm improving my serve with a tennis pro,
And I'm practicing verb forms in Greek,
And in Primal Scream Therapy all my frustrations are vented.
I don't have to ask what I'm searching for
Since I already know that I seek
To be good-looking, healthy, and wise,
And adored,
And contented.

I've bloomed in Organic gardening,
And in Dance I have tightened my thighs,
And in Consciousness Raising there's no one around who can top me.
And I'm working all day and I'm working all night

To be good-looking, healthy, and wise.
And adored.
And contented.
And brave.
And well-read.
And a marvelous hostess,
Fantastic in bed,
And bilingual,
Athletic,
Artistic . . .
Won't someone please stop me?

Jane Wagner
(Contemporary)

FROM *The Search for Signs of Intelligent Life in the Universe*

Judith

About a month ago, I was shown some products designed to improve the sex lives of suburban housewives. I got so excited,
I just had to come on public access and tell you about it. To look at *me*, you'd *never suspect* I was a semi-nonorgasmic woman. This means it was *possible* for me to have an orgasm—but highly unlikely.

To me, the term "sexual freedom" meant freedom from having to have sex. And then along came Good Vibrations. And was I surprised! Now I am a regular Cat on a Hot Tin Roof.

think of it as a kind of
Hamburger Helper for the boudoir.

Can you afford one, you say?
Can you afford *not* to have one, I say. . . .

Ladies, it simply takes the guesswork out of making love.

"But doesn't it kill romance?" you say.
And I say,
"What doesn't?"

★

Chrissy

A sobering thought, Eileen:
What if, right at this very moment,
I *am* living up to my full potential?

I've about reached the conclusion if I'm ever going to make
something of my life, chances are it won't be through work.
It will have to be through personal growth stuff.

Go for the burn!

I've been trying to get into positive thinking in a really big way.
Frankly, I think it's my only hope.

My seminar leader said to me, "Chrissy, you should learn
to be happy
one day at a time." But what I learned from that is that you can
also be *miserable*
one day at a time.

This seminar I'm in, Eileen, has opened me up like some kind of
bronchial *spray*. I got clear:
my expectations about life are simply way too high.
    So are yours,
I bet, Eileen, because we
are all being *force-fed* a lot of false hopes about romance,
success, sex, life—you name it.

My seminar leader said to me, "Chrissy, you are a classic
'false hope' case" . . . because not only do I not have a very firm
grasp on reality, see,
but I have sort of a loose grip on my fantasies, too.

We had this exercise, Eileen.
We played this mind game called

"We know everything we need to know
if only we knew it."
We were told to be silent and our minds would tell
us whatever we needed to know.

I flashed on the time I lost my contact lens. There I was
looking for my contact lens
which I couldn't find
because I had lost my contact lens.
I thought: Wow, the story of my *life*.

You can't expect insights, even the big ones,
to suddenly make you understand
everything. But I figure: Hey, it's a step if they leave you
confused
in a deeper way.

The seminar ends tonight. To get us to face our fears,
we're supposed to walk over this bed of really red hot coals—
barefoot. Quite a test! You name
 it; I've feared it.
Except walking over hot coals . . . I never had that fear
till just now.

I'm working on overcoming my fears, Eileen,
but it's not easy.
At the Phobia Institute once,
this guy in group told about a friend who was terrified
of driving on the freeway,
but finally she conquered her fear and got so she thought
nothing of driving on the freeway.
And guess what?
She died
in a freeway accident.
That story has always stuck with me.

But *my* fears are more subtle. Like I fear being out
    of work,
and yet when I'm working, I have this constant fear
of being fired. The worst fear I have
is that this feeling I once had may come back.

AT THE LOCKERS

Once . . . I've been wanting to tell someone this, Eileen . . .
once I came *this* close
to committing suicide.
That's how down and low I felt.
I would have, too. There was just one thing stopped me.
Fear. I was just plain too afraid.
So, if I ever did commit suicide, I'd have to be so desperate
I wouldn't even let fear of suicide
stand in my way.

And yet if I could overcome a fear like that
I could overcome
all my fears, I bet.

And then, of course—
and here's the irony—probably
if I weren't afraid, I'd really want to live.
Only, by then, if I'd really conquered my fear of suicide,
it might be too late.
I might already, you know,
have done it.

Life can be so ironic. Sometimes, to make any move at all seems totally pointless. I
bet the worst part about dying is the part where your whole life passes before you.

I hope I don't ever feel that low again. At the moment, I feel pretty up about the
work I'm doing on myself. I used to be so sensitive; sometimes I would think of
the Kennedy family and I would just burst out in tears. I'm not so sensitive anymore; I don't burst out in tears as much as I used to and I hardly ever think of
the Kennedys anymore. So these seminars have been good for me, Eileen, which
is more than I can say for any job I've ever had.

Course, *I* don't want to be a seminar-*hopper;* like this
ex-friend I used to know. She had no time for *anything* but
self-improvement. She felt she had outgrown everyone,
especially *me.* Behind my back, she told this person that *I* was
Upwardly
Immobile. Asshole. And then, to add insult to injury,
she said it to my face. That did it—
I get enough insults on job interviews.

Well, I guess I'll see you tomorrow. How they lied about
this health club! Talk about false hopes. "The *place* to get

thin and meet good-looking men." The good-looking men here
are mostly looking at themselves.

I have never gotten so much as a date for cappuccino.

Yet I keep coming. I'm keeping really fit, I tell myself.
But the truth is,
I pig out one week and starve the next.

I have gained and lost
the same ten pounds
so many times over and over again
my cellulite must have déjà vu.

And all that business about exercise releasing endorphins.
I have not felt so much as *one* endorphin being released. Once
more, false hopes.

But hey, if it weren't for false hopes, the economy would
just collapse, I bet. Oh. I better hurry. My job interview! This
time I could get lucky. Requires no skills;
I'll just be hooking people up to
bio-feedback machines. At least I won't be lying to them.
Well, slinkydinks, I'm outta here.

AT THE DOCTOR'S

Lyn

You're sure, Doctor?
Premenstrual syndrome?
I mean, I'm getting divorced.
My mother's getting divorced.
I'm raising twin boys.
I have a lot of job pressure—
I've got to find one.
The ERA didn't pass,
not long ago I lost a very dear friend, and . . . and
my husband is involved . . .
not just involved, but in love, I'm afraid . . . with this
woman . . .
who's quite a bit younger than I am.

And you *think* it's my *period*
and *not* my life?

Gene Weingarten
(Contemporary)

And So God Says to Charles Darwin: Let There Be Light in Kansas

COMMENTARY: THE EVOLUTION OF EDUCATION

MEMO TO: The members of the Kansas Board of Education
FROM: God
RE: Your decision to eliminate the teaching of evolution as science

Thank you for your support. Much obliged.

Now, go forth and multiply. Beget many children. And yea, your children shall beget children. And their children shall beget children, and their children's children after them. And in time the genes that have made you such pinheads will be eliminated through natural selection. Because that is how it works.

Listen, I love all my creatures equally, and gave each his own special qualities to help him on Earth. The horse I gave great strength. The antelope I gave great grace and speed. The dung beetle I gave great stupidity, so he doesn't realize he is a dung beetle. Man I gave a brain.

Use it, okay?

I admit I am not perfect. I've made errors. (Armpit hair—what was I thinking?)

But do you Kansans seriously believe that I dropped half-a-billion-year-old trilobite skeletons all over my great green Earth by mistake?

What, I had a few lying around some previous creation in the Andromeda galaxy, and they fell through a hole in my pocket?

You were supposed to find them. And once you found them, you were supposed to draw the appropriate, intelligent conclusions. That's what I made you for. To think.

The folks who wrote the Bible were smart and good people.

Mostly, they got it right. But there were glitches. Imprecisions. For one thing, they said that Adam and Eve begat Cain and Abel, and then Cain begat Enoch. How was that supposed to have happened?

They left out Tiffany entirely!

Well, they also were a little off on certain elements of timing and sequence. So what?

You guys were supposed to figure it all out for yourselves, anyway. When you stumble over the truth, you are not supposed to pick yourself up, dust yourself off and proceed on as though nothing had happened. If you find a dinosaur's toe, you're not supposed to look for reasons to call it a croissant. You're not big, drooling idiots. For that, I made dogs.

Why do you think there are no fossilized human toes dating from a hundred million years ago? Think about it.

It's okay if you think. In fact, I prefer it. That's why I like Charles Darwin. He was always a-thinking. Still is. He and I chat frequently.

I know a lot of people figure that if man evolved from other organisms, it means I don't exist. I have to admit this is a reasonable assumption and a valid line of thought. I am in favor of thought. I encourage you to pursue this concept with an open mind, and see where it leads you.

That's all I have to say right now, except that I'm really cheesed off at laugh tracks on sitcoms, and the NRA, and people who make simple declarative sentences sound like questions?

Oh, wait. There's one more thing.

Did you read in the newspapers yesterday how scientists in Australia dug up some rocks and found fossilized remains of life dating back further than ever before? Primitive multicelled animals on Earth nearly three billion years ago, when the planet was nothing but roiling muck and ice and fire. And inside those cells was . . . DNA. Incredibly complex strands of chemicals, laced together in a scheme so sophisticated no one yet understands exactly how it works.

I wonder who could have thought of something like that, back then. Just something to gnaw on.

Assuming the PLOTUS Position

Ordinary persons such as you probably don't realize it, but famous literary figures such as myself and the poet laureate of the United States often get together to discuss eternal verities. Recently, Poet Laureate Billy Collins and I traded insights about the human experience.

Me: Isn't Billy a stupid name for the poet laureate? Shouldn't you have a more dignified name, like Heathcliffe?

PLOTUS: Well, it's an antiliterary name. Literary names tend to use initials, like T. S. Eliot. Eliot didn't say, but it is clear to me that the "J" in "J. Alfred Prufrock" stands for "John." He was trying to hide the fact that he had a plain first name. I am the opposite. I would be Johnny Prufrock. Or better, Jon-Boy Prufrock.

Me: Most of us are first exposed to poetry in fourth grade when we are encouraged to recite this, in the following manner: "IthinkthatIshallneversee apoemlovelyasatree atreewhosehungrymouthispressed against theEarth'ssweet-flowingbreast. . . ." Now, aside from the bosom theme, can we agree that this is without merit, a total hack job?

PLOTUS: It's pretty dreadful. One of those poems that give poetry a bad name.

Me: So should we shoot all fourth-grade teachers?

PLOTUS: Many people hate poetry, and many of them teach English. You know, we're born as poets. The heartbeat you hear in the womb is iambic—dah-DUM, dah-DUM. So we've already taken a course in meter when we come out of the womb. Then we have the poetry beaten out of us by teachers.

Me: Your poetry seems shockingly straightforward and understandable and funny. Why haven't you been drummed out of the Society of Pretentious-Snot Poets?

PLOTUS: I used to be a member! I am a lapsed obscure poet. I committed acts of literature resulting in poems so obscure even I had no idea what they were about. One was titled "Before the Words of Yearning Waned, Yearning Waned."

Me: Wow.

PLOTUS: Yeah.

Me: Highly sophisticated literary persons such as you and I of course celebrate the liberation of poetry from the tedious confines of rhyme. But in a way wasn't it better before any moron could write some lowercase words with arbitrary punctuation and random line spacing, and call himself a poet?

PLOTUS: Yes, the good news is that we have put away the metronome. The bad news is that it has let loose on the world a vast number of people with no skill. Maybe we should have a poetry school, and it should be illegal to write poetry unless you've been issued a poetic license. This is a new use of the term, and I just invented it.

Me: Who would issue the licenses?

PLOTUS: The poet laureate of the United States.

Me: What is the best poem you ever saw on a bathroom wall?

PLOTUS: The best was in a bathroom in Ireland, when Miles Davis was still alive. It said, "Just remember that when Miles Davis dies, we all move up a step."

Me: What advice would you give a young American kid who really, really wants to become a big-shot poet so he can score with the chicks?

PLOTUS: Learn the guitar.

Me: Is there any subject inappropriate for poetry? Could you write a poem about, say, one of those cotton thingies women put in dresses to prevent underarm stain?

PLOTUS: The fact is, when poets write about things that are inappropriate, poetry moves forward. In the mid-nineteenth century, you were not supposed to write about machines, only nature. Then Whitman wrote about a locomotive in winter. It was an antidaffodil poem. It moved poetry forward.

Me: So you could write about the underarm thingie?

PLOTUS: I gave you a long answer to avoid that short answer. But I suppose so.

Me: Say something poetic about the Treaty of Versailles.

PLOTUS: Well, to me, when you say that, I hear the word "sigh" at the end of it.

Me: That's really good!

PLOTUS: You have to have a poetic ear.

Me: How about spanakopita, that bitter Greek spinach pie?

PLOTUS: "Bitter Greek spinach pie" has a poetic beat. It is sort of lovely. If you say it ten times in a restaurant, you'd have more than you could eat.

Me: Is it possible to accidentally write poetry? This column that we are creating together, might it be poetry?

PLOTUS: No.

Me: Why not?

PLOTUS: Because you'll go to the edge of the page. That's your mistake. We poets leave raggedy edges on our lines.

Me: That's the secret?

PLOTUS: That's it.

Mae West
(1893–1980)

One-Liners

Is that a pistol in your pocket or are you just happy to see me?

. . . Why don't you come up and see me sometime? Come up on Wednesday, that's amateur night . . .
Trust me, hundreds already have.

★

When women go wrong, men go right after them.

★

A hard man is good to find.

★

He who hesitates is last.

★

Give a man a free hand and he'll run it all over you.

★

Why should I be good when I'm packing them in by being bad?

FROM *Pleasure Man*

Dolores is learning the meaning of the word repentance. It is how you feel when you get caught.

★

Nellie knows people are divided into the goods and the bads. The thing is not to be caught with the goods.

★

Poor Mary Ann! She gave the guy an inch and now he thinks he's a ruler.

FROM *The Constant Sinner*

When Babe Gordon had told the Bearcat she had been to church, it never occurred to her that she was lying. That is, it had no moral significance for her. To Babe, a lie was simply something one told to gain an advantage, to get what one wanted by the shortest route. . . . Bearcat was now convinced that she was a good girl, had character; and now, no matter what Charlie said against her, if she were careful Bearcat would always believe in her.

Babe was the living example of all that is immoral, when viewed through conventional eyes. But she herself was unmoral. For her, morals did not exist. She would not have known what a moral was if it could be made to dance naked in front of her.

★

A distinguished-looking tall man, with snow-white hair and well-groomed body, got into the cab with a dame who was highly rouged and expensively attired from shoes to the beautiful summer fur-piece about her shoulders. He caught snatches of their conversation.

"But I don't want to stop at the Plaza for tea," the man was saying, irritably. "You just want to show off that new fur I bought you."

"Please, honey," the girl begged.

"No, no. I'd be bored stiff. Let's go up to the apartment."

"But I don't want to go up there yet. It's too early."

"What has the time got to do with it? We can't get anything to drink at the Plaza." . . .

"All right, then," the girl said. "If you don't take me to the Plaza, I won't be nice to you the way you like, any more."

"Oh, I say now, Zelda," the man argued. "That's not sporting, after I've given you so much."

"Well, I don't care," said the girl. "I just won't be nice that way any more, that's all."

"Oh, good lord!" the man exclaimed, anxiously. "Well, all right." He rapped on the taxi window with his stick. "I say, my man."

"Yeah?" the Bearcat answered as he choked down the speed of the car.

"Drive us to the Plaza—the Plaza!"

"Oh, you darling!" cried the girl.

FROM *A Bio-Bibliography*

I like movies about strong women. I was the first liberated woman, y' know. No guy was gonna get the best of me, that's what I wrote all my scripts about.

You must be good and tired.
West: No, just tired.

I'm not a little girl from a little town making good in a big town. I'm a big girl from a big town making good in a little town.

Hatcheck girl: Goodness, what lovely diamonds.
West: Goodness had nothing to do with it, dearie.

★

It takes two to get one in trouble.

★

I've been things and seen places.

★

When I'm good, I'm very good, but when I'm bad, I'm better.

★

I used to be Snow White but I drifted.

★

It's not the men in my life, but the life in my men that counts.

★

Too much of a good thing can be wonderful.

★

Keep cool and collect.

★

Between two evils I always pick the one I never tried before.

★

I always say keep a diary and one day it will keep you.

★

I generally avoid temptation. Unless I can't resist it.

★

If young girls knew more about love and didn't take it so seriously, it would be better for them.

I have never minded foreign films, but who needs dirty foreign films? We can do better dirty films ourselves.

Some mousy women have more oomph in their hip pocket than a lot of beautiful women have in their whole bodies.

★

Politics? I keep up with what's going on. Although I'm not much for politics myself. But I always know a good party man when I see one. . . .

Edith Wharton
(1862–1937)

FROM *The House of Mirth*

"Ah, there's the difference—a girl must [marry], a man may if he chooses." She surveyed him critically. "Your coat's a little shabby—but who cares? It doesn't keep people from asking you to dine. If I were shabby no one would have me; a woman is asked out as much for her clothes as for herself. The clothes are the background, the frame, if you like: they don't make success, but they are a part of it. Who wants a dingy woman? We are expected to be pretty and well-dressed till we drop—and if we can't keep it up alone, we have to go into partnership."

It amused her to think that any one as rich as Mr. Percy Gryce should be shy; but she was gifted with treasures of indulgence for such idiosyncrasies, and besides, his timidity might serve her purpose better than too much assurance. She had the art of giving self-confidence to the embarrassed, but she was not equally sure of being able to embarrass the self-confident.

She waited till the train had emerged from the tunnel and was racing between the ragged edges of the northern suburbs. Then, as it lowered its speed near

Yonkers, she rose from her seat and drifted slowly down the carriage. As she passed Mr. Gryce, the train gave a lurch, and he was aware of a slender hand gripping the back of his chair. He rose with a start, his ingenuous face looking as though it had been dipped in crimson: even the reddish tint in his beard seemed to deepen.

The train swayed again, almost flinging Miss Bart into his arms. She steadied herself with a laugh and drew back; but he was enveloped in the scent of her dress, and his shoulder had felt her fugitive touch.

"Oh, Mr. Gryce, is it you? I'm so sorry—I was trying to find the porter and get some tea."

She held out her hand as the train resumed its level rush, and they stood exchanging a few words in the aisle. Yes—he was going to Bellomont. He had heard she was to be of the party—he blushed again as he admitted it. And was he to be there for a whole week? How delightful!

But at this point one or two belated passengers from the last station forced their way into the carriage, and Lily had to retreat to her seat.

"The chair next to mine is empty—do take it," she said over her shoulder; and Mr. Gryce, with considerable embarrassment, succeeded in effecting an exchange which enabled him to transport himself and his bags to her side.

"Ah—and here is the porter, and perhaps we can have some tea."

She signalled to that official, and in a moment, with the ease that seemed to attend the fulfilment of all her wishes, a little table had been set up between the seats, and she had helped Mr. Gryce to bestow his encumbering properties beneath it.

When the tea came he watched her in silent fascination while her hands flitted above the tray, looking miraculously fine and slender in contrast to the coarse china and lumpy bread. It seemed wonderful to him that any one should perform with such careless ease the difficult task of making tea in public in a lurching train. He would never have dared to order it for himself, lest he should attract the notice of his fellow-passengers; but, secure in the shelter of her conspicuousness, he sipped the inky draught with a delicious sense of exhilaration.

Lily, with the flavour of Selden's caravan tea on her lips, had no great fancy to drown it in the railway brew which seemed such nectar to her companion; but, rightly judging that one of the charms of tea is the fact of drinking it together, she proceeded to give the last touch to Mr. Gryce's enjoyment by smiling at him across her lifted cup.

"Is it quite right—I haven't made it too strong?" she asked solicitously; and he replied with conviction that he had never tasted better tea.

"I daresay it is true," she reflected; and her imagination was fired by the thought that Mr. Gryce, who might have sounded the depths of the most complex self-indulgence, was perhaps actually taking his first journey alone with a pretty woman.

It struck her as providential that she should be the instrument of his initiation. Some girls would not have known how to manage him. They would have over-emphasized the novelty of the adventure, trying to make him feel in it the zest of an escapade. But Lily's methods were more delicate. She remembered that her cousin Jack Stepney had once defined Mr. Gryce as the young man who had promised his mother never to go out in the rain without his overshoes; and acting on this hint, she resolved to impart a gently domestic air to the scene, in the hope that her companion, instead of feeling that he was doing something reckless or unusual, would merely be led to dwell on the advantage of always having a companion to make one's tea in the train.

But in spite of her efforts, conversation flagged after the tray had been removed, and she was driven to take a fresh measurement of Mr. Gryce's limitations. It was not, after all, opportunity but imagination that he lacked: he had a mental palate which would never learn to distinguish between railway tea and nectar. There was, however, one topic she could rely on: one spring that she had only to touch to set his simple machinery in motion. She had refrained from touching it because it was a last resource, and she had relied on other arts to stimulate other sensations; but as a settled look of dullness began to creep over his candid features, she saw that extreme measures were necessary.

"And how," she said, leaning forward, "are you getting on with your Americana?"

His eye became a degree less opaque: it was as though an incipient film had been removed from it, and she felt the pride of a skillful operator.

"I've got a few new things," he said, suffused with pleasure, but lowering his voice as though he feared his fellow-passengers might be in league to despoil him.

She returned a sympathetic enquiry, and gradually he was drawn on to talk of his latest purchases. It was the one subject which enabled him to forget himself, or allowed him, rather, to remember himself without constraint, because he was at home in it, and could assert a superiority that there were few to dispute. Hardly any of his acquaintances cared for Americana, or knew anything about them; and the consciousness of this ignorance threw Mr. Gryce's knowledge into agreeable relief. The only difficulty was to introduce the topic and to keep it to the front; most people showed no desire to have their ignorance dispelled, and Mr. Gryce was like a merchant whose warehouses are crammed with an unmarketable commodity.

But Miss Bart, it appeared, really did want to know about Americana; and moreover, she was already sufficiently informed to make the task of farther instruction as easy as it was agreeable. She questioned him intelligently, she heard him submissively; and, prepared for the look of lassitude which usually crept over his listeners' faces, he grew eloquent under her receptive gaze. The "points" she had the presence of mind to glean from Selden, in anticipation of this very contingency, were serving her to such good purpose that she began to think her visit to him had been the luckiest incident of the day. She had once more shown her talent for profiting by the unexpected, and dangerous theories as to the advisability of yielding to impulse were germinating under the surface of smiling attention which she continued to present to her companion.

Mr. Gryce's sensations, if less definite, were equally agreeable. He felt his confused titillation with which the lower organisms welcome the gratification of their needs, and all his senses floundered in a vague well-being, through which Miss Bart's personality was dimly but pleasantly perceptible.

Mr. Gryce's interest in Americana had not originated with himself: it was impossible to think of him as evolving any taste of his own. An uncle had left him a collection already noted among bibliophiles; the existence of the collection was the only fact that had ever shed glory on the name of Gryce, and the nephew took as much pride in his inheritance as though it had been his own work. Indeed, he gradually came to regard it as such, and to feel a sense of personal complacency when he chanced on any reference to the Gryce Americana. Anxious as he was to avoid personal notice, he took, in the printed mention of his name, a pleasure so exquisite and excessive that it seemed a compensation for his shrinking from publicity.

To enjoy the sensation as often as possible, he subscribed to all the reviews dealing with book-collecting in general, and American history in particular, and as allusions to his library abounded in the pages of these journals, which formed his only reading, he came to regard himself as figuring prominently in the public eye, and to enjoy the thought of the interest which would be excited if the persons he met in the street, or sat among in travelling, were suddenly to be told that he was the possessor of the Gryce Americana.

Most timidities have such secret compensations, and Miss Bart was discerning enough to know that the inner vanity is generally in proportion to the outer self-deprecation. With a more confident person she would not have dared to dwell so long on one topic, or to show such exaggerated interest in it; but she had rightly guessed that Mr. Gryce's egoism was a thirsty soil, requiring constant nurture from without. Miss Bart had the gift of following an undercurrent of thought while she appeared to be sailing on the surface of conversation; and in this case her mental excursion took the form of a rapid survey of Mr. Percy Gryce's future as combined with her own. The Gryces were from Albany, and but lately introduced to the metropolis, where the mother and son had come, after old Jefferson Gryce's death, to take possession of his house in Madison Avenue—an appalling house, all brown stone without and black walnut within, with the Gryce library in a fire-proof annex that looked like a mausoleum. Lily, however, knew all about them: young Mr. Gryce's arrival had fluttered the maternal breasts of New York, and when a girl has no mother to palpitate for her she must needs be on the alert for herself. Lily, therefore, had not only contrived to put herself in the young man's way, but had made the acquaintance of Mrs. Gryce, a monumental woman with the voice of a pulpit orator and a mind preoccupied with the iniquities of her servants, who came sometimes to sit with Mrs. Peniston and learn from that lady how she managed to prevent the kitchen-maid's smuggling groceries out of the house. Mrs. Gryce had a kind of impersonal benevolence: cases of individual need she regarded with suspicion, but she subscribed to Institutions where their annual reports showed an impressive surplus. Her domestic duties were manifold, for they extended from furtive inspections of the servants' bedrooms to unannounced descents to the cellar; but she had never allowed herself many pleasures. Once, however, she had had a special edition of the Sarum Rule printed in rubric and presented to every clergyman in the diocese; and the gilt album in which their letters of thanks were pasted formed the chief ornament of her drawing-room table.

Percy had been brought up in the principles which so excellent a woman was sure to inculcate. Every form of prudence and suspicion had been grafted on a nature originally reluctant and cautious, with the result that it would have seemed hardly needful for Mrs. Gryce to extract his promise about the overshoes, so little likely was he to hazard himself abroad in the rain. After attaining his majority, and coming into the fortune which the late Mr. Gryce had made out of a patent device for excluding fresh air from hotels, the young man continued to live with his mother in Albany; but on Jefferson Gryce's death, when another large property passed into her son's hands, Mrs. Gryce thought that what she called his "interests" demanded his presence in New York. She accordingly installed herself in the Madison Avenue house, and Percy, whose sense of duty was not inferior to his mother's, spent all his week days in the handsome Broad Street office where a batch of pale men on small salaries had grown grey in the management of the Gryce estate, and where he was initiated with becoming reverence into every detail of the art of accumulation.

As far as Lily could learn, this had hitherto been Mr. Gryce's only occupation, and she might have been pardoned for thinking it not too hard a task to interest a young man who had been kept on such low diet. At any rate, she felt herself so completely in command of the situation that she yielded to a sense of security in which all fear of Mr. Rosedale, and of the difficulties on which that fear was contingent, vanished beyond the edge of thought.

The stopping of the train at Garrisons would not have distracted her from these thoughts, had she not caught a sudden look of distress in her companion's eye. His seat faced toward the door, and she guessed that he had been perturbed by the approach of an acquaintance; a fact confirmed by the turning of heads and general sense of commotion which her own entrance into a railway-carriage was apt to produce.

She knew the symptoms at once, and was not surprised to be hailed by the high notes of a pretty woman, who entered the train accompanied by a maid, a bull-terrier, and a footman staggering under a load of bags and dressing-cases.

"Oh, Lily—are you going to Bellomont? Then you can't let me have your seat, I suppose? But I *must* have a seat in this carriage—porter, you must find me a place at once. Can't some one be put somewhere else? I want to be with my friends. Oh, how do you do, Mr. Gryce? Do please make him understand that I must have a seat next to you and Lily."

Mrs. George Dorset, regardless of the mild efforts of a traveller with a carpet-bag, who was doing his best to make room for her by getting out of the train, stood in the middle of the aisle, diffusing about her that general sense of exasperation which a pretty woman on her travels not infrequently creates.

She was smaller and thinner than Lily Bart, with a restless pliability of pose, as if she could have been crumpled up and run through a ring, like the sinuous draperies she affected. Her small pale face seemed the mere setting of a pair of dark exaggerated eyes, of which the visionary gaze contrasted curiously with her self-assertive tone and gestures; so that, as one of her friends observed, she was like a disembodied spirit who took up a great deal of room.

Having finally discovered that the seat adjoining Miss Bart's was at her disposal, she possessed herself of it with a farther displacement of her surroundings, explaining meanwhile that she had come across from Mount Kisco in her motor-car that morning, and had been kicking her heels for an hour at Garrisons, without even the alleviation of a cigarette, her brute of a husband having neglected to replenish her case before they parted that morning.

"And at this hour of the day I don't suppose you've a single one left, have you, Lily?" she plaintively concluded.

Miss Bart caught the startled glance of Mr. Percy Gryce, whose own lips were never defiled by tobacco.

"What an absurd question, Bertha!" she exclaimed, blushing at the thought of the store she had laid in at Lawrence Selden's.

"Why, don't you smoke? Since when have you given it up? What—you never— And you don't either, Mr. Gryce? Ah, of course—how stupid of me—I understand."

And Mrs. Dorset leaned back against her travelling cushions with a smile which made Lily wish there had been no vacant seat beside her own.

Bridge at Bellomont usually lasted till the small hours; and when Lily went to bed that night she had played too long for her own good.

Feeling no desire for the self-communion which awaited her in her room, she lingered on the broad stairway, looking down into the hall below, where the last card-players were grouped about the tray of tall glasses and silver-collared decanters which the butler had just placed on a low table near the fire.

The hall was arcaded, with a gallery supported on columns of pale yellow marble. Tall clumps of flowering plants were grouped against a background of dark foliage in the angles of the walls. On the crimson carpet a deer-hound and two or three spaniels dozed luxuriously before the fire, and the light from the great central lantern overhead shed a brightness on the women's hair and struck sparks from their jewels as they moved.

There were moments when such scenes delighted Lily, when they gratified her sense of beauty and her craving for the external finish of life; there were others when they gave a sharper edge to the meagerness of her own opportunities. This was one of the moments when the sense of contrast was uppermost, and she turned away impatiently as Mrs. George Dorset, glittering in serpentine spangles, drew Percy Gryce in her wake to a confidential nook beneath the gallery.

It was not that Miss Bart was afraid of losing her newly acquired hold over Mr. Gryce. Mrs. Dorset might startle or dazzle him, but she had neither the skill nor the patience to effect his capture. She was too self-engrossed to penetrate the recesses of his shyness, and besides, why should she care to give herself the trouble? At most it might amuse her to make sport of his simplicity for an evening—after that he would be merely a burden to her, and knowing this, she was far too experienced to encourage him. But the mere thought of that other woman who could take a man up and toss him aside as she willed, without having to regard him as a possible factor in her plans, filled Lily Bart with envy. She had been bored all the afternoon by Percy Gryce—the mere thought seemed to waken an echo of his droning voice—but she could not ignore him on the morrow, she must follow up her success, must submit to more boredom, must be ready with fresh compliances and adaptabilities, and all on the bare chance that he might ultimately decide to do her the honor of boring her for life.

Frances Miriam Whitcher
(1812–52)

Hezekiah Bedott

He was a wonderful hand to mortalize, husband was, specially after he begun to enjoy poor health. He made an observation once, when he was in one of his poor turns, that I shall never forget the longest day I live.

He says to me one winter evenin as we was a-settin by the fire—I was a-knittin. I was always a great knitter—and he was smokin, though the doctor used to tell him he'd be better off to leave tobacco alone. When he was well, he used to take his pipe and smoke a spell after he'd got the chores done up, and when he warn't well, he used to smoke the biggest part of the time.

Well, he took his pipe out of his mouth and turned toward me, and I knowed somethin was comin, for he had a particular way of lookin round when he was a-goin to say anything uncommon. Well, he says to me, "Silly,"—my name was Prisilly, naturally, but he generally called me "Silly" because 'twas handier, you know—well, he says to me, "Silly," and he looked pretty solemn, I tell you! He had a solemn countenance, and after he got to be deacon 'twas more so, but since he'd lost his health he looked solemner than ever, and certainly you wouldn't wonder at it if you knew how much he underwent. He was troubled with a pain in his chest and mazin weakness in the spine of his back, besides the pleurisy in his side, and bein broke of his rest of nights because he was put to it for breath when he laid down. Why, it's an unaccountable fact that when that man died he hadn't seen a well day in fifteen year, though when he was married and for five or six years after, I shouldn't desire to see a ruggeder man than he was. But the time I'm a-speakin of, he'd been out of health nigh upon ten year, and, oh dear sakes! How he had altered since the first time I ever see him! That was to a quiltin to Squire Smith's a spell before Sally was married. I'd no idea *then* that Sal Smith was a-goin to be married to Sam Pendergrass. She'd been keepin company with Mose Hewlitt for better'n a year, and everybody said *that* was a settled thing and lo and behold! All of a sudden she up and took Sam Pendergrass. Well, that was the first time I ever see my husband, and if anybody'd a-told me then that I should ever marry him, I should a-said—

But lawful sakes! I was a-goin to tell you what he said to me that evenin, and when a body begins to tell a thing I believe in finishin on it some time or other. Some folks have a way of talkin round and round and round for evermore. Now there's Miss Jenkins, she that was Poll Bingham before she was married—but what husband said to me was this. He says to me, "Silly."

Says I, "What?" I didn't say, "What, Hezekiah?" for I didn't like his name. The first time I ever heard it I near killed myself a-laughin. "Hezekiah Bedott!" says I. "Well, I would give up if I had such a name!" But then, you know, I had no more idea of marryin the feller than you have this minute of marryin the governor. I suppose you think it's curious we should name our oldest son Hezekiah. Well, we done it to please Father and Mother Bedott. It's his name, and he and Mother Bedott both used to think that names had ought to go down from generation to generation. But we always called him Kiah, you know. That boy *is* a blessin! I ain't the only one that thinks so, I guess. Now, don't you ever tell anybody that I said so, but between you and me, I rather guess that if Kesiah Winkle thinks she's a-goin to catch Kiah Bedott, she is a *little* out of her reckonin!

Well, husband he says to me, "Silly." And says I, "What?" though I'd no idea what he was a-goin to say, didn't know but what it was somethin about his sufferins, though he warn't apt to complain, but used to say that he wouldn't wish his worst enemy to suffer one minute as he did all the time, but that can't be called grumblin—think it can? Why, I've seen him when you'd a-thought no mortal could a-helped grumblin, but *he* didn't. He and me went once in the dead of winter in a one-hoss sleigh out to see a sister of his. You know the snow is deep in this section of the country. Well, the hoss got stuck in one of them snow banks, and there we set, unable to stir, and to cap it all, husband was took with a dreadful crick in his back. Now that is what I call a predicament! Most men would a-swore, but husband didn't. We might a-been settin there to this day, far as *I* know, if there hadn't a-happened to come along a mess of men in a double team, and they pulled us out.

But husband says to me—I could see by the light of the fire, for there didn't happen to be any candle burnin, if I don't disremember, though my memory is sometimes rather forgetful, but I know we weren't apt to burn candles exceptin when we had company—I could see by the light of the fire that his mind was uncommon solemnized. Says he to me, "Silly."

I says to him, "What?"

He says to me, says he, "We're all poor creatures."

Herman Wouk
(Contemporary)

FROM *City Boy*

. . . they arrived at Golden's Restaurant on Southern Boulevard without exchanging another word.

Herbie's heart glowed within him at the sight of the steaks, fruits, layer cakes, and thickly creamed pastries in the glittering show window of Golden's, while Mr. Bookbinder, seeing Powers, Louis Glass, and Krieger seated at a table near the window, suddenly wondered whether bringing Herbie had not been a foolish deed. An impulse to honor the boy, a vague sense that he was in the habit of neglecting him, and an equally cloudy notion that the time had come to give his son the baptism of fire of a real business discussion had combined to cause his act. Now he sensed an urge to send him home. But Jacob Bookbinder was not in the habit of altering his resolutions. In fact, it was his way to quell his own hesitancy with grim pleasure. "Do it and see," was his favorite word to himself. He had invited Herbie to dinner at Golden's, and dinner at Golden's Herbie would have.

"Come, my boy, I see we're late," he said, and led his son inside.

Introducing Herbie was as awkward as his father expected, but he met the astonished glances of the others squarely and explained that he was rewarding his boy with a treat because he had skipped. Louis Glass, a fat, rubicund man with a black mustache, shook Herbie's hand and congratulated him. He had seen many youngsters ripen into clients yielding fees. Powers, already out of sorts at being dragged up to the Bronx after dark, permitted himself to look annoyed as he rapped the ash out of his pipe and thrust it into a pocket.

Krieger delivered his views as follows: "Same father, same son. Haybie big future. Maybe not go too fast better. Little fat boy in college better maybe not. Slow and steady turtle beat rabbit. Haybie different naturally. Smart is very fine—"

The table had places only for four. As Mr. Krieger rattled on, the waiter moved a narrow serving table alongside, projecting into the aisle. Here Herbie sat, looking like an extremely unnecessary appendage to the group. Menus were placed in the hands of the diners, and the men ordered their meals carelessly and quickly.

Not so Herbie.

"What should I have, Pa?" he said nervously, bewildered by the menu.

"You're old enough to order for yourself. Have whatever you want."

Herbie ran his eye up and down the page and got a confused impression of a meal composed of sponge cake, pastry, smoked salmon, goulash, vegetables in sour cream, roast chicken, chopped herring, prunes, and ice cream.

"I—I'm not very hungry," he faltered.

"Then skip down to the main course. That's all we're having," said the father, and indicated a section of the bill of fare with his finger.

This was a help. But having to choose among lamb chops, broiled chicken, roast duck, steak, and so forth was still torture—not less for the youngster than for the waiter, a squat, bitter-faced bald man in greasy black trousers and spotted gray cotton jacket. This functionary shifted from foot to foot while Herbie puzzled; he yawned, he rapped his pencil against the order pad, he went "ha-hem" several times, and he stared malevolently at the boy, obviously wishing him far away and in bad health.

"Come, Herbie, the man can't stand there forever," said the father.

Powers said, "The kid evidently doesn't know what he wants. Order for him."

"I'll have the boiled haddock," Herbie burst out all at once, picking the item under his eye at that instant.

Everybody, even the waiter, looked amazed.

"Don't be silly, boy," said Jacob Bookbinder. "Boiled haddock, with all those delicious meat dishes to pick from? Come, take a steak."

But Herbie felt that his self-respect, his whole grip on manhood, depended on his sticking to the haddock now, although he loathed it. "Can't a guy order what he wants?" he complained. "I ordered boiled haddock, and that's what I'd like."

"Give him boiled haddock," said his father with a shrug. The waiter pried the bill of fare out of Herbie's spasmodically clutching fingers and walked off. Herbie gloomily watched the stooped back disappear through the swinging kitchen doors, and cursed his own folly.

The consequences were worse than he imagined. Golden's was mainly a meat restaurant. The fish was a desultory item placed on the menu for the rare customer who insisted on fish. Soon the waiter reappeared with four sizzling steaks that smelled heavenly, and a plate containing a pair of round blobs, white and green. The white was the haddock, buried under a thick flour sauce; the green was an unexpected horror, creamed spinach, which came with the fish. As the waiter put Herbie's plate down he winked, and all the men laughed. Herbie felt a blush rise to his face.

"That fish looks disgusting," said his father. "Waiter, take that mess away and bring the boy some lamb chops."

"Pa, please, this is just what I want," cried Herbie angrily. He placed his hand protectingly against the plate, and the gluey white mass trembled a little. The boy's throat crawled at the prospect of eating it. But he was going to eat it or die.

"After all, Bookbinder, he's grown up," said Powers with a grin. "Didn't he just skip to the eighth grade?"

Herbie's father glanced at the young man from Manhattan with narrowed eyes.

"All right, my boy," he said to Herbie. "But as long as you ordered it, eat it."

And Herbie, who understood his father's appeal not to disgrace him, ate it, with all the men watching him. Not a morsel of spinach or haddock remained. Heroes in other books do more noble and colorful deeds, but Herbie Bookbinder stands or falls as a hero for swallowing down every trace of those two ghastly mounds, green and white, and smacking his lips over them.

"Well, Bookbinder," said Powers when the steaks were eaten, leaning back and packing his pipe from an alligator-skin pouch, "do we talk business or do you send the boy home first?"

"The boy's doing no harm," retorted Bookbinder, "unless you other gentlemen object to him."

There was a difficult pause.

"Why, I think," said Louis Glass heartily, "that it'll do Herbie good to hear a business talk. Hear a business talk. Nothing like starting early in life, early in life, eh, Herbie?" He slapped the boy lightly on the back, and lit a cigar.

The waiter brought dessert. It was a house custom at Golden's to serve French pastry on a little flat stand, which was placed on the table when coffee was served, and left there. The stand accommodated eight pieces. The waiter simply counted the number missing at the close of the meal, and charged for them on the bill. None of the men accepted a piece when the waiter offered it to them, so he set the little stand down before Herbie and departed. The boy felt his shattered appetite pull itself together as he surveyed the eight creamy pastries, all of different shapes and colors.

Louis Glass polished the pince-nez that hung on a black ribbon around his neck. "Well, gentlemen, I see no reason why we can't settle our business between the time we start our coffee and finish it. Start our coffee and finish it," he said.

"That'll suit me beautifully," remarked Powers. "I'm late for a theater party now."

Bookbinder and Krieger said nothing.

Herbie tentatively selected a chocolate-covered cylinder filled with whipped cream, and sank his teeth into it. He seemed to hear chimes of Paradise. By comparison with this, the frap itself sank out of sight.

"There's only one thing to be discussed," went on Louis Glass. "I've described to you, Bookbinder, the advantages that will accrue to both you and Krieger from a merger of Bronx River with Interborough. I've made it as clear as I can that Interborough, which is now the largest ice company in New York, will guarantee to give both of you top executive positions. As I happen to be their attorney, I am speaking with some authority, with some authority. I have also given you my opinion that the so-called blue paper is a totally irregular document, no more than a scratch-pad memorandum, in effect, which does not transfer in due and proper form any stocks to you, and have advised you that if you choose to stand on it your stand will be overthrown in court. Overthrown in court."

During this speech, Herbie finished the whipped-cream roll in three rapturous bites. He now chose a charming oval piece entirely covered with green and chocolate cream, and bit into it.

"Your decision, then, as I see it," proceeded the lawyer, waving away clouds of blue smoke from Powers' fast-puffing pipe, "must be the sensible one of accepting this great increase in your good fortunes—I refer to the merger—or the highly dubious one of a court fight as to whether you or Mr. Powers has control of the Place, which I have stated you will lose. Stated you will lose."

Herbie heard these words dimly through the fog of ecstasy conjured up by French pastry, and wondered why Mr. Glass had the habit of acting as his own echo. But he forgot the perplexity as the last bite of mint and chocolate vanished, leaving him with the urgent question, which cake to eat next. The boy was not aware that these things would have to be paid for. They had been set before him like a bowl of fruit at home, and so he regarded them. After the haddock horror, it seemed to him that the only way to retrieve the glory of a restaurant meal was to consume as many pastries as he could hold. So he selected a chocolate éclair, and went to work on it.

When the lawyer finished talking, Bookbinder and Krieger looked at each other. Herbie's father started to speak, but Krieger hastily and loudly broke in, "I say this way. Blue paper maybe yes, maybe no, who say for sure? I say peaceable. Executive position ten thousand a year very fine, maybe three thousand not so fine. But peaceable black and white on paper how much guaranteed? All gentlemen, word good as gold, but black and white on paper not yet. Thirty years in the ice business always black and white more peaceable. Mr. Glass very fine explain, everybody good friends all stick together. I say this way—"

(The éclair gone, Herbie commenced a rapid demolition of a round brown pastry that looked rather like a potato but was filled with exquisite orange-flavored cream.)

"If I understand you correctly, Mr. Krieger," interrupted Louis Glass, "I believe you need say no more. Interborough is prepared to guarantee in writing, as a condition of the merger, both of your salaries at"—he glanced at Powers, who continued puffing at his pipe and gave a tiny nod—"five thousand a year, merely as a beginning. Merely as a beginning."

"You understand him wrong, and what he said meant nothing," exclaimed Jacob Bookbinder, his expression so drawn and belligerent that he hardly resembled the man who had been smiling at his son a little while before. Herbie had seen this expression, which he thought of as his father's "business face," more than once, and it terrified him. He paid more attention to the talk now, as he absently began to eat a flaky yellow Napoleon. . . .

Herbie could not follow the duel and lost interest. For some reason the Napoleon did not taste as good to him as the first four pastries had. He finished it quickly and began on a cherry tart. And now he became aware of a new disturbing fact: the waiter was standing near by, staring at him with a mixture of horror and fascination. With each bite he took of the tart the waiter's eyes seemed to open wider. Herbie could not imagine what the man was looking at. He glanced uneasily at his suit to see if a blotch of food had fallen on it, and looked behind him, but evidently there was no marvel in sight but himself, a perfectly ordinary boy. The waiter's eyes made him self-conscious. He gobbled down the tart, not enjoying it very much, and reached for something he had been saving, a morsel consisting of four walls of solid chocolate brimful of coffee-colored cream. As he bit into it he saw with some discomfort that the waiter's jaw dropped open and he actually grew pale. He concluded the man must be sick—probably from the food in this miserable restaurant. Herbie was feeling none too well himself. The beautiful chocolate cake somehow tasted not much better than the boiled haddock had, and was just as gluey.

The conversation had jumped ahead several notches during Herbie's preoccupation with the waiter. He tried to pick up the thread, nibbling at the pastry more and more slowly. Powers was saying, "—certainly don't see why I had to come uptown at night to hear this same foolish story. I thought you men had come to your senses."

"I cannot help calling it most ill-advised, most ill-advised," the lawyer said, crushing out his half-smoked cigar. "I assure you the blue paper as it stands is worthless. In my opinion, Mr. Powers would be justified in proceeding to sell Bronx River Ice, but we must recognize that as the attorney for Interborough I cannot advise them to purchase a property, title to which is in any way doubtful. Any way doubtful. . . ."

"Yes, I'm a crazy businessman," Bookbinder shot back. "I want to remain a businessman, instead of becoming Burlingame's assistant."

"Pa."

The word came faintly from Herbie's direction. His father turned and looked at him.

"Pa, I don't feel good."

Herbie slumped in his chair, looking straight ahead with dull eyes. In one listless hand hanging at his side was a fragment of chocolate cake. The color of the boy's face was not unlike that of the creamed spinach he had eaten.

"Lord in heaven! He's sick. Why did you have to eat that rotten fish, boy?" said the father in great distress.

"Mister, don't you blame our food!" shouted the waiter. He advanced to the table and raised his right hand high. "I hope I drop dead if that boy didn't eat seven pieces of French pastry. Seven pieces, mister! I saw him with my own eyes. From that even an elephant would get sick. I personally don't feel good from watching him."

Herbie stood up unsteadily.

"I guess I'll go home, Pa," he said. His stomach seemed to him to be rippling like a lake in a breeze; he could see mistily before his eyes the colored images of all the pastries he had eaten, swimming slowly around; and the word "frap" kept repeating itself in his brain—frap, frap, frap—and was somehow the most loathsome sound that man had ever uttered.

"Come, my boy, I'll take you." Bookbinder jumped up and grasped the boy's arm. "Gentlemen, our business was finished anyway, so excuse me for leaving like this. Mr. Powers, believe me you'll live to thank me for keeping our business in our own hands. Krieger, pay my check. Good night."

He rushed the boy outside and stood with him at the curb, signaling for a taxi. But none came at once, and Herbert, teetering on the curb, endured all the agonies of a rough sea voyage and then suddenly enjoyed the sovereign relief that comes of leaning over the rail. His father sympathetically gave him aid, and then walked the pale shaky boy home. Fresh air was better for him, now, than a taxi. The walk gradually revived Herbie, and through the darkness of his discomfort the drift of the business talk began to come back to him.

"Pa," he said timidly, "can Mr. Powers really sell the Place and throw you an' Mr. Krieger out?"

"Don't you worry about that," said Bookbinder. But his face was tense and sad. "Forget everything you heard, Herbie. For you it's castor oil and bed."

And thus, with castor oil, bed, and a chilly awareness that he had failed to distinguish himself, ended Herbie Bookbinder's first evening as a man among men.

Author Biographies

Bud Abbott (1897–1974)
Lou Costello (1906–59)

William "Bud" Abbott was born in Asbury Park, New Jersey, and as a teenager entered the family business of running burlesque shows. Eventually he landed onstage as a straight man, most successfully with his wife, Betty, until meeting Lou Costello. Costello was born in Paterson, New Jersey, and had a brief career as an actor and stuntman in Hollywood before breaking into burlesque as a comic. In 1936, Abbott and Costello teamed up and went on to star in every available medium: stage, radio, film, and television. In 1957, their recording of "Who's on First" was inducted into the Baseball Hall of Fame in Cooperstown, New York, making them the first non-baseball-playing celebrities ever to receive that honor.

Scott Adams (Contemporary)

Born and raised in Windham, New York, Adams received a B.A. in Economics from Hartwick College in 1979 and an MBA from the University of California at Berkeley in 1986. His experiences in the workplace, particularly at Crocker Bank and at Pacific Bell in the San Francisco Bay Area, inspired his famous comic strip *Dilbert*. Adams has described his cartoon hero as a composite of many of his past coworkers. He has published more than a dozen collections of *Dilbert* strips, and *Dilbert* appears in 1700 newspapers in fifty-one countries.

George Ade (1866–1944)

George Ade was born in Indiana and read Mark Twain's books as a child. His first publication, a school composition titled "A Basket of Potatoes," appeared in the *Gazette* in 1881. He attended Purdue University on a scholarship and graduated in 1887. He moved to Chicago in 1890 and wrote for the Chicago *Morning News*, which changed its name to the *News-Record*, and eventually to the *Record*. He wrote columns in collaboration with John McCutcheon until 1897. A collection of Ade's "Artie" sketches appeared in 1896 under the title *Artie, a Story of Streets and Town; Artie* led to his "discovery" by William Dean Howells. Ade started writing his "Fables" in 1897; the collections *Fables in Slang* (1899) and *More Fables* (1900) followed. The Fables were soon syndicated and more than a dozen collections were eventually published. Ade also found some success as a playwright; he wrote *The Sultan of Sulu* (1902), *Peggy from Paris* (1903), *The College Widow* (1904), and *The Old Town* (1910), among other plays.

Louisa May Alcott (1832–88)

Louisa May Alcott was the daughter of Bronson Alcott, well-known Transcendentalist, abolitionist, and educational reformer; her childhood provided not only the material for much of her best-known work, but the experience of poverty that shaped her determination to be self-supporting. Her early positions as a governess, companion, domestic servant and Civil War nurse are treated in *Work: A Story of Experience* (1861); later, she was able to support herself and her family through her writing. Alcott is most famous for her children's novels, especially the classic *Little Women* (1868), *Little Men* (1871), and *Jo's Boys* (1886), but she also wrote sensation stories and gothic thrillers, either anonymously or under a pseudonym, as well as more "serious" works for adults. Her second novel, *Moods,* deals with adultery and divorce; *Transcendental Wild Oats* (1873) is based on Alcott's experience at Fruitlands, a short-lived Utopian community established by her father. She never married, but remained close to her family and devoted much energy to such causes as women's suffrage. Some of her other works are *Hospital Sketches* (1863), *An Old-Fashioned Girl* (1870), *Eight Cousins* (1875), and *Rose in Bloom* (1876).

Woody Allen (Contemporary)

Allen was born Allen Stewart Konigsberg in New York City. An extremely prolific screenwriter and film director, Allen began his career in show business as a comedy writer for television. His first produced screenplay, *What's New Pussycat?*, was made into a movie in which he starred in 1965. *Take the Money and Run* (1969) marked his debut as director of his own material. His major films include *Play It Again, Sam* (1972); *Annie Hall* (1977), which received four Academy Awards, including Best Picture; *Manhattan* (1979); *Zelig* (1983); *Hannah and Her Sisters* (1986); *Husbands and Wives* (1992); *Mighty Aphrodite* (1995); *Deconstructing Harry* (1997); and *The Curse of the Jade Scorpion* (2001).

Regina Barreca (Contemporary)

Hailed as "smart and funny" by *People* magazine, Gina Barreca is the celebrated author of the bestselling *They Used to Call Me Snow White . . . But I Drifted, Perfect Husbands (and Other Fairy Tales), Sweet Revenge: The Wicked Delights of Getting Even* and a collection of essays, *Too Much of a Good Thing Is Wonderful.* Barreca also edited the *Penguin Book of Women's Humor.* Her works have been translated into Chinese, German, Spanish, Portuguese, and Japanese. She edited *Don't Tell Mama: The Penguin Book of Italian American Writing* and *A Sit-Down with the Sopranos: Watching Italian American Culture on TV's Most*

Talked-About Series. Her book *The ABC of Vice: An Insatiable Women's Guide* was cowritten with cartoonist Nicole Hollander, and *I'm With Stupid: One Man, One Woman, and 10,000 Years of Misunderstanding Between the Sexes Cleared Right Up* was cowritten with Gene Weingarten, of the *Washington Post.* She is a professor of English literature and feminist theory at the University of Connecticut and an award-winning columnist for the *Hartford Courant.* She has also regularly published articles in *The New York Times*, *The Washington Post*, *The Chicago Tribune*, and dozens of magazines.

Dave Barry (Contemporary)

A celebrated syndicated columnist and successful humorist, Dave Barry was born in New York State. He won the Pulitzer Prize for Commentary in 1988. His titles include *Dave Barry's Guide to Marriage and/or Sex* (1987), *Dave Barry Talks Back* (1991), *Dave Barry Does Japan* (1992), *Dave Barry Is Not Making This Up* (1994), *Dave Barry in Cyberspace* (1996), *Dave Barry Is from Mars and Venus* (1997), *Dave Barry Turns 50* (1998), *Dave Barry's Only Travel Guide You'll Ever Need* (1999), *Dave Barry's Complete Guide to Guys* (2000), and *Boogers Are My Beat: More Lies, But Some Actual Journalism* (2003).

Lynda Barry (Contemporary)

Born in Wisconsin, Barry grew up in Seattle and became the first member of her Filipino-American family to go to college. She was a fine arts major at Evergreen State College in Olympia, Washington, in 1977 when she started drawing cartoons following a breakup with her boyfriend. Barry began her collaboration with *Esquire* in the early 1980s and her work was soon syndicated in weekly newspapers like the *Village Voice* and *L.A. Weekly* throughout the country. She adapted her novel *The Good Times Are Killing Me* (1988) for the stage in 1991. Barry's titles include *Girls & Boys* (1981), *The Fun House* (1987), *Heap Big Dysfunctional World* (1990), *My Perfect Life* (1992), *It's So Magic* (1994), *The Lynda Barry Experience* (1996), *The Freddie Stories* (1999), *The Greatest of Marlys* (2000), *Cruddy: An Illustrated Novel* (2000), and *One Hundred Demons* (2002).

Robert Benchley (1889–1945)

One of the most famous members of the Algonquin Round Table group, Benchley was born in Worcester, Massachusetts, and received a degree from Harvard in 1912. In addition to collaborating with numerous magazines in New York in the 1920s, Benchley worked in Hollywood as a radio and film actor, writer, and producer. He won an Academy Award in 1936 for his short film *How to Sleep.* His titles include *20,000 Leagues Under the Sea or, David Copperfield, Benchley—or Else, Pluck and Luck, Love Conquers All*, and *My Ten Years in a Quandary and How They Grew.*

Jennifer Berman (Contemporary)

Jennifer Berman is a nationally syndicated cartoonist whose work appears in both major dailies and alternative weeklies, as well as magazines such as *Ms., Harper's, Mademoiselle,* and *Glamour.* Her cartoons often appear for the first time in her line of postcards. Berman's books include *Adult Children of Normal Parents* (1994), *Why Dogs Are Better Than Republicans* (1996), *Why Dogs Are Better Than Kids* (2000), and *Why Dogs Are Better Than Men* (2001). She lives in Chicago.

Ambrose Bierce (1842–1913 or –14)

The man who would later be known as the "Wickedest Man in San Francisco" was born in Ohio, grew up in Indiana, and worked as a printer's assistant on the antislavery newspaper *Northern Indianian* between the ages of fifteen and seventeen. He studied at the Kentucky Military Institute in 1859 and enlisted for the Civil War, during which he was involved in most of the deadliest battles. Bierce was severely wounded and discharged in 1865. The following year, he joined a mapping expedition covering the territories between Nebraska and California. He began working as a professional writer in San Francisco in 1867; he quickly became well known for his weekly column, "The Town Crier," in the *Newsletter.* At the height of his popularity, he was famous for his humorous writings from San Francisco to London, where he lived between 1872 and 1875, and where his first three books appeared under the pseudonym Dod Grile. He was editor of the weekly magazine *Wasp* between 1881 and 1886. His books include *Tales of Soldiers and Civilians* (1891), *Fantastic Fables* (1899), *Write It Right* (1909), and *The Cynic's Word Book* (1906), later reprinted as *The Devil's Dictionary* (1911). Bierce died in mysterious circumstances in Mexico, where he was last seen on December 26, 1913.

Amy Bloom (Contemporary)

Amy Bloom's highly acclaimed first book, *Come To Me: Stories* (1993), was a National Book Award Finalist and was also a finalist for the *Los Angeles Times* Fiction Award. Her novel *Love Invents Us*—described by the *Los Angeles Times* as "lyrical and funny"—was also welcomed with considerable praise. Her most recent collections include *A Blind Man Can See How Much I Love You: Stories* (2001), which has also received wide critical acclaim, and *Normal: Transsexual CEOs, Crossdressing Cops, and Hermaphrodites with Attitude* (2003). Bloom's stories have appeared in such publications as *The New Yorker, Story, Antaeus,* and *River City;* they have been anthologized in *Best American Stories* of 1991 and 1992 and in the 1994 *O. Henry Prize Story Collection.* Bloom is also a contributing editor for *New Woman* and the *Boston Review of Books.* She lives in Connecticut.

Elayne Boosler (Contemporary)

Elayne Boosler, a popular comedian, has performed her stand-up routine in countless venues. Her first television special, *Party of One*, aired in 1986, and was followed by *Broadway Baby, Top Tomata,* and *Live Nude Girls.* She has also made numerous appearances on such shows as *Politically Incorrect, The Today Show*, and *Crossfire.* The *New York Times* once commented of her, "How refreshing, a woman who doesn't have to tear her own skin off for our amusement."

Mel Brooks (Contemporary)

Brooks was born Melvin Kaminsky in Brooklyn, New York. He served during World War II and organized shows for his fellow servicemen. He began working as a stand-up comedian in the Catskills when he returned to the United States after the war. In the 1950s Brooks worked as a television writer with Neil Simon, Woody Allen, and Carl Reiner. He teamed up with Reiner in 1960 for the popular routines called "The 2000 Year Old Man"; Brooks and Reiner made a hit record and appeared on numerous television shows to perform these routines. Brooks went on to win three Grammy Awards for this landmark role. In the late 1960s, Brooks turned his attention to movies. He won an Academy Award for his screenplay for *The Producers.* Brooks's films as director include *Blazing Saddles* (1973), *Young Frankenstein* (1974), *Silent Movie* (1976), and *Space Balls* (1987). His production company, Brooksfilms, is responsible for more serious movie fare such as *84 Charing Cross Road*, starring his wife, Anne Bancroft.

Claude Brown (Contemporary)

Claude Brown was born in New York City; his parents had migrated North from South Carolina in search of work. He grew up in Harlem and became a member of a street gang by the age of ten. He was sent to the Wiltwyck school for delinquent boys but at thirteen he was back on the streets and shot during an attempted bank robbery. Brown graduated from high school in 1957, played jazz in Greenwich Village, and received a degree from Howard University in 1965. That same year he published his highly regarded autobiography, *Manchild in the Promised Land.* The book met with instant success and turned Brown into a prominent voice in American letters. His second book, *Children of Ham* (1976), was less successful but Brown remains active in social causes.

Charles Farrar Browne (1834–67)

Browne was born in Waterford, Maine, and at the age of thirteen he became an apprentice at the *Weekly Democrat* in Lancaster, New Hampshire. He later wrote for the Boston weekly *Carpet-Bag*, then moved to Ohio and worked in the printing trade until he became an editor at the Cleveland *Plain Dealer* in 1857. He invented the persona of Artemus Ward in the pages of the *Dealer*. Browne left Cleveland three years later and began working as a regular contributor for *Vanity Fair*. He traveled extensively until his death, of tuberculosis, in 1867. He was an important figure in American humor during the Civil War era, and his lectures, which probably influenced Mark Twain, met with popular success from San Francisco to London. Browne's books include *Artemus Ward; His Book* (1862), *Artemus Ward; His Travels* (1865), and *Artemus Ward Among the Fenians* (1866). His *Collected Works* appeared in 1870.

George Carlin (Contemporary)

George Carlin's career in comedy began in radio, at age nineteen, while he was in the Air Force. He went on to make appearances on numerous television shows, including a number of HBO specials in the 1970s and 80s. Carlin is perhaps best known for his "Seven Words You Can't Say on Television" monologue; his often controversial humor is known for its intelligence and irreverence as well as its profanity. Carlin's 1972 album *FM & AM* received a Grammy Award; later recordings include *Class Clown* (1986) and *Parental Advisory—Explicit Lyrics* (1990). He won Cable-Ace awards for the shows *Doin' It Again* and *Jammin' in New York*—which also won a Grammy Award for best spoken-word comedy album. Carlin is also the author of *Brain Droppings* (1997) and in 2001 the CD version of the book received a Grammy. In 2001, he received a Lifetime Achievement Award at the Fifteenth Annual American Comedy Awards on Comedy Central. He is also the author of *Napalm and Silly Putty* (2001).

Roz Chast (Contemporary)

Chast was born in Brooklyn and decided to become a cartoonist after discovering Charles Addams at the age of eight. She received a B.F.A. from the Rhode Island School of Design in 1977 and published cartoons in *The Village Voice* and *National Lampoon* before finding a permanent home for her work at *The New Yorker* in 1979. Her cartoons have been collected in more than seven volumes, including *Proof of Life on Earth* (1991) and *Childproof: Cartoons* (1997). She has also illustrated children's books, including *Now Everybody Hates Me*. Chast's work also includes an introduction and illustrations for *The New Yorker Book of Kids Cartoons* (2001) by Robert Mankoff. Her most recent work, *The Party, After You Left; Collected Cartoons 1995–2003*, brings together the last nine years of her cartoons.

Margaret Cho (Contemporary)

Celebrated stand-up comic Margaret Cho was born and raised in San Francisco and began her career in comedy at sixteen, performing in a club above her parents' bookstore. Shortly thereafter, she won a comedy contest where the first prize was opening for Jerry Seinfeld. During the early 1990s, Cho performed on the college circuit and has subsequently become one of the most popular touring comedians of our day. She won the American Comedy Award for Female Comedian in 1994, and in 1999, she took her off-Broadway hit and one-woman show, *I'm the One That I Want*, on a national tour that resulted in rave reviews, and a feature film and bestselling book by the same name. In 2001, Cho's tour of her second show, *Notorious C.H.O.*, was a smash-hit national tour that was made into a second feature film. In March 2003, Margaret embarked on her third sold-out national tour, *Revolution*. The film version of *Revolution* was released in 2004 as well as a behind-the-scenes documentary of the tour. Cho has been honored by GLAAD, American Women in Radio and Television, the National Gay and Lesbian Task Force, the Asian American Legal Defense and Education Fund, and the National Organization for Women for making a significant difference in promoting equal rights for all, regardless of race, sexual orientation, or gender identity.

James David Corrothers (1869–1917)

James Corrothers was born in Michigan; his parents were of mixed African and European American descent. He attended Northwestern University and became a school teacher. His friend Paul Dunbar encouraged him to write poetry and his dialect verse was published in the *Century Magazine*. He wrote humorous "negro" reports for the *Chicago Journal* and other newspapers; these pieces were later collected in the volume *The Black Cat Club* (1902). He became a Methodist minister until he was unjustly expelled from his church; he later became a Baptist, then a Presbyterian. He published an autobiography, *In Spite of the Handicap*, in 1916. He was famous in his time as a spokesman for the black community.

Bill Cosby (Contemporary)

Bill Cosby's long and successful career began on the night-club circuit before Cosby landed a part on the television series *I Spy*, for which he eventually won three Emmy Awards for best actor. His later TV shows include *The Bill Cosby Show, Cos*, and the enormously popular series *The Cosby Show*. He has won five Grammy Awards for best comedy album; his albums include *Bill Cosby Is a Very Funny Fellow . . . Right?, I Started Out as a Child*, and *Wonderfulness*. He has also appeared in a number of feature films. His books include *Fatherhood* (1993), *Love and Marriage* (1989), *Kids Say the Darndest Things* (1998), and *I Am What I Ate . . . And I'm Frightened!!! And Other Digressions from the Doctor of Comedy* (2003).

Josephine Daskam (1876–1961)

Josephine Daskam, who occasionally published under her married name, Bacon, was a prolific author of short stories, novels, articles, and poems. She graduated from Smith College in 1898 and published her *Smith College Stories* in 1900. She raised three children while contributing to magazines like *Harper's Bazaar, Ladies'*

Home Journal, and the *Saturday Evening Post*. One of Bacon's most popular books was *The Memoirs of a Baby* (1904), her satire on baby care and child-rearing. In her serious fiction, Bacon dealt with the New Woman and her struggle to gain a more equal status in society. She wrote the words to the "Hymn for the Nations" for the United Nations and compiled the *Girl Scout National Handbook* (1920). Her works include *Fables for the Fair* (1901), *Domestic Adventures* (1907), and *Kathy* (1934).

Ellen DeGeneres (Contemporary)

Ellen DeGeneres was born in Louisiana and moved to Texas with her mother after her parents' divorce. She attended the University of New Orleans but left before the end of her first semester. She supported her struggling career as a stand-up comic by working as a hostess, waitress, oyster shucker, clerical worker, and house painter. Her first big break happened in 1986 when she appeared on the *Tonight Show* hosted by Johnny Carson. DeGeneres's television sitcom *These Friends of Mine* first aired in 1994; it was soon revamped and renamed *Ellen*. The show and its star made social history when the Emmy-nominated "coming out" episode aired in April 1997. DeGeneres became the first openly gay actress to play a gay lead character on American television. In addition to her stand-up and television work, DeGeneres has also appeared in several movies. Her bestselling *My Point . . . and I Do Have One* was published in 1995. Her most recent book is *The Funny Thing Is . . .* (2003). In 2003, DeGeneres became creator and host of her own syndicated talk show, *The Ellen DeGeneres Show*.

Joseph Dennie (1768–1812)

Known in the nineteenth century as "the American Addison," Joseph Dennie grew up in Boston during the exciting years preceding the Revolution. His parents were involved in his education and gave him free rein in their extensive library. He attended Harvard and began writing poetry and essays in 1788. He passed the bar examination in 1794 and opened a law office in Charlestown, New Hampshire. Despite his official career as a lawyer, Dennie found time to write essays for various papers like the *Eagle* and the *Boston Centinel*; the *Federal Orrery* published his satire in 1795. He also became involved with publishing as writer and editor for the *Farmer's Museum* magazine, published out of Walpole, New Hampshire. He wrote the regular *Lay Preacher* essays in the *Farmer's Museum*; these essays, inspired by Sterne's *Sermons of Yorick*, were later printed in two volumes in 1796 and 1816 and established his literary reputation. He moved to Philadelphia, then the nation's capital, and wrote regularly for the *Gazette of the United States*. His most lasting contribution to American letters may be his *Port Folio*, a weekly magazine patterned after the English *Tatler* for which he served as writer and editor from the first issue in 1801 until 1808. The magazine had a nationwide circulation; Dennie used it to spread his love of literature and to exert his influence on his country's budding culture. He died of cholera in

Philadelphia; his tombstone reads: "He devoted his life to the literature of his Country."

Phyllis Diller (Contemporary)

She was born Phyllis Driver, and at the age of thirty-seven, after raising five children, she became a stand-up comic. Her first success as a comedian came at San Francisco's Purple Onion club in 1955. She went on to star in three television series and in *Hello, Dolly!* on Broadway. She created a persona on stage very different from her real-life personality. In addition to her stage performances, Diller wrote several bestselling books, including *The Complete Mother, Phyllis Diller's Marriage Manual*, and *The Joys of Aging and How to Avoid Them.*

Ralph Ellison (1914–94)

Ralph Ellison was born in Oklahoma; his father died when he was only three but his mother, significantly, led protests and campaigned for black civil rights while working as a domestic servant. Ellison studied music at the Tuskegee Institute for a year and then went to New York in order to earn more money for college; there he met some of the people involved in the Harlem Renaissance, as well as Richard Wright, who encouraged him to write. Ellison worked for the Work Projects Administration as a researcher with the New York Federal Writers' Project from 1938 to 1942. In 1944 he received a Rosenfeld Fellowship to work on a novel, and for seven years Ellison worked on *Invisible Man*, which was published in 1952. The novel became a bestseller and won the National Book Award; it also established Ralph Ellison's position as an important American voice and enabled him to spend the ensuing years teaching and lecturing. He later published two collections of essays, *Shadow and Act* (1964) and *Going to the Territory* (1986).

Ralph Waldo Emerson (1803–82)

A poet, preacher, and essayist, Emerson had a tremendous influence on the works of nineteenth-century writers like Thoreau, Whitman, and Frederick Douglass, among many others. Born and raised in Massachusetts, Emerson was educated at home and at the Boston Latin school, and he attended Harvard on a scholarship. He trained as a minister at Harvard Divinity School, but resigned from the ministry after six years. Throughout his career as a writer, he supported and encouraged fellow authors like Bronson Alcott and Margaret Fuller, while publishing his own essays like the classic "Nature" and "The American Scholar." Emerson died of tuberculosis in Concord, Massachusetts.

Nora Ephron (Contemporary)

A journalist, novelist, screenwriter, and film director, Nora Ephron was born in New York City and grew up in Los Angeles, where her parents worked as a screenwriting team. She turned the story of her public divorce from the Watergate journalist Carl Bernstein into the novel *Heartburn* (1983), later made into a movie with Meryl Streep and Jack Nicholson. Since the late 1980s, Ephron has worked primarily as a screenwriter and film director. In addition to the script for *When Harry Met Sally*, her films as director include *This Is Your Life*, with Julie Kavner; *Sleepless in Seattle*, with Tom Hanks and Meg Ryan; *Michael*, with John Travolta; and *You've Got Mail*, reuniting the popular duo Hanks and Ryan. These films have established Ephron as one of the most powerful women directors in Hollywood. She lives in New York City with her husband, the screenwriter Nicholas Pileggi.

Blanche Farley (Contemporary)

Blanche Farley is coeditor of *Like a Summer Peach: Sunbright Poems and Old Southern Recipes* (Papier-Mache Press). She has been an art professor and a stay-at-home mom. Currently, she is a librarian at Middle Georgia College's Dublin, Georgia, campus. Her poems, stories, and essays have appeared in various publications, such as *Newsday*'s Sunday magazine, *Indiana Review*, and *The Flannery O'Connor Bulletin*. She was the winner of a PEN Syndicated Fiction Award and has been published in several anthologies and textbooks, including *At Our Core: Women Writing About Power* and *The Bedford Introduction to Literature*.

Fanny Fern (1811–72)

Fanny Fern was born Sara Payson Willis in Portland, Maine, and grew up in Boston. She attended Hartford Female Seminary and married for the first time in 1837. Her husband died without any money in 1846, leaving her with two children. She married a widower with two children of his own, Samuel Farrington, in 1849, but the marriage was a mistake and she left him in 1851 to earn her living through writing. Her first articles appeared in the Boston *Olive Branch* and *True Flag* in 1851. By the following year, Fern was working as a columnist for the *New York Musical World and Times*. She published her first collection of essays, *Fern Leaves from Fanny's Portfolio*, in 1853. Her autobiographical novel *Ruth Hall* appeared in 1854. She became a columnist for the New York *Ledger* and married James Parton in 1856. She wrote her columns, often on taboo or controversial subjects like prostitution and divorce, until her death. Her publications include a second novel, *Rose Clark* (1856), three children's books, and numerous essay collections.

Fannie Flagg (Contemporary)

Fannie Flagg began writing and producing for television when she was nineteen; later she began acting, as well, in television, the theater, and films. Eventually deciding that she had allowed herself to get sidetracked from what she really wanted to be doing, Flagg quit acting in 1980 and has devoted herself to writing ever since. Much of her writing is set in the South, where she grew up, although she now lives in California. Her novels *Daisy Fay and the Miracle Man* and *Fried Green Tomatoes at the Whistle Stop Café* were both bestsellers, and Flagg was nominated for an Academy Award for her script for the film adaptation of *Fried Green*

Tomatoes. Her most recent novels are *Welcome to the World, Baby Girl* (1998) and *Standing in the Rainbow* (2002). "I suffer from what most humorists do," Flagg has remarked, "a deep need to be taken seriously."

Jeff Foxworthy (Contemporary)

Foxworthy was born in Atlanta, Georgia, and attended the Georgia Institute of Technology for three years. He worked as a computer repairman before setting out to make it as a comedian. Foxworthy first appeared in an Atlanta comedy club in 1982; his first national exposure was a spot on an HBO special starring Rodney Dangerfield in 1989. By 1991, he was a regular on the Comedy Central program *Comics Only*. His first solo special, *Jeff Foxworthy:You Might Be a Redneck*, also aired in 1991. A live album of *The Blue Collar Comedy Tour* was released in 2000 and a feature film was made out of the highly successful tour in 2003. His publications include *You Might Be a Redneck If . . . , Red Ain't Dead, Hick Is Chic: A Guide to Etiquette for the (Grossly) Unsophisticated*, and *Games Rednecks Play*. He starred in the sitcom *The Jeff Foxworthy Show* from 1995 to 1997. The passage here first appeared in his 1996 autobiography titled *No Shirt, No Shoes . . . No Problem!*

Redd Foxx (1922–91)

Redd Foxx, a St. Louis–born African American comedian, began his career on the night-club circuit, taking odd jobs to support himself. By 1968 he had made a name for himself in Las Vegas. In 1970 Foxx appeared in a film called *Cotton Comes to Harlem*, which led to his being cast in the hugely successful television show *Sanford and Son*. The show ran until 1977, and Foxx followed it up with *The Redd Foxx Comedy Hour* (1977–78) and the *Red Foxx Show*, among others. In 1977 he coedited *The Redd Foxx Encyclopedia of Black Humor*.

Al Franken (Contemporary)

An Emmy Award–winning writer for the television comedy series *Saturday Night Live*, Al Franken is also the bestselling author of *Rush Limbaugh Is a Big Fat Idiot and Other Observations* (1991), *Why Not Me?* (2000), and *Oh, the Things I Know! A Guide to Success, or, Failing That, Happiness* (2003). In 2003, he served as a Fellow with Harvard's Kennedy School of Government at the Shorenstein Center on the Press, Politics, and Public Policy. His most recent book is *Lies and the Lying Liars Who Tell Them: A Fair and Balanced Look at the Right* (2003). He lives with his family in New York City.

Benjamin Franklin (1706–90)

The legendary author of the *Autobiography* was born in Boston and began publishing essays at age sixteen in his brother's newspaper, *The New England Courant*, under a pseudonym. Philosopher, inventor, philanthropist, pamphleteer, and politician, Franklin penned *Poor Richard's Almanac* (1733–38), *Proposals*

Relating to the Education of Youth in Pennsylvania (1749), and *A Narrative of the Late Massacres* (1764). He spent twenty years in London and wrote satires of England's low opinion of America. Franklin also served as minister to France during the American Revolution and returned to America in 1785. His most famous speech was written for the Constitutional Convention in Philadelphia in 1787. He died before completing his celebrated *Autobiography*, written and revised between 1771 and 1789.

Adrianne Frost (Contemporary)

Adrianne Frost is an actor and comedian living in New York. She has appeared on numerous television shows and off-Broadway productions and in comedy clubs all over the country. She believes it is her goal in life to bring people laughter.

Lewis Burke Frumkes (Contemporary)

Frumkes teaches at Marymount Manhattan College, where he is also director of the Writing Center. He contributes to numerous magazines and newspapers and hosts a weekly radio program featuring interviews with celebrities. His books include *How to Raise Your I.Q. by Eating Gifted Children* (1979), *Manhattan Cocktail* (1989), and *Metapunctuation* (1993). He is also the coauthor of the *Mensa Think-Smart Book* (2000).

Charlotte Perkins Gilman (1860–1935)

Charlotte Perkins Gilman was one of the most important intellectuals in the women's movement from the 1890s to the 1920s; she wrote and lectured on women's rights and other social reform issues. During her life she was best known for sociological studies like *Women and Economics* (1898), an ambitious analysis of the social status of women that promoted a radical restructuring of the public and private spheres. Now she is most famous for "The Yellow Wallpaper," a disturbing short story based on her experience of Dr. Weir Mitchell's "rest cure" following a bout of severe depression. Gilman was divorced from her husband and married her cousin, George Houghton Gilman, in 1900. Her works include *The Home* (1904), *Human Work* (1904), *Man-Made World* (1911), a magazine called *The Forerunner* (1910–16) for which she wrote all the copy (including the feminist Utopian novel *Herland* in 1915), and hundreds of short stories.

William Goldman (Contemporary)

Goldman was born in Highland Park, Illinois, and is most famous for his Academy Award–winning screenplays, *Butch Cassidy and the Sundance Kid* (1969) and *All the President's Men* (1976). His screenplay for the detective thriller *Harper* (1966), starring Paul Newman, gave him his first success in Hollywood, but he had been a published novelist since 1957. His novels include *Magic*, *The Princess Bride* (1973), which he adapted for the screen, *The Silent Gondoliers* (2001), and *The Temple of Gold* (2001). Goldman's publications also include humorous behind-the-scene books about the entertainment industry, *Adventures in the Screen Trade, The Season: A Candid Look at Broadway,* and *Which Lie Did I Tell? More Adventures in the Screen Trade.* He is also coauthor of *The Big Picture: Who Killed Hollywood? And Other Essays* (2001) with Herb Gardner. His most recent screenplays include *Misery* (1991), adapted from Stephen King's novel, and *Maverick* (1994), a western starring Mel Gibson. Goldman continues to work in Hollywood as an uncredited script doctor.

Mark Halliday (Contemporary)

Mark Halliday teaches creative writing at Ohio University. His books of poems are *Little Star* (1987), *Tasker Street* (1992), *Selfwolf* (1999), and *Jab* (2002). His study of Wallace Stevens, *Stevens and the Interpersonal,* was published by Princeton in 1991. Born in 1949, Halliday feels that a great deal of attention should be paid to poets born between 1945 and 1955. His work was influenced by the late Kenneth Koch. Halliday considers Bob Dylan a fabulous genius.

Margaret Halsey (1910–97)

Margaret Halsey grew up outside of Yonkers, New York, and entered Skidmore College in 1926 as a secretarial science major. Although she established a reputation as a humorous columnist on campus, she abandoned this pursuit after college, taking jobs as a stenographer, a dictaphone operator for a real estate company, and a secretary. A job in the editorial department at Simon and Schuster turned out to be the break she needed: the letters she wrote back to the publisher during a trip to England with her husband led to the commissioning of the book from which our selection is excerpted, and thus began her writing career. Margaret Halsey's work as a novelist, social critic, and humorist focuses on a wide range of social and political issues. She is the author of *With Malice Toward Some* (1938), *Some of My Best Friends Are Soldiers* (1944), *Color Blind* (1946), *This Demi-Paradise: A Westchester Diary* (1960), *The Pseudo-Ethic* (1963), *No Laughing Matter: The Autobiography of a WASP* (1977), and *Invisible Hands: Contract Clearing—A Theological Reflection* (1996).

Lynn Harris (Contemporary)

Lynn Harris is cocreator of the cybersuperhero *Breakup Girl* and author of *Breakup Girl to the Rescue!* (2000) as well as *He Loved Me, He Loves Me Not: A Guide to Fudge, Fury, Free Time, and Life Beyond the Breakup* (1996). A standup comic, Harris also delivers advice to the lovelorn in print, radio, and television. She is a regular contributor to the New York *Daily News* as well as to numerous national magazines.

Bret Harte (1836–1902)

Bret Harte dominated the literary world of the West and his publications are innumerable. As the founding editor of the *Overland Monthly,* he helped promote the careers of a generation of western writers. Harte was born in Albany, New York, and moved to New York City with his mother at age nine after his father's death. He quit school at thirteen to work as a clerk and moved to the San Francisco Bay Area in 1854. Harte wrote for the *Golden Era,* a literary weekly, and began writing a series of condensed novels in the burlesque style, taking as his satirical targets the works of Dickens, Wilkie Collins, and James Fenimore Cooper. He later moved to England, where he enjoyed a greater popularity than he did in his native United States, and where he died of throat cancer in 1902. His works include *The Luck of Roaring Camp and Other Sketches* (1870), *The Story of a Mine* (1877), *On the Frontier* (1884), and *Suzy:A Story of the Plains* (1893). *The Writings of Bret Harte*, in twenty volumes, appeared between 1896 and 1914.

Cynthia Heimel (Contemporary)

An American humorist and feminist, Heimel has published essays on gender relations and columns in numerous magazines. She is a regular contributor to *Playboy*. Her titles include *Sex Tips for Girls* (1983), *But Enough About You* (1986), *If You Can't Live Without Me, Why Aren't You Dead Yet?* (1991), *Get Your Tongue Out of My Mouth, I'm Kissing You Good-bye* (1993), *When Your Phone Doesn't Ring, It'll Be Me* (1995), and *Advanced Sex Tips for Girls: This Time It's Personal* (2003).

O. Henry (1862–1910)

O. Henry was born William Sydney Porter; he invented the pseudonym under which he became famous after being released from prison, where he had been serving a sentence for embezzlement. Before establishing himself as a writer, Porter worked as a pharmacist, a draftsman, a bank teller, and finally a feature writer for the *Houston Post*, where he wrote anecdotal sketches. He moved to New York in 1902, after his release, and for several years published a story a week in the New York *World*. O. Henry's first collection of stories, *Cabbages and Kings*, appeared in 1904 and was followed by such works as *The Four Million* (1906), *The Trimmed Lamp* (1907), *Heart of the West* (1907), and *Whirligigs* (1910), which contains the classic story "The Ransom of Red Chief." In all, O. Henry published ten collections and over six hundred short stories during his life, as well as several posthumous works; his stories range from tales of ordinary New Yorkers to tall tales and stories of Western adventure.

Nicole Hollander (Contemporary)

A cartoonist famous for her love of cats and her feminist humor, Hollander grew up in Chicago and studied painting at the University of Illinois at Urbana-Champaign. Her first cartoon strip, *The Feminist Funnies*, appeared in 1976. Her first collection of cartoons, *I'm in Training to Be Tall and Blonde*, was published in 1979. Hollander's cartoon alter-ego, Sylvia, first appeared in 1980. *Sylvia* is syndicated in over sixty newspapers and has inspired a line of greeting cards, a play, and more than a dozen books. Hollander's titles include

The Whole Enchilada (1976), *Female Problems: An Unhelpful Guide* (1995), *My Cat's Not Fat, He's Just Big-Boned* (1998), *Cats with Attitude* (2002), and most recently with Regina Barreca *The ABC of Vice: An Insatiable Women's Guide, Alphabetized* (2003).

Marietta Holley "Josiah Allen's Wife" (1836–1926)

A famous literary humorist often compared to Mark Twain in her time but largely forgotten until feminist scholars recently rediscovered her work, Marietta Holley was born on the family farm in Jefferson County, New York. At twenty-one she published her first story, "Piety," in the *Jefferson County Journal*. She first used the pseudonym "Josiah Allen's Wife" in her story "Fourth of July in Jonesville" published in *Peterson's Magazine* in 1869. Holley sent writing samples to the important publisher Elisha Bliss, who became her mentor and editor and encouraged her to write *My Opinions and Betsey Bobbet's* (1873). She created the persona of Samantha, the "rustic philosopher farm wife of wit and gumption," as a covert vehicle for her particular brand of feminist humor. Holley wrote a dozen Samantha books between 1887 and 1913, tackling in them feminist issues such as the economic dependence of women and their lack of political power, as well as social problems of her day like temperance, children's rights, and poverty. At the height of her fame, she commanded fees as high as $14,000 per book, and "Betsey Bobbet" clubs were created around the country to read and act out parts of her books. She died of cancer at home, in the fifteen-room Victorian house she built on her family's land.

Langston Hughes (1902–67)

Langston Hughes was born in Joplin, Missouri, and grew up in Kansas. He read the poetry of Paul Dunbar and Carl Sandburg as a child and he began writing poetry himself under the influence of their work. Hughes attended Columbia University for a year, then left to work on a ship and traveled extensively in Europe and Africa before returning to New York and establishing himself in Harlem, where he quickly became an important figure of the Harlem Renaissance. His first poem was published in the *Crisis* in 1921; his first collection of poetry, *The Weary Blues*, appeared two years later. His titles include the coming-of-age novel *Not Without Laughter* (1930), *The Ways of White Folks* (1934), and the poetry collections *Shakespeare in Harlem* (1942) and *Montage of a Dream Deferred* (1951).

Zora Neale Hurston (1891–1960)

Zora Neale Hurston, born in the African American town of Eatonville, Florida, went on to become one of the most important figures of the Harlem Renaissance. Her writing is dedicated to the preservation and celebration of African American culture, as was the very persona she created. Best known for the novel *Their Eyes Were Watching God* (1937), Hurston is also the author of *Dust Tracks on the Road* (1942), an autobiography; *Mules and Men* (1935), a collection of folklore;

Tell My Horse—Voodoo Gods, an Inquiry (1938), an anthropological work; and *Jonah's Gourd Vine* (1934), *Moses, Man of the Mountain* (1939), and *Seraph on the Suwanee* (1948), all works of fiction. Hurston spent her last years alone and in poverty, but her literary reputation was revived largely through the work of Alice Walker in the 1970s.

Molly Ivins (Contemporary)
A journalist, humorist, and political commentator, Ivins contributes to various newspapers, including the *Texas Observer* and the *New York Times*. Her collections of essays include *Molly Ivins Can't Say That, Can She?* (1991), *Nothin' But Good Times Ahead* (1993), *You Got to Dance with Them What Brung You* (1999), *Shrub: The Short But Happy Political Life of George W. Bush* (2000) (coauthored with Lou Dubose), and *Bushwacked: Life in George W. Bush's America* (2003).

Erica Jong (Contemporary)
Erica Jong grew up in Manhattan and studied literature and writing at Barnard College; she received her M.A. from Columbia University. She published two books of poetry, *Fruits and Vegetables* (1971) and *Half-Lives* (1973), before the appearance of *Fear of Flying* (1973), a widely acclaimed and enormously popular novel, which established her fame and reputation. The frank attitude toward sexuality and the interest in the female experience that mark her first novel continue to dominate Jong's work. Among her many other works are *How to Save Your Own Life* (1977), *Fanny, Being the True History of the Adventures of Fanny Hackabout Jones* (1980), *Ordinary Miracles* (1983), *Parachutes and Kisses* (1994), *Inventing Memory: A Novel of Mothers and Daughters* (1997), *What Do Women Want? Reflections on a Century of Change* (1999), and *Sappho's Leap* (2003).

Judith Katz (Contemporary)
Katz was born in Worcester, Massachusetts. She received her B.A. from the University of Massachusetts at Amherst and her M.A., from Smith College. She describes herself as a Jewish Lesbian Feminist and she writes: "My first novel sought to make heroes out of contemporary Jewish lesbian characters." That novel, *Running Fiercely Toward a High Thin Sound*, a appeared in 1992. Her other works include *The Escape Artist* (1997). She has worked as an Arts Administrator in Minneapolis and has taught writing at the Loft, also in Minneapolis, since 1988. She has received an NEA Fellowship.

Bel Kaufman (Contemporary)
The granddaughter of Jewish humorist Sholom Aleichem, Kaufman was born in Germany and emigrated to the United States at the age of twelve. She received her B.A. from Hunter College in New York and her M.A. from

Columbia University. Kaufman taught high school in New York City for over thirty years and has taught creative writing at the University of Rochester and the University of Florida. Her bestselling novel *Up the Down Staircase* (1964), from which our passage is excerpted, chronicles the bittersweet adventures of a young woman who teaches in an inner-city school. It remained on the bestseller list for sixty-four weeks, was translated into sixteen languages, and was made into a movie starring Sandy Dennis in 1967. She also published the novel *Love, Etc.* in 1979. Despite her novels and her numerous publications in periodicals and newspapers, including *Esquire, Ladies' Home Journal*, and the *New York Times*, Kaufman describes herself as a teacher first, and a writer second.

Garrison Keillor (Contemporary)

Keillor was born and raised in Minnesota, a state which has inspired most of his published work. He attended the University of Minnesota and began working in radio in 1963; his show, *Prairie Home Companion*, known for its blend of regional humor, musical guests, and audience participation, airs weekly on National Public Radio. His titles include *Lake Wobegon Days, Leaving Home, Happy to Be Here, Wobegon Boy, We Are Still Married, Good Poems*, and *Love Me*. Keillor lives in Wisconsin and New York.

Florynce Kennedy (1916–2000)

Florynce Kennedy, feminist essayist and lawyer, was born in Kansas City, Missouri, and raised by her parents to question authority. She received her B.A. and her law degree from Columbia University and devoted her life to fighting for civil liberties. Her memoir was entitled *Color Me Flo: My Hard Life and Good Times*.

Jean Kerr (Contemporary)

Kerr was born Brigid Jean Collins in Scranton, Pennsylvania. She received her B.A. in 1943 from Marywood College, where she met her future husband, Walter Kerr. The Kerrs collaborated on numerous plays, among which is an adaptation of Franz Werfel's novel *The Song of Bernadette*, in 1945. That same year Kerr received her M.A. from Catholic University. Kerr's first solo effort, *Jenny Kissed Me*, only ran for twenty performances in 1948. The playwright, unfazed by this setback, went on to write ten plays in the next three decades; two of these, *King of Hearts* (1954) and *Mary, Mary* (1961), were made into movies. Kerr also published humorous essays in a number of magazines including *Reader's Digest, Ladies' Home Journal, Harper's*, and *Saturday Evening Post*. Her collections of essays include *Please Don't Eat the Daisies* (1957), *Penny Candy* (1970), and *How I Got to Be Perfect* (1978). She has received honorary degrees from Fordham and Northwestern University.

James Kincaid (Contemporary)

Kincaid is Aerol Arnold Professor of English at the University of California in Los Angeles, where he teaches Victorian literature and cultural theory. He has written extensively on Dickens and Trollope and edited numerous scholarly collections of literary criticism. His titles include *Child-Loving: The Erotic Child and Victorian Culture* (1992), *Annoying the Victorians* (1995), and *Manufacturing Virtue: The Culture of Child Molesting* (1998).

Alan King (1927–2004)

Alan King has been a prominent figure in American entertainment for decades, as an actor, producer, and comic. He is the author of such works as the autobiography *Name Dropping: The Life and Lies of Alan King* (1996), *Is Salami and Eggs Better Than Sex?: Memoirs of a Happy Eater* (with Mimi Sheraton), *Help! I'm a Prisoner in a Chinese Bakery* (1964), *Anybody Who Owns His Own Home Deserves It*, and *Alan King's Great Jewish Joke Book* (2002). In *Chinese Bakery*, King writes, "If I can laugh at 'the system,' I can always keep it in its proper perspective. Then there may be hope for all of us."

Tony Kornheiser (Contemporary)

Tony Kornheiser was born and raised on Long Island, New York. He graduated from Harper College with a B.A. in English and Social Sciences and taught grammar school for a year. He began his writing career with features for *New York Newsday* until 1976, when he was hired by the *New York Times* to cover sports. Kornheiser has been a sports columnist for the *Washington Post* since 1979; he also writes a weekly humor column for the *Post*, which has been syndicated nationally since 1991. His books include *The Baby Chase* (1993), *Pumping Irony* (1995), *Bald as I Wanna Be* (1997), and *I'm Back for More Cash* (2002).

Fran Lebowitz (Contemporary)

Fran Lebowitz grew up in Morristown, New Jersey, but is generally associated with New York, where she now lives. She is a columnist, critic, and essayist whose humor is fused with social commentary. She is perhaps best known for her best-selling works from the 1970s, *Metropolitan Life* and *Social Studies*, reissued in *The Fran Lebowitz Reader* in 1994. She has made numerous talk show appearances—particularly on *Late Night with David Letterman*—and publishes essays in *Vanity Fair* and other magazines.

Jay Leno (Contemporary)

Leno is a stand-up comedian and host of the award-winning *Tonight Show*. He is the author, with Bill Zehme, of the autobiography *Leading with My Chin* (1996). Leno grew up in Andover, Massachusetts, and now lives in Los Angeles.

David Letterman (Contemporary)

David Letterman was born in Indianapolis, Indiana, and graduated from Ball State University. He began his media career as a weatherman and television announcer before becoming a radio host and stand-up comic. Numerous appearances and frequent guest hosting on *The Tonight Show with Johnny Carson* led to his first television show, the daytime *David Letterman Show*, which ran for only three months yet managed to win two Emmy awards. His next effort, *Late Night with David Letterman*, lasted slightly longer—11.5 years—and received five Emmy Awards. He is currently the host of *The Late Show with David Letterman*, which has received thirty-nine Emmy nominations and eight Emmys, including six for Outstanding Variety, Music or Comedy Program. From the start, Letterman has received critical praise for redefining the talk show genre. In 1992, he received the prestigious George Foster Peabody Award for taking "one of TV's most conventional and least inventive forms—the talk show—and infusing it with freshness and imagination."

Anita Loos (1893–1981)

Any biographical information about Anita Loos should be prefaced by a warning: the celebrated novelist, playwright, and screenwriter consistently lied about her age (usually subtracting five years) throughout her life. She performed on stage in San Francisco at the age of ten and sold her first screenplay in 1911. Loos wrote numerous screenplays for D. W. Griffith's company and articles for *Vanity Fair*. In addition to her modern classic *Gentlemen Prefer Blondes* (1925) and its sequel, *But Gentlemen Marry Brunettes* (1928), she wrote the autobiographies *A Girl Like I* (1966), *Kiss Hollywood Goodby* (1974), and *Cast of Thousands* (1977). Her most famous screenplays are *Red-Headed Woman* (1932), starring Jean Harlow, and *The Women* (1939), directed by George Cukor. Loos also adapted the Colette novels *Gigi* and *Cheri* for Broadway. She continued to write until her death from a heart attack.

"Moms" Mabley (1894–1975)

Born Loretta May Aiken, "Moms" Mabley was an African-American comedian, singer, and actress. She performed at the Apollo Theater and the Cotton Club in Harlem at the height of their popularity and appeared in movies such as *Boarding House Blues* (1929), *Emperor Jones* (1939), and *Amazing Grace* (1974). Thirteen of her comedy albums made the top two hundred on the Billboard Charts during the 1960s; among her biggest hits were *At the UN* (1961) and *Young Men Si, Old Men No* (1963). She was known for her fusion of bawdy humor with a female perspective.

Merrill Markoe (Contemporary)

Merrill Markoe taught art at the University of Southern California before she began writing for television and performing as a stand-up comic in Los Angeles.

In 1978 she met David Letterman, an alliance that led to a major development in her career: she became the head writer for *The David Letterman Show* and later for *Late Night with David Letterman*, winning several Emmy Awards for her work; she was the creator of, among other things, the ever-popular Stupid Pet Tricks. After leaving the show in 1987, Markoe became a regular contributor to *Not Necessarily the News* (for which she won Writers' Guild and Ace Awards) and appeared in a number of HBO comedy specials. She is the author of *What the Dogs Have Taught Me and Other Amazing Things I've Learned* (1992), *How to Be Hap-Hap-Happy Like Me* (1994), *Merrill Markoe's Guide to Love* (1997), and *It's My F——ing Birthday* (2002).

Julius "Groucho" Marx (1890–1977)
Adolph-Arthur "Harpo" Marx (1888–1964)
Leonard "Chico" Marx (1886–1961)
Herbert "Zeppo" Marx (1901–79)

The Marx Brothers were encouraged at a young age by their mother Minnie, herself the daughter of vaudevillians, to pursue show-business careers. The brothers conquered Broadway in 1925 with their play *The Cocoanuts*; this success led to a contract with Paramount in 1929 and a move to Hollywood the following year. They wrote three original films together: *Monkey Business* (1931), *Horse Feathers* (1932), and *Duck Soup* (1933). They began a productive and successful partnership with Irving Thalberg at MGM in 1934; before his early death the legendary producer teamed the Marx Brothers with writers like George S. Kaufman and produced the most successful films in the brothers' careers, *A Night at the Opera* (1935) and *A Day at the Races* (1937). The group eventually split up in 1941. Groucho remained the most visible member with occasional film appearances and a long career in television and radio; he received a special Oscar in 1973.

Julio Marzán (Contemporary)

Julio Marzán has published two volumes of poetry, *Translations Without Originals* (I. Reed Books) and *Puerta de Tierra* (University of Puerto Rico Press). He is the author of the groundbreaking study *The Spanish American Roots of William Carlos Williams* (University of Texas Press) and the novel-in-stories *The Bonjour Gene* (University of Wisconsin Press).

Jackie Mason (Contemporary)

Jackie Mason grew up on the Lower East Side of Manhattan and was once a rabbi; he went on to become a popular comedian. He won a Tony Award for *The World According To Me*, his highly successful first Broadway show, and an Emmy Award for *Jackie Mason On Broadway*, an HBO special. His Broadway success continued with *Jackie Mason: Brand New* and *Politically Incorrect*. His published works include *How To Talk Jewish* (with Ira Berkov, 1991), *Jackie Mason's America*,

The World According To Me, and *Jackie Mason and Raoul Felder's Survival Guide to New York City.*

H. L. Mencken (1880–1956)

Henry Louis Mencken, better known as H. L. Mencken, was born in Baltimore; he attended the Baltimore Polytechnic Institute before working in his father's cigar factory from 1896 to 1899. He then began working as reporter or editor for a variety of local papers. From 1914 to 1923, Mencken coedited *The Smart Set* with drama critic George Jean Nathan; the two cofounded several other publications, among them the influential magazine *American Mercury* (1923–1933). As a literary critic in the 1920s, Mencken's role was extremely important; he helped to establish the careers of such major authors as Theodore Dreiser and Sinclair Lewis, among others. He continued to contribute essays to numerous publications, including the *Chicago Tribune,* the *New York American, The Nation,* the *Evening Mail,* and *The Baltimore Sun.* No aspect of American life was safe from Mencken's satire. His work was collected and published in a number of volumes, including *Ventures Into Verse* (1903), *The Philosophy of Nietzsche* (1908), *Damn: A Book of Calumny* (1918), *In Defense of Women* (1918), *The American Language* (1919), *Notes on Democracy* (1926), *Treatise On the Gods* (1930), *Happy Days* (1940) and *Heathen Days* (1943).

Alice Duer Miller (1874–1942)

Unlike most humorists, Miller received a degree in mathematics from Barnard College in 1899. From 1914 to 1917, her column "Are Women People?" ran in the New York *Tribune.* She belonged to the group of radical feminists called Heterodoxy which met in Greenwich Village from 1912 to 1940. She was also a member of the Algonquin Round Table and the subject of a *New Yorker* profile in 1927. Although she wrote primarily about the upper classes during her career, some of Miller's earlier work appeared in the socialist magazine *The Masses.* She published regularly in the *Saturday Evening Post* from 1916 to the 1930s. Her novels *The Charm School* (1919) and *Gowns by Roberta* (1933) were adapted for the screen.

Dennis Miller (Contemporary)

Comedian, actor, writer, producer, and TV host, Dennis Miller's early success was as the anchorperson of *Weekend Update* on *Saturday Night Live* from 1985–91. He has written and produced numerous television specials, such as *Dennis Miller: State of the Union Undressed* (1995) and *Dennis Miller Live* (1994), and has received three Emmy Awards for writing in a comedy series. Widely known for his political and sardonic wit, his books include *Rants* (1997), *Ranting Again* (1999), *I Rant, Therefore I Am* (2001), and most recently *The Rant Zone: An All-Out Blitz Against Soul-Sucking Jobs, Twisted Child Stars, Holistic Loons, and People Who Eat Their Dogs!* (2002).

Margaret Mitchell (1900–49)

Born in Atlanta, Georgia, Margaret Mitchell was the daughter of a founder of the Georgia suffrage movement and the president of the Atlanta Historical Society, a pair of influences which certainly manifest themselves in her work. Mitchell's studies at Smith College were cut short by her mother's death, following which she returned home. Her first marriage ended in divorce after two years, and she married John Marsh shortly thereafter. Meanwhile, she had become a journalist, working as a reporter for the Atlanta *Journal* at a time when this was an unconventional occupation for women. She left after three years and began writing *Gone With the Wind*, on which she worked in secret for years; it was published in 1936 and won instant popularity. Movie rights were sold immediately, the book sold over a million copies in the first six months, and Mitchell received the 1937 Pulitzer Prize for the novel that was to become a popular classic. Although she wrote fiction from an early age, *Gone with the Wind* was the only book Mitchell ever published, and her life was cut short at forty-nine when she was hit by a car.

Pat Mora (Contemporary)

Mora was born and raised in El Paso, Texas. She has taught at high school, community college, and university levels. She considers herself Mexican-American and she has written extensively about the life of her family on the Texas-Mexico border. Mora has been called "one of the most significant Chicana poets of our time" by the *New Mexican*. Her titles include *House of Houses*, a family memoir; *Nepantla: Essays from the Land in the Middle; Agua Santa: Holy Water* and *Aunt Carmen's Book of Practical Saints*. Mora is the recipient of numerous awards, including a National Endowment for the Arts Fellowship.

Ogden Nash (1902–71)

Ogden Nash was raised in Rye, New York, and Savannah, Georgia, and attended Harvard briefly. His career as a writer began with a job writing ad copy in 1925; in the same year he published his first book for children, *The Cricket of Caradon*. He published his first poem in *The New Yorker* in 1930, and joined the magazine's staff in 1930. Elected to the National Institute of Arts and Letters in 1950, Nash published nineteen books of poetry in all. His works include *Hard Lines* (1931), *Good Intentions* (1942), *You Can't Get There From Here* (1957), *Marriage Lines* (1964), and *Bed Riddance* (1972).

Bill Nye (1850–96)

One of the most important humorists of the late nineteenth century, Nye was born in Maine and raised in Wisconsin. He later moved to Wyoming, where he became a successful writer and edited the *Laramie Boomerang*. Nye moved to New York in 1887 and wrote a humor column for the *New York World*. His genres of choice were the short comic essay and the sketch, but he also wrote two Broadway plays and two books of burlesque history. He traveled extensively throughout Europe from the late 1880s until his death and he used his travels as column material. He died in North Carolina, where he had lived since 1891. His titles include *Bill Nye and Boomerang* (1881), *Hits and Skits* (1884), *Baled Hay* (1884), *Bill Nye's Red Book* (1891), and *Bill Nye's History of the United States* (1894).

Dorothy Parker (1893–1967)

Dorothy Parker was born in New Jersey and attended the Blessed Sacrament Convent School in New York City until she was expelled for claiming that the Immaculate Conception was "spontaneous combustion." One of the most celebrated members of the legendary Algonquin Round Table in the 1920s, Parker was known for her acerbic wit and her epigrammatic style. She published reviews and articles in *The New Yorker* as well as poems and short stories. Her publications include volumes of poetry like *Enough Rope* (1926) and *Death and Taxes* (1931); and the short story collections *Laments for the Living* (1930) and *Here Lies* (1939). Parker was involved with the Communist Party in the 1930s and subsequently blacklisted. From 1925 to 1950 she spent much time in Hollywood where she wrote numerous screenplays, including *A Star Is Born* (1937), for which she received an Academy Award nomination. An edition of her *Complete Stories* appeared in 1995.

Samuel Pickering, Jr. (Contemporary)

The real-life inspiration behind Robin Williams's beloved teacher in the film *Dead Poets Society*, Pickering has been teaching children's literature and the familiar essay at the University of Connecticut since 1978. He has published numerous articles of literary criticism in academic journals, and his scholarly titles include *The Moral Tradition in English Fiction, 1785–1850* (1976). Pickering is most famous for his numerous essay collections, which include *A Continuing Education* (1985), *Still Life* (1990), *Trespassing* (1994), *The Blue Caterpillar* (1997), *Living to Prowl* (1998), *Deprived of Unhappiness* (1998), and *The Last Book* (2001).

Sylvia Plath (1932–63)

Plath was born in Boston and published poems and stories as an adolescent in numerous publications. She received a scholarship to attend Smith College, from which she graduated summa cum laude with a B.A. in English in 1955. In the summer of 1953, Plath served as a guest editor on *Mademoiselle*, and she would later use this experience as the basis of her only novel, *The Bell Jar* (1963). She attended Cambridge University on a Fulbright Fellowship and received an M.A. Plath lived in England with her husband, the poet Ted Hughes, until 1957 when they moved to the United States and Plath taught freshman English at her alma mater. The couple returned to England in 1959, and during Plath's most intensely creative period she wrote and published *The Colossus and Other Poems*

(1960) and *The Bell Jar*, and she composed the poems which would appear posthumously as the collection *Ariel* (1965). Plagued with depression throughout her life, Plath committed suicide in her London flat. Her *Collected Poems* (1981) won the Pulitzer Prize for Poetry in 1982.

Edgar Allan Poe (1809–49)

Poe was born in Boston and became an orphan by the age of two. He attended the University of Virginia and published his first volume of poetry, *Tamerlane and Other Poems*, while still in his teens. He worked as an editor for the *Southern Literary Messenger* in Richmond, Virginia, until he left in 1837 to go to New York, where he wrote *The Narrative of Arthur Gordon Pym*. He then moved to Philadelphia, where he worked as an editor on *Burton's Gentleman's Magazine*. Between 1839 and 1844 Poe composed many of his now famous tales like "The Tell-Tale Heart" and "The Pit and the Pendulum." He published *Tales of the Grotesque and Arabesque* in 1840 and *The Raven and Other Poems* in 1845. He moved back to New York and unsuccessfully edited a literary magazine, *The Broadway Journal*. The *Journal* quickly folded and Poe's wife, Virginia, died. He returned to Richmond and for a brief period he was feted and celebrated for his literary achievement. He was found dying on the streets of Baltimore, on his way to New York City.

Libby Reid (Contemporary)

Libby Reid is a nationally known cartoonist, author of the cartoon collections *Do You Hate Your Hips More Than Nuclear War?* (1988) and *You Don't Have to Pet to Be Popular* (1989). She has also collaborated with Linda Sunshine on the collections *101 Uses for Silly Putty* (1990) and *How Not to Turn into Your Mother* (1991). Her cartoon essays "City Woman's Home Companion" and "Dr. Trudy True, Cartoon Therapist" ran weekly for three years in the *New York Daily News*. She also creates cartoons and illustrations for magazines, greeting cards, and advertising.

Carl Reiner (Contemporary)

Reiner was born in the Bronx and performed in Broadway musicals before he began working with Sid Caesar on *Your Show of Shows*. He went on to receive two Emmys for Best Supporting Actor for his work on another television program, *Caesar's Hour*. In addition to his highly successful collaboration with Mel Brooks on "The 2000 Year Old Man," Reiner in 1961 created the popular *Dick Van Dyke Show*, for which he won seven Emmys in five years. Since 1967, he has worked mostly as a film director and screenwriter. His credits include *Enter Laughing* (1967), *Oh, God!* (1977), and four films starring Steve Martin, which include *The Jerk* (1979) and *All of Me* (1984). He is also the author of *Enter Laughing* (1958), *All Kinds of Love* (1993), *Continue Laughing* (1995), and *My Anecdotal Life* (2003).

Agnes Repplier (1855–1950)

Born in Philadelphia and raised in a well-to-do family, Agnes Repplier "learned [her] letters at the cost of infinite tribulation, out of a horrible little book called 'Reading Without Fears' " and attended two schools for girls from which she was expelled for rebellious behavior. She set out to educate herself and started writing stories and sketches for publication after her father's bankruptcy. Repplier contributed essays and stories to the *Catholic World*, among which was "The Good Humor of the Saints": the purpose of the essay, according to her biographer, "was to offer the point of view that a sense of humor is not incompatible with otherworldliness." She fulfilled her ambition to contribute to the prestigious *Atlantic Monthly* in 1886 when the magazine published her essay "Children, Past and Present." The monthly became a regular outlet for her writing. She also began lecturing in 1889 and this pursuit would take her traveling around the country for three decades. Over the next fifty years, Repplier became known for her incisive wit and published more than fifteen books. Her collections of essays and sketches include *Books and Men* (1888), *Points of View* (1891), *In the Dozy Hours* (1894), *Americans and Others* (1912), and *Counter-Currents* (1916). She also wrote biographies of distinguished religious figures, including *Père Marquette* and *Junipero Serra*. One of her last books published was a history of humor from the Middle Ages to the twentieth century entitled *In Pursuit of Laughter* (1936).

Chris Rock (Contemporary)

Chris Rock began performing comedy at New York's Comedy Strip when he was eighteen years old. Comedian Eddie Murphy was so impressed with the young comic and actor he cast him in *Beverly Hills Cop II* (1987). From 1990–93, he was a member of the cast of *Saturday Night Live* and also appeared as a guest performer on Keenan Ivory Wayans' *In Living Color*. In 1997, his scathing HBO comedy special *Bring the Pain!* (1996) earned Rock two Emmy awards. That same year, he also received an Emmy nomination for his work as a writer and correspondent on Comedy Central's *Politically Incorrect* with Bill Maher. Rock went on to have additional success with *The Chris Rock Show*, winning both Emmy and NAACP Image Award nominations for his work in 1998 and 1999. Rock garnered wide respect for his comedy regarding politics and issues confronting African-American communities. He continued to concentrate on acting and performing in television and films such as *Lethal Weapon 4* (1998). In addition to his television and film work, his first book, *Rock This!*, was published in 1998.

Will Rogers (1879–1935)

Will Rogers grew up on an Oklahoma ranch in the Cherokee Nation; there he gained the expertise in the use of the lasso that helped establish his early career in wild west shows and in vaudeville and shaped his popular cowboy image.

Known for his folksy brand of humor, Rogers went on to star in seventy-one movies; he was also a radio personality and newspaper columnist. He wrote six books, including *Not a Bathing Suit in Russia, Ether and Me or Just Relax*, and various collections of his essays and addresses.

Helen Rowland (1875–1950)

Born in Washington, D.C., Rowland wrote a satiric dialogue for the *Washington Post* at the age of sixteen. She left for New York City after the death of her father and wrote for the Sunday edition of the New York *World*. Her columns were quickly syndicated; in them she deals with issues of gender inequality, particularly the dependent status of women within marriage. Her collections of columns include *The Digressions of Polly* (1905), *Reflections of a Bachelor Girl* (1909), *The Widow* (1908), *A Guide to Men* (1922), and *This Married Life* (1927).

Charles M. Schulz (1922–2000)

Charles M. Schulz is the most widely syndicated cartoonist in history. Schulz's first success came in 1947 when he sold a cartoon feature called "Li'l Folks" to the *St. Paul Pioneer Press*. In 1948 Schulz began to sell cartoon panels to the *Saturday Evening Post*, and by 1950, United Features Syndicate debuted the *Peanuts* cartoon strip in seven newspapers. Today, *Peanuts* appears in more than 2,600 newspapers worldwide. In addition, he created the popular musical *You're a Good Man Charlie Brown*. In 1964, Schulz and fellow animator Bill Melendez created one of the most loved and watched televised specials of all time—*A Charlie Brown Christmas*. The team would later produce many animated productions together including *Charlie Brown's All Stars* and *It's the Great Pumpkin, Charlie Brown*. Schulz received Reuben Awards from the National Cartoonists Society in 1955 and again in 1964, and was inducted into the Cartoonists Hall of Fame. He was named International Cartoonist of the Year in 1978 by seven hundred cartoonists. He published more than 1,400 books and won Peabody and Emmy awards for his animated specials. The National Cartoonists Society honored Schulz with a lifetime achievement award in 2000.

David Sedaris (Contemporary)

David Sedaris was born in New York but spent much of his youth in Raleigh, North Carolina. He became a contributor to National Public Radio's programs *This American Life* and *Morning Edition* after being discovered at an open mike in a Chicago coffeehouse in 1993 by Ira Glass, the host of *This American Life*. His first book, *Barrel Fever* (1994), a collection of fictional prose and essays, included one of his most famous pieces "Santaland Diaries," which details his experience working as a Christmas elf at Macy's department store. Three other collections of his work followed: *Naked* (1997), *Holidays on Ice* (1997), and *Me Talk Pretty One Day* (2000). He has written numerous essays for publications such as *Esquire* and *The New York Times Magazine*, has continued providing commentaries to NPR, and has collaborated on several plays with his sister, Amy.

Henry W. Shaw "Josh Billings" (1818–85)

One of the most famous humor writers of the Civil War era, Shaw was born in Massachusetts and attended a preparatory school. He spent one year in college before setting out for the West, where he traveled and worked between 1835 and 1845. Shaw's first volume of sketches using his Josh Billings persona, *Josh Billings, Hiz Sayings*, appeared in 1865 and met with great success. Shaw's blend of aphorisms, puns, misspellings, and malapropisms was in part inspired by the essays of Addison and Steele. He settled in Poughkeepsie, New York, in 1867 and wrote a humor column for the *New York Weekly*. His annual series titled *Josh Billings's Farmer's Allminax*, published between 1869 and 1879, became his most successful literary endeavor. Shaw's titles include *Josh Billings on Ice, and Other Things* (1868) and *Josh Billings's Wit and Humor* (1874). His *Complete Works* (1888) appeared posthumously. Shaw died of apoplexy in Monterey, California, in 1885.

Jean Shepherd (1921–99)

Jean Shepherd arrived in New York City in the 1950s, and later made his name as a radio personality. His career eventually expanded to include theater, film, and television; he performed live at Carnegie Hall and many other venues. His short stories have frequently been published in *Playboy* magazine, and have received various awards for fiction. His works include *In God We Trust, All Others Pay Cash* (1966), *Wanda Hickey's Night of Golden Memories and Other Disasters* (1972), *The Ferrari in the Bedroom* (1973), *The Phantom of the Open Hearth* (1977), and *A Fistful of Fig Newtons* (1983).

Allan Sherman (1924–73)

A television writer, lyricist, and album producer, Sherman attended the University of Illinois where he wrote and produced the annual campus variety show. His specialty was the song parody and he produced three best-selling albums including *My Son, the Folksinger* (1963). His book *The Rape of the A.P.E.*—the American Puritan Ethic—appeared in 1973.

Betty Smith (1896–1972)

Betty Smith was forced to leave school early in order to support her family; nonetheless, she later went on to study at Yale and later to hold a fellowship at the University of North Carolina. She published over seventy novels and plays, including *A Tree Grows in Brooklyn* (1943), *Tomorrow Will Be Better* (1948), and *Joy in the Morning* (1963).

Gloria Steinem (Contemporary)

Gloria Steinem studied political science at Smith College and later attended the University of Delhi and the University of Calcutta, where she became involved in local peace activism. When she returned to the United States she became active in the civil rights movement of the '60s and worked as a freelance writer, co-founding *New York Magazine* in 1968. During this time her political interests increasingly focused on feminist issues, and eventually she found it difficult to publish her work in the mainstream press. This led Steinem to found *Ms. Magazine*, a groundbreaking feminist publication controlled entirely by women, in 1972. Steinem remains a prominent feminist, well known for her activism as well as her writing. Her works include *Outrageous Acts and Everyday Rebellions* (1983), *Marilyn* (1986), *Revolution from Within: A Book of Self-Esteem* (1992), and *Moving Beyond Words* (1994).

Pam Stone (Contemporary)

Pam Stone is an actress and stand-up comic whose credits include the ABC sitcom *Coach*.

Frank Sullivan (1892–1976)

Frank Sullivan, the well-known author of countless newspaper and magazine pieces, was born in Saratoga Springs, New York, where he began contributing to the *Saratogian* at an early age. After graduating from Cornell University, Sullivan was drafted into the army in 1917. After the war he moved to New York and began writing for the *Herald*, the *Evening Sun*, and the *World*; he also became a member of the notorious Algonquin Round Table, a group of writers who gathered at the Hotel Algonquin in the 1920s. The invention of a fictitious old woman he called Aunt Sarah Gallup, while covering the 1924 Democratic Convention, brought him national attention, and from that time on he was no longer a reporter, but a humor columnist. In 1926 he began contributing humorous pieces to *The New Yorker*, embarking on what would be a lifelong affiliation. Moving back to Saratoga Springs in 1935, Sullivan continued to contribute humorous essays to a wide range of publications for the rest of his life. Through the years his essays were collected and published in a number of volumes, among which are *The Life and Times of Martha Hepplethwaite* (1926), *Innocent Bystanding* (1928), *A Rock in Every Snowball* (1946), *The Night the Old Nostalgia Burned Down* (1953), and *Well, There's No Harm in Laughing* (1972).

Linda Sunshine (Contemporary)

Linda Sunshine is the author or editor of more than fifty books, including *The Family Dog: Celebrating Our Favorite Relative* (2003) and *The Family Dinner: A Celebration of Love, Laughter, and Leftovers* (2003), two in a series of books in collaboration with Mary Tiegreen. She is also author of *Women Who Date Too Much (And Those Who Should Be So Lucky): A Guide for Singles in Search of Significant Others* (1988). She often writes about the movies and has published books about *Stuart Little*, *E.T.*, *Frida*, and *Catch Me If You Can*. Her most recent work as an editor includes *All Things Oz: The Wonder, Wit, and Wisdom of The Wizard of Oz* (2003) a collection of excerpts from Baum's *Oz* novels, poems, short stories, and song lyrics mixed with art from around the world.

Judy Tenuta (Contemporary)

An improv artist and stand-up comic dubbed the "fun feminist of the '90s," Judy Tenuta has appeared on *The Late Show with David Letterman* and starred in her own specials on HBO, Lifetime, and Showtime. She was the first stand-up to win the "Best Female Comedian" prize at the American Comedy Awards. An animated version of Tenuta has appeared on the Comedy Central show *Dr. Katz*. A self-proclaimed "Multi-Media Bondage Goddess," Tenuta has produced an album, *Buy This, Pigs*, published *The Power of Judyism* (1991), and starred in the off-beat comedy film *Desperation Boulevard* (1998).

James Thurber (1896–1961)

James Thurber was born in Columbus, Ohio, and is most famous for his classic story "The Secret Life of Walter Mitty," which first appeared in *The New Yorker* and was made into a successful movie. His titles include *My Life and Hard Times; The Seal in the Bedroom; The Middle-Aged Man on the Flying Trapeze; Men, Women and Dogs;* and *My World—and Welcome to It.*

John Trumbull (1750–1831)

A famous satirist in his day and prominent member of the Connecticut Wits, John Trumbull was born in Connecticut and was remarkably precocious. He learned to read at two and passed the Yale entrance exam at the tender age of seven, although he had to wait six years before he was allowed to enter college. Trumbull received his B. A. from Yale in 1767, worked as a tutor on campus, and received a law degree. He passed the bar in 1773 and moved to Boston to work closely with John Adams. Trumbull was a prominent voice for educational reform. He wrote most of his satirical work in the 1770s and 1780s, when he published the poem *The Progress of Dulness*, the mock epic *M'Fingal*, and the *Anarchiad*. He also wrote a series of essays called the *Meddler* (1769–70) and the *Correspondent* (1770–73) with a fellow Connecticut Wit, Timothy Dwight. Trumbull died in Detroit in 1831. His *Satiric Poems* were reprinted in one volume in 1962.

Mark Twain (1835–1910)

The most celebrated American humorist needs little introduction. He was born Samuel Clemens in Missouri and at the age of twelve became a printer's apprentice for the *Missouri Courier*. He published his first piece of writing in a Boston magazine at the age of sixteen and worked as a steamboat pilot on the Mississippi from 1857 until the outbreak of the Civil War. Clemens was appointed secretary for the Nevada territory during the war and started using the pseudonym Mark Twain for his humor pieces. He lived in California, where he worked as a journalist and lecturer; the letters he wrote for publication during his trip around the Mediterranean and the Holy Land became *The Innocents Abroad* (1869). His most famous books include *The Adventures of Tom Sawyer* (1876), *Life on the Mississippi* (1883), *The Adventures of Huckleberry Finn* (1885), and *Pudd'n-head Wilson* (1894). His *Autobiography* appeared in 1924.

John Updike (Contemporary)

John Updike grew up in Pennsylvania and attended Harvard University on a full scholarship. He graduated summa cum laude in 1954 and began his fruitful collaboration with *The New Yorker* in 1955. The magazine regularly publishes Updike's stories, poems, and literary criticism. His major fiction titles include *Rabbit, Run* (1960), *Couples* (1968), *Bech: A Book* (1970), *The Coup* (1978), *Rabbit Is Rich* (1980), *The Witches of Eastwick* (1984), *Rabbit at Rest* (1990), and *Seek My Face* (2002). Updike has also published a memoir, *Self-Consciousness* (1989), and a volume of essays, *Odd Jobs* (1991). He has received many honors for his work, including the National Book Award and the Pulitzer Prize. Updike lives in Massachusetts.

Judith Viorst (Contemporary)

Judith Viorst was raised in suburban New Jersey and received her B.A. from Rutgers University. She moved to Greenwich Village after college and published her first volume of poetry, *The Village Square*, in 1965. She has published numerous collections of verse since, including *It's Hard to Be Hip over Thirty* (1968), *Forever Fifty and Other Negotiations* (1989), and *Sad Underwear and Other Complications* (1995). She has referred to her poetry as "aggravation recollected in tranquillity" and is well known for her humorous descriptions of women's anxieties. A popular author of children's books, Viorst also published *Alexander and the Terrible, Horrible, No Good, Very Bad Day* (1972) among others. She works as a columnist for *Redbook* magazine and published a bestselling self-help book, *Necessary Losses*, in 1986. She is the author of another self-help book entitled *Grown-up Marriage* (2002). Viorst lives in Washington, D.C.

Jane Wagner (Contemporary)

Jane Wagner was born in Tennessee. She is most famous for her longtime collaboration with actress Lily Tomlin on the play *The Search for Signs of Intelligent Life in the Universe*, for which she received a Tony Award and a New York Drama Critics Circle special citation in 1986. Wagner also received two Emmy Awards, in 1975 and 1982, for comedy-variety specials starring Lily Tomlin. She wrote the screenplay for the movie *Moment by Moment* (1979), starring Tomlin and John Travolta. Their most successful collaboration has been without a doubt *The Search for Signs*; it ran in theaters for two years, was made into a movie, and was also published in book form. In 1994, Ms. Wagner wrote and executive produced the first of three animated specials based on the child character Edith Ann, whom Tomlin made famous on the hit television show *Laugh-In*. Wagner earned her second Peabody Award for the third show in this series of specials, *Edith Ann's Christmas: Just Say Noël* (1996). She is also a codirector of the documentary *Question of Equality* (1999), about the struggle for gay rights in America.

Gene Weingarten (Contemporary)

Gene Weingarten writes the "Below the Beltway" humor column for the *The Washington Post Sunday Magazine* and is author of *The Hypochondriac's Guide to Life. And Death* as well as coauthor with Regina Barreca of *I'm with Stupid: One Man, One Woman, and 10,000 Years of Misunderstanding Between the Sexes Cleared Right Up.*

Mae West (1893–1980)

Born in Brooklyn, Mae West began her career as a child star in vaudeville and went on to produce, write, and star in numerous plays, films, and musical revues. Her first play, *Sex* (1926), led to her arrest for obscenity and corrupting the morals of youth. Throughout her life, the bawdy humor and frank sexuality that made her popular both as an actress and screenwriter also drew attacks from censors and moralists. Her works include *Diamond Lil* (1928), *The Constant Sinner* (1931), and *Go West Young Man* (1936).

Edith Wharton (1862–1937)

A best-selling author in her time and recognized modern classic in ours, Wharton was born Edith Newbold Jones in one of the oldest New York families. She married Teddy Wharton in 1885; the unhappy union would eventually end in a divorce that scandalized the bride's milieu. Her first story appeared in *Scribner's* in 1891 and she published her first book, *The Decoration of Houses*, in 1897. She suffered a nervous breakdown in 1898 and published her first collection of stories, *The Greater Inclination*, the following year. Wharton left America in 1911 and settled permanently in France. She organized relief efforts during World War I and received a medal from the French government for her relief work. Wharton is most famous for her short stories and her three major novels: the best-seller *The House of Mirth* (1905), *Ethan Frome* (1911), and the Pulitzer Prize–winning *The Age of Innocence* (1920). The contrast between American and European customs, the tribal rituals of Old New York families, and the inequality of women in a patriarchal society are recurrent themes in her fiction. She published her memoirs, *A Backward Glance*, in 1934.

Frances Miriam Whitcher (1812–52)

Born Miriam Berry in 1812, this pioneer of women's humor lived for thirty-five years in Whitesboro, Oneida County, New York, in the popular inn run by her family. Her extreme shyness kept her from boarding school but she educated herself with the local circulating library. She also joined the Maeonian Circle, a society of men and women who met for music, reading, and conversation. Whitcher contributed to the circle a literary burlesque read one chapter at a time and serialized in a local newspaper under the title *The Widow Spriggins*, with only the name "Frank" as author. She went on to publish her first sketch with the Widow Bedott persona in the *Saturday Gazette* in 1846, and the vernacular heroine Aunt Maguire first appeared in *Godey's Lady's Book* magazine in 1848; she published most of her work anonymously. She married Benjamin Whitcher, an Episcopalian minister, in 1846 and died of tuberculosis six years later. Her fame spread posthumously with the publication of her major works, *The Widow Bedott Papers*, in 1855. In the words of her biographer, "For more than fifty years, Miriam Whitcher stood alone among women as creator of vernacular humor that mocked not women, per se, but the way women behaved." In the 1870s, David Locke adapted selections from *The Widow Bedott Papers* for the stage; Whitcher's heroine was played by a man in drag, Neil Burgess. Whitcher's humor influenced later female authors like Marietta Holley and Fanny Fern.

E. B. White (1899–1985)

Born Elwyn Brooks White in Mount Vernon, New York, E. B. White is one of the most important humorists and essayists in American literature. After graduating from Cornell University in 1921, White worked as a reporter for the United Press, the American Legion News Service, and later the *Seattle Times*. Upon his return to New York, he began contributing pieces to the then-young *New Yorker*; by 1927, he was working there full time and became one of its most prominent figures. In 1929 he published his first two books, *The Lady Is Cold* and (with James Thurber) *Is Sex Necessary?* As time went on his writing became more political; he treated the issues of the day with irony and skepticism. In 1941 he coedited *A Sub-Treasury of American Humor*, a work influential in broadening and redefining the very concept of American humor. Among White's numerous other works are *Every Day Is Saturday* (1934), *Stuart Little* (1945), *Here Is New York* (1949), *Charlotte's Web* (1952), and *The Points of My Compass* (1962).

Herman Wouk (Contemporary)

Wouk was born in the Bronx, wrote poetry from the age of eight, and graduated from Columbia University with a B.A. in Philosophy and Comparative Literature in 1934. During college he contributed humorous columns to the *Columbia Spectator*. He worked as a gag writer for radio comedians from 1934 to 1941. He joined the Navy in 1941, served in the Pacific from 1943 to 1945, and spent some of his time aboard the USS *Zane* reading and working on his first novel, *Aurora Dawn* (1947). Wouk went on to publish *The Caine Mutiny* (1951), for which he received the Pulitzer in 1952, *Marjorie Morningstar*, which was made into a movie, and the bestsellers *The Winds of War* and *War and Remembrance*, dramatized as mini-series on ABC. The subject of Wouk's second novel, *City Boy* (1948), from which the passage in this collection is excerpted, is his childhood memories as the son of immigrant Jewish parents in New York City.

Grateful Acknowledgment Is Made to the Following for Permission to Reprint Copyrighted Material

M

Excerpts from *What the Dogs Have Taught Me* by Merrill Markoe. Copyright © 1992 by Merrill Markoe. Used by permission of Viking Penguin, a division of Penguin Putnam Inc.

"Groucho and Chico Make a Deal" from *A Night at the Opera* by the Marx Brothers. Copyright 1935 by George S. Kaufman and Morrie Ryskind. Permission granted courtesy of Turner Entertainment Co.

"Ethnic Poetry" by Julio Marzán. Used by permission of the author.

"Jackie Mason on Starbucks." Copyright © Jackie Mason. Reprinted by permission of William Morris Agency, Inc., on behalf of the author.

"The Blushful Mystery" from *Prejudices: A Selection* by H. L. Mencken. Copyright © 1958 by Alfred A. Knopf, a division of Random House, Inc. Used by permission of Alfred A. Knopf, a division of Random House, Inc.

Excerpt from *The Rants* by Dennis Miller, copyright © 1996 by Dennis Miller. Used by permission of Doubleday, a division of Random House, Inc.

Excerpt from *Aunt Carmen's Book of Practical Saints* by Pat Mora. Copyright © 1997 by Pat Mora. Reprinted by permission of Beacon Press, Boston.

N

"Not George Washington's, Not Abraham Lincoln's, But Mine" from *Good Intentions* by Ogden Nash. Copyright 1940 by Ogden Nash. First appeared in *The Saturday Evening Post*. By permission of Curtis Brown, Ltd.

P

"The Garter," copyright 1928, renewed © 1956 by Dorothy Parker, "Little Hours" by Dorothy Parker, copyright 1933, renewed © 1961 by Dorothy Parker, from *The Portable Dorothy Parker* by Dorothy Parker. Used by permission of Viking Penguin.

"Book Tour" from *Living to Prowl* by Sam Pickering. Copyright © 1997 by Sam Pickering. Used by permission of the University of Georgia Press.

R

"Low Self-Esteem" and "Mail Order Alternatives to Costly Psychotherapy" from *You Don't Have to Pet to Be Popular* by Libby Reid. "What's in the Refrigerator?" "Girl's Eye View" and "Virginity Recertification" from *Do You Hate Your Hips More Than Nuclear War?* by Libby Reid. Used by permission of the author.

Excerpts from *Rock This!* by Chris Rock. Copyright © 1997 by Chris Rock. Reprinted by permission of Hyperion.

Selections by Will Rogers reprinted with the kind permission of the Will Rogers Memorial Commission. © Will Rogers Memorial Commission.

About the Editor

Professor of English literature and feminist theory at the University of Connecticut, **Regina Barreca** grew up in Brooklyn and Long Island, received a B.A. from Dartmouth College, an M.A. from Cambridge University (where she was a Reynolds' Fellow), and a Ph.D. from the City University of New York. An award-winning columnist for *The Hartford Courant*, she has served as an adviser to the Library of Congress for work on humor and the American character, and was deemed a "feminist humor maven" by *Ms.* magazine. With Gene Weingarten of *The Washington Post*, she wrote *I'm With Stupid: One Man, One Woman, and 10,000 Years of Misunderstandings Between the Sexes Cleared Right Up* (2004). Barreca has appeared on scores of radio and television programs including *20/20, 48 Hours, Today*, and *Oprah*.

Barreca's works, which have been translated into Chinese, German, Spanish, Italian, Japanese and Czech, include the bestselling *They Used to Call Me Snow White . . . but I Drifted, Perfect Husbands (and Other Fairy Tales), Sweet Revenge: The Wicked Delights of Getting Even, Untamed and Unabashed: Essays on Women and Humor in British Literature, Too Much of a Good Thing Is Wonderful* and (as editor) *The Penguin Book of Women's Humor, The Signet Book of American Humor, The Erotics of Instruction*, and *A Sitdown with the Sopranos: Watching Italian American Culture on TV's Most Talked-About Series* (2002). With cartoonist Nicole Hollander, she wrote *The ABC of Vice: An Insatiable Woman's Guide* (2003). Her Web site address is www.ginabarreca.com.